Ziiza Moves to Beaverton

Ziiza

Moves to Beaverton

Fred Barrett

Bev + Bob
Enjoy!
Fred 02-27-04

Alder Press
Portland, Oregon

Alder Press
P.O. Box 1503
Portland, OR 97207-1503

503-246-7983
alderpress.com

Printed in the United States of America

* * *

Publisher's Cataloging-in-Publication Data

Barrett, Frederick Gould.
    Ziiza moves to Beaverton / Fred Barrett. – 1ˢᵗ ed.
        p. cm.
    ISBN: 0-9636614-5-0
    1. Northwest, Pacific – Fiction. 2. Beaverton (Imaginary place) – Fiction. 3. Families – Fiction. 4. Single mothers – Fiction. 5. Emigration and immigration – Fiction. 6. Business – Fiction. I. Title.

PS3552.A7342 Z55 2003
813'.54 – dc21

* * *

To purchase copies of this book, please see information on the last page.

Contents

1

Eyes in the Forest

ZIIZA FELT the creature's eyes, but did not turn around. She slid her bare foot across the beach pebbles and touched her son's leg. The boy, Edu by name, turned slowly, as if by prearrangement. She moved her head, signaling him to look behind her. He looked into the trees. He noticed nothing unusual. She signaled again. Finally, he saw the creature, sitting beside a dark-leaved salal bush, almost covered by a drooping cedar limb, head tilted quizzically – not an aggressive stance at all. Edu had never seen a creature like this before. Wolf? Right shape. But no. Its soft brown eyes, bent ears, and short muzzle were not those of a wolf. It was stockier, too. Or it would have been had it not been starving, which it obviously was, as Edu caught sight of its ribs through its tawny chest.

Ziiza smiled mischievously and tossed a piece of scorched deer meat over her shoulder. The creature left its cover, caught it on the fly, and swallowed. No rustling leaves or branches, no nails clicking on pebbles, no snapping teeth. One silent, fluid motion. And back, beside the salal bush, where its hungry eyes again bored into her back.

She turned and faced the creature for the first time. Her other children, sitting around their driftwood fire, were now staring at it, too. She flicked another scrap. Again the creature left its cover, swallowed, and returned. At that, Milli, her eldest daughter, giggled into her hand. Another son, Com, threw a chunk high in the air. The creature caught it and bolted it down. "Hungry tonight, dummy," Milli said, poking him in the side. "You threw it all away." The children laughed and threw more meat to the creature, who stuck to its routine, swallowing in one gulp, two if necessary, then returning – its eyes still as hungry-looking as if it had not eaten a thing.

Ziiza relaxed and leaned back. Her smile broadened. "We haven't had this much fun," she said, "since before. . . ." She clamped her teeth as if to bite off the words and began again: "We haven't had this much fun in weeks, have we children?"

Below them, MeTonn, canoe flotilla leader and headman of the band of travelers, heard them laughing. "Stupid woman. Stupid children. Stupid all of them," he growled, as he pulled a charred bone from his fire. "What do they think they are doing, wasting food?" he said to Hawl, his hairy, thick-wristed second canoe man. "The first meat we've had in days and days, since I can't remember when, and those *passengers,*" he spit out the word, "those passengers are throwing it away, feeding that mangy . . . that mangy, whatever it is. Why did I ever allow? Strange creature, though; I've never seen anything like it." Hawl grunted his agreement, accompanied by a broken-toothed grin, and, in the manner of the slow-witted, an exaggerated nod.

Grumbling and complaining, plotting and scheming – how to get rid of Ziiza and her six children – was nothing new for MeTonn and Hawl, they had been at it for weeks. The wasted deer meat, the improbable creature, the passenger family's levity, were incidental to his complaint, though, for it was MeTonn's raging complaint, not Hawl's. The muma, Ziiza, did not behave like a woman should, did not limit her speech to gossip-talk with the other women, or to controlling her children, and then, when among men, obedient silence. "This looks like an excellent campsite," she once had the effrontery to suggest. It was, but they had paddled on. And she was not his only problem.

"I hate the big one," MeTonn hissed, crunching the bone with the good side of his long-ago-broken and poorly-healed jaw. "I hate him. I hate him." He sucked burnt grease from his fingers, one, two, three, four, and his thumb. His silent paddling cadence – *I* (dip), *hate* (stroke), *him* (recover). *I* (dip), *hate* (stroke), *him* (recover) – was out and he did not care. Speaking the words even made his sour stomach feel better. For a while. The object of his hatred, Ziiza's eldest son, Org – tall, muscular, quick, confident – was growing into manhood before his eyes. Threateningly. When would he challenge him for leadership? Soon, MeTonn feared. Yes, feared. Could he take him? Twenty years ago. Probably. Possibly. Maybe. "It was luck. Just luck. I know it," he said, referring to Org's extraordinary kill that afternoon. "Luck. He could never do it again. Never." True, luck had played large. The feat could never be repeated. But the fact remained, Org *had* done it. And, equally embarrassing, everyone in the five canoes had seen him do it. The men's grateful smiles, the women's admiring glances, the long-dreamed-of meat feast he had no part in delivering, had cracked his confidence.

One by one MeTonn's travelers found their sleeping places, prompted by his glares, reminding them that, as always, late-night fires were for leaders only, meaning Hawl and himself. Senior paddlers squirmed under overturned canoes and wrapped themselves in fur robes. The others found the most comfortable spots they could: depressions in the sand above the tide line, stony nests farther up the beach. Later, when it rained, some scrambled under trees. Some did not bother; they pulled their robes tight and endured. Day and night in this saltwater and rain country, they were wet much of the time anyway. They endured. Or they gave out.

MeTonn hunched over the fire, as he would all night, his robe draped on his back, dozing, waking, thinking, dozing again. Hawl slept across from him. MeTonn trusted no one but Hawl and himself with the night watch. The others, he believed, with justification, were worthless.

Tired, satiated, and content, Ziiza and the children lost interest in the creature. They did not try to drive it away. Hungry as it was, there were far more threatening animals and creatures in the forest. They scooted close to their fire, now a pile of glowing coals, Ziiza in the middle, the youngest tight against her, the older ones tight against them. Not having robes for everyone, they shared, pulling them over their backs and heads, shelter-like, clutching the ends. Govvi, the youngest girl, who usually attached importance to such things, did not bother to build up the fire; she closed her eyes and let go. Ziiza kissed each one – a cheek, a nose, a forehead – and whispered, "Good night all." The children fell asleep immediately. Ziiza gave Org a proud muma's look, pulled Edu and Govvi tight, and closed her eyes. Before she drifted off, she recalled Org's feat that afternoon:

They were traveling a sheltered passage formed by a string of long narrow islands. Org, paddling bow-man in Hawl's canoe, had spotted a pair of deer browsing sea-grass in knee-deep water. Tiny waves lapped on the shore, making just enough noise to cover the bow wake's gurgle; the wind was in their faces. He raised his paddle – which by MeTonn's rules he had no right to do – signaling the others to stop.

Org thrust his paddle deep and pulled hard. Hawl did the same. The mid-canoe paddlers pulled their paddles, caught the drips in their hands, and bent forward. *Let them not look up, catch our scent*, Ziiza had pleaded silently. *Please. We have not had meat in so long*. Org and Hawl stroked again. Closed in in a slow glide. The doe raised her head, water dripping from her nose. Flicked her ears. She lowered her head and resumed feeding.

Two canoe lengths from them Org pushed his paddle away. Deer chewing. Glide slowing. He drew his knife. Crouched. Sprang from the canoe. He grabbed the buck by an antler, plunged the knife into its throat, and pulled up. Blood spurted, pulsed, and gushed.

Ziiza shivered with delight, opened her eyes, looked at sleeping Org, and closed them again.

Had it not been for the muddy bottom, the doe would have been off. But when she lunged, her sharp hooves stuck. Org splashed heavily through the water, twisting his feet to break the suction. "Ahhhh-yeeee. Ahhhh-yeeee," the people screamed, beating their paddles on the sides. The doe freed herself from the muck and bounded onto the beach. He threw his stone-headed club. One – slow – revolution. Thunk. Behind the eye. A step and her forelegs buckled. Org walked slowly to her. Finished her off. The people jumped from the canoes and ran to him, screaming, dancing, slapping his back. Had he been one to seize dramatic moments and revel and show off, this was the moment. But he was not. His only show was the blood on his hand as he gutted the doe. They camped on the island beach.

Twilight passed into blackness, clouds blotted the stars, the moon stuck behind the mainland mountains. The driftwood fire spit and flared in the breeze.

"Wake up, Hawl. Wake up," MeTonn said, pounding a fist on his knee. Hawl started, blinked, and raised his head from his rock pillow. "Listen, the big one will paddle in the bow. Your canoe. Tomorrow morning." Hawl grunted. MeTonn grabbed a clump of rotting seaweed, threw it on the fire, and shifted position to relieve his tingling bum. He inhaled the acrid smoke till it burned his lungs. Loved it. Inhaled again. And again. Pop. A spark shot into the air. MeTonn leaned forward, trying to catch it on his thick purple tongue. The spark expired and floated away like a miniature shooting star. Click. He snapped his yellow teeth – the few that met.

Again he leaned into the foul seaweed smoke, widened his eyes, and snorted. Waggled his head. Savored the pain. Deliriously blinded and gagging on smoke, he growled: "The – muma – she – is – mine." Hawl grunted obediently. MeTonn cupped his ear suspiciously – as if he could hear Ziiza listening. He turned his ugly, menacing face toward her sleeping family and their faintly-glowing fire. Still blinded, he cocked his head, and waited. No sound but the wind. And the water lapping on the protected shoreline. "This is the last of the islands," he said, leaning away from the smoke and prodding Hawl with his stick to make sure he was listening. "No more passage. After this one, nothing but open Sea. I smelled it this afternoon. I tasted the wind."

MeTonn rocked in and out of the smoke. He let the fire die. As the night deepened, he nodded into a smoke-induced stupor, mumbling, growling, coughing, and spitting. He slept and waked, slept and waked, until the moon brightened the clouds. Then he slept.

Edu woke first, as always. And, as almost always, he saw and felt a dripping gray fog covering the beach, hanging over the water, blocking the sunrise beyond the mountains. New days did not *begin* here as they did in other parts of the world. On this lonesome coast, nighttime gave way slowly, grudgingly. Beautiful in its way, since it was springtime and mild. Were it winter, another matter. Some mornings the sun overcame the fog, burned it off, leaving scattered low clouds over the Sea. That was his prediction for today.

After his weather analysis, which he did propped on an elbow, Edu sat up and scanned the sleepers – no one awake – and the canoes. He walked to the fire and poked below the dewy top coals for an ember. Finding none, he walked to the other fire. MeTonn slept hunched forward, under his robe, his face touching his knees. Hawl gurgled and snored opposite him. He probed for a live stick. Found one. As he picked it up a rock rolled under his foot and clicked on another. MeTonn jerked his head up, recognized the boy, and opened his mouth to speak. But he did not. Instead, he glared at now-awake Hawl and lowered his head. Edu tiptoed back to his family, waving the stick to keep it alive.

On reaching the fire he was startled to see – the creature – still there – sitting – at the edge of the forest. Sitting beside the salal bush. Under the cedar limb. Head tilted. Eyes filled with the same sad, hungry, quizzical look. Edu blew on the stick and it flared. The creature watched. "Muma, Muma," he whispered, leaning over and touching Ziiza's shoulder, "That thing. The creature. The one that ate our meat. It's still here." She groaned, drew her shoulder away, and tightened her eyelids.

"The creature's still here," Edu repeated the news to his brothers and sisters as he woke them. It continued to stare with brown, unblinking eyes. Intelligence? Cunning? Possibly. But he had seen that in creatures before: wolves, foxes, wildcats. This creature's look was not like that. Hungry eyes? Yes. But he knew that. What else?

Morning fires were not for cooking in MeTonn's camps, just warm-ups for the travelers, to ease their stiffness, pull the pain from their elbows, shoulders, backs, and knees. Now he was up and giving orders. Not that he had much to say; everyone knew his or her duties. The men carried the canoes to the water and positioned their paddles and weapons. The tide was out and the muck bottom that had slowed hunter and deer the day before was exposed, an odoriferous mixture of needles, twigs, sand, saltwater mud, and decaying seaweed. The women loaded the leftover meat, other food, robes, and the few cooking implements they possessed. Ziiza's five children – Org, the sixth, was considered a paddler, not a child passenger – were filling water pouches at a tiny spring leaking onto the beach north of camp. They ate no formal meals; last night's meat feast was as close as they came to that. Individuals carried personal food pouches, eating when hungry, on the water, during shore breaks, or in camp. When food ran low, they dug clams and pried mussels off exposed rocks at low tide, their staple foods. Or they worked the river estuaries on the incoming tide, for crab, perch, and flounder. They had no time for hunting unless an animal presented itself for a quick kill, such as yesterday's deer, or baby sea lions left on the beach, or the rare small creature that came within a stone's throw. After satisfying their immediate needs, sometimes cooking their catch, sometimes not, they gathered enough to sustain themselves for a few days and paddled on.

"Wet your paddles," MeTonn shouted. Foggy mornings were, for the most part, windless, and paddling was best. Get the distance in before mid-day was his rule, and his people – and unwelcome passengers – knew it to be a good one. After that, the wind generally rose, on good days creating gentle, easy swells, on bad days headwinds, crosswinds, and whitecaps, enough to stop canoes dead in the water and drive them to early camps (much to the flotilla leader's disgust). Spring and summer winds blew from the northwest, and, since they were traveling south, gave an assist. Rarely enough, however, to make sail-raising worthwhile.

The five steersmen pushed their canoes into knee-deep water and steadied the sterns while the others climbed in. The paddlers and the non-paddling children squirmed to adjust themselves, kneeling, sitting, or half-sitting against cross braces. The steersmen shoved the canoes out and jumped in. Bano led, followed by the second and third canoes. Then Hawl's. MeTonn trailed so he could keep an eye on things, as a good leader should, with harsh words for any paddler who slacked off.

They formed up single file and slid along the shore. The creature, still in position, watched. As they drew away from the smoldering campfires, it left the forest edge and walked along the beach. When the paddlers reached their rhythm, it broke into a run. Com, facing the stern, called, "Look. Look. It's the creature. Following us." The creature kept to its business, negotiating rocks, depressions, driftwood, checking the canoes to make sure it was keeping up.

At that, MeTonn turned toward the creature and glowered. "Faster! Faster! Dig! Dig!" he bellowed over the water. "Fast-tuh. Fast-tuh," Hawl echoed. The canoes surged ahead. But however fast the paddlers pushed their canoes the creature matched them. After their initial thrusts, the paddlers eased off. "Dig! Dig!" MeTonn bellowed again. He beat the canoe side. Boom! Boom! The creature broke into a flat-out run, flying over rocks, jumping driftwood, its feet sending up splatters of sand.

Bano's canoe reached the island's tip. Without hesitation the creature ran into the water and swam for the canoes. Swam? Hardly. It fought its way through the water, churning legs providing both floatation and forward motion. Bano's canoe left it behind. Number two slipped past. Number three. The creature persisted, angling toward Hawl's. "Ge-wa-way, beast," Hawl growled. Netti, amazed and delighted, urged the creature on – to what end she did not consider – slapping her hand on the water and crying, "Here, creaty-creature.

You can do it." Org, in the bow, said nothing, but, after looking over his shoulder, paddled slower. Still, the creature could not close the gap. The sisters waved laughing good-byes as their canoe pulled away.

With this, the creature sighted on the last canoe and paddled even harder, spreading a wake behind. MeTonn pried his paddle, trying to steer away, but the creature had the angle and intersected the canoe. "Off! Off!" he yelled. Com stuck out his hand to pat its head. MeTonn raised his paddle, ready to strike. But before he swung, Ziiza leaned over, caught the creature by its bony underbelly and lifted it into the canoe. MeTonn's bloodshot eyes bugged. His cheeks showed red. He screamed, but no words came. Rocked forward, then back, clutching his throat, apoplectic. "Get that – that – that – thing – out of my canoe." He sucked in a breath, then another. "How dare. How dare," he spouted, gagging on his words. The creature cowered against the side. Com reached back to pat it. It rumbled low in its throat and he jerked his hand away. Fixing its eyes on Ziiza, the creature lay still.

MeTonn dug hard, lifting his paddle on each return in exaggeratedly high arcs. Hawl, looking back, saw him and continued on. MeTonn scowled and held his paddle over his head with both hands, horizontal to the water. Hawl still did not comprehend. "Hawl!" MeTonn yelled in exasperation, waving his paddle in the air. Hawl looked hard as if to say, now?

Hawl stowed his paddle, crouched, and moved forward. On his touch, the paddler in front bent over to let him to pass. He gripped the sides, stepped over a bundle of robes, and pushed between the girls. The next paddler, now aware of Hawl's movement, fell back against the robes. Hawl threw himself at Org, crashing his head into his back. Jamming his huge paws into Org's armpits, he lifted, shouldered, and shoved him half out of the canoe. He reached down, grabbed a leg, and flipped him into the water. "Pad-dle! Fast!" he ordered. The girls sat rigid in disbelief. Hawl's enormous hand crashed into Netti's face. He jerked her up and tumbled her over the side. Milli yelled, "No!" and went limp. Hawl picked her up and dropped her in.

At the moment of Hawl's attack, MeTonn swung his paddle at Ziiza and hit her ear. He lunged forward, seized her waist, and threw her overboard. He turned, grabbed Govvi by the hair, and flung her in. Com followed his sister. Little Edu hung onto the cross brace in a grip of terror. MeTonn jerked him away and threw him over the side. To finish the job, he took the offending creature by a leg, and, ignoring its snapping teeth, flung it into the Sea.

"Out! Gone! Done!"

2

The Beach

ONE MOMENT Org was paddling, strong, confident, upright, looking ahead to the horizon, fresh to the day's work. The next he was shocked, disoriented, hovering upside down. He clamped his lips, expelled water, and opened his eyes. Above, blackness; below, a light green glare. He allowed himself a moment of suspension and swam for the glare, even though it seemed wrong. Breaking the surface, he spit salt water, gulped, and cleared his nose. He shook his hair, swiped his eyes, and scanned the water. Hawl's canoe, instead of turning around to pick him up, was pulling away, heading to the open Sea. Milli bobbed a few yards ahead of him. She gasped, sputtered, then inhaled, her eyes wild. Netti's head broke the surface.

Org swam to the girls. Decision time. Swim back to the island? Or to the mainland? Although the mainland was farther away, the mountains gave it a higher profile than the low island they had come from; it looked closer. At least it did to Org's water-level, bleary eyes. And it *was* the mainland. "Swim for it," he ordered, pointing to shore. Netti hung in the water, turning slowly. A swell flowed over her. She made no attempt to ride it. Org lunged, grabbed her hair, and, with a hard scissor kick, jerked her up. "Netti! Netti!" Her eyes stayed closed. He wrapped his arm around her waist, turned her face up, and side-stroked toward shore. Milli followed.

Ziiza's scream was cut short when she hit the water. A searing heat tore through her ear, as if it had caught fire. She surfaced, gulped, spit, blew, shook her head, and slapped her throbbing ear – anything to stop the pain. She tread water, circling slowly, until she saw MeTonn's canoe, now twenty strokes away. Com, an excellent swimmer, bobbed to the surface in front of her. Govvi? Edu? Not to be seen. She circled again, scanning the surface. "Dive! Now!" Ziiza shouted at Com. Not waiting for him to react, she ducked her head, tipped her feet, and swam herself under. Straining her eyes in the gray-green water, she saw neither child. She dove again. A third time. A fourth. And with each dive, she saw less and less, as her eyes began to cloud.

Don't panic. Don't panic.

On the next dive Ziiza touched something. Body-like? It had to be. Pawing frantically, she felt a head and grabbed a handful of hair. Lungs screaming, head aching, she kicked and pulled upward with her free arm. She kicked, raised a head out of the water, and pounded a back. A cough. Ziiza put her mouth to Govvi's and sucked. She spit and sucked again. Suck. Spit. Suck. Spit. That was all she could think to do. That was all she could do. She stopped spitting and yelled at Com, "Find Edu. Find Edu." Holding Govvi's wrist, she side-stroked toward the dark green shore.

After a half-hour struggle, Org stopped to rest and let Milli catch up. He lowered his feet to tread water. To his amazement, his foot touched bottom; he must have been half a mile from shore. "Milli! Milli! We've made it," he yelled. In a few minutes he was walking on a smooth, sandy bottom, pushing slowly though the water. When the water was chest deep, he stood Netti upright and shook her gently. Milli reached them and caught her sister by the waist. "We're safe, Netti," she said. Netti wobbled, half standing, half floating. "Walk her in," Org told Milli. "You've got to. I'm going back. Muma. The kids." Milli and Netti stood shivering, watching him swim out and away, fearing they would never see him again.

Milli pulled Netti's arm over her shoulder, turned, and splashed toward the still-distant beach. The water level dropped from chest deep to waist to thigh to knee. And up again, as the shore waves increased. Netti grew heavy. The water clung to her legs as if to pull her down, and out, and back into the Sea. Her legs gave. She sat in the water. "Netti, you've got to get up. I can't carry you. Any more. Netti! Get up!" Milli pulled. They stumbled ahead. More steps. Ankle deep now. They fell. Stumbled on. Fell again. But in the right direction. They staggered onto the beach. "Beach, Netti. Keep going." They dropped face down on the sand. Holding hands, they lay still.

"Muma! Muma! Stand up," Org shouted to Ziiza, when he was far enough out to see her stroking toward him. "You can touch bottom." She did not see him, did not hear. She continued side-stroking with Govvi in tow. He swam to them. "Stand, Muma. I've got her."

"I can't believe it," Ziiza exclaimed, her head above the swells. "We're still way out." She held Govvi up and slapped her face. "Govvi!" she yelled, spitting water and pounding her shoulder. She pulled her mouth to hers and sucked, then blew, then sucked, and spit. Govvi coughed again, gagged, and moved her arms.

"Edu. Edu. I couldn't find him," Ziiza said. "Com's looking. Happened so fast. Go. Go." Org dove and leveled out swimming. Ziiza pulled Govvi toward the beach. "Can you stand, Govvi? Can you walk the rest of the way?" Govvi looked at her, glassy-eyed. "Edu. Com. I've go to go after them."

Govvi felt for the bottom. Water washed over her face. Ziiza pushed her shoreward. "Go, Govvi. Swim. I've got to go back for the boys." Ziiza rose on her toes and scanned the horizon. Thought she saw Org's arms. Swimming. Nothing else. She dove into a swell and stroked.

Ziiza swam with the strength of desperation. Heading out. No idea where. Org out of sight. Her surge of strength turned to stiffness; her arms grew heavy; her legs resisted her commands to kick, kick, kick. She felt the Sea's clinging chill. Swallowed water with each breath. Instead of the smooth, one-armed strokes that had brought Govvi in, her arms flopped forward without direction, and returned without power. She gulped air and dove. Came up gasping.

Useless. Dumb. Where are the boys? I can't even see Org.

The island. Its tree-topped outline, barely above the waves. She fluttered her hands to stay afloat, made a desperate calculation, and swam west, toward the open Sea, south of the island. Every few minutes she stopped, kicked, arm-pushed herself up, and scanned the water. A dark spot rose on a swell, then fell away. It did not reappear. A jolt of hope. She swam painfully, sloppily. Her only chance.

When she reached the spot, where the spot should be, she stopped and tread water, turning slowly around. She saw something moving, swimming, paddling. It could not be. The creature?

A dark spot moving steadily toward shore, exposed between swells, covered while passing over. Legs churning. Tail behind. And something in its mouth. A stick. With a hand attached. She battled toward it. Grabbed the arm. The creature let go, stopped paddling, and sank. Ziiza kicked out, caught it on her foot, plunged her other hand down, and brought it up. She grabbed the drowning creature by its neck and shook.

Don't give up. Keep going.

She swam-struggled toward shore holding Edu's arm in a death grip. The creature paddled behind.

With so much open water to cover, Org, swimming straight out had missed them: Com, Edu, the creature, even Ziiza. He turned and swam a slow zigzag pattern. Shoreward. Steadily shoreward. This is hopeless, he thought, but I've got to try. Diving is useless. They've been down too long. Can't be alive. Don't waste your strength. He swam slower and slower until he was barely moving. Then he frog-kicked just enough to stay up. Will they blame me if I come in? he continued. I can't stay out here forever. But I should.

After minutes of float-stroking, trying to make up his mind, Org saw a spot at the peak of a swell. When he reached Ziiza she was treading water, spitting and puffing, gathering herself for the next thrust. "I'll take him, Muma," he said. He pried at her hand, but she would not let go. He hooked her free hand on his belt and swam.

But Ziiza let go, passed Edu's hand to Org's, and swam back to the struggling creature. When she reached it she grabbed its neck fold and side-stroked toward shore.

"Drop it," Org yelled, when he paused. Ziiza ignored him and kept on swimming.

When his feet touched bottom, Org stood, raised Edu, and forced his way through the water. At waist depth he held the boy upside down and thumped his back. Shook him. Thumped again. Swung him around. Put his mouth to his and sucked. Spit water. Sucked. Spit. Forced air. Sucked. Tried to fill his lungs. Edu did not respond. Org continued his on-the-splash resuscitation until he reached knee-deep water. He pushed through the surf toward the girls on the beach. Laying Edu on his stomach, he pressed gently on his back. Milli crawled over and rested Edu's face on her hand. "Water's coming out," she said. Edu coughed. He choked up more water, heaved his chest, and caught a breath through blue lips. Org held him up by his feet and the water drained out through coughs and sputters and sobs.

Ziiza splashed ashore with the creature in her arms, dropped it, and staggered toward the children. Her legs gave out. She crawled. "Edu lives?" she croaked.

"He's breathing, Muma," Milli replied. "Water's stopped coming out." Org pushed rhythmically on his back. Netti breathed into his mouth.

Ziiza's head dropped. "Everybody else?" she whispered with her cheek on the sand. "Speak your names to me. I want to hear them."

"Org's here, Muma. And me, Milli."

"Org, you say it," she whispered through stiff lips.

"Org."

"Yes, it's me, Netti," Netti said between breaths for Edu. "I'm okay, I guess."

Ziiza fought with her spinning brain, struggling to think. She raised her head and fixed her eyes on each figure, trying to recognize him or her, take a head count. "Yes, and yes. Who else? Help me. Please. Who's missing?"

"Com's not here, Muma," Milli said. "But I think that's him walking toward us on the beach." She pointed to a distant figure advancing from the south.

"Who else? Who else? Say it."

After a pause, Govvi said, "I'm here, too, Muma."

"Yes. Everyone," Ziiza said. She closed her eyes and blended into the sand.

When Edu's breathing steadied, Org's last strength drained away and he collapsed. Milli took over, rubbing Edu's back, fast-stroking his arms and legs. "He's breathing, Net," Milli said. "Help me rub." Netti stopped sucking and rubbed. Their strength, too, soon expired. They lay down, one on each side of Edu, letting what warmth they had flow into his body. Com staggered to the pile, and, seeing his family asleep, peacefully, it seemed, and unhurt, lay down next to Govvi, blinked, and fell asleep.

While they slept, the low clouds scattered. The sun rose bright over the eastern mountains and warmed the sand. And warmed the sleeping family with all of its mid-day, springtime warmth and energy. Small waves bumped the shore and fell forward. The salt-scented breeze, without its usual chill, wafted over them and dried their bodies. After the commotion of their self-rescue, life in the beach community resumed its timeless routine: gulls circling, squawking, searching, pecking; plovers and sandpipers skittering, poking, then rising en masse, flying off for no apparent reason only to land abruptly down the beach. They slept on a broad, sturdy, Sea-facing beach, not at all like the sheltered, stones-to-sand-to-mud-and-grass beach of yesterday. To the south, the only direction worth considering, the sand stretched without end. No lofty headlands jutting into the water, no offshore islands creating sheltered canoe trails or wind-protected beach walkways, not even an off- shore stack to break up the sameness. And no sign of humans.

A sand flea jumped from Ziiza's tangled brown hair onto her red and swollen ear, onto her forehead, onto her eyelid. Then onto her nose, where it walked over the end and entered her nostril, upside down. She snorted and shook her head. Her sand-covered hand twitched and lifted, as if to swat the flea – or dig it out of her nose. Her hand fell back. It would take more than a sand flea, or the dozens more jumping on her body, to wake her.

Compared to her sleeping children, Ziiza was the third tallest, topped by Org, her eldest, and Netti, her tall, large-boned, gangly, teenage daughter. Ziiza's shoulders were broader than most women's of her time, giving her a sturdy, solid look. She had a square face and a broad forehead. Cheekbones defined, but not sharp. Although middle-aged, her lips were rounded and full, covering a mostly complete, mostly unbroken, set of large white teeth. When awake and willing, her smile was attractive. To complete her smile, her eyes were large, well-spaced, intelligent, and friendly – playful and humorous, even. At times. When awake and willing. Not much chin, which added to her square face and the pronounced angles of her jaw.

Ziiza lay naked on her back, having lost all of her fur garments in the water; her skin the color of inner tree bark. She darkened slightly in summer and lightened in winter, but her garment-ending lines did not show it, as it was spring, the time of transition. Her hair did the opposite, streaked light in summer, then back to brown in winter. In keeping with her square face, her hands were broad, thick-fingered, and strong, a working woman's hands. As she lay on the sand, her slightly protruding abdomen and full breasts showed good body fat and good health – in spite of months of travel and subsistence living. Unlike the aforementioned children, Org and Netti, who had long legs, and Edu, who at age five gave every indication that he, too, would be tall, Ziiza's legs were proportionally shorter. Her thighs rounded and muscular. Her calves well-defined, running to not-so-trim ankles; legs built for travel and work, but not outright speed. She twitched her legs as she slept, pushing her heels into the sand. Nine toes pointed upward. Where her right big toe should have been was a jagged red and black scar, cracked, oozing, and crawling with fleas.

3

Tracing the Sea

IT WAS afternoon when Ziiza lifted Milli's arm off her leg and sat up. She brushed what sand she could from her face and lips, spit, swiped aimlessly at the fleas, rose to her knees, and shook her hair out. She scanned the children through gritty eyes. Org breathed deeply, noisily. Milli and Netti clung to Edu; no apparent problems. Govvi lay curled in a fetal position, her back pressed against Com. Yes, Com was there, too, on his back, legs apart, arms stretched out for maximum heat absorption. They were all there.

Ziiza surveyed her surroundings: beach, water, trees, foothills, white-peaked mountains, and the island, maybe a thousand paddle strokes to the northwest – one wanted to say uphill. When she finally realized that the dark spot at the water's edge was not a rock, driftwood, or a seaweed clump, she felt embarrassed, ashamed. She rose on stiff, unsteady legs and walked to it. Bent and touched. No movement. She stroked its head and ears, and, as it did not move, gave its chest a whack. The creature twitched, and, it seemed to her, struggled to open its eyes. She placed her hands on its chest. Press. Release. Press. Release. Water trickled from its mouth. When it recognized the strange touch it moved its legs in an instinctive attempt to run, even while lying on its side. Ziiza stopped pressing and leaned away. "So that's it," she said with a knowing smile, "you just want to run away. Well, you've certainly earned it. Go. With our thanks and our blessing." Possibly taking this as an insult, the creature struggled to its feet, and walked unsteadily, but proudly, down the beach. When it evidently felt a comfortable distance separated them, it turned, sat, and looked alternately at the one squatting human, Ziiza, then at the pile of prone, motionless humans, then back at the squatting one.

I've got to do this right, Ziiza thought, as she watched the creature watch her. One: I can't let the children know how desperate our situation is. Heck, I can't even let myself think of it. They'll figure it out soon enough. Two: I need time. I have to think. And, at the same time, I have to act like I know what I'm doing. Which I do not. Act like I have a plan. Which I do not. I have to have everything under control. Which it is not. So, I must act. Now.

"All up. Everybody up," Ziiza shouted. Six bodies on the sand. No movement. She walked closer. "Wake up! Wake up!" She lowered her voice. "Now. Now. Time for a swim." Still no movement, although Milli groaned in disbelief when her muma's shocking announcement registered. Ziiza tickled Org's foot. "Cut it out," he shot back with a snarl-plead-snarl. She tapped Milli's leg. "Up. Now." She pushed her foot under Com's back and lifted. Tickled Govvi's bottom. Govvi swatted and missed. One by one they sat up, shook their heads, and dug sand from their eyes.

"Okay, stand up," she said. "We'll all feel better after our swim."

"Swim?" Org muttered. "She must be out of her mind."

"Mu-ma," Milli said.

"Mu-ma," Milli and Netti whined together, rolling their eyes.

"Like we need a swim with a. . .," Com muttered into his hand. "Like we haven't just been – swimming."

"I heard that, young man," Ziiza snapped.

In spite of their grumbling, they followed Ziiza across the beach and into the surf. When they were knee-deep, she said, "Wash up as best you can. When we get to a freshwater creek we'll take a real bath." She turned to Govvi, hanging back in ankle-deep water and said, "Come on, Govvi. Come on, dear." Govvi shuffled backward, turned, and ran to the beach. She stood with her back to the Sea and her muma. "Govvi! Come! Now!" Ziiza ordered.

"I can't, Muma. I'm afraid."

"Well that's why we're doing it, dear. To show the Sea that, in spite of everything, we're not afraid of it. And to wake up and clean up." Govvi stood still; she was not coming in. Ziiza softened. "Okay, dear, find a pool and splash some water on your body. Good girl."

"Yes, Muma." She did not move.

After their swim and wash-up, and after making certain they had left nothing behind, they walked south. Time for Ziiza to walk, and think, and plan, and, most importantly, she thought, get out of sight of the island, put it behind. In a few hours they came to a large drift tree, half-buried in the sand. "Sit, please," Ziiza said, indicating the bare section between the massive root clump and broken-off branches. "Thank you," she said sweetly, but with firmness of tone and a touch of exaggerated formality. "Now, if you would be kind enough to arrange yourselves by age." Except for Com, number four, who was sitting next to Org, number one, they already were. He shifted into position between Netti and Govvi.

"Popa's dream," Ziiza said, "was to move to Beaverton. And mine, too," she added quickly, positively, and somewhat truthfully. "You know. Take us, his family, to what he believed, what he was told, was a special place. So here we are. Partway to Beaverton. And left to our own resources."

"The understatement of the year," Com said. Milli laughed. It caught, and her brothers and sisters joined her, guffawing and slapping their legs.

If you only realized the half of it, my boy. But you will. Nevertheless, your brashness is a good sign, all things considered.

"The problem is," Ziiza continued, raising her hand to quiet them, "our directions are sketchy. All Popa had to go on was this; call it a riddle: 'Trace the Sea. Then let it go.' If he knew more, he didn't say. 'Don't repeat this to anyone,' he told me, 'they don't want too many people there.' After.. . . ." She swallowed and began again. "After MeTonn picked us up. . . ." Org and Milli and Com cut her off, shouting epithets at MeTonn as if he were there. Netti, Govvi, and Edu sat in silence. Ziiza wanted to shout out a few herself, but instead said evenly, "I never discussed it with MeTonn, where he was going; how could I? He was traveling south and so were we. The others in his group? I doubt if they knew where they were going. Canoes are faster than walking, and that was good enough for me. Besides, not only was he the only one who offered us a ride – although he really wanted paddlers, not passengers – he was the only one we saw, the only one who *could* have offered."

That's the problem. We're late. If we don't make Beaverton before winter. . . .

"'Trace the Sea,'" Ziiza continued. "The beach. The edge of the Sea. What we've been doing all along. On foot. By canoe." Ziiza jerked her thumb toward the water. "'Then let it go.' Perplexing. Let go of the Sea? When? Where?" She paused and looked hard at the children. "But for now our goal is clear: proceed south."

Edu slid off the trunk, raised his hand as if in school. "Muma, what is a Bea-ver-ton, anyway?"

"I can't tell you exactly," Ziiza said. "All the food you want. That's what Popa was told. A friendly community. Mild winters – that was enough to interest me. Lots of rain, though. Always green. So desirable they try to keep it quiet, limit newcomers, hope most travelers to the New Side go someplace else. It's impossible to keep it a secret, of course; we found out, didn't we? Anyway, that's what Popa told me." She patted his head. "That's the best I can do for you, Edu."

She stepped back from the tree, forced a bright smile, and resumed: "Now I would like someone to tell me what we have to be thankful for." Six jaws dropped in amazement. Six minds, maybe five, thought the same thought.

Milli broke the silence, "Thankful? After what we've been through? We could have drowned. Edu saved in the nick of time. You, Muma. Your ear. All discolored and swollen. Thankful? Thankful?"

"Yes, Milli. What do we, you, I, have to be thankful for? One thing."

"That we're alive. I guess. That's obvious."

"Good." Ziiza said, ignoring Milli's smart mouth.

"The weather could be worse," Com said with another smirk, although weaker than his previous ones. "At least it's a sunny day." Milli poked Netti in the side and snickered.

"Very good, Com. What else? Anyone?"

"That we're alive," Org mumbled, looking at his feet and repeating Milli's answer. "And stuck on this beach with . . . with nothing."

"Quite right. Quite right."

"This might be a clam beach," Edu said, brightening. "And my stomach's rumbling. I'm hungry, Muma."

"No fresh water to wash them in," Govvi said glumly. "Or drink."

"That we're alive. We're all alive," Netti said. Then quickly, "Especially Edu."

"True," Ziiza said. "And for the benefit of those who haven't thought about it, the creature, yes, that creature over there." She pointed to the creature, sniffing by the water's edge, keeping a prudent, almost disdainful, distance. "Yes, that queer one held Edu up, swam with him in the cold water, until Org and I reached him. He, she, it, whatever it is, held him in its mouth, would not let him go down. Something of a miracle, I'd say. Something to be thankful for." Eyes shifted to the creature, which had tagged after them, always in "contact," and which, by any rule of the wild, should have disappeared from their lives hours ago, yesterday in fact. The creature, as if in response to their stares, raised a forepaw, licked it like a cat (which it definitely was not), cocked its head, and stared back at them, as if to say, okay folks, what's for dinner? What's my reward for saving the boy?

With that, Ziiza extended her arms. They came to her as they had many times and hugged.

"Feeling better?" Ziiza asked. Hints of smiles. "Please sit again. Same order on the tree trunk. We're almost finished with our talk," she added quickly. They arranged themselves. "Now for some unpleasant business. We must take inventory, take stock. We lost almost everything: our sleeping robes, the shelter skins, water bags. So what else have we lost? And what have we saved?"

"Food baskets, Muma," Netti said. "Our food baskets, our pouches, and all of our food. Including Org's deer meat – that I was looking forward to roasting this evening."

"And we're hungry. Right now," Edu said as he slid off of the trunk.

"You're right, Edu," Ziiza conceded. We can continue this later." Since the canoes had left the island, the tide had flooded, turned, and was now on the ebb, leaving vast stretches of dark sand with thousands of clam holes.

"Hop to it, everyone. Let's see if the clams are good." Org and Com paired up, as did the older girls. Ziiza took the youngsters, a wary Govvi, and a hungry, but subdued, Edu. They walked softly out to the exposed sand. Ziiza dug hard and fast, with experienced hands. Govvi and Edu leaned over intently, ready to grab. Slow going. Yells from the other groups confirmed that this was far from the best of clamming beaches; these clams were deeper, or quicker, or smarter, or something. After two hours of hard scooping, Ziiza signaled for a finger count from the teams. Org and Com: three. Milli and Netti: five. Ziiza and the kids: only two. Total: ten. With no fire and no fresh water to soak them in to expel the sand, they laid them on the trunk, smashed them open with rocks, and ate them in a few minutes, raw and gritty. Org could have eaten them all himself. The creature, who did not venture out with the diggers, edged closer as they ate. They tossed the necks, which it gulped, and broken shells, which it sniffed, licked gingerly, bit, and spit out, all the while keeping its calculated distance.

"Better than nothing," Ziiza said, throwing the last shell. "Now to continue our inventory. Then we'll walk a bit, find a freshwater campsite, if we're lucky, and spend the night."

"My club slipped out of my belt," Org began. "But look at this." He held up his glistening black knife.

"Great luck," Ziiza said, clapping her hands to boost morale. The others, catching the spirit and realizing how important this bit of good fortune was, clapped with her.

"All my clothes came off," Com said. "But I don't care."

"Mine, too," Ziiza said. "As you can see." No one smiled or laughed. "Girls?" she continued. Then, not wishing to embarrass them by making them report the obvious – the three girls had each lost parts of their clothing – she backed off. "Anything useful in your waist pouches? Turn everything out. I have to know."

Milli spoke first: "I have some bone hooks. And I know how to use them." Then, realizing this was no time for sauciness, held out the small hooks and added, "But not around here."

"Wonderful, Milli. Anyone else?"

"Flints," Com said, holding out three reddish-brown stones.

"And I have a flint knapper," Org added, holding up an antler tip.

"Anything else we might use? Govvi? Edu? Netti?" Nothing. Ziiza smiled and said, "A good knife, some hooks, flints, a knapper, and some clothing. Not much. What it comes down to, I think, is this: the best we have is the summer weather coming on. And our resourcefulness."

They walked on hard sand without speaking. All except Com, who ranged ahead, fell back, disappeared into the trees, then out again. "Find us a campsite," Ziiza yelled at him as he ran along the dry, slippery sand near the tree line. "With a good water supply. But don't get too far ahead." He sprinted away.

Com found a small stream with sweet-tasting water that cut through a bank, ran onto the beach, fought hard to reach the Sea, and did not make it. "Got one," he told them, pleased that he had been allowed to do what he liked.

Org splashed up the stream and found a clearing, far enough into the trees to cut the wind. Not really a clearing, just a level space under a spruce tree's drip line, covered with a thick bed of needles. He broke off two dead, moss-covered limbs and handed them to the girls. They stripped the moss, keeping the pieces as large as possible, their sleeping "robes" for the night. Not that they would be warm, but the moss might help create the illusion of warmth. Ziiza and the others pushed and smoothed the needles to form a seven-person nest. Edu rolled on it, picking out twigs and cones, anything that felt sharp.

"Muma," he said, looking up at her, "why don't you soak your feet in the stream. We'll take care of the camp. Sure, a camp." He laughed.

Ziiza took his suggestion. She washed her feet in the stream, splashing her legs, body, arms, face, washing off grit and salt, symbolically cleansing herself of MeTonn and Hawl and the canoes and sharp paddles and sullen traveling companions. Time for a plan, she thought. Springtime or no springtime, nights on this coast are chilly at best, freezing at worst. Soon they would have to find fire (unlikely in this wet country, where lightning was rare), borrow it (also unlikely because, even while with MeTonn, they had seen no one else on land or water), or make it (they had no equipment except Com's flints and were out of practice because MeTonn had had a designated live-coal carrier). They could subsist on raw clams and mussels from the salt water; fish and crawfish from the rivers and streams; crabs, oysters, and whatever else they could catch in the estuaries; and what they found on the beach. Berries? Eventually, as spring became summer. But not now. Roots? Swamp cabbage? Not to be counted upon. Honey, seeds, nuts, grains? Possibly, but they were strangers to the New Side.

"We've got some daylight left," Ziiza said. "Spread out and look for food. Org, take Com, Govvi, and Edu to the beach. Scour it. And stay together. Milli and Netti, give the stream a try. Anything we can eat. I'll sit here under our tree; I've got some thinking to do." When they had gone, she looked through the trees at the pink evening clouds, pulled the soothing, familiar smell of needles, moss, and decaying forest loam into her nostrils, savored the lull in the wind, and thought: it could be worse. "Yes, it could be worse," she said out loud. "And it probably will be."

Milli walked upstream looking for what pools and wide spots it offered. Netti followed. Milli crawled to the edge of a cut bank and stuck her slender, delicate hand in the water. Strands of her long hair spread on the surface. She turned her head up, closed her eyes, and waited. Milli, the fisher, operated by touch. When others attempted to copy her techniques, their results were what one might expect. Even when she fished the standard ways – hooks, hand lines, poles, dip nets – she out-caught everyone by embarrassingly large margins. So she had joined her too-intelligent, too-opinionated muma, and her too-strong, too-handsome, too-lucky, elder brother as fuel for MeTonn's rage. That she was lovely to look at made it worse. The slender, gray-eyed girl-woman who caught fish by sticking her hands in the water, he had concluded, must be a sorceress. That is what the ugly man had told Hawl, when he was not ranting about Org or Ziiza. That is what he had told himself between furtive, lust-filled looks and unfulfilled dreams. Evil must be destroyed, MeTonn had concluded. And he had tried.

Water flowed past Milli's fingers. She felt a fish tail fanning slowly, then saw the fish in her mind's eye, a trout, two hand-lengths long. She stroked the tail with her fingertip, then curved it under its belly, and stroked some more, gills to tail. She closed her hand, yanked the fish, and flipped it at Netti. It sailed over her head. Netti crawled to it on hands and knees and killed it with a rock. She waited. This was her part and she knew it well. Milli slid over the bank, waded into the center of the stream, squatted, stuck her hands in the water, and closed her eyes, trying to "see" what was there – hatchlings, fry, minnows. If anyone could catch them, Milli could. If there were any to catch. She moved upstream to the next deepening – it could hardly be called a pool – and continued her routine. Again and again, until the light faded. Three small fish and nine fingerlings. Not much of a catch. But amazing, considering the circumstances. Netti joined her and they walked downstream. They lifted rocks for crawfish. Where others had to wait for the black swirls to clear, Milli did not. Eyes half-closed, her deft fingers moved quicker than the crawfish as they scooted backwards, desperately seeking new hiding places. A dozen small crawfish. Together with the fish, not much for seven. Night fell, and although Milli could continue, and would have had they been starving, it was impractical. So they returned to the tree.

The beach hunters were back with their catch. Two dead birds found on the tide line, a seagull and a cormorant, so rotten no one was interested. They set them aside. Two washed-up crabs, surprisingly good. "We didn't see a person," Edu said. "Or an animal. Or the creature, either. I wonder where it went?" No comment. "Do you mind, Muma?" He rose and walked downstream in the dark, nibbling on his fish. Where the stream left the trees and met the sand, he placed what was left of his food on a rock.

They pressed together, burrowed into the needles, and covered themselves with moss. "What do we have to be thankful for?" Ziiza asked.

"That we're alive," came the answer in a singsong, but agreeable, fashion.

"And?"

"And we're a family. And we love each other."

"And?"

"And, I don't know," Com said after no one else said anything. "What do you want us to say?"

"I'm thankful it's not raining," Ziiza said. Scattered weak laughs in the dark. But enough. She squirmed around, felt for each child, kissed, and said good night, six times. Then she sat back against the tree, drew up her knees, and, stroking Edu's head, thought and sang her way to sleep.

4

Govvi's Fire

WHEN EVERYONE was awake, Ziiza announced, "No traveling today."

"Why?" Org said. "I'm ready to go, ready to get out of this place."

"It gives me the creeps," Netti added.

"Of all the things we lost in our liquid adventure," Ziiza continued, giving their comments only a flick of an eye, "what was the most important; what do we need most?"

"'Liquid adventure!'" Milli snapped. "This is no time to be funny, Muma. I'd hardly call attempted murder by that broken-jawed madman an 'adventure.'"

"Quite right, dear," Ziiza responded. "Sorry for my poor word choice. Sorry for underestimating you. You're tough and I'm proud of you. Now Edu," she said, shifting the subject, "you checked on the creature? Is it still on the beach? Did it take the food you left?"

"The food's gone, Muma," Edu said. "But it could have been taken by a bird, animal, anything. And I didn't see the creature."

"Okay," Ziiza continued, "I didn't sleep well last night. And not just because I was cold, and, well, cold. I was thinking, thinking about yesterday. That creature that seems to have attached itself to us – we'll know for certain when we begin walking – may have saved more lives than Edu's, miraculous as that was."

"Huh?" Com said.

"It may have saved all of us. Let me explain. I don't think MeTonn threw us overboard in a moment of rage because I picked the creature out of the water. I think he and Hawl had it planned. He knew we were reaching the end of the islands and the sheltered water. He was going to paddle offshore, far out to Sea, *then* throw us overboard. It happened too smoothly, too silently; it was all set up. Very unlikely *any* of us would have survived out there. We would have drowned. Vanished. It *was* attempted murder, Milli. That's my belief, anyway. Had that creature not run along the beach and paddled after us. Had I not picked it up. Had MeTonn not become enraged at that very moment. . . . Well, you see. A mile out, two miles out, in that cold water. Think of it. We've been given second lives, children. Let's make the most of them."

Each reacted to Ziiza's statement in his or her own way: Org and Milli with barely suppressed rage; Netti and Edu with shivers and arm bumps; Govvi with grim resolve; Com with a shrug, he was ready for another adventure.

"As I said, we won't be walking today. We have something more important to do: make fire. The sun is out, but it could start raining anytime. And last for who knows how long. This is a break and we have to take advantage of it. I know we need other things, but fire is our priority. We must all learn and practice, but one of us must become an expert, the fire builder. So we're all going to try. Call it a contest. Who will it be?"

"Excuse me, Muma," Milli said. "Aren't you forgetting something? Like, we're hungry. And that you know how to do it. We've seen you. Many times. So why don't you just make us a fire? And we'll search for food."

"First, Milli," Ziiza said, "I'm as hungry as you are. When the tide goes out, we'll take a break, and hope this stretch of beach is better than the last one. Second, it isn't so simple. To begin with, I'm out of practice. You know who did it before. While we were with the flotilla, we borrowed. And I've no equipment. What I'm getting at is this: what if MeTonn had hit me harder with his paddle? Knocked me out and I had drowned? Creature or no creature. Or he had killed me outright?" She pulled her hair back and showed them her ear. "What if I hadn't made it? And you children had? Or some of you did and some didn't? See what I mean? You've all seen fires made. In various ways. And you've all tried, from time to time. But are any of you proficient? No. Because you've never had to. You've always had someone to do it for you. This contest requires a winner. No prize for best effort. So I'll begin with you, Org. How will you do it?"

"I have my knife. I don't know. I'll have to think about it."

"Girls?" Ziiza addressed the two older girls, knowing they would respond together.

"I saw a woman with a stick. Way back," Milli said.

"Yes, I remember," Netti added. "She rubbed it between her hands, real fast."

Milli: "Then it began to smoke. Looked easy."

"Sounds good to me," Ziiza said. "Why don't you two team up, as if I had to suggest. Okay Com, you're next. How will you do it? And Com, if I have to remind you, this is serious."

"Easy," Com said, with a grin. "I'll use my flints and Org's knife. I'll strike and Org can blow. We'll have one going in minutes."

31

"Why don't you two find a spot and get to it. Govvi, any ideas?"

"I can make one," Govvi said evenly. "But it will take time." She raised her head and scanned the trees around their nest as if calculating each one's potential. "Maybe all day, Muma. Maybe more than a day. But I can do it. One thing. I'll need to use Org's knife. Not for long. Just a bit."

"That's it?" Ziiza said.

"Yes. I just need time."

Ziiza was taken aback by Govvi's reply, her self-confidence, her turnabout from yesterday's frightened, shaken child. She opened her mouth to say something, then changed her mind. Wasn't this what she had asked for? So what if it came from the one she least expected it from. "Edu," she said, "how about you?"

"I don't know, Muma. How about you?"

"Edu, this is no time for questions. We need answers. We need fire and a dependable person to make it. We need it for cooking. We need it for warmth. And we need it for protection."

"Protection? From what?" Netti said, turning around.

"Aside from the obvious," Ziiza said, "which you know very well, we can talk about it later. Fire first. Fire now. Edu, I've got an idea. You and I can work together. We'll be the support team, the supply team. Of course we'll try ourselves. But I like support. So Org and Com will strike flints. Milli and Netti will twirl a stick. And Govvi will try whatever she has in mind."

"Fine," Edu said, pinching off his next question.

Org motioned to Com and they moved under another tree. Click, click, click. Stone on stone. Netti and Milli walked back and forth, looking for something to use as a fire stick. Govvi moved around to the back side of their shelter tree and sat thinking. When the others were occupied, Ziiza said, "Edu, I suspect they've forgotten one thing. Can you guess what it is?"

"What is it?"

"Eee-yikes, Edu," Ziiza screamed. "Don't answer me with another question. Fire-building is a meticulous process. Everything has to be perfect: out of the wind, out of the rain, dry materials, and the builder has to know what he or she is doing. If anything is lacking, or just a bit off, it doesn't matter what you do, it isn't going to work. What the rest will need, whatever method they use, is tinder. Perfectly dry tinder. That'll be our job. Building a fire is going to be harder than any of them realizes. With the possible exception of one. But it's so important we're going to stay here until we do it."

Ziiza walked to a cedar near the stream. "Over here, Edu," she said. "Kneel down." She grasped a hanging strand of bark, passed it to Edu, and told him, "Pull away and jerk it loose."

"Now what?"

"Turn it over to the inside. Pick it apart in thin strands." He began. "Thank goodness it's a nice day. Otherwise, impossible." Ziiza rolled the strands, then twisted and crushed them between her fingers until she had a fluffy pile. She set it on a rock and placed a cross of sticks on it so it would not blow away. "Now, let's make some more," she said.

Com clicked halfheartedly over a small pile of forest floor twigs, bloody nicks on his hands. "Any luck?" Ziiza said.

"Not even a spark," Com said. "Whoever said you could start a fire with flints? Whoever said these *were* flints? Org lay on his back, staring at the sky and clouds through the tree limbs. He did not speak.

"Keep trying, boys." She walked to Milli and Netti. "How's it going?"

They, too, had a pile of twigs. And a punky cedar limb on the ground. And an arm-length shaft of alder. Milli spun it vigorously, working her hands down the slender shaft, keeping the pressure on. She had even worn a small hole in the cedar. "A suggestion," Ziiza said. "You might try a dry cedar stick for friction instead of alder."

"But alder is stronger," Netti said.

"Just a suggestion."

"How do you know, anyway?"

"I don't. And your starter twigs should be smaller."

"Come on, Netti," Milli said. "Do what she says. We're not getting anywhere this way.

Govvi had not moved. "Doing?" Ziiza asked.

"Thinking. Or trying to. Making a list in my head. A plan."

Govvi called to Com, who was by then chipping aimlessly, more for noise effect than expected result. "Can I borrow the knife now?" He tossed it to her.

On hearing the chipping stop, Milli stopped twirling and said, "Whew. I'm going fishing. Or crawfish catching. Or something. Come on, Net." Ziiza did not stop them.

"And Org," Govvi continued, "I need a strip of hide, since you're the only one with anything to spare. Just a thin strip, as long as you can make it." She held up her little finger. "This thick." She tossed his knife back to him.

When she had her strip and the knife again, Govvi walked the forest till she found an arm's length vine maple limb – strong, springy, and green – and cut it off. Two hours later, with the sun high, she had arranged before her in a straight line: two cedar boards smoothed with the knife, a split cedar shaft with the edges knocked off, the vine maple limb, Org's strip of hide, a pile of twigs that snapped when she broke them, and two handfuls of the finest forest fuzz she could gather.

The tide fell, the beach widened, and Ziiza, after a lack-of-progress report from all parties, took the other children clamming. Leaving her equipment in line, Govvi searched again, this time on tiptoe, as if the quieter she walked, the dryer the tinder she would find. Of course she would not find perfectly dry tinder in this heavy forest so close to the moist salt air. And Ziiza and Edu's pile was hours, if not days, away from being dry enough. She crawled into the rotted center of a ancient blow-down and clawed out chunks of decayed fiber. This was as good as she was likely to find.

After reviewing her plan – Govvi's way – she sharpened both ends of the split cedar shaft and gouged mating holes in the boards. She tied the hide strip to one end of the vine maple limb, making a crude bow. Instead of pulling it taut and tying it off, she looped it around the shaft and held the end with her hand.

It took many tries, many minutes, to control the drill, get it rotating properly; simply adjusting the bow string was a maddeningly slow learn. "Stay away. Don't look over my shoulder. Don't ask questions. I'll be okay," she said through her teeth. "Stay away. Dig lots of clams."

Mid-day passed into afternoon. The clam diggers returned with double yesterday's take, having spent double the time. "Nothing yet," Govvi said. "But I'm trying. And learning. No hint of fire, though."

The drill board's hole blackened and grew warm to her touch. Drill ends blunted. Govvi re-pointed them. She drew the bow back and forth carefully, praying the hide did not break. One knot, maybe two, and it would be useless. Org had only so much clothing. Milli and Netti, even less. Her muma, the young boys, and herself: nothing. Little by little she varied her technique – without knowing exactly what she was trying for, or how close, or how far, she was from success. She varied the point angles, moved the friction hole closer to the edge, carved a small collection notch for hot powder. Pressed harder, pressed lighter on the spindle block. No smoke. Something was wrong. An element missing. A secret passed from popa to son? Muma to daughter? Master fire builder to apprentice? A fire priest's blessing? She hunched over her work.

"Why don't you stop for a moment, Govvi," Ziiza said. "Take a rest."

"No."

"Walk over to the stream. Drink some water. Your knees, your arms, they must be aching."

"I'm so close," Govvi said. "So close." Milli gave her a clam piece. She took it and chewed. "Everything should be working," she said, clam juice running down her chin. "I feel the friction, feel it starting to take hold, then the bowstring stretches, slips, comes loose, or something."

34

Govvi kept at it until it was too dark to see. Before the family bedded down under the tree she accepted some clam chunks, together with cupped handfuls of water, but did not join them. She lay down, pulled her equipment under her, and slept curled around what should have been her new fire.

Next morning, Edu slipped from his muma's arm and peered around the tree. Govvi was already working. "Can I watch?" he whispered.

"Smell this," Govvi said. He crept around, bent over, and sniffed the sharp odor of smoldering cedar. "The drill tip smokes sometimes. I guess that's how it's supposed to work." Edu knelt beside her. "Isn't that the most wonderful smell," she said. "A baby fire about to be born."

Poor as her sleep had been, Govvi had woken clear-headed. She worked relaxed, did not force the bow; that was important. Slowly, easily, gradually, she increased pressure and speed. She was relaxed enough to let Edu look on, unusual for her, the quiet, independent one. The drill produced heat, smoke, and an accumulation of black dust in the groove.

Later, at Ziiza's urging – command – the teams made halfhearted attempts to continue. But the contest was over and everyone knew it. Either Govvi made fire her way, or it would fall to Ziiza, and she did not want that. There were lessons to be learned.

They formed support groups. Milli and Netti fed her crawfish and clams. Org and Com tramped the forest, searching for replacement materials. Ziiza and Edu waved finger pinches of tinder in the air, trying to speed up the drying. Govvi's technique improved to where she could produce tiny red coals almost every time. She moved around the tree to keep out of direct sunlight, the better to see the emerging coals. She knew now what the next great step must be – but could not take it. Without perfectly dry, properly fine tinder it did not matter how deft she was at producing smoke or coals. They had to be tipped onto something that caught. And breathed to life.

It took one more day. Ziiza and Edu found dry tinder, strangely *on*, not *in*, Govvi's huge blow-down. A lucky find in an always-damp forest. Inner bark shreds, dry enough to catch a coal, bloom into flame, and ignite Govvi's pile of fuzz, twigs, needles, and cones. The family hunkered around her to block the breeze. The tinder caught, burst into flame. They leapt with joy. They ran through the forest, cracking off dead limbs, smashing them against trunks. They built it higher and higher, till it licked the green branches. All in a mad fervor to keep it alive – forgetting that she could do it again. They let it die down, and, after a bountiful tide, ate roasted clams and burned fingerlings. And crawfish, steamed in moss. Com joked about deer meat and no one scolded him. Did not even get a sour look from Milli. They built the fire high again, stared into it, hugged it, far into the night, entranced, as if they had never seen fire before. And in a way they had not, not like this one, created with their own hands – yes, they had all contributed to Govvi's fire – out of what the forest had given them, a strip of hide, and a stone knife.

* * *

"Slow it down, Org," Ziiza yelled from the back of the line, "you're walking too fast. Pass it on, kids, if he doesn't hear me."

"Slow down. Slow down, Org," Netti picked it up, "we can't keep up with you."

Only when Milli ran ahead, shouting, did he stop and give her his pained, disgusted look. With his long legs and powerful build, a stroll for him was a walk, run, walk, run-to-catch-up for the others. Com the beach bug ran free – with Ziiza's encouragement, as if that were necessary – streaking ahead, zigzagging across the sand and into the trees, then running back at full speed to report his discoveries. Org, the straight-ahead trail breaker, planted each foot as if every step broke a barrier: hard-packed sand, foot-sliding dry sand, or the slimy, green-black seaweed that marked the high water line. A way back he had climbed up, over, and through the branches of a washed-up tree. Just for the challenge. Up and onto the trunk. Broke off a limb – not too long dead. Crack. Splinter. Crack. And another. Until he had created a triumphal opening. He threw his head back and bellowed at the sky, thrilled by it. Breaking through. Beating the tree. To relieve the accumulated boredom. Day after day of beach walking. When Ziiza and the children reached it, they simply walked around.

And yes, the creature was with them. Visibly, it seemed to be recovering from its sad state on the island. Not that it was gaining weight. As with the people, walking all day precluded that. Its pattern was somewhat like theirs: full of energy in the morning – it often ranged ahead of Com or fell behind Ziiza – resting on the warmer dry sand during mid-day breaks, then trotting along at their pace in the afternoons. Always the same position, walking along the water line on the hard sand, hanging behind Ziiza and Edu, as if calculated to tease; they could not see the creature, but it could eye them. Was it protection? If it hunted, or scavenged, or dug, or dove for food, no one saw it doing so. Edu collected scraps, and each night set them on a rock a good distance from camp. Each morning they were gone. But again, he could not tell if the creature had taken them. Although it never allowed anyone to advance on it, let alone touch it, it had earned a place with them, that was certain. And, if the entertainment it provided, the laughter it provoked – chasing shore birds, jumping wavelets, and rolling on every dead, foul thing it found – was any indication, it continued to earn it.

It was seven days since their "liquid adventure," and they still had no weapons except Org's knife, and the smooth rocks he flipped from hand to hand as he walked the beach, looking for crab shells or kelp bulbs to throw at, anything that would break. And Govvi's fire. Because of their vulnerability, Ziiza had insisted on an order of march, as she called it, in order of age: Org leading, she trailing, the others in between, closely spaced to create the illusion of a creature-beast-animal plodding along, instead of seven vulnerable humans.

Com's campsite choice had been made for him. A small river blocked their way, flowing backwards, as it were, the flood tide rushing in. It was to be a leisurely camp, since they had plenty of daylight left and tomorrow's crossing would not be until the mid-morning low. He led them upriver beyond a beach-grass-covered rise. If the weather held, as it had all week, this could be their best camp yet. "No crawfish or small fry for me," Milli announced after they had fashioned their nest and Govvi had built her fire. "I'm going crabbing in the river. Come on, Netti."

"You girls be careful." Ziiza cautioned. "The tide's coming in strong."

"Yes, Muma."

Their camp routine: Milli and Netti fished the nearby rivers and streams for whatever was in; Org, Com, and Edu dug clams; Govvi started the fire, tended it, and roasted the catch. Ziiza rested and looked after her foot. Clamming was poor, but the crabs were so plentiful and large the girls soon had a record number. Together with yesterday's leftovers, the beach travelers had their best meal since the deer feast.

While eating, Ziiza announced, "Time for another contest everybody. Pay attention. After fire, the best weapon I can think of is a spear. Anyone have a better idea?"

"Yeah," Org said, "a good club with a rock on the end. Better yet, a club with a sharp rock on the end. An axe. And this." He tossed a rock in the air, the one he had been carrying for days, a pock-marked piece of black basalt, and deftly caught it behind his back.

"Certainly," Ziiza replied, "But I was thinking. . . ." She stopped, and said, "Edu, did you put any food out for the creature?"

"Yes, Muma. Just like every night."

"Good." She continued: "I was thinking of a weapon we could all use. In addition to your rocks and clubs and whatever else. Those are a little beyond some of us. And, you must admit, when you throw a rock, that's it. If you miss, or it doesn't do the job." She held up her hand. "I know, Org. I know. You never miss." She smiled at him. "Okay, people. We need shafts. We'll split into two groups," Ziiza continued. "Org, you take Milli and Netti. Cut about two dozen long ones. Let's see," she scanned them, "about as big around as this." She put thumb to forefinger and made a circle. We want them fresh-cut, straight, and strong. A little whippy. Nothing brittle, nothing found on the ground. Spears. And walking sticks. And something I'll explain later. We've waited too long to do this, but this is the first place we've come to with small trees. Govvi, you stay and tend the fire." She sat. "Okay, Edu and Com, come with me."

"Our task," she told the boys, "will be easy or hard, depending upon how lucky we are. But either way, it's sure to be messy. We're going after our secret weapon, pitch, the amber-colored sticky stuff that oozes out of the big trees."

"Oh, fun," Com said.

They walked upstream and into the tidal flood plain to an inlet stream choked with skunk cabbage growing in the ankle-deep muck. The large, yellow flowers that had signaled the end of winter a few months before were wilted and brown, but the leaves were still broad and thick. They pulled the plants out by the roots and stripped off the leaves.

They made their way to an ancient spruce growing at the edge of the beach, which Ziiza had noticed when they passed. Most of its west-facing limbs were missing, blown off in winter storms over the past hundred years or more. It was so out of balance it was sure to topple in the next one. Or the next. Or the next. But for the moment it stood, proudly supported by its stout base. Because of its wounds and exposure to the springtime sun, rivulets of golden pitch ran down its rough cracked bark and puddled on the ground. They piled as much on the cabbage leaves as they could carry. Of course the boys had to give it the stickiness test. By the time they reached the fire their fingers were stuck together in a mass of pitch, dirt, needles, and sand. "Okay, you two," Ziiza said, "don't touch your bodies."

When the pole gatherers returned they bent each one against a tree, testing for strength and suppleness. Many broke, leaving about a dozen. "Pick the one you like," Ziiza said. "Org, cut them a hand longer than each person's height. Otherwise they won't fly straight. How is your knife holding up?"

"Getting dull," Org said. "I'm going to have to flake the edge soon. Better yet, replace it, if I can find some of this black rock. It can't last forever."

"Obsidian," Govvi put in.

"How'd you know that?" Edu asked.

Ignoring his question, Govvi stirred the fire and pushed a pile of coals together. Blew on them. Org whittled seven spear points. On Ziiza's instructions he split three of the remaining shafts, two hand lengths in from the end. Ziiza pried them apart with a stick. "Now we need some springy limbs and strands of cedar bark. Off you go." Com and Edu bounded away. Milli and Netti followed, walking and talking. "What is she up to now?" While they were looking, Ziiza pushed the cabbage leaves close to the coals to soften the pitch, taking care it did not catch fire. Org and Govvi flame-hardened the spear tips. Not that it did much good. Not that it actually made them harder or sharper. But they looked good, looked lethal, looked and felt like real weapons. Pointed walking sticks, really.

Ziiza wedged the limbs into the split ends and handed one to each girl. "Okay, girls, I want you to weave the cedar bark in and out and around, form a basket to hold the pitch." Netti finished first. When Milli and Govvi finished, Ziiza examined them. Finding them wanting in strength and uniformity, she undid them, and, trying not to hurt their feelings, handed them to Netti. "Here, you seem to have the knack," she said.

Ziiza gave the first one Netti finished to Milli, and said, "Roll the basket in pitch. All it can hold. Don't let it catch fire." As Milli rolled and daubed, Ziiza pulled the leaves away and threw them in the fire, where they flared up with the sweet, stinking smell of pitch and burning leaves. "I'd like more than three of these pitch baskets," she said, "but they're probably all we can carry, along with spears and food. Next time the boys will do it. I want everyone to learn."

Soon after midnight the stretch of good weather ended abruptly. Ziiza woke to the sound of rising wind. Rain slammed into their shelter tree. The branches shed it at first, and Ziiza nodded off. But soon the cold water ran down the trunk, down her back, and underneath. Then through the branches; they could only shed so much. Ziiza groaned and pulled Govvi closer. Robes. We need robes. Not to mention shelter. She reached for Edu, touched something strange, and jerked her hand away. "Oh! What?" She patted and felt. Slid her hand to a head, over ears, along a short-haired snout, to a cold nose. So, she thought, her surprise now under control as she continued to feel and pat – a back, a leg, a rough paw, then Edu. Your final step, creature. The big one. She poked her own wet middle as a point of reference in the dark. Then poked the creature. Then Edu. Back over to Govvi. She drew a breath through her nose and expelled, "Uh-oh," out loud; she did not care if she woke them. No one moved or spoke. She chuckled. Sniffed her fingers. "If you smell this bad in a rainstorm, what are you like in the hot sun? Oh, well, I should have expected. I guess. And welcome. I guess. Yes, truly." She patted the sopping fur then withdrew her hand, resigned to a cold, wet night. The head rose, nose pressing against her hand, twisting to keep contact. She slid her finger under its jaw and stroked. The creature relaxed and settled back, dropping its head, taking her hand down with it. She bent its ears and ran her fingers over its eyes and onto its head. Under its jaw again. Caressed with a finger. A warm tongue licked back. "Well, I'll be," Ziiza said, with the rain running down her face.

5

Rogue Wave

ZIIZA SAT under the shelter tree, still trying to sleep. "The creature likes me, Muma." Edu said. "He lay down next to me. Just after it started to rain. Pressed close. Stuck his nose under my arm. That woke me up. But I didn't say anything. He stayed with me all night long."

I know, Edu, he, it, woke me up, too.

The creature sat next to the pile of black slush and half-burnt sticks that had been last night's fire. Sat. And looked. Looked as if it did not consider for a moment that its self-invitation into their lives would be anything less than welcome. Edu walked to it and rubbed its head against the lay of its hair. "This is the creature that saved my life," he said proudly. Ziiza cracked her eyes, smiled weakly, and closed them.

How do you know it's a he, Edu?" Netti quipped, jumping up and down, shaking off what wetness she could, then stripping the water from her hair. "They have girl creatures, too."

"You could take a look," Milli said with a snicker.

"I guess I will," Netti replied, picking up on the challenge. But when she approached the creature it moved away. Did not run, just moved enough to keep its distance, keep its space. After making its point, that Netti was not going to touch it, it circled around and sat next to Edu. "What do you make of that?" Netti said. "And all the clam scraps I've saved for it. Ungrateful little. . . . Tonight I'll give it my clam shells. Yup. Clam shells for that one."

By this time all were awake and doing their best to get warm and dry: jumping, rubbing, slapping themselves. With varying degrees of waking up comprehension, they faced the creature and stared. Ziiza was the last to stand. She bent forward and shook her hair. Taking that as a cue the creature shook, too, showering everyone and ending with a massive shiver, starting at its head, working along its body, then, with a vigorous hip shake, sending its tail into whirling vibrations. "Eh, yuck," Govvi said, backing away. Ziiza blinked, rubbed her eyes, worked her jaw, and cleared her throat. She took a small step on the spruce needles. She stood still. Then another cautious step. Reaching the creature, she bent down and pulled its head against her leg. She scratched lightly as she assessed the morning. "I guess we're a family of eight, now," she said. "But it's not like we have another mouth to feed." No reaction from the children. "That was supposed to be a joke." Silence and blank stares from all but Edu, who smiled. "Oh, you're jealous," she continued. "Well, don't be."

"Why just you and Edu?" Com whined, speaking for the rest.

"Yes, Muma, why?" echoed Milli.

"I can't say. I don't know. But I have the distinct feeling, as I've indicated before, that this ragged fellow is one smart creature." That did not satisfy them, but they did not pursue it. "Okay, let's pack up and get out of this miserable place. I have a treat. This is game day."

"Another contest, I suppose," Org said glumly.

"Details later, when we're down the beach a ways. Let's go."

Although the rain had stopped, the sky remained overcast, the wind fresh. Org and the older girls smashed open some clams, which they nibbled raw as they walked. The creature stuck to its routine, lagging behind, zigzagging from surf to trees, then running up to, but not quite passing, Ziiza and Edu. The difference today: it stayed closer to the two, allowing occasional pats, while gobbling up sand-covered clam scraps tossed by those walking ahead. Ziiza was excited and pleased. She turned the game she was planning to spring on the children over in her mind, something she hoped would relieve the boredom of walking all day, reduce their bickering, and boost everyone's morale, including her own. Midday passed. The sky had not changed. Com swung back from his exploration. Before he could make his report, Ziiza said, "I want a nice place to take a break, Com, someplace where we can talk and think. Yes, think."

"No streams ahead," Com replied, "if that's what you mean. But there's a dead sea lion washed up. We can sit there, poke at it, see if it's good to eat. It sort of smells okay."

"That will have to do," she said resignedly. "Looks like the rain will be back by nightfall. Tough on fires, eh Govvi?" Then, giving Com a big smile, she said, "And by the way, I love how you pump that spear when you run. It looks so manly. Why don't you jog up the beach and signal us from the sea lion." Com sped away.

When they reached him, Com was bashing the dead animal's jaw with a rock. Crack! Crack! "I need a tooth for a souvenir," he said. Crack! No luck. The carcass was not old enough; the jawbone would not break.

"Org," Ziiza said, "if you will cut some blubber strips and pass them around, I'll begin. First off, I'm so proud of you. All of you. I want you to know that. We've made good progress."

I hope. Do they believe? Do I believe?

Ziiza plopped down on the sand and drew in her feet. She sat silent for a minute, absentmindedly massaging her foot, which was beginning to hurt earlier each walking day. And they had a whole summer of walking ahead of them. Hard walking if they were to reach Beaverton before winter. Which they absolutely had to do. She drew in a long breath, forced a smile, and looked around. "Your spears. They're good walking sticks, yes? They're not great weapons, I know. But better than nothing. You don't mind carrying them? Not a bother?" Positive murmurs and nods. "Org, you don't mind carrying the pitch baskets?"

"No trouble at all," he said, not knowing what she was up to and not wishing to show any sign of weakness. They were a bother.

"We have fire," Ziiza continued, nodding at Govvi. "What a blessing. And so far, enough to eat. Now sea lion meat and blubber. If we only had a way to render it and carry the oil. Of course we need more practice with our spears and pitch baskets. We've been lucky so far; no sign of the sita, no bear tracks, no strange animals and nothing dangerous from the Sea. We'll get to that. So let's have some fun. Here it is. As we walk this afternoon I would like each of you to think of something special to find or make. A useful tool, say. Or anything that strikes you as pretty. The only rules: they have to be small enough to carry, and each of us – yes, I think I'll try, too – has to have something different. Personal objects. Think about them. Talk about them. One more thing. All I'm asking for is a start. It need not be perfect on the first try. You can change your minds. Start over as many times as you like. Improve and refine." Ziiza stood, clapped her hands and said, "Let's do it!"

"We have to?" Govvi whined.

"Not really, Govvi. But yes. It's supposed to be challenging, interesting, and fun. Think about it."

Nothing more was said. When they had satisfied their hunger and the creature's sides were bulging, and they had slung as many strips of blubber and meat over their shoulders as they could carry, they began the afternoon march.

Late in the day, Com came racing back. "Trouble ahead, Muma," he reported breathlessly. "There's a river. Not a stream, either. A pretty big river. And on the other side. That cloud hanging over the beach. See that?" He pointed south. "Well, it's not a cloud; it's a mountain."

"A headland?" Ziiza said.

"If that's what you call it. And it drops straight into the Sea."

"Did you find a feeder creek? Any fresh water?"

"I didn't have time to look. I thought you'd like to know."

"You've done well," Ziiza said. "Now run ahead and find a campsite with water. And the best shelter you can locate. Tonight could be just as wet as last. And scout the river for crossings. And Com," she added as he sprinted away, as much for the others' benefit as for him, "have you thought about your object?"

That's the idea, give them something small to think about. Let me worry about the obstacles.

"Yes," he said. "It's a. . . ." But by then he was too far away.

When they reached the river, Com was waiting. Ziiza immediately concluded that crossing would not be a problem; just a matter of waiting for a low tide. Or, if necessary, a low, low. The river mouth was choked by a fan-shaped sandbar pushing far into the Sea; she could tell by the wave patterns as they rolled in.

The headland, however, was formidable. Near-straight walls of black rock rose directly out of the river. High above, they rounded, curving inward, holding patches of green and brown. Moss? Grass? Dry stalks? Too high to tell. Above that the lump rose into gray clouds, which broke open, but not enough to reveal the top, and closed in again. How tall, how long, how far inland it went, Ziiza could not tell. Looking back to the north, the flat, boring beach looked positively inviting. Was this the end of it? Was the headland mountain just that, a headland, something that could with planning and effort and luck be surmounted? Then more beach walking? Or had the coastline changed entirely?

Com had selected a campsite on a small stream a hundred paces inland. When they reached it, Ziiza was disappointed. Shelter was minimal, only a small grove of shore pine, minimum protection from wind and rain. But seeking another, walking back into the broad estuary full of bogs and marshes was more than she had strength or patience for. Besides, her foot had endured enough for one day. Govvi had a hard time with the fire, but got one going with her last handful of dry tinder. "I'm guessing," Ziiza said to her after the fire was burning, "that you've already decided on your object. You'll keep upgrading your fire kit, replacing each part with a better one, making it easier to use."

"You would be wrong," Govvi replied in her precise, clipped speech.

"Oh. And what would it be, then?"

"I'll make it when I find what I want. Then I'll show you."

"Oh."

Ziiza thought the camp was not only disappointing, it was terrible. Sand, wind, dripping clouds, and precious little shelter from the small trees portended a bad night. Plus, the headland, looming across the river, cast a wet-rock chill over them. The sea lion blubber, however, toasted on sticks, was delicious, a welcome change. Milli caught four crabs at the edge of the channel. She also hooked some sculpins, which no one would eat except Org, who bit off the heads, spines, and fins, and swallowed them whole. "Yuk, Org! Yuk!" Milli said. "I caught them to show I could. But I'd never eat them. Nobody should eat them. They're revolting." She and Netti covered their eyes in disgust. Edu and Com squirmed, giggled, and poked each other.

Their camping and sleeping routine was settled and refined. Rotating keepers were assigned to the fire. But, as MeTonn had complained, keepers sometimes fall asleep. Or, if they were diligent, their replacements would not wake up when shaken. Few could stay awake through a double watch. Or triple. All slept with their spears by their sides. Org and Com fancied themselves as the family's warrior-protectors, and never loosened their grips. Although not as formidable as real stone-tipped weapons, they gave each traveler a feeling of security and power. And a third leg during river crossings. The pitch baskets – Edu called them fire spears – were stuck in the sand, at the ready.

Unless totally exhausted, Ziiza habitually took an hour or more to get to sleep. The creature, confident of its status now, mostly wet, whatever the weather, always stinking, but always warm, lay between Ziiza and Edu. She enjoyed watching the fire, drew strength from it as well as warmth, strength for the next day's trial. Almost more strength than from sleep itself. Many nights she sat against a tree. Sometimes she sang the children to sleep. Sometimes she sang herself to sleep.

"I'm going to name him Dg, Muma," Edu said, patting the creature.

"What!" Ziiza shouted. Then, in a softer voice, as if she could erase the outburst, "I thought you were asleep."

"No, Muma, I was thinking. And listening to you sing."

"How on earth did you come up with a name like that?"

"I tried it out on him. I called, 'Here, Dg. Come on, Dg.' He didn't really come, but he looked pleased. Looked like he liked his name. I mean, that's how he looked to me."

"You're an amazing child," Ziiza said, reaching over the newly-named 'Dg' and smoothing Edu's cheek. "An amazing, dear child."

Ziiza's observations were correct. Soon after Edu's naming announcement the light wind grew into a steady breeze, then into a gale, whipping beach grass, shaking the small trees. Then it rained. Hard. Hard, driving rain, pounding the headland, slanting across the river, whipping over the dunes. Nothing to do but scrunch closer, pull their scanty garments over their heads

– those who had them – and wrap them around their shoulders. Wait out the night.

With the faintest hint of morning they rose, went through the routine of trying to shake and rub themselves warm, and left what would not have been a pleasant campsite in the best of weather. Feeling for their belongings, they gathered up spears, pitch baskets, food, and personals, and walked slowly downriver, through the grass, over the dunes, and onto the beach. The tide? Judging from yesterday it should be ebbing, near low. But it was too early to tell by sight. So Ziiza's family, now eight in number, stood, then sat, knelt, or squatted, not much worse off than under the trees, as the day tweaked open, minute by minute.

Edu knelt with an arm around a passive Dg, his enthusiasm as cold and wet as their drowned campfire. As it lightened, the rain did not let up, so it took well over an hour for Ziiza to gauge the crossing. It looked good, as far as she could tell. "Org," she said, "test the water, will you."

"But that's my job," Com said in a hurt voice.

"I know, dear, but Org's legs are so much longer. It's best." And to Org: "I'll hold the pitch baskets. Make sure you take your spear for balance. No heroics. Come back if the water is over your knees or running too fast. This is the ebb, you know. Very dangerous." He moved away, splashing through the water. "We can wait until it's safe," she followed. "All day if necessary." Org kept going.

In a few minutes he was back. "Give it an hour," he said. "Two at most. Then I think we can make it."

As the gray day opened, Org kept testing, each time reporting favorably. Finally Ziiza, anxious to get across, agreed. "Let's try it," she said. "I'll carry Govvi. Org, you carry Edu."

"What about Dg?" Edu said. "Who'll carry Dg?"

"What?" Com said.

"That's his name. Dg. I gave it to him last night."

"Little brother," Com said, "that's the stupidest name I ever heard of."

"Real-ly," Govvi added.

"Enough of that," Ziiza broke in. "We've got a crossing to make."

Edu wasn't fazed. "Well, that's his name. And he likes it. And I like it, too."

It was a good bet. They crossed easily, even though Org had to carry both Edu and the ex-creature, Dg. The deepest part was a slot where the water washed through, knee height to Org. After depositing the two, he stood in the middle like a secure post and handed everyone across. When they were "safe," Ziiza spoke her mind. "We have to choose: Travel upstream until the hills aren't so steep, over and through the forest, then down to the beach again. If there is a beach again. We have no idea how high it is, or how far inland it extends. But we do know the forest will be thick, difficult to get through. Could take a week or more. Or we can try to climb the head from here, over the tops of the cliffs. Or, our third choice, wait and see if the slack, which is upon us, opens up a passable strip at the bottom of the cliff. Your thoughts?"

"I'd try for the strip," Com said, evidently speaking for all, since no one else said anything. They had climbed tree-and-brush-covered outcroppings before, but nothing this large, this tall, with its peaks hidden in the clouds. A Sea-level run-for-it was by far the easiest. If it worked.

As they approached the headland, not only was it vertical, its looming black mass hung out and over the beach, undercut by thousands of years of wave action. Water dripped off overhanging lips and spattered on the sand.

Org went first, with Com hanging onto his belt. Order of march was suspended as they pressed together, making their way cautiously, but as quickly as possible, through ankle-deep water. They rounded a corner and found themselves in a cove with exposed sand. The hostile odor of wet rock, damp vegetation, bird droppings, and salt spray combined to overwhelm their noses. The rain had let up, but not by much. Capped by a dark sky, it still felt as if they were walking in a cave. The edge of the Sea showed them its unfriendly face.

Rounding the next outthrust, this one slanting back from the Sea, Com yelled, "Look out! A wave! A big. . . ."

There had been waves: scattered whitecaps, gentle swells, petering out on the sand, tumbling over, slapping against rock walls. But this one. It grew higher and higher, as if pumped from the depths, a monster wave, a never-cresting rogue. Ziiza dropped Dg and clung to Edu. "Tight against the wall," she screamed, frantically grabbing at the girls. Org did the same. A chest-high wall of water slammed into the cliff with a resounding thunk, shot up in a white-green sheet, and fell away. The backwash sucked at them. Ziiza drove her spear into the sand, hoping the others would do the same, pressed her back against the cliff, and slid into a sitting position, holding onto Milli. She dug in her heels and fought the water's terrible strength. Count one. Count two. And it slid away.

"Org! Org! Save Dg!" Edu cried. "He's going out!" Org looked at him blankly, not comprehending. "The creature, Org," he said, pointing at the receding wave. Org let go of Govvi, and, swinging a pitch basket around, plunged into the water. Dg paddled frantically against the pull, but was swept out. Org threw the basket at him, then dove in after it. Dg paddled toward it and bit into the pitch. Org swam a few strokes, grabbed the shaft and pulled him in.

"Let's get out of here," Ziiza ordered. "Netti, get up. Let's go." Netti lay motionless on the sand, her back against the wall. "Netti, get up; the next one might be bigger."

"Muma! Muma!" Milli cried. "Can't you see? Her head. She's bleeding."

"Run! Run!" Ziiza screamed. "All of you, run! Org, help me carry her."

They ran back to the river, turned the corner, ran upstream, and laid her down. Ziiza grabbed a clump of moss from the wall and pressed it to her head, just above her ear. The bleeding slowed, but Netti did not open her eyes. "Get me some more moss," Ziiza cried. "Warm it in your armpits; it's the best we can do."

Org held Netti in his lap to keep her off the cold sand. The others squatted and hovered, trying to block the wind and rain. Ziiza changed the moss, blew on her face, and rubbed. "She has a pulse," she said. She threw the moss away and clamped on a new bunch. "Still bleeding, but that's not what I'm afraid of. Inside-the-head wound." She scanned their faces. "Com, run upriver. Not too far. See if you can find a way out of here. Over the headland. Anything. Or we'll have to cross back before the tide comes in. Go!"

Com sprinted away gladly, after his feeling of helplessness leaning over Netti. Back in his element.

"You two follow Com," Ziiza told Edu and Govvi. "But slowly. Look for a path. Any way to get up to the top."

Milli held Netti's head, her hands shaking. Ziiza ran her fingers gingerly over her face and hair, closer and closer to the wound. When she touched it, Netti opened her eyes, pressed her hand to her head, and cried, "My head. My head. It hurts so much. I can't stand." She went limp.

"Great," Ziiza said, patting her. "Netti, my dear, wake up. Wake up." Netti rolled her head. "Netti. Netti." Ziiza slapped her face. "We're in a bad place. We've got to get going. Sorry to hit you, but I've got to keep you awake."

Org willed heat into her body. Ziiza and Milli stroked and massaged, keeping away from the wound. Upriver, Ziiza could see Edu and Govvi scurrying around. Com was out of sight. Netti shuddered, then spoke: "I'm so cold. Freezing cold."

It was still early morning; the dripping cloud-cover held. The black rocks at their backs, the wet sand beneath, sucked at their body heat, just as the wave had tried to suck them into the Sea.

"Org, we can't wait," Ziiza said. "Run upstream. What's Com found? Why aren't the kids back?"

Org and Com were a long time returning, but when they did they had a solution. Or so they thought. "Muma, I've found a deer trail," Com reported breathlessly. "Very steep. But there's a chance."

Org picked Netti up. Her face was bloody, her hair matted, but the bleeding had slowed. She lolled her head from side to side. "It hurts so much," she moaned.

"We have to push on," Ziiza said. "Com, show the way. The best you can think of. Quickly. She's got no chance here."

6

Climbing the Headland

I⟨T WAS⟩ to Com's credit that he even saw the deer trail; Org did not. From the beach, which would soon be under water, the wall rose smooth and wet, slippery green moss growing from the cracks. Org boosted Com up. Com went to his hands and knees and clawed his way higher. Ziiza and crew looked up anxiously. Com stopped climbing and slid partway back. "So far, so bad," he said.

"No time for. . . ."

Don't knock drollery in the face of misfortune. He has what it takes.

She tossed him his spear and gave a thumbs up.

Org boosted Ziiza onto the trail, then Edu, glaring at him because he would not let go of Dg. Then Govvi and Milli. He picked Netti up and leaned her against the wall. Ziiza and Milli grabbed her hands and pulled while he pushed. Up and over. "Milli, Govvi, Edu, you start climbing," Ziiza said. "Follow Com." Now Org. He ran at the cliff and leapt. Ziiza caught his hand and braced herself while he scrambled up.

"Ohhhh," Netti wailed. "Don't touch me."

"I have to, sis," Org said, sucking air through his teeth. As if Netti's dead weight wasn't enough, the trail rocks were sharp and loose. Org tried to carry her on his back, climbing on hands and knees, but he almost lost her over the edge. So he pulled her. Up. Up. Ziiza pushed and braced with her spear so they would not slide back. Netti stopped crying.

Gradually, the wall began to bend, tilt away from the river, and the trail grew wider and less steep. They rested at a switchback. The others were ahead and out of sight. "Com. Com," Ziiza called.

"Up here." Com's voice carried over the Sea sounds. "We're stopped."

Org carried Netti, taking a full rest count with each step. Ziiza walked with her hand on his back: still aware of the danger of stumbling, slipping back. Now high above the Sea, Ziiza blinked in the glare. She felt warmer than she had in days. They were almost on top of the clouds, almost out of the drizzling rain. The trail changed from loose rock to slick soil and the headland assumed a gentle roll.

After three more switchbacks, Org came to the youngsters. He lay Netti down and rolled over to rest.

"Her back," Milli cried, "it's all torn up and bleeding. What did you do to her?"

"Had to drag her," Org said matter-of-factly.

Following the curve of the hill as if it grew on the cloud line was a thick green hedge. The trail vanished. Into it? Around it? Com, Govvi, and Edu ranged along, looking for openings. "Deer can't jump it," Com reported. "And they can't thrash their way across the top; the branches are too tangled, too strong."

"But Dg can," Edu said, pointing to Dg as he popped into view. "He's found a tunnel."

Com squirmed in and disappeared. In a few minutes they heard his voice: "Come on."

Edu released Dg, who clawed his way in. Govvi, Milli, and Edu followed.

"Sorry, Netti," Ziiza said, "but we have to." Netti moaned. At least she had heard. The opening was so narrow Org had to roll Netti onto her side and snake her along. Ziiza reached ahead, holding her hand over broken-off branches to keep them from cutting her. Light filtered in from above.

Org pulled Netti out of the tunnel and collapsed beside her. Ziiza lay nearby exhausted, her hands stretched out.

"Do you think we've made it, Muma?" Edu asked as he picked pitch off Dg's teeth.

Not one of your better questions, Edu. But understandable, considering the circumstances.

"We've made it this far," she said. "And Netti's alive. I'm too tired and scratched up to think of anything else."

Com ran ahead and disappeared over a rise. After a brief rest, the others rose and walked slowly toward him. When they caught up he was sitting on the crest, arms around his knees, looking south. Silver-white clouds swept in from behind him, floated over the crest, curled up and out in swirling wisps, and disappeared: clouds into nothingness in the space of a few feet. Before them lay an undulating meadow covered with purple and blue flowers, like nothing they had seen before. No one spoke. To their right, toward the Sea, the meadow rolled over and down, ever so gradually, ever so invitingly – the deadly transition – and dropped straight down. Beyond, the Sea sparkled, deep blue, pea-green, and black, with far-away, evenly-spaced whitecaps. No hint of rogue and killer waves; this afternoon's Sea presented its now-serene, spring-into-summertime face. They drank in the sight. "Look," Com said proudly, as if he had created the sight, "way out." He pointed southwest. "Could be a whale spouting."

"If we find water," Ziiza said, "I'd say let's camp up here on the headland. Netti can't go much farther today. Maybe even if we don't find water."

Org and Ziiza walked on either side of Netti, steadying her, carrying her when necessary, down the gentle slope through the flowers. Com stayed back, admiring the view. "I'll be along," he told them. They walked easily, through the grass, the flowers, and scattered thistles. Then up the next rise. "Let's head for those alders," Ziiza said, pointing to treetops showing over a ridge. They dropped into a notch, fine for a campsite, all things considered: wind-sheltered by hill and trees, with a level spot, and a rill-fed pool. The water trickled over a barrier of rocks, twigs, and leaves, through the trees, out of the notch, through the meadow, and turned to mist as the wind caught it at the cliff's edge.

"Can you see me clearly?" Ziiza asked Netti when she was down. "Are you dizzy? Any trouble keeping your eyes open? Look out at the Sea through the trees. We're going to have a beautiful sunset."

"I'm all right, I guess," Netti mumbled. "If only this thunder and lightening in my head would go away. Owww! It's coming."

"How's your tinder?" Ziiza asked, turning to Govvi. "Can you start a fire?"

"I'm out. And I lost most of my fire kit. Couldn't hang onto it climbing."

"Uh-oh."

"The trees. Up higher," Govvi said. "I'll hike up and find the makings."

"Everyone go with Govvi," the muma ordered. "Wood gathering."

The camp in the notch was as good as any Ziiza could remember, made sweeter by their escape from the wave and Com's discovery of the trail; the scout had come through again. Ziiza's sunset prediction was more than fulfilled. A thin ribbon of cloud hanging over the horizon turned pink, then red, then fire red, then purple as the orb dropped. But for Netti's injury, they would have walked out and sat on the grass. Instead, Milli propped her up and held her head while they watched through an opening in the branches. Netti faced a painful night, even though it was pleasantly warm, dry, and near windless. Milli arranged what was left of their clothing under and over her. Ziiza and Org pressed against her to give her warmth. A fire would have helped, but Govvi had not had time to repair her kit. The ball of humanity was too much for newly-friendly Dg to snuggle into, so he excused himself and made a meadow-grass nest on the ridge top. Ziiza reminded Org that he had the first watch, but he was already asleep.

They woke to a clear day; the weather had held. Netti had moaned and cried her way through the night, which was good. Far better than the extremes: silent unconsciousness, or shrieking headaches. Ziiza examined her, sliding her fingertips gently over the wound. Netti took it well. "May I wash your face?" Netti's eyes said yes. "Can you eat?" Ziiza held out some meat. Netti pushed it away, so she handed it to Org. She doled out the rest of their food, not taking any herself. They had to get down to a good beach.

"I can travel. I can walk," Netti announced, anticipating Ziiza's question. She pressed her hands to her temples and twisted her head as if to loosen the pain and cast it away.

Govvi sat against the bank with a piece of wood on her knees, a thin smile on her face. When her siblings noticed, more or less at the same time, she waved a flat cedar slab, like her fire drill's base. "I have my object, Muma," she said. "My personal object. It's a tally board. I broke it off a split tree. Up the hill. I'm going to make a record of everything we have: food, clothing, spears, pitch baskets, tinder, everything. I'll smooth it later. I'm going to change it every day." None of them knew what to say, what to make of her "tally board," all the weirder because it seemed to involve constant work.

"Know sumpin'?" Edu said, with a self-satisfied smile. "I have my object, too. And he's sitting right there, looking at us."

"You can't have a live creature, for an *object*," Milli teased. "Can he, Muma?"

Ziiza was delighted, amazed in fact, at their creativity, but did not want to show it. How to answer without creating a can-you-top-this competition? Or appearing to chide the others for not coming up with anything. Or prompt them to make silly choices, make a mockery of her calculated exercise. She pulled at her chin, thought for a moment, and said, "How about this, Edu. You could make Dg," she was beginning to like the name, "a collar to wear. That's an object." That seemed to satisfy everyone. "Keep working," she said to the others. "I can't wait to see what you come up with." The best part of the little exchange, however, was Netti; she had joined in the laughter.

Instead of running ahead, Com held back again, as if reluctant to leave the high meadow behind. He fell into his place in the order of march, ahead of Govvi and behind Netti, who was walking with Milli's support. No need to scout this early in the day. Today's objective? Simple: get down to the beach and find food. The Sea sparkled – as different from yesterday's Sea as yesterday's was from the day before – crystal blue, flecked with white. As the meadow rolled on, more flowers presented themselves: blunt-petaled yellows, miniature pinks-on-white, low flowers hiding among the taller purples and blues. They had no idea what these flowers were called. As far as they were concerned they had no names; they were just overwhelmingly beautiful in their variety and abundance. Com saw an orange-and-black-striped caterpillar climbing a stem. He picked it off and threw it at Milli. "Stop that, you brat," she screamed in mock disgust, but delighted with his attention. Cliff swallows, far-away black dots, swooped up the edge and fell out of view again. Vultures circled high above. Far up the hill a white-headed eagle watched them pass through her territory from a broken-topped snag. Sea lions bellowed and barked on the rocks below.

"Well, Govvi," Ziiza said, mostly to make conversation at their first rest stop, "why don't you give us your report. Where do we stand?" It was obvious, but she was curious to hear what she would say.

Govvi came to attention, snapped her tally board up, and said, "Clothing: Netti, fully covered. Other females, including Muma, barely adequate. Males: practically nothing. But it doesn't matter, it's summer. Food: blubber and meat almost gone; not even a full meal left. Clams: none. Mussels: none. Tinder: a wet handful; I'm drying it in my hair. Weapons: two of seven spears left after the wave and the climb. Pitch baskets and shafts: none. Knife: one. Pouches: same."

"Thank you, Govvi," Ziiza said, taken aback by the girl's precision and grasp of their situation, but, again, not wanting to contrast her with the others. "We know where we stand. At our first forest camp, hopefully tonight, we'll make new spears, gather pitch, and look for cedar root. We're starting over. But, as always, fire is our first priority. Then weapons. Then food." Ziiza took their stares. "Maybe food first."

At the south end of the headland they stopped to enjoy a last look before their descent. This time the meadow sloped gradually to a rocky beach – no surprise cliffs – an easy walk down. The shallow-looking river below, half the size of the one they had crossed the day before, flowed lazily out of the eastern forest, meandered through a tall-grass flat, broadened into an estuary, then met the Sea. The broad beach ran south again, until it disappeared into a low haze. The same as so many miles before. Except for one thing. "What could that be?" said sharp-eyed Com, the first to spot it.

"You mean the shiny black thing rising out of the haze?" Milli said, squinting.

"Strange. Strange," Ziiza said. "Intriguing. How far away do you think? Com? Anyone?"

"Couple of days," Com replied.

With spirits uplifted and curiosity piqued they descended the headland, crossed the river, and began their march. Ziiza was frustrated with their slow pace, but Netti could not walk more than an hour without a break. They put their stops to good use, however, timing the tides, digging clams, and stopping by creeks to let Milli fish. Netti discovered, or noticed for the first time, a strong, supple water reed. At rests she gathered as many as she could carry, and was on the lookout for more. For her first project she wove a crude headband. "My headache remedy." Although it did not give inside-the-head relief, the pressure felt good, and it kept the wind out of her ears. And searching, gathering, planning, and weaving on-the-walk took her mind off of the dull throb that was with her even when the shooting pain attacks were not.

"Help you carry?" Edu asked, skipping ahead of Govvi and on to Netti. Then: "Do you think you might make Dg a collar?"

The weather held fairly well, standard summer: fog in the morning, clear by mid-day, wind in the afternoon. The beach held, too: broad and straight. Their spear-and-walking shafts were easily replaced, as were the pitch baskets. Food was boring but adequate, and they had fires to cook it. Com's "couple of days" to the knob proved overly optimistic. In fact, after dropping down from the headland and walking the beach, they had not even seen it, let alone reached it, in six days. What the shock of their narrow escape from the Sea, Netti's plight, their frantic climb, plus hunger, rain, and cold could not accomplish, boredom and the tease of the distant, mysterious knob did; the children behaved like . . . children. First joking and poking. Then tripping and shoving. "Enough of that!" Ziiza snapped. "Back in your places. Order of march." Org stomped ahead, driving his feet into the sand. Edu threw stones at shore birds. Dg chased. Govvi retreated into her silent world, occasionally scratching her board.

Ziiza took a chance and taught them a new song. Not only a new song, a new kind of song. She had each child – she thought of Org as a boy, even though he was surely a young man, and Milli a girl, even though she had clearly crossed over to womanhood – fall back and walk with her. She sang a rough version, then worked out the words to each one's lines. They practiced, accompanied by the musical wind and rhythmic surf.

Netti did well. She could not maintain their old ground-covering pace, but each day she walked faster and farther. Her headaches became less frequent, but longer in duration, and sometimes so shatteringly painful she rolled on the sand pounding her head. Or leapt out of her sleep, screaming. Gathering her reeds, her shoots, her grasses, became her passion, her passion to offset the pain. Not only headache pain but the pain of anticipation, the constant thought that time was running out; when would the next one begin? She twisted her reeds together; she loved it, had a talent for it. She made another headband: thicker, more pressure. And a collar for Dg. Not that he appreciated it. He set about rolling, twisting, pawing, rubbing against trees and rocks until it was destroyed. He seemed to sense what it meant, what it symbolized, and did not like the idea one bit. She enlisted Milli, Edu, and her muma to

help chew the reeds to soften them. For her first major project she wove –
fashioned? braided? twisted? – seven conical hats: good in the sun, fair in the
rain, bad in the wind, but a pleasure to wear and a pleasure to own.

Ziiza had tried to offset their bickering and boredom with singing, campfire
stories, and objects to find and fashion. What else could she do? "Now Org,"
she inquired, after they had plopped down on a dune to rest, "have you
decided on your object?"

Strong, silent, man-of-action Org almost smiled at his muma and said,
"I've got it." Then quickly, "Not the object, the idea."

"Can you tell us what it is?" she replied offhandedly, not wanting to push
him back into silence.

"Sure, it's a rock. A perfect rock. I'm looking. I've been looking all along.
Even climbing that gravelly, muddy deer trail, dragging Netti, I was feeling
for them. Got to be perfect. When I find it I might make another fish club.
Or maybe I'll just have it."

Quite a speech. This must mean a lot to him.

Unlike the previous two object announcements, this one pleased everyone.
Org was, after all, the man of the family, the tallest, strongest, their best hope
in a fight. His choice *was* perfect.

"Can we help you look?" Govvi asked.

"Nope. Not Muma's rules. Got to find it myself. Maybe I'll shape it myself,
too." Everyone remembered.

7

Decision at Way Rock

BY THE seventh day after descending the headland the children had stopped asking about the point in the clouds. Had it been a mirage, an illusion, something they had wanted to believe – so they did believe? Then, on the eighth day, it appeared in faint outline, so large in the thick, beach-hanging mist that it seemed to be of the mist. They rounded a low sandstone bank and there it was, tall, polished, and gleaming, as if a mile-long whale had washed up on the beach long ago. And all that was left was one black tooth standing upright in the sand. High up, birds circled round and round. No hint of a depression, crack, or ledge; no place for them to light upon except the top. So they walked around. How large was this rock? Fifty people holding hands might encircle it. One hundred people standing feet-upon-shoulders might top it. Maybe more.

Ziiza stared, transfixed. For a moment. Then the rock drew her irresistibly toward it. The sandstone bank broke sharply left, revealing a break in the forest that lost itself in the eastern mountains, the first such opening she had seen along the coast. Just beyond the rock, a good-sized but crossable river flowed through the break.

Com bolted and ran. Ziiza opened her mouth, raised her hand, and changed her mind. When he reached the rock he slid his hands up as high as he could, standing on tiptoe and moved them in circles as if polishing its seductive smoothness. As the others were drawn – Org, Milli, Netti, Govvi, Edu, Ziiza – they, too, were compelled to slide their fingertips over its surface, ever so lightly, barely touching. Could anything this large possibly be this smooth? What mysterious force made it this way? Dg, not awed, raised his leg and sent his steaming water against the rock. Shouldn't a rock like this be offshore, rising out of the Sea, Ziiza thought, not out of a sand beach at the mouth of a river? Shouldn't it be rough, jagged, pocked, undercut? It did not seem right. Then again, it was monolithically right.

The rock repelled them and drew them in, calmed and excited them, frightened and embraced them. Unthinking, they walked the big circle around it. Order of march. Order of wonder. When Ziiza reached the other side she was surprised to see, between the rock and the river, the remains of an enormous fire. Ceremonial? Sacrificial? Far too large for cooking or camping. What? This quickly resolved itself when she reached it. The prow of a well-formed canoe lay unburned at the edge. A paddle handle. A scorched bailer. So travelers turned inland here. Burned their canoes. A great many, Ziiza reasoned, when she considered the size of the ash pile. An ash pile this large, this deep, even if the result of many smaller burnings, should radiate some heat; something should be smoldering, unless the last fire was many days, even weeks, ago. They hadn't had rain in days, either, not real rain. She walked to the pile and kicked her good foot beneath the damp overlay. She wiggled it. Bent over, ready to dig with her hands. And stopped.

"What are you doing, Muma?" Edu, of course.

"Feeling for heat. And I'm not feeling any. This fire has been dead for a long time. If this is the flotilla ritual, burn the canoes and head inland, then the last one was some time ago. We're late in the season. Put differently, we're closer to winter than I had figured. If I figured at all."

I wonder if MeTonn's canoe is in this pile?

She gave a hoarse laugh.

They continued around the rock, then walked upriver and made camp beside the sandstone bank, as was evident – from fire rings, bones and shells on the sand, names and signs scratched into it – so many had done before. Govvi took unusual pleasure in feeding her fire with canoe parts pulled from the black heap, rather than twigs and sticks. She set a smooth paddle part aside. After the fire was blazing, she borrowed Org's knife and shaped it into an improved tally board. Then she carefully transferred her inventory, small as it was. Edu skipped stones on the river; one made it all the way across. Dg sat nearby, biting and tugging at the hair between his foot pads. Org inspected everyone's spears (without being told) and re-pointed and re-hardened the blunt ones. Then he leaned back against the cliff and stared into the fire, his second-favorite pastime (after throwing rocks). The flood tide turned the river back, forming a swirling, gurgling, knee-deep moat around the rock. Milli found a particularly beautiful shell and kept it. Com was unaccounted for.

No mystery: Com was off exploring. They had eaten, washed in the river, and were making their nests around the fire and he still was not back. Although his actions were not that unusual, Ziiza worried. It was almost dark. "Where could he be?" she asked. "Why didn't he tell us he'd be gone so long?"

"I'd better go after him," Org said.

As they spoke, Com appeared at the edge of the firelight. "I have news," he announced.

"Well?" Milli said, while the others made impatient, get-on-with-it motions.

"I found something very long," he said, obviously pleased with himself.

"Don't tease," Netti said.

"Give you another hint: It's wide." Silence. "Footprints," he said, after no one responded.

"A trail?" Ziiza asked.

"The widest, deepest-worn trail I've seen. Going east, up the river."

"That's where we're going, huh, Muma?" Edu asked. Ziiza made a non-committal mumble.

Darkness fell and they sat around the fire, feeding it with canoe parts. They pressed close together and went to sleep. Ziiza took the first watch, sitting with her back against the sandstone, staring at the rock she could sense but could not see. After waking Org for the second, she slept.

Morning was windless. A low, chilly fog hung over the river, blotting out all but the base of the rock. High above, it probably rose out of the fog, round and gleaming, as they had first seen it from the headland meadow. "We're leaving the beach," Ziiza said. "Gather as much food as we can carry. I don't care how long it takes." Then, "Yes, I do care." As she trailed the boys out to the clam beds she smiled back at Netti, who stood on the river edge, catching the crabs Milli pitched at her. Like before-the-wave Netti. Almost.

"All right," Ziiza said, after a delicious cooked lunch, "pack up and get ready to move." They picked up their spears, hoisted their bulging food sacks, and walked to the rock.

"For luck," Com said, slapping it and drawing his hand away slowly. They all did.

The sand ran out and they soon found the trail. This river had nothing which could be called an estuary. But it did have something Com had not mentioned, a thundering waterfall. And behind it a deep, narrow, raging-river canyon.

So that's why they burned their canoes.

Com's trail entered a low wood and wound upward to the canyon rim. Ziiza called a break. "How are you doing, dear?" she asked Netti, hands on her cheeks.

"Oh, fine," Netti said. Then, with fear Ziiza could see in her eyes, "The big one hasn't come today. But it will."

"I'm so sorry, Netti. Brave girl." Ziiza hugged her. Milli and Govvi joined in. Edu patted her arm.

They sat on the bluff, feet dangling. To the east, the direction they were headed, the mountains receded; not only were they farther inland than what they had been used to, they were lower, gentler, rounder. To the south the mountains rose up again, seemingly higher. So that was it, a low-level pass to the interior. Ziiza looked back toward the Sea. She saw the full rock for the first time that day, gleaming, black, symmetrical, with its white topknot of bird droppings. When they had eaten, and their usual break time was over, Org swung his pitch baskets and spear onto his shoulder and said, "What are we waiting for?" The other children made ready. Ziiza did not move. "Coming, Muma?" he asked.

"Rest some more," Ziiza answered. "Look around. Gather tinder. Anything. I've got to think." Which she did, for over an hour, never taking her eyes off the rock. *Tinder* set Govvi off on a run. Edu and Dg ran after her. Org gave his muma her thinking space and threw rocks, trying to span the canyon, which he did not. But he enjoyed trying. Milli, Netti, and Com set out to explore but were soon back. Ziiza sat.

Edu returned, hands full of cedar bark, surveyed them, and said, "We're going back, aren't we, Muma?"

"Yes," Ziiza said. "Yes, we are. For now, anyhow. Beautiful as this country is, clear as the trail seems to be, as many people who have walked it, it doesn't seem right. And the farther we go, the less right it seems."

They walked down the incline, away from the canyon's roar, and into the silent zone before the surf's boom. Once again they felt the rock, but were not as awestruck as before. Govvi found her coals and blew them to life. They plopped down in their old nest.

"Do what you will," Ziiza told them. "We've plenty of food, but we could use more." She walked out to the beach. Edu got up to follow. Dg, too. She waved them back. At the point where they had rounded the sandstone yesterday, she turned and walked to the rock. Touched it. Same way. Circled. Toes in ashes. Around again. To the river edge and looked south.

Com stood by the sandstone bank, examining it closely for the first time. It did not occur to him to think about the disparity between sandstone, as opposed to loose beach sand, and the hard, black, tooth-shaped rock a few footsteps away. One built up, layer by layer, squeezed solid by pressure and water over who knew how many thousands of years. The other, forged of molten lava, thrust out of the earth and polished by the elements over thousands of years – during which time the sandstone should have been reduced to beach sand. What fascinated him was the color. The exposed, nearly vertical face ran about fifty paces either way from where he stood, rising to three times his height at its highest. Viewed from the beach, one would not notice anything unusual; just another beach dune that fell away abruptly. To the east, upriver, it petered out. Green beach grass grew along the top edge, clumps leaning over ready to fall, just as trees lean over riverbanks, ready to topple and be swept away. The sandstone was, of all things, pale blue, unlike the tan-white beach sand the cliff rose out of. As his muma stared at her rock and wrestled with her question, Com stared at the bank and conjured up an idea that thrilled him.

"Org," Com called, "come over here, will you?" Org raised his head slowly, tried to think of a reason not to come, and failing that, ambled over. "Stand with your back to the bank, please." Com stepped away. "Good. But it needs something. Wait a minute." He walked to Org's spear and pitch baskets. "Let's try one in each hand. In the sand. Business ends up." He stepped back and shaded his eyes. "Now drop –"

"Where's this going, Com?" Org said gruffly.

"I'm going to immortalize you," he said with a twinkle. "Or at least do your picture. Drop the spear. Just your pitch basket." He outlined Org's legs, scratching and pecking with his spear point. Torso and head. "I changed my mind. Let go of the basket. Just the spear; it looks more frightening." Org sucked in his gut, puffed out his chest, and tried not to look pleased, tried not to let Com see that he was enjoying posing, looking important, being "immortalized." "Pretty crude," Com said. "I'll have to make some adjustments. Thanks. That didn't hurt, did it? Are you ready, Milli?"

Milli and Netti were watching and eager; there was no doubt in *their* minds. "We want to be drawn together," Milli said. "Like this." They flattened their backs to the bank and pressed close together. Netti, the taller, leaned over and touched Milli's head with hers. They made lip-curling, toothy smiles and held them.

"I don't do smiles, girls, but they're nice."

While he traced, Milli asked: "Are you going to do our crazy muma, too?"

"Yes, I am. Last. Just like order of march on the beach." He was now only poking and pecking dots, having given up trying to scratch accurate outlines with the spear.

"I don't think she's crazy," Edu said. "She's just not sure it's the trail to Beaverton."

"It's obvious," Milli said disgustedly. "How could a broad trail like that not be the way?" Org, the trail breaker, snorted in agreement. "Like, you know," she continued, "the secret words: 'Trace the Sea. Then let it go.' This is it, the place to let it go. But she can't."

"It could be the trail to someplace else," Netti said, talking through her still-frozen smile. "I mean, not Beaverton."

"Anyway," Com said, after finishing the girls, "I go right here, after Netti, before Govvi." He looked at Govvi, sitting by the fire. "Govvi, aren't you interested in having your picture done?"

"I guess so. I'll be there," she dragged her words, "when you're ready."

Away from them and out of hearing, Ziiza continued walking around the rock, sitting occasionally, with her back against it, looking off, as if she could see, sense, smell, or feel. . . . She glanced once at Com's drawing activity, but otherwise paid no attention. She walked back to where the trail began, turned and faced the Sea. She raised her arms, pointed them at the rock, and held them, slowly turning her hands, as if expecting them to vibrate – like a water witching stick – indicating the way to Beaverton. She turned, did the same thing facing east on the trail, away from the rock. No sign.

Ziiza walked back to camp. Milli and Netti were pecking Com's figure into the sandstone. "You're last, Muma," Com said cheerfully. "Just like on the beach."

"Fine," Ziiza said without stopping, "Let me know." She turned the corner, angled toward the Sea, and walked north. Dg joined her. After some distance, she raised her arms to the rock. She felt its power, or thought she did, but did not feel its message. She and Dg walked slowly back to camp.

"Can't do any more thinking today," Ziiza said. "I'm not getting anywhere. I've decided to cross the river. Alone. But the surf's rolling hard and the tide's wrong. So I'll wait until tomorrow." The children's eyes darted to one another, but they said nothing. "Until then, Com, I'm yours. What do you want me to do?"

"Govvi's next," Com said. "Then Edu. Then you, Muma. But I can mark where they go and do you right now."

"I can wait," Ziiza said. "In fact I'd love to wait. It's lovely to look at, Com. The color. Simply gorgeous. I hadn't paid much attention before." She looked back at the rock. "I've had so much on my mind."

"Thank you, Muma."

Com's own outline showed him with feet apart and hands on hips, spear-less. Govvi stood straight-faced, inwardly pleased with the attention and representation, but like Org unwilling to show it. She was the shortest and thinnest and stood rigidly, legs pressed together, holding her tally board. Edu's pose was as relaxed as Govvi's was stiff. Ziiza held Edu's hand, legs spread, slightly off balance, favoring her injured foot. Last, Dg, sitting, forelegs planted, head cocked, ears raised.

After he had pecked them in, Com connected the dots, varying the shapes according to his artistic vision – narrowing or widening faces, thinning arms, exaggerating feet and hands. The others fished and crabbed and wandered. Edu threw stones in the river. The black rock was a tempting target, but after his muma's look he thought better of it. One by one they returned to the fire to eat, rest, and talk. Talk of everything except what was on their minds. Unlike last night, when they felt compelled to face the black tower, they sat with their backs to it, watching Com work. One by one they fell asleep. All except Dg, who stayed up on duty alert, and Com, who was so excited he could not stop working, and thus became night artist, night watchman, and fire tender.

Next morning, after Ziiza had waved a silent good-bye and crossed the river, the brothers and sisters fell under the spell of the picture project. The next step would be dirty, Com told them. And lots of fun if they cared to help. Which he hoped they would, since he did not know how long they would be here and desperately wanted to finish. The figures would be outlined in carbon black, jumping out of the blue sandstone, figuratively speaking, even if they weren't in actual jumping position. All he needed was charcoal from the canoe pyre, water, and a clay binder. He led them upstream and into the forest, where they dug brown-red clay.

Milli slapped a handful of wet clay on Org's back and ran away. "Dare you," she said laughing. He halfheartedly tossed the clump he was mixing at her, halfheartedly because he thought of himself as her protector; she was not a target, even in fun. Milli stopped, planted her feet in the sand, and said, "She's already made up her mind, you know; we're not taking the trail." Com stopped working on Milli's figure and stared at the real her. As did the others; she had their attention. "Her little walks are all for show, pretending she's agonizing over her decision. But she's already made it. Or the rock," she pointed, "has made it for her." Milli stopped to let it sink in, screwed up her pouty-pretty face, and said, "She *is* crazy, you know."

"Yup, crazy," Org said. "What's to decide? There's the trail. We take it. Everyone else did."

"Exactly my point," Milli shrilled. Then, lowering her voice: "Any questions? Comments?"

Com spoke: "I've seen enough beach to last me awhile. I'd like to explore the trail, and the mountains, see what's out there beyond." He pointed east with a blackened finger. "But what I really want is to finish my picture. My masterpiece." He grinned, trying to make light of *masterpiece*. "We're leaving this place soon, whichever way we go."

"Netti? Govvi? Edu?" Milli prompted; she was not going to let it drop. "Govvi, what do you think?"

"I don't know," Govvi said, drawing out her usually clipped, precise speech. "I'd like to hear Muma out, hear her say it herself. Her reasons." Then, without the trace of a smile, "Even if she is crazy."

Netti, not wanting to but feeling pressure to respond, said, "The harder I try to think, the more my head hurts. I vote however you do, Milli."

"That's it!" Milli cried, "we'll vote on it. Refuse to go. She can't leave us and go on by her nutty self. And we don't have to do what she says, either."

Com worked on the figures, smoothing them flush until they appeared part of the cliff, just as naturally unnatural as the color itself: a family of figures facing – defiantly? – the shining rock across the way. To remove the spill-over smudged black he rubbed the outline with chipped-off blue sandstone. While Com was crouching, working on Dg's image, Org touched Milli on the shoulder and said, "She's coming."

"Everybody," Milli whispered, as if she had to. "You know my vote. And Netti's. Quick, before she gets here." Then she added, "We have to be unanimous."

"Mind if we vote before you give us the results, Miss Pushy?" Com said.

"Sorry, Com, but I thought you'd voted. Done with beaches and all that. Right?"

"That's right."

Milli continued: "Org? Still the same?" He signaled agreement. "That's four. Govvi?"

I don't know," she drawled. "How are you voting, Edu?

"Dg and I cast two votes for Muma. And she's not crazy."

"Little muma's boy," Milli taunted. "Can't think for himself. Wants her to carry him down the beach. All the way to stupid old Beaverton – which, by the way, she has no idea where it is. Or how far. Or anything."

"She's your muma, too." Edu said, plopping down on the sand, pulling Dg to him, his eyes filling. "Okay," he sobbed, "you can have our votes." He raised Dg's paw and waved it at her.

"That leaves you, Govvi. Hurry up, she's coming."

"Oh, I agree with you, Milli," Govvi said, back to her clipped speech, "in *every* way. I just wanted to see how everyone else voted."

"Then we're unanimous," Milli gloated.

Ziiza's face was firm and her steps purposeful as she approached. The children mumbled their guilty greetings, hardly looking at her. Milli was the exception; she stood firm, defiant, jaw set, looking straight at her.

It's not as if I didn't expect something like this.

"Hello, children," Ziiza said, "I'm glad to be back. And Com, your picture is beautiful. Something to remember. Something to be proud of. Something all of you can be proud of."

"Muma," Milli said, shrugging off the sweeping compliment, "we've something to tell you." Ziiza's eyes cooled. "We've talked it over. Taken a vote. It's clear that the big trail goes to Beaverton, and we're going to take it. Going to take it."

"What makes you so sure it goes to Beaverton?"

"What difference does it make, Muma?" Netti said, more out of loyalty to Milli than what she thought. She caught herself just before saying who cares about Beaverton, and continued, "It's the trail. Everybody takes it." Org and Com nodded in weak agreement.

"Well," Ziiza said, "I've given this much thought. Explored some." She scanned them, stopping at Com. "And I've decided that the beach is the way to Beaverton. Not the trail."

"You're forgetting about feeling the rock and talking to it," Milli shot back.

"No need to talk mean, Milli," Ziiza said, controlling her irritation. "But I must admit, the rock does exert an influence on me. It has a powerful presence. I'm surprised you don't feel it, too." She stopped talking. Gave them an opening. No one spoke. Continued: "The tide is right for a crossing and we've been here far too long. I propose we leave now. Walk till day's end."

Ziiza sat on the sand and pulled her legs together. She massaged her knees, calves, ankles, to arrive at her objective, her bleeding and aching foot. She set her eyes on the flat sand between them, drawing a line to cross, as it were. Waited. The space between her and her recalcitrant children grew.

Edu lifted his hand from Dg's collar to scratch himself. Dg got up and walked over the "line" to Ziiza. She wrapped her arm around his middle and hugged him. Not too hard, not too possessively, just a routine hug. She let go. He sat.

"That's the first one," Edu said with a laugh, breaking the tension, and, unbeknownst to him, losing the standoff. With that, he rose and walked to his muma. He knelt, patted the Dg creature, and looked at the sand, avoiding his brothers' and sisters' eyes.

Com was next, followed by Org. Having had their say seemed enough of a rebellion for them. Since they did not know where they were going, what difference did it make which way they went? Either way would be an adventure, and that was what interested them most. Not winter. Not survival. Not Beaverton.

Netti could stand it no longer and poked her sister. "Oh, I guess," Milli said disgustedly. They walked over together. Govvi followed.

"I have no choice, Muma," Milli said, her resolve shattered, her anger dissolving into sobs.

"That's right, dear," Ziiza said. "And neither do I."

8

Watabeast Attack

AFTER THEY were across the river, down the beach, and the rock was far behind, Com said, "So we're staying on the beach, Muma. But why'd all those people go the other way?"

And why are we going the wrong way, huh?

"Yes Muma, why?" Edu chimed in, not wanting to be outdone in the questions department.

Oh, well, that's life.

"I can't say for sure," Ziiza answered, "but once folks start walking in a certain direction, and the trail gets wider and smoother, and others see the trail, or the people, they tend to continue."

"You mean without even thinking?" Org asked, uncharacteristically.

"People come under irresistible spells that pull them along."

"Another example, please," Milli said.

"A crowd. People watching something. Curiosity takes hold. We're all like that, to one degree or another. Take a campfire at night. You're standing away in the dark. You're not even cold. You're not even invited. But you're drawn to it."

"You're getting closer, Muma," Milli said. "But you're not there."

"Maybe," Ziiza answered, "they don't have what it takes – to go their own way -- plot their own course."

"And we do?" Netti said, pressing her headband.

"It's the song, isn't it, Muma?" Milli said in soft realization. "You've been planning the song all along. Just in case."

Ziiza smiled and sang out, "*Whatever it takes*." Then, "Come on, Org, let's hear it."

"Do I have to?"

"*Whatever the breaks*," Ziiza sang in a raspy contralto. "Come on, Org," she prompted him again.

"*We're marching and walking, running and prancing*." He dragged the words.

"Prancing," Com said with a snicker, "Org prancing. I'd like to see that."

"Milli, you're next."

"Singing and tumbling, tripping and dancing."

"Tripping. You got that right."

"Enough, Com. Get ready," Ziiza said. "Netti."

"We've come a long way, such a short way to go."

Com sang out, arms waving, little fingers extended: *"Weeks on the beach, so much to show."*

Govvi, speak-singing : *"We're young and we're strong, in so many ways,"*

Edu: *"We'll knock off the miles in just a few days."*

Ziiza: *"Yes, yes, yes. We're a family united. We'll never forget. That —"* She pointed at Org to begin the second verse.

Org looked crookedly at Com for support and said, "Oh Muma, this is embarrassing." But after a drilling look from Ziiza he sang: *"We're stumbling and tripping, grouching and grumbling."* Then added: "That's for sure."

Milli: *"We're wobbling and falling, wet-over-alling,"*

Netti: *"We've come a long way, such a long way to go. Now."*

Com: *"Weeks on the beach, so little to show."*

Govvi: *"I'm tired and I'm hungry; the nights are so cold."*

Edu: *"My legs are so sore, my spirits so low."*

Ziiza: *"But. But. But. Children. We're a family united. We'll never forget. That —"* Come on Org."

Org: *"Whatever."*

Org and Milli: *"Whatever, whatever."*

Org, Milli, and Netti: *"Whatever, whatever, whatever."*

Org, Milli, Netti, and Com: *"Whatever, whatever, whatever, whatever."*

Org, Milli, Netti, Com, and Govvi: *"Whatever, whatever, whatever, whatever, whatever."*

Edu: *"Whatever?"*

Ziiza: *"Whatever it takes."*

All: *"Whatever the breaks."*

Ziiza: *"Whatever the aches and pa-ya-yanes."*

All: *"We're moving to Beaverton."*

They walked for a while. And for a while they really believed they were walking toward Beaverton. The sun dropped low on the Sea. Dg chased the peeping, skittering shore birds. The corny, catchy, patched-together song rolled around in their heads. "Whatever it takes. Whatever the breaks." They were so alone. What difference did it make if they sang it out loud? No one could hear them anyway. No one could laugh at them. Ziiza said nothing, letting the pressure build. Milli, of all people, was first. "Whatever it takes," she sang out in her clear sweet voice. Org joined immediately. Then down the order of march, each with his or her well-rehearsed line, always guffawing at Ziiza's "pa-ya-yanes." They walked into the darkness, singing it over and over.

The next day Ziiza pushed the pace, or tried to, but Netti still slowed them. It was not just her injury and lack of endurance, she was still poking around, collecting – new grasses, weeds, rushes, bark – and discarding materials that did not look pretty, broke when bent, or tasted bitter. Even with her help, Edu had not managed a decent Dg collar. Govvi scratched on her tally board as she walked. Simple as it was, and, in truth, unimportant as it was considering their meager possessions and always-low food stores, she seemed driven to put things in order, to record, to know, unusual in the extreme for a seven- or eight-year-old. Org shuffled along in the surf run-outs, always maintaining his lead position, picking up and examining every good-sized rock he spotted, throwing reject after reject into the Sea; he took as much pleasure in rejecting as in seeking. Or sharpening his aim, throwing at every target he could find: trees, logs, boulders, birds, even starfish and anemones exposed at low tide. Milli walked the wet sand with him, looking for smooth, shiny shells. After washing and rubbing the scum off, she tried to catch her reflection in their concave, iridescent surfaces. When she found one she liked better she spun the old one away, to Dg's delight, as he chased it on the beach, or ran it down in the surf, only to lose interest as soon as he reached it.

Their pursuit of objects, combined with bursts of the song Ziiza called "Whatever It Takes," good weather, and talks around the campfire, made Ziiza's crew a happy one – the squelched rebellion all but forgotten. But the "objects" game was also slowing them down. This Ziiza had not foreseen. Sooner or later she would have to tell them to wind it up. On the other hand, she could not push them much harder. They were a finely-tuned walking company, a successful team so far, negotiating the delicate balance between serious work and fun along the way; children, youngsters and not-so-youngsters, walking, walking, day after day. Another thing: Ziiza was not doing so well herself. Her bad foot was troubling her more than her "home" remedies – walking in the cold surf, feet close to the campfire, massages at night, anytime she thought no one was looking – could alleviate. She, her feet, her foot, needed a long break, a week without walking. Ideally, much longer. That, of course, was exactly what she could not do. The evidence at the rock only confirmed what she had believed all along: this year's migration had passed; they were not only last, they were very late.

Or were they? Those who chose Beaverton – whether from accurate information or the rock's mysterious influence – could continue south in their canoes, ahead of them, behind them, passing in fog, rain, or at night.

Only those bound overland had to abandon their craft, burn them in what must have been an emotional ceremony. But what was the split? It would appear from the trail that the majority headed east to the interior. The exact number Ziiza would never know. Likewise those for mysterious Beaverton. Surely it was possible there could be late starters and slow movers, possibly even major flotillas, indicating perhaps they were not so late after all. Nice thoughts. Comforting thoughts. And, Ziiza quickly concluded, self-delusional thoughts.

"How are you doing?" Ziiza asked Com, casually. After leaving the rock he had not been his front-running self. He fell into order and walked slowly, for him. Not that his scouting was needed. After the headland and rock the beach had been relatively clear. He had sung his lines but, she noted, not with his usual enthusiasm. Not even with sarcastically enthusiastic enthusiasm. He walked with either his head down or his eyes fixed on the horizon.

"I'm fine."

After an interval, Ziiza moved closer and tried again. "Do you mind my asking . . . is something is troubling you?"

"I'm really okay. It's my object. I can't seem to . . . Everybody else . . ."

"You can't find it?"

"It can't be found. I have to make it. But I don't know how."

"What does it look like? What does it do?"

"Something like a canoe rope. Or a lashing rope."

"Something woven, twisted?" Ziiza asked. "Like Netti makes with her grasses?"

"Yes, but stronger. And maybe with a throwing weight on the end. Strong enough to hold me."

"Let me think," Ziiza said, pulling him to her and patting his head.

Night camp. The broad beach climbed gradually, transforming itself into wind-blown dunes. Clumps of shore pine struggled to take hold in the depressions. The dunes themselves proved to be a narrow strip, behind which lay a shallow, fetid swamp, dark water covered with a layer of matted scum so thick it held animal tracks.

Dune pockets are sunshine collectors and wind protectors, fine for mid-day rest stops. They are, however, less than ideal overnight campsites; sand beds are cold, gritty, and hard. But it was late and, as Com reported, the dunes stretched on "forever and forever." So they picked a spot and made the best of it. During their afternoon approach the tide had dropped and they had veered out onto the hard wet sand, hoping for clams. Milli, using all of her considerable skill, had found two. Ziiza, one. The other five, none. A dead zone. They still had some carry-food; Govvi told them exactly how much. Rather, how little. Berries were ripening by the edge of the swamp, sour but edible, providing some moisture and a little sugar. The fire was good but difficult to keep going, pine straw, twigs, and cones burned up rapidly. Ziiza talked of food and rest and happy times without mentioning Beaverton once. Then she sang them to sleep.

Ziiza awoke to Dg's deep-throated rumble. My foot hurts, was her first thought. She felt his sides heaving as he pressed against her. She listened to the ever-present, booming surf sound floating over the dunes, dropping into their depression. Nothing unusual. Dg was up. She twisted around, sat up, and put her arm around the creature. He trembled. Growled. She looked and listened, straining her eyes and ears. The fire was out. A sliver of moon shone weakly. Dg barked. "Org! Wake up!" Ziiza said in a hushed, but urgent voice. Milli mumbled in her sleep.

"What is it, Muma?" he groaned.

Dg, barking now, twisted away from her and bounded into the night. "Something's out there." Ziiza shook Edu and Govvi. "Wake up! Wake up! Govvi, you've got to get the fire going."

"Yes, Muma. Yes, Muma," Govvi said as she crawled to the fire.

Dg gave a series of high-pitched yips. A branch snapped. Then a crunch-crash from the Sea side, so loud it sounded like a pine tree breaking in two. High above them, a drawn-out, mournful roar. "Spears! Spears! Positions, all," Ziiza screamed, pushing, slapping, and prodding the still-groggy children. "Govvi, get that fire going!" Govvi's probing hands touched a warm pine knot. She breathed on it. It glowed red. She sucked in a breath. It faded. She blew hard; no time for delicacy. A flame leapt. She swiped around, feeling for half-burned twigs on the fire edge. "Pitch-baskets, Org," Ziiza screamed.

The smell of wet fur sank into the depression. The animal hesitated, rose up, roared, and charged.

"Spears up. Spears up," Ziiza screamed. Growling and biting, Dg chased it down the dune. It swung at him with a giant paw; he jumped away just in time. The fire flared and Ziiza saw its gleaming white teeth and long claws. Org tipped his pitch basket into the flames. The children stood trembling, spears pointed at a monster they could hardly see. It rose up again, swinging its forepaws, knocking their spears away. "Run, children! Run!" Ziiza screamed.

Org raised his flaming basket and backed away, swinging it from side to side. The animal hesitated, then went for him. Dg kept at it, snarling, biting its legs. Ziiza grabbed a pitch basket and shoved it in the fire. It caught. She raised it up. The dark animal loomed over her. "Now!" she shouted. Org swung his fiery basket, slamming it against its head. The enraged beast swatted his pole away, but the flaming pitch stuck. It swiped and pawed and the more it did, the more the hot pitch burned and spread into its mouth, ears, and eyes. Its ferocious bellow-roar turned into a pathetic bawl. Ziiza swung her pitch-basket full circle till it flared bright. She jammed it into the animal's mouth and held it, twisting the fireball in its throat until its gnashing teeth crushed the pole. Pathetic bawl turned to plaintive yips, as it turned and lumbered up and over the dune, leaving the stench of burning fur and scorched flesh hanging in the air.

"It won't be back," Ziiza said to Org, trying to sound positive. "You were magnificent."

"You too, Muma. You've got guts." They hugged, both trying to stop each other's trembling.

Ziiza and Org spent the night tending the fire, gathering wood and pointing spears in case the animal returned, although they agreed it was unlikely. But another one? Certainly that could happen. It took three "Whatever It Takes" to calm the terrified children, but when they finally fell asleep, they slept the sleep of exhaustion.

Dawn came, but even early-rising Edu slept on. Dg, tight against his side, snorted, growled, and whined, as if vanquishing all manner of monsters in his dreams. "I'll take the fire watch," Org said to his muma. "You get some sleep." Her head wobbled, her eyes closed, and she tipped over.

After peering cautiously over the dune, they stepped onto a broad, clear beach. Clear except for the animal's enormous footprints. Milli and Netti shuddered and walked around them. Edu did the opposite, twisting his feet to obliterate them. At the water's edge he pulled up short, as if expecting something to emerge and gobble him up. He ran to the security of his family.

Com, back to his old energized self, zigzagged down the beach. He ran back. "I found it!" he said, panting, and very pleased with himself. "The monster., dead on the beach. At least I think it is; I didn't get too close."

A watabeast and dead. They poked with spears and it did not move. A strange beast indeed, the first Ziiza, Org, or any of them had seen close up, although, from canoes, they had seen a few heads bobbing in the Sea. Placid and solitary, watabeasts lived far from shore, floating, fishing, diving, coming on land only to give birth. Like grizzly bears, their smaller cousins, they were omnivorous. They had only two enemies, the orca or killer whale, and starvation. Their enormous bulk – they were probably the largest fur-coated animal on earth – required constant eating. When for whatever reason their aquatic food supply failed, they found themselves in a dead zone, they came ashore. A starvation rampage was just that; watabeasts consumed anything they could catch, squash, or strip from trees, as fast as they could.

The watabeast's bulk was strangely distributed. Its head and forelegs, especially its head, were disproportionately small; its shoulders comically narrow. In contrast, its bulbous lower body provided floatation and its large hind legs and oversized webbed paws gave it swimming and diving power. On land it could run short distances on its hind legs — at surprising speeds. As the children edged closer they were revolted by the animal's grotesquely burned head, especially its swollen tongue, forcing its mouth open, squeezing around its teeth. Even Ziiza could not resist stroking its honey-colored coat. And indulging in the celebratory satisfaction of kicking it. And wondering how it managed to get so far down the beach before it expired. As they patted and stroked and kicked, the watabeast's involuntary munificence dawned on them, the finest of furs: thick and lustrous. Clothing for all. Sleeping robes, too. And all the meat and fat they could eat and carry. It was that big.

9

Grand Muma River

THE DAYS were still sunny and warm, but the nights grew longer – clear, cold nights under canopies of stars. Wind gusts shook down brown-flecked alder leaves. Ziiza walked the beach lost in her thoughts, and, as she had every day since the canoes, posed the problem: autumn is upon us and I have no way of gauging our progress. If we do not make it, could the little ones, or Netti, or any of us, survive a cold, wet, windy winter on this coast? Anything is possible – she continued to herself, for she could not discuss her doubts and fears with the children, any of them, and still project the calm certainty her position as Muma-in-Charge required – we are, after all, trail-hardened and resourceful. Nevertheless the answer was sobering: highly unlikely. Besides, she thought, after surviving MeTonn's treachery, after the rogue wave, the slippery headland, the rampaging watabeast, haven't we used up a goodly portion of our luck?

The burned canoes by the rock, the sandstone graffiti, the beaten trail, were the last evidence of people they had seen. No flotilla sightings, far-off ants-at-Sea. No canoes drawn up on the beach. No spot-in-the-dark bonfires. No chattering paddlers in camp. No noisy children making games of wood gathering.

The fear of meeting up with another "MeTonn" had faded. *I'd welcome meeting up with anyone now,* she confessed to herself. And for the hundredth time she asked: *Did I choose wrong? Should I have given in to their vote? Should I have taken the easy way? Would we be there now, safe, secure, beginning our new lives?*

Although their fortunes swung from days of super-abundance, such as feasting on watabeast, to weeks of subsistence, the Sea never let them down. The animal had solved their clothing problem: skirts for the females, hip wraps for the males, and loose capes for both. Order of march was now order of march in uniform, the ultimate uniform: rich-looking, warm, and rainproof (although crudely put together). They now had better clothing and sleeping robes than before the fateful event that had set them on the beach.

Org thrived on each day's challenge, his strength and endurance increasing. After weeks on the walk, Ziiza still had to shout: "Slow down, Org; you'll leave us behind." Com, the scout, *was* slowing however, showing the wear of the miles. Instead of ranging ahead as earlier, he walked with the family. In mid-afternoon, sometimes only after Ziiza's promptings, he jogged ahead to find a campsite. His selectivity waned; anyplace with fresh water would do. Of course if something piqued his curiosity, that was different. Netti kept up, barely. Her headaches – one or two a day, about an hour long at peak intensity, then a gradual recovery – were not going to go away, Ziiza concluded, although she spoke optimistically. Although Netti was longer-legged and normally a faster walker than her shorter, more delicate, older sister, Milli was at least uninjured. Whereas they had previously walked together by choice, now they did so by necessity. Dour Govvi, the super-organizer, always found energy for the day's walk (but not a bit more), starting and tending her fires, and keeping her tally board current (which no one required of her). Edu was struggling, nearing the end of his endurance, although one would not know it from his cheerfulness and curiosity.

Ziiza walked through her pain, she had no choice, but it was growing worse. At first she had told herself: Get through the last few miles; make it to camp. As spring blended into summer it hurt from the first step: Just get through the day. Now: Get through the hour. Not only that, she had to concentrate on walking without limping. The missing toe threw her off balance, off stride. If she limped, the pain spread to her ankles, knees, and hips, especially her offsetting hip.

By mid-summer they had experienced just about everything the broad beach could throw at them. They were noticed by bears (and other large beasts they could not identify) but were not threatened; the animals seemed more interested in fishing and berries. Or perhaps seven people marching in line was a formidable enough "creature" to make them wary and lose interest. Evening fires were well-tended, night watchers alert, pitch baskets at the ready. The best watcher, of course, was Dg, who established territorial boundaries and fearlessly defended them by yipping, growling, and barking at dark threats "out there" that the humans could not see, smell, or hear. Just as he had alerted them to the watabeast.

Still, there were the daily obstacles: beach-blocking boulder piles to clamber over; grass-choked shallows to pick through; sucking mud flats to risk; and tangled driftwood piles to somehow get around. The most formidable obstacles were rivers. The smaller ones were routine. If the tide was right, they crossed on the sand fans at the mouth.

Sometimes the channel escape slots were so narrow Org could stand in the middle, as he had done before the wave, and hand them across. If that did not work, they walked upstream and waded or swam. Techniques were the same for large rivers, except they demanded greater caution, effort, and, sometimes, long waits for a turn. Rafting was out of the question. Although the rivers, estuaries, and beaches were littered with washed-up trees of all sizes, they were impossible to make into manageable rafts. Their compromise was to lash two or three small tree trunks together with Com's and Netti's crude ropes, tie their food and belongings on, and, kicking and hand-paddling, make their way across. Dg rode with the gear, but by mid-crossings always jumped in to swim the rest of the way; he could not stand not being first.

* * *

Edu woke, propped his head on his hand, and assessed another day's weather: chilly, some clouds, but otherwise every indication of a fine autumn day. After shaking himself awake, Dg ran into the trees after something. Govvi got her fire going, but only after a false start because she tried a heavy, red-barked wood that grew along the shore; it was so dense it would not support combustion.

Com went off exploring, but soon returned. "Look what I found," he said, holding out a handful of tiny oysters, his legs and arms dripping black muck from the tidal flat.

Netti woke clear headed and pain free – for now.

Ziiza had been awake for some time, feigning sleep, letting them run their accustomed routines so her announcement would have maximum impact. "Put out the fire, Govvi," she ordered. "We're leaving. Now."

"Huh?" Org said, pulling another robe over his head.

"I'm not warmed up yet," Milli said.

"These oysters are delicious, Muma," Com said. "You crack them with your teeth."

"Pack up. Let's go." They gathered up and set out.

As was her custom, Ziiza waited until mid-day to talk business. "Here are the hard facts, children," she began after they had stopped by a creek to refresh themselves. "We – okay, I – chose 'Trace the Sea,' for better or worse. Who knows, if I had stayed on the trail we might be there by now. But I didn't. And frankly, I'm not ready to say I made a mistake," the first time she had spoken of that possibility, "or that we are lost." She paused for emphasis and continued: "The days, as you well know, are growing shorter. Any morning we'll find frost on the grass. Then on the ground and on the bushes. The fact is, dear ones, we have only a few weeks till the first winter storms. Real winter storms, with real snow, like on the Old Side. But we were prepared for it then, had warm shelters, stored food, and a community of neighbors we could rely upon. Here, alone. . . ."

Ziiza's hard eyes passed from child to child. She continued: "The night watcher will wake everyone at first light. We pack immediately and go, eating as we walk. No morning fires; no cooking. Com will resume full-time scouting for food, water, rivers, and campsites. Limited rest breaks. Expect to be hungry. If a clam beach is poor, we move on; no more spending two hours per clam. We walk until dark. Past dark. If possible, Govvi, you will run ahead, join Com; have a fire going when we arrive, because we will eat what we have, quickly, then go to sleep. Org, you will pick up the pace, which should please you. When Edu slows down, you will carry him. Milli, you and I will assist Netti. We must make Beaverton. We *will* make Beaverton before winter."

"I thought we *were* walking fast, Muma," Com said. "As fast as we could."

"I'm not blaming you, Com. It's not your fault or anyone's; it's winter coming on." Then, in an attempt to finish with something positive, she said, "Keep working on your objects. Everyone's should be complete when we get to Beaverton, mine included." She pointed to Org, then down the beach. They walked south.

Throughout the journey Ziiza had enjoyed looking for colorful driftwood chips. She licked them for salt, then dried them. If they held their colors, did not go flat and dull, she kept them. When Netti began braiding cedar-root strands, she suggested Ziiza make a necklace (which eventually grew to two). At breaks, in camp, even on the walk, Ziiza smoothed and rounded the chips on flat stones of progressively finer grits, then drilled holes with broken shells. A simple, never-ending task, taking her mind off her foot, her hip, the children's questions and complaints, and the big problem. She strung them, alternating larger, smaller, darker, lighter, regular, irregular. As a final touch, she polished them with hair and nose oil. So her habit developed, fingering them, moving them around her neck, humming her made-up tunes, one chip, one tune.

Govvi's tally board grew more detailed. Each day she scraped away the previous day's data and started afresh, in a tight code only she understood. She even counted the pieces in Ziiza's necklaces. "Only add chips in twos," she admonished. "Odd numbers are unlucky."

Milli found, polished, and rejected shell mirrors. Org, his rocks. Netti wove shoulder baskets for herself. Refined and improved. Edu finally found a collar Dg would accept, a strip of watabeast fur. But only after he had run in the salt water and rolled in the sand, presumably to remove the beast's odor, to make it his own.

Which left Com. He had had so many rope-making failures that Ziiza gently suggested he try something else. A headband would look dashing and suit his personality, be it woven or fur. How about an antler dagger or a sharpened shell knife? No. The more he failed, the more he had to have a rope. It had to be strong, pliable, and thin, he insisted, demanding specifications from one with no tools and limited to the materials he gathered. It came down to, or back to, braided cedar root. The latest version did not come close to satisfying him, not as thin as he had hoped, not supple enough, not uniformly round. But strong it was; it held his weight. Org's, too. He wrapped it around his waist, tucked in the end, and wore it like a belt.

They passed a long island, so far offshore it did not cut the wind. Then an open passage to the Sea. And another island, this one with steep, jagged, snow-topped peaks rising out of black, green, and tan foothills. Only it was not an island. It was a peninsula, formed by a large inland waterway, salt water but without the smell of the Sea. And as if to balance the landscape, far to the southeast rose a mountain as different from the peninsula mountains as a mountain could be: immense, flat-topped, solitary, and white all the way down. So they walked a giant S, curving south, then west, then north – exactly the wrong direction – then west, and finally south again. All the while, the pressure mounted.

Three weeks had passed since Ziiza's announcement. Fortunately, food was more or less plentiful. Netti was coping. Org had little trouble assisting Edu. The children's grumbling was minimal, even as their muma pushed the pace. The old, sensible, order of march turned into a dogged forced march, one foot in front of the other. But however determined, however hard they tried, fatigue set in; they were a beach-weary band of travelers, endlessly tracing the Sea. Hasty meals, too little sleep, no rest-over days, the accumulation of miles; the more Ziiza tried to "pick it up," the slower they walked.

* * *

Com came toward them with his head down, shuffle-ran, then walked again, hastening, yet holding back. He stopped, turned away from his family, and stood, twisting his feet in the sand, looking south at the small headland he had just investigated. When they caught up, Ziiza put her hands on his shoulders and massaged them, running her thumbs up his neck. "What's wrong, dear?" she said. "What don't you want to tell us?"

He looked up at her and his eyes filled with tears. "It's the . . . It's the biggest river in the world, Muma."

No one spoke. No one, not even Ziiza, could think of anything to say. They just stared ahead, trying to imagine "the biggest river in the world."

When one is healthy, strong, and optimistic, he or she can toss off bad news with a laugh and push through it. When one is weary and down of spirit, bad news is tough to absorb, let alone deal with. But it must be dealt with. Ziiza sighed and said, "Well, we might as well find out." They trudged along the last of the sand and began climbing the headland. The surrounding trees grew shorter, bent and sculpted by the wind. Com followed a faint trail that ran through pocket meadows and shrub thickets, and in and out of low forest, none of which broke the wind that grew fiercer with each step toward "the biggest river." It turned their ears red and blew through their watabeast garments.

The trail dipped and turned inland to the east. Com did not take it. Instead, he led them single file up a side trail to the edge of a cliff. On a windless day, one could easily step off before he realized the trail had ended, it was that abrupt. He stopped them with a jerk of his spear. Then he stepped back from the edge, raised his arms, and leaned backward into the wind. It supported him. No need to say anything; no one could hear him anyway. One by one they struggled forward. Looked over and down. The wind tore at their eyes.

It might be a river. Should be a river. Probably was a river. Com pointed out to Sea, swung his arm wide to the south, and held it. He waggled his finger in a low flat motion, indicating the other side, a light brown strip, barely visible through the heavy air. Below them, the "river" surged into the Sea, which, instead of welcoming it as a proper Sea should; raged against its entry, as if a rival, a violator of its domain. Mountainous stand-up waves crisscrossed the surface, crashing into the cliff, slapping into each other, falling over. A twig-sized tree with still-green branches and red roots moved steadily toward the open Sea. Counting one. Counting two. Counting three. On each count, water enough to fill a lake surged into the Sea, like it or not. Ziiza gave Org a signal with a blue-cold hand: lead on. Then another to Com to fall into place; no more scouting today. After a few steps, and with the screaming wind at their backs, she gave Com a wink and a shrug. "Well done," she mouthed.

They filed downhill, leaving the huge bar waves behind, replaced by frenzied whitecaps and blowing spume. Org led them to the riverside, then up and over a rise which mercifully cut the wind. Just before nightfall a low black cloud swept in from the Sea. They were soaked before it rained.

The miserable camp reminded them of the one in the headland's cold shadow, the night before Netti's accident. It should have been ideal, a wind-sheltered hollow surrounded by tall trees. It even had people signs, a blackened-stone fire ring. But no fire for them. Org, true to his duty, selected the best shelter tree he could. They dropped down and huddled together. Edu tried to crawl under Dg.

This is it. Not chilly beach rain. Winter rain. Ice rain.

Every hour or so throughout the night Ziiza had them stand (she did not have to wake anyone) and jump and rub each other down.

"I'm starving," Milli said, opening her eyes in the dull early light. The rain continued, pounding them as it had through the night. She fumbled for a food bag, withdrew a clam chunk and gnawed at it. Govvi jerked the bag away, only to have it snatched by a quicker hand.

"Take it easy," Ziiza said.

"A couple of more bites and we won't have anything," Govvi said. She was right, of course. A couple of bites to Govvi meant exactly two.

"Can't be any worse upriver," Ziiza shouted over the rain. "And we have no other way to go. Order of march. Let's get moving."

But it was worse. Not just the cold rain, sometimes mixed with sleet; they were out of food, and away from the Sea with its bountiful clam beaches and mussel-covered rocks. This river presented no placid, life-generating estuary teeming with frogs, crabs, and fish. This river never slowed down. The salmon runs were over, or so they seemed. No rotting fish on shore. Just an occasional skeleton working its way into the sand, picked clean by animals and birds. "Chew grass and stems," Ziiza told them to take their minds off their hunger. "Suck pebbles."

On the third day of their inland march the rain stopped and the wind eased off – to just about what they were used to on the beach. Sleepy gray clouds hung close to the river. It seemed warmer, but it was not. In fact, it was colder. Getting ready to snow. Were it not for Ziiza's desperate timetable, they would have stopped, rested, built a fire, dried out and, with Milli leading the way, fished and turned rocks for crawfish. Instead, they dried out as they walked, albeit slower and slower. Islands in the river, large and small, appeared on their right. At first they were grass-covered mounds and flats that disappeared under each tidal surge. Farther upriver they were more substantial, cut-banked, tree-ringed islands, or long, stringy sand heaps.

We can't cross, even when the river narrows for islands. Too much. Too swift.

The trail was relatively good, mostly along thin dark sand beaches, sometimes over high cliffs and rises. It showed signs of use, although nothing like the broad trail from the rock. Coastal spruce, cedar, and alder had long since given way to interior fir, maple, willow, and cottonwood.

They camped on the edge of a small feeder river, too hungry and exhausted to cross. Govvi managed a fire. She and Com, the thinnest and coldest, lay down and curved around it, just shy of scorching, trying to soak up enough warmth to get through the chill, foggy night they knew was coming. Edu lay with Dg tight against him.

Ziiza walked to the big river's edge and surveyed its powerful flow, finally running smooth. She looked up at the gray clouds and sniffed the air.

Snow coming. I can smell it: moist, with the faint scent of fir needles. Before-the-snow air. Reminds me of home.

Org, Milli, and Netti followed the feeder river the other way, upstream, searching for food. Dg joined them. When it broadened and pooled, Milli exclaimed, "Look! Fish!" Dozens upon dozens of large fish languidly circled the pool, some with grotesquely hooked jaws, all with mottled sides; they looked diseased. She waded in. One hit her leg and hung in the slack current. Seemed not to notice. She scoop-threw it onto the bank. Dg sniffed, nipped, and held it down with a paw. After a few feeble flops it lay still. Milli waded in farther, expecting the other fish to spook, scurry away upstream, or down. They paid no attention and circled slowly, dorsal fins cutting the surface, swinging wide, bellies scraping gravel in the shallows. The swimming dead. She drove her spear through one. Too easy. It hardly wiggled. She flipped it up. They watched in silence. "We'd better take them back," Netti said calmly, as if it was a routine food-gathering event. Org and Netti jaw-hooked a fish with each hand, carried them to camp, and cleaned them as best they could. Milli, the fisher, continued, scooping and pitching until she tired. She kicked one onto the bank and stopped. It was too much.

The meat was soft and pasty white. As it cooked, instead of a delicious fish-roasting smell, the smoke was so putrid the warmers backed off. It tasted worse than it smelled. But they ate it gladly. "Slow down, now," Ziiza said. "I don't want anyone getting sick." But it was no use; even the most self-controlled eater, Govvi, gorged herself on the oily, repulsive, half-cooked fish. They sprawled around the fire, stuffed and exhausted, and fell asleep. Edu dreamt of fresh clams, broad sandy beaches, and summer breezes. Ziiza dreamt of wide, hard-flowing rivers, and snow.

Edu vomited first and oftenest. Dg hacked and gagged throughout the night, then lapped up what he and the others had expelled. Only Ziiza and Govvi kept theirs down. The night watchers assisted the retchers, leading them away from the fire, holding their heads.

Ziiza held out her hand to the morning. Giant snowflakes floated down, came to rest, and melted.

If we were settled in, had a snug, well-stocked shelter, this would be the loveliest of sights.

Her hand grew cold. Flakes piled on. She licked them. Lovely sight, yes? Big-flake snowfalls in springtime are one thing, usually gone by afternoon. But wet ones on the new side of winter are quite something else. These snowflakes lacked only wind to make them deadly.

Before they left Camp Stinky, as Edu called it, Ziiza had everyone scout around for anything good to eat. "Quickly, we have to get going." They found nothing, not even crawfish or minnows (and they weren't ready for slugs and worms). So they filled their bags with the rotting fish and promised themselves they would eat sparingly. Ziiza wrapped her fur tightly and cinched up her cedar bark belt, out of habit, because it did not feel cold. Netti walked without assistance. Bad fish and vomiting had produced an unexpected bonus: no headache. As they filed along Ziiza dropped back, stopped, and looked at her footprints in the snow.

How horrible. Is that really my foot? It never looked that bad on the beach. Or it didn't seem to.

Brown prints in the mud, outlined in white, revealing everything. Multiplied over and over.

What if someone saw them? What would they think? What kind of deformed person would they think I was?

She shuddered at the thought and walked on. Then she recovered and smiled.

At least I'm walking. And doing quite well, thank you.

10

The Crossing

THE PATH along the big river continued level and reasonably clear. Hour by hour, the temperature dropped. Snow stuck to the fir limbs. At mid-day the terrain changed, the forest receding from the river, replaced by a broad plain. On their right, the river ran cool and blue, and broadened to almost as wide as at its mouth. The trees on the opposite side stood thumbnail high on Ziiza's outstretched hand. Upriver, to the east, rose a solitary, point-peaked mountain, proudly displaying a mantle of new snow. As they walked on, another mountain showed itself on their left, larger-appearing than the other because it was closer. And different: perfectly symmetrical, with a broad level top and a column of smoke rising from it. They walked along a thin sand beach, enjoying the mountain views and the gentle snowfall, trying to keep their minds away from hunger.

"Isn't that a canoe ahead?" Org said, pointing to a dark object perpendicular to the water. He ran. The canoe was medium sized (considerably smaller than MeTonn's), smooth-sided, and expertly made. The edges and cross pieces held fluffy ridges of snow. Three paddle handles stuck up and out at an angle, also holding snow. But unlike any canoe he had seen before, this one had words chiseled into its sides and colored red: "Prong's River Transport."

Org stared at the canoe and its advertisement. Milli and Netti joined him. They could not resist swiping at the snow and tasting it — as if snow on a dark canoe with red lettering should taste different from the snow falling on their heads and shoulders. Then Govvi and Com. Finally Edu, Ziiza, and Dg. "No, Dg," Ziiza commanded, as he headed for the canoe. "Hold him, Edu."

Just then a man emerged from a thicket of stunted willow along the river edge. "My, my," he said, "customers." He was a finger taller than Org, and slimmer: hips, shoulders, waist. Arms sinewy, powerful, and long, the arms of a professional paddler. His sun-bleached hair, trimmed neatly and evenly all around, brushed his shoulders.

This man is something of a canoe man, if I say so.

His face was an unusual combination of chiseled features, smooth skin and a hint of "baby" fat. He appeared not to have facial hair. Body hair, either. He ambled to the canoe, leaned stiff-armed against the prow, and looked them over. His intense brown eyes darted to Milli, to Ziiza, to Netti, and back to Milli, where they stayed. A self-satisfied smirk crept to a corner of his mouth, as if to say: I know, I know, ladies. I can hardly believe I'm this beautiful myself. He wore only a lower garment, so loosely fitting it might have been a shortened version of a female's skirt – except for the very un-female, pole-like protrusion from the crotch.

"We. . . ." Ziiza stopped, forced her eyes back to his face, gathered herself, and continued: "You're the first person we've seen in a long time." Then, "Where are we? Can you tell us, please?"

"Prong's the name," he said, passing on her question. Then, attending to first, or perhaps second, things first, "I run the river service." He flipped a hand toward the river. "The only one, I might add."

"Can you tell us where we are?" Ziiza repeated.

"Where you are?" he said with a sneer. "You're standing next to the Grand Muma River. What did you think it was, Blackberry Creek?"

"What's that big mountain doing?" Edu asked.

"Hush, Edu," Ziiza said, "This is business." Then to Prong: "Beaverton. We're moving to Beaverton."

"Beaverton." He laughed. "You people really are out of it, aren't you. You're at Beaverton. Or close to it. Just over there. On the other side of the river."

Seven pairs of shoulders sagged. Milli and Netti slid to the ground and sat cross-legged, their mouths open. Dg sat, as if he understood, but kept eyeing the man. Edu knelt, put his arms around Dg's neck, and hugged him, hard. Ziiza looked across the big river and fingered her necklaces. Tears welled up and she did not even try to stop them. She turned away, pinched her nose with her fingers, and blew onto the ground. Swiped her eyes. Govvi's tally board swung in her hand. Com looked alternately from mountain, to shore, and back again. Org stood.

Com broke the silence. "I don't see anything. Any village or settlement or town. No smoke rising."

"You can't see it. . . ." Then, not wishing to insult a potential customer's child, he swallowed *stupid* and substituted, "It's on the other side of the ridge, sonny. A day or two's walk from here." He smiled, thumped the lettering on his canoe, and added, "Correction: from *there*."

"Will you take us across?" Ziiza asked.

"Of course. Of course. That's my business." Then, with a hip twitch and a lascivious look at Milli, he added, "For a little price."

82

"Never," Ziiza snapped.

Don't blow this, Ziiza. We have to get across.

"We have fish," she told him. "That's as close to money as we have to offer. Org, show him." Org held one up.

"Spawned-out trash. Wouldn't touch it."

"Our sleeping robes?" Govvi said hesitantly. "Watabeast. Pretty new."

Prong's lips curled into another of his now-familiar sneers. "Watabeast fur is illegal in Beaverton, dearie. Clothing, robes, or anything. You'll find out soon enough. If that's where you end up. And you will, because there's no place else to go. Less you want to – keep – on – camping – and walking – and camping – and walking. Or camping – and not walking." His last comment struck him as particularly funny and sent him into such a fit of laughter he slipped and fell backward into his canoe.

Ziiza was speechless.

"Think about it," Prong said, pushing himself up and scratching his member. "See you in the morning." He disappeared into the willow thicket.

Doubly shocked and left to themselves, they retreated from the river and made a slow camp inside the tree line at the edge of the plain. After gagging down some fish – it was past repulsive – they sat around the fire, each trying to make sense of the situation in his or her own way.

On the plus side, they were finally here, or so they had been told by a man they did not trust. The snow continued, not a snowstorm, just a snowfall. The temperature: cold enough to snow, but just barely. The night was windless, lit by the fuzzy-glow of a three-quarter moon. All things considered, it was as good as they could expect. And, as far as expecting, Ziiza half-expected Prong to join them around the fire. Or invite them over; they could see his fire though the trees. He never did. A wife? A woman in there? On the minus side: how to get across without paying his price? "We can overpower him," Edu whispered, apparently reading her mind. "We all have spears. And Org. He's tough, stronger. Even without his rock." Then louder, "Org, you hear me?"

"That I do, little brother," he said. "Take that pretty boy guy all by myself. Borrow his canoe for a bit."

"He might have friends," Com said. "Besides, we can't all fit in. We'd have to make two or three trips. How would we do that?"

"Friends?" Milli said, sneering. "I'll bet his vanity, and his, ahem, are the only friends he's got." Netti joined her.

Gosh, it's great to see them laughing again.

And so it went, back and forth, with no solution. What should have been a night of celebration – Beaverton in a day – was instead gloomy and song-less. One by one they gave in to sleep. Except Ziiza, who sat, her legs pulled tight under her robe, massaging her foot. Late at night, with the sounds of the river running strong and thoughts of Beaverton over the hill, Ziiza curled around Edu and Dg and closed her eyes.

"Trace the Sea. Then let it go."

They woke to far-off scratching and scraping, Prong dragging his canoe to the water. Leaving the stern on shore he stood, feet wide apart, looking at their camp.

Ziiza rose stiffly, shook herself out, and walked to him. He smiled as cordial a smile as he could manage. They talked. Ziiza shook her head "no" again and again, refusing whatever he was offering – or demanding. Finally, she nodded agreement and returned. "Org, you and Milli and Netti will go first. He's ready to leave. Now." Then, in Org's ear: "You have your spear and your rock. If he makes a move toward Milli – or Netti – use them. I'm depending upon you."

With Org in the bow and the girls in the middle, all with paddles, Prong lifted, shoved the stern off the gravel beach, guided and waded until he was knee-deep, and climbed in. Ziiza waved them away – with flash memories of their last canoe trip. Once away, Prong chatted cheerfully; he was in his element, and evidently satisfied with the bargain he had struck. They quartered hard, paddling upstream against the current. Then, to everyone's surprise, he stood, held his paddle flat to the water as if to catch snowflakes (for it was still snowing, but tapering off), and boomed:

"'To him who in the love of Nature holds
Communion with her visible forms, she speaks.'"

Netti poked her sister. "What's he talking about?"

"I don't care," Milli whispered. "I just wish he would sit down. It's freaky em-bar-ras-sing."

He recited more lines. Then he did sit down, abruptly, evidently figuring they had slipped too far downstream from his sight point. He dug hard in the water and ordered them to do the same. When they had gained enough on the current, he stood up and continued:

"'The all-beholding sun shall see no more
In all his course; nor yet in the cold ground.'"

And so they zigzagged across the big river, more properly the Grand Muma, most assuredly not Blackberry Creek, taking twice the time they should have. When they reached the far shore he had intoned, shouted, or mumbled dozens of incomprehensible lines, none of his fares knowing, or caring, what prompted the outburst. He offered no explanation and they did not ask. It obviously gave him pleasure and perhaps helped restore his strength for the tough solo return trip.

With Ziiza paddling in the bow and Com in mid-canoe, along with Edu, Dg, and Govvi who provided no paddle power, and a not-so-energetic Prong in the stern, the second crossing was even slower. Since Prong had now affected a reasonably courteous demeanor toward his customers, Edu asked his mountain question again.

"You mean that one?" Prong said, pointing upstream and east. "That's Morning Spire. Sharp as a knife edge on top. Although I've not been up; nobody has. Not that I couldn't."

"Thank you, sir, Mister Prong," said the inquirer. "What about the other one? Over there." He pointed at the flat-topper behind them, barely visible in the falling snow.

"Smoke-storm. And when she blows, you'd better be far away from here."

"What about you?" Edu quipped innocently. "How will you know? How will you be far away?" He got no answer as Prong stood and recited more lines for his second load of customers:

"'The venerable woods, rivers that move
In majesty, and the complaining brooks
That make the meadows green.'"

Again the canoe slipped downstream, too far and too fast for Prong, so he gave it up and sat down, revealing much more of what Govvi had not seen before. Sitting backward in the canoe and facing him, she covered her eyes. As they approached the south shore, Prong continued paddling, up what was obviously a large tributary river, one they had not noticed from the other side.

"Why don't you put us off over there?" Ziiza asked nervously.

"In the first place," Prong replied, "that's not where your kids are. In the second place, it's an island; you'd be stranded." They continued, eventually passing an inlet on their right. "That's it, the channel that makes it an island," he said. "Few minutes more."

Ziiza spotted the three waving at her. When the bow hit the snow-dusted, mud-and-sand beach, she got out, and, with Org's help, pulled the canoe part way up. Dg squeezed between Edu and Govvi and jumped. Ziiza and Org held the canoe steady while the children moved forward and out. "Okay, Org," Ziiza said, "lead off. Com, you scout the trail." She pointed to a worn slot in the riverbank leading into the trees. "I'll catch up."

They clawed their way up the slippery bank and disappeared into the trees, as the two below watched. A few yards down the trail Org stopped, put his finger to his lips, and led them back, where they crouched and peered between the evergreen limbs. Edu held Dg's collar.

At least it isn't snowing as hard over here, Ziiza thought, as she stood ankle deep in the water, waiting. Prong, after laying his paddle in the canoe with exaggerated care, straightened up and smiled crookedly. Then, in a burst, he tore off his "skirt." Whap! He slapped it against the canoe.

I could run. I could scream. But I bargained.

Again, with exaggerated slowness, he splashed toward her, twisting his hips, his engorged member swinging and jiggling with each step.

It will be quick. Then over.

He lunged, grabbed her shoulders, pushed her back on the canoe. He tore at her cape, grabbed her breasts. Lowered his hand. Lowered himself.

"Now!" Org yelled. Dg tore away from Edu's grip, leapt the bank, and ran at them, ears back, eyes wild. The six ran from the trees, spears in hands, sliding and stumbling down the bank.

Dg launched himself at Prong. Bit. Clamped. Twisted. Released. And bit again.

What's happening?

Dg fell away, shook his bloody muzzle, tilted, gulped, and swallowed.

Ziiza pushed, twisted away, and sank to her knees. Prong clutched his crotch and rolled on the canoe in speechless agony. He gasped for air, fought for words, and finally squealed: "Owwwwwww! Yowwwwww!" A red blotch spread on the water. "I'm . . . I'm dying."

"You should die," Org yelled, the first to reach them. He helped Ziiza up, slowly, gently, and walked her away. Dg shifted sideways, positioning himself between Ziiza and the moaning, screaming, stony-eyed Prong. Only then did he allow himself the luxury of a good "grrrrr."

"Edu, hold onto Dg," Org shouted, after turning his muma over to Milli and Netti. Prong wavered back and forth, ready to faint. Org grabbed his arm, pulled him up, and dumped him into the canoe. He flipped his legs in and shook the canoe to shift him to the middle. He yanked the canoe from the shore, and, kicking and splashing, ran it into the river. He drew the canoe back and pushed.

Just get away from here. From the sight of him.

Ziiza sucked air and pointed toward the trail. "Let's go," she breathed. They scrambled up.

"Come on Dg," Edu shouted. Dg bounded up the incline. Edu pulled him in by his collar and hugged him.

Ziiza patted the creature's head. "Good Dg. I think."

The canoe floated downstream, rider-less it seemed, except for Prong's foot sticking over the side. Snowflakes continued falling. The wide tributary glistened and rolled in its final glory, till it joined its Grand Muma. The current caught the canoe, turning it round and round in lazy circles. It bumped a wooded point of land and stopped. The river caught the end, swung it free, and, as far as Ziiza and the watchers were concerned, it was gone.

11

Welcome to Exciting Beaverton

T HEY HURRIED along the trail as if speed and distance would erase what they had witnessed. The children understood that they should not speak until their muma broke the silence. Which was fine with her, for she was a cauldron of emotions: rage to relief, teeth-shaking fear to exaltation over Dg-to-the-rescue. His loyalty, his understanding, his action; simply amazing when she thought about it. When anyone thought about it, which was all the others could think about, too.

Self-defense, wasn't it? Will he recover or bleed to death? Do I care? Should I care?

By mid-day the sun was out. Melting snow slid off the tree limbs, releasing them to snap up and shower the walkers with super-sized "raindrops." Sun-charged vapor rose and hung over the trail, so thick Org punched through it with his fist. Fun. They all did. Smiles. Looks. Silence. Ziiza was not ready.

Ziiza thought the nameless tributary to be about one-third the width of the "Grand Muma River." From what she could make out, the terrain on the opposite side was as densely treed as this, but rose ever so gently, interrupted by small, widely-spaced knobs, into a range of substantial mountains, the most prominent being "Morning Spire." Easy walking on a gentle up-and-down trail that swung away from the river for stream crossings, then back along the bank.

With daylight expiring and the close-in west hills casting early shadows, Org raised his hand signaling a halt. Just ahead the trail entered a small, half-circle-shaped clearing covered with lush grass and divided by a creek tumbling into the river. On the other side of the creek, next to a fire ring with no visible fire, two men engaged in vigorous discussion, shouting and waving their arms. They did not seem angry, ready to fight, just overly-enthusiastic debaters. Since he had little choice, Org revealed himself and walked toward them. As he drew closer, one of the men flipped a small object in the air, caught it, slapped it on the back of his hand, and shouted "Popville."

"Gimme that," said the other. He grabbed the object, and, after balancing it on his thumb, flipped it high in the air. He let it fall to the ground and examined it. "Jayberg," he exalted. "Mark one for Jayberg."

They flipped and called, flipped and called, sometimes scraping a mark on the ground, sometimes not, oblivious to Org and company walking toward them. Only after splashing through the creek, hopping onto the mud bench, and almost surrounding them, were they noticed.

"Well, how-dee-do." said the man closest to the riverbank, his eyes twinkling. "Late arrivals off the Sea Trace, I'd say. Anyhow, welcome to Popville."

"Popville, my foot," the other man shot back. "My *big* foot," he repeated for emphasis. "Welcome to Jayberg."

"No, it's not."

"Yes, tis." Then, "Or it will be."

A hundred more flips before it's settled," said "Popville." "Maybe a thousand. Don't be so impatient." Then, "And who might you folks be?"

"I'm Ziiza, and these are my children." They shifted uncomfortably as she introduced them by name, mumbling their greetings, wondering whether these two were more of the Prong-sort they had left behind. "We've come a long way," she continued. "We understand we're almost to Beaverton. That's where we're going."

"Everyone who gets this far has come a long way, that's for sure. Anyway, I'm Pop, and this here is Jay. Our friends call us Pop&Jay. Together like." Then, under his breath, "Or they would, if we had any."

"We're pleased, ah, Pop . . . and . . . Jay," Ziiza replied.

"You're welcome to spend the night in our fair city," Pop said, "as it's about dark. Say, you don't have anything to eat in those fine-looking pouches and baskets do you?" He sniffed the air and rubbed his greasy stomach.

At an eye signal from Ziiza, Milli lowered her pouch and Netti opened her basket. Each withdrew a fish and held it up. "They taste awful," Milli said, "but they're all we have left."

"A teeny sample?" Jay said, holding out his hand.

Milli passed him the fish. He picked at it greedily.

"I could start a fire," Govvi said shyly.

"By all means," Pop&Jay responded in unison. "By all means."

"We have a song that goes sort of like that," Edu said, trying to make conversation. "'Whatever It Takes.'" The girls groaned.

"Not now, Edu," Ziiza said softly.

"You can have that lot for the night," Pop said, pointing to the edge of the clearing. "Or that one." He waved toward the riverbank. "Great view. Or any one of them."

Only then did Ziiza notice the wooden stakes sticking out of the grass; the clearing was marked off in a grid of rectangles. Pop&Jay were halfway through the raw fish and looking longingly at Netti's. She quickly restored it to the security of her basket.

"We're building a city, you see," Jay picked it up. "Right here on the banks of the beautiful North-flowing Son. Sell you a shelter lot. Cheap. You don't want to go to Beaverton anyway."

"North what?" Ziiza said.

"Name of the river," Pop said. "That river," he jerked his thumb, "the Grand Muma's North-flowing Son. Get it?"

"Got it," she said, not wanting to go further.

Ziiza played their game – it was, by all intents and purposes, their "city" – and busied herself arranging the family's belongings within the confines of four stakes. Since none of the "lots" had trees, she chose one by the riverbank. Both men were elderly and had friendly, if somewhat slippery, smiles, and bad teeth. Pop's hair was well on its way to white, albeit a dirty, yellowish white. Jay looked younger, his face covered with a full, still-dark beard, revealing only an oversized, veined nose and claw marks around his eyes.

Govvi's fire building fascinated them, although not enough to prompt them to help gather firewood; they left that to the other children. They hovered around her as if they had never seen it done before. "How'd you ever figure that out, Little One?" Pop asked, feigning amazement.

"So decidedly deft, isn't she, Pop-ol-buddy," Jay added, all friendship and partnership now that they had stopped flipping and arguing.

"I taught myself," Govvi replied cautiously. "Way up the beach. After we were. . . . It's my job. I do it every night, except when the weather's bad. Then we sleep without one." Flattered by their attention, she started a second fire nearby. Pop&Jay skewered the remaining bits of fish on sticks, roasted them briefly, then, with huge smiles, gulped them down without chewing – reminiscent of a certain creature's actions way back when, a certain creature that happened to be sitting nearby, in the same position as he was way back when, wet nose shining, tongue protruding, head cocked hungrily. Govvi picked up her tally board and scratched off one fish.

"What's that, Little One?" Pop said.

Govvi explained how she maintained the family records. This time their amazement *was* genuine; "Little One" had something special going for her.

"You won't mind if we roast our *smaller* fish on the fire," Ziiza asked, leaving no doubt that, since the two of them had consumed over half of their remaining food, there was to be no more sharing. They nodded resignedly.

In the morning, Pop&Jay, considerably better fed and in better spirits than Ziiza and company, and having had no trouble holding down the rotten fish, cheerfully made their pitch. "One lot for the price of two," Pop said.

"Two for the price of one, you numskull," Jay corrected. "Special deal for big families." They were talkers for sure, natural salesmen, and, once started they could not shut themselves off. Popville or Jayberg, Pop City or Jaytown, or whatever it was to be called, was to rival, nay, outshine Beaverton on the other side of the hill. Why? Right by the North-flowing Son River. Easier access to the Grand Muma. Loads more firewood. Splendid view of the Spire.

Again, why? "Don't like Beaverton a-tall." More accurately, Beaverton didn't like them a-tall. Asked them to leave. Kicked them out, truth to tell. Again, why? Guy who runs the place, Mistermayor, thought they were trying to take over. Malicious lies. Traitors, he had called them. Public hearing at the town council. Banished for life. Humiliated.

"We'll show 'em," Pop said. "Found a new town. A real city. Overwhelm Beaverton. Sink it." As their story spilled, Pop&Jay's countenances turned black and their eyes flashed hatred. But only for a moment. They brightened, salesmen-like, and Pop said, "You could pay us later. Anytime. Anything. How about three lots for –"

"No, thanks," Ziiza said. "We've gone through more trouble than you can imagine to get this close to Beaverton and we're not stopping here." Pop&Jay's shoulders drooped as they felt their last prospects for the season slip away. "That, I assume," she continued, pointed to an opening in the trees, "is the trail to Beaverton." They nodded reluctantly. "Thank you for your hospitality," she said in a thanks-for-nothing voice. "And thank you for the offer. We'll think about it."

Org started up the trail and the children fell in. Ziiza waved at Pop, who stood absentmindedly flipping the object, and Jay, who was picking his nose. Com sat with his feet over the bank, looking across the river. "Com," she called, "we're going. Big day ahead. Come on."

Com rose slowly and came to her, slapping Pop&Jay's raised hands in farewell as he passed. "Sorry, Muma. I was just staring at the Morning Spire. It has to be the most beautiful mountain I've ever seen, all sharp white, and alone, rising out of the hills."

As they filed past, Jay touched Govvi's arm, pressed the object in her hand, grinned, and said, "Hang onto this, Little One, it'll be valuable someday." She smiled weakly. He backed away, waved, and added, "And come visit, will you?"

The trail was reasonably good, considering the size of the trees: broad-based, heavy-rooted, some toppled, requiring twisting detours. Because they were so old their lower limbs had long since dropped off or were blown off, creating a high canopy through which shafts of sunlight ran to the forest floor. But strangely, instead of following what appeared to be the cut between the hills, the trail continued upward. Org led them onto a brown meadow, and after a few steps they stood on the gently rounded hilltop. Directly ahead to the west lay a broad valley with a thin river, silver bright in the morning sunshine, meandering south, then turning east. A strip of low mountains in the west ran north and south, blocking any view of the Sea – if they could have seen that far. Just below them, a smoky haze covered the valley. "Cooking fires," Ziiza said, pointing at the obvious, she was so excited. "Hundreds of them. Thousands, maybe. You're looking at Beaverton, children. I'm sure of it." She pulled Govvi to her and patted Edu on the head.

Turning around, they saw Morning Spire, the high point of the eastern range. Below them, the Son ran out of a broad valley. Pop&Jay's clearing, their would-be city, was hidden by the trees. Left and north they were high enough to glimpse portions of the appropriately-named Grand Muma, "the biggest river in the world." The green ridge they stood on curved northward, then northwest, then west, enclosing the valley. Across the Grand Muma stood serene-looking Smoke-storm, its white mantle trimmed with black – at the same time threatening, pouring gray smoke straight up. East of Smoke-storm rose a another white, flat-topped peak, similar to the one they had seen during their maddening detour around the inland sea.

And so, with their bearings clear for the first time since the beach, Ziiza, her six children, and Dg, started hesitantly down the hill to Beaverton, their home-to-be.

When they came to a noisy stream, Ziiza said, "Cleanup time, kids."

"Aw, do we have to?" Com said. He was by far the dirtiest.

"Strip off your furs and jump in. Don't forget your hair. And Edu, give Dg a good rub-wash."

After their baths they beat their furs against trees, raising clouds of dust. Thistles and burrs were not hard to find, so they combed each other's capes and wraps and hair. Edu tried combing Dg, but his fur was so matted a light touch on his head and ears was all he could manage.

"Line up," Ziiza said. "Order of march. And we're going to sing our song."

Six faces turned toward her. And, in differing volumes, depending upon age and temperament, six groans rose from their mouths.

"Come on, I've limped a long way for this." She gave a self-deprecating laugh. "And one more thing. I'm going to ask you to do me a favor. We've been alone for a long time. Now we're going to be with people. Much has happened and we have many stories to tell. But please, don't tell one. When people ask about a popa, just tell them we don't have one. No details. Nothing more. Do this for me?" All nodded. "Thank you." She smiled, trying to make light of what was important to her. Then, grinning, she said, "But that doesn't excuse you from singing."

The trail meandered downhill, emerged from the trees, and took a straight line across a mixed meadow of autumn browns. They crested a rise and Beaverton lay before them.

Instead of the tent-like shelters on the Old Side, these had straight sides and almost-flat roofs; few appeared tall enough for an adult to stand up in. And colors. Each had a slightly different hue – pale blues, salmon pinks, field-flower yellows.

Not exactly awful, my dear Prior. But not impressive, either. Your dream. Our dream. Now only mine. Would you have been disappointed?

The trail crossed a broad, dusty, curving pathway that appeared to be the town's circular boundary, as all the shelters were on the inside of the curve. A crudely-lettered wooden sign on a splay-topped post read: Welcome to Exciting Beaverton.

"Ready, now," Ziiza prompted, as they crossed the curving pathway and continued on a smaller path running between the shelters. "Heads up. Spears up. In step. Here we go." She sang:

Whatever it takes,
Whatever the breaks,
Whatever the aches and pains.

She waved a let's-go to Org.

We've been marching and walking, running and prancing,
Milli: *Singing and tumbling, tripping and dancing,*
Netti: *We've come a long way, such a short way to go,*
Com: *Weeks on the beach, so much to show,*

A red-faced woman lifted her shelter flap, poked her head out, and gave them a you-folks-must-be-crazy look. Ahead on the path a man turned, made a sour face, and walked faster, as if to get away from an encroaching pestilence. "Govvi, you're up."

"Do I have to?"

"Yes. Now."

93

Govvi: *We're young and we're strong, in so many ways.*
Edu: *We've knocked off the miles in so many days.*
Ziiza: *Yes, yes, yes, we're a family united. We'll never forget. That . . .*
Org: *Whatever.*
Org and Milli: *Whatever, whatever.*

"Oh! Shut! Up!" yelled a grizzled man bending over a fire, without even bothering to look at them. Then, for emphasis, "We keep the peace and quiet around here." Neighborhood eyes glared.

"I guess that's enough for now," Ziiza said.

So this is exciting Beaverton.

The path broadened and straightened. It was so straight, once Ziiza thought about it, it must have been sighted or lined. Unusual. After they stopped singing and calling attention to themselves, except for a few "strangers" glances, no one paid attention; they blended in with the path walkers, most of whom were going in their direction.

"I'm hungry, Muma," Edu said, pulling on Ziiza's cape. With that statement, coupled with the letdown – obviously the finale to their move rather than their grand entrance into Beaverton – hunger swept over them; they hadn't eaten today, hadn't had a full meal in two days, and hadn't had a decent meal in over a week. And by their definition, raw clams were a decent meal.

"We'll find something," Ziiza said reassuringly. But she had no idea what or where. Another change: as they walked, the shelters, dwellings, or whatever they were called, on either side of the path, or whatever it was called, became more elaborate and substantial. Some appeared to be near-squares, or near-rectangles, honest attempts anyway. More than tall enough to stand up in. Most had front yards enclosed by neatly trimmed shrubs or expertly laid rock walls and covered with grass cropped close to the ground. Here and there were stone pots that had held decorative flowers or plants in season, but were now bare or filled with dead stalks and dried-up leaves.

After some time (the path was long), the walkers speeded up, as if in anticipation, and they heard the buzz of a crowd ahead. And other noises. Music? Chanting? Singing?

Singing? Fine here, but not back there. I see.

The path ended abruptly, disgorging its followers onto another curving path enclosing what appeared to be Beaverton's central hub and commercial center. Ziiza and crew crossed the path and found themselves among vendors' stands, so close together there was almost no way to get past them. This *was* exciting. Some were covered with brightly-colored woven canopies; others were open-air. Many had poles flying hand-dyed streamers or flags advertising the products they sold or the owners' names.

Merchants hawked their goods with voices and musical instruments: wood-over-earth foot drums, skin-covered and bent-wood drums of all sizes, pebble-and-bone rattles, wooden castanets, rocks, anything to attract attention. A small woman dressed in a dark cape stood next to a fallen tree reciting what Ziiza took to be the news of the day. A yellow-headed wood pigeon perched on her shoulder, shifting its weight, seemingly in cadence with her words.

The people appeared to Ziiza to be clean and well-groomed, although she spotted an occasional smudgy, smelly type, possibly a less affluent fringe dweller. She had never seen this many people in one place before. Dg trotted close to Edu. He, along with the bird, appeared to be the only non-humans in the heaving mass. They smelled food – meat roasting, meat smoking, roots boiling and baking – and their hunger became acute. A vendor passed out samples of a berry concoction. He placed one in each child's mouth, in Ziiza's mouth, then, with a smile, the first they had seen in Beaverton, flipped one into the air for Dg, who snapped it up with his usual alacrity.

How do you buy this stuff? Barter? Trade? What?

Before she could ask the vendor, she heard a deep, warm, elderly voice behind her. "May I . . . May I . . . May I be of assistance?" Ziiza turned to face a tall man leaning on a cane. He moved the cane, and making certain he did not stumble, took a short step backward, as if to reassure her of his good intentions – he had obviously performed this move before – and bowed a stiff, abbreviated bow. Not stiff in an arrogant or dismissive way, but stiff as if his back pained him. Slowly he resumed his upright position while brushing back his long white hair, which had fallen in front of his shoulders. He was dressed in full-length trousers and a hide cape that touched the ground, once fur-covered but now smoke-blackened and smooth. Looking into his watery gray eyes, Ziiza saw warmth and friendliness. And behind that, the firmness and resolve of a lifetime of leadership. And behind that, the weariness of a man ending his run. "My name is Popamayor," he said, "and it is my pleasure to welcome you to Beaverton. Unofficially, of course." He paused, then said: "Not to be discourteous, but you are late. So very late. The last party of travelers arrived weeks ago. Last, that is, until you folks. Pardon, but I assume you are off the Sea Trace."

Ziiza and children stood in the path with the noisy crowd surging around them, and slowly extended their hands to Popamayor, so overwhelmed by everything, especially his friendliness, that they could not speak. To loosen them up, Popamayor looked down at Dg and said, "And who might this strange fellow be?"

"That's Dg and he's mine," Edu said. "See his collar."

"Ah, yes," Popamayor said, "his collar. And your clothing: watabeast. We can deal with that later. Would you folks be hungry after your, I presume, lengthy journey?" The children smiled too hard. "Follow me," he said.

Instead of continuing on the circle path, he led them between the vendors' stands and through open spaces with people talking and eating, and past what appeared to be more substantial places of business, some fairly elaborate structures, comparable to the elaborate shelters they had passed on the walk. Popamayor moved right along, considering his age and back and cane, nodding, greeting, acknowledging people but not stopping to talk. They came to the source of the music they had heard earlier: three men – one playing a hollow-reed flute; another drawing a stick across, then plucking, a five-stringed instrument in his lap; the last playing an assortment of percussion pieces: drums, sticks, clatter-stones. The string player sang in a twangy voice: "You'll never know how much I miss you, 'cause I'm never comin' home." Older people and families with small children sat on the ground or stood listening, eating, drinking, clapping hands. Popamayor stopped, leaned over to Ziiza, and, as if confiding a secret, said, "These gentlemen have been playing at H&G since it began. Call themselves Skedaddle. The band, that is."

"What is H&G, Popamayor, sir?"

"Oh, I'm sorry," he answered Edu. "Hunters and Gatherers Market. H&G for short." Skedaddle finished the piece and stopped for a break. "Off we go. Off we go."

Holding hands, and with Dg tight behind Edu, they plunged through an even thicker crowd. Popamayor stopped them with an upraised hand before a small vendor's stand (which, Popamayor explained, people in Beaverton called "vends") with a pennant reading Trace End Café. A slender, middle-aged woman, her hair wound up in a bun with a wooden spike through it, who appeared to have been quite beautiful in years past, bent over a raised cook-fire. Trace End Café had no customers. "Sister Sissi," Popamayor said, "I would like you to meet Ziiza and her family of six. Ziiza, this is my dear friend and associate, Sister Sissi."

"Seven," Edu corrected, pointing at Dg. Popamayor laughed heartily and thumped his cane. Sister Sissi looked at the odd creature in surprise, then laughed, too, putting them at ease.

Popamayor continued, "They have completed the Sea Trace and wish to settle in Beaverton. Yes?" He turned to receive Ziiza's confirmation.

"We have beaver tail soup on the menu," Sister Sissi said. "And roast beaver tail. And raw beaver tail. And water in the stump. That's it. We'll skip the small talk and get down to business. What would you like?"

Ziiza had to slow the children, they ate so greedily. Sister Sissi filled their platter-bowls again and again, with double helpings for Org; she understood. Then she served Popamayor roast beaver tail, well done, and herself a small bowl of soup. After Ziiza, the children, and Dg were reasonably satisfied,

Popamayor and Sister Sissi talked casually of themselves and Beaverton. Popamayor had founded Beaverton many years ago, she told them. Retired now, his title was Mayor Emeritus. He used to welcome and help newcomers as part of his official duties, but now he did it as a hobby, a charity. She, his longtime collaborator in this endeavor, had dedicated her life to helping Sea Tracers get started in Beaverton. Her husband and children, Popamayor had informed them earlier, had been killed by robbers on a mountain trail east of town. As their eating slowed, Ziiza and company lay on the ground or sat on the café's split seats, listening.

"What about that sign at the start of the path," Edu asked.

"Oh," Popamayor said, "that was one of Mistermayor's big ideas when he took office. He figures if he says Beaverton is exciting, then we'll believe it is. Want to stay. He wants everyone to stay. But only if they're the *right* kind of people, of course. And you folks seem to fall into that category, the right kind of people, Beaverton people. Mistermayor, by the way, is my successor. There have been only two mayors of Beaverton: me, for longer than I can remember, and Mistermayor, for the last five years or so."

Sister Sissi took their bowls, scraped the scraps onto the ground for Dg, and filled them with water, presumably her method of washing.

"He didn't want those two gentlemen on the other side of the hill to stay though, did he?" Edu said.

"Not now, Edu," Ziiza said, quietly but firmly.

Before we know it, you'll be asking about river man erectus. Worse yet, river man post erectus.

"Now," Popamayor said, winding things down, "you can spend the night at the café. Bed yourself down. Eat what you like. Sister Sissi and I live elsewhere. Separately, I might add; I'm married. But before we part for the day, we have a small matter to attend to. Your clothes. Your clothes."

"What's wrong?" Ziiza asked.

"Watabeasts are protected animals under Beaverton law. No one is allowed to kill them."

"It attacked us at night in our camp," Milli said tartly. "Org and Muma set its head on fire with burning pitch baskets. Otherwise it would have eaten us up. Right out of the Sea on a starvation rampage. Up and over the dunes. We were asleep."

"Its fur saved us, too," Netti added. "We lost our clothing and robes. And we ate its meat."

"True?" Popamayor asked Ziiza with a demanding look.

"I'm shocked," Ziiza said. "We thought it was quite an accomplishment to defend ourselves with such crude weapons. No stone spear heads. Nothing but our ingenuity and courage. Org and I were, and are, proud of ourselves."

Popamayor nodded and said, "Follow me, everyone. I'll bring you back."

He led them to a partitioned-off space labeled Town Hall that they had passed earlier and "turned them in." The man receiving the news was one Constable Barclaw, tall (about Org's height), bearded, thick-chested, and muscular, although going a bit to fat with advancing age and a presumably easy life. "Wal, wal, watabeast hide," the constable said, "and a mighty fine specimen at that. Looks like you're all outfitted from the same beast. I killed plenty of 'em away back, afore I turned my hand to beavers." He tugged proudly at the dark, blue-stained fringe on his top garment, waiting for them to be suitably impressed. "But I gotta tell you, it's agin' the law now. Not many left. The council figured if they made it illegal to wear 'em it would shut off the hunting."

"Self defense. On the Sea Trace," Ziiza said. "If we hadn't killed it, or driven it off, we wouldn't be here today."

"I'll vouch for that," Popamayor said. "I believe her story." Barclaw acquiesced immediately, and, without a word, picked up a small stone with a block B standing in relief, dipped it into a greasy green liquid, and placed a mark on each piece of clothing. Popamayor pointed to Dg's watabeast collar.

"Wal, I don't know. I never certified a creature's collar afore."

"Go ahead, Barclaw," Popamayor said, with a touch of authority. "Bend a little. The creature seems to be one of the family."

"He's my very own, my object," Edu said, looking up at Barclaw with wide eyes. "He saved my life, too."

Barclaw motioned to Ziiza to put her hand around Dg's muzzle, then gingerly made the green mark on its collar. At his touch, Dg rumbled. He yanked his hand away.

"Not that I'm a-feared of any creature," Barclaw said in mock seriousness. "Or any man, for that matter." He laughed again and said, "Now you're official ta Beaverton."

"Thank you for your service, Barclaw," Popamayor said. "You perform your duties admirably. Just like the old days – when we founded this town – together." Then, with a wistful glance at the bustling H&G, he added. "So, so long ago."

He led them back to the empty café – Sister Sissi had closed up and gone home – and said goodbye. As he was walking away, Ziiza called to him, "Popamayor, Popamayor, thank you. How much do we owe?"

"Take care of your splendid family, friend Ziiza, that's what you owe."

12

The Lots Plus Real Estate Company

IRREPRESSIBLE COM did not return from their meeting with Barclaw at Town Hall. He hung back, then slipped into the crowd to explore. After they reached Sister Sissi's and ate some more, the others were eager to explore, too. Ziiza excused them. Org walked slowly into the crowd, not terribly interested in anything. In a short while he returned, hungry again, since, although many vendors sold food, he did not have anything to purchase it with. Milli and Netti set out for the music. Govvi headed across H&G to the western side, the part they had not seen, stopping at each place of business, sizing it up, and moving on. Edu, overwhelmed by the day's events and the contrast between Beaverton and life on the beach, had had enough newness for one day and did not want to go anywhere. He lay on his back next to the fire with his hand on Dg, watching the sky. Ziiza sipped water from a leaf cup. Org sat on a log, turning his rock in his hands.

It happened so suddenly.

Edu saw it first, in the clouds, before it hit. He was savoring the white bulbous shapes floating past, moving slowly, west to east. In a blink they darkened, speeded up, and turned north. "Look at that, Muma," he said, pointing. The market hubbub ceased, and a heavy stillness took its place. The dark sky lowered. A whistling noise spun up the valley. The tips of the few trees standing in the marketplace shook, then bent, then whipped. The black sky slammed down on Beaverton, lifted it up, and tore it apart.

"Stay here," Ziiza screamed at Edu as she crawled toward him. Then, "Come on, Org, we've got to find the children." Org stood. The wind caught him and knocked him over. Ziiza ducked as a massive fir limb flew over her, crashed into a vendor's booth, tumbled along the ground, and imbedded itself in a mound. Skins, food, clothing, swirled in the sky. Shoppers hugged the ground and their children. Some crawled into runoff ditches. That, in the first few minutes. That was only the beginning.

The wind howled and whined through the valley, a brown, dirty wind filled with needles, leaves, twigs, limbs, and fire ashes. Ziiza crawled on top of Edu and Dg, then clawed the earth. Org twisted around, head into the wind, wiggled over tight against them, and clapped his hands over his ears. The three gasped for breath as the wind sucked the air from their mouths. Above the roar, came an ear-splitting CRRRR-ACK as a tall tree broke off at mid-trunk. It hit with a thud, its broken-off limbs impaling those unlucky enough to be near. Once it was down, people crawled to it for what shelter it offered, and to comfort the injured and dying pinned underneath.

Daylight faded and so did the storm's fury. Still air. Two hours to wreck the town.

When the stars came out and they could orient themselves, shoppers and vendors tried to make their way home to what was left of their shelters, if anything. Instead of hundreds of cooking fires that would normally be burning, there were but two or three, most welcome sentinels. Ziiza, Org, Edu, and Dg set out to find Com and the girls, but with so many people wandering about, they realized it was hopeless and stopped. As did almost everyone else who did not find whomever or whatever they were looking for. They lay down where they happened to be, a few to sleep but most to whimper and shiver and get through the night. The moon rose, tempting some to begin searching again, ghost-like figures walking in circles, calling, whispering, mumbling to themselves. Govvi found them after midnight.

Next morning Sister Sissi arrived just as they were setting out to search for Milli, Netti, and Com. Popamayor and Wife Popamayor were alive, she told Ziiza, doing as well as could be expected. He would not be in today, perhaps not for many days. His shelter, being the oldest in Beaverton and survivor of many storms (but none like this) was in fairly good shape. But he was depressed over what had happened to his town and his people. She then told them that newcomers off the Sea Trace were welcome to camp in the small grass plot next to the café or in the temporary campground on the edge of town. But not in the meadows outside the circle path. Where you could or could not camp or settle was strictly regulated by the town council.

Com found them first, of course, a few minutes after they began. He hailed from a distance, then jogged up as casually as if back from a scouting mission down the beach. Scared? No, he told them; he was thrilled. Oh, it was dangerous, he guessed, and terrible for Beaverton. Poor people, especially the dead ones. But it was the most exciting night of his life. No, he had not seen Milli or Netti, but he had an idea where to find them: go to the music. He led them toward the circle road, roughly the reverse of Popamayor's route yesterday. Amazingly, a few vendors had already rebuilt and were open for business. Others were walking in from the north side of town, carrying armloads of skins and grass mats, the ones that had been caught on bushes and trees, had not blown away. If they were lucky enough to find property they could identify, they used it to rebuild. Very considerate, very responsible. What they could not identify they carried to Town Hall and spread out. The businesslike calmness with which the Beavertonians went about the clean-up and fix-up amazed Ziiza. No looting. No thieving. No taking advantage. It was as if natural disasters like this were regular occurrences. But how could they be? This, by any reckoning, and from bits of talk she had heard, had to be a "hundred-year" storm. Folks were cheerfully setting up as best they could, then helping their neighbors do the same. Some even helped their neighbors first.

After the blown-away shelters and vends, the most visible damage was to the fir trees: limbs cracked or whole trees broken. Few were uprooted though, as the winter rains had not set in and the soil was firm. In H&G, all of the tall trees were down, waiting to be hacked into firewood. In the residential areas outside the circle, most of the supple, shorter, deciduous trees had survived, just stripped of their fall leaves a few weeks early. But most of the evergreens were damaged.

Com was more than right. The Skedaddle musicians were hard at it, with tip-food thrown on their spread-out instrument bags. Same as before. Milli and Netti sat tight before them, knees drawn up, arms wrapped around, listening to the music, which was quite different from yesterday's. When Ziiza and crew greeted them – "Milli! Netti! You're safe!" – they hardly moved, hardly raised their eyes, they were so hypnotized by the sounds. Was it a funeral dirge, a lament? Or was it the slow-beat accompaniment to Beaverton's resolute rebuilding? Ziiza could not tell. "Coming with us?" she asked. No answer. "Hungry, girls?" No answer.

Milli looked up, continuing to nod her head with the music, and said, "Aren't they simply wonderful?" A white-bearded Skedaddler thrummed a mournful chord. "Can't we stay?" Ziiza was about to insist they come with her when she realized she did not know what they should do next, any of them. So, just to say something, she told them they could stay, but to return to Sister Sissi's before dark.

Walking among the vends, rising again in H&G's circle, a woven-mat sign strung between two poles jumped out at Ziiza. In barely readable washed-out letters, it read: Lots Plus Real Estate Company. Hanging beneath it was a split board with Agents Wanted scratched in charcoal.

She stood in the crowd, evaluating the signs and the establishment – consisting of a pile of stake-signs, a plank counter, a small shelter behind the counter, a three-legged stool, and a man sitting on the stool. Spotting them, the man, dressed in a chalk-white tunic and a broad-brimmed, smooth-skinned hat, also white, smiled and rose. He caught Ziiza's eye, took his hat off, held it over his head, and twirled it. Holding his smile, he launched his voice over the crowd noise. "Be of service to you, ma'am?" Not being prepared to do or say anything, Ziiza continued staring at the sign. "Come right on over. All you nice folks."

Ziiza stood firm. He held his smile, never removing his eyes from her. Finally she walked to the counter, followed protectively by Org and the children. "I'm new to Beaverton," she said. "We're all new to Beaverton. Yesterday, as a matter of fact. Storm. Shocked by it all. Tired out from our long walk on what people around here call the Sea Trace. I haven't had much time to settle in and think about it, but sooner or later I *will* need a job."

"I need help," he said. "Lots of help. Right now. I mean this very instant." He twirled his hat again, put it on, and held out his hand. Ziiza extended hers hesitantly. "Deal closed," he said. "You're all hired. Whoopee!" He tossed his hat into the air. "Wiggi Bub's the name. Lots Plus's the business. Used to be Lots-a-Lots. But I changed it because now we're selling vacant lots and lots with shelters already up. Beaverton's changing and so are we."

"Ziiza. And this is Org and – "

"Pleasure to meet you all," he said, cutting her off. "All my new employees."

Wiggi Bub picked up a stake-sign which read: For Sale: Offered by Lots Plus. Their jobs, he told them, were to spread out and place a sign on each vacant lot they found. Vacant, Wiggi Bub explained, meant any lot that did not show signs of activity at the moment. Evidently he was not concerned with technicalities; if the owners showed up and demanded possession, take the sign down. If frightened owners who had fled during the storm showed up a few days from now, that was another matter. They would have to buy their lots back from him, Wiggi Bub. Well, not from smiling, friendly Wiggi Bub himself, from the impersonal real estate company, Lots Plus – which Wiggi Bub happened to own. And if he hadn't mentioned it before, they would report, that is be under the direct supervision of, Gstan, his sales manager, who was presently out of the office.

After telling Wiggi Bub how pleased and grateful she was to have the job, so pleased and grateful she forgot to discuss the matter of pay, Ziiza explained that the children would not be available for long, as she intended enrolling them in school. That was if Beaverton had a school; she had not had a chance to investigate. Wiggi Bub waved this objection away with his hat. He wanted all of them, today, and today only. Ziiza, if she proved herself, might, just might, be hired by Gstan as one of his full-time salespeople.

"All the signs you can carry," Wiggi Bub said, pointing to the pile. "For the glory of Beaverton. And the glory of the Lots Plus Real Estate Company."

They walked back to the circle, then took a spoke path. Com stopped in front of a seemingly abandoned lot. How to tell? Nobody was present and no repairs had been made. The shelter had been hit hard, more than just wind, perhaps knocked down by flying limbs, only two corner posts standing, the rest of it down and the coverings stripped away. On the other hand, the lot was surrounded by a neatly-built rock wall. Behind the dwelling was a recently-harvested garden and some leafless berry bushes. This indicated solid lot ownership. Wiggi Bub did not hesitate. He grabbed a sign and jammed it into the ground in front of the wall. "Let's go," he said. Govvi raised her tally board, and, out of habit, marked a new column.

Wiggi Bub wanted them to separate, spread out, cover more of the town. "Faster, faster, faster," he said. Ziiza demurred, saying she had had enough of storms and lost children for now, and wanted to take it easy. After posting about half of their signs, and swinging by Sister Sissi's for lunch – Wiggi Bub eagerly partaking – and leaving Edu, Dg, and Org to take naps, they continued until they ran out of signs.

"Gstan," Wiggi Bub said when they returned to the office, "this is Ziiza." Ziiza extended her hand. Gstan gave it a squeeze. He was a smallish man, a notch shorter than Ziiza, even narrower at the shoulders and hips. One would be tempted to describe him as wiry, sinewy, that sort, except upon closer examination his bare arms revealed no muscular definition; he was not physical or athletic in any way. His eyes sparkled as he smiled, a mixture, it seemed, of friendliness and shrewdness.

"This is Com. And Govvi," Ziiza said, pulling her hand from his overly-long squeeze. "I have four more, but they're scattered all over town."

"My gosh," Gstan said. "And your husband?"

"I have no husband," Ziiza replied flatly.

"Ah, yes."

Ziiza and the children spent the rest of the afternoon making yard signs. Wiggi Bub and Gstan dealt with customers (if one could call irate people slamming yard signs on the counter, customers). A tall man, who Gstan pointed out as Mistermayor, Beaverton's mayor, walked along the circle path, accompanied by Barclaw and five long-faced dignitaries, giving encouragement, inspecting damage, and assessing the town's rebuilding efforts. Whether Mistermayor was giving them any direct assistance was difficult to determine. Later in the day, the woman with the wood pigeon stopped in front of Lots Plus. She stood on a tree round, and, in a voice that belied her size, shouted out the news. Bitta, Gstan informed Ziiza, was the town's independent reporter. The pigeon's name was Hobart, he told her disgustedly, as he pointed to the white drippings on her hair and shoulders and down her back.

"Fourteen dead," was Bitta's attention-grabbing opener. "Worst storm in memory. Uncounted injured. Hundreds of trees down. Shelters ruined."

"She has an uncanny nose for news," Gstan told Ziiza, who was trying to listen to Bitta, "sometimes before it happens. And she never forgets; she's the repository of Beaverton history." Gstan obviously admired her ability and dedication, but wondered aloud how she made a living, as she did not charge for her services. It was rumored she had a wealthy backer down south in Big Bay, but he did not know for sure.

At Sister Sissi's that evening, Ziiza told her of her new job. Gstan wanted to hire her, train her, give her a chance, she said. Just like that. Her second day in Beaverton. Sister Sissi was not impressed but congratulated Ziiza anyway, as she was obviously happy. But before she began, Ziiza had arranged with Gstan to take tomorrow off to enroll the children in school. "Grassy-something, isn't it?"

"Yes. Grassyknoll school," Sister Sissi said, looking pleased with the opportunity to become involved. "I'll take you over tomorrow morning."

Next morning, Popamayor, who was supposed to be taking the week off to restore himself, showed up at the café. Leaving him stirring beaver tail stew, and expecting few customers, Sister Sissi led Ziiza and the children across town. On a rise at the edge of a medium-grade residential neighborhood – more accurately one attempting to regain that position – was the school. And on the top was Addle, as Sister Sissi explained, owner, schoolmaster, and dispenser of wisdom. The students, about twenty-five, ranged in age from about Edu's (five or six), to Milli's (seventeen or eighteen). Org, pushing twenty, would if accepted become the oldest student. No matter, he had catching up to do. They sat on the top of the grass-covered knoll, Addle addressing them from below, gesticulating, pacing, stamping, his long hair swinging as he shook his head for emphasis. Ziiza, Sister Sissi, and the children stood off to the side, listening respectfully. From what they heard, he was telling them of his travels. He had allowed himself to be captured by some "rough customers," as he put it, so he could learn their language, then civilize them. At that he said something in an incomprehensible tongue, which impressed the class immensely. As they clapped, whistled, and yelled their approval (whether sincerely or to play up to him was unclear), Addle raised his hands in proud acknowledgment, and, practiced orator that he was, ended class on the high. Placing his thumbs in the armpits of his ground-length academic robe – which, Ziiza noted, bore the watabeast exemption stamp – he strode to the top of the knoll. The students queued up below him. He motioned each one to approach, and, after a brief conversation, they walked or ran away.

"Addle," Sister Sissi said, after the last student had left, "I would like to introduce Ziiza and her children." She swept her hand around. "They would like to attend Grassyknoll."

"Pleased, to be sure," Addle said. "And they might be?" he continued in a condescending tone.

"Well," Ziiza started off, "we've been on the Sea Trace for most of the year."

"And they might be?" Addle said sharply, eyes narrowing.

"Oh, yes. Org is the oldest." Org stood in back, fingering his rock. "He was our trail breaker, first in the order of march. Pretty much by age. Next is Milli." She touched Milli's shoulder. "She's older than Netti, here" – Ziiza shifted her hand to Netti's arm – "but a bit smaller. They're only a year apart, almost like twins." Milli and Netti held hands, smiling weakly. "Milli's a talented fisher and Netti's an equally talented weaver and basket maker. Very accomplished, in my opinion. Both of them."

Get your tongue under control, Ziiza.

"Impressive," Addle said, drumming his fingers on his arm. "And the others?"

"Com was our scout, our campsite, food source, and barrier finder. He probably covered twice the miles we did." As she spoke, she passed her hand over his head. She shifted to Govvi and took her hand. "Govvi built all our fires and kept our inventory on her tally board." She raised Govvi's arm and the board. Addle stroked his beardless chin. Ziiza continued: "Edu's the youngest. He keeps everyone honest."

"This is Dg," Edu said, reaching down to pat him. "Do you allow creatures in your school?"

"And how does he do that?" Addle asked Ziiza, ignoring him.

"Oh, I don't know. He has a knack for asking questions, the right questions, young as he is."

"I ask the questions in this school," Addle harrumphed. "I try to keep the class size below twenty-five. Individual attention, you know. But since this is the only school in Beaverton, I suppose I'll have to take them."

What does he want, more students, or no students?

"I lecture in the morning," Addle continued. "Then each student spends the rest of the day on what I call Individual Studies. Personal enrichment, if you will."

"Why so few students?" Ziiza asked. "I mean, Beaverton seems to be a large town; there must be hundreds of children."

"A variety of reasons, my good woman, the main one being that life in Beaverton is so easy, for now at least, most parents don't see the need for it. A few interested parents such as yourself, enroll their children, support them, and encourage them to keep at it. Occasionally a curious and industrious child comes of his or her own accord. But there is no law. Even with your six children raising the class size to more than thirty, dropouts will soon have it back down. Now, if you or your precocious son don't have any more questions, I'll be retiring. I'll expect them here tomorrow. Early. Proof of their commitment to education."

"Thank you," was all Ziiza could manage as Addle strode down the knoll, his robe swinging behind him. Then, turning to Sister Sissi, she said, "It's free, and nobody sends their children?"

"You have a lot to learn about Beaverton, Ziiza," she said with a grin. "And you will."

They had a pleasant walk back to the café. After turning the children loose, Ziiza, Popamayor, and Sister Sissi fussed with food and straightened things up – after a day with no other "customers." Sister Sissi repaired the modest tent-like shelter with some materials Popamayor had brought, and, after repairing the sign, they were back in business. Terrible as the storm had been, H&G seemed as busy as before.

On their third day in Beaverton Sister Sissi packed beaver-tail lunches for the children and looked on jealously as Ziiza kissed them goodbye – except Org, who would not let her kiss him in front of anyone except his siblings. Com led; he had found a shorter route than the way Sister Sissi had taken. He had also followed the trail Addle had taken down the knoll and located his shelter. "Not much for such an illustrious schoolmaster," he told them as they walked along, proud of this new type of scouting information.

Ziiza washed her face, combed her hair, brushed her clothes, and said goodbye to Sister Sissi, who wished her luck on her first real day on the job. The pleasant fall weather had returned and although the nights were long, they were less windy, and considerably warmer than on the Grand Muma, just over the north ridge divide. Although the snowfall seemed a long-ago memory, Prong was not; Ziiza could not get the vision of pink water and his canoe spinning downriver out of her mind.

Gstan's job, as he described it to Ziiza, was doing legwork, showing lots, convincing prospects they couldn't live without such and such property, then enticing them back to Lots Plus. And training, inspiring, and supervising the sales force, which as far as Ziiza could determine consisted of one, herself. Once he brought in a prospect, "primed and ready to buy" was the way he put it, his part was over. And so would Ziiza's be when she got "up to speed" (more real estate lingo). Wiggi Bub was the closer, the master closer: tall, big hat, effusive, domineering, tough as tough when tough was required. That was the company line. When Wiggi Bub stepped away for a moment, Gstan said, "His closing record *isn't* that great, not even fifty percent. But he has a way of remembering only his successes and forgetting all the deals he's let slip away – or outright blown." His words were clipped, measured, and spaced, leaving no doubt he believed he could do better.

The storm had created a great opportunity, Gstan told her. Normally, as they entered the slack winter season, Lots Plus would be laying off salespeople, not hiring them. Her timing had been perfect. Right place, with kids, at the right time. And she was qualified. Meaning she took care of herself appearance-wise, was articulate, resourceful (having completed the Sea Trace), responsible (with what seemed to be a functioning single-parent family), and, if not desperate for a job, without many opportunities at the moment. Any opportunities at the moment. Wiggi Bub had figured that out and meant to take advantage.

Step two in her training was walking around with Gstan, learning the town, meeting people, and following up on the signs they had planted. He set a fast pace, but Ziiza, fresh from the Trace, and with legs as long as his, matched him easily, bad foot and limp notwithstanding. They had done quite well with the signs; only a few were gone, thrown into the road or burned by owners who had returned. Walking the east side they came upon a couple with two children looking at a vacant lot with a Lots Plus sign stuck in the yard. Gstan grabbed Ziiza's arm and stopped her. "I know 'em, the Pokos," he whispered. "Live on the outskirts. Other side of town. Watch this." He walked over, and standing behind and off to the side, said, "Lovely lot, don't you think?"

"Urm," said the man.

"A little far from Grassyknoll school, to be sure," Gstan continued, nodding at their seemingly school-age children. "But a fine neighborhood and just a few minutes to H&G."

"We're not interested in no schools," said the wife, a short woman with too many chins under her real one and too few hairs on her head. "We want the fast life. The good times. Shopping. Excitement. H&G every day."

"You've got it all right here. And very reasonably priced, too. Our after-storm special."

"Hey, who are you?" the man asked.

"Gstan, at your service. Marketing manager, top producer, and executive training director of Lots Plus Real Estate Company, located in the very heart of Hunter and Gatherers Market. One of Beaverton's oldest and most respected businesses, I might add. May I introduce my friend and associate, Ziiza." Scruffy-bearded Poko kicked mindlessly at a rock and said nothing, his resistance building. Gstan stepped away and put his hands behind his back to wait them out. No one spoke.

Finally the woman could stand it no longer and blurted: "The neighborhood where we're at is a bunch of thieves. Always stealin'. Can't turn your back. Beaverton ain't supposed to be like that. I've told Barclaw a hundred times. He don't do nothin'. Just give me crow-pucky, that man. Mistermayor, too." She raged on, then turned to her husband. "I want out, Poko. I want to buy this place."

Still staring at the ground, Poko said, "How much?"

"I'd like you to meet Wiggi Bub, our owner," Gstan told him. "He'll have you folks all moved in by sundown." Gstan pulled the sign out of the ground, and, with a flourish, motioned them to follow. Which they did, muma beaming, popa frowning, dirty-faced children trailing behind.

"Wiggi Bub," Gstan said when they reached the office, "this is Mister and Missis Poko and family. They're interested in the eastside property." He winked. "*Very* interested."

Wiggi Bub twirled his hat and launched into a recitation of the property's – which he had not seen – advantages, attractions, low price, for which, he reminded them over and over, Lots Plus retained the smallest of commissions (while, in reality, he would keep the entire purchase price, since the lot was presumably abandoned and the owners got nothing), its proximity to H&G (which they knew very well) and on and on. As he babbled, Gstan ground his teeth so loudly Ziiza felt one of Netti's headaches coming on. Inexperienced as she was in the ways of real estate, she knew all these people wanted to do was pay their money – it appeared they had money or something of value – and leave. Move in. After twenty minutes, the Pokos' eyes glazed and rolled, the children whined and wiped their drippy noses. Poko said, "Eh, we'd like to think about it. We'll let you know tomorrow." And they left.

"They'll be back," Wiggi Bub said, with a closed-sale smile, slapping his fist into his hand. "Crawling back."

Gstan did not speak. Ziiza stared across the path. Gstan recovered. "Take you to lunch, Ziiza," he said.

Invitation? Or command?

13

Barclaw Saves the Town

GSTAN TRADED a polished shell for take-out beaver tail, which he and Ziiza ate leaning against a storm-downed fir's rough bark. Ziiza had so many questions she did not know where to begin. Besides, she didn't know her place, didn't know what a real estate employee's place was; she had never worked for anyone before. Gstan talked about business in a friendly, get-acquainted, chitchat extension of sales training. Ziiza stuck to the basics, too, just a sketchy outline of her "story." No mention of the MeTonn affair, just that they had been in canoes and ended up walking, which Gstan did not pursue. Or the Prong affair, although she wondered when word would drift into town, and what that word might be. Or the watabeast affair, although for a different reason. Sometimes it's good, she thought, to stretch things out, save some of her better stories and anecdotes for later. If he asked about the green watabeast exemption marks on her garments, maybe she would tell him.

She was curious about how real estate salespeople were paid; that had not been mentioned by Gstan or Wiggi Bub. She did not know how to broach the subject, so she went at it obliquely, playing it shy. "For the life of me, Gstan," she said, "I don't understand the money system around here. Where do all the beaver tails come from? They are quite tasty, I must say, but how do people buy them? How do they pay for them? How do they pay for lots, for that matter?"

"I'm amazed," Gstan replied. "Do you think people come to Beaverton for the climate? Well, some do, on second thought; there are worse places. Anyway, wait until the winter rains start, which they will soon. This is a beaver tail economy, makes the whole thing run. If you don't know about beaver tails, why did you come to Beaverton?"

"For one thing," Ziiza replied, filtering out what she did not wish to say, "I'm not a crowd follower. And my children aren't crowd followers, either. I'm bringing them up that way, as hardy individuals who think for themselves."

"I do admire you for that."

"From the bits and pieces I heard, way back," she fibbed, "I just knew. I knew there was no other place for me and my family. The fact that 'nobody' went to Beaverton made it more appealing. As I said, I'm contrary. If the crowd goes one way, I'm repelled, not attracted; I go the other. But I never heard about this 'beaver tail economy.' Not a word."

"That pleases me," Gstan said. "You might call it Beaverton's tasty little secret. Remember Mistermayor's sign on the edge of town? Makes no difference. The people who come here have already made their choices, 'exciting' or not. They can't change their minds, run across the Sunup Range, all the way to Swarm City. Too far. Too difficult."

So that's it. It's starting to make sense. Way Rock, that's what they call it, sends you to Swarm City – or to Beaverton. Depending upon what? What it "thinks" of you? A rock? Sends you merrily up the big trail like a herd of animals. Or down the coast – "Trace the Sea. Then let it go" – to Beaverton.

"They're committed," Gstan continued. "They have but two choices: stay in Beaverton or try to make it on the outside, in the vast country beyond the Valley of the Beaver – the hills, the forests, the mountains, back to the coast, or down to Big Bay. But, as I said, not Swarm City, way to the east. Impossible. They can't get to us and we can't get to them."

"Swarm City?" Ziiza asked. "What is it? Where is it?

"Big. Mayor's an all-powerful guy named Sac. Sac the Magnificent, he calls himself. That should give you an idea. Beavertonians hate him, hate his city. Or we're supposed to. That's all I know."

"Well," Ziiza said, "I guess that will have to do for an answer. But what's the secret?"

"Simple. Valley beavers aren't ordinary beavers. Their tails are larger, and, as you know, very tasty. Beaver tail supreme, you might say." He patted her shoulder and laughed. "If you chop them off just so, leaving more than half, they grow back. Quickly, I might add. The best tasting, most nutritious food in the world. It's unlimited and almost free. That's Beaverton's not-so-secret secret. Best of all, it's not salt water victuals; you don't have to live by the Sea." Ziiza did not mention that "salt water victuals," in her opinion, were not that bad, they had sustained her on the beach.

After lunch, they walked the town, prospecting, posting new signs, checking old ones. Most of the owners who had run away after the storm were reclaiming their properties, regardless of Wiggi Bub's best laid plans. What had started out as a huge inventory of "abandoned" lots, both improved and unimproved, was now reduced to a few. Prospects were fewer. Sales were nil. The Pokos had returned to their old digs, determined to tough it out. Nothing Gstan could offer or say could change even the missus's mind. On Friday afternoon Gstan politely reminded Ziiza that real estate salespeople worked a seven-day, not a five-day, week. People had time to look around on weekends, and that was what they did, whether they were serious about a new lot or not. They looked. They shopped. They talked. They listened. He was showing a prime lot adjacent to Inner Circle. She could, if she would, show the east property, if not all weekend – he was trying to be as accommodating as possible – at least Sunday afternoon. Wiggi Bub would, of course, handle office inquiries and any closing opportunities they brought in.

Also on Friday, after their first full week of school, the children told Ziiza they liked Grassyknoll. Rather, they found little to dislike. Addle did not divide the students by age, ability, or anything like that. There weren't enough, and he was the only teacher. The day's lesson was the same for everyone. This week he had concentrated on his travels and adventures, interesting in their way, but delivered in a dry, humorless, and self-congratulatory manner (according to Milli). Each day, after the others students' Individual Studies consultations were over, he met with Ziiza's six, beginning with Org, of course. He was intrigued by their objects, he told them.

Popamayor could not stay away from the café, fussing, rearranging containers, tightening up the shelter for winter. Sister Sissi had plenty of beaver tail, delivered by a town employee. She repeated her invitation to live at the café so often Ziiza realized it was more than her hospitable nature; she was lonely. Moreover, she had a deep need for someone to care for, not just to feed. This vibrant, once-beautiful woman was sliding into despondency. For the time being anyway, hosting Ziiza and family was helping brake the slide. Ziiza's relationship with her was cordial, but for some reason Sister Sissi did not seem like someone she cared to get close to.

After standing on the east-side lot most of Saturday and Sunday, watching streams of disinterested people pass by without so much as a nod, Ziiza had a nibble. A tall woman with long, thin arms and sharp elbows walked past, abruptly left the man accompanying her, entered the property, knelt down, and began rearranging the decorative stones around a crematorious bush. When she finished, they formed a perfect circle. Not only that, but the stones were graded by size, the largest on the north, then successively smaller around both sides to meet at the south. The few that were not smooth enough or round enough to satisfy her, she tossed aside. While she worked she talked continuously, carrying on a conversation, presumably directed at Ziiza, but never acknowledging her as anything other than another inanimate object, one of the stones. The substance of this one-way conversation was that this was the most unsatisfactory lot she had ever seen; everything was wrong. But she might consider buying it if the price was right and if seller would "bring it up to standard" before closing. The husband stood off, back on the path, stroking his chin, saying nothing, seemingly not caring whether she bought it or not. After demanding to know the price – so she could begin haggling? – and being told sheepishly by Ziiza that she did not know what it was, they marched off to Lots Plus and Wiggi Bub.

The Lots Plus sign sagged on its poles and Wiggi Bub sagged even more; he was asleep on the ground next to his stool. As Ziiza bent over to wake him with a touch on the shoulder, the woman kicked him in the back. Wiggi Bub rubbed his eyes and looked disapprovingly, first at Ziiza, then at the woman.

"Wife Dragga, here," the woman said. "Rise and shine Wiggi Bub, you old thief."

"Oh, hello, Wife Dragga," he said. "Bargain hunting after the storm?"

"I might be interested in that terrible lot on the east side." With that, both talked at once, she ranting about the lot's bad points – compromised view, water in the fire-pit, lack of privacy, tasteless rock-scaping – he extolling its presumed virtues. Ziiza and the man, now identified as Husband Dragga, stood off, listening to the combatants. Finally, after talking themselves out, and never coming close to discussing price or closing, Wife Dragga turned, wrapped her talon-like fingers around H's arm, and stalked away, pulling him after her.

Wiggi Bub smiled, scratched his side, and lay down again, seemingly pleased with his day's work. "She'll be back," he said as his face touched the ground.

"What is the price, Wiggi Bub?" Ziiza asked in exasperation. "Gstan doesn't know." No answer. She lifted her foot to nudge him, then, thinking better of it, leaned over and tapped his shoulder. "How much for the lot?"

"She owns more property than anyone in Beaverton," Wiggi Bub said wearily. "And she's got her eye on the lot. Price doesn't matter. She wants it, she gets it. I'll handle it."

"She wants to know. I want to know." No response.

Disgusted, Ziiza did not return to the "open" lot. Instead, she took a meandering walk through H&G, which, even though holding to its shortened Sunday hours, was still bustling. The crowd buzz and the shoppers' smiling faces helped revive her spirits. She stopped at Skedaddle, half-hoping to see Milli and Netti, but they were not there. She passed Town Hall, which was closed, except for Constable Barclaw, who had a dozen or so children sitting in a semi-circle in front of him. Curious, she stopped.

"Now gather round close, my little friends," Barclaw told them. "And hold onto each others' hands. A-cause this tale's a little on the scary side." He checked his listeners. "All set? Wal, many years ago, before Popamayor's hair turned white . . . and how long ago do you think that was? Yes. You with the rosy cheeks."

"A hundred years ago, Mister Barclaw?"

"That's *Constable* Barclaw, young-un. Anyway," he continued, "that's a good answer, because it just might have been a hundred years ago. Anyway, it was a long time ago, and Beaverton was just a-starting. Popamayor and me and a few other folks found this Valley of the Beaver where you sit. And we said to ourselves, this is the finest, most beautiful valley we ever saw, Old Side, New Side, anywhere we been. Sweet weather, sweet rain, sweet beaver tails, sheltered from the wind, and snow-free, nearly."

"What about the big windstorm we just had, Mister Barclaw?" asked the rosy-cheeked girl.

"Wal, that's what they call an exceptional, which you will learn about when you go to that Grassyknoll school up there. Exceptionals, they do happen. But not very often. I happen to be something of an exceptional myself. I led the very first party down the Sea Trace. Fought everything that walked, crawled, or swum in the water, I did. Sometimes I had to fight my own people just to keep 'em in line." He chuckled. "That's why I got this job of *constable*." Barclaw stood, stretched, turned around, and sat on the ground facing the children, eye to eye, storytelling level. "Wal, my children," he placed his hand beside his mouth for a confidential whisper, "would you like to hear how old Barclaw fought the most dangerous beast on the New Side or any other side, and saved Beaverton in the bargain? Would ya?"

He's good. Gets them excited and curious, then hooks them.

Ziiza smiled at Barclaw. He noticed her and winked.

"Please, please Mister Barclaw."

"Wal, he's a big cat, name of Sita. A big, big cat with long sharp teeth." He held his forefingers down from his mouth. "That long. Enormous feet, too. Claws so long he can't pull 'em in. Punches holes in the ground when he walks. No mistaking old Sita's tracks. But quiet." He lowered his voice again. "Oh, so stealthy quiet. Quieter than a little ant." He wet his finger, swiped the ground until an ant stuck to it, and placed it on the tip of his tongue. When it moved, he sucked it in, chewed noisily, and smacked his lips with theatrical relish. The children started looking and feeling for ants. "Keep on holding hands. We ain't come to the scary part yet. Sita, he's long and low and powerful. Shiny black all over, except for a white stripe runs right up his nose and 'tween his eyes. And a white tip on the end of his tail. And what does old Sita eat? Anyone know?"

"Springers? Bears? Fish?"

"Yor getting close, my friends."

"Beavers?"

"Co-reck," he boomed in his heavy-gravel voice. "Beavers and anything else he fancied was tasty. But mostly beavers. So many beavers he et there was hardly enough left over for us. Cause old Sita was a little on the mean side; he killed more beavers than he et. Just for the mean fun of it. Those were the hard days for Beaverton, just getting started. Old Sita's what made them hard." He leaned forward, checked every eye, and went on.

"Wal now, one night way back, when Beaverton only had a few families and a few shelters, Popamayor had just appointed me to be *constable*. My first night on the job, fact to tell. Winter. Terrible pounding rain coming down. I just stood out in it, so proud of my new job of *constable*, but not seeing anything because it was wet and dark and black. Only sound, the rain banging into the puddles, sloshing away in the ditches, wherever it could go. I was walking around, slow, it was all I could do, checking shelters, soaked, but determined to do my job, when, just like that, appears a shaft of light. Then a scream, cutting though the sound of the rain, the unmistakable scream of a child."

Oh, no, he wouldn't tell a story like that to little ones.

"What it was – are you holding on tight? – was a boy screaming. A boy name of Little Binni. Cute little boy. I knowed him. Lots of hair hangin' down over his eyes. Course I didn't find out it was him till later. And what made that shaft of light? Not a big light, just a little one. Anyone guess?"

"Tell us, Barclaw. Was it Sita?"

"You sure guessed right on that one. Old Sita had crept into town in all that dark and rain and slashed open Little Binni's shelter with those big claws of his. And out popped this shaft of light from his muma's cook fire. Just enough for me to see a flash of white, as he bounded off with Little Binni in his mouth; going to have him for dinner. Splash. Splash. His big pads hit the puddles. What did Barclaw do? All in an instant, when I didn't even know what was happening, what was going on," he held up his hand for silence, "I grabbed my knife, the only weapon I had, and, for good or ill, I flung it at the white flash. Hard as I could. A screeching yeeeee, yaaaaw, howwwl was what I heard. Then nothing. Couple more splashes and old Sita run away in the dark.

"By now Little Binni's muma and popa are up and out and screaming for their boy. Then the others. Screaming and yelling. But they don't know what to do. When I finally got everyone shut up, what did I hear but Little Binni weeping and crying and splashing in a mud puddle just a ways away. I ran, picked him up, and took him back to his muma, none the worse for it except for a couple a holes in his arm where Sita's teeth had gone right through and out the other side. All right children, you can let go. The scary part's over. Little Binni recovered quick enough. Tough one he was. Just like you kids, huh? Tough." Clapping and cheering.

"Wal, the men got their spears and clubs and stood out in the rain all night. Even though I told 'em *Constable* Barclaw was on duty and had everything under control. So how did I know it was Sita what done it? Found his tail in the mud. Knife flying through the air took it clean off. Right where it met his be-hind. That's what caused him to howl and turn loose of Little Binni. Call it luck. Call it skill. Call it whatever you want. But Little Binni was as sure as et till I saved him.

"So how did you save Beaverton in the bargain, Mister Barclaw?"

Edu's question exactly, except he would have said Constable.

"Wal, old Sita, he must have been so shamed a havin' his tail cut off he never bothered us again. Not only that, he never killed another beaver. No hide nor hair of him, ever again. Some say he might a gone ex-stink. A-cause if he'd a kept on the way he was going he'd a killed 'em all long ago and there wouldn't be no giant valley beavers today. And no Beaverton."

"Ohhhh."

"You and I'd be scattered all over the New Side, fishing the rivers to keep ourselves alive, traipsing off to the coast for crabs and clams and such, bashing animals and creatures on their heads, picking berries and plums." He paused. "And chawin' on worms and slugs."

"Yuck, yuck, yucky."

"And so the giant valley beavers, they multiplied and multiplied, year after year, and built bigger and bigger dams, which made bigger and bigger lakes. And they grew more and more baby beavers with tasty little tails. Which grew into bigger and bigger beavers with tasty big tails. We tried to keep it quiet, keep it all to ourselves. But word gets out. And Beaverton grew and grew, as more families plucked up the courage to 'Trace the Sea.'" Another pause. "Instead of? Instead of what?"

"Swarm City," the children cried, shaking their fists. "Booooo. Swarm City. Booooo." Parents, standing behind, waiting to pick up their children, joined in, adding sharp hisses and hearty boos.

"And that's all for today. Thanks, children. Thanks, folks." Barclaw pushed himself off the ground, stood, and bowed. "Oh, and I almost forgot. Next week's story: 'Barclaw meets Stomp, the man-creature.' Don't miss it." He grinned dark-stained teeth through his bushy beard and bowed again.

So how much of that is true? Is any of it true? I'll have to ask him someday. Still, that was a pretty strong story for kids.

Ziiza resumed strolling and browsing, now enjoying herself. Entering the southwest section, she came upon a vendor who called to her, invited her to sample a new beverage. Slooze, he called it. Dipping a bent-leaf cup into an enormous stone crock, by far the largest she had ever seen, he filled it with a dark, odd-smelling liquid. She sipped. Drank. Awful, she thought, and thanked him perfunctorily. But as she walked, the aftertaste was strangely agreeable.

Ziiza's next work week passed much as the last. There was plenty to do, in a busywork sort of way. Although she and Gstan were doing essentially the same things, they seldom crossed paths during working hours; how amazingly large Beaverton was. They met for lunch each day at his invitation. They did not discuss sales or training; it was clear that her training period was over. He did not give her any hint of a sales quota or his expectations; she wondered if he was as upset at Wiggi Bub's bungling business ways as she was. They chatted pleasantly, avoiding the hard subjects – her compensation, the real estate slowdown in general – while maintaining a polite, junior-female-employee-to-senior-male-supervisor relationship. Gstan was, however, interested in her reactions to his jokes and stories. He would pause, look for approval, and continue. He never told the same story twice, never reprised a punch line; he was too good for that. It was obvious that he liked her, wanted to impress her. But behind his bluster and bravado and authority, she felt, she knew, he was unsure. Maybe only with women. Lifelong bachelor, he had told her. Said it with pride? Or shame? Or defeat? Well, she thought, if not an old pro with women, he was an old pro joke teller and salesman.

Ziiza and Sister Sissi readied the children for school each morning, sometimes with cold lunches, sometimes not; they could always stop at the café for a hot noon meal before tackling the afternoon's Individual Studies. Popamayor rigged an open-front tent for them beside the café. Just in time; the rains started Sunday night. Not rain as in "it rained last night," but rain as in permanent winter wet – low, dark, marine clouds oozing over the Sundown Range, flowing into the Valley of the Beaver, spreading out and pressing down like a gray stone lid. The rains varied, of course. Downpours soaked them straight on. Wind-driven drizzle-mist slipped inside their watabeast furs, soaking them from the inside out as well as the outside in. As they slept, the smoke of hundreds of Beaverton fires mixed with the rain and mist, sometimes creating a friendly, homey, welcoming smell, and sometimes a thick, oppressive, choking fog, an inescapable fog that squatted in every depression and wafted through every shelter, dwelling, and place of business. Nothing dried out. The only good of it: on occasion, when the rain let up and the fog/smoke lifted, usually in late afternoon, the valley filled with the piquant scent of winter fir.

Yes, the rains slowed things as Beaverton hunkered down for the winter. The seasonal vendors – berry, shoot, cress, grape, and plum – slipped away, went somewhere, leaving bare poles and vacant spaces in H&G. But Basic Business Beaverton remained active, retreating into low-ceilinged vends. Instead of the vendors standing outside hawking their wares and services to passers-by, potential customers had to know what they wanted, and step inside. Or call them out. The effect on the real estate business was, in a word, depressing. The effect on Ziiza was the same. She could have stayed home in bed. Wiggi Bub would not have cared; sleep was what he liked best. Gstan, however, was different. As the weather worsened, his cheerfulness and optimism increased. He worked harder. He laughed more. He smiled more. He had the combative spark.

After working through the week Gstan told Ziiza to take the weekend off; that was what he was going to do. Maybe she and her children would like to join him for a walk in the hills, listen to Skedaddle, sit around the fire. Anything. She smiled, thanked him for the invitation, and reminded him she had not made a sale. "Don't worry," he said. "Selling is like fishing; sometimes landing a big one right off gives you the wrong idea, makes you think it's simple. Anyway, in case you're interested, most of us real estate professionals take it easy till the summer-run Sea Tracers start swimming into town. By fall, we've caught a bunch."

Nevertheless, early Saturday morning Ziiza was in the front yard of the east side property, rain running down her face, smiling at walkers, touting the lot, complimenting mumas on their babies – as if she were running for office. As the crowd swept by, an elderly couple stood on the opposite side of the path, off at an angle, their eyes fixed on the For Sale sign. They took their time, scanning Wife Dragga's meticulous rock work, what was left of the shelter, and finally Ziiza herself. After a few breaks in the crowd, when they could have hobbled across for a better look, they hung back, perhaps trying to place her, perhaps out of pure shyness, perhaps because she struck them as too smiley, too greety, too real-estatey. Trying too hard. The crowd surged again, then thinned, and Ziiza saw them. She stopped talking, dropped her hands, let her shoulders down. They walked slowly across the path, two antique miniatures, wizened, white-haired, no more than two-thirds Ziiza's height. They were dressed in skins cut exactly the same. Were they an old man and an old woman, two old women, or two old men? Not wishing to startle them, scare them off, Ziiza fingered her necklaces. This seemed to ease their wariness.

The tiny woman, as she turned out to be, withdrew a pouch from under her cape and held it out. Ziiza took it, knelt, and, removing its contents piece by piece, lined them up on the path: six beaver tails (smoked for trade purposes and moldy), three small stones (possibly unpolished agates), a smaller pouch containing a mix of sun-dried berries and fruit (huckleberries, sour cherries and blueberries), and a few seashells (edges chipped, obviously carried for a long time). Raindrops splattered on the dried food, threatening to ruin it. Ziiza continued looking down, thinking, pretending to appraise their meager offering. When she rose she saw the fear in their eyes: not enough, turned down again. She placed a hand on each bony shoulder and said, "It's yours."

After explaining that she would clear up any formalities with Lots Plus Real Estate Company, whatever they might be, Ziiza refilled the pouch and left them, standing on the lot, shocked at their good fortune.

Wiggi Bub leaned against his counter, blinking and rubbing his eyes, as if he had just woken up. When Ziiza gave him the pouch and told him what she had done, he really woke up. "You! Sold! A! Lot!" he exploded. "They've moved on? You closed the deal yourself? For this?" He pushed the pouch across the counter, caught a breath, and continued, "Take this worthless barter, throw it at them, and throw them off the lot."

"I won't."

"Then I'll do it myself," Wiggi Bub snarled. He grabbed his big hat, pushed it tight on his head, and stepped around the counter.

Ziiza cut in front of him. "You won't, either," she said through her teeth. He drew himself up and thrust his arm out to push her aside. She lowered her shoulder, dug her feet into the mud, and got ready to fight. "I've had enough of your endless talking. Talk, talk, talk, till they go away. Gstan and I bring them in, ready to buy, ready to close, and you talk the deals away. Every time. Anyway, the old folks are desperate for a home lot and I'm desperate for a sale. I'm happy for them. Now I want my commission."

"I'll commission you, Miss Smarty," Wiggi Bub said with a sneer. "You've earned no commission. And if you had, Lots Plus doesn't pay commissions till month's end." He thrust his jaw at her. "And you won't be around —"

Ziiza clapped her hand over his mouth, and said, "I quit."

14

Sita's Lair, a Pleasuring Establishment

POPAMAYOR AND Sister Sissi gave Ziiza the usual expressions of sympathy when she told them what had happened. But they soon turned chatty and cheerful as they prepared the evening meal. Instead of disappointment, Ziiza felt a loss-cutting sense of relief. What to do now? She would have to think this through and make a correction in course. The other two had known all along that Wiggi Bub was a scamp, that it would end something like this. But they had not been asked, so they had kept quiet. They couldn't offer her a job at the café because it was slack season; there was hardly anything for *them* to do. And they were getting to know Ziiza; simple chores at a charity café would never satisfy her ambitious nature.

During her break, Ziiza asked the children for a report on Grassyknoll, something she had glossed over during her short real estate career. Their consensus: Addle was, to put it politely, Addle. Only Edu genuinely enjoyed his rambling stories; he couldn't get enough. Same with Dg, according to Edu, patting his head as he spoke. Org put up with school, but gave all of the signs of a captive animal about to break out of his enclosure and run for it. "He's okay," was his sullen comment. Milli: "He's from another world, I guess." Her brothers and sisters laughed in hearty agreement. Netti: "He gives me a pain in the head. Right here." More laughter. Except from Ziiza, who wondered whether she was joking or if her headaches were worse. Com, the doer, had gained popularity with the other students, especially Torc, a skinny uncoordinated boy who attached himself to him, followed him on his hikes across fields, along creek-sides, and into the hills. Com said he enjoyed his cheerful company and would bring him around, introduce him sometime. Govvi's Individual Studies were actually individual and actually studies. Tally board in hand, she spent every afternoon walking through H&G, evaluating vendors and businesses, noting everything she saw, sometimes questioning owners and clerks. Information-filled boards piled up in the shelter.

Monday morning, to clear her head and think things through, Ziiza took a walk. The rain had eased off to a drizzle. It was not too cold and the wind was down, which, compared to the shore-walking she was used to, made for downright pleasant weather. She headed out the western path, into the Valley of the Beaver, into a topography she had not seen before: rolling meadows with occasional stands of fir. The perimeter trees were mostly storm-shattered, broken off midway up, but the interior trees were relatively undamaged, giving the appearance of massive stockades filled with green soldiers. The path was broad and well-traveled, leading to the Ever-faithful Daughter, the medium-sized, silver-bright river that drained the valley and joined the North-flowing Son a few miles upstream from Pop&Jay's.

On a high bank well above the spring run-off level was a large-scale commercial enterprise: men and women cleaning and cutting, stacking and storing beaver tails. It was presided over, she found out, by Castor, a name she remembered hearing before, Beaverton's licensed beaver hunter. His crew of deputy hunters, he told her – visitors and wanderers were checked on immediately – stalked the giant valley beaver in its many ponds and lakes on the Daughter and its feeder streams. Aside from the discomfort of always being wet, it was easy work: sneaking up on snoozing or gnawing beavers, then whacking off chunks of their oversized tails. Easy work because they were fat and slow. If his rules were followed, and his hunters always followed his rules, tail-whacking was little more than an inconvenience to the beaver. And painless at that. Or so they believed. The rules, as Castor explained: Never take more than half a tail. Always cut on a slant, never at what would be a right angle to a stretched-out beaver. If done this way, tails grow back in a few weeks, most of the time larger and fatter than before, making that particular beaver all the easier to "tail" the next time. And so on. The Daughter and its streams, Castor told Ziiza with evident pride, was the only place in the world home to the giant valley beaver. The impossibility of verifying this claim did not seem to faze him. His deputies, he confided, as if she were an old-timer, were more game wardens than hunters; joy poaching was the problem. Tails are so plentiful they do not have much value, he told her with a sigh; they are practically free at H&G. Poachers do it for sport, the fun of it, and ruin many a beaver in the process. But he had it under control, he claimed. Maintained this way, beaver tails were an endlessly renewable resource. They were versatile (tasty, cooked or raw), nutritious (people could survive for long periods on tails and water), and stored well (dried and bundled). And beavers weren't affected by hundred-year windstorms.

After examining a monstrous dam across the Daughter (which Castor bragged about as if he had constructed it himself), walking up to a sleeping beaver, which she estimated was as long as Govvi was tall, and the tail of which was twice as heavy as the now well-fed Dg, Ziiza decided she had seen enough of "beaver country." She said good-bye to Castor and headed back to town. Six men bound for H&G were leaving, so she joined them on the path. Her curiosity aroused, she had planned to follow them to the tail vendors so she could learn the complete process, how Beaverton's economy worked. Instead, she found the slooze vendor, Biber, scrubbing his brew-crock. "Hi. How's business?" she said, making passing conversation.

"Terrible," he replied. "Best slooze anywhere, but nobody's interested." He gave a lick with his stick-and-moss scouring pad, and added, "The *only* slooze anywhere, for that matter." This struck the misery-loves-company drum in Ziiza's head and she stopped to commiserate. After telling him that her own situation was not so fine, either, he poured her a sympathy drink from a small bowl set back from the crock, and, as every professional drink purveyor should, one for himself. So instead of learning more about beaver tails, she learned about slooze, and, of course, Biber himself.

He was fresh from the Old Side, like herself. Fresh from the Sea Trace, like herself. He had come all of the way by water, brought his brew-crock – he glanced at it, lovingly – on a specially-made barge. Paid the crew extra to roll it across the point at the Grand Muma's mouth, drag the barge across to safe water, then paddle it upriver. Then up the North-flowing Son. Then the Daughter, to the first dam. There, with the last of his savings, he had hired some idlers to boost the crew and they rolled it to this very place. He had arrived a few weeks before Ziiza. Another late one off the Sea Trace.

Biber appeared older than herself, Ziiza observed, but how old she could not be certain. Five years? Ten? Twenty? His drawn, sallow face and hunched shoulders could show age, or hard work, or worry. Or all three. Like Gstan, he was not married, had never been. He had learned slooze making, saved his barter goods, and taken a chance on the New Side. "Like yourself?" he asked, winking, probing, enhancing his question with a rare smile.

Ziiza did not bite. "What is it, this slooze? How's it made?" she asked, turning his question back on him as she was so used to doing with Edu. He did not answer, but sat licking the inside of his leaf-cup, carefully weighing what he would reveal and what he would not reveal. He took so long Ziiza thought he was not just agonizing over what to tell, but whether to say anything at all. She was, as it turned out, correct. All of his formulas and processes were secret; he had never told anyone. Never had a partner. Never let anyone watch. She sat, waiting patiently, looking straight ahead, turning her cup in her hands.

"The name, slooze," he said, as if they weren't three words, but three teeth being wrenched from his mouth, "is a combination of *sludge* and *ooze*. Slooze." He glanced sideways to see what impact this information had on her. Maybe she would stop prying, change the subject, and walk away. Or, on second thought, maybe he would like her to stay. She stopped turning her cup and waited. "From swamp bottoms," he said. She flinched, then cocked her head and let her wide eyes speak for her. Satisfied, he said, "Don't worry, it's heated and cured." With that, he went back to his cleaning. Taking her signal, Ziiza tossed the cup, thanked him for his hospitality, wished him well, and left.

He waited for maximum impact until she was almost out of hearing. "And, if you haven't noticed," he shouted, "it gives you a bit of a buzz."

She answered with a wave and an exaggerated leg wobble.

Gstan found Ziiza in front of the Willow Tree, a dried flower, grass, and knick-knack vend. "I've been looking for you," he said, panting. "Running all over Beaverton. Sister Sissi's. Skedaddle. I even checked with Barclaw. Missing persons, you know."

"I quit," Ziiza said. "Just quit. He didn't care. I took a long walk to cool off. A long and interesting walk, I might add."

"*I* care. Why didn't you talk to me first?"

"Spur of the moment. I sold the lot and asked for my commission. He refused to close. No commission. That was it. I just quit and walked away."

"Great," he said. "That's what I wanted to talk to you about. I'm ready to ditch the sleepy old has-been myself, go on my own, form my own business. I've just been waiting till the time was right. I'm this close." He held thumb to forefinger. "Can I trust you on this? Keep it quiet?"

"Certainly you can trust me."

"There's a new area opening up over northwest. I'm going to develop a subdivision. Not lots, but – get this – burrows, holes in the ground. Lot and shelter all in one big sale. I call it Hill Burrow. Clever, what?" He jumped, turned in the air, and landed with a plop, holding his finger up like a performer ending a song.

"Wonderful, Gstan," Ziiza replied, as if responding to one of Edu's fanciful tales.

"And I want you to come with me. Work for me. No, work *with* me. Be part of it. You'll be terrific."

She knew her answer, but hesitated out of respect for the offer and his enthusiasm. "Gstan," she said deliberately, "that's so nice of you. But I think not. I want to take some time before making my next move. With six kids to support, I simply can't afford to make another mistake like Lots Plus." She hoped he would smile.

He did not. Instead, he continued, paying no attention to her turn-down. "Hey, that's not all I have to tell you. Are you ready to learn another one of

Beaverton's secrets? How Beaverton really works?" He grinned in anticipation.

Evidently today is secrets day.

First Castor and beaver tails. Sort of a secret. To her, at least. Then Biber. If not an entire secret, part of one. Now what?

"Lots are free," Gstan said. "To the first owner, anyway. Only after that do they become valuable. Then the owner can sell for what whatever he or she can get. Sell it themselves. Sell it through Wiggi Bub. Or me. Sell it through you, Ziiza. Or abandon it. Then it's free again. See where I'm going?" Ziiza shook her head. "The Beaverton town council controls the whole valley, including the beavers. And a good ways beyond, I might add. All the way to the coast. They say, in effect, you want to live in our fair valley and eat our tasty tails, you play by our rules. Of which there are two. Two big ones, anyway. First, kill no beavers. Tails only. Castor and crew enforce it, conserve them, make them last. They, together with Barclaw, are the closest thing Beaverton has to an army or a police force. But it works. Second, if you want to live in the valley and partake of the food, you must live in Beaverton town. Everywhere else is beaver breeding territory and open spaces. The town boundary is Outer Circle. Obvious. And if you live in town, you must live on a designated lot. Or something the council says is a lot. Such as the Hill Burrow development." His eyes brightened. "That's the hold cheap and easy beaver tails has on us. So why am I telling you this, Ziiza?"

"Because you think I'm naïve."

"Quite the opposite, or I wouldn't have asked you to join me at Hill Burrow. Anyway, if you don't want to join up because you don't know me well enough, I understand. Think it over."

"You were leading up to something, Gstan. At least I can see that. You have something else in mind."

"Yes, I do."

While he talked Ziiza looked him over, trying to get beyond her first impression: older, skinny, and her boss. His face was covered with tightly-stretched, nut-brown skin, not unusual even among Beaverton townies, as everyone spent most of his time outside. She re-checked his arms and legs, as much as she could without staring. They were straight and smooth on either side of elbows and knees, which were wrinkled and loose, the limbs of a man, as she had noticed before, who had talked rather than muscled his way through life. She wondered whether he could have kept up on the Sea Trace, paddling or walking, let alone have been much good in a fight with, say, a watabeast. Or a fight with a man. On the other hand, his large eyes sparkled with intelligence and enthusiasm, and possibly sincerity, causing her to question her original take on him as simply a smooth-talking real estate sharpie.

"I know of an abandoned lot," Gstan said. Ziiza's head jerked up. "How

Wiggi Bub and you and the kids missed it I don't know. But you did. All you have to do is claim it. Put your own sign up, so to speak. Not for sale, for possession. And it's a beauty. I was thinking of claiming it myself, selling it after I quit. But I'll have my hands full. So let's take a look. If you're interested."

"You know of a lot?" she said. "My head's swimming. I need time to sort this out."

"Sort while we walk." He took her hand to get her started, then let go.

The lot was oversized and high. Water drained away in all directions, a bonus. She saw immediately why they had overlooked it. It was close to H&G, southeast side, in a more expensive neighborhood. Relatively undamaged by the storm, it did not appear to be abandoned. "See, I told you," Gstan said, beaming. Then, anticipating her question: "The neighbors think the owners are up the Grand Muma, sturgeon fishing. Back in a few weeks. But they're gone, gone, gone. I'm not saying where they went, but I know for a fact. Send the big kid, Org, over to camp on it tonight. That's my advice. Move the family in, gradually, orderly. Everything easy and natural, not to get the neighbors asking questions. Say you're lot sitting. Anything. A couple of days. A week. Amble over to Town Hall. See Barclaw or one of clerks. Register it in your name. Just to be sure." He smiled, saluted, and having made what he hoped were big points, left.

A few days after they had claimed the lot, Ziiza, while heading back to Sister Sissi's, found herself drawn in another direction. Are things falling into place? Or am I falling apart? True? Or too good to be true? Why, for instance, didn't that old shrewdy Wife Dragga find the lot with her long pointed sniffer? Well, she couldn't own everything. Ziiza found Biber closing for the night, covering his giant brew-crock with a skin and pegging it down; evidently he crawled under the edge to sleep. "I have an idea for you, Biber," she said after they had exchanged pleasantries. "It's not completely formed, but if I talk it over with you maybe it will make sense. It could be the answer to your problems. And mine."

"How so?" he asked glumly.

"I think people would love your slooze if it was served it in a different setting. A different way. Not this outdoor, walk-by vend or enclosure – not that there's anything wrong with it, except that nobody comes – but a place where they could sit, relax, and enjoy themselves. Out of the rain. A little food. Some music, maybe. Cater to single folks who have nothing to do and nowhere to go after H&G closes."

Biber leaned against his brew-crock. "I'm listening," he said.

"I've been thinking about this since the first time I met you, took a drink, felt the warmth in my belly and toes. All nine of them," she added, trying to lighten things up. Biber looked. She saw him cringe and covered her right foot with her left. "Sorry."

"Got the buzz, eh?" he stammered.

"Got the buzz." She gave him a sly, bonding look. "A place with a fire. Warm, bright, cheerful. And I have the location for it."

"You do?" he said. "In H&G?"

"No, not H&G. That's the point. I don't want it there. I – we – want it in a neighborhood, where people can drop in casually. Not tied to H&G's rules and hours. I even have a name for it. Popped into my head. Sita's Lair. After the legendary cat Barclaw tells the children about in his tall tales. Has a ring to it, don't you think?"

"Well, Ziiza," he said, smiling a full smile for the first time since she had met him, "at least it's a chance. Couldn't do worse than I'm doing here."

Ziiza stuck out her hand. "We'll pursue it, then."

Govvi picked up on the idea immediately. She sorted through her tally boards and found the one she wanted. "Biber," she reported. "Stone crock. Capacity: two thousand and fifty cups. Brewing time: undetermined. Product potential: good to sensational."

What kind of a child do I have here? She's never said anything was sensational in her life. Sensational. Truly amazing.

Sister Sissi and Popamayor were not as enthusiastic. Not because she would be leaving, taking away the children's lively company which they obviously enjoyed; it was just a matter of time before all newcomers set their courses and moved on, and they knew it. But to move out and open a place with a name like Sita's Lair. And introduce a disgusting-sounding drink called slooze. Cater to singles. For the sole purpose of having fun. Why, there was too much fun in Beaverton already. And not nearly enough honest toil.

Fortunately Biber had not burned the rollers he had used to roll the brew-crock in from the river. That was the first step; get it in place, then build the shelter around it. Org held back while Biber, Ziiza, his brothers and sisters, and every passer-by they could enlist tried to get the dead weight moving. Then, after a dramatic and uncharacteristic display of deep breathing and muscle flexing, he put his shoulder to it and pushed. It did not move. He stood back, picked another spot, and strained. "Eeee-yaaa," he yelled. The huge brew-crock moved and began its painfully slow journey. It was especially painful to Biber, watching a new batch of slooze slosh up and over the sides and waste away on the ground. Until, that is, the volunteer pushers began licking the sides. Pay for their efforts. Good advertising, too.

Ziiza and Biber finalized Sita's Lair's layout and settled the operating particulars. Ziiza would own and operate the drinkery-eatery (for lack of a better term). Biber would continue to own and operate the brew-crock. The secret recipes and procedures would, of course, remain his. Ziiza would have exclusive rights to all the slooze he produced, to mark it up, and sell it. The price? Whatever Govvi approved.

After school, Ziiza sent the children to the north side of town to hunt for shelter mats missed after the windstorm. Surprisingly easy to find, even after the rebuilding. More than they could use. The pitch-covered mats went on top, supported by poles; sloping gently for runoff and maximum headroom, with openings over the fire pits. The vertical hanging sides were in so many different hues it looked as if each shelter in Beaverton had contributed. They spent the remainder of the week lining fire-pits and building seats and serving stations. They accomplished all of this with their own labor and materials they scrounged. Biber was excused from construction; his sole task was to produce a batch of slooze for opening night. "Might as well go all out," Ziiza told him. "If Sita's Lair catches on, we'll need it. If it doesn't. . . ."

That night Biber feigned sleep. After midnight he gathered his pouches, left the shelter, and stole out of town, taking the wide path to the Daughter. Just before Castor's tail works he cut through the forest, then across the meadow, till he reached a large beaver pond. He lay on his pouches and tried to sleep, but could do no more than close his eyes, he was so excited. This shallow mucky beaver pond, and a few others nearby, held the finest slooze ingredients he had ever found, better than anything on the Old Side. He discovered them his first day, passed them while rolling his brew-crock in from the river. Not by chance; he was always looking. And sniffing. One sniff with his trained nose, and he knew: stink-lovely. No one else had any idea of the sublime treasure lying under the water. Just for the taking. He returned that night to confirm it, not that he had had to. Patrol patterns? Easy to figure out. Too easy, almost. They were so lazy. So complacent. So interested in other things? When patrols passed while he was mucking and scooping, it was easy: slip under the water without a ripple, just like a beaver.

Carefully, he half-swam, half-waded across the pond, pouches tied to his waist, pausing to smell gas bubbles as they popped to the surface. "Too clean, not rotten enough," he mumbled. He turned and worked his way along the shore, just far enough out to avoid the brush and toppled trees; beaver doings. He stepped into a hole and dropped to his neck. While fanning the water to keep upright and easing his foot out of the goop, he caught the scent. "Sludge in, slooze out," he said. "Should be my company motto." He took a breath, dove, dug his hands in the bottom, and crammed a pouch full. He waddled to the pond's edge and laid it on the ground allowing the water to drain away. When he had filled all his pouches, he waded back, savoring the night-pond stench. Only he, Biber, knew how to refine it, transform it into wondrous slooze.

Dawn came. He was lucky: none of Castor's men this morning, just a few beaver swimming around, not caring how much sludge he took out of their pond; they treated him as one of their own. Avoiding the wide path, Biber carried his load through-woods and cross-country. Just before Outer Circle, he hid the pouches in the trees, far enough away so the they couldn't be smelled. He would wait until later to bring them in, create an aura of mystery, the secret ingredients appearing magically, as if from nowhere.

The children were bolting breakfast, late for school as usual, when Biber sauntered up, chewing on a stick of dried tail, dirty, but no more so than usual; smelly, but no more so than usual, looking as if he was coming back from the leak pit.

"Morning, Mister Biber," Edu said. "I missed you when I got up." Dg advanced on him and sniffed his legs for the longest time.

"I think we're on target for a Saturday night opening," Ziiza said. "Think you can have a batch worked up by then?"

"Not only that, it will be my finest ever. I have a feeling."

"Don't you mean the stinkiest ever?" Ziiza said with a laugh. He forced one in reply, wondering how much she knew. Had she followed him? She continued, "I've got one more problem to solve: food. We need a snack, something as unique as your slooze. I'm going to talk to Sister Sissi and see if she has any ideas."

Unfortunately, lack of a signature snack was not the problem. Friday afternoon, Constable Barclaw knocked on the front post. "Anybody here?" Thinking it a friendly, walk-by call, Ziiza waved him into the dark, sprawling shelter, and, since that was what was on her mind, eagerly explained her concept, the need it would fill, and how she and Biber were going to operate. "Sorry, Ziiza," he said, "that's just it. I have a Stop Work order and I'm going to have to post it right here."

"Stop what? What do you mean?" she said in a voice loud enough to turn Biber's head.

"Yor planning to conduct a commercial business, in this case a pleasuring establishment, in a residential neighborhood. They're only allowed inside the Inner Circle pathway, in the H&G itself, if they're allowed a-tall. And besides being in the wrong place, you've got yourself no permit."

"Permit. I'll get one. Where do I go?"

"Too late for that. Construction already started. Vi-o-la-tion. Appeal town council's the only way. I *am* sorry for the trouble, Ziiza," he added. "Sounds like a good idea. Sounds like someplace I'd like to visit myself. After duty hours, of course. Oh, yes, council meeting's Tuesday evening at Town Hall."

"Well, Biber," Ziiza said after Barclaw had gone, "it looks like a slow Saturday night."

15

Tip-n-Dips and Slooze

THERE BEING no old business, Mistermayor began the council meeting with the state of the town report. "Maybe I should call it the slice of the beaver report?" he said, smiling broadly and chuckling, scanning the overflow audience and council members for laughs or looks of approval. There being none, he stood up slowly, as if gathering himself for a major effort. When he unfolded to his full height he was as tall as Popamayor, Ziiza observed. Or he might have been in his youth. Was being tall a prerequisite for the job? "Smoke-storm's behaving," Mistermayor began in a honeyed voice with an odd twang. "Our monitoring crews have found no new vents. Just normal rumbling. Nothing to worry about." Applause.

"Save the beavers." A shrill voice from the back. "Eat no tails." Ziiza turned to see an older woman shaking a ragged umbrella and glaring fiercely at Mistermayor.

"Not now Mizpark," Mistermayor said, stroking his jaw, "you know my position on that. Come to my office. We'll talk."

"Talk, huh," Mizpark shouted. "We want action, not talk." Some men in the audience hooted and booed and laughed; evidently they had heard this before.

"The beaver population is up ten percent, according to Castor's latest count," Mistermayor continued. "Tail harvest is steady. No winter food problems anticipated." More applause and cheers. "Now, on the question of expanding Outer Circle to accommodate Beaverton's growth, we expect to have our study complete by early spring." At this, some whooped and cheered, while others shook fists and yelled at Mistermayor, calling him a traitor and sellout. Mizpark's shrill voice cut the air; she was very much of the latter view.

"Order! Order!" shouted Polcat, the senior council member, his face reddening. "Quiet down!" The spectators quieted a bit, and as they did, rearranged themselves creating an aisle, a division between the two factions.

"Ah, sorry, Mistermayor," he said. "Back to you."

"That's about it for the report," Mistermayor said. He sat.

The meeting continued with Mistermayor and Polcat (the other council members said little) talking on subjects ranging from crows stealing dried beaver tails, to draining water off the town's pathways, to appointments of minor functionaries, to plans for sprucing up Beaverton. Unlike the boundary study, nothing said or proposed aroused controversy or discussion, and everything put to a vote passed. During all of this the audience members slipped away in ones and twos. Looking pleased with themselves, Mistermayor and the council members stretched and yawned. "Do I hear a motion to adjourn?" Mistermayor asked.

"Wait," Ziiza said. "I have some business here. I need a permit. At least that's what Barclaw told me I needed." The council members groaned, making no effort to hide their disappointment, and sank into their seats.

"Oh, yes," Mistermayor said, "he mentioned something about that. Pleasuring establishment, isn't it? Outside of H&G. Quite unorthodox. Quite illegal. Well, quickly, it's late."

Ziiza explained Sita's Lair, told them of her life-long dream of owning her own business (which she had dreamed up for the occasion), of being a single muma with six children to support. The yawns stopped; at least they were listening. Biber explained his slooze, somewhat, and how integral it was to Ziiza's plan. Rather, her dream. Had any of the council members had a chance to sample his slooze, Ziiza asked after Biber had finished. No one had. "Well," she said, in another flash of inspiration, "why don't you stop by on your way home and we'll treat you to the best drink you've ever tasted. No obligation."

Constable Barclaw appeared early next morning. With a flourish, he tore down the Stop Work order and replaced it with a slab titled: Conditional Use Permit. Below, it read: Permission granted to operate a pleasuring establishment on this lot as long as the neighbors don't complain. By order of the Beaverton Town Council. Then Mistermayor's flowing signature. Barclaw gave Ziiza a smile, a hand-to-mouth drinking motion, and walked quickly away.

On a hunch, and since he had the time, Biber doubled his batch. He emptied his finished slooze into pouches, pots, and bowls, anything he could find. Again he went diving in the pond. And again he toted, blended, and stirred. Since the crock was in Sita's Lair, also Ziiza and family's home, one of his secrets could no longer be hidden: dropping hot rocks into the roily slooze, the final curing, blending, and thickening step.

Aside from neighborhood talk and a makeshift notice Govvi had scratched onto a board and hung above the entrance, publicity had slipped to the bottom of Ziiza's checklist. How to get the word out? One answer came from Gstan when he stopped by to chat, help a little, and brag about Hill Burrow (which was not selling, but not to hear him talk). "Bitta's been telling the Sita's Lair story every day," he said. "Just pay her a little something to embellish, give out the details, invite everyone to your grand opening. She's awfully poor, you know."

Ziiza found Bitta in front of Town Hall next to Barclaw's outdoor office, too close as far as he was concerned. He looked pained as he raised a finger to Ziiza in greeting. It took a while for Bitta to wind down, but Ziiza waited her out. When she stopped, Ziiza thanked her for mentioning Sita's Lair – as news. What were people saying? Any feedback? Was anyone coming? Could she purchase a longer, more detailed, announcement?

"Happy to," Bitta replied. "Anything you like – as long as it's true. No charge. Do it for nothing. My calling. My reason for living, actually. So what do you want me to say?" Ziiza gave her the specifics: Saturday night. East side of town. Close to H&G. A new pleasure beverage. (Better go easy on the name, slooze, Bitta suggested; it might scare them.) Food. And loads of fun. Every Beaverton adult welcome. Bitta reached up and poked Hobart. "Stand still, you silly bird." Hobart slipped off her shoulder, caught himself, and flapped up. She stepped onto her round, and, after reciting the council agenda, which she had already done a dozen times, launched into Ziiza's message.

On Thursday after school, Ziiza lined the children up in the old order of march and gave them their assignments. All, that is, but Govvi, who assigned herself. She would stand at the entrance, she announced, and collect admissions. For opening night she felt it would be best not to set a fixed amount and accept whatever was offered. She had earlier decided it would be impractical to charge by the drink, at least for the time being. Neither Ziiza nor Biber questioned this. Govvi would keep a customer count, a receipts count, a payables count, and an inventory of everything, including brew-crock contents, measured hourly with a marked pole. (Actually, the "accept anything offered" idea came from Gstan who was trying to launch Hill Burrow the same way. And, if one wished to push the point, from Pop&Jay, too.) Govvi also made it clear that she had graduated from fire building and fire tending. The job now fell to Org, and it was a big one, with three fire pits and two dozen torches to tend. Milli and Netti would be serving girls, which pleased them; they could stay up late, interact with the customers, and share in the fun. Com would assist Biber at the slooze station, filling cups and running errands. Ziiza would stand by the entrance, greeting customers, then circulating through the crowd (assuming there was one) in the proprietress-hostess role. Edu and Dg drew cleanup duty.

During all of this, curious neighbors stopped by. "What exactly is going on here?" Ziiza proudly showed them her permit, told them how much Beaverton needed such a place, and introduced Biber, who ladled out samples of slooze for all but the children. This seemed to dampen their objections. Some even said they were looking forward to opening night. "Sounds exciting." After what seemed endless rehearsing, and endless counting by Govvi, and endless stirring and tasting by Biber, the food question was still unresolved; Sita's Lair needed a signature taste treat. Not beaver tails, Ziiza had decided; they were too common. Too late for salmon, as they had discovered. Too late for fruit or nut gathering, although Netti offered to try. Sister Sissi's recipes and suggestions proved uninspiring. And, as Govvi reminded Ziiza again and again, their credit with vendors was "stretched pretty thin." Gstan donated a large basket of dried blueberries for slooze-drinking munchies as an opening night present. That was it in the food department.

Until Saturday morning, when Ziiza took Org on a fast tour of H&G, desperate for ideas. Passing a beaver tail vendor, she noticed him throwing something onto a garbage heap. "What's that?" she inquired.

"Them's tail tips. We trim 'em off. Too hard to chew."

"May I have them?"

He looked surprised, but said, "Take 'em away."

They returned to Sita's Lair with all they could carry. Ziiza sent the boys and Dg back for the rest. "Hurry, before they bury them."

"What are these gross looking things, Muma?" Netti asked when they returned.

"Tail tips; they throw them away. I've got an idea how to use them. We open in a few hours. The pressure's on. So it's idea time. Not perfect idea time, any idea time. You boys," she said, "run out and cut some willow branches. Arms length, green, thin. As many as you can carry. Off with you." Caught up with the urgency and excitement, Edu, Com, and Org ran to Beaverton Creek. "Here it is, girls," Ziiza said. "We'll have a basket of these tail tips next to each fire-pit. Our guests, our customers, can spear them with sticks, roast them, then dip them in our secret sauce."

"Secret sauce?" Milli, of course.

"We're going to make it, the four of us." Now the girls were interested. "Milli and Netti, run over to H&G, please. Buy every flavor root, spice, seed, strong berry, medicine herb, dried flower petal you can find. On credit, of course. If they refuse credit, ask again. Then cry, beg, anything to get them. And Sea-salt. Ask vendors for ideas. Flatter them. Taste everything. The stronger the better. Hurry."

When they reached H&G Milli and Netti decided they could cover more vends if they separated; they would meet at Skedaddle in an hour. Netti took the circle path to cover the periphery. Milli headed for the center. As she stopped to sample some dried chokecherries she heard music. It came from Skedaddle's direction, but this sound was definitely not Skedaddle. Not at all. The cherries were bitter enough, she concluded, so she bought a sack full with her muma's few remaining trade items; she was not about to beg for credit.

Boom! Boom! Boom! A drum thundered over the crowd noise. Seductively-spaced beats. Boom! Boom! She walked, rather was drawn, toward the sound. The drummer's shaggy hair flew as he swung his head to the beat of the largest, most resounding drum she had ever heard. Next to him a younger man played a small hard-covered drum, his fingertips a blur. In addition, he tapped a hollow log with a stick held between his toes. Click. Click. A larger man, older and taller, stood off to the side, eyes closed, strumming a small stringed instrument. "Woo, doo. Woo, doo," he moaned in a bass voice, almost matching the huge drum's carrying power.

"Where's Skedaddle?" Milli inquired of the boy standing next to her.

"Don't know. Don't care," he said, snapping his fingers to the beat. "Call themselves Screaming Indifference. Came from somewhere. Best thing's happened to H&G. To Beaverton. Ever."

Evidently they were introducing a number, because a fourth man ran out from behind the backdrop, leaped into the air, and began playing a larger stringed instrument hanging from his neck, and singing words Milli could not understand. He could not have been more of a contrast to "Woo Doo": skinny, narrow-faced, and with straight yellow hair. He screamed and bounced for a few minutes, then hunched over his instrument and backed away from center stage with exaggerated steps. The audience, which Milli realized was almost entirely youngsters her age or younger, clapped and cheered as if they knew what was coming. The background musicians played faster. "Twigg! Twigg!" the audience members screamed.

The backdrop parted, revealing a medium-height man, about "Woo Doo's" age. He stood with legs planted, hands on hips. No instrument. He was bare-chested, as were the others. Unlike the others, his chest was smooth and hairless – reminding her of someone – his face soft-looking and round, his hair cropped close. He advanced with the same heavy steps his predecessor had used in retreat, his mouth fixed in a cocky half-smile. Milli tingled at the sight of him. She did not know why. He took a breath, raised his arms, and screamed:

Got ten days more,
Baby,
For you and me,

To hop on top,
This stinking world,
And shake, shake, shake.

The youngsters screamed too, drowning him out. They shook their fists, jumped, kicked the mud until everyone's legs were splattered. He lowered a hand, index finger extended, commanding silence. The noise level dropped to a rolling throb. He gave them a haughty look that forbade further interruption, jerked his head to the side, and continued.

And shake, shake, shake
This stinking world,
Till it gasps
And pants
And rolls over
Upside down
And dead, dead, dead.

He raised a finger. Not yet.

Got ten days,
Baby,
For you and me,
To finish
Shaking up
This stinking, stinking world.

He stepped back and raised his hands, palms out, accepting their applause. Then palms in, inviting them to sing along. Milli could not take her eyes off of him. She tried to join in, tried to sing, rather shout, the incomprehensible words, but her mouth was dry. She stood with her arms crossed over her chest, swaying with the music, thrilled by the rebelliousness of it all. Where did these people come from? Her kind. Finally. They certainly weren't Grassyknoll students. More to the point, who was *he*? Where did *he* come from? Twigg allowed them to sing along until they lost it. He raised his commanding finger, sang one more verse, and disappeared backstage. "Twigg, Twigg, we love you," they screamed. "Come back, Twigg." Milli swallowed, found her voice, and joined the chant. Evidently this was the final number. The support musicians followed him in. They screamed for an encore, but their demands were ignored. Evidently they had had the screaming portion; this was the indifference.

Netti found Milli sitting, fixated, near the empty stage, chokecherries spilled in the mud. "Been waiting long?" she asked. "What'd you find?"

After a pause, Milli said, "Netti, you won't believe what I've seen. What I've heard. *Who* I've seen. *Who* I've heard."

"Skedaddle? I mean, they're good, but. . . ."

"No. A new band. A band that spoke to me. Rushed my soul. And their lead singer. He spoke to my heart." Then, quickly: "I shouldn't have said that."

"And?"

"That's all. You'll have to hear them yourself. When they play again. If they play again." Then, remembering their errand, Milli said, "I hope you've got enough stuff for both of us. Muma will kill me. All I have are these chokecherries." She began plucking them out of the mud and wiping them off.

Ziiza did not even look at what they brought; it was less an hour till opening. She spilled everything onto a stone slab. They pounded it fine. Then they heated and stirred and mixed it with root starch, wood ash, and thickened it with sand. It tasted awful, grated their teeth, but she was out of time. It would have to do.

Govvi forced on her best smile, tucked her tally board under her arm, and positioned herself at the Sita's Lair entrance. Ziiza stood at her side and slightly behind, nervously stroking her fur and clicking her necklaces. Milli and Netti primped by the serving station. Org fed each fire till it blazed with welcoming brightness. Edu stood at attention, wiping mat in one hand, a bundle of roasting sticks in the other. Dg pressed against his leg, every bit as nervous as his family.

Biber stirred, tasted, ladled, and worried out loud whether he would have enough. He was the only one who had any idea of the risk; opening a new place based on an untried idea. So many untried ideas. What if no one comes? What if everyone comes? What if Castor shows up and accuses him of trespassing? Stealing muck? Poaching beaver? What if the wardens were watching? What if he brings Barclaw to arrest him? He was sweating now, wiping his face as his imagination ran faster and faster. He trotted around the brew-crock, patting, talking to it as if it were alive, pleading with it to come through for him. For Ziiza. For all of them. He ran outside for a breath of cool air.

The neighbors across the path came first, "We're just here for a bit." Then more neighbors. Barclaw came, congratulated Ziiza and Govvi, but did not enter. Instead, he positioned himself across the path, standing as close to attention as an old beaver hunter could, wishing he was off duty. He was soon joined by Bitta. Since she, too, was working, gathering news, gossip, and everything, they stood together, chatting, looking, sniffing. Then Gstan. He presented Govvi with a pile of tails, reasonable admission for ten, and hugged Ziiza. He pretended to look around, surveying the Lair, although he had seen it many times before. "Coming along nicely," he told Ziiza, referring to Hill Burrow. He lowered his voice. "I'm just about ready to leave old you-know-who." It was obvious that he wanted to talk more, but she turned away to greet customers. So he smiled and flowed along with the crowd toward the brew-crock and its slooze. Strangers came, both smiling in anticipation and hesitant, not knowing what to expect. "Why, Wife Dragga," Ziiza said, trying to conceal her surprise. "Welcome."

"Wouldn't miss it for anything, Zi-iz-ahh dah-ling," Wife D said with spiked sincerity as she wrapped her bony arms around her. She brush-kissed Ziiza and whispered, "Success," in her ear, as if they were the dearest of friends. "I'm single tonight," she added, releasing her. "*He* doesn't like these social things. *He* might have to say something." With Wife Dragga, and those streaming in after her, Govvi gave Ziiza a wink and nod. Sita's Lair's admissions had reached the critical number. Opening night would not be a flop.

Nor would the slooze. Milli and Netti, and soon Ziiza, Org, and Edu – all but Govvi – were soon pouring and serving and running for refills. Customers bypassed the servers, went directly to Biber and Com. Some dipped from the great brew-crock itself. Likewise the tail tips. Skewering them onto the sticks and roasting proved to be great conversation starters. Neighbors who had not spoken in years found something to talk about. Who said Sita's Lair was just for singles? Dipping, then eating, sauce dripping down arms and fronts, provoked round after round of elbow pokes and laughter. The more they laughed, the more they enjoyed. Fires and body heat warmed the droopy shelter. The conviviality level rose. Then something magical happened. Biber caught it first. Then Ziiza. Slooze, plus Tip-n-Dips – as they came to be called – along with the lively, active atmosphere they created, were greater than the sum of their parts. Slooze tasted great – all the way down. Tip-n-Dips tasted terrible. But nobody cared. Maybe it was the Sea-salt. Maybe the sand. Maybe the devil-may-care idea of consuming something so outrageously bad-tasting it tasted good. Along with plenty of slooze. Eat Tip-n-Dips. Get thirsty. Drink slooze. Get hungry. Eat more Tip-n-Dips. Drink more slooze. Laugh. Sing. Have fun. Not exactly as Ziiza had anticipated, but what a fantastic formula for filling the place and selling Biber's slooze.

They kept coming. Those who "came for a minute" stayed. A chill evening fog formed in the pathway outside, but inside, with the press of people and three tall fires fed by Org's wood and tail tip fat, it grew uncomfortably hot. Customer's faces glowed, assisted by slooze. Barclaw and Bitta abandoned their detached, professional stances and came in to get warm, mingle, and pick up information.

"No more wood on the fires, Org," Ziiza said, "It's too hot in here." Then to Biber: "How's the slooze holding out?"

"Good," Biber said "But I'm glad I doubled the batch."

"We're almost out of tails, Muma," Edu said, yanking on Ziiza's shawl to get her attention.

Ziiza thought for moment, then took his hand and pulled him through the crowd. "Govvi, have many paid in beaver tail?" Govvi did not have to answer. She bent over her collection baskets and handed pieces of fresh and dried tail to Ziiza and Edu. One fell on the ground and Dg snapped it up. Not that he was hungry; he had already snapped up so many Tip-n-Dips his sides were bulging. At the fire, Ziiza told Org, "Cut these up. Small pieces. Make them last. If we run out of dip, that's it."

Ziiza pushed her way to the center pole and beat on it with a stick until the closest people noticed and turned. "Hello," she said, as loudly as she could without screaming. "Greetings, everybody. Your attention, please." Customer nudged customer, neighbor nudged neighbor. Ziiza stepped on a tree-round and waved. "Thank you for coming," she said. Cheering and stomping. "Are you enjoying Biber's slooze?" She pointed at him leaning against his brew-crock. They raised their leaf-cups as if in a toast and cheered again. "Sorry we have no music tonight; it was all we could do to put this much together." No one seemed to care. She continued: "However, as an alternative," she paused, letting the anticipation rise, "I challenge every guest in Sita's Lair to an arm-wrestling contest." Except for a blink or two, no one reacted. "To an arm-wrestling contest. Anybody. Against me. Right here. Across this round."

A husky voice from the back called: "You mean women only, don't you?"

"No. Anybody. Who's first? Beat me and win free slooze and tips for a month."

The space around Ziiza opened as the crowd moved away, pressing back against the shelter sides. Men stood, mouthfuls of Tip-n-Dips unchewed, leaf-cups of slooze spilling down their fronts. Women's jaws hung open while they searched through the dim light for another woman. When they found one, their eyes locked in disbelief. "Come on," Ziiza urged. "This is supposed to be fun."

Barclaw leaned against the shelter side, sweating. There must be something illegal about this, he thought. Arm-wrestling? Woman against woman. Woman against man. Bitta moved forward, positioning herself for a better view, her mind in fast-recording mode, tasting the story. Hobart snapped a Tip-n-Dip scrap tossed in the air. Gstan pushed closer. Org moved in, too. His muma? Shouldn't *he* be the one challenging? He took his rock from its belt pouch and squeezed. Hard. The rest of the family, Milli and Netti, Com and Edu, gaped, not knowing whether to be shocked or proud or worried – that their muma was going to make a fool of herself. Govvi, at the entrance, willed the next customer inside, even though there was no room to sit or stand.

Ziiza knelt next to the tree-round, grasped a protruding chunk of bark with her left hand, and placed her right elbow on top. "This is how it's done, folks," she said. "Anyone?"

Dompa, a large woman, wife of one of Castor's wardens, dropped to her knees and locked hands with Ziiza. "Easy drinks. Easy eats," she clucked.

Ziiza looked up at Gstan, who was staring at her, open-mouthed, and said sweetly, "Gstan, would you give us a ready-set-go?"

"Ah," he stammered, "Ready. And a set." He paused, as if working up courage to take her on himself. "Go."

Ziiza slammed Dompa's arm down on the tree-round. "That hurt," Dompa cried, tears jumping from her eyes. One person clapped politely.

Wife Dragga, obviously sloozed, came forward, pirouetted, and said, "Not so rough this time, dearie." Her arm was so long Ziiza had to grab her forearm; her fingers met easily around it. After phony facial contortions, Ziiza slowly pressed Wife Dragga's arm to the round, taking care not to break it, which she easily could have. This was more to the crowd's liking. Not many – any – liked Wife Dragga, the lot owner, rent collector, and richest woman in town. Perhaps the richest person in town. Rhythmic clapping from one person. Others joined. Men urged their wives and girlfriends to try, pushing them forward. The women, caught up in it, were quite willing now, and queued up. Ziiza devised handicaps: pretending not to hear Gstan's "go," looking away, not holding with her left hand; she even let smaller opponents use both arms. She dispatched them, one by one. The laughter and clapping continued. Ziiza played to the crowd, groaning, faking pain, rolling her eyes, allowing opponents to bend her arm back, ever so close to the round – but not close enough. The more women she beat, the more the crowd urged the remaining ones to compete. Ziiza realized one thing: Beaverton women were soft. She was hard, fresh off the Sea Trace, and it showed.

When she had beaten all of the women who were willing to step up and be beaten, Ziiza rose, stretched, shook her hand out, and thanked everyone. "Slooze for everyone. Biber, if you please. Folks, let's party."

A voice called out from the dimness: "A man. Can you put a man's arm down?"

Ziiza had no choice; she had started this. Clapping and chanting. "A man. A man." No man volunteered. Gstan looked around, embarrassed; he surely wasn't going to arm-wrestle her. He did not even want to say "go." With a slight wave, he faded into the crowd. From the back, the same voice growled, "How about Blotto?"

"Yes!" The crowd picked it up. "Blotto! Blotto!" Then, "Blotto, Blotto, he's our man." Ziiza turned to see the crowd part and a bear of a man walk to the tree-round. He was half a head taller than Barclaw and twice as wide. Thick, dirty, matted hair covered his head and merged into a long beard, leaving an opening for a nose and two dull eyes. His arms and legs were tree-trunk thick, but so hairy it was difficult to tell how thick. But his hair could not disguise his enormous protruding belly. That was real, the obvious processor of endless beaver tails, and tonight, many dripping handfuls of Tip-n-Dips. And many cupfuls of slooze. He bowed as low as his belly would permit, extended his arm to Ziiza, and said, "La-dies first, ma'am." Ziiza knelt, grabbed the round, and raised her arm.

Haven't I seen this guy before? Ziiza thought. Yes, she had. He was more or less a fixture in H&G, sleeping beside paths or in the bushes. He closed a huge hand over hers and smiled. Then he pressed against hers, in what he assumed would be an easy pin. Ziiza locked her arm. He relaxed, then pushed harder. She clenched her teeth and concentrated. He gave a quick burst. Not that easy. He gathered himself and tried a long, slow push. He got her two hands from the round. One hand. But no farther. He panted, eased off, and her arm popped up. Although she had never arm-wrestled before – the idea had come to her out of nowhere – Ziiza was learning fast. This was indeed a mental game as well as a physical one. This guy was huge and powerful, no doubt about it. But if she could hang on a little longer . . . a little longer . . . he might spend himself.

She felt his arm vibrate. Sweat streamed out of his beard, dripping onto the round. She held on. Her arm vibrated, too. Ziiza moved her right foot around and touched his foot. He blinked. She ran her foot up his leg. She slid it down. He had to look. He did look. Looked down and saw – four red-painted toenails and a grotesque scar. He roared like a speared grizzly and lost his concentration. With the last of her strength, Ziiza pushed his arm down till his hairy knuckles touched the round. She let go and fell away.

Cheers and cheers. Customers slapped Ziiza on the back. Milli and Netti shrieked with joy. A man yelled, "Way to go, Blotto!" without meaning it. Another: "Nice try, old boy." He didn't mean it, either. But most were silent, not knowing what to say.

The broken bear of a man rose to his feet, turned, and without taking his eyes from the dirt floor, shambled past Govvi and into the night.

16

Screaming Indifference

ZIIZA LOOKED up from chopping Tip-n-Dips to see a petite young woman standing in front of her.

"I heard you singing sings," said the woman. From her posture it seemed as though she had been watching her for some time. Although she appeared to be about Org's age, her eyes were large, dark, and adult-like: sharp, penetrating, and intelligent, and, at the same time, warm and friendly. And compassionate, if one could read that much in a first glance. Her wraps could have used a brushing. They hung on her as if she had never given them a thought. "I'm Litti, your neighbor," she said. "Last night I heard you." Before Ziiza could respond, she said, "Would you join me for a cup of tea? Only rose hip, I'm afraid."

"Why, that would be nice. Litti."

"My little place," Litti said when they reached her shelter. "Sit down. I'll pour. It's already made." Ziiza had not noticed it before, small as it was, hidden behind a larger one. She had not noticed Litti, either.

"I'm sorry," Ziiza said, as politely as she could, "I don't believe I've seen you before. Not on the path. Not in H&G. Are you new to Beaverton?"

"No, I was born here," Litti said. "I spend most of my time walking, in the fields, in the forest. Many nights I bed down on the ground. Wherever I find myself. That's probably why you did not see me. I volunteer at the daycare center in H&G, though. Part-time. A few hours a week. My good deed." She sat cross-legged, smiling pleasantly, holding her tea to her lips but not drinking. "Today is my shelter cleaning day. You sing beautifully."

"Not really," Ziiza said, wondering if Litti had picked up her exact words. "A habit of mine. It's helped me through some rough nights. I sing the children to sleep, let my feelings run. Sing whatever I want to express: joy, sorrow, hope, thanks. Helps me unwind after a hard day's work. And I work hard."

"I sing sings, too," Litti said. "To myself. Just like you." Her voice drifted off; she did not expand.

They chatted amiably for a few minutes. After Ziiza finished her tea, she thanked Litti, expressed pleasure at meeting her, and went back to work. She was about to toss her an automatic invitation to the Sita, but thought differently.

That afternoon, Ziiza had an appointment with Addle. On the way to Grassyknoll, she passed Sister Sissi's and paused to chat. Popamayor, Sister Sissi told her, was doing poorly, had not been at the café for some time. Last week he had taken to his bed. This might be his last illness, she told her, almost choking on the words.

"If I didn't have to see Addle," Ziiza said, "I'd visit him right now. Parent-teacher dialogue, he calls it. I'll get over as soon as I can."

Addle sat, god-like, on the knoll, his robe attaching him to the ground. The good weather had firmed its muddy slope, temporarily negating the students' behind-his-back nickname: Greasyknoll. Unsmiling, he motioned Ziiza to approach.

"Muma Ziiza," he intoned, "please seat yourself." She did. "I suggest we go over the reports in descending order of age. Shall we begin with Org?"

Yes. Order of march. And I know what descending means.

Her children of whom she was so proud, not only for their perseverance on the Sea Trace, and their help in the Sita, but for being just plain good kids, were not so outstanding in Schoolmaster Addle's eyes. Of course some of them possessed more than a modicum of native ability. But, with one or two exceptions, they were not utilizing the gifts they had. Org, when questioned after morning lectures, never recalled anything. He was tall, well-proportioned, and sturdy (evidently Addle could not bring himself to say handsome), all to the good. But he had no appreciation for the abstract or artistic side of life. This did not surprise Ziiza; she knew he was physical and direct, not subtle in any way. What surprised her was Addle's dismissal, treating him as a throwaway, not worthy of his time or attention. He did in fact throw him away, telling Ziiza he would find life more fulfilling as a "transporter of firewood or dicer of beaver tails."

Ziiza saw him differently, of course, her strong-armed, first-born son, loving and loyal in his own silent way, the trail breaker, literally, without whose efforts they would not have made it. Simply would not have made it. But that counted for nothing now.

Milli, Addle continued, was the school flirt. Again, no surprise. And again as with Org, he could not bring himself to say the word: pretty. Yes, pretty, Ziiza thought, now that she was not walking all day and getting enough to eat. Too outspoken, abrasive at times, preoccupied with herself, he opined. Has strong views on everything, including things she knows nothing about. More listening and less talking was his prescribed remedy.

All things considered, he continued the "dialogue," Netti was doing well, if one took her "handicap" into consideration.

Schoolmaster-speak for what?

Ziiza braced.

"She is capable of academic work," Addle continued. Ziiza breathed again. "But I wonder whether she might be happier as a craftsperson. A highly-skilled craftsperson, to be sure. Her ever-present shoulder basket, for instance, is first rate work."

Can't say beautiful work, can you? Always faint praise. Everything a notch below or a finger shy. I hate to admit it, though, but you may be right. I've never thought of her in that light. She is so different from Milli, and not only in appearance. Sisters. Best friends. But other than that, they're opposites. You may be pompous and arrogant, Schoolmaster Addle, but I have to give you this: you're insightful. Milli's the leader. Netti's the tag-along: shy, reticent, dependent. But what a worker.

They, the older two girls, were welcome to continue at Grassyknoll, he pronounced, on three conditions: First, their Individual Studies had to become individual; no more joint projects. Second, studies reporting on the "dreamy" music in Hunters and Gatherers Market were no longer acceptable, not even for extra credit. Third, no more "sick" days. It was so obvious when both were absent at the same time.

For a school that attracts only a small percentage of Beaverton's children that's pretty assured.

Ziiza nodded and said nothing.

Com and Govvi were bright, exceptional in their ways. But inattentive, sometimes disrespectfully so. Com made friends easily, was popular with the students, and asked good questions. He lacked focus, however, was interested in too many things, skipped from flower to flower, the hummingbird, so to speak. Did Muma Ziiza realize how far away from Beaverton he and his odd friend, Torc, ventured each afternoon, the dangers they exposed themselves to? (She *had* noticed how late he was getting home and that his duties at the Sita were slipping.) His classmates, Addle continued, found Com's Individual Studies reports more interesting than anyone else's. He conceded that. But one adventure after another. That was not the foundation of a Grassyknoll education.

"And what," Ziiza asked when he paused, "does a 'Grassyknoll education' consist of?"

"A Grassyknoll education, my good muma, consists of. . . ." He fingered his chin, grappling with the impossibility of bringing it down to her level. "Let me put it this way, the objective of a Grassyknoll education, a classical education if you will – the terms are synonymous – is to enrich and develop the whole person – in heart and mind. We strive for the higher sensibilities. I give my students the benefit of my extensive experience and scholarship in my morning lectures. In the afternoon, they develop into unique individuals. Thus Individual Studies." He moved his hands together as if in a washing motion and smiled condescendingly.

"Well, what do they learn?" Ziiza asked, looking perplexed. "Specifically? I mean, whatever happened to the three Ts: Thinkin', Throwin', and Thwackin'? How will they defend themselves, feed themselves, make their way in the world?"

Addle drew himself up. "Grassyknoll does not concern itself with the three Ts, as you put it. Besides, they went out years ago. Grassyknoll's mission is to develop Beaverton's future elite. We do not train common H&G merchants and vendors, for example. They exist to serve us."

"Do the other students' parents share this view?"

"It is understood. It is understood. You are, in fact, the first to ask. Shall I continue?" Ziiza rubbed her nose, oiled her finger, and polished a necklace chip. "Govvi is possibly the brightest of the lot." He caught himself and rephrased. "Of your children. She has an amazing facility with numbers. Truly amazing. But it goes beyond that. I would say she's obsessed. Obsessed with recording. Recording everything. Knowing everything. She bears watching. Careful watching.

"Yes," Ziiza said, "she's my record keeper at the Sita. Invaluable."

"Knows everything," Addle continued, "about every business in H&G. If her I-S reports are correct, and I have no doubt that they are, I wonder what she's found out about Town Hall's numbers." He chuckled to himself without sharing. "But unlike Com's, her reports are of no interest to the other students; they cannot understand a word she says. More accurately, they cannot understand a number she says. In short, her problem is the opposite of her able brother's; her focus is too narrow."

"I don't know what I can do," Ziiza said. "That's just the way she is. He is. Both of them. They've been that way ever since they were little. Govvi, on the Sea Trace: she won my fire building contest. We always knew exactly how much food we had. Timely reports. She just told me; I never had to ask. And Com: he ran ahead, scouted the beaches, the rivers, the barriers, found our campsites, reported on everything. How much time he saved, the mistakes we avoided, possibly fatal mistakes. . . . Without Govvi and Com's contributions I don't know. I really don't know."

And, of course, Org's, and Milli's, and Netti's, and Edu's, and Dg's. But why bother?

"The little boy, Edu." Addle continued, smiling down at Ziiza, touching each fingertip to its opposite, forming a peaked shelter. "His pet creature sits beside him in lecture. He drapes his arm around its neck and strokes, under its chin, its ears, its belly. Odd creature."

Does he have any idea of the bond those two share?

"A future scholar," Addle continued. "Where his considerable abilities will lead him, only time will tell. He is attentive, has an excellent memory, answers all of my questions. Correctly. And *his* questions after lecture: so far-reaching, so penetrating. For someone so young. His Individual Studies are lagging a bit, but they will, I am sure, improve. And he appears to be shy outside of the academic environment."

Ziiza knew Edu's qualities, as she did her other children's. She had just never heard them expressed this way. She was proud of him, of course. But then, were Addle's comments pure praise for Edu? Or was he simply building him up to diminish the others? Because he did not cause trouble, hung on his every word, asked endless questions, giving him, Addle, opportunities to expound at even greater length. Was that it? One promising scholar – praised. One steadfast, physically powerful non-academic – dropped. Two teenage girls struggling to find themselves – grudgingly allowed to continue. Two bright but eccentric youngsters who did not fit into his woodpecker holes – tolerated, with suspicion. One out of six, Ziiza concluded. Not good. Two out of seven, if she counted Dg; at least he wasn't ousted. Better. She chuckled.

That evening, Ziiza said as little as possible about the "dialogue" to the children. She gave Org the news. He shrugged, seemed relieved. Edu questioned her, but she limited her response to, "Fine." To the others: "Fine."

Next morning Ziiza visited Litti, and while sharing tea, recounted the Grassyknoll report. Litti listened attentively but offered no comments. What could she say? Besides, Litti, as Ziiza was finding out, was a woman of few words, a natural and sympathetic listener. Ziiza appreciated this.

Sita's Lair's business fell off after the big, more or less free, opening night party. Then, week by week, it began to build. A few customers became regulars, so regular Ziiza had to shoo them out at closing time before they slipped into sloozy stupors and slept where they fell. In this she and Org were assisted by Dg, who appointed himself watch creature when the pleasuring establishment – as good a description as any – was closed, and assistant bouncer when open. On a word or a look by Ziiza or Edu, but not Org or the others, Dg would growl and nip at the offender's legs, working him down the path until he was out of sight. If the undesirable resisted, Dg nipped him higher and higher up until he got the message. Blotto, a potential regular one would think, was so humiliated by his arm-wrestling defeat that he hid out in the forest. Bitta told the story so many times that Ziiza begged her to stop, offered to pay her not to say anymore. Too late. It was part of Beaverton lore.

Gstan was a regular, too, but different. He liked slooze, but not in excessive amounts; he was a sipper. A few Tip-n-Dips satisfied him, too. A spare man, he was not interested in food. Ever the salesman, the talker, he enjoyed the can-you-top-this competition of joke- and story-telling. He joined in the raucous songs. (Even though Ziiza did not expect it to be this way, most of the weekday customers were men. Most of the women came on weekends, and many came escorted.) But it was clear Gstan did not want to be treated as just another customer. All of the above was incidental; he came to see Ziiza. For all of his business wiles, he was clumsy in man-woman relationships, did not know how to express himself, show his interest, his affection. And, to be fair, Ziiza was taking her time deciding how to respond. Whether she wished to respond. It had been so long. She was busy with the children and the Sita. Soon to be busy with the Sita and the children, in that order. He came early, offering to set up, cut tails, mix, pour, anything to be close to her, to be involved in her life. While she worked, he told his stories, a little too loudly, glancing her way, checking her reactions, which, if she had any, she attempted to hide – although he sometimes caught her smirking at his more outlandish ones. After closing he stayed on, chatting, helping, until, worn out from the day's work, she gently eased him out and away. On his long walks home he dropped the garbage off at the dump, thus gaining favor with Edu and Org.

Biber constantly improved his slooze, tasting, testing, and searching for new and exotic ingredients. His brew-crock developed an interior patina, some would call it a scum, that he was convinced added to the unique flavor; he never scraped or scrubbed it again. Castor's wardens did catch him in a pond; that was inevitable. But after he explained that he was taking nothing but bottom sludge, and offering them free drinks on weekends, they left him alone. Some even lugged sacks of sludge to the Sita for him. (He played along, letting them believe it was the true ingredient, then dumped it in Ziiza's garden.) So the base secret was out. But it did not matter. His formulas and methods were so refined that no one could duplicate them. Not even Govvi, with her furtive glances, calculating mind, and attempts at ingratiating conversation. And no one else had a huge stone brew-crock.

Likewise, Ziiza, Milli, and Netti worked to improve Tip-n-Dips. They had an easier time of it, in a way. Biber had already perfected slooze; his improvements were incremental; sometimes change for the sake of change, to add variety. Tip-n-Dips had worked because of slooze, and because of the excitement of opening night. They *had* to change. Govvi recorded everything on her board: measured amounts, temperatures by feel, taste, grading by letter. When they finally got it right, they had to be able to duplicate it, she told them. Ziiza had stumbled onto the two critical ingredients right off: Sea salt for taste and sand for bite. Interestingly, the A recipe called for double the amounts of each. Beyond that, it was a process of elimination; many of the opening night's ingredients added nothing. To keep ahead, they prepared sacks of dry base mixture – root powders, spices, flower stems, and herbs – and packed them away. Water and bulky ingredients: salt, sand, and a nameless round red fruit that formed on ground vines, was added when needed. And, as with slooze, the longer it cooked, the more it was stirred, the better the result.

It was through Biber's experimenting with slooze, and her own with Tip-n-Dips, that Ziiza found a way to make amends with Blotto. After fleeing and hiding, and after the reporter and her yellow-headed cohort had finally stopped talking and coo-burping about him, he returned to his old haunts. But not to Sita's Lair. He could not face the teasing and taunting, however good-natured. Ziiza spotted him sleeping beside a fallen tree in H&G, one of the few not yet burned. She apologized for tricking him and said she knew he could beat her. That statement took him by surprise. She even stuck her right foot in the mud so he did not have to look at it. Did he wish to return to the Sita? He was welcome. He shook his large, furry head. Didn't he enjoy slooze? Tip-n-Dips? He did not speak, but his sad eyes said yes. "Let's make a deal," Ziiza said. "Be our sampler and taster. Come to the back entrance whenever you like, night or day. Tell me whether you like the latest Dips, the latest slooze." Before he could respond, she turned and left.

Ziiza had little trouble with town hall after the Stop Work order was replaced with the Conditional Use permit. Barclaw saw to that. He shifted his night rounds to include the Sita. Stood outside, a handy listener to any neighbor's complaint. Bouncer in reserve. Peacekeeper. Was he there, Ziiza wondered, on his own volition, or on orders from Mistermayor or Polcat? Although he never took more than a complimentary taste of slooze or a handful of Tip-n-Dips, he seemed to enjoy being there. Did Barclaw have one of those marriages where he found more pleasure in being away from home than in it? Bitta often joined him, but she had a reason: she was older, children gone, husband dead or gone, and was a news hawk. Whenever Barclaw went in to help Org stop an altercation, she followed him, her eyes bright with anticipation. All to the good, Ziiza thought; Bitta's our publicity arm.

When Milli and Netti skipped school three days in a row, and Addle said nothing, they knew where they stood. If he did not want Org, he did not want them, was how they saw it. Each morning they walked their three younger siblings to the bottom of the knoll to keep up appearances. After good-byes, they strolled in the woods. This innocent activity took the edge off their guilt

– guilt vis-à-vis their muma, not Addle – and killed time before H&G grew busy. Busy enough to blend in with the crowd. Busy enough not to be recognized. "Addle, Addle, Addle," Milli was fond of saying. "Why doesn't he change his name, anyway?" It was always good for a giggle. As if making fun of him excused their actions.

Leftover Tip-n-Dips gave them basket money, trading material, for any baubles that struck their fancies. Sister Sissi enjoyed seeing them, as customers were few and Popamayor was sick. Skedaddle, the old-timers, played until mid-afternoon, then went home for their naps. The girls liked their soft, plinky-plunky melodies, their scratchy voices, their down-home jabber, their corny jokes. They were only a warm-up, of course, an appetizer, preliminary to the real thing. Screaming Indifference was now performing regularly, the slot between Skedaddle and closing. Each day the audience grew, mostly teenagers but adults were showing up, too. Again, Milli and Netti wondered where they all came from. As they talked to more and more fans the answer was simple: everywhere. Some youngsters had run away from home (not that their parents went looking for them), camping in H&G to be near their beloved S-I, as they called it. Barclaw did not allow that of course and ran them off. So they shifted to the Sea Trace arrivals' temporary camp.

One drippy, overcast day, as Twigg began his opening number, the sun dropped into a crack between the clouds and the Sundown Range. The crowd jumped and screamed. He ranted, ran down everything and everybody: Beaverton, parents, working, school. They loved it, roared for more. Milli held up her shell mirror, caught the sun, and aimed a shaft at him. It jumped across his chest. Steadying her hand with the other, she jiggled the light up his leg, up his body, onto his face. A few in the audience caught on and clapped, trying to get in synch with the bouncing light. She wiggled it in his eyes. He blinked, frowned, and raised his hand. The sun slipped below the Sundowns.

Milli thought mirror flashing was fun, daring in a way; it drew her into the music. More particularly, she was making a connection with *him*, and, however conscious she was of it, that was what she wanted. That was what all of the girls wanted. After that, whenever the sun shone, Milli and her mirror were part of the show. They expected it. Twigg expected it. Not that he liked it. He put up with it until, one performance, he stopped in mid-song. "You," he said, "shining that mirror at me. Stand up." Milli pushed off the ground and stood before him, winsome, frightened, and excited. Twigg was talking to *her*. She moved the shell behind her back. The kids roared. He smiled and motioned her to come forward. Those sitting in front leaned away to let her pass. When she reached the stage he put his hand on her shoulder, turned her around until she faced the audience, and shouted, "This little lady wants to be part of the show. Let's see if she can sing." Applause. Then politely to Milli, "Join me?"

She knew the words, but her voice was drowned out by the band and his bombastic delivery. Milli thought she was flubbing it, playing the fool; she stepped away and stopped singing. Twigg took her hand and pulled her even with him. "Now, take a breath," he said, leaning over, touching his lips to her ear. "Keep going; you're doing fine." They began again. In the middle he stopped, motioned the band to tone it down, and the audience to do the same. "It's all yours," he said. She finished the song in her clear soprano voice. "You know this one," he said. "I know you do." They sang "Forever," in duet, one of the few romantic songs in S-I's repertoire.

Tell me you love me.
Tell me you're mine.
Tell me you're with me.
Forever. Forever.

They blended perfectly. The audience caught it. They were *hearing* something.

That was enough. Milli pulled her hand from his and jumped off the stage. She pushed her way through the crowd and headed home. Netti ran after her, tears flowing.

17

The Kenni Mann Trio

ZIIZA CONSIDERED meeting bright-eyed Litti a surprise bonus. Although half her age, just a few years older than Milli, she was the first person since her husband that she could talk to, confide in without reservation. Partly, she concluded, because Litti did not seem to know anyone else, seemed the perpetual outsider. By choice. Ziiza could talk freely and know it was not going anywhere. And in spite of the Sita's modest success and the children's incorporation into Beaverton life, Ziiza saw herself as an outsider as well. They met most mornings, except when Litti was on one of her woodland rambles, which had become longer and more frequent as the weather improved. She was the perfect listener, and made wonderful tea, but was slow to open up about herself, preferring to let Ziiza talk about her incredibly complicated life, with Sita's Lair to run, six fast-growing children to raise, and an admirer to fend off, maybe. Litti was not interested in the Sita or slooze, had never visited. All the better for their relationship, Ziiza thought; keep things separate. Litti's purity and strength of mind made her all the more intriguing.

But one day Litti did open up. A little. She smiled shyly, looked down at her cup, and said, "I've met a someone, Ziiza." She had not, it turned out, met a someone, she had seen a someone. In the forest. More than once. And she had no idea who he was. She shook her head in giddy embarrassment.

Well, her solitary walks are getting interesting.

More than a few of their tea-time conversations involved Gstan. His help around the Sita continued; he came every evening. With springtime's arrival, he had brought flowers: crocus, trillium, camas. "Touch of color for the place," he had said, handing them to Ziiza, not able to say they were for her. This continued through summer, as long as he could find them. He invited her for walks, even tried to hold her hand. They walked over to Hill Burrow. He expounded on his plans. A wee bit like Pop&Jay, she thought. She saw no workmen, no residents, and many For Sale signs. Maybe living in a hole in a hill was ahead of its time. He talked a good line, but rumors were about.

With the Sita's Lair going well, he hadn't mentioned partnership in Hill Burrow in months. Curious as he must have been, he did not press Ziiza to talk about her past, did not ask about her children's popa. Or where, for instance, she had lived on the Old Side. Why she was so driven to succeed in business. Why she wasn't content to float along in Beaverton's easy swim like everyone else.

Popamayor died in the spring, half a year after he had "rescued" Ziiza and the children in H&G. Sister Sissi got word to Ziiza just in time. He lay with his hands folded on his chest, lucid, but ready to go. Wife Popamayor – who seldom showed herself outside their shelter, did not like politics or celebrity – sat on one side of him. Sister Sissi, his partner in charity, sat on the other. Ready to go. But not quietly. In a burst of bitterness and disappointment, he erupted: "There's nary a person in Beaverton I have not helped. One time or another." He fought for breath with filled-up lungs. "When they came in from the Sea Trace, exhausted and hungry, I gave them food, shelter." He expelled noisily. "I showed them around, told of the beaver's bounty, settled them onto a lot, the best one I could find. Who's come to say good-bye, pay their respects?" Sister Sissi could not handle it and stepped outside. "Darn few," he continued. "Mistermayor and Polcat, Esqq and Font. For show. For politics, I suspect. Oh, not Mistermayor, he's a true friend." He closed his eyes, gathering the last of his strength. "But the regular people, the heart of my Beaverton, where are they? I'll tell you. I'll tell you where." He coughed and rattled; this outburst was going to be his last and he did not care. "They take and take and take from an old man who gave and gave and gave. I founded. . . ."

Popamayor was right. Ziiza, her children, and Dg attended his funeral, the last newcomers he had welcomed to his beloved town. Gstan came, but Ziiza wondered whether it was for Popamayor or to impress her. The deathbed bigwigs came, along with a sobbing Barclaw. He had paid his respects, but Popamayor had forgotten to mention him in his rant. Two council members came to make it look official. Wife Popamayor. Sister Sissi, of course. Bitta and Mizpark: they had known him in the old days; loved and respected him; their tears were sincere.

Barclaw dug a grave for him in front of Town Hall, at the corner of the cross paths. Everyone knew about his funeral, Bitta had made certain of that, but no one else took the trouble. Passers-by did not even acknowledge the ceremony, let alone stop. Not to speak of. An older man doffed his hat, swung wide, and kept on walking – acting as if he had owed Popamayor money. Which he probably had. A woman carrying a shopping sack stopped to watch them lower him down. Mistermayor said the words. Sister Sissi laid his cane on his chest, positioning it under his hands. Barclaw took up his wooden shovel and let the black dirt dribble down. Slowly, out of respect for the great man. The woman shuffled on.

Along with Popamayor's passing, spring brought a slump in the Sita's business. This lasted until mid-summer, when the first of the Sea Trace migrants came in. That helped. Their first stop was Sister Sissi's, of course; she carried on. But just as Ziiza and the children had, they soon tired of handouts and being fussed over. Sita's Lair, people told them, had a new drink called slooze – "You'll never believe how it lifts you up, then smacks you down." And a new taste treat, Tip-n-Dips, a spicy change-up from mussels and clams, clams and mussels, on the Sea Trace. But not for the weak of constitution. Convivial atmosphere. Leave the kids behind. But Beaverton people were outdoor people, so the business gains from newcomers and curiosity seekers were offset by the loss of the regulars, off and away on summertime activities.

To combat the slump Ziiza removed the center roof mats, transforming the Sita into what Biber called a "slooze garden." Govvi's financial reports showed a bare profit and expenses kept climbing. "My next Individual Studies project," she told her muma, "will to be to find out why tail prices keep rising. I should know already, but I just don't." Ziiza immediately rejected the two promotional ideas she was playing with: Free Tip-n-Dips night and Two-fer slooze.

Keeping good help was becoming harder, too. *Help* being the children. With the long summer evenings, Milli and Netti came home later and later, skipping work as well as school. But with business slow it didn't matter, so Ziiza didn't call them on it. She was pleased they were happy in Beaverton, fitting in. But what about fall and winter, when hopefully business would pick up? Milli was becoming something of a regular with the band. Netti had hinted that she might even be offered a full-time job. She was beyond sing-by-invitation jump-ups; she even practiced with them. Twigg introduced her as "lovely and talented." And the way he looked at her, held her hand when they sang, it was obviously more than a professional relationship. Govvi and Com were mildly interested in S-I, but mostly out of pride in their sister, not from an interest in music. Edu did not like it, did not get it. Dg could not stand the noise. He either whined Edu away or ran back to the Sita by himself. Org, however, caught S-I fever, loved it, standing in the back by himself, swaying, tossing his rock to the music. When he found the gumption to tell Milli how much he liked the band and her singing, it was the first time brother and sister had connected. She was touched.

Expiration of the summer fun season – forest and field wandering, garden tending, fishing, picnics, games, swimming in the Daughter or Son, general outdoor laziness – plus the new arrivals off the Sea Trace, finally ratcheted Sita's Lair out of its doldrums. So much so that Ziiza hired a young man named Sufx, a "pouring guy" as he called himself. He was on the short side, compact, with unkempt hair and dark, shining eyes that, until one knew him, might have been confused with angry eyes, they were so intense. He brought to the Sita a quality the serving girls, Milli and Netti, lacked; he was personable and chatty with the customers, whereas they were dutiful and reserved. A little afraid of the sometimes-rowdy men, they delivered, quietly accepted thanks and tips, and retreated. Biber liked him, began taking him along on his pond visits, first as a carrier, later as a diver. Within a few weeks he had confided more slooze-making secrets to Sufx than he ever had to Ziiza or Govvi.

To celebrate summer's end and Sita's Lair's first anniversary, Ziiza and Biber decided to throw an "event," marking its "making it," passing the critical point when most new businesses folded. Privately, it would celebrate Ziiza and family's making it as well. And Biber's rescue from the depths. There was a market for slooze after all. He had just needed something. The something was Ziiza's imagination, guts, drive, wile, and out-of-a-job desperation. All of the time, effort, and money he had spent to bring the brew-crock from the Old Side had been worth it.

Mistermayor and some of the council members were, if not Sita regulars, stop-in-occasionally customers. Barclaw and Bitta still performed their nightly duties – as they saw them – although they often skipped the slow evenings. Ziiza did not anticipate town hall trouble this time, but to be certain she took out – they had a name for everything – a Special Events permit. As with the Conditional Use permit, upon which the Sita's Lair's continued existence depended, this one came with conditions as well. With the advent of so many new residents, the beaver tail supply was "tight," Ziiza was informed. But as always, "No problem," Mistermayor had assured the council, and therefore the populace. "Things will turn around next year. Just as soon as the baby beavers are birthed." Ziiza, however, had heard rumors that Castor's reports were so pessimistic they had been suppressed. But she had not taken it too seriously. Maybe she should have. Poaching was up; everyone knew that. But was it the usual sport poaching? Or was it the result of rising prices? Hard to tell. Nowadays poachers openly bragged about how little it took to bribe the wardens. And what of the wardens themselves, their after-hours "recreational" activities? Litti, who passed the beaver ponds on her walks, confirmed the poaching part. Tail tip leftovers, throwaways that Ziiza had turned into the Tip-n-Dips sensation, were now sold and traded along with the choicer cuts of beaver tail – centerline, skinless, and chopped-with-herbs. People were even making their own Tip-n-Dips, albeit vastly inferior to Ziiza's. The permit's condition was: Ziiza and Govvi would have to wait until H&G closed Saturday before they could buy tails. She pleaded with Mistermayor, Polcat, and the council, but they would not alter the condition. Were they waiting for something? Bribes? The old ploy, free drinks after the meeting, did not work – although they accepted the drinks. She visited Mistermayor in his office. She pumped Barclaw and Bitta for ideas. Aside from the time bind the deadline put them in, quality would suffer; the Tip-n-Dips would not have time to soak, to cure properly. They would not taste right. Nevertheless, Ziiza and Biber had their permit.

"What can I do to help?" Gstan asked Ziiza, when he heard about the big doings. "We could go for a walk together, gather some flowers."

"It's fall, Gstan," she said, "there are no flowers.

His face went blank. But just for moment – during which Ziiza realized she had been curt. "Well then, how about decorating with those bright red leaves, vine maple, I think. Dry cattails. Brown thistles."

"I don't know. I'll be so busy with everything. Just before. . . . "

"They're dry, Ziiza," he said with a twinkle. "We can do it anytime."

Biber was truly excited. For one thing, he was free of self-doubt, not at all like last year. With Sufx around he felt more like an independent businessman and less of a back-of-the-Sita accessory. His brew-crock was performing better than ever. Her – being a vessel, he always thought of "her" that way – inside patina scum grew thicker with each batch. And each batch was that much smoother and refined. At least to Biber. And increasingly to Sufx, who was developing a discriminating taste. (Unlike the official taster, Blotto, to whom each batch was: "Just great. Keep it coming.") And to Mistermayor and a few other educated tongues. The majority of customers did not care as long as it tasted good, loosened their inhibitions, got them tipsy, and helped with the laughs.

One afternoon Biber motioned Ziiza into the back yard for a private talk. "This," he said, "is my plan. I'll make up a special batch of slooze, just for the party. Sufx and I've been working on it for weeks. Secret." He would, he whispered, as if anyone could hear, store as much slooze as possible in waterproof baskets, crocks, and skin bags; run the crock empty. Hopefully that would carry them until Saturday. In the meantime, he would blend his masterpiece, the pinnacle of the slooze-maker's art. Fill it to the rim. Overflowing. "Special name, too," he told her: "Biber's Obtuse."

"Obtuse? For a name?" Ziiza exclaimed. "Aren't you insulting our patrons' intelligence, in effect calling *them* obtuse?"

"Of course I am," he said, patting his crock, "and they'll love it. Contradictory product names are in. Stupidity is splendid. Banality is beautiful. Disgusting is dazzling. Haven't you been to H&G lately? Skunk cabbage soup. Essence of vomit perfume; Idah's selling it. You think those are bad? Prudence and my respect for you prohibits me from repeating the bodily-function-inspired names I've heard. See for yourself. They're all the rage."

"If you say so. Anyway, it's the taste and the kick they're after."

So slooze was covered. Food was taken care of, as best it could be. Help was covered, with Sufx, and with Milli and Netti under orders to "Be here." Govvi would cover the entrance as usual, take payments, and keep count. Ziiza paid Barclaw to not only be there, but to give Org lessons in crowd control. She considered hiring Blotto as another bouncer, but rejected the idea. In spite of their understanding, and his role of taster, which he performed regularly, he had not been inside Sita's Lair since *that* night. She doubted he would attend. Com would make emergency runs and help wherever needed. Like the older girls, he was under orders not to roam. Edu and Dg were given a choice. Since the regular customers knew the routine and required less service they could attend if they liked, or stay the night with Sister Sissi. Come back Sunday morning to help with the clean-up. (Although Sister Sissi and Ziiza remained friends, and Ziiza had invited her many times, she, like Litti, had never been to the Sita. Evidently she had no interest in drinking or meeting eligible men; she was content with, or resigned to, her widowhood.) What remained was entertainment. A year ago the novelty of the opening, slooze, and Tip-n-Dips had carried the evening. Arm-wrestling could certainly not be repeated. What then?

Music? Skedaddle was out of the question. Nothing special about them. Everyone had listened to their songs for years. Besides, Sita's Lair's hours were past their bedtimes. When Ziiza asked the girls whether Twigg might be interested, their rolling eyes gave her an immediate answer. Just as well, she thought, kid's music. It also ended thoughts of Milli singing solo (although Ziiza thought her voice beautiful and her on-stage appearance sublime). She flirted with the idea of the family singing "Whatever It Takes," all in a line, arms swinging, feet stamping. Loud. Bouncy. Patriotic. Then she remembered their reception that first morning. No. Anyway, the children would refuse. She had to admit they were not the same tightly-knit family they were a year ago. Trace the Sea, order of march, and all that, were long past and long forgotten as far as they were concerned. For better or worse. Probably for better. Town kids matured fast.

A week back, Wife Dragga had walked past the Sita with a rental prospect in tow. Ziiza hailed her and invited her in for a slooze after she finished. They had had a nice chat. More than a chat. Wife Dragga unloaded more business advice on Ziiza than she could absorb. It seemed, in her estimation, that Ziiza had passed through the stage of "mere small vend operator," as Wife Dragga put it, and was now on the threshold of cracking Beaverton's power establishment. "Con-grad-u-la-tions."

Watch out. Too friendly. Too aggressively helpful.

Beaverton needed more women entrepreneurs, and she, Wife Dragga, would become her mentor.

Whether I want one or not.

In the course of her mentorship lecture, Wife Dragga had mentioned a man to whom she had shown a rental, a musician named Kenni. "Kenni Mann, if I recall correctly." (No doubt of that; Wife Dragga recalled everything correctly.) He had his own group, she told Ziiza, the Kenni Mann Trio.

So Ziiza sent Com to ask Wife Dragga if Kenni was still around. Com walked to her shelter. Not there. Husband Dragga, stooped over, clearing leaves from his garden patch, told him Wife D would get back to him when she returned. She did not. Ziiza forgot about it.

On Saturday morning, party day, Ziiza's best entertainment idea was group singing, hardly an idea at all. Then Wife Dragga came round. "I found him," she called to Ziiza as she strode down the path. She leaned on Sita's entrance rock to catch her breath. "He's been out of town on a gig. Or something. Would love to play tonight. So," she said, beaming, "I said, 'Kenni, you march right over to Ziiza's and give her the big audition.'"

Audition, that's a good one; I'll take anything that walks, talks, plays, or sings.

"Do you know what he charges?" Ziiza asked.

"If I'm not mistaken," Wife Dragga replied, "he doesn't charge anything. Works for tips. And food and drink. Can't beat that, can you?"

"Well," Ziiza said skeptically, "that's strange, to say the least. I'll discuss it when I see him."

"Of course, there's my finder's fee," Wife Dragga said, her long fingers caressing the rock. Then, quickly, "Just kidding, Ziiza, old dear." She reached over and pinched Ziiza's cheek.

If those nails were any sharper she could slide them down and slit my throat.

154

Biber's crock was so full each time he dipped and ladled, slooze sloshed over and down the side. "Terrible waste," he moaned to Ziiza. He and Sufx had been sampling and fine-tuning all morning. "As promised, my lady. Maximum slooze. Biber's Obtuse – black, thick, and frothy on top. Goes down like lava from Smoke-storm's belly." She noticed his hand shook as he emptied his cup, his eyes a happy dull. Sufx leaned against the brew-crock for support, glowing with goodwill.

Org kept the fires low, just hot enough for roasting Tip-n-Dips. If the crowd was large, and there was every indication it would be, body heat would be enough to overcome the fall evening chill. Late afternoon, Ziiza lined her crew up for inspection, as she had done so many times before. Their watabeast outfits were holding up, although Barclaw's approval stamps had long since disappeared. "Nicely brushed," she told them. Milli's newfound success – or was it something more? – translated into a self-possessed and radiant beauty that took her muma's breath away. Netti, too, looked better than ever, proud to be standing in her sister's light. Her headaches, she insisted, stopped when she listened to Milli and Twigg sing. Followed by twenty-four pain-free hours, guaranteed. Com moved his feet in place, swinging his arms, ready for any job, any errand. Govvi almost smiled as she showed her muma and siblings her latest invention. Next to the entrance she had dug a storage pit and covered it with a wooden slab. When admission fees piled up, she would drop them in and stand on the cover. Convenient and secure. Edu and Dg had, of course, declined the offer to go to Sister Sissi's. He stood at stiff attention, head thrown back like a boy soldier, ready for anything. At Edu's pat, Dg tilted his head back and gave a mournful on-duty howl. All was ready.

First the neighbors. But this was different, not like last year's opening night shindig; they were here for the evening, the haul. Then the regulars; they had been talking about it all week, dying for a taste of "Ob-toose." And to let go: sing, dance, kick some mud. Stuff themselves. Get sloozed. Within a half hour Sita's Lair proper was filled. And they kept on coming. Biber and the girls worked the inside. Sufx passed slooze out the back entrance. Who should appear but Blotto, who plopped himself down in the back yard and pronounced Biber's Obtuse the finest yet. (He had been "testing" all week.) Mistermayor brought Wife Mistermayor, and, towering over everyone, called for quiet, raised his cup, and made an eloquent toast to the memory of Popamayor. The drinkers applauded politely – as if they remembered – and resumed their partying. Polcat did not bring his wife, but he brought his council buddies. Was it for fun? Ziiza wondered, cynically. A conditional use inspection? Or to press hands for the coming election?

The path filled with drinkers. The Sita's backside, closest to the brew-crock, jammed up. Someone threw a side mat up, then another, until Sita's Lair was just a roof covering with smoke holes. Barclaw stood his ground across the path for a while, until the crowd pushed him into a neighbor's yard. Bitta retreated with him, continuing her on-the-spot reporting, singing out names of distinguished arrivals (with emphasis on who was escorting whom), tartly appraising their dress (with sniffs of approval or disapproval), commenting on revelers' scuffles and slooze-induced arguments, and ranking dancers according to their abilities. It kept her going. But not Hobart, who dozed on her shoulder.

A slender, bald-headed man of medium height made his way through the noisy crowd toward Barclaw, evidently because he was taller than everyone else. "P-pardon me," he said. "C-could you p-please direct me to someone called Z-Ziiza. I think."

"Straight ahead and inside, stranger," Barclaw said. "If you can get inside. Standing next to the girl that's a-takin' admissions." He pointed across the path.

The man nodded, twisted through the crowd, and found Ziiza. "K-Kenni," he said. "Kenni Mann at your s-service."

"Finally," Ziiza said. "I'm so relieved. Some of them are getting vulgar and abusive, yelling for the entertainment. The show. We never promised entertainment, just food and drink and fun, and lots of it. But word leaked out. Where are the others? The trio?"

Kenni grinned sheepishly. "Worry not," he said, "the Kenni Mann Trio is ready to per-f-form."

"Well, I guess," Ziiza said, leading him to the stage, a hastily-erected platform by the entrance. She rapped with a firewood stick. Only when the children took it up did the revelers quiet down. "Folks," she said, "this is Kenni Mann and his trio – although how he's going to manage that is beyond me." She laughed. Nearby people laughed. "He's fresh off the trail from. . . . Where you in from Kenni?"

"The c-coast. Rain Coast Resort and C-campground."

"The coast," Ziiza said, resisting the urge to mimic his stutter. She laughed and waved her arms. "Where all the Beaverton drop-outs go." Many laughs. "Kidding. Just kidding. You're welcome here, Kenni." She leaned close and said, "You don't know how happy I am so see you." Ziiza passed her hand over his bald head, down his slender nose, over his chin, and down his pinched, bony chest. The crowd roared. He shrank back in embarrassment, trying to hold his stage smile. He wore a loin-wrap and a blue-purple collar. A personals pouch swung from his belt. He rocked on his feet, snapping his fingers to a silent beat. His eyes matched his weak smile, shining with a vagabond minstrel's feigned enthusiasm. "You settle yourself down," Ziiza said, chucking him under his chin. Then to the crowd: "And you folks, fill your cups, grab yourselves a handful of Tip-n-Dips, and —"

"You've been out of Tip-n-Dips for an hour."

"Yeah, we're hungry. This better be good."

"Milli. Netti. Org. Sufx." Ziiza called around, "Hustle, now. Fill 'em up. Show's about to begin."

"How about it."

"We're waiting."

"Let's go."

Outside customers pressed in, lifting roof mats, trying to get a look and a listen.

"Yeowww!" someone yelled as they stepped in a fire-pit.

Kenni raise his arms, then lowered them slowly. The crowd obeyed and quieted. Ziiza breathed a sigh of relief. He spoke-sang in a nasal voice:

I'm Ken, Ken, Kenni.
I'm Ken, Ken, Kenni.

He stopped, snapped his fingers, playing for approval, and continued; evidently the act of singing, or what he called singing, cured his stutter.

I'm Ken, Ken, Kenni.
I'm Ken, Ken, Kenni.

The men stamped the dirt floor and whistled. Their ladies screamed encouragement, swung their pouches.

Ken, Ken, Kenni.
Mann, Mann, Mann.
I'm Ken, Ken, Kenni.
Mann and Mann and Mann

They picked it up, over-shouting him.

He's Ken, Ken, Kenni.
He's Mann, Mann, Mann.

He spoke-sang back.

Yes, Ken, Ken, Kenni.
Yes, Mann, Mann, Mann.

Kenni removed a pair of castanet-like stones from his pouch, and, clicking them rhythmically, shuffle-danced in a circle.

My, my. So this is the Kenni Mann Trio – singing, dancing, and stone-clicking. The fake. Three performers, huh. Oh well, we do the best we can in a pinch.

He stopped abruptly, threw his hands in the air, and held them up, grinning – the mediocre performer's stock applause-getter. And he got it. "Isn't he great," Gstan said. He had pushed his way to Ziiza's side. "He's got the crowd in his hands."

Kenni banged his stones on the pole in faster cadence, his other hand inviting the revelers to scream to the beat.

I'm Ken, Ken, Kenni.
I'm Mann . . .

Raised-hand clapping stopped. Shouting ceased. Feet grew roots.
"Get on with the show."
"We know. We all know you're Kenni whatever."
Kenni grinned and began again.

I'm Ken, Ken . . .

Splat. A clod of mud hit him in the face. Ziiza jumped onto the stage. Gstan followed. "Folks, folks," she shouted. "Give him a chance. Let him show what he can do."

"He can't do nothing." They picked it up, chanting, "He can't do nothing. He can't do nothing." Cups, hats, pouches, tramped-in-the-dirt Tip-n-Dips, flew onto the stage, hitting Ziiza, Gstan, and Kenni. A big, sloozed-up rowdy hugged a shelter pole and rocked. They pressed around the stage, shaking fists, screaming, pawing at Kenni, who cowered behind Ziiza and Gstan.

"They're out of control, Gstan" Ziiza said. The shelter shook. A side-pole fell. That's it," she screamed, "he's on his own. Get the children." They dove into the mass of bodies.

A burning stick flew through a smoke hole and landed on the roof. The pitch-covered mat caught fire and spread, mat to mat, around the edges and underneath. Sita's Lair filled with smoke. "Fire! Fire!" Customers clawed and pushed each other, trying to get out. With the fire cry, a burly drunk climbed into the brew-crock and dunked himself for protection – or so he believed. A flaming roof mat tore loose and landed in the slooze. Biber and Sufx tried to fend off the other idiots trying to join him. The half-full crock of Biber's Obtuse burst into flames. "I'm going to die. I'm going to die," the drunk screamed, splashing and blowing in the slooze. He beat his stone club on the side – thud, thud, thud, thud – in out-of-control desperation. And thud. The blow hit a seam, a fault-line in the stone, and Biber's treasured brew-crock split in two. Dg and Edu, who had been hiding behind, were swept away in a river of slooze. Biber was not so lucky, part of the crock half rolled onto his leg, trapping him.

Constable Barclaw did everything he could – which was almost nothing. They poured onto the path, battering their way out of the collapsing, burning Sita's Lair. Some, when they got out, ran. But most stopped to watch the spectacle.

Kenni crouched behind the stage, his only protection. When a flaming mat brushed him as it fell, he ran outside. Hands over his face for concealment, he picked his way through the crowd, his sweat-covered head shining in the glow. "There he is! Get him!" Kenni lunged, but they blocked his way. He turned. More enraged customers came at him. Turned again. An opening. He ran. "After him! Don't let him get away!" He was a fast runner and pulled ahead of the sloozed-up louts. "Catch him!" A spear flew. Hit him in the hip. He swatted at the spear, stumbled, and went down. He pulled, but the point stuck. He twisted and wrenched in desperation. The point broke off. Kenni struggled to his feet and took a step, flailing his arms at his attackers. A jolt of pain shot through his leg and through his body. He fell again. Realizing he had to get away or be killed, he forced his way up, shook off the grasping hands, and, clenching his teeth against the pain, ran and ran and ran.

18

Water Child

AFTER THE fire, after the rampage, Ziiza, Biber, Sufx, and the children spent the night in Litti's yard. They would have preferred going to Sister Sissi's, to get farther away from the smoking ruin, but it was too late. Ziiza tied Biber's leg to a stick, just enough repair to hold him until Provido could set it in the morning. He moaned and cried and swore through the night, whether from leg pain or the pain of his split-in-two brew-crock she could not be sure.

Most of the children took it well, perhaps too well, the excitement overshadowing the loss. Only Org and Govvi were visibly upset: Org because he had been powerless to stop them, an affront to his pride and manliness, Govvi because, even before Ziiza, she knew they were broke. They had bet everything on the party, trying to kick-start a new, bigger-than-ever season. The admission fees in the pit were secure, but they were pledged to creditors. If her tally boards were destroyed in the fire, it did not matter, she knew the tally: less than zero.

Dg, carried away with the spirit of the evening, had spent the night with the drunks on the path. Instead of helping Org and Ziiza keep order, nipping misbehavers where it did the most good, he had taken to Biber's Obtuse as enthusiastically as did the patrons. In the rush of business, when the regulars began dipping directly from the brew-crock, so much ran onto the ground Dg felt it his duty to lap it up, keep the place clean. When Kenni fled, he joined the chase, helping run him out of town. But he was soon winded, just like the humans, his too-round belly swaying, threatening to topple him. The fermented slooze had had its way and he slowed to a walk. Lurched. Peed against a tree. Then his legs gave and he rolled under a garden bush, panting. But Dg was a tough, resilient creature. When, after a night of retching, he appeared at Litti's next morning he was fine, the sturdy, smelly sloozer.

Sita's Lair party report: One broken leg. (Crushed, as it turned out. Very serious.) One Dg, in need of a bath. One split brew-crock. (Whether it could be repaired was questionable. Seal the crack with pitch and lash the halves together? Sink it in a hole in the ground to hold its tremendous weight? Might work. But in any event, Biber told them, his fabulous brew-crock, brought from the Old Side at such great cost, would never be "right.") Nine dejected people. The establishment itself: a stinking ruin, smelling of wood-ash and charcoal, smoldering mats, and slooze-created mud. No profits. No slooze. No Lair. Remaining on the plus side: What Govvi had stashed in her pit. Ziiza's ownership of the lot and her Tip-n-Dips recipe. Biber's slooze formulas and techniques. And the business experience they had gained. Remaining on the minus side: Debts to creditors. Complaints from twenty-two neighbors, resulting in a visit from an apologetic Barclaw and his posting a Violation of Conditional Use notice on a charred support pole.

"Let me show you my world," Litti said to Ziiza later that morning, "show you why I love the valley so." And that was about all she said as they walked toward the Ever-faithful Daughter River. Ziiza, with so much on her mind, was thankful for her uncomplicated, undemanding companionship.

But when they passed the last of the ponds, quite beyond poachers and wardens and harvesters, Litti's steps quickened. She straightened, seemed taller. It was, Ziiza thought, as if she had broken through a curtain, passed into another territory: her own. They walked under high, late fall clouds. The early morning drizzle had stopped, but the tall grass they pushed through was still wet. Litti playfully slapped at the brown tops, sending up droplets. It did not matter, they were soaked to their waists anyway. Ziiza caught her spirit and joined in, kicking the grass with the sides of her feet so it would not rip through her toes.

Litti led her south across the expansive meadow, away from the broadening river, sometimes breaking into a trot. Although it was obvious to Ziiza that she meant it to be a relaxing, therapeutic walk after last night's disaster, it was also obvious that she had a specific destination in mind; this was not an aimless ramble. Ahead, on a slight rise, a broken-topped fir tree grew out of a ring of brush. As they approached, Litti glanced at Ziiza, taking her reaction. Then she looked away to hide her excitement. As they drew closer, the "brush" became a stand of brown-leaved scrub oaks and maples. Closer yet, the trees were full-size, and they, in turn, were filled with blackberry vines arching and twisting high above the two women. So it was an illusion, created by the largest tree Ziiza had ever seen, larger, even, than any on the Sea Trace, where all of the trees were enormous.

Litti lifted a spiky trailer with a stick, bent forward, took Ziiza's hand, and drew her into the barest of openings through the vines and branches. Bobbing and twisting, they made their way into a clearing that extended to the huge tree's drip line. Litti ran to the tree – so large in circumference, that once she reached its base, it appeared flat, not round – and pressed her arms to its thick black bark. She spun around, eyes flashing with delight, and said, "Great-great-great-grandpopa Monumentree, please welcome my dear friend Ziiza." Ziiza was taken aback, never having heard anyone talk to a tree before. Litti smiled, her white teeth gleaming, first at Ziiza, then at Great-great-great-grandpopa Monumentree, as if she expected him to reply. And he did, in a way. A puff of wind showered them with brown needles, covering their heads and shoulders. Ziiza wanted to laugh, in a friendly, nervous way. Instead, she shook her hair. "Don't mind him," Litti said. "He's a bit of a crosspatch. He does have rights to be at his age, don't you think?" Ziiza smiled. "I come here when it's storming storms," Litti continued, "to listen to his branches snap and whistle, to hear him moan in the wind. He would never drop a branch on me. He promised." Then, with a toss of her head, indicating they should be on their way, and, perhaps, that she had revealed more of herself than she had planned to, she led Ziiza carefully through the opening.

They continued walking south, toward a wall of trees at the edge of the tall grass. In the few hours they had been out, the clouds had broken apart and the sun warmed their shoulders. Litti fluffed her hair, stopped, caught a meadowlark's song, and headed in its direction. "Are you thirsty?" she asked Ziiza. The meadowlark sat singing and swaying on a thin bush next to a muddy, low-water pond waiting for the winter rain. As Litti approached the bird she hunched her shoulders, fixed her eyes on the horizon, and adopted a rolling gait, smoothing her motions. Ziiza, noticing her change of pace, stopped, and watched. At the pond, Litti stood arm's length away from the bird. It continued singing. "Good morning to you Buckibird," she whispered. Buckibird stopped singing but did not fly. "Or is it afternoon?" Litti said, raising her voice. The bird flew away, not, it seemed to Ziiza, in fright, but because it was ready to go.

"Buckibird's pool is too muddy to drink," Litti said. "No matter. In a few minutes you'll have the best drink of water you've ever tasted." They entered the forest where a creek emerged and flowed west toward the Daughter along the tree line. She led Ziiza over sections of animal paths and around trees with roots so large they had to climb over them. The trees grew in clumps of three, four, five, so tightly they must have made each other uncomfortable. If it wasn't for the fallen trees to detour around or climb over – some blown down in last year's storm; others hollow giants, down for decades; others down for centuries, nurse logs supporting the forest's endless cycle – walking would have been easy. Ziiza fell into the swing of it, her feet sinking into the damp, springy floor of needles, moss, and cones; stepping on twigs that snapped and crunched; coming to black sinks, having to back away and skirt around; feeling fern clusters pick at her bare legs like summer mosquitoes; vaulting broken-off limbs the size of residential trees in Beaverton. Litti was in charge, and, in spite of their zigzag course, she never lost contact with the creek. Neither woman spoke. They had a simple job to do, and the light was so subdued, not gloomy, just subdued, and the forest so silent that along-the-trail chatter seemed inappropriate.

The ground rose, the trees thinned, walking became easier, and Ziiza fell into her old Sea Trace reverie, luxuriating in the beauty of her surroundings, the joy of the moment, and still grinding away at her problems, worrying about the unknowable. Ahead through the trees, shafts of sunlight played in the mist rising from the forest floor, a sight common enough in morning but not in afternoon. As it grew lighter still, Litti veered back to the creek and led Ziiza to a clearing the size of nine or ten Beaverton lots. Unlike the expansive meadow they had crossed, and in keeping with its size, the ground cover was grass, still green, cropped short by springers, elk, and deer. Across the clearing, just as it emerged from the forest, the creek slid over a gently rounded boulder, the height of a tall man.

Litti walked to the water slide and sat by the pool. Could she have timed this more perfectly Ziiza thought, as she knelt beside her sipping water from cupped hands? Two bright green, moss-covered rocks – such a contrast from the forest darks – channeled the water through an age-worn slot. How extraordinary. So this was her secret place. Litti lay back on the grass. She closed her eyes, inviting Ziiza to do the same.

"You may sing sings if you like," Litti said much later, nudging Ziiza.

She sat up. "How long have I been asleep?"

"Or talk talks. This is Water Child." Litti glanced upward, indicating there was still light, and, ignoring Ziiza's question, continued, "Water Child will talk back to you. Or sing back to you. Both."

"Ah, what should I talk about?"

"Whatever is giving you bothers. Or whoever. Whatever is giving you joys. Or whoever is giving you joys. Like this." Litti stuck her feet in the water. A fingerling darted out of the grass along the water's edge. "First listen to Water Child."

"Do people come here? I mean, from Beaverton?"

"Your son, Com, did come to this place."

"No! He never told me."

"Of course not. Now sit next to me, please. We'll listen and learn together."

"What?"

"Quiet, please."

At first Ziiza heard only the water splashing into the pool, a ragged staccato after it ran through the slot and fell free of the back-curving boulder. Then

Water Child's infinite vocabulary. Or was it singing? The water calmed itself in the pool, then, gurgling and tinkling, talked and sang its way over the rock-and-pebble bed, never stopping, never repeating. All she had to do was listen, Ziiza concluded. As for the business of the day, sitting with her feet in the pool, between the creek's baritone and tenor sections, Ziiza talked. Litti knelt behind her, rubbing her back and neck, kneading her shoulders. Massaged her temples.

Ziiza spilled it to Water Child: the Sita's burning, Govvi's bleak report, Govvi herself, Biber's leg, the brew-crock, Gstan's friendship, Gstan's intentions, making it in Beaverton, not making it in Beaverton, Gstan again, Milli and Twigg, Com's far-ranging adventures, Org's aimlessness, Netti's headaches, Netti herself. Making it. Not making it. Starting over. Kenni. The fire. The end of it. A happenstance? Or a confirmation of dark forces working against her?

"Is that all?" Litti said, when Ziiza stopped talking.

"I guess so."

"Nothing good? Nothing positive?"

"What do you mean?"

"Well, dear Ziiza, the Sita's Lair, I know how important it was to you. Very important. But it's only a business. You've been in Beaverton a year and you've accomplished more than most people do in ten years. Ever. Isn't that something? Isn't that positive? Isn't that *enough*?"

"No."

Litti knew when to stop. "Come, my friend," she said, tossing her head, "Water Child will be here, listening, talking, singing, anytime you like. We should get back before dark. Unless you'd like to spend the night in the open." She eyed Ziiza. "I thought not."

Next morning, Ziiza, Litti, and the children visited Biber at Provido's convalescent center. He had received many visitors the day before: Mistermayor, Sister Sissi, Barclaw, and, of course, Bitta. He was cheerful and chatty, the result of a somewhat pain-free night and Provido's prediction of a complete recovery: "Just give it time." This, of course, was just what Biber and his friends wanted to hear, even though they were well aware of Provido's reputation for exaggeration; if his effervescent optimism was medicine, he would cure everyone instantly. As they filed away, Biber leaned off of his robe and motioned to Ziiza. When they were alone, his eyes filled with tears and he asked about his brew-crock. As if anything had changed. As if it had taken a miraculous turn for the better and had restored itself. Ziiza leaned over, kissed his cheek, and said, "She'll be all right, Biber." All she could think to say.

Before visiting Water Child, Ziiza had told the children to take the day off, do what they liked, not to bother with the mess. Ziiza did not ask how they had spent their time, she fairly well knew what their habits were. Edu told her anyway, and, like all of his sibling reports, he began with Org. He had moped around H&G, with frequent stops at the beaver tail vendors. That was it. Milli and Netti had spent all day listening to Skedaddle, then, of course, Screaming Indifference. Milli did not perform. Com and Torc had gone exploring. No surprise. Govvi had stood guard over the smoldering "establishment" and her safe pit. "My duty," she said, coming up behind them. "Someone's got to do it." Then, with her shoulders back and her hands pressing her skirt, she said, "I was on duty all day yesterday, Muma. I would like today off. All day. If you please."

"Of course, Govvi. What will you be doing?" Ziiza answered, not choosing her words carefully.

"Visiting friends," she said. "I have an invitation." Ziiza smiled and patted her arm. Govvi walked quickly away.

Although it had not rained hard since the fire, last evening's fog and this morning's mist had dropped enough moisture to almost extinguish Sita's Lair's smoldering remnants. Ziiza, Org, and the older girls worked through the morning. Com, Edu, and Dg joined them after school. The brew-crock lay in two, like giant xoa nut halves. What to do? Build a park or a playground with it as the centerpiece? Start Beaverton's first art museum? With a sculpture commemorating Ziiza's failure to make it in Beaverton? "Ha!" Ziiza shouted, her anger-and-tears stage over. She could almost laugh. Litti's introduction to her secret world – Great-great-great-grandpopa Monumentree, Buckibird, and Water Child – had done the job. The fire, less than forty-eight hours ago, seemed a distant memory, as if they had chanced on this lot and were hired to clean it up. Ziiza placed what were left of Biber's supplies and belongings beside the brew-crock halves and covered them up. Org used the charred tent poles and Kenni's smashed platform to start a trash fire. They tossed in all of the refuse they could gather. That left a few good poles, which Org and Netti stacked in a pile. Pitch-sealed mats? Not one remained. Didn't anyone foresee their flammability? Tonight, they would sleep on their own clean lot, a small step up. Tomorrow's project: build a new shelter.

* * *

165

Govvi's request had been truthful, if not complete; she had been invited. Not to see friends from school or H&G, as was implied, but to visit Pop&Jay. And not through a one-time invitation for today, as her muma had hastily assumed, but a standing one; she had been there before, enough times to develop a routine.

"Welcome to Popville, Little One," Pop said when he saw her emerge from the trees and into the clearing. (And except for their crude shelter, it was a clearing, because in the past year while Govvi had been working the accounts at Sita's Lair, Pop&Jay had not sold a single lot in their yet-unnamed community. Their flipping and arguing continued.)

"A visit from our fair Govvi," Jay added with a toothy smile. "Where've you been keeping yourself?" But before Govvi could begin to account for her activities, let alone tell them about the fire, they propped their fishing poles in forked stick holders and faced her, standing shoulder to shoulder. "Present yourself," Jay said in a play gruff voice. "Come forward to receive the Scepter." Govvi grinned and walked toward them with hesitant steps. They nudged each other. "Isn't she the prettiest one you've ever seen," Jay said to Pop in a stage whisper. "Yup, she sure is," Pop replied. When she reached them she knelt and bowed her head. Jay tapped her lightly on each shoulder with a polished stick and said, "With this Scepter, I proclaim you Princess of River City. That's our name for today." He presented the Scepter. Govvi pressed it to her cheek and smiled demurely.

"And," Pop followed up, "your first princessly duty is to build us a fire."

Govvi expected this; she would have been disappointed if they had not "commanded" her to build one, strange as the whole procedure was: two nobodies tapping a princess, then giving *her* orders. But it too was part of the routine: she always brought her old fire building equipment and they always commanded. (She was not sure whether they truly could not make fire, or if they were too lazy to try, but they never seemed to have one burning when she arrived.) "Now, Mister Pop," she said regally. "And now, Mister Jay, why are you standing there? Hustle off and fetch me some firewood." She could have started the fire in minutes. Instead, she stretched it out, pointing and re-pointing, drilling, resting, drilling some more, while they stood over her – between fetching, oohing and aahing, and clapping their hands – as if they had never seen a fire started before. As if she, Govvi, Princess of River City, holder of the Scepter, was the only one who could possibly do it. Two jolly rogues and their princess for a day.

"Will you never learn?" Govvi chided, tossing away the green and soggy sticks they dropped next to her tiny fire. They danced away, giggling, loving the lively interplay with the bright young girl. Incompetent as they were, or pretended to be, they did possess a just-caught, late-run fish, not bright, but edible. Govvi roasted it – after they had finally collected enough dry wood to raise the fire – and they enjoyed a tasty luncheon, a most welcome change, she thought, from her diet of beaver tail in all of its variations.

Pop&Jay had an abiding curiosity about Beaverton. Why, Govvi did not understand, since they were banned for life, professed hatred of the place (and everyone in it), and were building their rival town. Along with her fire building kit, she had brought a few unburnt tally boards, ones hidden in the safe pit. And, as always, by the drawn-out meal's end they had quizzed her on all of the news: from Mistermayor and the council, to Font and his bank, to Castor and the beavertail market, and, of course, her tally boards and the amazing details they held. They made an after dinner game out of her numbers, laughing, forgetting, confirming, repeating, playing the fools, an extension of their fire building amazement act. Govvi loved it, loved getting caught up in it, loved their attention, the respect they showed her, their joviality and friendship. She did not have many, if any, friends, not even, to be blunt, among her brothers and sisters. Pop&Jay were the best of friends.

"Getting late," Govvi said. "Thank you for the Scepter and lunch, but I must be home soon."

Pop reached into his pouch and extracted one of the flipping objects. "For you, Princess. And thank you for your company." He placed it in her hand. She started up the trail, alert for Jay's admonition that was sure to come. When she was almost out of sight, he yelled, "Hold onto that, Little One. It'll be valuable someday."

* * *

When Govvi returned, Ziiza and Gstan were sitting in front of the old Lair entrance, talking. The lot was clean, and, except for the split brew-crock, a stack of poles, and their surviving belongings, it looked almost as it had last year before they had built the "pleasuring establishment." Being Govvi, she could not help comparing their present inventory to that of the day, a year and a half ago, when they escaped from the Sea with just the clothing on their bodies, and not complete sets at that. "Hi, Govvi. Enjoy the day?" Ziiza called. Gstan waved. After a pause to allow her to elaborate on her day, which she did not do, she continued, "Everybody's at Litti's; we'll spend one more night there."

At Litti's, her brothers and sisters were bunched together, talking excitedly. Even Dg looked excited. "They've been together all day," Netti said breathlessly. "We think he's proposing." Govvi looked back and her mouth fell open. Gstan was holding her muma, *her muma*, by the hand. Or it looked that way.

"Ziiza," Gstan said, nervously looking around to make certain no one had moved up within earshot, "I've liked you since the day we met. You know, when that jerk, Wiggi Bub, introduced us. Me, the boss. You, the neophyte, the trainee. Seems silly now." He laughed. She smiled, laughed, not a full smile, and certainly not a full laugh, not enough to place Wiggi Bub and Lots Plus in the category of treasured memories, not encouraging him but not discouraging him, just enough of a smile and a laugh to keep him going. She *was* curious about what he had to say. And surprised. No, not completely surprised.

Since the Wiggi Bub, Lots Plus move did not segue into the nostalgic, bonding, shared experience he had hoped for, something that would make it a two-way instead of a one-way conversation, Gstan tried the sympathy approach. "You know, Hill Burrow has not done as well as I had expected." (An understatement to be sure.) "A good start, yes. My place. And Old Man Haracosh's. He has a large burrow with a view. Nice place if you don't look inside. But he lives alone, no wife, no kids running around. Selling to him was a mistake; I know it now. But sometimes you do things early on, just to get rolling. You have to. Know what I mean? But now every time I show a burrow to a family, they take one look at his and leave." Ziiza nodded.

Dg sat apart from the children, scratching himself. Gstan spotted him, and anxious for anything to establish a connection, slapped his leg and called, "Here Dg. Come on over here, boy." Dg cocked his head to let him know he had heard, and waited, making certain Gstan knew he was in control and would come if he darned well pleased. "Come on, boy," Gstan said again. Dg sat next to him. It was Gstan's turn to hesitate. He looked down, back at Ziiza, then reached his finger under Dg's chin and scratched. Evidently this met with Dg's approval, because he closed his eyes.

"Speaking of burrows," Gstan said, continuing to scratch (although they were not, strictly speaking, speaking of burrows), "I built a gazillion of them. Twenty-six to be exact. Taking away mine and Old Man H's leaves twenty-four. That I've paid for." His voice rose, "And are unsold." Then, loud enough for the attentive ears at Litti's to hear, he boomed, "Totally unsold." He glanced at Ziiza, and, detecting a glimmer of sympathy, and, being the cagey old sales pro that he was, shouted again, "Totally unsold." He shifted into confidential mode, "But I have a way out. Have it all planned," he whispered, leaning over and patting her on the shoulder.

"If only," he said. "If only, Ziiza, you had come in with me, joined the business when I asked you before. You're talented. Savvy." He was floundering. "You proved it. The Sita's Lair. Great business move. Resounding success. Kenni, the . . . , the rampage, the fire. That was a fluke, no fault of yours. I've never been married. You have. Six children. Six wonderful." His words flopped like a caught fish on the bank. "I like you, Ziiza. I've liked you since we met."

"Go, go, go!" came a shrill cry from the pathway. "Go, man!"

"What's going on?" Ziiza said, jumping to her feet.

Another voice: "Run hard! Run hard! You've almost got him."

Ziiza ran to the path. Two young men raced toward her – straining so hard it seemed each step would be their last. Sweat gleamed on the leader's forehead as he ran toward the sunset. Red sweat. Bloody sweat. His rival, tall and slender, surged, trying to pass, and pulled even, his neck veins stretched tight as roots. Pulled even, but not ahead. The leader clenched his jaw, sucked air through his teeth, and fought him off. They ran down the path and out of sight.

Org and Netti joined Ziiza. Then the other children. Gstan remained seated, not believing she had simply walked away from him. For as trivial thing as a race. Then the pack, eight runners fighting it out for third place. After a twenty-step gap, a pair, followed by single runners with larger spaces between them. Only when the slower runners, walkers actually, began passing did Ziiza notice details, such as charcoal numbers on their arms and thighs. "They have rocks on their heads," she shrieked, pounding Netti's shoulder. "What on earth are they doing that for?"

"It's rock running, Muma," Org said.

"Rock?" Ziiza said incredulously.

"Running?" Netti finished.

"Latest thing," Org said, proud of his inside knowledge. "I might enter the next race. And by the way, did you notice who was leading, the guy in first place?"

"Why no, they went by so fast."

"Sufx."

"Our Sufx?" Ziiza said as she joined the crowd following the runners. The children fell in with her. Gstan put his arm around Dg and held him, but he squirmed away and ran after them. When they reached Inner Circle, the few runners remaining turned right, but the spectators, quickening their pace, headed straight into H&G. At Town Hall they gathered around what appeared to be the finish line. Ever-present Barclaw was on duty. "Keep off the racecourse, now. Stay back. Stay back. They'll be a comin' any time now."

Ziiza touched Org's arm. "So that's why Sufx was coming to work all sweaty and dirty. Now I know. That was blood in his hair. From those rocks. Rocks on their heads. I can't believe it."

"That's right, Muma."

What had been a neck and neck battle earlier was a letdown at the finish. Sufx not only won, he came in alone. His gangly rival, having spent everything on the surge as they passed Ziiza's place, did not finish. As he crossed the line Sufx hoisted his rock and pitched it forward in triumph. Spectators jumped aside, dodging it as it rolled. He took two steps on unsteady legs, stopped, rested his hands on his knees, and breathed deeply. The crowd was on him. "Stand away. Stand away," Barclaw boomed. "He's all done in." But Sufx's fans pressed even tighter, pummeling his back and yelling "Fantastic race!" and "Way to go, Sufx!" Bitta was there, trying for a finish line interview, but she was not strong enough to push through the crowd. She would get to him later.

The spectators dispersed, happy, excited, and with something to talk about all week. Ziiza and her children held back. "That was a splendid performance, Sufx," Ziiza said. "I don't understand it, but it was splendid."

"Thanks, Ziiza."

"Can I carry your rock for you Sufx?" Edu piped. Sufx, who was cradling it against his belly, smiled and handed it to Edu – who dropped it immediately. Com picked it up and staggered for a few feet. He, too, could not hold it. "See, Com," Edu said, "it's a lot heaver than it looks."

Netti touched Sufx's neck. She licked her finger. It was blood. "I'll clean you up," she said as a sister might, "if you don't mind." Ziiza was, of course, about to say the same thing.

When they arrived at Litti's, tired, content, and proud of Sufx, Govvi and Litti were there to meet them. Gstan was not.

19

Milli's Pledge

ZIIZA LOOKED up from her garden patch to see Milli and Twigg standing on the path.

"Hi, Muma," Milli said.

"Hi, Milli. Hello, Twigg."

They walked toward her, hand in hand, stopped a few feet away, and stood stiffly. Milli dropped his hand, withdrew her shell from her bag, and held it with both hands.

I don't like the looks of this.

Ziiza's face froze; she could not help it.

"Twigg and I have something to tell you," Milli said. "No, we have something to ask." She hooked her arm in his. "Well, rather, Twigg has something to say, to ask you. Don't you, darling?"

Twigg composed himself and took over. "Muma Ziiza. Milli and I love each other. Very much." Milli looked up at him, smiled, and rubbed her shoulder into his arm.

They're more intimate than I'd imagined.

"Screaming Indifference. My band. Our band, I should say, is going on tour. Beaverton isn't the only place. A band has to reach out."

With all of the terrible things you've said about Beaverton, I'm not surprised.

"Well, that's not the point," Twigg continued. "We're deeply in love. We want to get pledged – Barclaw could do it, Mistermayor, if he has the time – and leave together on tour. Tomorrow morning. I'm asking for your blessing."

"Me, too, Muma," Milli said. "You see, it's so right."

"Leave Beaverton?" Ziiza said blankly, as it sunk in, after they had said what she had known was coming. "I don't know."

"Muma, please. The Sita's gone."

"Milli's a natural performer," Twigg said. "She has a beautiful voice. You've heard her. You've seen the audience's reaction. They love her. I love her. It's what she was born to do."

This was too much after the fire. And Milli herself; Ziiza had never heard her talk like this, not even at Way Rock. Not that she hadn't always had strong opinions and had never hesitated expressing them. It was her intensity. This was a grown woman addressing her, frank, intelligent, and forceful. Ziiza pulled her shawl.

I see so much of myself in you, Milli.

"Oh, please. Your blessing?"

"Let me think about it."

After a pause to give her time to reconsider, Milli said quietly, "We leave tomorrow, Muma."

Ziiza fussed around her fall garden pulling dead plants, throwing them in the compost pile. Not that she had to do much pulling; they were trampled flat. She walked to Litti's, but she was not home. Netti showed up. "You know?" Ziiza asked.

Netti slid her finger under her nose and wiped the drip on her fur. "I've known for a long time, Muma." Tears erupted and she pressed her fists into her eyes. "I wish them well. I do. I really do. I'll go to Barclaw's with them. She asked me to stand by her while she takes the pledge." Netti dropped to her knees alongside Ziiza, and continued, "I don't know whether to be happy or sad. To wish her well. Or wish her ill. For choosing – him."

"I couldn't have said it better, Netti."

Org bounded into the garden. In a rare show of exuberance and, ignoring their hugging and weeping, he said, "Hey, Muma. Hey, Nettie. How's this for style?" He stood grinning, naked above the waist (his watabeast fur draped over his belt), holding a rock. When he had their attention he ran in place, stamping his feet, faster and faster, harder and harder. When he got "up to speed," he hoisted the rock over his head, lowered it till it touched, and held it with both hands. He slowed his running-in-place and said, "I'm ready. I'm ready to take him. Ready to kick his tail end."

"Ready for what?" Ziiza and Netti asked, almost together. Two tear-covered faces looked up at him, then down, as they covered their smirks with their hands. Then up again, as straight-faced as they could.

"Not exactly ready. I'm getting ready to get ready. I'm starting to train for next week's rock running race."

"Oh. And who's the *him*?"

"Sufx. Everybody's out to beat him." Org ran in place again. "Oh, I like the little guy. Great to work with at the old Lair, you know. But he's been so cocky lately. I think he needs to be taken down a chip or two." Then, as quickly as he had arrived, he turned and ran east on the path. "Twice around Outer Circle," he shouted. "Three times tomorrow."

"Ridiculous." Govvi's voice came from behind. The three younger children had returned from school.

"What's ridiculous?" Ziiza quipped, snapping out of her funk. "Milli's wanting to get pledged – I assume you know – or Org's rock running?"

"Ridiculous. Both of them," she said again in her clipped imitation adult voice.

"I think it's neat," Com said. "I'm already a runner." He touched his chin. "But I don't know about running with big rocks on top of my head. Why deliberately slow yourself down? Why not get rid of the rocks and just run the race?"

"Dg doesn't like the rock runners," Edu put in to be included in the banter. "He thinks they're stealing them, running away with them. So he's going to chase them and bite their feet till they give them back. He told me so."

"Ridiculous," Govvi said for the third time. "And that's that."

"Yes," Ziiza said, "it is ridiculous, I suppose. But interesting at the same time. Very interesting."

Org returned in an hour, so wet with sweat it might have been raining. He walked into the garden. Bending his knees, he boosted the rock into the air and jumped away. He winked at his muma as the rock thumped on the ground.

Truly, I haven't seen him this animated, this excited, about anything since the Sea Trace, since smashing through branches, or fighting the watabeast, or swimming against a tide.

"What is it, Org?" Ziiza asked. "What's the appeal?"

"Oh, I don't know." Org struggled for words, wanting to give her a proper answer. "Anyone can run. Anybody can race." He brightened. "But rock running is different. Not everyone can do it. Run so long. Stand the pain in your head. In your arms. Blood running into your eyes."

"The pain," Ziiza said. "Of course, the pain. And the blood, although you don't seem to have cut yourself this time."

"Practice run, Muma."

Ziiza asked more questions, but Org was not a details man and she knew it. Sufx had moved away, where to she did not know. He came by every day to check on Biber and his crushed leg, but he had to find another job, he had told her. She found him in H&G. "Congratulations again on your race, Sufx," she said in greeting, leaving no doubt in what direction she wished the conversation to travel.

"Hi-ya, Ziiza."

"I have a question, if you have a minute. Several, in fact."

"A minute? I'm unemployed and broke. I have all the minutes you want."

"I can relate to that." They laughed.

"The rocks," Ziiza asked. "Why so big? Who organizes the races? Who can enter? Who says how far? Who started this, anyway? Does the winner get a prize?"

"Come on, Ziiza old thing, one question at a time."

Sufx told Ziiza everything he knew, topping Org by a large margin. Rock running, it seemed, began with a dare, a spur-of-the-moment idea. A group of boys and girls were idling in H&G, when a boy, to impress the girls, picked up a rock, raised it over his head, and challenged the others to match him. To his disappointment, and to the girls' delight, they did. So he started running with it. To make it more difficult, he balanced it on his head. He ran out of sight and returned ten minutes later with blood streaks down his neck. The girls ran to him, stroked his hair, and cleaned him up. The other boys took distinct notice of the attention he received.

Impromptu show-off races ensued. The boys used whatever rocks were handy and ran short distances. After that, and it did not take long, a contagious rivalry began, spreading beyond the teen-age idlers to include boys and men of all ages. Although a few girls tried it, the prevailing view was that it was a "crazy boy thing," interesting to watch, but not worth doing.

Sufx continued: A competitor's popa, Quord Senior, soon broadened his interest beyond cheering for his son, to encouraging all of the runners. He was probably the first person to take it beyond a simple amusement and view it as a sport, Sufx surmised. Racers and spectators began to take it seriously, too. Path-side spectators now included runners' friends, parents, and relatives, plus casual bystanders. Sufx told of a race that had ended in a fistfight between Quord Junior and a rival who claimed he bumped him, cut him off, then tripped him. Runners and spectators took sides and threw stones. Junior took a bad one in the thigh. That was all Senior needed to take action, to take over rock running.

The fundamental rule of rock running, Quord Senior had decided, was: rocks had to be held above or balanced on competitors' heads throughout the race. Carrying them on a shoulder or holding them low in the hands, for instance, meant disqualification. A sanctioned race consisted of one lap around Outer Circle. The start and finish line would be in front of Town Hall. The problem, Senior concluded, was rocks. Must they be round and smooth like black-and-brown-speckled river rocks, hard to hold onto but easier on the head? How about slabs of sandstone, smooth, but brittle on the edges? Red lava rock presented another problem; it was full of holes and deceptively light for its size. Also, it crumbled easily; runners could break off pieces as they ran, giving unfair advantage. Basalt – shiny, black, dense – presented the opposite problem; runners liked it for its compactness, but its sharp edges inflicted more cuts on head and hands than other rocks. He pondered all of this, spurred by his son's injury, and his interest in what he saw as a new first-class sport.

Senior's decision was not popular, but it was a decision, and the beginning of a set of rules to run by. And it was only through the force of his personality, his physical strength, and that he now "ran" the races, that he prevailed. After testing many rocks on many runners, he declared that all must be smooth and weigh at least as much as his Master Rock. He created an ersatz balance scale by placing the Master Rock on his left shoulder. (He sometimes left it on his shoulder throughout the race as a badge of authority.) Prospective contestants then set their rocks on his right shoulder. He "weighed" them by bumping them into the air with a shoulder hunch. If he said "Pass," they did. This was his great innovation, and what caused him to become known as the Popa of Rock Running, which, of course, he was not. That honor belonged to the idle and nameless boys trying to impress equally idle and nameless girls; they were the real popas and mumas of rock running. The girls created the name, rock running, however, loved screaming it from their raspberry-stained lips.

"Thank you, Sufx" Ziiza said when he had finished his history. "Very interesting. Very interesting."

"You're welcome, Ziiza." Then, he added, "I don't suppose Sita's Lair will be opening up again? The fire, the brew-crock, Biber, and all."

"To be frank, Sufx, I can't see it. But if we do, you'll be the first to know, the first one we'll hire back. You know how Biber and I appreciated your cheerfulness and good work. How many people entered the last run?"

"I'd say fifty or more. I don't know." He shrugged modestly. "Not everyone finishes."

"Can women enter?"

"Of course. Some have. It's just that I haven't seen any lately. Have to ask Senior, I guess. You thinking about it?"

"Maybe yes. Maybe no. But I'm definitely thinking – about rock running."

As Sunday's race approached, Org trained harder. He had no training schedule or coach to give him one. Straight-ahead trail breaker that he was, his approach was simple: run longer, run harder, and run with more weight than required, the make-the-practice-harder-so-the-race-is-easier strategy. He ran Outer Circle two or three times without a rock, as fast as he could. Then he did sprints with his big rock on his head and his object rock in his waist pouch. He found Ziiza a rock, noticeably under the Master Rock's weight, but heavy enough, he told her. They started on a practice run together. She made it a third of the way around Outer Circle and panted to a stop. "You're doing good, Muma," he said. "You have to start easy and work up to it. This isn't arm-wrestling you know, over in a few grunts." He laughed. "It's an endurance thing, plus strength and speed. Everything you could ask. Why don't you walk the rest of the way?" And he was off in a burst. When she arrived home, her head was sore, her back was sore, her legs were sore, and her feet, especially her right foot, were sore. She slid to the ground and asked Govvi and Netti to give her a rub.

"You could at least take your necklaces off when you run, Muma," Netti said. "Flopping around so."

"They don't bother me."

When Org returned, the girls offered to rub him, too. He refused with a grunt, mumbling, "Real rock runners don't need rubdowns."

Ziiza raised her head off the ground. "Where do the others train?" she asked.

"Here and there. Different places. Some train at night."

"Really?"

"Sufx, he trains a lot," Org volunteered, thinking that was where she was going. "Up in the hills, along the north ridge trail I think. I've seen him headed out that way. Always alone. He doesn't want anyone to see how he trains. And since no one can keep up with him, no one has. But that's about to change."

Milli did not wait for Ziiza's blessing; Barclaw pledged them in a minute. It was all Netti could do to witness, but she did. Where was the band going, she had asked, as she hugged and kissed her "big" sister good-bye. South, Twigg had told her, way south. There were scattered small settlements along the inland trail that followed the North-flowing Son, then crept over the mountains, he had heard. If they got nibbles of interest they would stop and play. But he doubted it. They would probably have to travel all the way to Big Bay, the only other sizeable settlement west of the Sunups. Who knew how large it had become. All he knew was he was through with Beaverton, with its rain, regulations, and dampy-dull people, as he called them. Big Bay, if it worked out. Someplace else if it did not. Maybe Swarm City.

20

Rock Running

ON RACE day, as agreed, Com met his pal, Torc, at Mistermayor's Welcome to Exciting Beaverton sign. They walked briskly along the trail toward the North-flowing Son and Pop&Jay's camp. "What do your muma and popa think of your rambling around with me?" Com asked, making idle conversation.

"You know I don't have a popa," Torc said. "And my muma don't care."

"You should say, doesn't care, not don't care," Com corrected with a smirk. "Addle wouldn't approve."

"You know how much I bother what he thinks."

"I've no popa, either," Com continued. "I've kind of adjusted, probably like you. My brother, Edu, hasn't, though. I don't think he ever will. If he didn't have Dg I don't know what he'd do. But I've got a great muma and she cares a lot about me. And my brothers and sisters, too. She's all broken up about Milli right now, getting pledged to Twigg. Caught her by surprise. Doesn't know what to do about it. She's in denial; that's what Addle calls it. See, I've learned something in school. And she's upset about the fire that burned our place down. We're out of business. More than upset. Tries not to show it, though. Now goes Milli. I think she expects it won't last. That's why she's not running after her, making a big fuss. No matter. They won't make it to Big Bay, I think. Too far away. Come traipsing back to Beaverton. Go back to playing in H&G where they belong."

"I hope something doesn't get 'em along the trail, is what I hope," Torc said. "Bears and gazors, for instance. One pounce and that's it. Or one of those snakes I've heard about. Big around as your waist. Poison fangs that get you all dead. Have they thought about that?"

"Probably not," Com said. "Newly-pledgeds don't think about stuff like that." He rolled his eyes. "All they think about is luuuuv. Besides, we've never seen one of those snakes and we've been just about everywhere."

"Not to Big Bay and the hot country."

"What do you know about it, Torc?"

When the trail left the Valley of the Beaver and rose up the hill, Com veered north and plunged into a thicket. Torc held back. "Come on," Com said. "Time for some heavy bushwhacking."

"Well, the trail is over there. Why don't we take it?"

"You'll see, my friend. You'll see."

Com aimed a straight line to the top, deviating only for insurmountable obstacles: cliffs, fallen trees, boulders. He threw himself at the hill with such ferocity Torc could not keep up. "If you want to go crazy, why don't you take up rock running?" Torc sputtered. Com split an opening through giant ferns with his arms. As the hill grew steeper, he kicked his toes into the earth and pushed on his knees to keep going. When Torc fell too far behind, he returned, took his hand, and pulled him along.

As they approached the crest the trees thinned, then ended, replaced by a tangle of thornberry bushes. Com plunged in, beating the bushes. This did little good; they sprang back, slashing him. Clumsy as he was, Torc struggled on.

They crested the top on hands and knees and lay still, exhausted. It had not taken long, less than an hour, but it was brutal: scratched legs, torn furs, bleeding feet, and broken fingernails. Com pushed himself up, walked through the grass, and looked east, over the treetops, across the Son, over forested flatlands punctuated by small, dormant, volcanic peaks. As he had expected, the mountain was *out*, gleaming white on the horizon. Torc caught up. "Morning Spire," Com said. "Sharp as a newly-chipped blade." He rested his hand on Torc's shoulder. "I'm going to stand on top someday. Not too many days from now, either. You, too. You and me, Torc. Top-of-the-Spire. But don't tell anyone. Not anyone, hear me. Promise. Promise?"

"Well, I promise."

* * *

Ziiza counted seventy-three runners at the starting line. The majority were young men and boys, the average age being Org's and Sufx's. A few older athletic hunter types. A handful of boys down to Edu's age. One woman, Ziiza, herself. Quord Senior was feeling expansive and generous, thrilled, actually, by the number of entrants and his sense of rock running's (and his own) growing importance. Except for Org and Sufx, and a few he called "serious contenders," he had relaxed his standards for today's run. The kids could use whatever rocks they chose. Ziiza was peeved when he waved her through without shoulder-jouncing her rock, but did not say anything.

Bitta was hard into it, too. This was every chronicler's dream: a new event, a new sport to talk about, as exciting for spectators as for competitors. Add an undefeated champion and a tall, muscular challenger, and she had a *story*. Hobart flapped his wings and jumped from her white-speckled shoulder onto her head. "Attend your eyes on Sufx," Bitta told her audience. "Crouching at the starting line, like a gazor about to spring on its prey. Boulder-weapon resting at his feet. He straightens up, elevates his arms, and claws at the gray sky, checking the wind. He glances toward Smoke-storm, its black column spreading wider, wider, over forest and plain, almost to the Valley of the Beaver, threatening to choke off life itself. But our champion fears nothing. A raindrop lands on his hand. He tilts, lets it drip down his finger. Holding it to his tongue, he savors its life-giving sweetness. He rubs his forehead and cheeks, anointing himself, anticipating his victory to come." Bitta's sharp eyes scanned the assemblage, gauging her hyperbole's effect (it was not even sprinkling). Smoke-storm was, however, smoking, threatening to be sure, but no more so than usual. No matter. "But will victory be his?" Bitta continued. "Org, mighty Org, the contender, the challenger, stands next to him, hatred steaming from his eyes." (Org was twenty steps down the starting line doing lifting exercises with his rock, not paying attention to anyone.) 'I'll crush you, little man,' Org says, his words flying like flint chips. Sufx glares at him and responds: 'I'll be so far ahead, you'll trip over your tongue, big guy.'"

Bitta's fantasy report was interrupted by Quard Senior bellowing: "Just about starting time. Counting down." The experienced runners, self-seeded in front, jumped up and down, flopping their hands to stay loose. The fun runners stood behind, toeing their rocks, not moving. Ziiza stood behind all of them, alone and tense before her first race, and at the same time, analyzing, taking everything in. Netti, Govvi, and Edu, waved from the path edge. Dg strained at his new leash. Edu yanked him back.

"Rock runners, step to the line," Senior said. He inspected the line for cheaters (as if it mattered). "Everyone understand the racecourse?" he asked. "Out East Path. Turn left on Outer Circle. Once around. Back in on East Path to the finish. Right here. Got it?" The competitors crouched. "Raise! Rocks!" They picked up their rocks and held them over their heads. The spectators cheered, loving it. Slowly, dramatically, they lowered them to their heads.

"Get set!" Deep breaths. "Go!"

Four teenagers burst into the lead and were soon out of sight. The more experienced runners, including Org, Sufx, and the almost-healed Junior, fell in behind. Although she started in last place, Ziiza moved up quickly. As soon as the runners were out of sight, the spectators walked in the opposite direction, down the west path.

By the halfway point, the four boys had dropped their rocks and dropped out. Org, Sufx and one other now formed the lead pack, if it could be called a pack. A secondary pack ran a few paces behind, about a dozen, including Junior, showing blood streaking down foreheads and faces, necks and shoulders. Then the rest, drifting farther and farther apart. Ziiza stuck with it gamely, jogging, then walking, then jogging again, a trickle of blood running down her forehead, into her eye and down her cheek. She tried holding the rock up and away from her blood-matted hair, but her arms could not take it. The gashes grew deeper and longer and the blood flow increased. Other non-competitors, such as herself, walked with their rocks cradled in their hands, too proud to drop them, too determined to give up.

At the three-quarter mark, Org trailed Sufx by a few steps. He made his move, swinging wide to pass. Sufx dug deep and held him off. Org surged again and drew even. They matched each other stride for stride, all the way to East Path. As they rounded the corner, Org faltered. His legs wobbled; it was all he could do to run in a straight line. Sufx pulled away and finished well ahead. Disgusted, and hearing the cheers for Sufx, Org considered tossing his rock. But he pressed on, now blinded by sweat and blood, taking second place. To his surprise the spectators cheered him as lustily as they had Sufx. And they continued to cheer every runner as he crossed the line. Evidently there was more to this than he had imagined; finishing, sticking it out, counted for something, too. You did not have to win to get respect.

Not only that, but after they had finished, the runners gathered at the line to cheer. Ziiza finished on willow legs, weaving from one side of the path to the other, holding her rock at waist level. The crowd let loose with the grandest cheer of the afternoon, much louder than for Sufx, as if they had been saving it all for her. Ziiza let go of her rock as she crossed the line, dropped to her knees, and sucked air. Her children rushed her. All except Org, who stood away, pleased with her effort. (He was thankful he had not succumbed to pride and quit. There would be other races. Sufx would be beaten. By him.) And they continued to cheer, until every runner, or more accurately, walker, came in.

"I know one thing," Ziiza told Org at home, "some things have got to change in this rock running game. The sport is growing. Everyone's excited. It has a great future. Yet . . . it's running itself into a rock wall, so to speak."

"What do you mean, Muma?" Org said. "It's going great. There's only one thing wrong as far as I can see: I haven't beaten Sufx."

"Feel your head, Org. Look at the cuts on your hands. You and your tough guys will put up with it. For a while, anyway. But not the regular folks who would like to participate. They see rock running as a way to make

Mistermayor's Exciting Beaverton sign mean something. I can smell it." She looked up at an overcast sky as if to make a forecast. Edu looked up, too, making an instant calculation to match against hers. He sat back, waiting for her pronouncement. "It's so clear to me," she said. "If we can eliminate the cuts and the blood and the headaches, we'll open this whole thing up. We need some sort of protection between rock and head."

"What are you talking about?" Org said. "That's the whole idea, get cut up, spill blood, and win. It's called competing, beating your opponent, overcoming obstacles. Remember the Sea Trace, Muma?"

Ziiza did not press. She did not forget, either. That night she sang for the first time since the fire. An avalanche of thoughts kept her awake far into the night. At dawn she attended to herself briefly, then took Litti's route out of town. Dg fell in behind. "Here's the problem, Dg," she said, leaning over and patting him, "we need something strong enough to protect, but soft enough to feel comfortable. Take ferns. Too flimsy, wouldn't you say? But let's not reject hastily. They could make excellent padding if supported by something else. Get the idea?" Dg wagged his tail. "Good. Now examine everything around us like we've never examined before."

Ziiza reached up a cedar trunk and chipped at the bark. She pulled it halfway down, and then placed the end in Dg's mouth. "Now Dg, pull away." He backed up, twisting and snarling, till it peeled to the ground. She chopped it off and tied it to his collar. He dragged it along proudly. No other barks seemed promising, at least for the moment. Neither did evergreen limbs. They walked to the beaver ponds and gathered reeds and rushes. Supple willow branches held promise; she cut some of those. When she and Dg had all they could carry and drag, they returned home.

The children were up when she dumped her load in the yard. Govvi took a quick inventory, more from habit and to keep in practice than interest. Edu started to ask a question, but caught on and stopped. Org pretended disdain; he suspected what she was up to but watched anyway. Ziiza's first move was to balance a thick pad of ferns on her head. "Netti, dear, would you hoist my rock?" Netti set Ziiza's modest-sized rock on her head. "It's a start, but not much of one," Ziiza said. "Have to be much tougher to support race rocks."

Ziiza worked on her project, using up all of her materials, then sending whoever was handy to gather more: Edu and Dg for cedar bark, Com for rushes, Netti for willow. She used great amounts of willow, twisting, and interlacing, in tight circles. Her best effort was a thick ring that sat on her head and held the rock high enough so it did not touch, a bird's nest without a bottom. That was a step, but not a solution; the tightly-wound branches were too scratchy and uncomfortable. She sat with the willow ring on her head, her small rock balanced on that. Sat for an hour, ignoring passerbys' glances and her children's snickers.

"Have you thought about a basket?" Netti asked. "Not a basket, but woven like a basket. In the shape you have on your head."

"Would you try?"

As the week progressed Netti wove version after version. Ziiza kept her supplied with fiber, working it to Netti's specifications: cutting to length, pounding, chewing to soften, drawing over hard edges to straighten. She took test runs. (Org considered the idea silly and would not help.)

On race day, Ziiza and the children approached Senior at weigh-in time. "Here, Netti," Ziiza said, "hold the protector out of sight while I get my rock weighed. I don't want Mister All-powerful to say no before I've had a chance to try it out."

Same race result: Sufx won easily. Org found himself battling it out with Quord Junior for second place. He beat him, but, relative to Sufx, he had nothing to brag about.

Ziiza found herself in a different race, a product development race. Speed, personal records, and passing runners did not concern her. A few minutes into the race she stopped, took the protector out of her belt, pressed it on her head, and replaced her rock. She settled into an easy stride, long, strong, flowing, holding with the mid-speed runners, still all male. At halfway, she realized she was running comfortably, with a heavier rock than the week before. She was breathing hard; she had never run this far before, so she slowed to a speed she thought would carry her all the way. It did. She ran smoothly across the line. Maybe only her children noticed, but unlike most, she was holding her rock with only one hand to steady it; the protector did the rest. And unlike almost every other racer, she was cut-free. At least her head was; she had a few hand nicks. Another thing: she did not pitch her rock to get rid of the painful burden. When out of the crowd's way, she simply lowered it to the ground. Her arms did not ache. Why? Because she had been able to switch off. By all accounts, she had run a satisfactory race. Her last race. Her bad foot told her that. She saw a bigger, far more interesting race for herself. "Count the runners, Govvi," she had asked her before the race. "Count the crowd, too." Govvi's report at the finish line: more runners than Ziiza's quick count, and twice as many spectators as last week.

* * *

Monday morning Netti walked Com, Govvi, Edu, and Dg to school, then, mumbling an excuse, left them just before they reached the knoll. She kept walking on West Path, toward Castor's beaver works. She did not go far; solitude was not what she wanted today. She turned back, and keeping wide of Grassyknoll, entered Hunters and Gatherers Market. Where else? With her basket swinging at her side, she walked to the Trace End café. Sister Sissi was not there, but had left a sign on a round, reading: Help yourself. Donations gratefully accepted. Netti picked up a piece of dried tail, raised it to her mouth, then realizing she was not hungry, put it back.

Idah the scent vendor, peering out from under a conical hat festooned with dangling jewel-stones, called, "Netti, how nice to see you this gorgeous morning. Give to me your wrist, dear: morning glory and wild cucumber." Netti waved her off politely, and, after managing a weak smile, dropped her head and walked on. She caught Skedaddle's strains in the distance, the very sounds she did not wish to hear. She walked on and found herself in a sea of footprints in the mud. She found a pair that fit her and stood in them, facing the empty stage. Did she feel worse here? Or better? Screaming Indifference could have played here last evening. Twigg, with his deceptively cherubic face, would have ranted about Beaverton's conformity and pretense – all for the kids, not to be taken seriously. And at the center of it all (as far as Netti was concerned), Milli, lovely Milli, sister and friend, would have surpassed him, her lilting voice giving wings to her songs. But she did not sing last evening. Nor would she this evening. Maybe, Netti thought, she would never hear her sing again.

Across the way, a pair of teenagers paused opposite her, at the edge of the listening ground. Hoping? Paying their respects? Then, without acknowledging her presence, or she theirs, they continued on. Netti sniffed, wiped her eyes, and walked quickly away. By the time she was out of sight of the stage she was sobbing out of control. She sat and held her face in her hands.

"My poor lady."

"You sound heartbroken, dear."

Talking to me? She raised her head and blinked through her tears. A man and a woman stood before her, short of stature, ample of girth, whose shortness of stature made their girths appear very ample indeed. They wore identical knee-length, blueberry-dyed tunics, belt-less, open in front, revealing – everything. Netti did not know whether to look away in embarrassment, or laugh. She bit on a finger joint to forestall a reaction. They smiled at her, then, as if on cue, stepped back together. Their faces were round and full, as would be expected; their cheeks showed red and were brushed with a bluish makeup, as if to match their tunics. Each had wide-gapped upper front teeth and closely-cropped hair, hers not much longer than his. If it weren't for their parted tunics, they could have passed as twins. At least at a distance.

"A bit of Mire-root? Cheer you up," the man said, holding out a length of finger-sized, brownish-gray-colored root.

Netti stared at it.

"Or these," the woman said, extending a handful of smaller roots. "New gathering."

Netti's mouth sagged.

"Oh, I know," the woman exclaimed, nudging him. "We haven't introduced ourselves."

"You know," the man said affably, "you're right. I *will* correct that oversight immediately. Young lady, may I present my wife and professional associate, Mu Mire. And myself, Po Mire. We are proprietors of the Center for Enlightenment and Communal Contentment, known as the Mire.

"The what?"

Ignoring her query, they held out their roots and held onto their gap-toothed smiles. Netti relaxed, smiled back, and took a small one out of politeness. "Thank you, ah, Mu Mire," she said. She chewed slowly. It had a carroty crunch and a combination crabapple-tart and honey-sweet taste, unlike anything she had ever eaten.

"Give her some more," Po Mire said. Mu Mire pulled open her tunic, exposing herself, and dipped into an inside pocket.

"Here you are," she said, handing them to Netti. "Enjoy."

"We come to H&G every Monday," Po Mire said. "Land just about this spot. With more Mire-root, too. You like?"

"I do like," Netti said hesitantly.

"Po Mire and I want you to know," Mu Mire said, "want you to very well know, you are welcome to come visit the Mire any time. We have dozens of young people just like you."

"Dozens? Like me? What do you mean?"

"Well, what's your name?

"Netti. Netti, I'm called."

Well, Netti," Mu Mire continued, "we could tell you were troubled. We saw you from afar. No doubt about it. Lonely. Disappointed. Sad to the world. You were crying your eyes out, weren't you? The Mire, we run it, is a turn-around place; enlightenment and contentment is what we offer. Sum it up in one word and that word is: happiness. You're welcome to visit us. Any time."

"Thank you. How much do I owe?"

Mu Mire and Po Mire flashed their smiles and spun around. Their twirling tunics rose up, revealing, for an instant, their bare bottoms in good-bye. They walked quickly away, seeming to float over the muddy ground.

21

Gstan's Journey

"'Zi – THAT'S what I call you when I think about you, which is just about all of the time – I love you. So let's get pledged. Just like Milli did to her guy, Twigg . . . just go over to Barclaw's and do it.' Nope. Not good. Try again. 'Ziiza, you've got the most wonderful set of children I've ever met. They're growing up good. Seem to like me, too. My gosh, Dg – I count him as one of the set – has even stopped biting me.'" He stopped to visualize Ziiza laughing at his joke (Dg had never bitten him). "'Well, I was thinking they might like someone to be a new popa for them. Oh, I know I could never replace their real popa, the one you never talk about. But they must want one, must miss the one they had.'" He paused. "'More than one?'" He grinned; he could not help it.

"This isn't going right. Not right at all. New approach. 'Remember the flowers I brought you? You stuck them all over the Sita. Looked so pretty till they wilted from the slooze fumes. Hey, Ziiza, they weren't for the establishment, they were for you. Didn't you see that? I was saying I loved you, cared for you. Sorry, but I haven't had much practice at this. Heck, way back when I asked you to be partners in Hill Burrow, I loved you then. Look, aren't you lonely like me? Sick of it? Oh, maybe not, with your kids and all your customers and friends. But that's not the same. Let's be partners in life, all of us: you, me, Org, Milli – well, she's gone – Netti, Com, Govvi, and Edu. And Dg. The biggest, happiest family in Beaverton. It doesn't have to be Beaverton, either. You want to move? The coast? The valley? The hot country? We'll all move. Anywhere you like. Except Swarm City, that is.'"

He sat in front of his burrow looking at the Sundown Range, where mountains should be, where the sunset should be, but were not because of the gray-black hanging clouds. He cupped his hand around his ear, waiting for her answer. Looking for her smile. Waiting for her to lean into his arms and kiss him, push him away, and say, softly, deliberately, as if she had been anticipating his proposal and did not want to answer too quickly, "Yes, Gstan, yes. I love you. I've loved you from the first."

"'Oh, I see. You want to think it over. I can understand that.'" He flipped a stick at a bush. "'I'm no prize; don't think I don't know it. Probably can't compare to the first guy,' – boy, I've got to get this out. 'I mean he must have been something. Your sons are big, Org and Edu. Com's not so big, but he's lithe and strong. Tall, he must have been tall. I'm no taller than you. But that's all right, isn't it? Brains. They've got brains, plenty of brains. You, him, smart as all get out. Passed them on to your kids. Govvi, she explodes brains. Edu, too. Don't think I haven't noticed.

"'Me? You think I'm a pessimist, don't like it when I say Beaverton's star has reached its zenith and is heading down. I've been here longer than you have, Zi; I've got some perspective. Anyway, I like to think of myself as a realist. After all, you can't be a pessimist and sell real estate, now can you? No way. Tough, hard-headed realist.'" Gstan scooted into the opening to get out of the sprinkles starting to fall. "'Tough, hard-headed realist. How does that square with what you think of me?'" he repeated. "What I think," he softened his voice, "of myself?"

With that, Gstan rested his chin on his hands. "Let's face it, Mister Realist," he muttered, "it's not working. Ziiza's not working. Hill Burrow's not working. Maybe I was too early. Maybe too late. With her? With it? I don't know. I do know this development is sucking me dry. Financially. Emotionally. I'm linked to failure. Is that it? Is that it? She doesn't respect me, doesn't think I'm of any consequence? Thinks I'm just another Sita's Lair sloozer, all talk and no beaver? Well, I've got a string of successful ventures behind me. Oh, a few reversals along the way. Some bad luck. Anybody can have that.

"Maybe I'm out of touch. Rock running? Have you ever seen anything so pointless, so absurd? But the fools love it. Running themselves sick. Bloodying their heads. For a few cheers. A slap on the back. Proves my point, Beaverton's lost its purpose and is on its way down. And that's not pessimism, Ziiza!" he screamed at the dark clouds, shaking his finger. He shook it again, slower this time. Thought for a moment. "Let's face it Gstan, you've run out of excuses. No more of this slow-time-of-year, money's-a-little-tight, the-old-man's-hurting-sales kind of stuff. Hill B's a dump and Ziiza don't want you. I never thought I'd say this out loud, Gstan old boy, but you're through around here. Through with Beaverton. And Beaverton's through with you. You need a serious change of landscape. Complete with a serious head tightening."

Even in the fullness of youth Gstan had not been what one would call an outdoorsman. He had hunted some, fished when he had had to. To him the outdoors was something to get *through*, not to be *in*, certainly not to enjoy. He was a settlement man, the larger the better; a people person, he preferred jawing for his dinner. His journey from the Old Side to Beaverton had been relatively easy, all things considered; he was never tested. A large flotilla had held try-outs for paddlers. (His reasons for coming? Curiosity and to make his young man's fortune.) Although inexperienced and on the small side he was selected because he was single and had a small kit. Amazingly, nothing went wrong: no storms, upset canoes, creature or animal attacks, illnesses, fights, desertions, split-ups. Their leader, Jacobez, was an energetic, intelligent man, the "Beaverton type," later a respected vendor and close friend of Popamayor's. Gstan worked hard enough to earn a sleeping place under a canoe, thus avoiding the night wind and rain. On the first day at Sea he willed himself into a trance-like state, pushed his paddle, and, in due time, "woke up" to find himself in Beaverton. In short, his journey could not have been more different than Ziiza's. He had hardly been outside of Beaverton since.

That night, however, he broke with his habit, his preference, his very nature, and slept outside. To confirm my commitment, he told himself. When the cold drizzle finally soaked through his robe, then dripped into his ear as he pulled it tighter around him, he did not move, although he was next to his burrow opening. "Might as well get used to it."

He woke to the faint morning light, stripped water from his face, shook his robe, and bellowed, "Good morning, Hill Burrowers. Meet the new Gstan, the travelin' man. I'll be gone before you can blink an eye." Of course no one heard. There weren't any other residents of Hill Burrow except Old Man Haracosh, and he was away fishing or something.

He stuffed his shoulder sack – dried beaver tail, pressed berries, wet sleeping robe – stuck his knife in his belt, donned his rain hat, slung his cloak over his shoulders, and, without bothering to cover the entrance, jumped down from the ledge. He walked Outer Circle to its intersection with South Trail without meeting a person. By full daylight he was out of sight of Beaverton. By mid-morning, he was farther from Beaverton than he had been for years.

The first few days of a journey set the tone, or seem to: pleasant or unpleasant. If a sign was needed, Gstan got one. Late in the morning of the third day, while he was stopped to chew some dried tail, the sun came out and lit up a small woodland pond. The evergreens reflecting on its surface changed from black-on-gray to green-on-silver before his eyes. That was enough to put a smile on his face and confirm his hasty decision. And confirm his direction: south. South for the sunshine. South to escape the rain's chill. South for adventure. South to reinvent himself. And south to forget Ziiza. Forget loving Ziiza.

South Trail was narrow and appeared little used by the time he was a couple of weeks from Beaverton. But that was deceptive. Rather than hug the banks of the North-flowing Son as the Grand Muma Trail hugged its river, this one ran far back along the low valley-forming hills, grass-covered on the warm sides and dotted with widely-spaced oaks. An all-season trail along the river was impossible, anyway. The heart of the valley was a labyrinth of islands and lakes, thickets and sloughs, through which the river flowed and overflowed, a game haven in drier months (although with their crude weapons and the easy availability of beaver tails, only a few hardy out-settlers hunted), and impenetrable swamps during high water. He met no one on the trail, although he passed many side trails. Whether these were animal runs or led to isolated camps he did not bother to find out.

Food soon became a problem. No inexpensive sliced beaver tail from H&G vendors. No giant valley beaver. This was mountain beaver country, a different animal: small, slippery, and intelligent. Catch them barehanded as Castor's men and the poachers did? Forget it. But when food is short, being a small man has its advantages; scant rations power many footsteps. Birds saved him, swans and geese. The waterways were covered with them, thousands upon thousands. It took him days to learn. But a hungry man learns – or he starves. It was a matter of getting close, close enough to throw a rock as the geese sounded the alarm, ran on the water, and rose in a clamor of honking and wing beating. Fist-sized rocks were ideal, small enough to throw a distance, large enough to knock a bird down. Sometimes. Then the cold swim to retrieve. Gstan was a fire borrower, not a fire builder, so he ate the birds raw. He did not mind. On sunny days when the pine pitch flowed, he rolled a stick in it and sucked as he walked. Better than sucking a stone.

In time the valley narrowed, then expired. South Trail rose gradually and the hills grew more pronounced, until some could be called mountains. Although heavy evergreen forest stood above him, the trail wound its way through grassland – kept down by lightning-caused fires – and scarred and blackened oaks. Up-rises, created by tributaries of the Son, provided splendid vistas. The mirror pond sign had been true. As he walked south the weather improved; instead of walking into winter as the season told him, he seemed to be walking into summer. He had still not seen a person, and, as he walked out of mud country, noticed no footprints in the dusty trail. He encountered no dangerous animals – bears, cats, gazors – although they were certainly around, and in great numbers. Perhaps the abundance of grazing animals – deer, elk, springers – satisfied their appetites.

But it was not summertime, as Gstan was about to discover. The trail wound down into a broad, sun-filled bowl. Then rose, steeper and steeper, higher and higher, colder and colder, even in daytime. He was down to his last goose wing and the hard climb made him ravenously hungry. Strangely, however, he was enjoying himself. As he hardened to the trail and outdoor life, he took great satisfaction in his accumulation of miles. To keep himself company, he carried on a running conversation with Ziiza, as if she were his traveling companion. No more proposals or whiney excuses, just along-the-trail banter, sharing observations of the moment: a perching eagle, a woodchuck sticking his head out of his hole, a cloud formation – "Does it mean rain?" – even animal tracks.

He walked up, past the tree line, then over hard-packed snow, which supported his weight most of the time. Late on the fourth day out of the sun bowl he reached the crest, the crest being a leveling out. Ahead was a slot in the rocks through which he saw blue sky instead of more mountainside. High up, the walls held hundreds of menacing icicles; the floor was ankle deep with their smashed pieces. He stopped talking to himself and pushed his feet through the loose ice that would not support him, like wading through water that clinked, crunched, and tinkled. The close-in rock walls sucked at his warmth. Crack. An ice spear crashed to the floor and shattered. I have to get out of here fast, he thought as he kicked through the ice. When he reached the far opening, he stopped, panting. The sun hung low in the west. He held his arms high to absorb what warmth he could. Ahead, to the south by the sun, the mountain fell away in a long gradual slope, not nearly as steep as the one he had climbed. To the east and west he saw more mountains, mostly snow-covered, but a few showing rock gray and tree green. He examined the trail route again, planning. What's this? Spaced depressions in the snow. Could they be. . . .

"You made it." Gstan's heart thumped, his knees buckled, and he went down. "Congratulations." A laugh. Prickles ran up Gstan's back into his neck. He turned. The voice was a lump of fur sitting in a wall recess facing the sun. Gstan realized that if the voice had not spoken he would never have noticed; he was completely in this person's power. Shaggy black hair and a puffed-out beard blended into a fur hood, revealing only large shining eyes and a long nose. A large pack lay next to him. Some distance away, not within easy reach, a long spear or walking stick leaned against the wall.

Gstan gulped for air. "You startled me," he said, gripping his knife. The fur lump did not move. He relaxed, realizing that if the lump had meant to attack him, it would be over by now. The lump smiled, revealing large, white teeth. "I haven't heard a person's voice in weeks," was all Gstan could think to say.

The lump pried itself away from the wall as if it had been frozen to it and unfolded, slowly, stiffly, revealing a man, who at full height towered over Gstan. "Leegs," he said. "You've probably heard of me. Leegs's Delivery – Beaverton to Big Bay, Big Bay to Beaverton – if you're from Beaverton or thereabouts, which, from the direction you're heading, I assume you are."

"Yes, yes, Leegs," Gstan said. "Yes, I've heard of you. I've never used your service, though. I'm in real estate. Doesn't move much, you know." He extended his hand. Leegs wrapped his fingers around Gstan's and squeezed. Gstan winced. Leegs relaxed his grip and pumped Gstan's arm. The message was clear.

"And you?"

"What?"

"Your name? Who are you?"

"Oh, sorry," Gstan said, clenching and unclenching his fist behind his back. "Gstan. Long of Beaverton. Currently taking a break. A ramble, you could say. Going south for the sunshine. South to clear my head."

"Well, Gstan, my man," Leegs said, "it's a good thing you found me. If you don't mind a word of advice from someone who's traveled this route many a time, stop right here for the night. Too exposed on the trail you're headed down. Not enough time left today. Wind rises when the sun sets. No place to get out of it. Not even a boulder to hide behind. If you think it's cold now, wait until midnight. Or later. I have an extra robe, so you'll be all right. Got any food?"

"A little," Gstan said, stretching it.

"I have some extra tail," Leegs said, reaching for his pack, "and you're welcome to it."

The sun slipped away and they moved inside the notch. No fire, of course; not a twig to be had. Leegs was a man born to his job, though not unfriendly he was a loner who thought of it as a calling, a daily challenge to get through in all kinds of weather, "except in the worst of snowstorms." Leegs slept sitting, with his back to the wall, his arms wrapped around his legs, pulling them tight for warmth. He's *all* legs, Gstan thought, observing his knees sticking above his shoulders. A good candidate for rock running. Twice Org's stride. Three times Sufx's. No, not him; he's probably not that stupid. Then again, with this senseless job, maybe he is. The wind came up strong and swept through the notch. Gstan was cold even with Leegs's robe. That, together with icicles crashing down all night, made real sleep impossible.

If Big Bay was his destination, Leegs told him in the morning, and it ought to be since he had come this far, he had completed the hard part. Right here. Although a long way off, it was "more or less downhill all the way." Big Bay was the second largest settlement west of the Sunups, he told him –

Gstan knew that – second only to Beaverton, as much smaller than Beaverton as Beaverton was to mysterious Swarm City far to the east, on the other side of the Sunups. Or so he was told; he had never been to Swarm City. The delivery business was bad, he added.

"Join the club," Gstan replied, "Mine's terrible, too. One of the reasons I'm here. One of them."

Not that way, Leegs explained patiently. *His* business was bad all of the time. Most of his runs were empty, but he went anyway in case someone at the other end had a shipment waiting for him. Animal problems? Gstan inquired. No better or worse than on the trail he'd covered was Leegs's reply. He added a final bit of advice: "Before you come to the valley you will have to traverse a narrow trail, so narrow there's no place for two people to pass. This is Splat's territory. Splat the footpad. Splat the trail thief. Let him take what he wants. Resist, and you're a dead man. Repeat: let him take what he wants and you'll be on your way."

"How do you get through with *your* shipments?"

Leegs showed his oversized teeth. "Splat and I have what I'll call an understanding. We arrived at it some time ago."

"Uh-huh."

As Gstan hurried down the mountain the snow on the trail grew thinner and slushier until Leegs's tracks were no longer visible. He soaked in the sunshine in the crisp morning air. Just below the snow, the trail narrowed to a line so thin he had to place one foot carefully in front of the other. To his left the mountain rose straight up. Below him the canyon was so steep and narrow he could not see bottom. After awhile he heard water. Rounding a corner he saw a spring gushing from the wall twenty feet above the trail. Or where the trail should have been. The water tore through a cut, spun over the edge and plunged into the canyon. When Gstan stopped to assess the situation – he could not jump across the cut – he felt a sharp point in his shoulder. "Ouch!" he said, flailing his arms to keep his balance, to keep from falling into the torrent.

The point was withdrawn. Then thrust again, lower down, harder, into the small of his back. "Drop your pack behind you. Drop your weapons behind you. Do not move. Do not turn around." The unseen man spoke in a pleasant civilized voice, just loud enough to be heard over the sound of the water, a Saturday morning voice that could just as well have been saying, "Two handfuls of beaver tail, please," to an H&G vendor. Gstan did as he was told. The point was withdrawn and he heard his pack scritch away on the gravel. Jab again. A spear, not a knife, he concluded, as he did not sense Splat, it had to be Splat, that close to him.

"No good," said the voice. Gstan saw his knife sail over his head and disappear silently into the canyon.

"Why don't you give it back if you don't want it?" Gstan said. "It's life or death for me."

Whap! The spear shaft stung his shoulder. Whap! Whap!

"What do you want?" Gstan cried, chopping off a provocative *now*.

The spear prodded him toward the thundering water. Whap! A slender tree trunk he had not noticed spanned the cut, slimy and black. He stepped down and onto the trunk. It twisted in its moorings, threatening to spill him. The spear point pushed him on. Gstan flung out his arm, tried to grab hold of something, anything to steady himself. His hand found rocks behind the cascade. Two terrifying steps and he was across. He hurried on without looking back.

He was starving, eating whatever he could find. And learning. Pitch-covered sticks drew crunchy ants from their hills. They were best, but any insect would do. As would snakes, caught sunning themselves on the trailside – if he was quick enough with a stick. Fish? Impossible to catch. Rotten plums? Sun-dried berries? Too few. He made his way south.

A late afternoon thunderstorm drove him into the cave. He would never have found it but for the lightening flash that lit up the entrance. He clambered up a pile of sharp rubble and collapsed inside. How long he slept he had no idea, but it was a sleep of total exhaustion. He woke to the smell of food cooking, so delicious it pained his stomach, started it churning. He rolled over, blinked his crusty eyes, and rubbed them open. He saw a fire and crawled toward it on hands and knees.

The coals glowed softly in a pit lined with smooth stones sloping to the fire, covered with popping, roasting meat. Gstan slapped his hand on the nearest piece, pulled it to him, and ate ravenously. The best tasting meat and sauce since Tip-n-Dips. Perhaps ever. He tossed the bone into the fire and took a new piece on the return pass. Again and again. Only the thirst-provoking salty taste made him stop.

Thirst and the faint light he saw farther back in the cave. This is a big one, Gstan thought, even before his confused mind registered that someone must have prepared this food. Someone nearby. He stood and hugged his belly with both hands, as if to cover the evidence of his excess. His second thought was to leave immediately, take as much food as he could carry before anyone noticed. But the light enticed him. He entered a narrow corridor. Not one light but many, evenly-spaced along the sides. Not only that, as he walked closer, he saw that each light was a different softly-glowing color: blue, green, orange, yellow, purple. And another thing: after a dozen steps the odor shifted from that of delicious roasting meat to that of a nauseous something or other.

Gstan tiptoed to the first opening and looked into what appeared to be a small sub-cave. A thin figure with pale white arms sat on the floor holding a rectangular object. He jerked his head away in surprise when he realized that the bluish light this sub-cave cast came not from a fire but the object itself. For it was bluish, not blue, not sky blue, not Sea blue, not even bluestone blue. Here was the most beautiful blue color he had ever seen, probably the most beautiful *thing* he had ever seen – in the worst-smelling place that could possibly exist. His own bachelor burrow-keeping, even Old Man Haracosh's, could not compare. The man – he assumed it was a man but could not tell – was talking. Talking to himself. Or talking to the object. Gstan withdrew, pressed his back to the wall as if to make himself invisible, and listened. "Ya, ya, ya, yoo, ya, yoo, yoo, yoo. Yoo, yoo, ya, yoo, yoo, yoo, yoo, yoo." The talker, or chanter, continued, varying pitch, inflection, volume, ever so slightly with each series of yoo-yas and ya-yoos.

Along the corridor and on the opposite side, an orange glow drew him to it. A look inside revealed another chanter rubbing a similar object. He spoke-sung his peculiar version: "Ya, yoo, ya, yoo, ya, yoo, ya, yoo. Ya, yoo, ya, yoo, ya, yoo, ya, yoo." That's the first one that's made sense, Gstan mocked, chuckling to himself. As the first chanter was thin, this one was the opposite. Pendulous arms slapped his mountainous form as he stroked the object, which appeared to be a simple stone polished flat with parallel cut sides. It glowed orange, as beautiful and seductive in its way as the bluish one. Compared to Blue's cell, Orange's smelled worse if that was possible. The cause? The huge mound-of-a-man's sub-cave was crammed with rotting meat and unidentifiable trash, leaving only room for him to sit. And a path to the opening. He might even be sitting on the stuff, Gstan thought, as he withdrew.

Holding his nose, Gstan passed several openings glowing green, yellow, purple, and bluish again. He had to get out of there, he knew it. Just one more look, in this sub-cave. Different from the others. No glow. Dimly lit by an oil lamp. Gstan peered. The man inside appeared to be like himself, except for his bleached arms. Instead of chanting yoo-yas, this man was singing to a pair of stones, which he rubbed together, possibly grinding or polishing them. As with the others, his sub-cave was heaped with garbage. Foul dark liquid leached onto the floor. Oblivious to all of this, the man sat in the puddle rubbing his stones. Gstan looked up and noticed for the first time that the walls and ceiling were polished and flat and met at right angles. Flat walls and sharp corners! Gstan pressed his fist to his forehead in amazement. Along with every other weird thing in this weird place, these sub-caves were perfectly-formed rectangles in the rock. The effort to carve them! The precision! Why?

The man clapped his stones together, set them down, and stood up. Gstan froze. The man turned, saw Gstan, and shrieked, "Yoo, ya, yoo, ya! No, that's not it," he corrected himself. "Help, help! Intruder! Help me!" He flung himself at Gstan, flailing at him with open hands, slapping, pummeling, inflicting . . . no pain, no damage, no result. Gstan pushed him away with an easy shove. The man's a weakling, no strength at all, he thought. Disgusting. He doesn't know how to . . . Uh-oh. The corridor filled with men. They advanced on Gstan, ghost-like shapes in the colored lighting, circling him, cursing without conviction. They seemed confused, seemed to know he should not be in their cave but had no idea what to do about it. Gstan swung at a head. Head and body dropped to the floor. He popped a nose. "Owie!" squealed the recipient. His hand came away bloody. Soft hands pit-patted his head, his face, his back, his chest. Gstan brushed them away. This is laughable, he thought; I'll just slap them down and walk out of here. "Hey-eeeeee," he yelled. The slapping stopped. "Ha!" he jeered. "No guts! No fight!"

"I'll get him!" boomed a voice from behind. Orange had moved his ponderous bulk to the fray, taking up most of the passageway. "Out of the way brother Hieyeques," he said. They pressed against the wall as he waddled toward Gstan. With great effort, or, perhaps for the intimidating effect, he raised his meaty arms over his head and toppled onto Gstan – taking the Hieyeques unfortunate enough to be standing nearby with him. Crunch! Snap! Gstan waited for the pain, but there was none. Must be them, he thought. Orange's blubber flowed out and over him, sealing him to the floor. He tried to breathe. "Call Silvoo," was the last thing he heard before he blacked out.

Gstan woke, or, more accurately, regained consciousness, in a dark room. His throat screamed for water. He tried to move, but his arms were tied securely in front of him, his back against a cold, flat surface. When he leaned forward to test his bindings a rope around his neck choked him. He cocked his head to look sideways, trying to kick in his night vision. A faint light outlined a rectangular shape. I must be in one of those sub-caves, he thought. As he struggled to free his hands, he heard voices. The opening brightened. A face appeared at the side, apparently to check on him. Pulled away. Two men with torches entered and stood at attention on either side of the opening. Gstan shut his eyes to block the light's sting, then squinted to see what was going on. A man appeared between the torchbearers, so close he could make out only smooth-hide leggings, feet spread apart, and hands placed authoritatively on hips.

"So this is the stranger," the man growled, "who has entered our cave, stolen our food, and stolen our secrets. I will deal with him. Now."

The man turned and left the sub-cave, followed by the torchbearers. Another entered, untied him and jerked him to his feet with the neck rope. He pushed him out, marched him down the corridor, made a sharp turn and entered a large, rough-walled, high-ceilinged room lit by two fires. Except for a narrow walkway, it was filled with robed men sitting on the floor. The ceiling danced with color from the varied and moving stones.

When the leader reached the mid-point between the fires he turned to the men, and said, "Who will tell the story?"

Blue began, followed by Orange. Then a small man called Cook.

"Hieyeques," the leader said, glaring at Gstan, "I have made my decision."

"Hey, wait a minute," Gstan yelled. "Don't I get to say anything?"

"You do not." The leader slapped his face. Gstan's head popped back. This one hurt. Ceiling lights jiggled faster as the men laughed.

Gstan plunged ahead desperately: "I'm a traveler from Beaverton. I don't even know where I am. I crawled into your cave to get out of the storm."

"I know of no storm."

"Of course you don't, you guys never go outside, from the looks of you." The torchbearers lowered their fires menacingly. "Well, most of you, anyway."

"You ate our food," the leader said. "You stole our secrets." Then to the men, "Hieyeques, I say again, I have made my decision: the thief must die. Are we agreed?"

As he struggled to rise, Orange screamed: "Yes, Silvoo, glorious leader, yes! Yes, all-knowing Silvoo, yes! Death! Death! Death to the thief. Death to the one who stole our secrets." He dropped, exhausted.

"Death! Death! Death!" the men shouted.

Silvoo's mouth formed a cruel, self-satisfied smile, made the more menacing by the firelight and glowing stones. His left eyebrow fluttered in a high-speed tic. He calmed it with a finger. After surveying his men he raised his hands, palms out. Quiet. Quiet down, the hands commanded – but not too fast, his expression said, I'm enjoying this. Silence, except for Gstan's heavy breathing. Silvoo spoke: "In the morning, he dies."

22

The Mire

MONDAY MORNING Netti went to H&G and waited. Since meeting Mu Mire and Po Mire a week ago, she had thought about them constantly. They were so pleasant, so friendly, so different. And Mire-root. For the first time since the fire, and especially since Milli had left, her headaches were under control, sometimes reduced to a dull, manageable throb, sometimes gone altogether. She liked to nibble root chunks while lying under a big, low-limbed fir, out of the way where no one could disturb. Although she was pleased to help her muma with her rock running experiments, flattered that her weaving and basketry skills were of value, the idea of yet another family-style job – she could see it coming – did not thrill her. (School? Grassyknoll was a distant memory.) If Mire-root wasn't bringing actual relief and actual happiness, it was a very good substitute. Yet, there was a downside. When the Mire-root's sweet bliss wore off, the headaches returned, and she plunged deeper into despair – all the more reason to nibble the good stuff. "Why are they so late?" Netti asked herself when she arrived. "This is the same place, isn't it? They come here Monday mornings. They said so."

H&G began its business, filling with noise, smells, and activity. By mid-day Mu Mire and Po Mire had not appeared. Netti fidgeted and paced, checking and rechecking her memory – and her diminishing supply of Mire-root. This had to be the place. Had to be. The more anxious and upset she became, the more her head throbbed. She pressed her hands to her temples and walked. Then ran. Past Sister Sissi's. Around to Skedaddle. Even to S-I's empty stage, painful as it was to her.

Tuesday morning she slipped out of her muma's temporary shelter even before Edu was up. She had not slept. It was unlikely they would show up until next Monday, she thought, but she could not risk missing them. What else to do? She massaged her head and prepared for a long wait.

"Netti, Netti, my dear." Mu Mire came toward her, followed by Po Mire. They stood side by side, twirling their tunics, flashing their bottoms, evidently their signature greeting and parting display. Netti smiled and laughed a weak laugh; she had to. "I'll bet you came yesterday, didn't you, dear," Mu Mire continued, "We're so sorry." Netti nodded, revealing all. "Big business. Big business to attend to. But we came as quickly as we could," leaving *we knew you'd be waiting* unspoken.

Po Mire dropped a small root in her hand. Netti popped it into her mouth and chewed. They backed away and waited, smiling serenely while they rubbed each other's thighs. Her headache did not stop immediately, but it was about to, or it felt like it was about to. So, so good.

"Have you thought about it?" Mu Mire broke the silence. "What we discussed last week? We've just had an opening at the Center. It won't last long."

"I don't know," Netti said. "I don't know what Muma would think. After the shock of Milli's going away."

"It isn't a commitment or anything," Po Mire said. "If you don't like it, you're back the next day. Right here. On this spot. Guaranteed. Just like that."

"I'd like to, but I don't. . . ."

"We know how difficult it is," he said. "Tell you what. We'll do our errands and return at sundown. If you're here, you're here. If you're not, you're not. Fair enough?" He smiled.

"I'll try," Netti said weakly, then added, "Could I have a few more until then?"

As the sun fell and H&G emptied, Netti waited, clutching her basket. The Mire sounded interesting, even exciting. Where is the Mire? she wondered. After all, she wasn't moving away like Milli. Forever. It must be nearby, else how did Mu Mire and Po Mire – such nice folks – visit Beaverton each Monday? And Mire-root: where did it come from? The headache was gone, replaced by a serene feeling like the one she got sitting on the grass, legs crossed, fingers tapping, listening to Milli singing with Twigg.

Po Mire came to her, passed a handful of root, and in a low voice said, "Come along, Netti, we have a good walk ahead of us." A business-like walk evidently, sans twirling tunics and bare bottoms. When they reached Outer Circle they stopped. Although it was dark, Mu Mire tied a headband on Netti and pulled it over her eyes. "Just a little security measure," she said, "until we know you better. Now turn around." She and Po Mire twirled her around and around until they were certain she did not know which direction she was facing. Mu Mire took her hand and guided her, blindfolded, along a trail.

After they had walked a few miles on fairly level ground, crossing no rivers, Po Mire jerked her blindfold off and said, "No need for this anymore. Sorry for the inconvenience, my dear; we must take precautions."

A sliver of new moon cast a faint light in the east. Netti tried to orient herself. We are probably going south on a trail near the North-flowing Son, she surmised, although it did not greatly concern her. The trail curved along the edge of a good-sized lake, its still water gleaming in the faint moonlight. Po Mire hurried along. Mu Mire panted to keep up. When the trail left the lakeside, Po Mire headed into the trees. "We'll take a break here," he said in an exaggerated whisper, as if the moonlight would amplify his voice. "In case anyone's following us." He passed her a chunk of Mire-root.

Mu Mire sat and pulled Netti down with her. Po Mire slipped down to the lakeside, squatted behind a bush, and waited, peering through the branches. Netti yawned, leaned her head against Mu Mire's shoulder, and fell asleep.

When Po Mire nudged her awake, the moon was directly above, peeking between slow-moving clouds. "Trail's clear," he said. "Let's be off."

As they walked, the trees thinned and became smaller, as elderberry and wetland bushes replaced the scrub oak and cedar, which had replaced the thick firs. Long stretches of trail were under ankle-deep water, and the parts above water were a squishy mix of needles, leaves, and mud. They picked their way along until at first light, the trail, more accurately the muddy slot, stopped at the edge of what appeared to be a large, pale green meadow. Po Mire took Netti's hand. Mu Mire took the other. They stepped forward onto the softest, moss-like growth Netti's feet had ever touched. "Woooo," she said, almost losing her balance. "What's going on?" They stiffened their arms to steady her.

"You, my dear," Po Mire said proudly, "are entering the Mire. Hold on tight and do exactly as I do." With each step the surface quivered and sank. Each time she lifted a foot, the depression remained momentarily, then broke free with a gurgle-whump, as if a sucking force below was resisting its return to form. Ripples rolled out in ever-expanding circles. She fought for balance, and were it not for their assistance, would have gone down. As they made their way slowly across the undulating mass – to what destination she could not tell, except that they were heading toward low trees – Po Mire recited numbers aloud. Louder than necessary, Netti thought, as if high volume validated them. At intervals, when he reached a certain count, he turned: left, or right, slightly, or sharply, once so sharply they almost doubled back. They were following an invisible but very definite pathway.

They worked their way toward the low trees, which as they drew closer were taller than she had thought. Po Mire led them up a rise and through a narrow opening in the trees. Netti took a breath, relieved to be back on steady, if damp, ground. "This is our home, Netti," Mu Mire said, squeezing her hand. "Mire Island. Now it's your home, too." They walked a few steps to a clearing. Mu Mire dropped her hand and stepped onto what appeared to be the same surface as the Mire, except this one had bits of grass growing out of the moss and did not move. Two rows of small woven-mat shelters, about twenty in each row, ran down the middle of the clearing, set so close that their edges touched, giving the appearance of rows of pointed teeth. Each shelter, if that was what they were, was barely large enough for a person to slide into. Beyond and in a direct line with the shelter rows were two larger shelters, head high, and of the same shape and material. Behind the large shelters was a lumpy pile covered with Beaverton-style woven mats. If this truly was an island, Netti thought, and if it was completely surrounded by the sucking Mire, it made a perfect hideout. Mu Mire led her to one of the low shelters. "It's been a long walk, Netti dear. Crawl in and get some rest. Sleep as long as you like." She helped her slide in.

Netti woke to a mid-day sun filling the shelter with its warmth and the pleasant smell of reed matting, moss, and clipped grass all around. She also woke to the thumping of hand drums, the shrill sound of reed flutes, and the tinkle of sticks on shells. And voices, calling her name, "Netti, Netti, come out, we know you're in there." She rubbed her eyes and wiggled out of the shelter. A line of men faced her. Behind them a line of women. All close to her age, give or take a few years. As they talked and played (each had an instrument), their Mu-and-Po-Mire-style tunics swung with the beat and they twisted their toes in the soft, wet ground. A smiling young woman with plump braids hanging to her waist handed Netti a stick-and-shell instrument. The women's line joined with the men's and they circled the shelters, dipping, twirling, singing:

Welcome, Netti,
Welcome, Netti,
Welcome, Netti.
Welcome.
Welcome to the Mire.

After two revolutions, they stopped in the space between the two large shelters and the smaller ones and arranged themselves in a line. Braids took Netti's hand and led her to a position facing the middle of the line, about ten paces from the people. She returned to the line, gave a hand signal, and they sat. She motioned to Netti to do the same. They sang:

It is the Mire's desire.
It is the Mire's desire.

At that, Mu Mire and Po Mire leapt from the large shelters, burst through their line, halted in front of Netti, and flung open their tunics – which, although she had seen this move before, caused her to cringe with embarrassment. Po Mire sang:

Your welcome here is most assured.
We trust you'll feel at ease.
I'm Po.

I'm Mu. Mu Mire added, as she pirouetted clumsily.

Taking it as their cue, the others screamed:

And we're the Mirees.
The Mirees.

Po Mire, after their "spontaneous" declaration of identity, cleared his throat, and continued:

And together we
Will blend in like a breeze.

Mu Mire picked it up in a quavering voice, head tilted, hands pressed to neck, spacing her words:

A breeze to carry love across
Our refuge in the Mire.
This tiny island Paradise

Po Mire joined her in duet:

Far from those who never tire,

With rising indignation:

Of trampling on our feelings hard.

So hard we cannot breathe.
No more we'll have our spirits crushed.
No more we'll have to seethe.

Mu Mire took over, solo, chin up and arms swinging, marching in place:

With pride we cast them all aside.
They shall not interfere
With this, our sweet Society,
Where everyone's a peer.

The "Mirees" jumped to their feet and burst into chorus:

It is the Mire's desire, my dears,
It is the Mire's desire.
That everyone, especially you,
Be happy in the Mire.

The females sank to the ground. The males stepped forward, closed ranks, approached Netti, and sang:

Our precious roots grow deep and long,
Within the Mire, well hidden.
We plant, we pick, we cultivate,
Meet every quota bidden.

The men backed away, merged into line, and sat. The women rose, advanced, and continued:

With gentle care we scrub and clean – and chop and top, and dry and store, and pile,
and pack.

Laughter.

Prepare our roots for chewing,
And best of all, throughout the day – and night.

Giggles.

We love what we are doing.

The women backed into line, locked arms with the men, and marched in place. Po Mire stepped forward and sang:

I travel far and wide,
My clientele to serve.
Once hooked on Mire-root, you see,
I have them – I have them – I have them – where I want them.

"I know it doesn't rhyme," Po Mire confided, "but you get the idea. Present company excepted, of course." Knowing laughter. He looked at Mu Mire. She raised her eyes and trilled:

And so,
And so,
Each week we walk between the lines,
Dispensing Mire-root ration.
One handful, choice grade, per good and willing worker.

The Mirees extended their hands and cheered.

And picking out, with greatest care.
Two Mirees for duration.

More cheering. Mu Mire, Po Mire, and the Mirees in chorus:

It is the Mire's desire, my dears
It is the Mire's desire.
That everyone –
Especially you, Netti –
Be happy in the Mire.

After repeating the chorus they surged forward, surrounded Netti, and hugged her. Mu Mire slipped behind her shelter and returned with a basket of Mire-root. "Double-root celebration," she cried. "You first, Netti. Hold out both hands."

* * *

"Govvi," Ziiza yelled, "find Netti for me, will you. I can't seem to get this rock cushion thing to stay together."

"She's gone."

"It's come down to this: I need a good basket maker. I've got to come up with something that looks good and holds together. Otherwise, why would anyone buy it? Anyway, I should have asked her before, except I like to work things out myself."

"She's gone, Muma."

"Well, go get her. Bring her here. I need her."

"I mean she's disappeared," Govvi said with exasperation. "I haven't seen her since yesterday. Neither has Edu. Anybody."

"Why didn't someone tell me?"

"We were waiting for her to come back," Edu said. "Except she hasn't. It's only today."

Ziiza dropped the mass of sprung reeds and snarled, "Where's Com? Where's Org? I can't keep track of everyone all the time."

"Org's out running," Govvi replied in a subdued voice.

"Com's exploring, I guess," Edu said. "He sure wasn't in school today."

"This is what we're going to do," Ziiza said, as if she were back on the Sea Trace. "Govvi, you stay here. When Org and Com come around, grab them and don't let them get away. Edu, you and Dg trot around the Circle. Ask questions. Find out all you can. Then return here. I'm going over to H&G. Something's not right. I should have figured when she left so early."

Ziiza headed straight to Bitta: information central. She was standing on her usual round, quiet at the moment, swatting Hobart who had jumped on top of her head and was shifting his weight from foot to foot, his tail shielding Bitta's eyes like a visor. "Back on my shoulder, you dreadful bird," she said in mock disgust.

Under any other circumstances, Ziiza would have laughed, Bitta and Hobart looked so silly. "Bitta, Bitta, have you seen my daughter, Netti? She's gone." Bitta shook her head. After listening to Ziiza she walked with her to Town Hall where they consulted Barclaw.

"Today's Wednesday," Barclaw said, pulling on his beard. "That part fits."

"What do you mean?"

"Don't rush me, please," Barclaw continued. "Next question: Was she acting unusual in any way?"

"Well, she's been in a funk ever since Milli left," Ziiza answered. "But that's not surprising, they were so close."

"Hanging around H&G?" Barclaw's eyes narrowed. He turned to Bitta, as if to say: I'm surprised you're not onto this.

"Yes," Ziiza said, "but she and Milli always spent time here. All of the kids do. You know that."

"One more question," Barclaw said. "Think back to last week. Did she seem groggy? Sleeping more than usual?"

"I don't know. I've been wrapped up in my new project. I suppose she might have been."

"I'll meet you back here," Barclaw told them. "And don't follow me."

Barclaw walked west, toward Sister Sissi's and Grassyknoll. He walked fast until he spotted someone he wanted to talk to. Then he shifted into constable's saunter. He hardly stopped, just long enough to exchange pleasantries – "Sales picking up?" "Nice day we're having." "Glad to see you back in town." – and ask his question. Casual, cover-the-possibilities pauses. He continued to the far side of H&G, to a shabby bead-vendor's stand. "Day to you, Wyaa," he said to an older woman. "Any action lately?"

Wyaa straightened, raised her head, looked at him, then sagged again, as if her heavily-beaded shawl was crushing her. "Yes, Constable," she said, "I do believe."

"Any customers?"

"Do beavers chew willows? Ha, ha," she cackled. "Sold everything they had. Quick, too. Slept the rest of the day."

"Appreciate it, Wyaa," Barclaw said, pressing something into her hand. He walked quickly away, not wishing to be seen with his west-side eyes and ears.

"Okay, step one's taken," Barclaw told Ziiza and Bitta when he returned. "Step two is to hold a think session, pool everyone's information, and plot our course of action. Invite everyone you can think of who might know something or have ideas to offer.." Barclaw turned and stepped away, eyes twinkling, delighted with the suspense he was creating, delighted to be the center of attention.

Ziiza asked Bitta to come, and sent Com, who had returned early, for Sister Sissi and Gstan. She asked Litti. Biber was home but would have little to offer. Sufx was gone. Com could not find Sister Sissi or Gstan.

When Barclaw arrived, he quizzed each adult and child. He put on his official face and said, "Have any of you heard of the Mire?"

Govvi, sitting with her hands folded primly in her lap, said, "Certainly." Barclaw's eyes widened. "Mu Mire and Po Mire," she said. "They sell their Mire-root on the far side of H&G. The kids buy it. Get zonked." Ziiza stared at her daughter, open-mouthed. "Well, Muma, not exactly all of the kids,"

Govvi said, flashing a haughty, insulted look. Then, reverting to form: "Yes, Po Mire sells between two- and three-and-a-half basketfuls a week."

"How do you know that?" Barclaw sputtered.

Ziiza, having regained her composure, cut in: "She knows many things, Constable Barclaw. Many things. I'm not surprised, now that I think about it. And she is seldom wrong. Never, actually."

Barclaw rubbed his hands together, trying to regain the initiative. "By any chance," he said, looking straight at Govvi, "do you know where the Mire is? It hasn't been going that long, and they've taken great pains to keep the location secret. I've never had time to track it down." He paused for effect, and said, "Until now."

"No," Govvi answered, "I don't."

"I have an idea. Sort of an idea," Com said. Eyes shifted to him, sitting off to the side. Hearing no comment he continued, "Down south, I think. Forks off South Trail. I've done a lot of exploring."

"Could you lead us there?" Barclaw asked.

"Wait a minute," Ziiza said, "We don't know she's there, with them, in that Mire thing."

"Do you have a better idea?" Barclaw said with satisfaction. "A more likely answer?"

"Like Com, I too have many explores," Litti said, speaking for the first time. "And I agree. I have seen footprints leading away from South Trail."

"That's all I need," Barclaw said. "I'm forming a searching party. We leave early tomorrow morning. Who's with me?" All raised their hands.

Barclaw did not lead the search. When he returned he told Ziiza that Mistermayor had refused permission for him to go, said he could not spare him. Mistermayor, Barclaw explained, did not think Netti had been gone long enough to be a "missing person." She'd probably come home tomorrow. Just a kid off on a lark with some other kids.

Netti doesn't go on larks with other kids.

"Okay," Ziiza said, "If it's up to us, it's up to us. And I don't propose waiting until morning. We leave now. Cover as much trail as we can. Govvi, you stay here, our home guardian. If she comes back or you get a lead, send someone down South Trail after us. Com, Org, Edu, grab your packs; take some food. Oh, and Edu, find something of Netti's to take along for Dg to sniff. As if he needs it. But we'd better make sure. Litti, are you with us?" Litti nodded and went to her shelter to pack.

Within minutes they were striding along Outer Circle. "We've got a little more daylight left," Com said when they reached the South Trail intersection.

"Not much light tonight with the new moon, so we'll probably have to stop. But that's good because we don't want to miss the side trail, overrun it. If it is the Mire, and if it is a wet sort of place. Which it sounds like. . . ." He looked at Ziiza, then Litti, for confirmation.

Litti's eyes brightened and she continued for him, "Then it will be east of South Trail and down toward the Son River bottoms."

They slept head-to-toe on the narrow forest trail. Rather, they lay on the trail, too excited to sleep. Ziiza spent the night listening to owls and wolves, real and imaginary, and imagined a bedraggled, homeward-bound Netti stumbling over her in the dark. She rose before dawn to a reasonably warm morning and ground fog over the trail. After standing with Dg until light, she nudged Edu awake. "Let Dg sniff Netti's fur," she said, "See what happens." Dg barked and ran south. "Everybody up," she ordered. "Dg's got a scent."

Whether Dg had a trail scent soon became questionable; he returned as fast as he had left. Then he ran away again. What was he following, if anything? At each side trail, even the uphill ones, Ziiza sent Litti or one of the boys in, while she stood guard at the intersection. Her rule: never let anyone get behind the leader, just as on the Sea Trace. They found no tracks or signs.

When the sun was up, Com ran to Ziiza who was standing by a side trail waiting for Org to search it thoroughly. "Muma, Muma, come quick, I think Dg's got something."

Ziiza yelled, "Org, come back." When they reached Dg, Edu was holding him by his collar. He stood growling, his head poking into a rhododendron hedge beside the trail. The only evidence of a trail, or an opening in the hedge, were two broken-off leaves on the ground.

Org pushed his way though the stiff branches. Dg squirmed past him and was soon running and barking. "Footprints," Org called, after he had taken a few steps, "I've got footprints." Ziiza leaned into the rhodies to open them up and helped Litti, Com, and Edu through.

They picked their way along the sloppy trail. Dg barked at the trees by the lake. Com, first as usual, walked onto the Mire's deceptive green carpet. Two steps and he sank to his chest. Had he not been the experienced scout and swimmer that he was, he would have disappeared, the Mire swallowing him with only bubbles to mark the spot. When Org reached him he was feathering his arms slowly. "Org, stop! Stop now!" Com said, sputtering, as Org reached the invisible edge. "Now get me out of here." Org lay on his stomach, extended his arm and caught Com's greasy hand. The Mire released Com with a hungry slurp; another missed meal.

They arrived to find Com stripping slime from his body. One by one they stuck their toes in to test, like touching the irresistible sticky pitch. As Ziiza rubbed Com warm, she looked across the surface and scanned the distant tree line. She hushed everyone and listened. Nothing but a faint breeze and an occasional gas bubble belch. Finally she said, "So this is the Mire. It's got to be. But how on earth are we going to get her out? If she's over there. I've got to think. We've got to think."

Ziiza led them away to a point where she thought they were out of sight and hearing, but could observe the trail from both directions. They rested and ate and tested ideas on one another, eliminating them as fast as they spoke them. As the day drew to a close, Ziiza said, "Litti, you have been a great help. But I'm afraid this is going to take a while. Go back if you wish. As I said, I'm not giving up until we have Netti safely back in Beaverton." Litti shook her head. "Thanks, Litti, I can't tell you how much I appreciate, we appreciate, your help. I wish I had a great plan, but I don't. We'll just have to wait. Com, you take the first watch. Org, you next. Then wake me. Of course Edu, you and Dg will be on duty all night." Again they slept on the trail, not because of darkness or thickness of growth but because it was the driest place available.

23

Silvoo and the Hieyeques

"READY TO die?" taunted a Hieyeque.

"I hope it hurts. A really lot," said another, sticking his head between the guards.

Gstan was tied as before, his back against the cold vertical stone, rope around his neck, not choking this time but tight enough to irritate. How long have I been here? he thought. More particularly, how close is it to morning? When *was* morning inside a cave? He was not hungry, although they had not offered him food. But the salty meat taste lingered, reminding him of Ziiza's salty Tip-n-Dips. Which reminded him how fine an Obtuse would taste right now. Or a drink of water; he could drink a pouch full. Or a hand lap from a creek. A drop in his dry mouth. He would lick the walls if he could.

"Away!" Silvoo's unmistakable voice. "I want to be alone with this man." The guards stepped back and Silvoo entered, a torch in one hand, a pale green glowing stone in the other. He was dressed simply, the same as during the "trial:" leggings and bare above the waist. His black hair was trimmed even at his shoulders. Unlike his followers, he seemed to be in good physical shape, although not overly large – Gstan took him to be about a hand taller than he – or overly muscular. His skin color was healthy; he obviously spent time outside the cave. He stood before Gstan, taking his measure. His dominance established, Silvoo relaxed and smiled at his captive. "You've passed the test, my man. You didn't beg. Didn't beg for water. Would you like some?" Gstan nodded. "Guards," Silvoo called, "bring water." He untied him, talking as he did. "I've decided to postpone your execution," he said in a casual voice. "Postpone it from morning – right now," he added for emphasis, "to evening. This evening. Don't get your hopes up. I love evening executions. Although I have nothing against morning ones, either. I can see you now, outlined against the sunset, taking your punishment like a man. Splendid sunset. Splendid execution."

"I suppose," Gstan said, "you've composed something for your guys to chant while they slap me to death?"

"Don't push my good nature," Silvoo snapped. Then, shifting back, said, "I like you. What's your name?" A guard set a bowl of water in front of Gstan.

Gstan drank, sighed, and hesitated. "Gstan," he said finally. "From Beaverton. Up north."

"And your profession? . . . Gstan."

"In a few hours, corpse."

"You've made your point. Don't you get it? I'm trying to be nice to you. In fact," he smiled a smug, satisfied smile, "I was thinking of inviting you to lunch."

"Well, I've been just about everything: trader, real estate salesman, burrow developer. But like I tried to tell you, I just took a long walk, to get away for a while, to forget about some disappointments – which I'd rather not go into. I'm not a criminal. Yes, I took the food. But honest, I was starving. A guy on the trail took my knife and I was down to eating ants and bugs. But secrets? I didn't steal any secrets. I have no idea what you people are about. Heck, I don't even know where I am. Location-wise, I mean." Then, smiling weakly, "I can't even pronounce Hi-whatever-you-are."

"Ever the wise guy," Silvoo said, sighing resignedly. "Well, I can set you right on where you are. You're in the Noro Hills, north of Big Bay. I suppose that was your destination, Big Bay. Nice town. Nice bay. Too bad you'll never see them."

"That was cruel," Gstan said, pushing Silvoo's brittle good nature.

"I suppose it was, but that's my prerogative. The power thing, right? Anyway, let's have lunch. Outside, if you like. See you in a while."

"Some more water, please," Gstan said. Silvoo walked away without answering. The guards returned but did not retie him. Evidently his holding space was the Hieyeque jail, or simply an unused sub-cave, because it was clean, completely free of garbage. Not that it mattered. Gstan passed the time feeling the walls, tracing the finely-cut corners with his fingers. "Amazing workmanship," he said, trying to get the guards talking. No response.

The guards pulled away and Silvoo stepped in. "Hungry?" he asked. "Something special on the menu. Our food procurers have picked some strawberries to go with our standard fare, roasted meat. A last meal treat. And yes, I know you've been searched for weapons, but I must make certain." Silvoo patted Gstan's garments, then ran his fingers through his hair. "No guards. No tie-downs. Don't try to escape and we'll have a lovely time. Run for it and you'll wish you hadn't."

They sat near the cave entrance with a large wooden bowl of early-season strawberries and another piled high with slabs of steaming meat between them. The strawberries, none larger than a thumbnail, were inexpertly picked, Gstan noted, ranging from hard, flecked, unripe white ones, to pink, to just-ripe red, to rotting black. A depression in a rock held enough rainwater to satisfy. The sun shone overhead in a cloudless sky, the mid-day heat tempered by a slow breeze. Silvoo looked west and smiled, presumably gauging Gstan's placement against the sunset. "Go to it," he said, "I'm not particularly hungry."

Gstan slurped water, popped a strawberry in his mouth, and spit out the crown. "Delicious."

"Yes, I'm sure." Silvoo paused, then continued: "What we do here, if you're interested . . . are you interested?"

Gstan saw in his gleaming eyes that the man was bursting to tell him something, begging, in fact, behind his proud and odious facade. And he had determined the perfect way to do it: tell, then execute. "Why, yes," Gstan said, trying to sound casual. "I'm very interested." He bit into a ripe berry.

"We are the Hieyeques," Silvoo said, "and I am the unquestioned leader. We came from the Old Side, escaping persecution and other matters which, to use your phrase, I'd rather not go into. We chose to locate here for the salubrious climate, and to be left alone. That is, to work in secret. Then we discovered this cave with its special stone. Yes, I know about the broad trail that begins at Way Rock. And yes, I know about your beaver-infested paradise. And your love-hate relationship with Swarm City. Or, should I say, your inferiority-superiority ambivalence. And your Grand Muma, the greatest river that flows. And all of that." He smirked, as if his contempt for both Beaverton and Swarm City was not clear enough.

Gstan picked up a rotten berry, placed it between his lips, and squeezed. The juice ran down his chin. His luncheon companion's eyes darted.

"The Hieyeques," Silvoo continued, straightening his back, then letting his shoulders down, "are creators of the first order. A group apart. Inventors, if you will. Old Side's loss. New Side's gain. Abstractly speaking, of course; we do not share our secrets with anyone."

Get ready for a discourse, Gstan thought. I've never met anyone so full of himself.

They were run out of their old home, Silvoo told him, for pushing fists into still water, withdrawing them, and by sheer force of mind willing the depressions to remain; pointing to tree limbs and dropping them with finger snaps; spitting on stones and having the spit burst into flame. Conjurers, that's what the boneheads had called them. The Hieyeques saw it differently. Yes, they were tricks, but only to sharpen their minds, help them rise to the next level. And they had risen. Many levels. Silvoo assured Gstan of that.

Gstan listened intently, ignoring the meat, eating only strawberries. When he finished the last one he picked up the bowl and slurped the juice. Silvoo called for more. Gstan lifted the newly-filled bowl and inhaled: strawberries, the delicate smell of springtime and rebirth. What a fiendish choice for a man's last meal. He wanted to ask how they would do it: rock on the head, torture fire, spear in the heart, slow bloodletting? How did the sunset figure? He knew he should not be feeling this chipper, but it was so absurd it seemed funny. His mind leaped: suffocation under Orange's blubber? Throat cut by a sharp-edged, glowing stone? Burial under garbage? He wanted to ask about the sub-caves' too-smooth walls. Gstan grabbed the handful of rotten strawberries he had set aside and squeezed. Dark red juice ran down his arm and dripped from his elbow onto the ground. Silvoo winced. Gstan suppressed a smile, scooped up another handful, and squeezed again.

"I have an idea," Silvoo said. "Let's go inside. I'll show you the latest, what's really going on. We still have a few hours before . . . ah . . . sunset."

If this isn't the wildest, Gstan thought, he's looking forward to savoring my execution, but he can't stand the sight of make-believe blood.

Silvoo turned and walked into the cave, not bothering to look back to see whether Gstan was following. He led through the long corridor. Silvoo seeming to have no trouble adjusting to the darkness. All Gstan could make out were faint, shimmering colors as he passed the sub-caves. The large interior room, scene of last night's proceeding, was dark. Silvoo clapped his hands and the torch-carrying guards appeared. They walked through an opening, which instead of a being a sub-cave proved to be another corridor. Gstan coughed on the dusty air. Bang! Bang! The noise came from a large cave at the end of the corridor, lit by a small fire. Twenty or so workmen with hammers and wedges split rock slabs from the walls. "This rock," Silvoo said, "in this cave, is unique as far as we know. Special properties. Our mining operation. You are the first outsider to see it. You, because of our. . . . Come."

They walked back through the corridor to the large room, then entered another. Gstan covered his face, tried to breathe through his nose, avoid the airborne dust. Tried to bring up saliva. Almost spit, but thought better of it. Swish. Scratch. Swish. Scratch. A rhythmic grinding noise. This cave had openings all around. More sub-caves, but rough-sided. Silvoo motioned to one and a guard poked his torch inside. A man sat rubbing two stones together. He was white with dust and his eyes were closed. "He's an apprentice," Silvoo said. "Younger Hieyeques do the grunt work as part of their training. Mornings, they attend classes. Afternoons, while they mine and shape the stones, they memorize their lessons and think great thoughts. The glowing sub-caves, the ones you violated, are occupied by chanters, those of the highest rank."

Gstan coughed violently, trying to catch his breath. "I'm impressed, Mister Silvoo." He coughed again. "But I'm afraid I don't understand. What are you making? Sure, the glowing stones – and I must say I've never seen anything so beautiful – are the final product, I guess. But what are they for? What do they do?"

Silvoo drew himself up – this was it – and sweetly, condescendingly, as if it should be obvious to anyone but a simpleton, said, "Everything. Anything. Anything we want them to."

A few hours till sunset, Gstan thought, and I don't feel the slightest bit of fear. "For example?" he asked, not expecting an answer, not believing there was one.

Orange sat in his sub-cave, his mountainous flesh pushing the refuse hard against the walls and into the corridor. One hand held a flat stone, elbow-to-fingertip in length, one hand wide, and two fingers thick. The opposing sides were parallel but the finish dull. It exuded no color. He plunged his other hand into his garbage heap, again and again, until he extracted what he wanted, a large bone covered with rotting meat. He stuck it in his mouth and sucked, slurping, licking, slobbering. Silvoo and Gstan stood behind him watching. Strange, Gstan thought, while strawberry juice freaked out Mister Sunset Execution, this revolting display, this slob wallowing in his cesspool, doesn't bother him at all. Pop! Orange blew the bone out of his mouth and onto the heap. He chanted: Yoo, yoo, yoo, yoo. Ya, ya, ya, ya."

"Just warming up," Silvoo whispered.

"Yoo, ya, ya, yoo, ya, yoo, yoo, ya. Yoo, yoo, yoo, ya, ya, ya, ya, ya." Orange continued chanting.

"I could let you hear the whole thing and it wouldn't make any difference," Silvoo said. "You'd never understand."

"Then why was I stealing secrets?"

"The intent, my man. The intent."

"But I told you. . . ."

Orange's stone flashed faint orange and went dark. It flashed again, brighter, but not enough to light the sub-cave or corridor. "That's enough," Silvoo said. He took the stone from him and handed it to Gstan. "Ask a question. Ask the stone a question, if I must be so specific. Out loud. Or just think it. All that matters is that you are holding it. Squeeze a little. Come on, we're running out of time."

Beaverton's population was the first question that came to Gstan's mind. "Nothing," he said.

"Try again, you," Orange said testily. "And squeeze harder, it isn't finished."

Gstan squeezed and the stone glowed so brightly he almost dropped it. He asked again. He spoke a number: "Six thousand, eight hundred, and fifty-one. Well, I'll be. I don't know if it's right, but it sounds close. It sort of took over my mind. I couldn't say anything else."

"It's right," Silvoo intoned. "Ask it to remember your trail route," he prompted. Gstan asked. No result. "Trick question. You haven't put any information in on that subject, so it can't give it back to you. Ha, ha." He took the stone from Gstan and handed it to Orange. "That about wraps it up. We could show you a lot more, couldn't we, Orange?"

"You bet we could, Silvoo Master," Orange said, slobbering with delight and squeezing the stone till it pulsed bright.

"Come along, Gstan," Silvoo said, "we have business to attend to. And remember, Orange, all Hieyeques *will* be present to witness execution." The delight in his voice sounded like hollow-gourd wind chimes.

"Well," Gstan said, "you've shown me what they do, but what do you do with them? What's the point?"

Silvoo shrugged. "Do with them? We compete. Each chanter works to see how far he can advance his stone. We hold contests. It's about prestige within Hieyeque-dom. Pushing the limits of our creative abilities. After a winner is declared, mostly by vote, but occasionally by me, we break the stones and start over. For goodness sake, you saw them at the cave entrance, broken on the slope. You climbed right over them."

Silvoo's through with me now, Gstan thought. Last chance. "I could make you rich and famous," Gstan whispered, trying to make his desperation sound knowing and seductive. "Rich and famous."

"Rich. What do you mean by rich? Famous. What do you mean by famous?"

"Have you though of selling your stones? I mean, you just throw them over the edge and break them. Other people might like to use them, pay money for them. If it isn't just a trick, if all you really have to do is squeeze them like I did. Everyone in Beaverton, for instance. All six thousand, eight hundred, and fifty-one of them. Times whatever you want to charge." Silvoo looked at him blankly. I'm not reaching him, Gstan thought. My gosh, these guys are inventing geniuses and business ignoramuses. The chance of a lifetime. Literally. Ziiza. Everything. And I've only got. . . .

"Sell them, Silvoo Master, if I may be so bold as to call you that." Salesman Gstan moved in for the close. "Not only for money beyond your wildest dreams, but that you, and only you, will be known as the finest mind on the New Side. Singular. Unique. Incomparable. Not only the unquestioned leader of the Hieyeques, but the unquestioned smartest man in the world. How would you like that?" He saw a flash in Silvoo's eyes and a thin smile creep across his lips. Silvoo's eyebrow fluttered. He clapped his hand on it. Gstan finished: "No doubt word of your preeminence would reach the Old Side as well."

Silvoo led Gstan to the sub-cave jail and said, "Make your peace." He motioned the guards to block the opening and disappeared.

The multi-colored glow faded in the corridor as one by one the chanters stopped energizing their stones. Feet padded past Gstan's sub-cave. Whispers. He asked the guards for water. No answer. No water. They placed the rope around his neck and led him outside. Tied him to a stout tree. So this is it, he thought, spears or something like that. And I can't even see the sun drop into the beautiful Noro Hills. Slowly, singly, and in pairs, the Hieyeques walked out of the cave, many carrying hunks of roasted meat. They sat or stood, staring at Gstan, chewing, munching, slurping. He saw no spears or weapons of any kind. Was Silvoo Master going to order them to gather firewood and burn him? Stone him to death? He remained composed.

Dusk, accompanied by a satisfactory sunset, if the oos and ahs of the assembled, along with some confused yoos and yas, were any indication. Silvoo made his entrance, turned his back to Gstan, planted his feet, and said, "Brother Hieyeques, I have come to a simple, straightforward decision. The execution is off." Rumbles of surprise. Rumbles of protest. But before the rumbles could swell, Silvoo continued in a deep voice: "I have special knowledge. This stranger from Beaverton may be of more value to us alive than dead. Besides, he did not steal much. You," he said to one of the guards, "untie him." And to Gstan: "Come, we must talk." They walked quickly into the cave, followed by the Hieyeques, grumbling and grousing, but happy to go inside, radiant sunset or not.

Silvoo and Gstan talked so long Gstan sensed it was dawn or close to it. When they concluded Silvoo offered him food, water, and a comfortable place to sleep. Gstan declined. "I should be leaving. I've miles to cover and no time to waste eating or sleeping." At the same time he thought: I want to get out of here before you change your mind. Silvoo waved his assent. "And thank you, Silvoo," he was about to add *Master*, but thought better, "Thank you for sparing. . . . You won't regret it."

24

Netti's Rescue

AFTER TWO days of waiting, Ziiza and crew grew hungry, bored, and irritable. But somewhat encouraged. Each morning, as the gleaming top-lit mist hung over the dangerous green surface, they sat at the end of the trail and listened to hints of voices, tinkles of laughter, and – could it be? – music and singing. The fog, it seemed, acted as a transmitting medium. Never clear enough to understand the words, but unmistakably, they concluded, the sounds of humans.

Org and Com asked permission to explore along the edge, look for an opening, a passageway, get a better view, get closer to the voices. "Calm down," Ziiza told them. "I know you're anxious, but we can't risk being seen. We can't risk your being sucked in again either. And we don't know what they might do to Netti if they knew we were here. We just don't know." She patted Com on the shoulder. "Lay your rope on the trail, will you. I want to see how long it is." Com uncoiled his rope and ran it out. "Great," Ziiza said, "It's longer than I had expected. Have you lengthened it?" Com nodded. Ziiza motioned them to come close. They knelt as Ziiza whispered her plan – as much to find out how it sounded to herself as to inform them. They rehearsed their roles and waited.

By morning, Org could stand it no longer. "Muma," he said, "I've had it. This place is driving me crazy."

Ziiza could tell by the others' looks, even Litti's, that they were thinking the same thing. "One more day, people, please. Then you can. . . . What was that?" "Two, three, four, five," came a faint count from across the Mire. She turned to see two distant figures walking on the green carpet. "Go," she whispered to Edu. He ran up the trail, Dg with him. He skirted around the largest puddles, trying not to splash, then disappeared into the scraggly swamp growth. Com's rope lay coiled on the trail. Org stepped into the sloppy ditch beside the trail and sat in the scum-covered water. Ziiza tied the rope around a bush and handed the other end to Org. He put a hollow reed in his mouth, pinched his nose, closed his eyes, and sank into the water. Ziiza pushed floating scum over him to "cover" him up. "Right turn, three steps." The voice was closer. Likewise, Com and Litti sat in the water, mouthed their reeds, and pinched their noses. Ziiza joined them underwater.

When Po Mire's foot touched the rope, Org jerked and he went down, his basket of Mire-root spilling in front of him. Org rose up, splashing and struggling to gain a footing. He rubbed the mud from his eyes. Mu Mire screamed and dropped her basket. Litti and Com splashed out of the ditch and ran to the Mire's edge. Po Mire floundered and sputtered, rocking on his belly in the mud. Ziiza struggled to get out of the ditch; her necklaces entangled on something. She jerked, her head popped out of the water.

"Oh, my," Mu Mire croaked and passed out, not being able to handle another slime-covered apparition.

Org jabbed his reed into Po Mire's back. "Don't move mister, or you'll get a rock to the head."

Com and Litti moved to Mu Mire and stood over her. "So these are the famous roots," Com said, picking one up and sniffing.

"Drop it, Com," Ziiza ordered. "Don't even touch those things. They're evil." Then, turning to Po Mire, lying rigid as Org ground his rock into his hair, she said, "I'm Netti's muma and I want her back. Now!"

"We have no Netti."

"Clip him, Org," Ziiza said. He glanced his rock off Po Mire's head, stepped on his shoulder, and held the rock menacingly in front of his face. When Po Mire's eyes focused on the tuft of hair stuck to the rock with his own blood, he winced, but held firm. He grabbed spilled Mire-root from the mud and held it out to Org. Org sneered and gave him a face full of jagged toenails.

Mu Mire came round. Litti helped her sit up.

"Okay, woman," Ziiza said, "how about it? The big guy standing on the man here is Netti's brother. And he's awfully angry. As we all are. Great thing about that rock of his, he can use it over and over. Org!"

"Stop! Don't kill him!" Mu Mire shrieked. Then slyly, patronizingly, as she pointed across the Mire: "Netti's over there. Lovely girl, if I do say. But you'll never get her. Nobody can get across. Except him."

"You're wrong there," Ziiza said. Everyone's head swung round, except Po Mire's, who was blowing bubbles in the puddle Org had pushed his face into. "You're going across that Mire thing, whatever you call it, and you are going to deliver my Netti back to me. Unharmed. Just the two of you. Nobody else."

"But I can't," Mu Mire squealed. "I don't know the pathway. I don't know the count. Can't ever remember. I'll be sucked under and drown."

"Org, drag that man to the edge," Ziiza said. Org slid his fingers into Po Mire's hair, closed his fist, and lifted him up. He half-carried, half-pushed, the pudgy man to the end of the trail, then spun him around so he faced the island. Po Mire rubbed his neck. "Guide her across," Ziiza ordered. Then, quickly, "No you're not going; you're staying with us. Our insurance. Call out the numbers, however you do it. Get going, woman! And come back immediately. With my girl. Got it?" Mu Mire stood blubbering on the edge.

"Walk out five steps, my dear," Po Mire began. "Then turn left." Fortunately, Mu Mire and Po Mire were about the same height, had the same stride, or it never would have worked. As it was, she twice slipped over the edge and had to roll onto her stomach and pull herself up. Ziiza shuddered as she struggled, not in sympathy, but imagining Netti in the same fix on the return trip. Po Mire continued shouting directions – "Ahead seven." "Right and four." "Just keep walking" – louder and louder as Mu Mire got farther away. Until she stepped onto the island and vanished into the trees.

While she waited, Ziiza quizzed Po Mire: "Is it an island? How many people? Any other access?" He glared defiantly, his jovial, fatherly exterior, the one he presented to customers and his worker-captive Mirees, replaced with the hard face of the Mire-root dealer.

In a few minutes, two figures materialized out of the foliage line, a Mu Mire-sized short one and a Netti-sized tall one. "Out seven. Out seven," Po Mire shouted, prompted by Org's rock bumping on his head.

Ziiza counted to herself, one, two, three, four, five, six, seven.

So far so good.

Walking with Netti made Mu Mire even more nervous and hesitant. When they finally crossed, Litti and Ziiza handed Netti up and hugged her. Netti mumbled a soft, "Hello," but was otherwise unemotional, not seeming to understand, or care, whether they were rescuing her or capturing her.

"On your way, swamp scum," Ziiza said, pushing Po Mire toward the island. "You, too." Mu Mire lurched after him, crying, her knees shaking.

"Friend Ziiza," Litti said, "I think I'll take these Mire-roots along."

"What? Why?"

"If you don't mind, dear friend. However many pains to you, we may need them." She picked the roots from the mud.

Dg ran to Netti when they approached the hiding place by the lake, as if he knew. He licked her legs. She stood, looked ahead with unblinking eyes. "Hi, Netti," Edu said. "Glad you're safe. This is so weird. What happened?" Netti did not answer.

Next day, Ziiza told Barclaw the story. "Worst kind of evil," he said. "Come on to the young folks, real friendly like. They don't know. Eager to try something new. Have an adventure. All the better if they think their parents don't approve. 'Try this little piece of root,' they tell them. 'See how you like it.' Whatever happens, they win: gain a casual customer, gain a steady customer, find a recruit for the Mire. Even those who refuse, help with word-of-mouth advertising. I have my sources. I know how it goes. So you found it. Congratulations. And you got her back. For now."

"What do you mean, 'for now?'"

"You're a very smart woman, Ziiza, but you still – how shall I put this? – have your blind spots. Anyway, if I had the time and the manpower, I'd wipe the place out. As it is, Mu Mire and Po Mire won't be selling roots in H&G for a while. I'll see to that. Won't stop them, though. They'll find the kids or the kids will find them. Older folks, too."

Ziiza was amazed; Litti knew exactly what to do. At least she sounded and acted as if she knew. Netti's recovery, Litti explained, would take a good long while; it was a gradual process. She would live with Litti across the way, to get plenty of sleep and have fewer distractions. With Ziiza's permission, of course.

"Shouldn't we send for Provido?" Ziiza asked. Litti rolled her eyes and laughed her musical laugh. The process, she told her, was mental as well as physical. Netti would have to shed the liking for Mire-root. If she had been there much longer, it might have been hopeless. This would demand constant attention: talking, walking, sleeping long hours. Litti explained the Mire-root's addictive properties as compassionately as she could. Ziiza was aghast. This was why she needed the roots she had gathered from the mud, Litti explained, "to gradually reduce her likes for them." Family visiting time would be in the afternoon, while she rested after the morning treatment; she would need all the love and support they could give her. In a few weeks if all went well, Ziiza's part would begin. That would be what Litti called "work therapy." Netti's weaving talent – perfect. Rock running head cushions – perfect. Working with her hands, doing something creative and useful, being part of a family business again – what could be better?

Convinced that this was the best course of action (and not understanding the depth of the problem), Ziiza put her trust in Litti and returned to her experiments. Her first move was to get organized. To do that, and make up for the rescue-caused delay, she and Govvi walked to H&G looking for Bitta. They spotted Hobart circling over her, coo-burping to attract listeners. As they approached, the bird glided in and lit on Bitta's head. Bitta was about to begin when she saw them.

"Congratulations, Ziiza," Bitta said in greeting. "No outsider has gotten that close to the Mire before, let alone recovered a daughter or son."

"Oh, thank you," Ziiza said. "But I don't think it's over. As I think you are aware. Now Bitta, could you refresh me on last week's race? How many entrants? How many finished? Tell me everything. Please." Hobart flapped, impatient for the news work to begin.

"You know who won." Ziiza and Govvi shrugged. "It's big. Rock running is big and growing. Over two hundred runners. Officials couldn't handle them at the finish line; some of the places got mixed up. Quord Senior took some heat for that. This thing may be running away from him." She giggled into her hand.

Hobart tugged on Bitta's hair. She turned to address her impatient audience, beginning with the town council report. Although Govvi could have told her the news, Ziiza stayed.

Beaver tail prices were at an all-time high, Biita announced, the result of higher than expected demand. Friends of the Beaver, a conservation group formed by Mizpark, was proposing a summer moratorium on beaver tail cutting. And, in a politically risky move, Mistermayor had offered a motion to do just that. Died for lack of a second. But after Castor's report that poaching was up, Polcat, not to be one-upped if this turned out to be a real issue, moved to appoint a special committee to look into it.

Banker Font and lawyer Esqq, who seldom attended council meetings, Bitta noted, gave a joint report on Beaverton's monetary system. Tightening of beaver tail supplies was affecting the system beyond the potential shortage of food; the barter and tail method was breaking down. Why? Because people were eating most of the dried beaver tail "float," as they put it, instead of using it for savings and exchange. They heartily agreed with Polcat's special committee idea, and, in fact, would have suggested something like it if he hadn't. Both had agreed to serve.

Even though Font and Esqq's report seemed to support everything Mistermayor, Castor, and Friends of the Beaver were trying to get across, it provoked no comments or questions from Bitta's listeners; they had obviously reached their attention limit. Put differently, they were ready for what they had been waiting for, the real news. Smoke-storm still threatened, Bitta told them as a warm-up. The standard bad news. Faces turned north, noting the smoke column rising over the hills, then turned back, saying, in effect, get on with the good stuff. She reviewed the coming elections – elections were always coming – who was going after whom. Good for a titter. She told of the new businesses opening in H&G, always of interest. And, of more interest, the ones that were in trouble. She continued with the Battle of H&G, as she put it, a hair-pulling, vend-wrecking fight over alleged jewelry design copying. She saved the juiciest bit for last: Castor and Barclaw's shouting match over their respective jurisdictions, a tug-of-war over some poachers Castor had caught and refused to turn over to "the proper authority." Plus their vocal assessments of each other's law enforcement prowess. Or lack thereof.

"Well, Govvi," Ziiza said, as they walked home, "do you want a new job? Full-time, maybe?"

Govvi's look asked the question.

"You and I both know you've learned everything Addle has to teach you."

"Long ago," Govvi put in.

"So forget about Grassyknoll. This rock running, what I see coming, could be ten times Sita's Lair. More. Head protection. Everybody needs it. We have to get in quick with the best product, before anyone else does. I'm really excited. Are you?"

"Yes, Muma, I am," Govvi said flatly.

"Do you have a materials report? Did you do any investigating while we were gone? Like I asked you to?"

"Yes, Muma, I did," she said in the same voice. Govvi reviewed every material Ziiza had suggested or experimented with: thirty-eight reeds, weeds, grasses, supple limbs, woods, roots, and ferns, each evaluated as to availability, season, gathering difficulty, transport problems, weight, storability, flexibility and cost if there was one.

"Thanks, Govvi, you are amazing," Ziiza said. "No one else could have put together a report like that. In a week. Or a month. Or at all."

"I know, Muma."

25

Climbing the Spire

"WELL," ZIIZA said to Litti over morning tea. "Netti? What do you think?"

Litti smiled. Ziiza smiled back, relieved. "Good progress," Litti said. "Yesterday I forgot to give her the Mire-root and she didn't ask." Litti winked. "That's the best of things. Her weaving is steady and imaginative. You've seen the results."

"Yes, I have," Ziiza said. "Outstanding. Just in time, too, because I need her badly. In fact I would like her to train one or two assistants. I need protectors that are good enough for a trial. Then I want at least twenty-five ready to sell at the next race. So my question is, when will she be able to work full-time? I want her to be in charge of production. Govvi will handle the numbers, of course. I'll do the marketing and designing. I'm having trouble with Org. He loves the sport, but he won't try a head protector." Ziiza waited for Litti's assenting nod and continued. "Wants to beat Sufx 'pure,' he says, with no gimmicks. I really need him as my tester. And once I get them right, I want him to run with one, win with one. Then everyone will have to have one. That's my strategy."

"As to Org," Litti sighed, "I would not know. As to Netti, I think I know. Take it easy and she should work into it. Training others is a good idea. It will give her pride and raise her self-confidence. What she needs. And now, my friend, if you don't mind, I also have needs. I have been with Netti for many days and nights and I am wanting to get back to my walks. You don't mind my leaving our dear girl with you for a day or so?"

"Water Child?"

"Perhaps."

"Thank you so much, Litti," Ziiza said, leaning over and hugging her, "for going to the Mire with us. For sticking with Netti. For everything. Enjoy your walk."

The spring air was warm as Litti walked Outer Circle. She could have shortened her walk by cutting through H&G, but, as was her habit, she avoided crowds whenever possible. She glided past Castor's works, following the tree line, speaking to no one, meeting no one's eye. Once onto the south meadow she headed for Great-great-great-grandpopa Monumentree. She approached slowly, reverently, head bowed, as if about to drop and crawl to him, ask forgiveness for her lengthy absence. When she reached his massive trunk she flattened herself against it, touched her forehead, and moved her arms over his rough bark. "Did you miss me, Great-great-great-grandpopa Monumentree? Well, I'm back. It's just . . . that I had some important work to do. For some friends of mine. Thank you for being patient. I am happy to see you, touch you, feel your strength." She retreated. Then, instead of heading across the fields and into the forest, she veered southwest, toward Water Child's merge with the Ever-faithful Daughter.

"I almost missed your season, precious ones." Litti spoke to a circle of purple-blue flowers growing on slender, knee-high stalks. They grew in depressions, flooded in winter, dry in summer, ringed with cracked earth and newly-sprouting grass. She brushed the flower tip with her finger, then one of its splayed-out leaves. Bending over, she sniffed, a ritual gesture as the flowers had no fragrance. "You did not wait for me, did you? You're dying." She plunged her fingers into the black earth and felt for bulbs. She found a large one and gouged it out. After peeling the outer layer, she popped it into her mouth, rinsed with saliva, and chewed. "I know, little bulb, I should not be eating you raw like this, but I cannot wait."

Careful to take only one bulb from a clump, Litti ate four, then walked along Water Child's north bank. When it turned into the forest she took her accustomed trail. Although it was mid-morning, and the day promised to be sunny, the forest was dark and wet and quiet, broken only by Water Child's running. At the clearing, her eyes went first to the waterfall. Then to the green, moss-lined chute. Down to the pool. And to – the figure of a man – hunched over – reaching into the water up to his shoulder. "Whaa?" Litti said, and covered her mouth. She stepped behind a tree. Not large enough to hide her. She shifted behind another and listened. Intermixed with Water Child's noises, she heard whistling, the contented sounds of a man enjoying his work. Or play. Or whatever it might be.

Litti pressed against the tree, just as she had against Great-great-great-grandpopa Monumentree before. The whistling stopped, or if it continued, the tree blocked its faint sound. She crouched, leaned around the tree, and looked again. He had waded across to her side of the Child and was again probing the pool. He withdrew something, held it close to his eyes, examined it, and laid it on the bank. He plunged his arm back into the water and swished it around, seeking. He seemed smallish: compact and narrow-shouldered. Medium-length hair. Bare, except for a loin wrap. As the light caught his shoulders and neck, Litti sucked in her breath and retreated again, pressing against the tree. She sneaked more looks, longer looks, as he continued collecting, working around the pool's periphery, eventually standing in the falling water, reaching in, feeling behind.

Litti peered again, exposing an eye. He was standing in the middle now, facing her, holding a fern frond close to his face, turning it slowly, as if to catch the light. He shook the water off. Held it up again.

She snapped her head back and flattened against the tree. The man had stepped out of the pool and was walking toward her, listening intently, his hand cupped around his ear – as if he had heard her talking or singing.

"Hello, hello," he said in a friendly voice. "Someone over there? Someone behind that tree?" Instead of making for the tree he cut a wide circle until he had an angle. She wished herself into the tree, but since she could not, closed her eyes tightly. He kept his distance and said, "I thought your song . . . very pretty. Even though I couldn't make out the words. Sound of the waterfall, you know."

At that welcome information, "couldn't make out the words," and his disarming, just-long-enough hesitation, Litti pulled away from the trunk, wiggled her shoulders, and swiped her cheeks. The urge to flee drained into the earth and she stared at him, wide-eyed. He met her stare with silence, betraying his own unease.

"What's your name?" he said. "Don't run," he followed up quickly.

"Litti," she said, eyelashes flicking. "Litti from Beaverton." From forest and meadow really, she wanted to say, but held back. "And I wasn't singing. I thought I was perfectly quiet."

"Well," he said, searching for the right words, "Excuse my error. I meant no disrespect." Then, "I'd be pleased to show you what I'm doing."

He was Arbo. A collector, he described himself, a collector of nature's wonders: animal, plant, rock, everything. Like everyone else, he came from the Old Side. Unlike everyone else that Litti knew, or knew of, he had taken a long time to do it, years in fact, wintering on the Sea Trace, pursuing his collecting in all but the worst of weather. He had thought about heading inland at Way Rock, he told her. But something drew him south. He smirk-smiled as he said this; she didn't know whether he was praising the non-Swarm City part of the continent, or mocking it. He hadn't been to Beaverton, he admitted, but he'd seen it, seen its hanging smoke when he crossed the hills and skirted the valley. He would visit sometime, sometime soon, but he was not much of a town person. She smiled at that.

Litti could not tell if he was slightly older than she or slightly younger, and was reluctant to ask. His smooth, hairless chest, she noted, attempting to avoid outright staring, was taut, his ribs prominent yet with a trace of softness. Her heart pounded. The harder she tried to calm it, the harder it beat. Her color rose and she felt he could not help but notice – this observer of nature, this beautiful, roving boy-man with his beguiling smile and penetrating gaze. The meeting of woodland innocents.

He expressed no surprise when she told him Water Child's name, thought it perfectly fitting: the name, and the fact that it had a name. Did she name it? Yes, in a way, she told him as if considering it for the first time. It came to her. More accurately, it came out of her when she had first walked the stream, along its banks, over its slippery stones, and seen its verdant-framed waterfall in the now-not-so-secret glade. Rather than creating names for the trees and birds and animals she loved – his face showed he understood – she felt she was something of a conduit, a medium of appropriate expression; animate and inanimate things revealed their personalities through her. He nodded just enough to encourage her to continue. She would introduce him to all of them if he liked, she told him diffidently. He would like that very much. They could meet. Tomorrow? Later that week? Arbo gave her space and time. Himself as well.

"Litti, there's something about you," Ziiza said as they drank sweet tea. She reached over and squeezed Litti's hand. "Look at me. Let me see you," she said, the older-to-younger-woman's command. Litti raised her head slowly and met her with lively eyes. "I don't believe I've every seen you look so lovely, so pretty – dare I say it? – so rapturous. Not that you're not pretty; you've always been pretty, one of the prettiest women I've ever known. But today . . ." Litti stared into her cup. "If you have something to tell me . . ."

Before Litti could answer, could think how to answer, Com ran up to Ziiza and said, "Torc and I are going to explore the Spire. Okay?" Torc stood away, looking on from the edge of Litti's lot, his pack slung over his shoulder.

"You mean the mountain, Morning Spire? Why are you asking me? You never ask, you just go."

"Oh, we might be a few days. It's across the river. We might climb it."

"Sure, have a good time."

"Bye, Muma. Bye, Litti."

Ziiza turned to Litti. "You were saying?"

Litti told of meeting Arbo, described him in detail, more detail evidently than she realized: his soft-hard physique, his hesitant smile, his collecting, his solitary life – as if it was perfectly normal.

Poor woman, she's fallen for this man of the woods. Brilliant woman. Brilliant in so many ways. But. . . .

Ziiza rolled Litti's fingers in her hand.

Oh, well, she's filling the empty spot in her heart – and she doesn't have a notion.

Ziiza's mind twirled, searching for a just-right response; it should be warm, understanding, encouraging, but short of outright congratulation.

Flighty as a doe, this one. Don't upset her.

"What a wonderful experience," Ziiza said.

Disappointing word choice, but at least I did not mention him.

Litti refilled their cups. Ziiza felt privileged to share the moment.

* * *

"See this, Torc?" Com said as he pulled up a black stem. "Deep-wood trillium. Flower's gone. You know what that means?" Torc shook his head. "You do, but you're playing dumb. Try another. Pull a deep breath through your nose, as much as you can. What do you smell?"

"Fir needles, I guess."

"The most delicious smell in the forest. And why is that?" Torc trudged along without responding. "Because the trail is dry," Com answered, poking his companion. "No more sloppy trails. Shuffle up the needles and dust, old buddy. Crunch 'em and kick 'em and smell the smell of summer coming on." They walked the trail out of town, through shafts of sunlight, back into the shade, and out again. Sweaty, they removed their fur tops and tied them around their waists. Com had told Torc to bring all the clothing he had; it was bound to be cold. Foot covers too, if he could find them. And plenty of food, preferably dried tail.

Pop&Jay seemed uncommonly civil, greeting them warmly when they reached their camp – or town, or subdivision, or whatever it was at present. When Com told them he wanted to go all the way to Morning Spire it was all Jay could do to keep from laughing out loud, so he turned around and giggled into his hand. When he hinted they might try to climb to the top, Pop spit out, "Derned fools," then clapped a hand over his mouth as if to push the words back inside.

"Never been done; never will be done; shouldn't be done," Jay echoed, jamming a blackened stick into the ground with each admonition. Com scanned the two outcasts through narrowed eyes and twisted his foot in the grass. "Well, I ain't your popa," Jay continued. "And I sure ain't your muma." Everyone laughed and the tension eased. "So how can we help?" He lowered his hand with exaggerated formality.

"Can you tell us the route? Is there a trail?"

"See over there?" Jay said, pointing at the Spire with his stick. "Head that way." With that, Pop&Jay doubled up, fell over sideways, and rolled on the ground. When Jay saw Com and Torc staring at them straight-faced, he jumped up and said, "You're serious, aren't you? Want to be the first to do it and all."

"We got a canoe; take you across," Pop cut in. "Maybe all the way to the Twisted Uncle. You heard of that one? The river? Follow it as far as you can and you'll be pretty close by. How you travel after that, I don't know. Hey, you're welcome to stay the night. Start off in the morning."

"We'll leave right now, if it's all right with you, Mister Jay&Pop," Com said with a grin. Their reversed names set them off again. Jay pitched headfirst onto Pop and they rolled, laughing and pounding their sides, ending up in the fire pit.

"That," Pop said proudly, after many hours of paddling, "is the great falls of the North-flowing Son. Or maybe not so great, but a falls just the same." Upstream, barely visible in its mist, the Son thundered over a rock bench, three, maybe four, men high. A tree-covered island split the falls in two.

"We've seen it before," Torc said dryly. "We've seen just about everything around Beaverton. And the valley. And the rivers." Pop&Jay were plainly disappointed.

"What we haven't seen," Com said, "is the Spire. Close up, that is."

They did not approach the falls, although it was evident that had Com and Torc been properly impressed, Pop&Jay would have paddled up to it. Instead they turned east into the Twisted Uncle and ran the canoe onto a sand beach littered with trees, driftwood, and packed grass strung high in the bushes. "As far as we go, boys," Jay said. "Wish we could help you more, but we've got some important business to attend to in Jayberg." Pop groaned and rolled his eyes at the well-worn line. Com and Torc jumped out of the canoe and tossed their packs on the sand. "Now follow this big fellow river," Jay said. "You might run into a man hides out up there, big fat one called Blotto."

"You mean Blotto of Beaverton?" Com said. Jay nodded. "I know him. Muma liked him. Kinda felt sorry for him. He was our slooze tester at Sita's Lair. So that's where he went."

"Well," Jay continued, "he's pretty close-mouthed about it. But we think he's got some sort of apparatus up there. For the making of intoxicating liquids, if you know what I mean. Anyway, he's the only one we know lives up there. Just speculating on what he does, though. We've never gone up to check him out."

As Jay spoke, he and Pop back-paddled away from the beach. Pop pried the canoe around so the bow faced downstream. The Uncle's powerful current caught it and swept it down to the Son. In a few minutes they were out of sight.

The Twisted Uncle was a mean river, running through tough country. The Ever-faithful Daughter valley, the territory Com and Torc were used to, had a softening mixture of trees and rolling grass-meadows. The Uncle flowed fast, deep, and cold, fed by the Spire's glaciers and snowfields. The spring runoff was strong and rising. Unlike the other rivers and streams they had explored, this one had no paths or animal trails alongside. As they walked upriver the thin sand beach ran out, replaced by thick trees and every kind of vegetation, tight up against high rocks or steep mud banks. Worst were the toppled-over trees, lying every which way, sometimes on top of each other, sometimes sticking out in the river, bare roots high in the air, impossible to climb over. Had they had a canoe it would have been of no use; the two boys could not have paddled against such a current. The only reasonable solution, Com concluded, was to listen for the sound of the river, in from the bank. When that failed, follow specks of light shining through the trees.

That must have been Blotto's method, too, for it led them to his flop-down; it could hardly be called a camp. On their second day of forest-whacking they came to a high wall angling toward the river, forcing them into a canyon through which the river charged. Most likely they would have to climb over, Com thought, but he decided to explore a possible lower route. They stopped to drink from a spring, as cool, sparkling, and good-tasting as any they had discovered on their adventures. As they drank, they heard a rumbling, "Snaach. Snaach." Turning, they saw two sets of dirty toes sticking out from a snowberry bush. Blotto lay on his back, his giant belly heaving, sucking air, then belching it out; he sounded like clamshells grinding between stones. As they stared, he lifted his hands and waved them wildly, as if slapping away demons. Com bent over to wake him, caught him on the exhale, and gagged. Slooze breath smelled like mint leaves in comparison.

"Tickle his feet," Com told Torc. He did. No change. Torc laughed, then launched himself through the air and landed seat first on his belly. Blotto expelled gas in a thunderous belch and an equally explosive fart. Torc bounced off and ran to escape the rolling, ground-hugging stench. Com followed quickly. Blotto's hands stopped waving and fell to his sides. His mouth filled with a thick, yellow-brown liquid which rose and fell and bubbled, as he attempted to breathe. He retched and the liquid gurgled out of his mouth and onto his beard, ending in a slow-growing puddle around his head. He snorted it into his nose. Fearing that he, their one source of information, would choke on his vomit, Com and Torc ran back and tried to roll him over.

No use; he was too heavy. Blotto blew the rest of his vomit into the air, swiped his mouth and nose with a giant paw and cried, "Waaaa. Waaaa."

"Waaaa?" Com said. "Does he want water?" They ran to the spring, cupped their hands, and spilled it into his mouth. Blotto gurgled and spit. His arms fell limp. He breathed a sigh of what appeared to be final relief and resumed his snoring. "We might as well camp here," Com said. "He might know something. But I doubt it."

Blotto showed them his setup next morning: a hollowed-out tree half, a stirring stick, pulverizing rocks, and piles of makings; it was as if a child had watched Biber brewing slooze and tried to imitate him with the toys in his sand pile. Not having access to Biber's swamp sludge or formulas, of course, Blotto evidently threw in whatever he could find: rotten fish, ground-up beetles, ants and spiders, stump rot, animal fat, berries when he could find them, all mixed into the sweetest-tasting water east of Water Child. When thoroughly stirred, he let it "settle," he told them, until he could wait no longer, then drank the whole batch as fast as he could, the idea being to get as sick as possible. Since it would not ferment he did the next best thing, conjured up a sick-over hangover as bad as if he had gotten drunk on slooze. Poor man, Com thought, everyone else, including his muma it seemed, had gotten over the fire and rampage, had put it behind them. Except Biber. And old Blotto, evidently.

"What do you know about the mountain, Mister Blotto?" Com asked. "What's the best way to get there? Right up to it." Blotto had no idea; he had never ventured past the spring; did not even know whether they could get through the canyon. "Would you like us to wash you up?" Com asked, knowing his muma would want him to offer. Blotto shrugged, not caring whether they did or not. So they washed him with spring water, shook his hand, and said good-bye. He sat in the sun beside the Twisted Uncle, unblinking, clearing his head, contemplating his next Blotto-sized, make-believe drunk.

They followed the river on the canyon rim without seeing the mountain until it turned in what Com felt was the wrong direction. Then, after they climbed a heavily forested ridge, Morning Spire smacked them in the face, forcing their heads up, their mouths open, filling their vision – not with, as from the valley, a shimmering white spike rising out of black-green forests, a mere finger poking into the sky – but with broad sloping snow fields flecked with gray boulders. All mountain. It filled Com's vision as it had filled his dreams. They took it in, then dropped into a ravine.

The land turned upward, ever so slowly. The mountain *became*. The two were so fit from their rambling and exploring, they adjusted easily to the elevation. As they climbed, the trees grew smaller and farther apart: fir, to alpine larch, to mountain hemlock. They stepped over fallen trees without breaking stride. Much of the snow was gone, at least in the sun-warmed places. Water trickled through the grass and ran through the gullies; they sunk knee-deep in the bogs. They walked backward in the seasons, leaving spring-summer behind, entering winter-spring. Tiny blue and pink flowers shining in the grass gave way to spring crocuses poking through the snow. Com picked a flower, chewed it, and swallowed. "Live off the land," he said with a laugh. Torc grabbed a handful and shoved them in his mouth. As he did, he saw a feathery cloud run under the sun. Instantly the air turned cold. They pulled their furs tight around their chests and continued climbing. That night they slept fireless, tight against a boulder, and shivered through it.

"This is it, Torc," Com said as he rose and stretched next morning, "the big one, the big mountain. Are you afraid?"

"Not me. I'm with you."

Far above lay a narrowing sheet of snow, ending in Morning Spire's peak. Whereas from the ridge the day before the mountain had seemed so close it could topple onto them, from this angle the distances seemed longer, almost forbidding. Clouds had moved in during the night, taking away the sunshine's sparkle on the snow, replacing it with muted colors and shadows: dull whites and grays. They munched dried meat and surveyed the vast tilted landscape before them, almost certainly a landscape no one from Beaverton had ever seen. Eastern slopes drifted off to brown. To the west, the direction of home, they saw dark green waves of trees. South, due south, white island peaks poked up here and there. North, due north, Morning Spire rose, majestic, compelling. "We got a break with the cloud cover," Com, ever the optimist, told his pal. "We won't sweat so much while we climb."

"Couldn't those clouds mean bad weather coming in?" Torc asked. "Doesn't it get a lot colder the higher you get?"

"Naw. Not this time of year. Winter's over. But we probably should get some walking poles from lower down. They'd come in handy."

They walked back down into the scraggly trees. The poles they found were sturdy, rough-barked and short. They bashed them against a boulder to test them and snap off the twigs.

For the rest of the morning they placed one fur-wrapped foot in front of the other. As they climbed higher they slowed their steps and took deep breaths between each one. When they reached the rock ledge jutting out of the snow which had been his sight goal, Com said, "Let's take a break." To their surprise, they were thirsty, not hungry. And more to their surprise, melting snow in their mouths did not satisfy their thirst. Dried beaver tail's salty taste did not help, either. They cooled down quickly, too quickly, as they sat on the cold ledge. "A good thing we brought extra wraps," Com said, as he pulled his second fur around him. Torc had already done that. A shaft of sun broke through. The boys faced up, drank in its warmth, then shivered when it disappeared. No wind. Not a breath. But fast-moving thin clouds circled Morning Spire's peak.

They exchanged few words; there was little to say. Because of the cloud cover, the snow's crust held firm and they walked with relative ease, always upward in the thinning air. Had the sun been out for an extended time, it would have softened the frozen surface, and light-footed as they were, each step would have been a punch-through, then an energy-sapping liftout, over and over until they were worn out. As it was, they broke through the crust with their poles and sucked flat pieces of it as they climbed.

By mid-afternoon the snowfield had narrowed to a slot with jagged outcroppings on either side. Com stopped and sniffed. "Smells like rotten seagull's eggs up here," he said. "Anyway, we're almost up." They were at the foot of a spine, the point of transition where the mountain rose sharply. The magnificent view behind them was gone, obscured by dark clouds. Com started up the spine, poking holes in the crust with his pole, then wedging his toes into them. He leaned forward, balancing himself with his hand. "Owwww, I'm falling," Torc said, laughing, after sliding back a few feet and stopping himself with his pole.

"Maybe we'd better use my rope," Com said as he descended to meet him. He uncoiled it, and not knowing a better way, tied one end to each of their waists, leaving the maximum length between. He pulled it over his shoulder and took up the slack. They walked into chilled air. Com heard no sounds except for occasional rolling rocks dropping onto boulders below. The clouds, however, were streaking around the mountain top. Not the soft, white-to-gray clouds of a few hours ago, but torn-apart, gray-to-black streaks. Com reckoned that in spite of the darkening sky, they had four or five daylight hours left. They would top out in an hour or so, then scurry down to the tree line, where they would spend the night. Although the rope was good, Com felt Torc tiring; he felt as if he was pulling him along.

After an hour of cold, painful, stepping, the spine ran out and the slope grew steeper yet. "Uh-oh," Com muttered as he looked into a deep blue crack. He studied it, taking up rope as Torc struggled to him. The crack ran horizontally, perhaps twenty paces in either direction. "We can't jump it, that's for sure," Com said. "Looks better if we go left. It runs into that wall the other way." Torc stood, wheezing and puffing, holding Com's arm to steady himself.

Com walked carefully along the lip, sliding one foot, then sliding the other to meet it, slack rope in one hand, pole in the other, tip bouncing on the ice. Torc followed

CRACK. The lip edge gave. "Falling!" Com yelled, "Hold on." Torc reacted fast and well. He dropped to his knees, jammed his pole, and bent the rope around. The rope whizzed over the ice and snapped taut. Torc held. Both climbers hung on, gasping for breath – from altitude, from exhaustion, from fear.

Cold as it was in the eerie blue chamber, Com was sweating. Dangling in the air, he swung his feet around, desperate for a foothold. Nothing. He felt a slender ledge with a crack behind. He wedged his hand in and yelled, "Hold fast! I'm climbing!"

Torc flattened himself on the slope and held. Two, three, four pulls, and Com was up.

Torc lay ten feet down the slope, rope shaking in one hand, pole chattering on the ice, knees jerking uncontrollably. Then, battered and cold, he stopped moving, and lay exhausted and terrified. Com blew on his hands and shook his head. "Only a short way to go," he said. Torc did not move. "Torc! Coming with me?" Torc stared with uncomprehending eyes. He lowered his cheek to the ice. "Okay, you stay there," Com said. "Couple a minutes. I didn't come this far to turn back now." He untied his rope and left it with Torc.

Com worked along the edge on hands and knees, and sometimes on his stomach. At the end of the crack he attacked the final pitch. Punching in foot and handholds was out of the question; this was solid ice, not crusted-over snow. He pulled himself up with freezing fingers. Slipped back to the edge. Pulled off his foot wraps. Shoved them inside his fur. Attacked the slope again.

Pain shot through his fingers, up his arms and into his neck. Instead of discouraging him, it energizing him. If my hands are alive, he thought, I'm alive. And I'm going to make it. He clawed his way up.

Com flung his arm over the crest. Then his head. Wind bursts threw frozen knives in his face, tore at his mouth, rattled his lips. He tried to breathe; his lungs refused air. He eased back, clinging to the ice. What's happening? he thought. Why didn't I hear this before? The wind moaned, then increased to a high-pitched whine. Snow and ice shot straight up, and, twisting and swirling, turning everything white. "Well, Mister Freezing Wind," Com said, "this is my moment and you're not going to deny me." He kicked his leg over the crest, pulled himself up, and lay prone on Morning Spire's peak, his hand covering his windward ear. "One on top. Two on top. Three on top. That's all I ask." He loosened his grip on the ice.

He stopped sliding when his feet hit the crack, ripping his knees, tearing his fingers on the way down. Had he not hit the narrow end he would have gone in – again. Blinded by whipping snow he slid along the crack on his belly, hanging on with his hands until he thought he was above Torc. He let go and slid down braking with fingers and toes. "Torc! Torc!" he yelled. His foot touched fur.

Com felt till he found a face. Slap! Slap! "Talk to me, Torc!" he screamed, punching his arms and beating his shoulders. "Hey, I made it! I made it! But we've got to get out of here!" Com reached inside for his foot wraps. Gone. Got to save the rope, he thought. He pulled it from Torc's hand and looped it over his shoulder. He grabbed his friend's arm and slid him down the spine.

They crashed into an ice pile and stopped. "We've got to get down, get out of this storm! You've got to get up and walk, Torc!" No movement; no sound but the screaming wind. Com rubbed Torc's arms. "That help?" He could barely form words on his lips. He slid his hands down Torc's legs. "Ow!" A jagged bone slashed his hand. Torc's leg twisted back on itself.

Com grabbed Torc around his chest and forced him downhill. They fell and rose, slid and stopped. The white wind screamed at them. Com leaned into it, trying keep from being blown over.

The crust gave way and Com dropped out of the wind – into silence – or what seemed like silence as the wind roared above. Torc landed on top, now come to life, shivering violently, gasping for breath. Com dug in the snow with unfeeling hands. When he could dig no more he flopped into the depression and pulled Torc in after him. He felt Torc's hand bump weakly against his side. Once. Twice. And he knew what it meant.

"I'm not leaving you, pal," Com said through unmoving lips. "We'll get through this together." He pressed his shoulder into the warm snow.

26

A Rope in the Snow

BEAVERTON HAD taken a spring chill, and Netti had moved her work on the head protector into the family's shelter. Ziiza's latest idea was to create a ring of interlaced reeds, or some such material or materials, fat enough to fit comfortably on a runner's head, hold the rock a finger width above, and give it some sideways support. This had conjured up an elegant picture in the mind – that had proved to be completely impractical. Simply put, to achieve the desired cushioning effect, the ring was so large that the poor test runner could not reach over and around to steady the rock; very few were going to be able to balance rock and cushion while running as fast as they could on Beaverton's muddy, rutted paths.

Adamant Org still refused to test one, let alone race with one. Suffx, too. When Ziiza showed him her crude, oversized prototypes he laughed. Netti, with her headaches and recovery program, was out of the question as a tester (but vital as a maker). Com could have signed on as a tester but he had no interest in competing. Edu was willing. Govvi was not. No matter, both were non-athletic and too small to handle the hefty rocks. That left Ziiza. The plus: the inventor is the best evaluator of her own invention (at least in its early stages). The minus: her foot bothered her frightfully during and after any lengthy run. Although she had given up competing in favor of enterprise and the lure of wealth, testing was different; she could run far enough to make a quick evaluation and stop when the pain became unbearable.

"Toss them," Ziiza told Netti as she limped up to the shelter covered with sweat.

"All of them?" Netti's face pained.

"Every one."

"You mean into the fire, Muma? After all this work?" She teared up.

"Oh, Netti, it isn't you. Your work is fine. The problem is my design."

"Can't we save them? To sit on or something?"

"Trust me, darling, we have to get that design out of our heads. They don't work and they don't look good. I have this feeling, same as I had with slooze and the Sita." Ziiza looked up, as if success was hovering above, ready to float down and land in her hands. Netti stared at her over the fire with dull eyes. "No guarantees about this rock running thing," Ziiza continued. "It could be a fad. Could fade tomorrow. I don't think it will, but it could. That's not the point, however. The point is, if it does take off – I've said this before – we have to be first in line, first with the best. Not only that, we have to convince everyone they can't win without them. Whether it's true or not," she added, quickly. "But it will be. Just saving their bloody heads is enough. See what I mean, Netti? I'm talking about a vision here, a potential empire. Sita's Lair was a toad stool by comparison. I have no interest in starting that place up again. If Biber wants to fix his brew-crock and start brewing slooze after his leg heals, it's fine with me. But I'm through cooking and serving and pouring slooze. I just thought you'd like to know." Netti rubbed her temples with her thumbs.

Starting over is discouraging, but it can lead to better things. As in this case. Ziiza had learned a valuable lesson at the Sita: innovative ideas come from motivated people. Simply asking folks, surveying them for ideas, seldom if ever produces anything other than perfunctory lists – of the same old thoughts. So she spent the next few days walking around H&G, listening to Skedaddle from a distance, casually fingering vendors' wares, snacking on dried tail, and thinking. Litti was scarce; no mystery what she was up to. Sister Sissi was busy making the café ready for the Sea Tracers, but was delighted to chat. Ziiza stopped to listen to a Barclaw story, but found herself enjoying the children's actions and expressions more than his outlandish tale. Stepping over the finish line in front of Town Hall thrilled her. She *saw* her sales booth next to officials' stand. She *heard* herself describing her sensational new product – what to call it? – to customers. She *felt* the piles of barter and tail grow against her leg, so fast Govvi could not keep her tally board straight.

If asking people to do your thinking and inventing for you is a futile exercise, discussing your ideas with a knowledgeable, trustworthy, and sympathetic person is not. After her amble through H&G, she walked around Outer Circle against the flow of the oncoming practice runners. A few weeks ago she would have seen only serious runners training: Org, Sufx, Quord Junior, the leaders. Now it seemed everyone in Beaverton was training. Or exercising for the fun of it. And it was fun; the more bloody sweat blinding them, running down faces and necks, the more fun they were having. Badges of honor? Wrong. Ziiza knew it could not last. The blood had to go, or all but the hard-core enthusiasts would soon tire of rock running. A bloodless, comfortable head protector. But how?

The answer, or the first part of the answer, was simple. Forget about the space. Forget about the ring. Rest a protector on the runner's head. Rock balanced on top. Or held steady by hand or hands. Or a combination of both. In the abstract, it had to be compact, resilient but not too resilient, and good-looking. Especially good-looking. But there are different degrees of *simple*. Simple in concept does not mean simple in construction, else it can be copied too easily by hornsy-insy competitors, or, forbid the thought, fashioned at home. The esteemed customer must believe he is getting his money's worth. In addition, the product must eventually pass beyond good-looking and take on a cachet of exclusivity. Yes, even in a sport as crude as rock running. That was the point. Ziiza, Biber, and the kids had already done something similar with the Sita's Lair. (But that was history.) Ziiza was so close her teeth hurt.

Although Sufx often ran in the hills, he usually finished his week's training on Friday by running around Outer Circle one-and-one-half times the length of the coming race, at eighty or ninety percent of racing speed, his final tune-up. (Then an agonizing Saturday of idleness, nail-biting, fighting the urge to get out and run himself out, blow off his nervous energy. Essential idleness to avoid "leaving your race on the practice course," as he reminded himself again and again.) "Sufx," Ziiza called, as he ran passed, "I'd like to talk to you. Stop by when you're done, will you?"

"How 'bout now?" Sufx pushed his rock up and walked out from under it without looking, his crowd-pleasing finishing move. Thunk. "I'm done for the week," he said. "Ya doin', Ziiza?"

"Fine, just fine."

"Miss the old joint?"

"I'm over it, Sufx, believe it or not. All behind me. You, too, from the looks of it."

"Yeah, with rock running keeping me busy and all. I just wish Biber could get his leg together and start making the stuff again. Maybe in small batches. I could use a good sloozzle now and then. Have to replace my bodily fluids, you know." He laughed his deep, good-natured laugh.

"Talk seriously, Sufx."

"I *am* serious."

"Sufx, you can help me," Ziiza said, eyes alight. "I'm this close." She held her thumb to her forefinger. She spit on his wiping fur and cleaned his face – something Org would never allow. "Beaverton's ripe for this thing," she said. "Big time potential. Big time. But the blood must go." Sufx listened. "My designs are terrible. I've thrown them out. Netti's crushed, of course. All of her work for naught. I need a new direction. I've been thinking *flat*."

"Moss."

"Moss?"

"Try moss. See what you come up with."

"Will you test it for me?

"You know I'd do anything for you, Ziiza, after all you've done for me. But I have to tell you, it's got to be good. Not just look good. Really *be* good. Help me win races." He stopped short of *keep on beating Org*. She patted his arm. They sat. "Now I've got a problem for you to solve," he said. "Since you're so interested in seeing rock running go big time, someone has got to address the fairness issue. It isn't fair the way runners grab any old rock that Senior says is okay and off they go. I'm just a little guy. Why should I have to run with something the same size as – a bigger guy? I'm winning now, but later on, when they get better. . . ." He trailed off. "Since you're interested, Ziiza."

"I've mentioned it to Senior."

"Don't mention it, solve it," he said wearily. "Senior looks at any change as a threat to his authority. Besides, he's got Junior running with a lava rock full of holes. Nobody dares complain or he'll give them a hard time. I gave you *moss*. You give me *fair*."

"I'm on it. Believe me," Ziiza said, with a friendly nudge. Sufx walked away with his rock bellied in front of him, his knotted muscles standing out on his shoulders. "You're my tester," she shouted.

Ziiza could not wait to work with moss, did not even bother to attend Sunday's race, which Sufx won easily. Org, bothered by a slow-healing head cut, finished a poor-for-him fourth, still respectable considering the size of the field. She sent Edu and Dg to report, which, together with Bitta's news, provided more detail than she wanted or needed. Netti was delighted to hear the magic word, *moss*; her headache vanished. Litti appeared that morning, still glowing but not eager to talk. She joined Ziiza, Netti, and Govvi to scout for moss. Not that there was a shortage in or around Beaverton. But it had to be the right kind.

Fourteen varieties of moss in fourteen piles were lined up in front of Ziiza's shelter. Govvi registered each one on her tally board. Netti pulled the fibers apart and stretched them. Could they be twisted or woven together, made into a yarn or thread? Edu waved a puff on a stick over the fire, drying it, trying to change its properties. Dg tugged at his fur top, growling playfully.

"Not now, Dg," Edu said. Ziiza sat, thinking, evaluating, taking in every move and comment.

"Miss Ziiza! Miss Ziiza!" Blotto's bloated hairy figure lurched into the yard. "Miss Ziiza," he said, sinking to his knees, trying to catch his breath. "I'm worried about the boys. Your Com and the other one."

"Torc?"

"I guess. They found my camp, stayed the night, cleaned me up. Off to climb the Spire, they said. But I was pretty well . . . well . . ."

"Blotto?" Edu said, with a snicker.

"Right. At the time. It's been days. Never come back through my place. I was wondering if they were home already. Maybe took another route back."

"Omygosh," Ziiza said, and the breath went out of her. "I've been so preoccupied. I'm so used to him just going off exploring. A few days more than usual. The time got away from me. What do you mean, *climb* the Spire? I don't understand."

"It means walk all the way to the top, Muma," Govvi said. "Or try to."

"It's never been done, Miss Ziiza," Blotto said. "That's what I'm told. I have a feeling. And I'm worried."

"Well, is it dangerous?" Ziiza asked.

No one spoke. Finally Govvi said, "It's all white, Muma, covered with snow. And ice."

"I'm going to see Barclaw," Ziiza snapped. "Maybe he knows something about the Spire. They followed her to Town Hall.

Barclaw had not been on the mountain, he told them. But he had been a ways up the Twisted Uncle. That was the extent of his knowledge. He did not think Castor knew more. It had been so many years ago that it was difficult for him to fit the pieces together in his mind: how fast Com and Torc might have traveled, their route, the weather. It could be serious. Or they could be wandering around, exploring, enjoying themselves. The only thing they knew for certain was what Blotto reported and that they had been gone an unusually long time. "I'm going to ask Mistermayor for time off," Barclaw announced. "And if he turns me down this time, I'm going anyway."

"Thanks, Barclaw," Ziiza said. "I couldn't ask for more. I just don't know what to do."

"I do," Barclaw said. "We have to go up there and find those boys."

Org, stung by his fourth place finish, was training harder than ever. "My good blazes," he said, "another rescue? Didn't we just get Netti out of the Mire?"

"I didn't plan on this, Org," Ziiza said, clenching her teeth. "You don't have to come. He's only your brother."

Barclaw took charge. Pack and be ready to leave as soon as possible, he told them. Get over to Pop&Jay's. Did anyone know where the boy, Torc, lived? Anything about his parents? Not even Govvi could answer that one. No time to hunt for them, even to ask Bitta. The real question, he mused, picking his teeth with a splinter, was whether his old enemies would ferry them up the Twisted Uncle, or failing that, lend them their canoe.

But when they reached "Popville," Pop&Jay greeted everyone warmly, even shook Barclaw's hand. They recounted giving the boys the ride and expressed concern for their safety. "Nice boys," Pop said. "Very polite. Very knowledgeable."

The problem was the canoe; it was not the largest. When Jay offered to go up to the Grand Muma and hire Prong, or at least borrow his canoe, Ziiza cut him off: "We can manage without his assistance. Do not *bother*."

Org took the bow, his old position. Behind him: Ziiza, Edu and Dg, Blotto, and their gear. Then Barclaw, steering. Govvi was a tight squeeze so Ziiza kissed her good-bye and told her to go home — although she suspected she wouldn't. The canoe rode badly, but, given Blotto's enormous weight and his minimal paddling skills, it was the best arrangement Barclaw could devise.

Except for her venture to the Mire, and her walks with Litti, Ziiza had not been out of Beaverton since she had arrived two years ago. As the canoe crossed the river, then hugged the far shore to minimize the current, she felt as if she was slipping into another world, wilder than the Sea Trace. Which indeed she was.

* * *

Govvi waved good-bye, standing with Pop&Jay. When the canoe reached mid-river, she said quietly, not to either man in particular, "I'll bet if I was lost up there she wouldn't be going after me." Their eyes locked in amazement.

Jay took a deep breath, dropped to a knee, and said, "Chances are your brother and his friend will be fine; they're just off exploring, lost track of the time. Anyway, there's nothing we can do till they get back. Sooooo," he said with a grin. "Do you have any tricks for your old friends? Better get going if you do, Little One, because we've got something for you."

She built a fire, of course. They clapped and cheered. They laughed off her weak protest to be on her way — "I have to get back to work. Look after Netti." — with an invitation to join them craw-fishing in the stream. "Kicking over rocks and getting your fingers nipped," Jay said, "is the most fun ever. Besides, they're tastiest best right now. Roast 'em on sticks till their shells peel and flame up. Yuuum." He followed with the never-fail clincher: "You got to eat, don't you?"

After a friendly afternoon of stream wading and a delicious dinner of crawfish tails, Pop said, "Little One, how would you like to become someone very special? Not that you aren't already princessly special; we know that. But have a special job, join a special team." With each *special*, Govvi's eyes grew rounder. Pop continued: "No secret we're not too friendly with Mistermayor and his crew over there." He pointed west over the hill. "You know all that. How it came about is no matter. And as a smart girl like you has already figured out, this Popville or Jaytown layout here is nothing but a ruse." Govvi opened her mouth to speak. Pop put his finger to his lips and continued: "Fact is, we don't want anyone buying our lots. We wouldn't part with one if a person climbed right up that tree and dove headfirst to claim it for himself. Cried out in pain. Offered us double. Threatened to whack us up the head. We still wouldn't sell." Thinking he had outdone himself, Pop snickered, grabbed Jay and rocked him back and forth. As usual they fell over laughing. After their self-congratulatory celebration had run its course they lay sprawled on the grass, heaving and panting. Jay ran for the trees to relieve himself.

"The question is," Jay said, taking up Pop's line when he returned, "does a special position, a special task, interest a very talented, very energetic, and, if I say so, under-appreciated and under-rewarded, person such as yourself?"

"It might," Govvi said, her eyes sparkling, "if I knew what you were getting at."

They talked till the fire burned itself out, and what they were getting at interested Govvi very much indeed.

* * *

"Org. Ziiza. Ease off. Slow down," Barclaw said, trying not to order. He did not have to tell Blotto. "We're all worried and want to get there as fast as we can. But we have to pace ourselves for a long trip. We're bucking the runoff current, and it's as strong as I've ever seen." Instead of paddling straight against the flow he eased the canoe around deadly strainers — fallen trees, almost submerged, hanging onto the bank — and under riverside branches, close in to take advantage of every snatch of slack water, no mean feat with an overloaded canoe.

Ziiza's rush of frantic paddling expired, not because of Barclaw's nagging but because of what he said when, tired-armed, they turned east into the

Twisted Uncle's onrush. "The distance we've come on the Son," he told them, "well, it will be five or six times that to get up this one." Blotto grunted his agreement as he dipped his paddle daintily in the water. As Ziiza eased into a rhythm she thought of Com, along with Netti, her overlooked middle children. She pictured his wide smile as he stood before her proudly reporting his discoveries – on the beach, or around Beaverton. She thought of him running up to her, clutching her hand, telling her he was going to climb Morning Spire – and a chill ran up her back. How could I have been so thoughtless? So eager to get back to Litti's tantalizing narrative. Said yes so casually. But he had planned it that way. Set her up for an automatic. Up and gone before she had had time to think. Adventurous boy. Wily, too. Nothing stood in his way, not even his muma.

Barclaw stopped counting cadence with a, "My jaw's tired." Ziiza raised her paddle and aimed it at a solitary cloud. An osprey dropped out of the sky, splashed into the river, and flew off with a fish flopping in its talons. She stroked deep, dragged her left hand under, and lifted her paddle. The cold water ran down her arm, inside her loose-fitting wrap, down her side, and collected on the canoe bottom. She shifted the paddle to her right and repeated the move. She worked the raise-and-drip into her stroke. The sun grew hot and the water chilled her skin. Barclaw hummed to himself, pretending not to notice. "Is that a kingfisher?" Edu asked, pointing to the blue and white bird rubbing its beak on a branch. Dg lapped at the water Ziiza had run into the canoe.

It took two- and-a-half days of hard, steady paddling to reach the canyon. They pulled out at Blotto's camp, drank his spring water, and thanked him for his concern. "My heart goes out to you and the boys, Miss Ziiza," he said as they parted. Ziiza hugged the docile man-bear. With a few hours of daylight left, they plunged into the forest, leaving him to look after Pop&Jay's canoe.

They made their way up Morning Spire's shoulder, shouting "Com! Com! Torc! Hello!" Whapped sticks against sticks. Clapped. Anything to make noise. The only response: chattering chipmunks and squawking jays. Barclaw halted at the vast, up-tilting snowfield. "Now I've been after lost ones afore," he said. "We'll start here." He pointed along the ragged tree line. "We spread out and walk from one side to the other. Not that there is an end to the snow, but it's the best we can do. Then we all move up and do it again. So Org, why don't you start over there. Then Edu. Then you, Ziiza. Then me."

"If they were climbing to the top," Ziiza said, looking through Barclaw, "where would they start?"

"Look at what we're standing on," Barclaw said. "Clean snow. No dust. No bark shreds. No twigs or needles or cones sinking into sun pockets. Not only that, the surface is soft. Why we're sinking in. Struggling to walk. All points to a recent snow. There's been a second winter up here."

"Where would they start?" Ziiza pushed her point..

"I have no idea," Barclaw said. "But if they were going up this side, the gradually sloping side, I'd say they'd start right about here."

"Sorry to nix your plan, Barclaw," Ziiza said softly. "But I don't have time to waste down here." She turned, faced the peak, and walked straight up the snowfield. The three stood in place, watching her go.

"Muma," Edu yelled, "I'm coming with you." Dg bounded after him.

"I can't argue," Barclaw said, turning to Org, "we have so little to go on. Come on. You walk that way. I'll go over here. Then turn back. We'll meet, move up, and do it again. Frustrating. Pointless, really. But we've got to do something. " Org nodded and obeyed.

Ziiza, Edu, and Dg walked resolutely up the slope until Barclaw and Org were specks below. The sun rising in the cloudless sky glared harshly off the snow. They covered their faces and peered through finger slits. After hours of climbing in silence, the thin air and slippery surface slowed Ziiza. "Come on up, Edu," she called to the boy struggling below. "Let's stop and catch our breath." She scooped up a handful of crystallized snow and sucked. When he reached her they melted snow in their mouths and chewed dried beaver tail. Edu tossed some tail to Dg. He bolted it and ran off.

They sat in the snow with their hands over their eyes till the pain abated. Then they surveyed the most beautiful view they had ever seen – but did not want to admit it. The faint smell of sulfur stung their noses. Org and Barclaw had disappeared. Dg worked his head between Ziiza and Edu. He nudged again and Edu patted his head. Dg whined as if asking for food. Edu slid his hand under his chin and stroked and felt – a rope. Dg was holding it in his mouth; it trailed off behind. Edu took the end, examined it, and passed it to Ziiza.

"The rope," Ziiza screamed. "Could it be? His rope? Com's rope?" She leapt to her feet and followed it. The end was free. "Dg, where did you find it? Did you pull it out of the snow?" She ran up the slope. "There must be a hole. Did he pull it out of the snow? Edu, come help me look for it." Edu ran to her. Dg followed. "I can't find it, can't find anything. Dg! Dg! Show me! Show me where you got it! My boy could be buried in there!" She grabbed Dg and pushed him ahead of her. "Find him! Find him!" Dg stood. "Why, why did you pull it out?" Ziiza screamed. "Now we don't know where to look, to dig, anything!" Dg cocked his head and came to her. Her kick caught him in the chest and tumbled him over. "Bad, bad creature. Our one chance to find him and you've ruined it." She ran at him. Kicked again. Dg shifted to the side and she missed. She slipped in the snow and sat down, splay-legged, sobbing. Dg backed out of range and eyed her.

Edu ran to Dg and threw his arms around his neck. "He can't talk, Muma." Now Edu was crying. "Dg's sorry, sorry about the rope." After a pause, he said, "It is Com's rope, Muma."

Ziiza ran up the slope, punching holes in the snow. When she could run no more, she dug, frantically plunging her hands in the snow, throwing it up, and away, behind. She felt a layer of ice and bashed it with her heel. Pried up a piece and tried to use it as a shovel. It broke on the first scoop. She threw it as far as she could. She dug with her hands, scooped with her arms, moaning and wailing. Edu sat stroking Dg, looking away. With stiff red hands, Ziiza made the hole grow. Her frozen fingers hit another layer of ice. She walked down to the weeping Edu, and knelt. She threw her arms around him, drew in the shaking creature, and hugged them both. "It's over," she said. "If he's up here, he's gone." She pulled away, slid her finger under Dg's muzzle, and stroked. "Sorry, old friend. I didn't mean it. It's just that. . . ."

"It's time to go, Muma," Edu said, when their crying had slowed. "Time to go home."

"Wait here," Ziiza said. She walked back to the hole, coiled the rope, and dropped it in.

27

The Original Z-sport Company

ZIIZA SLOUCHED in the canoe, legs straight ahead, dragging her hands in the water. Since it was a downsteam run all the way and Blotto had stayed at his camp, her paddling was not needed. Org in the bow scanned the river for below-the-surface rocks and submerged trees, standing occasionally to look ahead. Barclaw dragged his paddle, exerting himself only to alter course. Edu sat in her lap, back pressed tight against her, hanging onto Dg as if to crush him. She plunged her arm into the cool water past her elbow. She withdrew it and skimmed her fingers on the surface, creating intersecting Vs, their ripple-sounds overridden by the gurgle-splash of the blunt bow. They made it to Pop&Jay's in a day. On the river, no one said a word.

Govvi and Netti were standing beside the shelter when they arrived. From their expressions, Ziiza's one fragment of hope vanished: that Com and Torc had somehow made it back, that they had crossed, simply missed each other, that Com's rope on the mountain had been just that, a lost rope. She staggered to them, weak-kneed and fuzzy-headed. They embraced. She dropped to her knees, crawled inside the shelter.

Ziiza dreamed of a slender, weather-skinned boy running away from her on the sand. He ran down the beach in exaggerated slow motion, made slower by his crossing back and forth in front of her, running from forest edge, across the beach, into the surf, then back, and across, and over again. The sun rose and he kept on running, gradually increasing the distance between them. She called, waved her arms, and called again, but did not hear her own voice. He turned his head as if *he* had heard, smiled back at her – she thought she saw him smile – and disappeared into the gray-silver mist rising out of the sand. She sat up with a jerk; it was morning.

From the earliest, neighbors on their way to work stopped to console Ziiza and her family. Addle canceled school and walked home with Edu and his classmates. Ziiza was touched by the gesture; how unlike him. Or, possibly, how like him. Had she misjudged? He and his Grassyknoll contingent stayed on, standing off to the side, sober-faced, while others talked, patted, and pressed Ziiza's hands. Barclaw brought Wife Barclaw. Stepping out of his constable and search leader roles, he hugged her, smoothed her hair, and chucked her chin. As with Addle, so unlike the everyday man. Bitta was another early visitor. Hobart wobbled on her shoulder, unusually quiet. "Will you be having a memorial service?" she asked. Ziiza shook her head and mumbled, "Evidently this is it." Bitta slipped away and went back to work.

Org excused himself to go running; he was not one for gatherings and small talk and Ziiza understood. He was never particularly close to his creative, adventurous, younger brother, either. Even in running, the one interest they shared, their goals were ever so different. The only sibling he played with was Edu, whom he occasionally threw around. Although Edu was in no way athletic, he liked it. And, with his sometimes silly questions and loquacious nature, Edu carried the conversation and made Org laugh. But however slowly it came, when his grief over Com's unfinished life finally hit him, it hit him hard. He dealt with it by running, rock cutting into his head, blood running over his face, his dim penitence for ignoring his brother while he was here.

Ziiza had half-expected a few friends stop by: Sister Sissi, Sufx, Litti of course and a few others; Biber was already there. How wrong she was. Mistermayor led a delegation, everyone from Town Hall. He stood towering over her, tears streaming down his elongated cheeks, and dripping from his river rock chin, seemingly on the verge of a speech. But he stopped open-mouthed, evidently thinking better of it. Polcat and the council arrived shortly thereafter. Neighbors who had never so much as nodded on the path or said "Hi" from their yards sidled up, squeezed her hands, and stepped back to become part of the ever-growing multitude. H&G vendors closed up early and came singly or in groups. Skedaddle set up, and without invitation or permission, played softly for what turned out to be an all day and into the night celebration of Com's life. Ziiza, Govvi, Netti, and Edu stood stiffly, receiving their hugs and handshakes and words. Dg, sitting respectfully beside Edu, sniffed everyone's legs as they passed, as if authenticating their sincerity.

At first Ziiza was shocked at the idea of music; Com may have been artistic but he was not musical. Bitta's doing? Then the familiar soothing sounds seemed only too appropriate. Old Sita's Lair customers, quite a few of them, recounted tricks he had played, drinks he had spilled, jokes he had embellished and passed along. How they would miss him. And how they missed the Sita. And Biber's Obtuse (as they glanced at the split-in-two brew-crock yawning behind the shelter). And Ziiza's to-drool-for Tip-n-Dips. People who had never known Com brought food, left food, and stood around eating food, passing and sharing. They talked to one another, caught up on Beaverton gossip, exchanged pleasantries, even jokes. And who should arrive, but Wife Dragga. She encircled Ziiza with spindly arms, bussed her, and said, "Want to wrestle?" Her timing was right, and Ziiza, try as she might, could not suppress a chuckle.

The second night Ziiza dreamed the beach dream again. In the morning the thick pain in her chest was gone – replaced by a different pain, a hollow pain lurking in the back of her neck, that bloomed whenever she tried to forget. Yesterday's people, however well-meaning and compassionate, had simply helped her through the day. One day gotten through. But she was grateful for that. How, she wondered, would Com's brothers and sisters handle it? They had faced many dangers. Death could have come to any of them on the Sea Trace. Netti for one could easily have died from her head wound. In fact, in fact. . . . But they had made it to Beaverton.

Litti was waiting with hot tea when Ziiza hobbled over. They faced each other. Stared at their hands. After minutes of silent friendship, Litti said softly, without looking up, "Have you needs for Water Child?"

Ziiza responded with a question of her own: "Do you meet him there?" Litti nodded and her color rose. "You can smile, Litti," she said. "You can show it. My loss should not diminish your happiness. Quite the opposite; sharing your joy diminishes my sadness."

Yes, Litti told her, they met most mornings at Water Child. Spent days together, walking, searching, and collecting. And yes, she confessed, as if Ziiza needed to be told, they were in love. "Water Child should be a happy place, is a happy place," Ziiza said finally. "And it's your special place. I will not go there. I would be intruding. Besides, I have a grand plan. I'm going to bury my sorrow in my work. If you thought I worked hard at the Sita, well, you haven't seen anything. Rock running is going to be big in this town. And if it doesn't get big on its own, I'm going to make it big. I felt it before and I feel it stronger now. That's how I'm going to push away the pain of losing my boy. Not to mention the ache of Milli's leaving. Netti's problems. Org's turning away from me. And Govvi acting so, I don't know, weird. Edu and Dg seem to be the only ones left with level heads. And you, Litti; I don't forget. I so appreciate your counsel and friendship. I don't know what I'd do without you. I hope you understand, Water Child is not mine. It's yours. And Arbo's. My answer, my only hope of an answer, is to create the biggest moneymaking enterprise this place has ever seen. Astonish Beaverton. Pull the family together again, maybe even bring Milli back. Order of march, you know. Just like the Sea Trace. We fought for our lives, over and over. A race against winter. And yet, as I look back on it, they were simple, happy times. We were all together. Moving to Beaverton. Strange, huh?"

"That would be Com's wants?"

"Absolutely."

* * *

Gstan's excitement gave him the courage to go directly to Ziiza on his return. Yes, the same man who had given up on her and had slunk away on that long-ago morning with no idea where he was going except south to the sun.

"Hi ya, Ziiza," he said, approaching the shelter.

"Oh, Gstan," she said, giving him a sisterly hug. "You just disappeared. Where have you been all winter?" He shrugged. Netti, sitting nearby, pressing handfuls of moss into woven rings, smiled. Govvi sat in the shelter entrance, bending over the tally board in her lap. She looked up and gave him the smallest of waves.

Gstan reached into his pack and withdrew a sharp-edged rectangular stone two hands long and a thumb thick. "This, Ziiza and lovely daughters," he said, turning it slowly, "is the most amazing stone ever seen in Beaverton. Heck, the most amazing stone seen anywhere."

"So?" Govvi said.

"ThinStones, I'm going to call them. I've had a long time to think up a name. Rather like it, don't you? The name. ThinStones."

"And?" Govvi again.

"Watch this." Gstan crouched, motioned Govvi aside and squeezed into the shelter. The ThinStone glowed soft yellow-green, bright enough to throw a faint light on his face and flow throughout the shelter.

"Wow!" Netti said. "Just wow!"

"And what, you ask," Gstan said, looking squarely at not-impressed-enough Govvi, "does it do? As if a glowing stone isn't enough, isn't the most amazing thing you've ever seen." He stuck out his jaw, demanding agreement. After a glimmer, he continued: "What does a ThinStone do, you ask? Everything. Anything you can think of: remember things, improve your mind, play games. Anything with numbers."

"Ge-Stan," Ziiza chided.

"Try this." He pushed past Govvi and handed the ThinStone to Ziiza. She bobbled it in her hands. He caught it before it dropped and held it still while she got a grip. "See, it's not hot. The glow is perfectly cool. And this isn't the only color they come in. Well, try it, Ziiza." She looked at him in wonderment. "Just ask it a question. Like, two times twelve? How much? You don't even have to say it, just think it."

"That's silly," Ziiza said. "I already know the answer: twenty-four." Netti tittered and Govvi rolled her eyes.

Gstan's face grew stern. "Five hundred and seventeen times thirteen equals? Say it, quick."

"Five hundred and seventeen times thirteen equals?" Ziiza looked at him. "Well?"

"Oh, yeah, I forgot to tell you. You have to give it a squeeze while you're asking."

Right, Gstan.

"Not hard, just enough to make solid contact. And don't hurt your fingers on the edges."

Ziiza held the faintly-glowing stone in one hand, pressed with the thumb and forefinger of the other, and said, "Five hundred and seventeen times thirteen equals . . . sixty-seven hundred and twenty-one."

"Well! Well!" Gstan said, jumping up, dancing a tight circle, and thrusting his fist in the air. He jerk-stopped in front of Govvi, busily scratching on her tally board. "Is she right? Is she?"

"Seems to be," Govvi said, twirling her blackened stick. "Should we tell him, Muma?" she continued. "Tell him about the rock running revolution? *Our* new venture? *Our* products? *Our* ideas? Tell him about something *really* big?"

Ziiza's mind flooded. While he was away, she gushed, rock running had exploded in popularity, just as she had anticipated. More and more people, she told him, were running, racing, even people who had never thought about running for fun. Even in winter. Rock running had thumped the drumhead of Beaverton's consciousness. Why? Folks are bored with easy living. They craved physical action because they seldom hunted, fished, or gathered anymore. Needed an outlet for competitive urges that trail-way fisticuffs did not satisfy. Something different. Anything different. Ziiza saw money in it. Big money. She and Netti, she continued her harangue, had designed and built new head protectors. Tested them in races. Tore them apart. Rebuilt them. Or burned them and started over.

"How about calling them Ziis, or Zees, or something like that. Z-something," Gstan said, with a mischievous smile. "After yourself. In all modesty of course. Strictly for marketing reasons."

"I've already thought of that," Ziiza said coolly. "I forgot to tell you; they're called Z-Zs."

Is he mocking me, helping me, putting me down, or what?

"Pardon me, Ziiza," Gstan said, backtracking, "but I've had a lot of time to think, especially about naming things. Naming products that need selling, to be exact."

That was all Ziiza needed to keep spilling. Org was not cooperating, and her bad foot hurt too much for her to continue running, she told him, so she had been forced to hire Biber's assistant, Sufx, to be her tester. Quite a rivalry was developing between the two young men, each representing a different philosophy – if that was not too fancy a word to appear in the same sentence with rock running. Anyway, Org, stood for – ran for – rock running purity: straight ahead, brute strength, blood-in-the-eyes, crash-the-finish-line, rock running. Sufx was the opposite: short, swift, strong, the crowd pleaser, grimly determined while competing, but smiling, jovial, and gracious in victory. He was well on his way to becoming Beaverton's first athletic superstar. (He had had a few close races, however, and Ziiza had not figured out whether they were legitimately close or if he was holding back to create excitement, get the spectators going. She had declined to ask.)

When Ziiza stopped to catch her breath, Gstan eased back to his ThinStone story as if he had not heard a word she had said. He told of his long walk to the sunshine south, omitting her part in the despondency that had prompted it. If this new tack did not impress her, he felt, nothing would. It was an exciting story, and she and the children *did* pay attention as they passed the glowing ThinStone from hand to hand. It ended with Edu, who turned it over and over. Dg licked it as if trying to lap up the light.

Gstan told them of the thunderstorm, of finding the cave, of the food that had saved him from starvation, of the odd men who called themselves, of all things. . . . He paused, and, hoping they did not notice the pause, began editing his story, veering further and further from the truth, avoiding the details of rubbing and shaping the stones in the cave's depths, of their transformation into magical ThinStones by the unfathomable chanting, of his narrow escape, of the deal. The gifted Hieyeques became a nameless few who lived in the cave – too late to reverse that one – and made these things. Their egotistical leader, Silvoo Master, with the high-speed tic, was passed over, as was the cave's location in the Noro Hills above Big Bay. No one would believe such a person existed, anyway. And the cave was better "located," he thought, somewhere in the vast unknown south of Beaverton. At this Gstan hesitated to reorganize his thoughts. Much of what he had said did not even make sense to him.

After Edu and Dg had allowed the ThinStone to continue around, Ziiza balanced it on her hand. Gstan indulged her, remembering that he had a few more at Hill Burrow. She passed it to Govvi, who passed it to Netti. Ziiza gave Netti an overly-encouraging smile. She's doing well, she told Gstan.

Very well. Thanks to Litti. She, Netti, with her basketry skills, would become chief fabricator of her new company. She already was, you could say. As they progressed, Netti would hire, train and supervise other weavers and makers. And, yes, Milli was still away; they had not heard. Govvi would be the financial manager, of course, just as she had been for Sita's Lair. She already had tally boards full of statistics on rock runners: age, sex, residence, number of races run, finishing places. And race spectators: races attended, favorite runners. She spent most of her time with what she called her projective tally board, which, Ziiza confessed, baffled her. Govvi could calculate potential profits after applying all the variables: number sold, selling price, cost of materials and labor, selling expense, and more. Then she scratched everything out and started over, changing one number, till she arrived at what she called "optimum strategy." "Tedious as the process was, it fascinates her," Ziiza told him. "She repeats it constantly, variation after variation, calculating while she eats, while she relieves herself, while she walks, even takes her boards to bed with her." Gstan looked, and indeed, Govvi was sitting hunched over her board, her nose almost touching, scratching away with blackened fingers.

Gstan opened his mouth, ready to continue the ThinStone story, when Ziiza confessed she had two problems, one she could solve and one she could not. The missing element, the impediment to the sport's taking off, was Sufx's "fair rock" problem. She could handle that one herself, she thought. The other was start-up financing; she was short of barter and tail after the fire and would need a backer, or backers, a partner, or partners, to get going. Govvi looked up, her eyes popping: Shut up, Muma, this is confidential family business.

Gstan felt the tension. He had no faith in rock running, no interest in it, even if it turned out to be more than the silly fad he thought it was. Especially since he was about to visit the ThinStone Revolution on Beaverton. Yet, Ziiza – here she was talking to him, was confiding in him, had hugged him, and was asking, if not for barter and tail, for help. If not for help, for advice.

He smelled her smoky scent as she sat cross-legged, juggling the precious ThinStone. He smelled her avarice, her need to win. It rolled out of her eyes, over her full lips, over her contours, over her legs, and enveloped him. His hand quivered, longing to touch her hair. He formed a fist and jammed it in the ground. She was wrong for him. But. . . . The memories of his humiliating departure that clammy morning fought with the now of it. Was she asking for a business partner, just as he had asked *her*, back in the heady stupid days of Lots Plus and Hill Burrow? Govvi's seething ruled that out. He was not part of the Ziiza family. And Ziiza was *all* family. No partners in Sita's Lair, not even Biber. Remember? Besides, he had his own big dream. Was she asking for something else? No, not in front of her kids. Impossible. Or? Was she as tentative, as shy, as he? How could she be; she had had a husband once. And six kids, for gosh sakes. Stymied. No quippy, Zee-style answer to this one.

He sat thinking, and as many do when faced with an important question they have no answer for, he shifted direction. "Govvi," he said softly, "I can't say for certain, but I think my ThinStone could help you with your tallying. They do just about everything mathematical. Not that I pretend to understand, of course." Govvi did not favor him with a glance or a word. "Anyone?" he said, palms up, scanning the circle, trying to regain lost ground.

Ziiza eyed him. "Gstan," she said, "I'm asking for your help. I need money, barter and tail. This is the opportunity of lifetime and I need the wherewithal to get going."

"Why don't you drop over to Font's and take out a loan?"

"Govvi, what do you know about this Font?"

"He's wealthy, possibly wealthier than Wife Dragga. No one knows. Made his money in furs, food, shells, gambling, transporting. Maybe legal, maybe not."

Ziiza had the feeling Govvi was not telling her all she knew. "Thank you, Gstan," she said, looking appreciatively. How appreciative he could not tell.

Govvi drilled her eyes into Gstan, but spoke to Ziiza, "Loans you have to pay back, Muma."

"That's right," Gstan said. "And if it's of any interest, I'm thinking of visiting old Font myself."

"My boy is dead," Ziiza said, dropping the ThinStone. She pulled her arms around herself, rocked, and cried. "My dear Com is dead. My dear, dear Com."

"Com?" Gstan said, eyes wide with astonishment. "Com? Dead, you say?"

"Lost climbing Morning Spire," Netti explained, her voice barely audible. "Lost with his friend, Torc. Muma and Org and Edu and Dg. They searched for him. Barclaw, too. Dg found his cedar root rope, way up on the mountain. Had to be his. No other like it. They gave up."

"We had to give up," Ziiza sobbed.

"Come inside and rest, Muma," Netti said. She and Govvi helped her into the shelter.

Gstan dropped to his knees and looked inside. "I'm sorry. I've been away so long. Just got back. I didn't hear about it. I'm so sorry."

From within the dark shelter he heard Ziiza say, "Thank you, Gstan. Come back soon." That is what the muffled words sounded like to him. The ones he wanted to hear.

Although she had cried herself to sleep, Ziiza slept well and long. When she woke the children were gone, about their business for the day. She lay on her robe, looking at threads of sunlight shining through the shelter mats. Saw a chickadee hopping, searching for food. Heard crows caw-cawing. Things she would not normally pay attention to on a summer day. And it was a real summer day; she could feel the heat. How late had she slept? Mid-morning on a glorious-to-be day, she thought, stretching her arms. Best of all, she had not had the dream.

She dipped into the water bowl, moistened her eyes, and washed away the night. She rolled over, took a small piece of dried tail from the food bag, and nibbled. Then she fell back on her robe, stared at the roof, savored the smell of the sun, and began sorting out her life. Gstan was back. Nice man. Interesting. But not that important. His slim stones or thin stones were simply too revolutionary to waste time on. Anyway, numbers were not her thing – except money numbers. She cupped a hand and raised water from bowl to lips. She felt no urge to use the night pot; she must have cried it away. But maybe he was important. He had mentioned Font's bank for barter and tail, or whatever he lent. That was what banks were for, weren't they, to help get businesses going? She and Govvi would see about it. She rolled onto her side. Rested her chin in her hand. It hit her; she felt good. But she should not. How long should she properly be in mourning?

"Com, dear," she said out loud, knowing no one was near, "I have to get on with it. You understand, don't you? Of course you do. You're an adventurer, a seeker like me. It's going to be great. And it's going to be in your honor. I promise."

For some reason Govvi did not want to go to Font's bank with Ziiza, said she was busy tallying Netti's new batch of moss, or pitch, or reeds. Something like that. Essential that she do it. She did however give her directions to what she described as a modest vend on the southwest side of H&G. "You'd never see it if you weren't going there."

As Ziiza walked in that direction she looked for Bitta. At Town Hall she found Barclaw slouched on his seat, staring at the ground; no stories today. Ziiza patted his shoulder. He gave her a weak smile and touched her hand. "Thank you again for the search, Barclaw," she said. Then, "Is Bitta around?" He pointed down the path and they parted without the usually voluble constable speaking a word.

She saw Bitta before she heard her. Rather she saw Hobart wobbling on her head, flapping his wings, and draining a thin white stream down the back of her already-soiled wrap. No one spoke of this hygienic outrage to her face, knowing, feeling, realizing that the bird was more than a pet to her, more than an obnoxious, attention-grabbing, coo-burping crowd-puller. Bitta was Bitta. With her nose for gossip and news, and her sea-cave-sized memory, she was a vital player in the Beaverton scene, and in spite of her caustic put-downs, judgmental turn of mind, and eccentricities, she was a devoted Beavertonian, an old sort from the Popamayor era. Hobart, alas, came with the package.

Good thing she cuts her hair short.

"Smoke-storm's about to blow," Bitta cackled in her high-pitched voice, putting maximum urgency into it. "Blow! Blow! Blow!" Her listeners, an unusually large group, raised hardly a murmur; they had heard her Smoke-storm alerts before. "Mistermayor's asked the council to pay for a watchman. Camp near the mountain. Warn us when she begins to rumble and shake."

A listener smiled at the man standing next to him and feigned a yawn. "Next subject," he said in a too-loud voice.

"Beaver tail prices will rise this summer. No doubt about it. If there are as many Sea Tracers as usual, that is." Murmurs and groans. "Polcat's called a special meeting next week to discuss beaver problems. Tuesday evening. Seven o'clock. Everyone's invited. Arrive at a meeting of minds. Alleged minds, that is." She chuckled. Hobart coo-burped. No one laughed.

"Now for the personals," she continued. The crowd buzzed with anticipation.

Thank goodness she won't be reporting on Com. I think I'd have to run.

"Son Hornshuker was arrested for stealing earrings in H&G. Barclaw caught him in the act. Walked right up behind him. He wouldn't say whether they were for his girlfriend," Bitta paused, grinning mischievously, "or for himself. Mistermayor gave him two days community service in the Town Hall latrine." Laughter; they loved it. "Husband Dragga, manager of his wife's extensive real estate holdings, evicted some tenants on Outer Circle, a young couple expecting their first child. Reason given: yard maintenance not up to Wife D's standards." Stomping and hoots. "Reason suspected: a certain person's jealousy of the expected event. Have to be careful here," she added, winking at her audience. Clapping and cries of: "Hear, hear," and, "You've got it right this time, Bitta, old girl." She curtsied, acknowledging the applause, while Hobart shifted and flapped. Bitta continued, "Wife Alggard's runaway ended yesterday when she tearfully embraced her husband and three children, saying, 'I'll never. . . .'"

Ziiza walked out of hearing range, continued down the main path and turned on the narrow sub-path Govvi had told her about, little-used, with widely-spaced vends, most of which appeared to be unattended or abandoned. The bank consisted of a counter with a board sign above reading Font's Bank in small letters, and an enclosure behind it that, from what Ziiza could see, had no roof. There was no one at the counter, but, as she reached it, she heard voices from within. She waited respectfully for a minute or so. The talking continued and, even though it was quiet in the area, the voices were so low she could not understand a word. Rap! Rap! A man pulled the flap open and poked his head out. "Ah, yes," he said in a business voice, "I'll be with you shortly." He withdrew. The whispering continued. Then both flaps were flung back, revealing two men. They walked to the counter, almost in step, and placed their hands on it.

"I am Font," said the man on her left, "and this is my attorney, Esqq." Esqq leaned forward in a just-to-make-sure bow (just to make sure he wasn't brushing off a potential client). He was as tall as Org, and in his youth must have been as powerful. He wore a lush, white, untrimmed beard, and still had a full head of hair. His eyes could have sparkled with intelligence and humor, had he chosen to present himself that way. But they were deliberately dulled by the aforementioned condescension – but not so much as to camouflage a touch of connivery.

So this is the famous – or infamous? – lawyer Esqq.

Ziiza stuck out her hand. He shook it softly, touched his eyebrow with a finger, and left.

"And how may I be of service?" Font asked, leaning forward across the counter, giving her his banker's smile. He was probably as old as Esqq but appeared younger: straight and spare, with a narrow handsome face, beardless, slicked down black hair. *His* eyes, even when focused directly on her, had a dreamy, faraway look, and were such a light blue they were almost colorless. Ziiza hesitated, not knowing how to proceed. "Oh, a private matter," he said. "A loan, perhaps? Won't you step in, Miss? Wife?"

"Widow, actually," Ziiza said, "with six – rather, five – rather, four – children. But I don't think of myself as a widow; it's been awhile. Ziiza's my name. I'm starting a business and I'd like to borrow some barter and tail. You do lend?" He encouraged her to elaborate with a smile and a hand move, which she did.

Yes, he knew about rock running, how popular it was. He had even seen a race or two come by, although he had not paid much attention. And yes, he was aware that she had founded the pleasuring establishment over on the east side of town. Quite unique. Sita's Lair, wasn't it called? Served – what was it? – slooze and something to eat. He had not patronized it, he was sorry to say.

You think I don't know that?

He was duly impressed with her personal history: the family's Sea Trace travails, her desire to become a productive citizen of Beaverton. He expressed sympathy for Com; he brought it up himself. But when she told him of her invention, a head protector for rock runners, he fidgeted. When she repeated how big, how really big, she believed rock running was going to become, and how much money there was to be made, he covered his mouth with his hand and willed his eyes not to betray him.

"What I want, banker Font," Ziiza said, "is. . . . Oh, I don't want it all now. I wish my daughter Govvi were here. She's my financial person."

"I know Govvi," Font said matter-of-factly.

"You what?"

"I know Govvi. She comes round. I just didn't know she was your daughter. Most inquisitive child I've ever met. Hardly a child, now that I think about it. Astonishing facility for numbers. A bit pushy, too, if you don't mind my saying; she won't take no for an answer."

Ziiza smiled knowingly.

So this is why she didn't come with me.

"Anyway," Font continued, "I think what you want is a line of credit. The bank grants you so much, an upper limit. You draw what you need for the week, say, paying interest only on what you have out. Pay down your balance as you are able. Draw again. You see?"

"You mean I have it? That's all there is to it?"

"Unfortunately, no. I'll have to discuss it with the loan approval committee. I'll need a record of your financial history. I believe your daughter should have no trouble with that. Then a detailed business plan, your company name, and. . . ."

"Z-sport."

"Z and sport," he said. "How nice."

"My children call them Z-Zs, the head protectors, so I'll call my company Z-sport. Simple. It just came to me. Right now. We're in the sporting business: Ziiza, Z-Zs, Z-sport. At least we want to be," she added deferentially.

"Good. Z-sport it is," Font said. "And?"

"I'll get them. I'll get the history and plan right away," she said, pulling so hard on her necklaces the chips bit into her neck. Then, to part congenially, and perhaps regain a splinter of control, she said, "Your bank, your office, is very pleasant. So light and airy. Not like the stuffy old shelters we're used to. But why no roof? Don't you mind the rain and cold? Don't you put a roof on in winter?"

"No," Font said, "I don't. I'm a waterman, used to the wind and rain and the sky overhead. I may be ashore, far from the gull's cry and the salty air, but if I can point my eye to a cloud above, I'm content."

Waterman. MeTonn's soot-blackened, misshapen face came to her mind. Then Hawl's rank ugliness. Then Prong, the river letch, and his ever-present smirk. Font did not look like a waterman – lake, river, or Sea – he was too fine-featured, and, at present, too well-groomed. Too dignified. They shook hands and she went.

Govvi acknowledged meeting Font, but did not admit to knowing him well. Met him doing Individual Studies, she told her muma. She worked up the business plan so quickly that Ziiza wondered if she had known all along, had prepared it in advance.

Again, Govvi declined to accompany her. Ziiza, feeling confident, tossed it off.

Font spread Govvi's tally boards on the counter – no need for back office formality this time – glanced at them and said, "Congratulations, Ziiza, your credit line has been approved."

Ziiza choked back a comment on loan approval committees and said, "Thank you so much. Such a load off my mind. Now I can get to work. We can get to work. My family."

"Sign at the bottom," Font said. He indicated lines at the bottoms of two boards he had produced from under the counter. "Thank you."

"Thank *you*."

As Ziiza started away, Font called: "Ah, one more thing. A condition, really. You can read your board copy when you have time." He paused and forced a smile. "Lawyer Esqq is preparing a petition for the special council meeting. About beavers. The giant valley beavers that everyone eats – the tails, I mean – and uses for everything. Including lines of credit. Nothing much, but we, the bank that is, request, require, that is, your support. At the council meeting. Tuesday. Your active, vocal support. Do I make myself clear?" His eyes had lost their faraway waterman's look and were slicing into her.

"Sure," she said. "I'll be there." He nodded his approval. "Well, good-bye."

28

Errix Enterprises

OLD MAN Haracosh stared into his Hill Burrow dwelling. Looked back at Gstan uncomprehendingly. His burrow was to become a warehouse, a storage facility; he understood that. He was going to work for Gstan, be the first employee of his new company. He understood that part of it, although he did not know what an employee was exactly, had never heard the word. Something about pay. Gstan called his new venture Errix Enterprises, another name he had dreamed up on his long walk home. Unlike Ziiza, who had had to come up with a quickie name, Z-sport, for Font and his business plan request, Gstan had led with the name when he applied for *his* credit line.

Old Man's job, Gstan explained, was to guard slabs of valuable stone that would be stored in his (more or less commandeered) burrow. Since he was already here, the first and only Hill Burrow purchaser, and as Gstan was converting the remaining burrows into manufacturing facilities, and because he trusted him, knew he could depend upon him, knew he would lay down his life in defense of a burrow full of ThinStones (another new word), he was honoring him with the position. Hearing *trusted*, Haracosh rubbed his eyes and smiled his toothless smile. He was touched and, not used to compliments, embarrassed. He clucked his lips and waggled his tongue, but no words came. He turned his head aside, composed himself, swallowed, and finally managed a spittle-ejecting "Thank you very much, Mister Gstan, sir," not understanding whether he was gaining more than he was losing, but honored just the same.

They sat in front of the burrow, gazing at the Sundowns, passing a sack of dried tail between them. Ironic, Gstan thought, I'm sitting where I said good-bye to this place months ago. Now I'm back and ready to turn Beaverton upside down, kick her in her fat old be-hind. "Ha!" he said out loud. Old Man H started, then continued gumming his meat. He thought of Ziiza. Gosh, it was good to see her. She almost seemed glad to see *me*. Really glad. Like she missed me. Until thoughts of Com overcame her. Boy, that was a shocker. What to do? What *can* I do, besides sell ThinStones like crazy. Make a success of Errix. Make her take notice of me. Make myself worthy. Come on now, Gstan, let's not get sloppy again.

"Here's the plan, Haracosh," Gstan said, looking up at a cumulus sky. Old Man followed his look, as if expecting to see The Plan appear imprinted on the side of a cloud. "I've got it all worked out." He spread his arms. "I've got this franchise. From this weird guy, Silvoo, truly weird, he and his Hieyeques. Genius types. But not a whit of common sense. Zilch of the practical, if you know what I mean." Old Man nodded solemnly. "So I wangle this franchise out of him. Saved my life, but never mind about that. Well, Errix is the Beaverton branch, the marketing branch. And the stone-shaping branch. They, Silvoo, the Hieyeques, down there," he pointed south, "are the development branch. The chanting branch. Give ThinStones their amazing powers." Gstan glanced at H. I'm giving too much away here, he thought. Nah, he doesn't understand.

"Here's the beautiful part." Gstan spit out a wad of tail he could not bite through. It landed on a Beaverton grape leaf, slid off, and hit the ground. Old Man's eyes fixated on the wasted meat. "Since I sell 'em, I control the money. Sure, I've got to pay Font his interest, but I'll ditch him as soon as the profits come rolling in. Can you believe, those cave dwellers do it all for fun, the competition, the intellectual satisfaction of developing their chants and stuff? Ya, ya, yoo, yoo. My chant is better than your chant. Yoo, yoo, ya, ya," he said in a mocking, singsong voice.

Gstan wiggled his bare toes in the grass on the incline, nudged Old Man in the ribs, and continued: "Now if that was the beautiful part, this is the secret part. I've not told anyone, not even Ziiza. But you, Haracosh, Errix's first employee." Gstan's mouth was running, just like the old times at Sita's Lair, when he was tipsy on slooze, bragging and lying about his business ventures. Except this afternoon he was tipsy on dreams – just as a certain someone was tipsy on her own dream. "The secret, Haracosh," he continued, "since you'll be part of it. The secret is this: We're going to control the stones. All of these burrows that nobody wanted to buy – in spite of their superb location and spectacular view of the Sundowns, I must say – will be put to good use. A higher and better use, if you will. Errix will hire workers. Pay them good. We'll grind the stones, flatten them, shape them, and polish them. Do all of the grunt work. Gradually, gradually, gradually, their people, the Hieyeque apprentices, will lose the ability to do the hard physical work. Heck, you can't believe how weak and puny they are now. I mean, just nothing. After a few months on the trail, I was a giant, ready to take them all on. Me! Little Gstan! And you, my man," he slapped Haracosh on the shoulder, "will guard them. Guard the unfinished stones. Guard the chanted ones, the really valuable ones. Although, on second thought, maybe I'll stick those inside my own burrow. But you'll guard my burrow. At all times. With your life."

Old Man Haracosh shifted position so he could lean against the opening. "So how, you ask, can this possibly work? With all of these separate operations going on down south, and here in Hill Burrow, and back south, and up here again?" Haracosh breathed heavily; he was asleep. "My second employee, Leegs. Well, he's not exactly an employee, he's too independent for that. Independent contractor is more like it. We have an agreement. A transportation agreement. ThinStones have first priority. Everything else comes last. 'ThinStones comin' through,' is what he'll say. He's due in tomorrow or the next day with the first shipment. No more empty runs for ol' Leegs." Old Man snored loudly. "Is this sweet or what?" Gstan gloated. "We'll see who's the smartest one on the old New Side, Mister Gen-i-us Sil-voo or Mister Reg-u-lar G-stan. Now your first job, Haracosh, career challenge you might put it, is to smooth the sides of these burrows a bit, flatten the ceilings, straighten the walls, sharpen the corners. You might as well have something to keep you busy till Leegs pulls in. Right, Old Man?"

* * *

Ziiza flung the sack of credit line barter and tail over her shoulder and headed for H&G. At Inner Circle she turned and walked to Lots Plus. The vend was the same, except the sign hung loose.

Very sloppy, but good for me. Brings the price down. No new businesses close by. No parts of the lot have been sold off. Very good. Perfect. Is he here?

She weaved through the crowd. She had not stopped here in weeks, just walked by in a hurry, or ran past with a rock on her head, hardly a time to notice, let alone evaluate Wiggi Bub's place of non-business. He was sleeping under the counter. At least he had exerted the effort to shade himself from the mid-day sun. She tiptoed past and pulled the closing room curtain open. Everything the same. That was good, too. She walked back to Wiggi Bub, maneuvered herself into position, held onto the counter for balance, and extending her right foot, wedged the V of her missing toe tight against his nose, and pressed her foot on his mouth.

"Ah! Ah!" Wiggi Bub sputtered, slapping at her leg and rolling his head. "Who? What? What's this?" Then, "A deal?"

"No deal, Wiggi Bub," Ziiza said. "Not that kind, anyway. How are you doing, boss? No hard feelings, huh?" Ziiza chuckled and wiggled her second toe in his ear.

"Yeeee! Get that thing away from me." Then, comprehending who she was: "Oh, sorry, Ziiza."

"That's all right, Wiggi Bub. Joke's on me. Here, let me help you up. Or would you rather do business lying on the ground? Because we *are* going to do business."

"That's good. At least I think it is."

They compromised by sitting, Ziiza cross-legged, Wiggi Bub with his legs straight out, leaning back on his hands, the counter blocking them from the eyes of passers-by. "Here it is straight," Ziiza said, "I'm going to buy you out." Wiggi Bub straightened, rubbed his eyes, and opened his mouth. "Maybe I should put it more diplomatically: I want to buy you out. I need this location. And none other. For my new business."

"Oh," he said, "you mean for a new Sita's Lair? Opening up again, huh?"

"No, Wiggi Bub, a completely new venture. Rock running. You've seen them run by. Rocks on their heads, sweating, groaning, throwing up all over the place." She laughed. "Haven't you? Or do you sleep through everything? Sorry, I didn't mean that. You know, location, location, location. This place is perfect for Z-sport; that's my new company. We'll be making a line of rock running accessories called Z-Zs. Perfect place to make 'em. Perfect place to sell 'em. They practice on Outer and Inner Circles. The races turn in here, right at this corner, and on to the finish line at Town Hall. It's a one hundred percent location if I've ever seen one. I've got to have it, WB. And I'm going to stay right here tickling you with this ugly foot of mine until I get it." She stuck her foot in his face and laughed. Wiggi Bub pushed it away with an exaggerated expelling of air.

"I dunno, Ziiza," he said. "I'll have to think about this. So sudden. Maybe sleep on it. I'm not ready to retire just yet; *retire* retire, I mean." He permitted himself a chuckle. "And Lots Plus is well established here."

You retired in the head years ago, you dimwit. This location is all you have left and I want it. And I'll get it.

"Tell you what, Wiggi Bub," Ziiza said, "I'll leave this over-stuffed sack of goodies beside you. Reach in. Rustle your hand around. Take a taste. Whatever you please. Sort of an earnest money. Down payment." Wiggi Bub pushed the sack away, but not out of reach, did not give it back to her. Then, mustering up all the sweetness she possessed, Ziiza said, "May I call again, Wiggi dear? Will you be in the office, say, tomorrow evening? After business hours," she added with a touch of sarcasm which she could not resist.

* * *

259

Litti left her shelter before sunrise, walked through town, over the meadow and approached Great-great-great-grandpopa Monumentree. "Good morning Great-great-great-grandpopa Monumentree," she said. "May I sit here with you and welcome the new day?" She extended her arms as if to hug the tree, but of course that was impossible, so she patted its bark with her small hands. She worked her way around the north side and then to the east side and sat with her back to the tree. She could not quite align herself with Morning Spire (which she could not see as it was hidden by the eastern hills), over which the sun would rise, because the ground around full half of the giant tree was covered with a glacial-like flow of pitch. Rivers of pitch flowed down the trunk's south side through the cracks and scars in its black bark, turned at ground level and spread, catching, holding and covering insects, needles, cones, grass, twigs, limbs, and feathers, even whole creatures unfortunate enough to have ventured onto it: birds, snakes, field mice, even larger creatures who had stepped into it while going for the trapped ones. When the meadow burned the pitch caught fire, wounding Monumentree again, causing more pitch to flow. And so it went, through the years. On a hot summer day when the pitch was flowing strong and sticky, even Litti would have a difficult time extricating a foot, and she knew it. But she enjoyed its piquant smell, its spectrum of colors – pale, translucent amber to rich, wavy, yellow brown – and sat as close as she dared, giving in from time to time to the urge to touch it with her fingers, feel how sticky-thicky dangerous it was.

Litti had watched sunrises, sunsets too, from under Great-great-great-grandpopa Monumentree's sheltering limbs many times before. In winter when the sun's arc was low, she sat on the pitch flow, cold-hardened and covered with needles. This time she had a double purpose: her traditional welcome-of-the-morning, and to wait for Arbo. They could be living together by now, pledged, even; they were that committed. But they had chosen not to. They had a better arrangement. At least for now. She had never been to his camp, deep in the forest; she referred to it as his private ground. He had not seen her small shelter in town, hard by Ziiza's, never set foot in Beaverton itself, for that matter. "Can't stand the people pressure," was how he put it. "My life's in the wild and I have no time to waste." This was not a problem for Litti; her work, her delight, was in the "wild" as well. They had developed a routine that suited them, blended their desires, their natures, their passions so well that they never spoke of changing it, as if discussing any aspect would upset the rare magic they had achieved. It went like this: They met beneath the giant tree at sunup, walked tight against each other through the still-dark forest to Water Child's clearing. They made love – under robes, on top, depending upon the weather and their desires – until hunger overcame them.

Ate. Loved again till full daylight, so much more exciting and satisfying. Then they roamed: he searching and collecting, she observing and singing. Being together. Doing together what each had done separately before they met.

Water Child's meadow was abloom. Litti and Arbo rolled apart, lay on their backs, and looked up. "Going to be a beautiful day, my love," he said, squeezing her hand. "Throw something in the air, will you? We'll take the direction, follow the wind today."

Litti snuggled close, kissed his forehead, and said, "There are no blowing winds today, silly; it's a perfect summer day. But I'll try anyway. For you." She plucked a handful of grass and sprinkled it on his chest.

"Quit it, that tickles."

She selected a thin blade and flung it into the air. It was too small, too lightweight, to go anywhere, and fluttered into the grass beside her. "West it is," she said jokingly, patting the ground as if she could recover the blade and make a calculation. "What's this?" she said. She patted the grass, ran her fingers over it lightly. She went to her knees and bent over, spreading the grass. "Arbo," she said. "A depression. My finger goes right in. And another next to it. If they weren't so large I'd swear they were animal tracks. Claw marks." Arbo rose and knelt beside her. "Right here," she said. "Put your finger in here."

Arbo poked his finger through the grass, tracing the outline. He clipped the grass with his knife. "Oh, my," he said. "My, my, my. This is amazing. First of all, it's the largest paw print I've ever seen or felt – other than a hoof print of some lumbering creature, I mean." He leaned closer, squinted, and poked his fingers into the depressions, one by one. "Okay, it should have gone this way." He crawled off the robe on hands and knees, spreading the grass, looking for more holes. He whistled. "Litti, look how far I've crawled." He whistled again, and said, "The stride. The holes. I'll tell you, if I didn't believe they were long gone from the valley, this whole territory, I'd say you've discovered a sita track. A sita! Unbelievable! Unbelievable!"

Litti stared at him with frightened eyes. "At Water Child?" she said. "Drinking from our Water Child? Here, in our glade?" She crouched on the robe, shivering, slowly turning her head, scanning the forest edge, imagining the mythical giant cat crouching, ready to pounce. "I'm fearing fears, Arbo," she said, transformed from confident, passionate lover to frightened little girl. "We've got to get out of here."

Arbo jumped up and yelled, "Yes, yes, drinking at Water Child! This is the greatest thing that's ever happened. To me. To us. If this is true. If this is true, Litti, if I can get a sighting, some evidence, my reputation's made. I'll be the greatest collector in history! Respected. Everywhere. We can get pledged.

Do what we want." Litti lay on her side, arms drawn around her knees, sobbing. He walked back to the robe, knelt, and stroked her shoulder.

"I thought we *were* doing what we wanted, Arbo. We must warn Barclaw. Mistermayor. Someone in Beaverton."

"No, no, this is my chance. Don't tell anyone. A collector only gets one chance like this in a lifetime. If that. I don't want those town blunderers messing things up. Promise me. Besides, think about it, Litti, if the sita was going to attack us it would have done so already. It would be over."

* * *

Font's bank was closed, so Ziiza and Govvi waited. Presently Font appeared, accompanied again by lawyer Esqq. "Oh, hello, Ziiza," he said, almost bumping into her, they were so intent on their conversation. "And yes, Miss Govvi, too." He nodded. "Good morning to you both." Esqq touched his forehead and smiled his smile. "Let me guess," Font said.

"I'm trying," Ziiza said. "No, not just trying. I'm going to buy out Wiggi Bub's Lots Plus Real Estate Company. Know him?"

"By reputation," Font said solemnly. "You need more barter and tail? Your credit line?"

"Yes, it's the perfect location for Z-sport and I have to have it. I'll pay whatever it takes."

"You have great faith," Esqq said, "in an enterprise that has yet to sell a single, ah, head protector."

"Don't pay attention to him," Font said, "he's as enthusiastic about your prospects as I am. It's just his lawyerly sense of humor. If you can call it humor. How much? One sack? Two? Three? I'll have them delivered this afternoon."

"I hate to over-borrow, but this is critical. Three sacks, please."

"Consider them delivered. Now if you will excuse us, Esqq and I must prepare for the council meeting tomorrow night. You haven't forgotten, have you?" Ziiza nodded, meaning she had not forgotten now that he had reminded her. "If our proposal passes, and it will pass, it must pass, eh, Esqq?" he looked at the lawyer sternly, "messy sacks of barter and tail will be things of the past. Beaverton will have a new form of money, a totally new monetary system."

Govvi's eyes flashed. Then, by force of will, she tightened her jaw and stripped away whatever hint of emotion might have appeared on her face.

"What?" Ziiza asked.

"You'll find out. Attend the meeting, with your entire family and all of your friends — remember our agreement? — and cheer our proposal like you've never cheered anything before. We don't want those honorable council members to even consider voting no. Understood?" He waved her off.

"Thank you, Font. You, too, Esqq."

Walking back through H&G, they found Bitta in high form, bobbing among the walkers, shoppers, and browsers. Her report was brief and sensational: everyone come to the meeting to hear Font and Esqq's monetary proposal. "I know, I know," Ziiza said, pushing gently past her. "Thank you, Bitta. We'll be there."

After some shopping, Ziiza and Govvi reached home. Edu was chasing Dg around the brew-crock halves. Or was Dg chasing him? Netti frowned as she struggled with weaving materials. "Delivery for you, Muma," she said, rubbing her head. "Three sacks. Over there."

"Another headache, dear?" Ziiza asked. "I'm so sorry." Before Netti could answer, Ziiza yelled, "Edu, come over here, please. Stand behind your sister and give her a good head rub. Govvi and I have some important business that can't wait." Ziiza picked up two sacks, and said, "Come on, Gov. One for you. Two for me. Let's go."

"Good," Ziiza said when she and Govvi arrived at Lots Plus, "you're awake."

But not up, you lazy lout.

"Oh, sorry," she said as she stepped into a mud puddle and splashed Wiggi Bub's arm. She bent over to wipe him off.

"Thought you said this evening," he said, pushing her hand away.

"I took a chance that you weren't busy." Ziiza squatted and leaned the sacks against him. He did not protest. Made no move. Did not acknowledge Govvi's presence. Govvi lowered her sack next to her muma and moved, by increments, to position herself behind him. "Ready, my friend?" Ziiza said.

"Yup."

"Good. You've got one sack. Like it?" No reaction. "Two for the works."

"Nope."

Govvi raised her eyebrow. "Three." Ziiza said. Then, quickly, "That's two. Plus the one you have."

"Nope."

"Come on now, Wiggi Bub. That's more than you make on any ten deals. Twenty. Be reasonable."

"Not interested."

Govvi shrugged at her muma.

"Okay, my last offer. Last offer, WB. The one you've got plus three. Four sacks, straight from Font's bank. Certified."

Wiggi Bub yawned, patted his mouth, and lay back. He looked at Ziiza, then closed his eyes. It was stare-down time, or, with Wiggi Bub, sleep-down time. Govvi settled in. This did not bother her a bit, she rather liked games with rising tension. The children's rebellion at Way Rock, for instance. Ziiza fidgeted. Ran her nails on her teeth, cleaning dirt, spitting it out. Wiggi Bub opened an eye. Ziiza slapped her hands on her thighs. Bent over till her necklaces touched her hands. Felt a chip. Pulled to the next one. Rubbed. Pulled again. Halfway through the necklace, she could stand it no longer. "What do you want, Wiggi Bub?" she screamed. "What do you want? What *is* your price?" Wiggi Bub did not move, did not raise an eye, did not fake a snore. "I'm going to wait you out. You'll see."

Govvi gave her muma the hard eye. Ziiza flashed anger and frustration back at her. "What, Wiggi, what?" she screamed again. He sighed contentedly. "What will do it?"

Govvi came close to a smile and said, "You don't see it, do you Muma. He wants the lot, the shelter, the broken brew-crock, and all." Wiggi Bub raised a finger.

"You mean my home? Our home? All we have? And up to my ears in debt, too?"

"Yes, Muma, our lot and the four sacks, too. It's the price of ambition."

Wiggi Bub half-opened an eye, curled his lip in a victory smirk, which he did not trouble to hide, and said, "Just leave the sacks inside. I'll see Barclaw in a bit. Take care of the transfer. Nice doing business with you, Ziiza. You too, sharp little lady." With that he was snoring before Ziiza got off her new property.

* * *

Polcat and the council members seated themselves on a peeled tree trunk in front of Town Hall. Mistermayor stood off to the side, smiling and nodding, acknowledging friends and supporters. Constable Barclaw stood opposite him, chest puffed out, arms folded, surveying the crowd with no-nonsense eyes. His friend Bitta joined him, quiet for once, totally engrossed in the news-gathering phase of her work. They waited five, ten minutes.

Mistermayor rapped his stick and said, "The Beaverton town council will come to order." The talking and laughing continued; no one paid attention. After repeating his command and rapping his stick again, he said, "Barclaw, do your duty."

Barclaw waved his arms and yelled, "Quiet! Quiet everyone!" A few paused and looked, but most ignored him. "Quiet down folks," he bellowed, "What do you think you're here for?" He plunged into the crowd, hushing people individually.

The crowd spread across the main path in both directions. People stood on vends and whatever else they could find to raise themselves up, trying to see. But most were simply too far away to see or hear. Not that they cared. Although they came because of the publicity Bitta and others had so competently produced, a goodly number came because they were paid, came early, positioned themselves in front. Ziiza and crew were late, but holding hands, they worked their way in. Gstan sat himself on a fat tree root, off to the side, high enough to see over the crowd, angled so he could survey faces, and tight against the tree so he could not be shoved around if it should come to that. He caught Font's eye. He waved at Ziiza, but she did not see him.

Mistermayor gave his Smoke-storm report: threatening as usual. Although Sea Trace immigration was expected to be large this season, he was against expanding Outer Circle to create new lots. Make better use of the ones we have, he told them. Wife Dragga stood smiling in back; a tight lot supply made hers the more valuable. Then paths. Then water. Then firewood. The fur market. The obligatory dig at Swarm City. Mention of Groopland, the new resort and casino opening on the coast. Plans to tax it. Mistermayor liked to talk, and when he started in on the beaver report, Polcat reminded him that that was the reason for the special meeting, and that he had agreed to let him have this one. Mistermayor reluctantly sat down.

Polcat raised his arms as if blessing the attendees, glared at Barclaw, waited for the noise to abate, and said, "Fellow Beavertonians, thank you for coming tonight. I shall not elaborate. I shall not expound. I shall not deviate from the subject at hand." Laughter and hoots. "I shall not delay the discussion of the momentous proposal before us."

"Get on with it."

"Yes, yes. I am pleased to introduce Esqq, Beaverton's most distinguished lawyer."

"Beaverton's only lawyer," a heckler yelled. Laughter all around.

"Esqq," Polcat continued, "who has spent many hours of his valuable time preparing a proposal which he has titled: 'Beaverton: A New Beginning.' People of Beaverton, please welcome, and give your undivided attention to one of our own. Esqq, if you please."

Esqq lumbered up to the tree trunk, lowered his head as if in prayer, then slowly straightened up to his considerable height. With his broad shoulders, large head, and snow-white beard and hair, he was a commanding figure.

Talking finally stopped. "People of Beaverton," he began. "My good friends. I came as a young man over the Sea Trace. My muma and popa, now departed, were close friends of Popamayor, helped him found this town. That's how far back we go. I have seen Beaverton then. And I see what Beaverton has become. What it is today. And let me tell you, things are very different. From the little settlement in our lovely valley we have grown into a thriving town. A place apart. Unique on the New Side. Unique in the bounty of giant valley beaver. Unique in its citizenry. The largest and most successful town west of the Sunups."

Esqq paused, bowed to the raucous, paid partisans in the front, and continued: "We are blessed, it is true. But with blessings come responsibilities. In short, my friends, we have outgrown our primitive barter and tail system: a handful of berries for a piece of beaver tail, a year or two's accumulation of everything for a small lot to live on." He waited for the demonstrators to quiet. "Why back at the Sita's Lair, what did it cost for a leaf-cup of slooze?" He reverently placed his hand over his heart in memory of the Sita (which he had never patronized). Many in the audience bowed their heads and did the same. "Whatever you could get Ziiza and her servers to accept," he continued. "That's what." Hoots and stomping. "And it isn't right. It's got to change."

Esqq swung round and looked at Polcat and the council members. Then Mistermayor. Then Bitta. He turned slowly back to the audience; the noisy ones hushed on the prearranged word *change*. "What we are proposing, dear friends, is to simplify your lives and increase the prestige of Beaverton. Adopt an official standard: beaver pelts."

Those who could hear gave a collective gasp of astonishment as the implication sunk in: killing giant valley beavers, next to murder, the worst thing a person could do. Hands went up. People jumped, shouted, "That's illegal." "Against everything Beaverton stands for."

On Font's signal, rhythmic stamping and chanting drowned them out:

Pelts in; barter out.
Pelts in; barter out.
Exciting Beaverton.
Town of the future.

They repeated "Pelts in; barter out." until the cadence wore into the crowd. Swept along, or in sheer self-defense, they chanted, too. Font joined Esqq at the speakers' place, and together they led the simple, but effective, chant. Over and over. Polcat and the council members looked at one another in disbelief, but were frozen by the enormity of the proposal. Barclaw eyed

Mistermayor, seeking instructions. Mistermayor shrugged, as if to say: They're not destroying anything. Not breaking any law. Just exercising their rights. Besides, what can we do?

Govvi applauded wildly, even chanted, surprising her muma and siblings; she seemed deliriously happy. Org clapped his hands clumsily. Ziiza prodded him when he lagged. The noise was too much for Netti. Dg, tight on Edu's leash, squirmed to be set free; he could not take the noise either. Seeing Dg tugging, Netti leaned over and said, "Let's get out of here, Edu." They turned and pushed away. Ziiza did not call them back.

Font raised his arm and the demonstrators fell silent. He signaled his key man, who yelled, "Vote! Now! Vote! Now!" His cohorts picked it up. Font and Esqq stepped into the throng, leaving the council exposed. "Vote! Now!" they continued. Polcat cleared his throat, struggling to regain his composure and control of the meeting, which had long since passed from his hands. "Do I hear a call for a full reading of Esqq's proposal?" he said.

"Vote now!"

"Any discussion?"

"Vote now!"

Polcat relented. "Mistermayor, will you accept a motion?"

"I guess so."

"Move to accept proposal," a senior member said, taking care to avoid looking in Font or Esqq's direction.

"Second the motion."

"Vote of council," Mistermayor said glumly. Polcat and the two senior members raised their hands. The junior member looked at them and slowly raised his hand. "I abstain," Mistermayor said. Then, "Motion passes four votes to none. One abstention." The crowd erupted with cheers and screams. They would have time to reflect on their actions later.

29

Amazing Z-Zs, Miraculous ThinStones

"MORE TEA?" Ziiza said, as she faced Litti across the morning fire. Litti passed her a dark-stained cup. Ziiza balanced a hot stone on a wooden spoon and dropped it in the water. When it bubbled, she smiled at Litti. Litti avoided her eyes. "I rented my lot back from Wiggi Bub," Ziiza said. "That's what he wanted. I know it. Wanted the rent. Wanted *me* to be paying rent to *him*. Took Govvi to figure it out, though. I was too slow. Anyway, moving the family over to Z-sport would have been tough, even if Town Hall had allowed it. You know how that is."

"Here's to a cheerful day," Litti said, raising her cup as if in a toast. They sipped tea in comfortable silence,

"Govvi, I don't know," Ziiza said at last. "She roams. In H&G, mostly, checking businesses I suppose, just like her old Individual Studies reports for Addle. Hikes over the hill to the North-flowing Son. Likes to watch the water from the high bank, she says. I know she's friendly with those two old scalawags. But she's on her own time, doing what she likes. And she's got everything under control at work. On top of it. All she can do until we get rolling." Ziiza wanted to ask Litti what was wrong, but did not think the time was right. So she chatted casually. Finally, she said, "And how is Arbo?"

"Wonderful," Litti said, her eyes betraying her. "His collecting is going well. What he's going to do when he's got everything, I don't know. But he's happy. We're happy, doing. . . ."

Ziiza did not press her. "I'm not dreaming about Com so often." Ziiza said, offering something of herself. Litti fidgeted with her cup. "Org hardly talks to me," she continued. "Sullen. Spends most of his time training and hanging out with his friends. A good thing in a way, because he never had many friends before. Whether they are the right kind of friends is another matter. I wouldn't be surprised if he moved out. That would be three children gone, one way or another. I don't know what I'd do without Edu to hug before he goes off to school. At night. Whenever I can grab him." She smiled, waiting for Litti's reaction. "He's doing well in school. Very well. You know what? Milli still bothers me. So unlike her. Not the running off part. I know she was infatuated with Twigg, maybe really in love with him. And caught up with the band and all of their anti-Beaverton rebelliousness. And singing: the attention and applause. Who wouldn't like that? Kids have to reach out, make mistakes sometimes. Big ones. Part of growing up. I sure did. But not hearing anything, not knowing where she is, if she's even alive. I can't search for her; I wouldn't know where to begin." Ziiza raised her eyes, gauging Litti. "Anything you would like to talk about?" She was about to add *dear friend* but decided against it.

Litti shook her head. Then, as if to take it back, shook it again, slowly. "They shouldn't have done that, the council," she said. "Mizpark and Friends of the Beaver are going to organize a protest, try to get them to reverse themselves." She sounded more dejected than angry. "So unwise," Litti continued. "So short-sighted. Killing beavers. Killing them for body meat and pelts. Don't you agree?"

"I don't know," Ziiza said. "Makes sense to me. They're practically limitless, I'm told. And beaver pelts as money. And for wear. Seems like a normal evolution. Progress. Getting rid of barter and tail is a step up. They say Swarm City has something like that."

"This – is – not – Swarm – City." Litti said, through clenched teeth. Ziiza had never heard her speak so forcefully. "The giant valley beaver," she continued, "is unique, found nowhere else in the world – that we know of. An amazing bounty. Unlimited food with virtually no effort. The tail restores itself, bigger than ever. After a few trims the beaver gets so large . . . But you know all of that. All we have to do is take care of the them. But no. That Esqq, he's a crafty one. Rammed it through the council. Had the crowd rigged. Probably some of the council members, too. Made it sound so plausible, so logical, so easy. No time to think. Just rammed it through."

"Litti," Ziiza said, "If you don't mind my asking. Were you at the meeting? I didn't know you were interested in Beaverton politics."

"No, I wasn't; I heard it from Bitta. As soon as I heard I went over to Mizpark's and joined. It isn't politics, you know. It's something more. It's Beaverton's integrity. It's Beaverton's future. Sorry, I don't mean to be preaching," she added quickly. "You will join us, won't you Ziiza? Mizpark is an old hand at this sort of thing. We have to stop them."

"I'll sleep on it, Litti." Ziiza said, smiling weakly. She put her cup down. She tried to think of things to say to change the subject, but could think of nothing except, Litti, this is so unlike you to get involved. She did not speak the words.

* * *

"No, not that way," Netti said sharply to one of her weavers. "Here, let me show you." She took the roll from the woman and tucked in the sharp ends sticking out of the enclosure. "That's how. Z-Zs have to look good as well as support the rocks, or they won't sell. Understand?" The woman, one of five she was training, was catching on slowly. What's she been doing all her life? Netti thought. Isn't every woman supposed to know *something* about basketry? This is just a variation on the same old thing. You don't have to be an expert. Should I continue trying, or find someone else? She rubbed her head. It was early in the day and she was still headache free, but this wasn't helping. The fact that they were opening Friday and Ziiza – it wasn't Muma on the Z-sport premises – wanted five dozen Z-Zs ready to sell, wasn't helping, either.

Ziiza had moved the Lots Plus vend tight against the corner of Inner Circle and Town Hall Pathway. Runners could touch it as they rounded it. "Location's the thing," Ziiza said. "Fond memories of my real estate days, now that I'm not living them anymore," She laughed for the umpteenth time at her worn-out witticism. She turned the Lots Plus banner over, lettered The Original Z-sport Company on it, and stepped into the busy pathway to admire. Just as she had when Sita's Lair had opened. Or so she remembered. She *was* developing a history in Beaverton. Wiggi Bub's closing office became a storage facility and rainy-day manufactory. Plenty of room for expansion. Which we will need very soon, she thought.

Sufx leaned on a mechanical device: a fresh-skinned, slender beam placed crosswise on a larger but shorter beam on the ground. Together they made a lowercase t. And like a t, the slender vertical portion was longer below the intersection than above. He had been working all week, chopping, forming, testing, balancing. He placed his running rock in a depression at the end of the slender beam, then lowered himself onto the other end. The rock rose, bobbed, quivered, and balanced. The problem, the reason it took so long to build: he was creating a lever with a five-to-one ratio. Empty, without rock or person, the beam had to balance. Much trial. Much error. Much kindling. "Hey Ziiza! Hey Netti! Govvi!" he called, as if he had just completed the work, "I'm ready." Govvi stood in the pathway, appraising it critically.

Ziiza's solution to the "fair rock" problem, which she had been pondering for some time, was to standardize weights for all runners. Thus the device. Not the same weight for each runner, but proportionally the same; every rock one fifth the runner's weight. Each runner would have his or her personalized rock. But it was more than that. Sufx, now a full time Z-sport employee – Z-Z salesman, rock certifier, competitor – had set the ratio himself, five-to-one, what seemed most comfortable to him. A fine point to be sure, but important

270

in high-level competition. The next step was Quord Senior's blessing, to make Z-sport's balance beam the official certifying instrument. More than that. Certification, done in Z-sport's vend, by Z-sport employees who could custom chip and balance rocks, along with custom fitting Z-Zs, would not hurt sales one bit.

"Now Sufx," Ziiza said. "Play with it, get it right; everything must work perfectly tomorrow. Then take the rest of the day off, do whatever you like."

The schedule: Thursday morning, tomorrow, Quard Senior's inspection. Friday: preview sale for invited runners, dignitaries, and friends, all of whom would get attractive discounts. (Or, if they preferred, custom Z-Zs made by Netti herself.) Saturday morning, afternoon, and evening: grand opening to the public. Sunday, race day: open for business except during the race itself.

Quord Senior passed his hand over the seat, over the notch that fixed the balance point, down the slender beam, and into the rock-holding depression, making continuous sounds of approval. Ziiza, Netti, and Govvi watched nervously as Sufx placed his rock on the long end, then sat on the other. (The workers had been given the day off, as inventory was complete, and because Ziiza did not want them distracting Senior. Or revealing any secrets.) "Very interesting," Senior said.

Quord Junior stood nearby, his rock at his feet. "Looking fit, Junior," Ziiza said. "Doesn't he, Netti?" Netti kept her eyes on the balance. "The point is, Senior," Ziiza continued, taking a chance. "For rock running to grow, for it to become the true sporting phenomenon it deserves to be – and is on its way to becoming." She stopped to let Senior translate her words into his self-interest. "To be a credit to Beaverton," she continued, "it has to be seen by everyone as a fair competition. One can't beat another just because they carry a rock that *looks* heavy. It isn't fair. And that's what's happening." She let her voice trail off. Netti, Govvi, and Sufx nodded obediently. "I believe this is an elegant solution."

Sufx motioned to Quord Junior. (Junior was tall and a bit gangly, a dedicated, determined runner, a "respectable finisher," encouraged to the extreme by Senior, who was living his dreams of athletic glory through his son and by his control of the sport.) "Put your rock on it, Junior," Sufx told him. "Oh, this is a heavy one." His look said: how could you run with such a heavy rock? I could never manage. Junior sat on the beam. The rock did not rise. Not even when he jiggled. "Exactly what I thought," Sufx said. "I'll have to chip some away." Both Quords smiled as Sufx hammered, rock against rock, making as many chips as he could to heighten the dramatic effect. "Okay, Junior, try again." As the rock rose, Sufx continued chipping until runner and rock balanced. "Look at all those chips," he said. "Now heft your rock." Junior hopped off, picked up his rock and placed it on his head. "Oh, here," Sufx said, "try one of these." He handed him a Z-Z. "And keep it. Compliments of Z-sport."

Is this guy, Sufx, a natural salesman or what?

"Feels good," Junior said. "Lighter rock. Z-Z cushion. I like it. I like everything about it. What do you say, Popa?" Senior walked to the balance and leaned against it. He continued smiling, at Sufx, at Junior, at Ziiza, at everyone. Smiling, just smiling. Govvi looked at her muma. She squeezed thought waves through tight black eyes: On this very spot, Muma. Wiggi Bub. Remember?

Ziiza was on target this time. "And if it becomes official, we'll need someone to operate the balance tester or whatever you want to call it," she said, greasing her words with disarming imprecision. "Maybe just on race day. Maybe full-time." She looked from balance beam, to Junior, to a large pile of rocks – which, after custom fitting and certification, could be *sold* to runners – to Sufx, and finally to Senior.

"Rock running competition," Senior said in his most official voice, then, after an Esqq-like hanging pause, "must be fair in every way possible. I say pass. With one condition."

Always a condition. Just like the conditional use permit for the Sita. The business plan for the credit line. Wiggi Bub and my lot. And everything. Everyone in a position of power has to have a condition, an and-by-the-way, to push you down, keep you in your place.

"I would suggest," Senior continued, "in the interest of fairness, that we phase it in. Make it voluntary for the first month or so. Not everyone will be chipping rock, decreasing weight, like Junior, here. Some will need heavier rocks. We don't want to discourage them, scare them off, now do we?"

That's a surprise. He's on our team. Along with his son. A condition I can live with.

"Offer a discount on Z-Zs if they certify early," Netti said.

"Brilliant, Netti," Ziiza told her. "Brilliant." Netti beamed, and the weariness of weeks of hard work and aggravation, teaching and re-teaching her fumble-fingered workers, fell away.

* * *

"Where is he? Where the heck is he?" Gstan fumed, as he paced Hill Burrow's pathway, waiting for Leegs. Inside, he heard Old Man Haracosh scraping and patting the walls of his residential burrow. "Water those walls, now," he said. "Smooth them down. That's a good boy." Down the row, in front of the newly-remodeled burrows, men sat, eating, drinking, rubbing their bellies with muddy hands, muddy from the make-work of smoothing the walls for the third or fourth time. Something to keep them busy till the un-polished stones arrived. Morning clouds rolling in from the Sea had not reached Beaverton; an azure sky covered the valley. Today would be warm-going-to-hot, tempered by a thin breeze, reminding Gstan of the Noro Hills far to the south. In short, it was a perfect day for his employees to be hard at work in their dark burrows, grinding and polishing stones for shipment back to Silvoo's chanting minions.

"Okay, take a break," Gstan called to Old Man. "Lunch time. Might as well. Nothing else to do." Then, not caring whether the lounging workers heard him or not, he added, "I'll send everyone home if he doesn't show up soon."

Leegs did. As Gstan and Old Man, who was proving to be a reliable worker, passed a plank of now-legal beaver meat between them, Leegs appeared in the distance, a dot with stick legs. He loped along Outer Circle, stopped at the pathway, and scanned the area. "Over here! Over here!" Gstan yelled, running to him. Leegs's pack was a hump, riding high over his head and far out behind, forcing him to bend forward. He held large sacks in each hand, so full they dragged on the ground. Gstan offered to carry a sack but Leegs shrugged him off. "Hope they got this right," Gstan said impatiently when they reached the burrows. Old Man held the plank out to Leegs. Leegs took a piece of meat. Then another. And another. Until it was empty.

"The finished ThinStones should be in here," Gstan said, opening the pack. "Ah! Ah! That beautiful glow. So many colors mixed together. I've never seen. This pack must be worth. . . ." He caught himself and started over. "I know, I know. I should have trusted them. Yes, they got it right." Not able to contain himself, Gstan danced around the pack, waving a blue-glowing ThinStone over his head. He stopped and toed the unopened sacks. "Rough sides mean unfinished stones. Break's over," he yelled down the line. "In – to – your – burrows. No. First over here to get your stones. Jump!" The workers shuffled toward Gstan and accepted their allotments of raw stones; workers who had already agreed to unite in a common goal: to slow down, stretch out the work, maximize the pay, and minimize the effort. Haracosh looked at Gstan as if asking permission, then offered the water sack to Leegs, who drank it all.

"Now look here, Leegs," Gstan said, when they were alone, "I want to get a few things clear. I have to, so Errix Enterprises can move forward. First, how did the trip go? What I'm getting at: Was the load too large? Too heavy? Could you handle more? Do you need help?"

Leegs replied with a toothy smile from deep within his beard. "I am so happy," he said. "So happy to be working, carrying a legitimate load over the mountains. Nothing can stop me."

"Not even that strange fellow who hides on the narrow ledge? The one who robbed me – in spite of your warning. What's his name again?"

"Not a problem."

"Did you find the drop-off spot all right? Were they stacked and ready to go? Are you holding up? Ready to make it a steady run?" Leegs nodded in vigorous ascent. "That's good, Leegs, because you stand to make a mountain of pelts on this. You know about Beaverton's new monetary system, don't you? It's okay to kill beavers; they call it 'harvesting.' They don't just slice tails anymore. Leegs shook his beard. "You'll be paid in meat and pelts. And dried tails, of course, as long as they last. But none of that other junk; barter's out. Unless, of course, folks want to do it amongst themselves. Unofficially." If Leegs was following this, he did not show it.

"Excuse me if I sound nervous and prying," Gstan continued, "but I have a lot riding on this, more than you'll ever know. One thing I can tell you; I drew big on my credit line at the bank, took a long-term lease on a vend in H&G. Got to sell these beauties fast, and what better place to do it than the best location in Beaverton, corner of Inner Circle and. . . . What I'm getting at is we'll be right across the path from Ziiza's new business, Z-sport. You know her?" Leegs said he had heard of the proprietress of the Sita's Lair, but had never met her. "Well, she has this daughter, name of Milli. Ran off with a local singer and head of a band. Screaming Indifference. Popular with the young crowd. Just disappeared. Over a year ago. Ziiza, she's a friend of mine, is worried sick over it, but too proud. . . . You see what I'm getting at? Will you do me a favor and ask around Big Bay when you're down there? I never did make it that far. The way I figure, it's the most likely place for them to be. Swarm City is a possibility. Anyplace. But I doubt if they went to SC first thing. Doubt it very much. Ask around, will you?"

"I never spend much time in Big Bay," Leegs said. "Just do my business and turn around. But I'll give it a try. It might delay me some."

"I'm relying on you, Leegs. You know this better than anyone, but few people take the trail south. And almost no one who takes it returns to Beaverton. This is important to the muma. And important to me." Leegs spun the implications around in his mind, but asked no questions. "Thanks," Gstan said. He warily shook Leegs's enormous hand.

* * *

Ziiza thought the preview sale went well. But since she had never held a preview sale for a sports company before, she had no standard upon which to base her opinion. Barclaw stopped by several times on his rounds. He would have brought Wife Barclaw, he told her, if he weren't on duty. But they were both coming to the race Sunday; both were becoming fans. Most of the invited dignitaries were no-shows, except Mistermayor who stopped by on his lunch hour. He declined to try on a Z-Z.

Wife Dragga came, of course, dragging a reluctant Husband D. "Wouldn't miss it, dearest darling." She poked her nose into the storage shelter, ran her long fingers across the counter, and touched every Z-Z piled up for sale, as if accurate tallying could be achieved only by touching (as accurate reading could only be achieved by moving one's lips). She stepped back onto Inner Circle, surveyed the set-up, drew her conclusions, and took Ziiza aside. "Well, darling," she said breathlessly, as if her inspection had taken as much out of her as running a race, "we must do something about that sign. Letters too small. Too far above eye level."

None of her business, but she may have something.

"Inventory's the thing," Wife Dragga said. "I always keep plenty of lots vacant, ready to rent. Lots to choose from. That way I never miss a deal. You *must* do the same."

Is she my boss, my mentor, or my best friend? Anyway, wouldn't she be better off if her lots were rented all of the time?

"Stack them on the counter," Wife Dragga continued. "Don't hide them in back. Let the people fondle them, try them on. That's half the sale, darling." She patted Ziiza's shoulder with a bony hand. "And that trash over there, that rock pile. Get rid of it. Classy vends simply do not *have* rock piles." Satisfied with herself, and deeming it unnecessary for Ziiza to respond, she marched off. Husband Dragga fell in behind.

"Bye, Wife Dragga., Husband Dragga," Ziiza called after them. "And thanks for everything."

Did you notice what business we're in, darling? *Rocks. As in rock running. As in rocks on top of the head. Custom-chipped, custom-balanced rocks. But at least she came. And I'll see her tomorrow.*

Bitta, who had been retained to publicize the preview sale and grand opening, stopped by to check. "I swear, Ziiza," she said, "I talked to everyone on the list. In person. Isn't that right, Hobi?" She tugged at his leg as if he would drip out a report the way he was dripping down her back. "Tomorrow's the big day and I'm off to tell everyone. Again."

"Don't bother, Bitta. You did your best. It's not your fault."

Sister Sissi, whom Ziiza had not seen for some time, was a surprise visitor. She brought four friends, all women her age, all interested in rock running. "We've been practicing with light rocks," Sister Sissi said, "anything we could find. Sunday's our first race. The most exciting thing we've done in years." They pranced nervously in place, holding their rocks at shoulder level with one hand, as they had seen the runners do. Sufx tossed their rocks aside and balanced them with beginner's rocks, as he called them. "Come back in a month or so," he instructed, "for regulation rocks. When you're really into it. Custom balanced." Netti, Govvi, and Ziiza fitted them with top-grade Z-Zs. Ziiza wished Sister Sissi had come alone, but since they were together, she graciously refused their proffered payments. She told Govvi to tally the lost income under "opening costs."

Saturday's grand opening was more encouraging. And again Wife Dragga was involved. Or would have been, had she been prompt. "You must have a ribbon-cutting ceremony," she had gush-ordered Ziiza a few days before. "And I'd be delighted to do the honors. Thank you so much, darling."

Owning real estate makes you a celebrity? Over Mistermayor? Over Polcat? Over a senior council member who could do me some good someday?

But Wife Dragga was late. So after waiting, and sending Edu and Dg to her shelter to check, Ziiza invited Senior, who was there early preparing to make a day of it, to snip the cedar-bark "ribbon," officially opening Z-sport for business.

Wife D did arrive, eventually. She launched into a fast-flowing apology before her foot left Inner Circle. "Some horrible renters to evict for non-payment," she whined. "Ugly business. Shouting. But I've taken care of their likes before. Threaten Wife Dragga, will they? Let them try to find a place to rent in Beaverton again. Ha!" Then, without so much as acknowledging their existence, she brushed past Netti and Govvi and began rearranging the Z-Z display they had gotten up early to construct. Sufx and Junior bent over, touching heads, snickering.

"Why don't we cut the ribbon again?" Ziiza said, looking around at the less-than-enthusiastic handful of lookers and might-be customers. "Wife Dragga, please?" She did and left. After that they took turns cutting the ribbon again and again: Netti, Govvi, Sufx, Junior, Ziiza herself, Quord Senior again, and Edu, who held Dg up to chew through it. Org, running past on a practice run, stopped. "Just passing," he said, as if he had to introduce himself to his own family. Ziiza re-connected the ribbon and invited him to "have a whack at it." He couldn't think up a fast-enough excuse, so he did. "Thanks, Org," she said, hugging him before he could get away. "That was splendid."

Govvi gave Ziiza a sales report for Friday and Saturday up until noon: "Six Z-Zs sold for real money: beaver meat, beaver pelt, or old-fashion dried tail. This did not surprise Ziiza. What surprised her, shocked her, was that as simple a gizmo as a Z-Z required so much detailed explanation and strenuous selling.

Isn't it obvious? A carefully-woven circle of reeds stuffed with layered moss. Place cushion on head. Add rock. No more blood or bruises. No headaches. Absorbs sweat. Lightweight. Attractive-looking. Cools you off on hot days; just dip it in water. And because of all that, you run faster, place higher, and (possibly) win races. Sufx runs with a Z-Z and he wins. And you can, too – or at least finish closer to him. Why don't they understand? They're not buying a high-priced lot near Inner Circle, the investment of a lifetime. Not even back-to-Grassyknoll outfits for the kids. They're just Z-Zs. And I'm practically giving them away.

Ziiza instructed her people to be flexible. "Quote the price," she said, "one dried tail or a quarter pelt, but accept any reasonable offer. Same as on the Sita's opening night." People looked, fingered, hefted, picked, and poked, but were reluctant to try them on. Ziiza had Sufx take short runs on the path, then jump up and down with his head protected by a Z-Z. He would toss his rock, remove his Z-Z, and bend over. "Here, touch my head," he told prospects, some of them serious competitors. "Not a cut; not a drop of blood."

Maybe tomorrow. Maybe more excitement on race day.

Having given the employees and "celebrities" as many ribbon-cutting opportunities as they wished, Ziiza invited a customer, a trim, athletic young woman. "You're our hundredth customer," she lied. But as she cut, from across the way, on the opposite corner, Ziiza heard a booming carnival voice.

"Introducing. I say, introducing. To Beaverton. To the valley of the beaver. Yes, I say, ladies and gentlemen, girls and boys." The speaker stood on a flattened tree-round holding a colored object. He continued: "The most revolutionary stones ever seen on the New Side. Old Side, too, for that matter." He paused for effect. Ziiza's customers turned to look. Shoppers at nearby vends dropped their robes, trinkets, vegetables, and greens. Listened and stared. Traffic on pathways slowed; people bumped into backs. The speaker pulled a similar object from his belt and held both over his head. The original shone soft green, the second, cerulean blue. As he turned them slowly the lights appeared to pulse with life, over-shining the sun. He beckoning with them. They walked slowly toward the man.

Ziiza did not. She stood stiff, blocking her children, Sufx, and Junior with outstretched arms, as her customers left Z-sport and walked across. She rose on her toes and squinted. "It's Gstan," she said. "And those things. How dare he? On my opening day." But she could not take her eyes off of him.

"Yes, my friends," Gstan continued, "possibly the most beautiful stones you've ever seen." He raised his voice. "Possibly?" He raised it again, "Possibly? Did I say possibly? These *are* the most beautiful and amazing stones you've ever seen. Or ever will see. Come closer, my friends. Closer, so everyone can hear. Even Hobart," he said, spotting Bitta and bird. Laughter and side-poking. Gstan smiled and took a satisfied breath. He had them.

"ThinStones. ThinStones. Miraculous ThinStones. That's what they are. You, sir," he said, pointing to a well-fed man in front. "Take hold of this." The man shrank back into the rapidly increasing crowd. "No, no, they're perfectly safe. They emit no heat. Do not burn. Cool to the touch, as a matter of fact. He held it to his cheek, and, smiling, turned a circle on the tree-round. The man touched it with a fingertip to make sure, then took the ThinStone and held it over his head. People breathed a collective sigh, some with relief, some with disappointment (that he did not get burned). "Now, sir," Gstan said to the volunteer, "pick a number, if you will. Don't tell me what it is. Don't tell anyone. Just pick a goodly-sized number, three or four digits, say, while giving the ThinStone a squeeze." The man closed his eyes, squeezed, and opened them, looking sheepish. Gstan reached down and took the stone. "Thank you, sir." As he rose, he spotted Ziiza across the path, apart from the crowd. He winked, smiled, almost called to her, then changed his mind when she did not return his look. "A lady, a lady," he said. "A lady volunteer." No hands. "You'll be making history," he said enticingly. Still no volunteer. "Bitta?" he said. Hearing her name, Hobart flapped and coo-burped. With him as a talisman, or more likely because of her reporter's curiosity, she moved forward. He handed her the ThinStone which she accepted without hesitation. "Squeeze it, Bitta, if you will. No, you don't have to close your eyes." Easy laughter. He paused to play the crowd. "Now, Bitta," he roared, to make certain everyone heard, "what's the number?"

"Five, four, nine, one."

"Now, sir," Gstan said, looking intently at the man, because everything hinged on this first public test. "What number did you impart to the ThinStone?"

"Five thousand, four hundred and ninety-one. Five thousand —"

"Quite enough, sir," Gstan cut him off. "No explanation necessary. Thank you very much." Gstan raised his fur, showed his bare belly, and swiped the sweat from his face; he could not help it. This brought a laugh, so he did it again.

By this time, Ziiza's crew had moved into the crowd; she could not hold them back. She even thought she saw Govvi raise her hand when Gstan had asked for lady volunteers. But Gstan had not seen her and had asked Bitta.

Ziiza scowled. She had hardly given ThinStones a thought since his demonstration on that awful day after Com's memorial, she had been so preoccupied with Z-sport.

What's with this man who professes to be my friend? More than a friend. Couldn't he have waited? Did he have to pick this very day, our grand opening day? Do it on the same corner, right across the path from Z-sport? I hope he doesn't intend to make it his permanent vend, because I can't afford to move. And I'll be darned if I'll move for the. . . .

Ziiza was not given to swearing, or even harsh language, but she came as close to it as she ever had, she was so furious.

So this is what he wants. Friendly competition. Fair enough. Unfriendly competition. Fine, too. But public humiliation. The nerve. The gall. The man.

Gstan hushed his audience with a hand wave. He lowered his voice so that all but the closest had to strain to hear. "Friends —"

"How much, Gstan?" yelled a tall man dressed in a new beaver-pelt coat.

"Ah, but a minute, good sir. There is so much to tell. The marvels of ThinStones." He held up the blue one and performed a mathematical calculation similar to the one he had done for Ziiza. Did it again with an audience volunteer. People passed from interested, to fascinated, to amazed, to stunned into reverent silence. Money time. He raised a sack over his head to provide shade from the sun. Inside, a deep purple ThinStone pulsed as if alive. He turned around. Waves of "ahhhs" rose and fell. He switched from pitchman's sweetness to authority voice. "You thought that was something. That's nothing. For every person who cares about numbers, there are hundreds who care about words — am I right?" The people roared their approval; by now it would not have mattered what he had said. He asked a matron to be a witness; he helped her onto the tree-round. He squeezed the ThinStone, grimacing as he did, and spoke so only he and the matron could hear. He called for a youngster. Handed the ThinStone to a girl. She took it without hesitation, squeezed, and said, "Everyone in Beaverton needs a ThinStone." Wave after wave of laughter. The witnessing matron patted the girl's head in confirmation, then glowed as if to say, I did it all myself.

The tall man stripped off his beaver-pelt coat and threw it at Gstan. "That one! I'll take that one! I want the purple one." Gstan gave it to him and kicked the coat behind him. "Careful now; don't drop it." The bag of ThinStones emptied as fast as he could pass them out. No bickering, no haggling, he never had a chance to quote a price; the people thrust everything of value they had with them, which was not a problem because every offer was for more than he had expected. Much more. "Sold out," Gstan said, stepping off the round. "And thank you very much."

"What about us?"

"When will you have more?"

"Next shipment expected in a few weeks," Gstan said, hopping back on the round. "Listen to Bitta for the date. And thank you again."

Most of the people moved away. A few stood staring at Gstan and his pile of skins, furs, clothes, meat, and tail. Disappointed buyers offered new ThinStone owners more than they had paid.

Gstan left his pile, no one would touch it, and walked across the path to Z-sport. "What do you think?" he started to say. Then he saw Ziiza's face. He nodded to Netti and Govvi. Touched his forehead in greeting. Then to Sufx and Junior. Smiled at Edu. "Did pretty well for a first crack at it, wouldn't you say, Ziiza?"

"How could you?" Ziiza said. "How could you, Gstan? Ruin my grand opening like that. Take away my hard-won customers. Just suck them away."

"Ziiza . . . I mean . . . I had no idea they would go over so well. Wow the folks like that. You weren't impressed when I showed you. None of the others I've shown them to. Old Man. Leegs. I had no idea. Of course I sure hoped they would. Speaking of Leegs, he's my overland delivery. . . ." He stopped short, realizing she wasn't buying any of it. He walked back to his pile, picked up what he could carry, and started across H&G toward Hill Burrow.

Edu looked at Gstan, then the remaining goods, then back at Gstan. "I'll help you, Mister Gstan," he shouted across the path. "I'll help you carry them."

Gstan looked back. Before he could answer him, Ziiza said, "Not today, Edu. You have plenty of work here." Gstan resumed walking.

Thanks a lot, Gstan.

30

Blood Camp

ORG LAY with his head propped on his rock. Gestured with his hand. A sweet-faced girl ran to him and stuck a piece of beaver meat in his mouth. She wet her finger and drew it down his bare, dark-streaked chest. She licked it, then ran giggling to the clutch of girls she had left. Her name was Hid, the same as all of the girls in the clutch, short for Hideous. Of the present eleven, she was the seventh to join, so became Hid Seven, but she answered to Hideous, Hid, or Seven. The boys in the camp, fifteen in number, had their own clutch, and not to be outdone by the girls, had adopted Gruesome, a more male-sounding name they thought, but equally debasing, which they shortened to Grue: Grue One through Grue Fifteen.

Blood Camp lay southwest of Beaverton in the big-tree woods by the Daughter River, the one Biber had sneaked through in early mornings with his sacks of pond sludge, the one Litti skirted on her way to Water Child, thick woods so close-in most town-dwellers never thought about them. Many Bloodies were on-the-rebound Screaming Indifference fans, devastated after they had left town. All had a fascination with blood. Especially Org's blood. They mobbed him after his training runs, rubbing his sticky hair, shoulders, chest, and back, covering their hands with as much blood as they could. Then they worked on each other's hair. The girls' hairdos were identical: a slicked-down top, which broke at right angles just above eye level. Stiffened with dried blood and pressed between hands, it stood straight out. In a ritualistic "biting off," a higher ranking (lower numbered) girl bit off the projecting ends which were then savored and swallowed. They never washed their hair – or bathed their bodies, for that matter. Hairdos were reinforced with new blood whenever possible and the girls had to sleep face down without moving, lest they ruin them – losing face and possibly membership. The boys' version started out the same, pressed flat on top, but continuing down, over face, ears, and back, parted for eyes, nose, and mouth, as long as their hair ran. Both males and females added their own blood to Org's, for as often as he bled, and as much as he bled, there was never enough. Their individualistically uniform clothing consisted of loin covers, smocks, and shawls, slashed to achieve a scruffy chic effect.

Org's blood-and-sweat rock running style appealed to these non-athletes; were it not for him they would never have thought of attending a race, let alone running in one. Their adulation sealed his decision to forsake Z-Zs, his siblings, and his muma. Org the trail breaker. Org the rock runner. Org, king of the Bloodies. They fed him, sheltered him, massaged his sore muscles, treated his head wounds in their peculiar ways, and cheered him when he ran. Winning was of no interest to them; he could finish second or second last. Did not matter. They measured success in blood seeping, blood dripping, and blood flowing. Org did not disappoint. He in return accepted the girls' favors, ruled over them (although he had no interest in ruling per se), and put up with their stench, their fleas, their lice-infested hair, and the aggressive flies that circled their heads. Blood Camp was a springtime, summertime affair. What would become of the Bloodies, their hairdos, their loose camaraderie when the rains came, was anyone's guess.

But today was today. And today was Sunday, race day.

Well before starting time the Bloodies formed up on the trail, tight enough to touch, Hid Eleven leading, followed by the girls in descending numbers, Org in the middle, then Grue One, and so forth ending with Grue Fifteen. Org hoisted his rock with a grunt. They cheered and were off, a quivering caterpillar encased in flies. They filed along the forest trail, over roots, through patches of Solomon's seal, across brooks, and around blow-downs. They turned onto Outer Circle. Rock runners jogged by, heading for the race; the caterpillar did not have to sound off for them to give way. They marched, more or less in step, around Outer Circle, turned on a residential path, onto Inner Circle, and continued until they came within sight of Z-sport's manufacturing facility, sales emporium, and rock balancing station.

Ziiza gasped.

So this is what he's up to.

Customers stood in open-mouthed astonishment. Edu bent over the balance scale. "Org, Org, what now?" he said, his back rising and falling as he laughed into folded arms. Dg ran to the caterpillar, barked once, and backed away.

"Where's Sufx? Where's Junior?" Org snarled, looking through his muma, his sisters, and his little brother. He stepped out of line and walked toward Edu and the balance.

Thank goodness he hasn't put on one of those ridiculous hairdos or slit his furs like the rest of them.

The stench of twenty-six Bloodies plus Org rolled from the caterpillar and broke like a wave on Z-sport's shore. Ziiza and crew covered their mouths, pressed their noses, and stood their ground. Customers slipped away. Org gave Ziiza an arrogant look. Holding his rock in one hand, he thrust the other defiantly in the air for the Bloodies. Foul words, cheering, and screaming. He kicked a customer's rock off the balance and replaced it with his own.

"Hi, Org," said Edu, hesitantly. "How's it going?"

"Balance me," Org commanded, and sat on the other end. The rock did not move. Org jiggled and bounced. It still did not move. He smirked. Edu advanced with Sufx's tool and began chipping. "Stop that, Edu!" Org yelled. "I came here to show Sufx I'm running with a rock that's way over his puny limit. And I'll still beat him."

"Yaaaa, Org," screamed the Bloodies.

Ziiza came to him with a Z-Z in her hand. "Here, Org, compliments of Z-sport. Netti made it especially for you." Org took it from her with a contemptuous look and returned to his place in the caterpillar. On a signal from Grue One they marched past Z-sport and turned onto Town Hall Path toward the starting line. As he passed the corner, Org flung the Z-Z high in the air.

And best of luck to you, too, my boy.

* * *

"One announcement before the race," Quord Senior said to the runners strung out far beyond his sight and out of the sound of his voice. "Minor rule change. All rocks must weigh at least one-fifth the runner's weight. You have four weeks to comply. So please stop in at Z-sport and balance up. And now, our honorary starter for today's race. I present Mistermayor." Cheers, whistles, and nervous foot flopping.

Ziiza had been correct in her predictions, mostly. Rock running was booming. A sizeable percentage of Beaverton's population was present, as runners or spectators. As many runners practiced on Outer Circle each day as used to compete. Attending Sunday races was becoming the socially correct thing to do, the place to be seen. Bitta reported race results. Folks discussed their favorite runners throughout the week. Would gritty Sufx *ever* be beaten? Would Org, could Org get any stronger, any faster before he "ran his rock into the ground?" Wasn't Quord Junior a disappointment to his popa, since he was finishing farther and farther back? (The discouraging fact: Junior was improving. But the competition was improving more.) Betting on runners, although discouraged by the council, was growing. Barclaw's periodic "crackdowns" were laughed off. Groopland casino was giving odds and accepting wagers – on human beings, who could think, talk, plot, and "adjust" their performances in endless ways. What next?

However controversial, Esqq's forced-through move away from barter and tail had smoothed the channels of commerce to the advantage of all – except the beaver. A few wrinkles remained to be worked out: how best to divide pelts to make change, whether it was more advantageous to keep pelts as money than make them into clothing as they wore out and lost value. And the question of how long this practice could continue. Yes, everyone knew the giant valley beavers were unlimited, a renewable resource. But how unlimited was unlimited? Should alternative food sources be developed, just in case? Should hunting, fishing, and berry, seed, and fruit gathering be given a look, a serious look as food staples, not just garnishment and snack offerings at boutique vends?

Ziiza liked being paid in beaver pelts, they thrilled her. She liked to stroke them, lie on them, roll on them; they made her feel wealthy and successful, even if they soon passed out of her hands – to Font for interest and pay-downs, to employees for wages, and to suppliers for everything else. The fair rock rule change and locating the certifying balance at Z-sport had helped business, it could not but help. Although far from a majority of runners were wearing Z-Zs in today's race, they were becoming conspicuous. Sufx kept on winning, using a new Z-Z in each race. Ziiza's constant question: Will they buy Z-Zs because they think they will help them "win" like Sufx? Or will Sufx's continued winning become routine so nobody will want to watch the races anymore for lack of excitement? Will they have the patience to watch race after race, hoping for the big upset? She was not worried about the runners losing interest. With the exception of Org and a handful of other top runners, they did not expect to beat him. Ever. They were thrilled to say, "I ran against Sufx last weekend." Or, "I kept contact with Sufx for the first half."

"Isn't this great," Ziiza said, turning to the children and giving each a playful shove as Sufx ran past. This was going to be an easy win for him, she calculated. Org passed in third place. Ziiza winced. Sweat-diluted blood dripped from his hair, streamed down his face, down his chest and back; his oversized rock seemed to be grinding a hole in his head.

The pain; how does he stand it? If he weren't so obdurate he might have a chance with a Z-Z.

Org's chest heaved as he sucked air for his sprint to the finish. Z-sport corner was where they made their moves – for second, third, fourth, and so on. She knew he would not catch Sufx, but secretly hoped he would. Just once. This rude, sullen, boy-man who was still her son.

Next came the lead pack. Then the lead-pack challengers. Then the surging, bumping, and sometimes stumbling river of runners, which grew until it filled the path. Runners with wobbly knees, glazed eyes, and arms no longer able to hold onto rocks. Spectators clapped, cheered, shouted names. They kept on coming, thick and steady. Then gaps. Then the stragglers, some running backwards, or sideways, or walking. The late finishers. The gut busters. Ziiza saw Gstan through a break in the stragglers, across the path, sitting on the tree-round in the Errix vend. He waved and smiled. Ziiza waved back, more in recognition than welcome.

Gstan walked to the path, stood for a moment waiting for an opening, bounded across, and walked slowly to Ziiza and Edu. Govvi and Netti stood behind, watching the last of the race. Sales-wise this was the dead point; no customers, everyone occupied with the race. The rest of the day would be critical, more critical than yesterday's not-so-grand opening. Would they remember Senior's announcement to have their rocks balanced and chipped? Or exchanged? Sufx would win as usual – with the aid of a Z-Z. He and Junior were expected back soon; slower runners would still be finishing. Would competitors stop by to shake his hand? The fans? Would they buy Z-Zs?

"You're looking good, Gstan," Ziiza said – because she thought his new clothes required it. He was dressed in black beaver pelt with a high-grade sheen. Tight-cut leggings. He sported a vest trimmed with what could only be a thin, in-your-face-illegal strip of watabeast fur. Three polished agates perched on each shoulder (how attached she could not tell), giving him a look of . . . dignity? authority? pretentiousness? She would decide later. It was the first time she saw him wearing a head cover, a beaver-skin cap cocked jauntily to the side. The tip of a blue ThinStone glimmered above his belt. Fashion accessory? Advertising his stock-in-trade? He looked good. Gstan, the unkempt bachelor who had never given clothing a thought, now had an image.

"You're looking swell yourself, Zi," he said in an offhand manner that came across as flippant, but was not intended as such.

"Don't 'Zi' me after what you did yesterday." Edu looked up at his muma, then at Gstan, then back at his muma. Govvi and Netti stepped back, fearing a fight, then seeing it was not going to happen, advanced to listen.

"Now, Ziiza. Like I said, how could I have predicted? I sold out, and they were gone. Made more money than I ever imagined. That's good, isn't it?"

You're so blind, Gstan. So blind. You think I share your success, your happiness, when it was achieved at my expense. You are not a stupid man, but you act that way. What's next, flowers?

Not flowers. Gstan held the ThinStone out to Ziiza. "It's for you. Like the one I showed you before. We did the numbers. It's the only one I have left until the next shipment comes in. And that won't be for weeks. I won't be bothering you across the way. I've nothing to sell. And I have to supervise my workers over at Hill Burrow. Remember Hill Burrow?" He smiled.

Ziiza turned the ThinStone over and handed it back. "I couldn't," she said. "It's too expensive."

Govvi stepped up. "We could use it, Muma. Use it in the business. It's the most wonderful. . . ."

"We'd like to play with it, learn how to do it," Edu said. "Gstan could teach us. Govvi and me. We could do it together." He patted Dg. "Dg wants it, too," he said, trying to add weight and humor to his request.

"Yes, yes, take it," Gstan sputtered. "I would be a poor choice for a teacher, though, being more the salesman type. I make no claim to knowing the ThinStone's finer points. I only sell 'em. But keep it, Ziiza. Please. It's for all of you."

Ziiza looked at Gstan, then at Govvi and Edu's pleading looks; she was trapped. "Okay," she said, "I'll trade you. Your ThinStone for a complimentary Z-Z." She walked to the display, selected one his size, and handed it to him.

"Pleased to accept it," he said, "even though I'm not much of a rock running man. And in all honesty, I don't plan on becoming one."

"Just hang it on your wall. And thank you for the ThinStone. Now, if you'll excuse us, we have a big day ahead."

I hope.

Afternoon sales were, to use the retailers' euphemism, mixed. Sufx drew his crowd of well-wishers and autograph-seekers. Junior balanced and chipped and juggled rocks till he was worn out. Z-Zs sold steadily but not easily. Ziiza still sensed an undercurrent of resistance. She had to do a little too much talking, explaining, convincing, to close each sale. Why?

Toward the end of the afternoon, with only two lookers in the vend, passers-by, really, Govvi gave Ziiza the totals and asked for the rest of the day off.

"You're not going over the hill to see those two, are you?"

"Mu Ma," Govvi said, in sham exasperation, "It's been a hard week. I'd like to walk around H&G. Relax. Catch up on things. Maybe see if Skedaddle is still playing."

Highly unlikely, this late on a Sunday afternoon.

"These folks aren't going to buy," Netti whispered. "They're just lookers. I agree with Govvi. I'm worn out. I'd like to go home and get some rest."

"Edu and I will close up," Ziiza said quickly. "Off you go."

Govvi took Town Hall Path to the center of H&G, cut across, walked Outer Circle to the Welcome to Exciting Beaverton sign, then climbed the hill. Pop&Jay were not in "town" when she arrived, so she sat on the riverbank and waited, looking at the water, then east toward the mountain that had taken her brother. Then quickly away.

Scratch. Scratch. Thump. It sounded like rock against wood. Govvi rose and walked toward the sounds. Scratch. Scrape. Scratch. An angry voice. Govvi followed the sounds into the trees.

Jay held a wooden shovel and looked into a grave-sized hole between two fir trees. Pop's upper half protruded. He, too, had a shovel and was leaning on it. "Ya danged fool," Pop sputtered. "If ya hadn't started this thing so close to the trees we wouldn't be hitting so many roots. I can't cut through 'em and I can't dig around 'em."

A smile crept onto Govvi's face. Same old Pop&Jay. She listened to them argue for a minute, then advanced past a large pile of sacks. "I would have come earlier," she said.

"Uh, what?" Jay sputtered. He dropped his shovel, ran, and hugged her in a fumbling greeting designed to stop her progress. Pop jumped out, dragged a heavy sack to the hole, and shoved it in. Then another. And another. Then the two men, realizing the futility of trying to hide their secret, turned, looked at each other, and laughed heartily.

"Well, Little One," Pop said, "ya caught us down in our hole, so to speak." That brought on more waves of laughter and thigh-slapping. "Caught us with our secret out in the light of open daytime. If you'd come an hour earlier, nothing. An hour later, not a trace. But since it's you, and since it's now, maybe it was meant to be." Jay let go of her and nodded his agreement. "C'mon over here. We were going to show you eventually, anyhow."

Pop opened a sack and withdrew a yellow-colored object about the length of his middle finger. He placed it in Govvi's hand. It was oval on one end and curved and flattened to a chisel point on the other. "This is easy," she said. "It's a beaver tooth. The upper incisor. The one they cut with. I have some myself. You gave them to me. For building the fires."

"That's right. That's right," Pop said, jumping and squealing with delight. "And that's wrong. That's wrong. Figure that one out, smart little miss."

"Well, this one's bigger."

"Yes. Yes."

"And it's the wrong color; mine are different."

"Why? Why? Why is the color wrong?"

"From the giant valley beaver?"

"Yup," Pop said, "two big teeth per dead one. We've been collecting them."

"But you're not allowed. . . ."

"True. True," Jay said. "But we have our ways." He gave Pop a knowing wink. "Why don't you sit here until this lazy one finishes the hole and we bury the sacks? Better yet, why don't you build us a nice sparkly-warm fire so we can roast us some tasty giant valley beaver meat for supper. None of that blah river fish for us. Then after we're filled up, leanin' back, and content, we'll tell you about it."

Govvi was out of practice and it took her a long time to start the fire; she was glad they were off digging and burying so they did not see her struggle. While they ate, they quizzed her on Beaverton news, with extra interest in Z-sport and the rock running phenomenon, and Errix and the ThinStone phenomenon. When she mentioned Ziiza's dealings with Font their eyes lit; they could not feign casual interest any longer.

"It's simple, Little One," Pop said, pointing a tooth at her. "Simple as can be. I'm sure you've figured it out." He paused, waiting for her answer.

"Money?"

"I told you. I told you," Pop chortled. "Told you she was better than all the rest of them over in Beaverton. Pick of a mighty big litter." Govvi lowered her eyes. "It's just a matter of time before they tumble to it. But we beat 'em. Perfect money. Ultimate medium of exchange. One big yellow – that's what we call 'em, big yellows – represents one-half of a giant valley beaver pelt. None other. Big yellows are larger than those tiny mountain beavers' teeth and a different color. Can't be faked. Smaller than pelts. Easy to carry. Easy to hide. And, unlike pelts, big yellows don't wear out. Indestructible. That is, unless you throw them in the fire. First barter. Then barter and tail. Then pelts and meat. Now big yellows. All the rest will be – just food, and clothing, and small change."

Govvi thought for a moment and said, "But they're not doing it, not using them. And besides, you have all the big yellows, as you call them."

"Not all of them," Jay said, his eyes shining in the firelight. "Just enough. Enough to do the trick. You're awfully bright, Little One, but maybe you still have a few things to learn. Like the power of the word *enough*. Pop&Jay know the power of *enough*. You will, soon. But the fools on the other side of the hill. Ha! They'll have to learn the hard way."

"But?" Govvi said.

Pop&Jay looked into the fire, raised their eyes as if in a rehearsed motion, fixed them on Govvi, and smiled like two beavers contemplating a riverside cottonwood.

"Me?" she said with a shiver. "Me?"

31

Lazy Grape

MONDAY MORNING. "I don't think we need to open today," Ziiza told Edu. She had finally admitted to herself how exhausted she was, with no successes to compensate.

"Lots of vends close Mondays," Edu said sympathetically.

So after sending him off to school, and with Netti and Govvi sleeping late, Ziiza walked over to Litti's. Litti stood next to her tiny shelter, beating a robe with a stick. She held her breath, closed her eyes, hit three times, then walked away from the dust cloud. She smiled when she saw Ziiza. "One more robe and I'll make tea."

Ziiza had plenty to talk about, plenty of problems to spill, but, after a few weather words, she sat quietly, sipping. Litti said little. Looked into the fire. When courtesy and friendship insisted, she looked at Ziiza, forced a smile, and tried to brighten her eyes. Ziiza waited her out.

"He swore me to secrecy," Litti said, "but I simply have to tell someone. And the only one I would tell is you. Promise me the greatest of promises?" Ziiza nodded. "He thinks he's found a sita. Yes, a live sita." She put her hand to her mouth and whispered, "Comes to Water Child." Litti told her of the morning, of finding the huge footprints in the grass, the finger-sized claw holes, and wishing she never had. "He's thought of nothing else since," she said. "He makes blinds to hide in, sits in trees, looks for tracks, tufts of fur, anything. He has no time for me, he's so obsessed. He invites me to go searching with him, but I can't. He has no idea how powerful and dangerous a cat that size is. Or if he does, he doesn't care. Everything is 'my career' and 'my reputation.'" Litti sniffed, dropped her head, and wiped her cheeks. Ziiza felt there was more to come and did not want to break in. "I still love him," Litti continued. "More than I ever realized. I guess that's natural when you're feeling yourself dropping into second place. Or maybe no place at all."

By the time Litti finished, Ziiza was weeping, too. Maybe it was too perfect a romance, she thought, too good to be true, to last. Then again, maybe Arbo will realize the ridiculousness of his chase and stop. And realize how exceptional this young woman was. And not toss her away.

"I feel better," Litti said, snapping her head up. "I really do. I had to tell someone. And you are the only one I can . . . trust to. . . . Well, you know."

"Thank you, Litti. I just wish I could offer something other than my wish that it works out. I think it will."

Ziiza started in slowly on *her* troubles; they seemed insignificant compared to Litti's, but once she got going she found it difficult to stop. So it was to be a commiseration session with little good news. Ziiza was worried about Govvi. She wasn't absolutely certain she was visiting Pop&Jay, but she was suspicious. Of course she would never have her followed, spy on her. Not on Govvi. She was doing so much for Z-sport, so valuable, so on top of everything, even more so than at Sita's Lair. She wished she had not used *suspicious* and *spy*, but they were out.

She brought Litti up-to-date on Org. Why would the son who had performed so magnificently on the Sea Trace turn on her like this? Yes, he was the strong, silent type, to use the cliché, but that is what he had always been, strong and silent, a boy of direct action, a young man of direct action. She had given him his head, praised him often, asked little of him except to try a Z-Z, which was to his advantage, for gosh sakes (as well as hers). Litti had no more of an answer for Org than Ziiza had had for Arbo.

"And our dear Netti?" Litti inquired.

"Hard work agrees with her, such as I can tell. She supervises five workers, does not even have to touch a product. She buys supplies, improves the designs here and there, and stocks the store. Sells a little."

"And?" Litti probed.

"She seems to have overcome the craving for Mire-root. Perhaps hard work and plenty of it is the answer. She has simply been too busy to think about anything else."

"Headaches?"

Ziiza doubted they would ever go away, just a matter of how often and how hurtful. She felt the conversation should shift back to Litti, but continued. The business was growing, she told her, but not anywhere near as fast as she would have predicted, given the popularity of rock running and the sheer logic of her invention. She could not help but mention Gstan, his audacity in setting up across the path and his astounding success. Litti nodded. Business was something far removed from Litti's world; she did not pretend to understand. In way of reply, she brought Ziiza up to date on Mizpark and Friends of the Beaver. Membership was building; she was certain they would prevail. She did not mention Ziiza's non-membership.

So they laid out their troubles, one to another. They talked through tea, through a mid-morning meal and into the afternoon. Heavy matters disposed of, they drifted into pleasant chitchat, the highlight of which was Edu's achievement in school and his willingness to help out at Z-sport without being asked. Dg's antics: chewing on Z-Zs, chasing runners, sniffing customers' legs.

"Anything from Netti's sister?" Litti asked as they were parting, trying to complete the conversation. Or extend it.

Ziiza walked back, wrapped her arms around Litti, and hugged her. "Nothing," she said. "Milli's stepped out of my life. Another empty place in my heart."

* * *

Leegs trudged up to Hill Burrow with the long-awaited shipment of ThinStones. As he bent to unload, Gstan grabbed his arm and said, "Not here, we're going straight to H&G and sell 'em."

Leegs pulled off his straps and lowered his pack. "Sorry, Gstan," he said, "but this is as far as I go. Not that I can't handle the job or anything, but you program yourself to go just so far. You get there and that's it. Everything goes out of you. I'm here. I'm through."

"Haracosh!" Gstan shouted. Old Man touched him on the shoulder. "Oh, Haracosh," he said, lowering his voice, "you're right here. Call out the workers and load them up; we're going to set this town on its ear."

Leegs wobbled into Gstan's burrow and sank down on a robe.

Cutting across H&G carrying a glowing yellow-green ThinStone, Gstan found Bitta in front of Town Hall. Hobart had drawn a large crowd and stood stiffly on her shoulder, finished for the moment. Barclaw sat at his station, waiting for the news. Mistermayor leaned against a pole.

Gstan pushed through the crowd, pumping his ThinStone up and down like a baton, his workers trailing him. "New shipment of ThinStones, Bitta," he said without stopping. "Spread the word." Not that she had to. Most of her listeners fell in behind Gstan. As did Barclaw, Mistermayor, town employees, and after a moment's hesitation, Bitta and Hobart.

"Oh, no," Ziiza said to Govvi when she saw them coming. "Here we go again."

When he arrived at the Errix vend, Gstan jumped onto his tree-round and said, "Ladies and gentleman, mumas and popas, girls and boys. Our shipment has just arrived. I mean *just*." He looked down. "You, sir," he said, addressing a man pawing a bag. "There are enough for all. No need to hurry."

The crowd grew. Vend owners and customers joined. Walkers on Inner Circle stopped, just as before. Word spread through H&G; Bitta was not needed. People clogged the paths, flowed into the surrounding vends, then into neighboring yards. And of course, into Z-sport and beyond; it was all Netti could do to keep them out of the work area. Ziiza fumed and stood guard over her display. Govvi and Edu looked anxiously at their muma, at Gstan, and back, until her look released them. Hand in hand, they wiggled into the crowd.

"Before we begin our auction," Gstan said, smiling expansively. He caught himself in mock surprise. "Did I say auction? I believe I did. Before we begin, I would like to let you in on a secret. He waved the yellow-green ThinStone in one hand and a bright red one in the other, back and forth over his head. The crowd throbbed.

"The secret, you said?"

"Yes, the secret. The secret law." He allowed the suspense to build. "Gstan's Law," he said, dropping his voice, "modestly named after yours truly. And what is this secret law? ThinStones get thinner and lighter by the week. And increase in power. And speed. And capacity." No response; it was beyond them. "Yes, ladies and gentlemen, Gstan's Law is the secret. I've done it all for you. Along with a little help from the workers in Hill Burrow. And down south."

"So, my friends," Gstan continued, his face flushed, "the ThinStones you bid on this morning will be far superior to the ones of a few weeks ago. Operate faster, hold more words and numbers. Plus. Now listen to this. Plus."

A beaver pelt sailed through the air and hit Gstan in the face. "Opening bid," said the man who threw it. Many laughs.

"Thank you, sir," Gstan said. "Plus, we've added a new household and business inventory feature called ThinStuff. Incredibly easy to learn. Powerful. And listen to this: new models include a game. You know it as toes and bones. Now it's ThinStone Amuse. Same game. More fun." Gstan raised his hand to hold the man's bid and said, "Next bid on this gorgeous, power-packed beauty?"

Because of the bidding, and a greater number of ThinStones to sell, it took over an hour to sell out. Govvi and Edu twisted and crawled through legs until they reached Gstan's tree-round, where they listened spellbound to the auction. They made themselves useful, stacking payment pelts and delivering ThinStones to winning bidders. Govvi the organizer quickly took over from the dull stone polishers and organized the pelts, meat, and barter, all the while pinching her ThinStone as she tallied them up. Edu helped, trying to listen to Gstan at the same time.

When they were all auctioned off, Govvi squeezed her ThinStone to confirm the numbers she already knew and reported them to Gstan in her most crisp businesslike voice, so as not to betray her astonishment. And not to raise the thought that she should not have been doing it at all.

But the auction was not the end of it. A goodly portion of the crowd stayed on, mostly men, older men, affluent men, the ones who had been doing the bidding. They formed into groups at first, then circulated, so the groups were constantly changing. The aftermarket. Quietly, carefully, they examined and tested each ThinStone offered up, appraising its strengths, weaknesses, and miniscule differences. And the differences were many; different Hieyeques (although unknown to them) in different moods or states of enlightenment, had chanted each ThinStone, imparting not only color but their idiosyncrasies. Those judged superior were resold and resold again in an informal on-going auction that would progress from the Errix vend to other gatherings, to H&G vends, and into private shelters. Another thing: some of the men did not care about speed, capacity, extra features, or power, did not try to operate them. They were the mint condition collectors, bidding, trading, conniving, (and sometimes more) to acquire the rarest of all ThinStones, those called Brilliant. Appearance, glow, and rarity of color mattered. Performance did not. Cost did not.

He drew a crowd, Ziiza had to admit. But not her kind of crowd. After Gstan and his workers marched away loaded with riches – he did not make the mistake of stopping by this time – she sold exactly one Z-Z in four hours. Thank goodness this only happens every few weeks, she thought as they closed for the day. She could not have been more wrong. Open or closed, from then on, the Errix Enterprises vend was the ThinStone exchange.

Sister Sissi, sensing a shift H&G's center of business, sub-leased a corner of the Errix location from Gstan and opened Konka Sanctuary number one. (With rock running, new friends, and expansion, she was no longer the repressed, depressed Sister Sissi of old.) She sold fast beaver and an experimental drink she called Konka, made from the pulverized pits of the konka fruit tree. Like Biber, she revealed as little of its formulation as possible. All people knew was that she boiled it until it turned a thick dark brown. Ziiza had to admit it was nice to have her nearby. The dark drink was a welcome alternative to tea, especially on chilly mornings. Sister Sissi and her friends drank it before their morning training runs; she claimed it improved their performances. Ziiza sometimes joined them (drinking, not running) along with some of the Z-sport workers. The children did not. Like slooze, it was considered an adult drink. Netti, who was almost an adult, still did not care for it.

* * *

"Look at this!" Wife Dragga's voice lashed across the garden and bit her husband's ear. Husband Dragga turned slowly from cultivating his celery and stared at her with dull, droopy eyes, his cheeks sagging like a starving squirrel's. "Well," she demanded, "what do you think?" It might have been a Z-Z. He got that far. Except it was held on with a thin strap around her chin, which allowed her to wear it at a jaunty angle. And of course there was no rock on top. Not only was she not dressed in running attire (she did not have any), she was in her best go-to-H&G outfit. But most startling, it was colored an unusual purple color. "You're wondering about the color, I know." Husband Dragga made a slow move to return to his work. She yanked him back verbally and continued: "Lazy Grape, I call it. The most disgusting color I could concoct, together with the most disgusting name." Husband Dragga raised his eyelids. Wife D walked to him. She turned full round, checking for peeping neighbors. She bent low and whispered, "I'm going to get her this time. Bring her down."

"Who?"

"Ziiza, of course. Who did you think?"

"What's she ever done to you?"

"Oh, my dear Dragga." She patted his bald spot; he was considerably older than she. "I suppose I must explain. Do you realize what will happen if that Z-sport business of hers takes off? It's at the critical point. I don't even need to know the numbers. I can tell by the smug, knowing look on that smarty-brat daughter of hers' face. Gov-vi. And Ziiza: she keeps on plugging no matter what, overcoming one obstacle after another – thinks she's still battling her way down the Sea Trace or something. Pretty soon Z-sport will turn the corner and become profitable. Then watch out."

"For what?"

"For Ziiza to take over this town," Wife Dragga hissed. "Become the most powerful, influential woman in Beaverton. I can't let that happen. Not after all I've worked for. I *won't* let it happen. Period." She glanced around, lowered her voice, and laughed sardonically. "I bought it from her daughter, Netti the weaving drudge, said it was a gift for a friend, made up some name, told her he was taking up rock running. Had it dyed at one of those kid culture boutiques." She looked at him for a glimmer. Seeing none, she said: "The power of perfidious flattery, my dear Dragga, is the power to destroy."

Wife Dragga flounced along the pathway, twitching her hips, holding onto her "hat" with her right hand, her sharp bony elbow threatening to impale anyone who came near, her other hand catching up her skirt. She got immediate results – exactly the opposite of what she wanted. "Good morning, Wife Dragga. Lovely hat." Everyone she passed, old, young, female, male, looked. And looked again. Yes, yes, I agree, she said to herself, smiling and nodding, Isn't it just awful. Then a perplexed look. Can they mean it? Lovely hat? Were those really admiring looks?

Entering H&G she heard a whistle. "Look at that doll," screamed a boy. When she reached Skedaddle, heads turned and the band switched to a faster, livelier tune: "Crickets in the Grass." The audience clapped. This wasn't turning out right. In her plan, she had been prepared to sacrifice her dignity, briefly, for the greater cause: bringing Ziiza down. Now her vanity was being stroked beyond anything she had ever experienced. Over a disgusting-looking, rock-protecting head cover. She hated it. She loved it. She hated it. She would see it through.

Walking toward H&G center, she picked up some teen-age girls. They were not giggling or pointing; she had been prepared for that. They were admiring, trying to get closer. She gripped the hat tightly and quickened her pace. At Town Hall, Barclaw stopped his storytelling, stood up, and bowed to the crowned goddess. "Bitta's missing a scoop," he said.

Wife Dragga approached the Z-sport/Errix Enterprises corner, stiff-legged. A few minutes more, she thought, and I can throw this thing away and go home. The ThinStone traders saw her, saluted with Konka cups, and cheered. Wife Dragga fixed her face into a smile for the last of it, walked slowly past them, and turned in front of Z-sport.

"You look absolutely ravishing, Wife Dragga," Ziiza shouted in greeting.

Wife Dragga stopped, bent her legs, and gave Ziiza a face full of teeth. She was surrounded in an instant: Z-sport customers, traders, walkers, shoppers, even rock runners. Ziiza stood back, thinking fast. But not fast enough.

"I want one just like that," shrieked the woman who had been talking to Govvi.

They pressed closer to Wife Dragga, reaching up, trying to touch the hat. "I call it Lazy Grape," she said weakly. "Isn't it dis –."

"Love it!" screamed one of the teenagers, pawing the air

"Lazy Grape! Lazy Grape!" Her friends joined in. "Lazy Grape! Lazy Grape!"

Ziiza pushed in and took Wife Dragga's arm. She led her past the vend and behind the manufacturing screen. Wife Dragga followed reluctantly. "I think," Ziiza whispered. "No. I know. You are onto something, my friend. Colored Z-Zs. Fashionable hats. Do you realize the market this opens up for Z-sport?" Wife Dragga flicked her eyelashes, fought the tears. "Of course you do," Ziiza answered for her. "You're so smart, so far ahead of everyone.

What a dear friend." Ziiza hugged her bony form. "I can't thank you enough."
Then she added, "What do I owe you? For the idea? The color? The rights?
For the hat? For the name: Lazy Grape? A grabber if there ever was one."

Wife Dragga may have been beaten, but she was a proud, determined
fighter. "Take it, it's yours. Run with it, Ziiza." She laughed her tight, haughty
laugh. "The color? I had it dyed at one of those adult-child vends over on the
fringe. Narda, I think her name was." She twirled around. "Busy day ahead.
Much to do." She stalked away.

"Govvi! Netti!" Ziiza yelled. "Over here. Now! Company meeting. Maybe
the most important meeting ever." She tossed the Lazy Grape in the air,
caught it by the edge, and twirled it.

*Thinner. Smaller. Different colors. Change them often. Not only do Z-Zs wear out,
requiring constant replacement – if I can get enough out there to replace – we now have
fashion obsolescence. Just like Gstan and his ThinStones. Always changing. Always
improving. Keep them guessing. Keep them buying.*

Ziiza lowered the Lazy Grape and opened the meeting.

Ziiza and Govvi ran into Gstan in front of Font's Bank, he leaving, they
arriving. Both on the same errand: money, he a depositor, they borrowers. He
touched his fur cap and greeted them with a knowing smile. "So that's the
hot new item," he said. "May I try it on?" Govvi handed him the Lazy Grape.
He put it on and walked around with mincing Wife Dragga steps, his hand
flopping.

News travels fast.

Font came out when he heard them.

Ziiza had to admit Gstan could be funny at times, at other times infuriating.
She stiffened, waiting for him to start bragging about his money. Or
ThinStones. Or their incredible aftermarket trading; he was buying them for
speculation himself. But he did not. "Lend her anything she wants, Font, old
boy," he said, in the manner of a substantial depositor. "From what I've
heard, this could be very big." Then with a smile for Ziiza and Govvi, he
said, "Good afternoon, girls."

"You're pushing your credit line to the limit, Ziiza," Font told her after
she had explained.

"Don't you *see?*" Ziiza sucked the too-shrill word into her mouth and
started over. "Don't you see? A whole new market. Twice, three times the
rock running market. The fashion market. The replacement market. The repeat
business market."

"How many have you sold?"

"None, yet. It just happened today. But you should have seen the reaction.
Heard the people. All kinds of people. Konka drinkers. Teenage girls. Men.

Women." She twirled the hat in her hands. "Lazy Grape," she said in a throaty voice, emphasizing each syllable as if the not-too-flattering name would produce a seductive effect, "is just the first of many colors."

"But how many have you sold?"

"I'm out of money: pelts, meat, barter and tail, everything. I've spent it on wages, real estate, and materials. You know that, Font" Her voice took a whiny edge. "Don't you?"

"Yes, I do," he said. "And I think it's a wonderful idea. You've laid all the groundwork. A considerable effort. But that's not the problem. The problem is, even with Gstan's considerable deposits, I'm short of lending capital." He placed his hands on the counter with finality. Ziiza's mind raced.

"Would you consider a new idea, Mister Font?" Govvi said softly, filling the void. Hearing no objection she continued. "A very new idea?" Font arched his eyebrows. "One that could make you and lawyer Esqq a great deal of money?"

"Continue."

"Well, I've been thinking," Govvi stretched. "If one beaver pelt represents one beaver, why can't something else represent one beaver pelt? From a banker's point of view, of course."

Font waved his hand in a keep-it-up manner. Ziiza's eyes drilled into her daughter. Then she relaxed.

Govvi doesn't say much, but when she does, I'd better listen.

"I'm talking about the beavers' incisors," Govvi continued genially. "The big upper ones. Castor, or whoever, can save them when the beaver are killed. Then it's easy. Instead of using bulky old pelts for money, you use teeth, each one representing a beaver pelt."

"Hold it," Font said. "To the best of my recollection, beavers have two upper incisors and only one pelt. Don't you mean half a pelt per tooth?"

"Possibly, Mister Font," Govvi said, with a coy turn of her head. "If you want to give up most of your profit." Font leaned forward. "Do all of your depositors come in for their valuables at one time? A big yellow," she segued into Pop&Jay's term, "is nothing more than a promise, your promise to exchange them for beaver pelts. Or whatever. You can issue as many big yellows as you can cover. Calculate the odds and I think you will find them in your favor." Govvi walked around Font and Ziiza, letting them think. She had nothing more to say. For now.

"Compact, durable, storable, portable," Ziiza said.

"Interesting, Miss Govvi. Interesting," Font said at last. "I'll have to think on it, though. Discuss it with Esqq. Can't do anything illegal, you know."

Can't get caught doing anything illegal, you mean. Leave it to Govvi to think up something like this.

Ziiza risked pushing it. "Do you think there is a good enough chance you'll convert to this big yellow system that Z-sport could begin manufacturing Lazy Grape-style Z-Zs? Go ahead in anticipation of available money and an expanded credit line? Just a bit?"

"Check back tomorrow," Font said. When they were out of sight he closed up and took the back path to Esqq's. After a brief conversation, Font and Esqq walked over to the Ever-faithful Daughter. Castor was supervising the day's kill. "Castor, we'd like to have a word with you," Esqq said, his hand on his shoulder.

The transition to big yellows went smoothly. As a banker, the only banker, all Font had to do was announce it and begin redeeming pelts and meat for big yellows. Within a week it was as if it had always had been that way. The reason: big yellows were used for large transactions and banking. Day-to-day trading – food, trinkets, clothing – was still conducted the customary way. Moneyed ThinStone speculators especially loved big yellows. Their novelty and ease of use helped raise asking prices. And brought in more speculators, the artless to be fleeced by the artful. And around it went. Bitta's report of Mistermayor's comments gave it a de facto imprimatur, even though he had not committed himself. Polcat mumbled something about bringing it up at council, but at the next meeting said nothing. Neither did anyone else.

Ziiza got her expanded line. She sent Govvi to buy Narda's dying formulas, and, if available, Narda's personal services. When offered a choice between a short stack of old pelts or new big yellows, Narda sold out without hesitation, opting for half-and-half, to be sure.

Netti hired six more weavers and two dyers to be supervised by Narda. For the first time since Z-sport had opened, weekday sales were strong. To avoid making change, and because she was falling in love with big yellows, Ziiza introduced them with a special sale: two Lazy Grape Z-Zs for one big yellow. This was not necessary; she could have sold them for a big yellow apiece. Not only did non-running customers buy them, runners traded in their old Z-Zs for Lazy Grapes. That Sunday, after Sufx won wearing a Lazy G, as he called it, the Original Z-sport Company was out of stock.

32

Fishing for Friendship

"WHERE'S GSTAN?" Leegs shouted at Old Man Haracosh, "I have to see him. Have to see him right now." Something was wrong. Leegs was early. Leegs was empty. Leegs was stark naked. "Come on, Old Man, where is he?" Leegs screamed. "This is an emergency. Can't you see?"

Haracosh spit, dribbling it onto his beard. Fastened his eyes on Leegs's bony feet. Ran them up his long form. "Been swimming?" he asked.

"No, I haven't been swimming. I've been robbed. Where is he?"

Haracosh touched a finger to his lips, thought for a moment, and said, "Over at the Errix vend, I believe. Having a Konka drink. Swilling the speculators. Waiting for you. Waiting for the ThinStones."

"I'm off," Leegs said, jumping down the bank.

"You're very welcome, young man," Haracosh said, grinning a black-gummed grin.

Leegs strode across H&G, so purposefully, and with such enormous strides, that, except for disapproving glances from two elderly lady shoppers, he attracted no attention. He bent his elbows and pumped his arms, making no attempt to cover his nakedness.

"Leegs!" Gstan shouted when he saw him. "You're here!" Then, "At least I think you're here. Where are my men? Where are my ThinStones? Where are your furs?"

"We must talk," Leegs said. He walked to the far side of the vend and sat. Gstan followed. "Splat. I'll tell you right off, Gstan, he got them all. The new super-thin ones. Robbed me. I didn't have a chance to fight. Or anything."

"I thought you had an agreement for safe passage." Leegs shook his head. "Well, let's go after him. Get them back."

Leegs wrapped his arms around his legs and pulled them in close. He rested his long face on his knees and spoke through his beard. "No chance, Gstan," he said. "None at all. Jumped, you see." Gstan opened his mouth, then closed it. "He caught me before his usual hangout. Ran his spear into my side." Leegs lifted his arm to reveal an oozing puncture wound. "'Drop your bags and strip,' he says. When I refused, tried to say something, he jabbed me the harder. Twisted his spear in my side. I set my hand bags down and lowered my pack. Peeled off my furs. All the while he had this wild-eyed look on him. Told me to back down the trail or he'd finish me off right there. When I did, he kicked my furs over the edge. Then he pushed the hand bags over, too. Without even looking inside. Seemed to know they were just raw stones." Gstan thought of his precious knife sailing through the same air, into the same canyon. "Then," Leegs continued, "he dragged this big sheet of skins out from behind a boulder. All stitched together. He slipped his arms into some loops, picked up my pack with the finished ThinStones in it, and jumped. Over the edge. Into the canyon."

"Is the guy crazy?"

"*Was* he crazy. Can't say for sure, but I think it was some sort of air sail he'd devised, going to float him down to the canyon floor. Maybe land him in the river. I shouted for him to stop. Anyway, the air sail just bunched together. Never opened up. If that was what it was supposed to do. He dropped – like a stone." Hurt, naked, and embarrassed as he was, Leegs could not suppress a smile at *stone*. "Clouds hanging low in the valley. Disappeared like a huckleberry into a kid's mouth. And gone. Just like that. Could not have survived. Could – not – have – sur – vived." Leegs caught the disbelief on Gstan's face, saw his anger rising. "ThinStones, too. Must be shattered. I'm sorry, Gstan. You trusted me and I've failed." Leegs looked Gstan square-on, tears streaming.

I may be a fool, Gstan told himself, but can this man be lying? First off, I don't think Leegs is smart enough to dream up such a fantastic story: air sails, jumping into clouds with loads of ThinStones, the foolhardiness of it. If he stole them, with or without Splat's involvement, why come back and tell me? Just take off with them. But where would he go? Who would he sell them to? My friends the speculators, the collectors? A possibility. Gstan looked suspiciously at the traders, talking, joking, sipping their Konkas almost within hearing. To some joker in Swarm City? He, or they, could probably get there. But does he have the know-how? Strange business. Strange business. I'll have to give this some thought. Many angles to consider.

Leegs *was* smart enough to keep quiet while Gstan pondered. He cleared his eyes with a crooked finger and stroked his beard, giving Gstan all the time he needed to grind his teeth, harrumph with a boss's superiority, and test him with dark accusatory looks to see if he would change his story. When Gstan stopped huffing long enough to give him an opening, Leegs said, "I have news from Big Bay."

"Big Bay?"

"The young woman. The singer. Down there. You asked me to find out about her. And I did."

Gstan brightened and looked at his new best friend. "Well?" But before Leegs could begin, Gstan said, "Wait. She's right over there." He pointed to Z-sport across the path. "You can tell her direct. She'll be thrilled." He paused. "If the news is good. It is good, isn't it?"

"Sort of good, I guess," Leegs said. Then, to himself: Good compared to what I just told you. Good if you still trust me. If you ever did trust this long-legged old loner who was so thrilled to get your hauling business – and Splat had to break our agreement and mess it up, leaving me looking like a featherless old buzzard.

"Wait here, Leegs," Gstan said, "I can't have you talking to Ziiza naked like this. I'll scout around. Find you a robe or something." He scooted into H&G.

Gstan returned carrying a flexible roofing mat. "Wrap yourself up, old boy, it's the best I can do." Leegs wrapped it around his middle; he looked like a stick man ready for burial.

"Ziiza," Gstan said, "may I introduce my business associate, Leegs." He smiled at him as if Splat's crime had never happened. "He's my overland delivery contractor."

Ziiza leaned against a stack of extra-small Z-Zs. She glanced nervously at Sufx and Junior, who were serving a line of balance beam customers. Business was good; Gstan had but a fraction of her attention. Everyone, it seemed, was trading up to Lazy Grapes. She shifted her eyes to Netti. She and her makers – sixteen when they all showed up – sat hunched over their work in the morning sun. Even though Netti had what amounted to two full-time jobs, supervising and teaching, a partly-finished Z-Z hung from her hip so she could work on it as she spoke. Edu, school out for the summer, ran finished stacks to Narda and her dyers in the back. With each delivery, Dg followed him with one in his mouth. More unpaid help. Ziiza made rough calculations: Lazy Grapes completed, Lazy Grapes drying, Lazy Grapes available for sale, Lazy Grapes sold.

She needn't have. Govvi had every number in her head and in the ThinStone she held. In addition, Govvi had developed into a more-than-adequate salesperson. She manufactured a professional smile that did not hurt too much and found that outwitting customers was stimulating enough to overcome her natural reticence. Their questions and objections were so predictable, she thought. She sized them up by customer type, anticipating their objections, and devising responses to overcome them, which she tested, revised, and refined. It got to the point where she had to force herself to wait for them to finish. To offset her severe demeanor and disturbingly penetrating eyes – frightening to some – she had affected a winsome little girl act. Clutching her ThinStone, she would press her elbows to her side, turn her head, tuck her chin, and flutter her eyelashes. Bold. Phony. So un-Govvi. But it worked. Worked so well that her customers often closed sales for her; she did not even have to ask. One thing did not change, her love of money in all of its forms. If she had enjoyed getting, tallying, and hiding the Sita's barter and tail, she enjoyed getting, tallying, and hiding Z-sport's pelts and big yellows even more.

The rush to Lazy Grape styling had brought technical problems. Ziiza dealt with them one at a time. Dying was expensive, but drying time was the stickler: it took at least two days, sometimes three. But Z-sport sold out each day. This created a most pleasant problem, but a problem just the same. Her solution, in addition to pressing Netti to hire more workers and up production, was to offer a slight discount for the "home drying" plan, as she called it. Another pleasant problem: requests for new styles. Since a growing percentage, soon to be a majority, of Z-Zs did not have to withstand the impact of actual rocks on heads, all sorts of shape, size, and color options opened up. Ziiza faced a major decision: should all Z-Zs be rock ready? Or should the Lazy Grape fashion line, and others to follow, be designated for dress wear only? Should standard Z-Zs be a separate line for athletes, the real rock runners? A delicate question she, Govvi, and Netti had discussed many times, for if they were wrong, and Z-sport faltered, lost leadership momentum, they sensed competition. More than sensed; it was a sure thing. Sharp eyes sat across the path, drinking Konkas, watching her business grow. Thinking. Thinking. She decided to stick with the formula: every Z-Z, whatever style or color, had to be rock sturdy. But the temptation to save time and material lingered.

"Ziiza," Gstan said again, "Leegs here asked around Big Bay, asked about Milli. And the band. And all."

Ziiza spun around; he had her attention now. "You have news?" she said. "Yes? Yes?"

"You tell her, Leegs," Gstan said. Leegs had not been embarrassed by his nakedness while on the trail, it was summer and it felt good, or while walking through H&G, but trying to hold the floppy roof mat tight around himself made him nervous. Gstan pushed him forward. "I haven't heard the story myself, Ziiza. Brought him right over here. After his other news." He gave Leegs a sour look. "Go on. Go on, Leegs."

"It was tough locating her."

"Is she all right?" Ziiza asked shrilly.

"Why, yes. She's fine," he said, taken aback, as if that should have been obvious.

Ziiza and company exhaled with relief. Netti's knees buckled; she began to sob. Gstan smiled, proud of his part in the wonderful news.

Leegs continued: "They, the band – what's their name? – reached Big Bay some time ago. Played a few times. Well received. But Big Bay was not big enough to support them. The bay itself is quite big, you see. Yes, very, ah, big. But Big Bay, the town. Not nearly as . . . big . . . as Beaverton."

"Very good, Leegs," Gstan said impatiently. "Enough 'bigs' and 'bays.' It's Milli we're interested in."

"Right. Well, it couldn't support them. And other problems."

"Problems?" Ziiza said. Customers and speculators were listening now.

"She had this baby."

"Yes, yes," Ziiza said. She pulled his arm and he let go of his mat. "A baby boy? Baby girl?"

"I don't know. Forgot to ask. Too young for me to tell."

"You mean you . . . ?" Ziiza screeched. Then, composing herself: "Continue, Mister Leegs, if you will."

"So she couldn't perform with the band with the little one, and being in a childrenly way again . . ."

"Do you mean she's expecting another child?" Ziiza said in exasperation. And before he could answer: "I must say, you are delivering news I have been aching to know, but you certainly have the priorities mixed up."

Gstan intervened. "Leegs is just Leegs, Ziiza, the delivery guy. He carries things over the trail. That's all he does. And he's had a bit of bad luck himself. Got robbed, as a matter of fact. Weird guy named Splat. My whole ThinStone shipment."

"The whole shipment?" said a bushy-browed speculator, fingering a pouch full of big yellows with one hand and squeezing a chartreuse ThinStone with the other. "That's the worst news. I don't. . . ."

Eyes turned back to Leegs, but he said nothing, as if waiting for respect – in the form of a chunk of uninterrupted time. A customer was about to prompt him, but caught himself before he spoke. After Leegs had made his point, he looked down at everyone and continued: "And the guy, her husband, the leader of the band, he wasn't feeling so well, either. The band broke up. No band now. Hasn't been for all that time. People hardly remembered. That's why I had so much trouble finding her. They live outside of town." He paused again, daring anyone to interrupt. "Something wrong with his chest. Coughing all the time."

"Sick. That's terrible," Ziiza said. "Did Milli have a message for her muma?"

"Said she loved you and missed you. And her brothers and sisters. And especially her sister. Netti, I believe." His eyes roamed until it was clear who Netti was. "She was sorry no message before. Didn't know about me. I'm the only one who travels the trail regular. And I don't go into Big Bay anymore. Not with the Errix contract. Not unless I have a delivery or a pick-up there. And I never do. Gstan asked me to find her. And to report."

Ziiza draped her arms over Gstan's shoulders and pulled him close. Netti would have too, but she could not move. "Thank you so much, Gstan. I thought I'd lost her." She turned to Leegs. "Sorry for my behavior, Leegs. I hope you understand. Anything else?"

"I don't think they'll be coming back. Said they had to stay in a dry climate. Beaverton's too damp for. . . ."

"Twigg," Ziiza said softly.

"Twigg's chest," Leegs continued. "They're thinking about moving east. New country opening up. Hot and dry, but river water, too. Good place to grow healthy, grow tubers, grow kids."

"Thanks again, Gstan," Ziiza said. "And thank you, Leegs." She looked at Govvi. "Will you take over? Netti and I are going home. We've had enough news for one day." She helped Netti up.

I wonder if he told her about Com?

She waved the question away.

* * *

Rather than harming Errix, the stolen shipment enhanced the ThinStone mystique. If anyone in Beaverton was not aware of them, they were now. Bitta made certain of that. The Leegs and Splat story had all of the elements: exotic location; daring, if stupid, criminal; truth stranger than fiction. People loved hearing it. Over and over. All that remained was to send a search party to scout the canyon. Many talked of going. Some started. All returned within a few days.

None of this solved Gstan's immediate problem: how to deal with the egotistical and mercurial Silvoo. Whatever had actually happened to the ThinStones, one thing was incontrovertible: they were gone. With each return shipment of cut and polished stones to be chanted, Gstan had always included Silvoo's payment. This time, no ThinStones. No sales. No profits. No royalties for Silvoo. (Gstan never thought for a moment that he shared the royalties with his Hieyeques.) The raising of the problem brought its immediate solution: pay him anyway.

Likewise, Leegs. Gstan paid him as if he had delivered, advanced him enough for a new summer-weight outfit, and sent him south. The test. If Leegs was telling the truth, Gstan wanted him down there on schedule. And back in Beaverton as soon as possible. If Leegs was lying, he could steal one more shipment, and Gstan would never see him again. He had no choice, had to chance it, because Leegs was so fast, strong, and dependable. Up until now. He did not want to try anyone else. At best a new man would take twice as long and carry half the load. If he could find one to try. So he swallowed and acknowledged his dependence upon this unusual man until he proved himself untrustworthy.

As the Splat story elevated, so did the price of ThinStones. Gstan was making money speculating, even if Errix at the moment was not. Leegs would be back in a few weeks, if he showed, and everything would be normal. Normal being a speculative fever unlike anything Beaverton had ever experienced. Would it have have happened if ThinStones were not so beautiful to look at, so sensuous to hold? It was almost as if the throbbing light set the stones in motion. Would it have happened without the constant improvements: thinner, lighter weight, Gstan's Law? Altogether, what? Progress? Or speculative bubble?

So Gstan, out of inventory and being bored with speculating, and having nothing for his workers to polish and trim, shut Errix down and went fishing. He had not fished since food duty on the Sea Trace, but since Old Man Haracosh seemed to enjoy it, he thought he'd give it a try. Of course he was too proud to invite Haracosh along to show him how; bosses did not do that. Besides, Haracosh had work to do: guarding Gstan's valuable ThinStone collection. As Gstan turned to go, he noticed Old Man's pole leaning against his burrow. "Mind if I borrow this? You won't be needing it today."

Old Man handed him his long, whippy pole with a gut line wrapped around. A bone hook stuck in the handle end kept the line from unwinding. "Heading over to the Daughter?" Haracosh asked.

"Sure, that's where I'm going," Gstan said. (He had no idea where he would go before Old Man mentioned the Ever-faithful Daughter.) But he could not resist checking today's ThinStone prices, so he walked over to the Konka Sanctuary to chat with the speculators and take a hot cup.

Trading was brisk and prices were up. Z-sport's business across the pathway was heavy, too. But not so heavy that Edu did not spot Gstan's pole on his shoulder as he walked away. He hurried after him, followed by Dg. "Where are you going, Mister Gstan?"

"Why, Edu. And Dg," he said, feigning surprise. "Good morning to you both. I'm taking a break, going down to the Daughter to catch a fish dinner. Rumor is that beaver tails are going to be in short supply. Ha, ha. So I'd better practice up." Edu stared at the pole with longing eyes. Dg leaned against his leg. Edu said nothing. "Like to come with me?" Gstan said, getting the message.

"Dg and I both would."

"I'd be pleased to have your company. But first we'll have to ask your muma."

Ziiza and Govvi each had a customer. Three more waited in line, Lazy Grapes in hand. None had rocks. After waiting through two sales, Edu pulled his muma's fur and pointed to Gstan. Gstan raised his pole, pointed west, and mouthed *fishing?*

Ziiza excused herself, walked to him, and said coolly. "What do you want, Gstan? I'm kind of busy."

"Edu. He wants to go fishing with me. And I'd love to have him."

"You want to go?" she asked. Edu nodded vigorously. "All right."

Gstan, Edu, and Dg walked quickly through Hunters and Gatherers Market, then cut across the meadow. Great-great-great-grandpopa Monumentree was so far away that they did not notice it. They walked easily along a worn riverbank path past the last beaver dam and pond to where the Daughter flowed free. Had they walked a little farther, they would have come to a feeder stream called Water Child.

A large fish hurled itself out of the water and splashed down. Rings spread across the surface. "What was that?" Gstan said. They walked to the sharp bank and stared down. At first they saw nothing. Then they noticed fin tips, tails, and black backs stirring the surface.

"Will you look at that, Dg," Edu said, now on his stomach, looking into the dark water the sun had not reached. "There must be dozens."

"Here we go," Gstan said. He poked a piece of meat on the hook and swung the line out from the bank. It hit the water and sank. "We'll share the pole. After I catch one, you catch the next one. Then me. Then you. And so on, till we have all the fish we can carry."

They fished and waited. Every few minutes the bait disappeared. Gstan or Edu re-baited. But they never felt a nudge or a nibble. The sun rose and warmed their backs. It grew hot. They moved downstream and sat in the shade of a solitary alder. Few fish broke the surface now. Those they saw through the clearer water hung still, hugging the bottom.

"Why don't you take it," Gstan said. He pushed back and leaned against the tree. "Done much fishing?" he asked him again, to start a conversation. Edu shook his head, keeping his eyes on the line, gripping the pole with both hands. "Anybody in your family?"

"We all fish one way or another. It's just that we fish for different things, you could say."

"How's that?"

"Milli, she was a real fisher, the only one of us who took to it – for more than getting food to eat. She loved it, had what people call 'the touch.' If we kids fished all day and caught nothing, she always caught something. But she's gone now, run off with Twigg. Like Leegs said. Even has a little baby. Netti gathers fruits and berries and things. She's never without her basket. You might call that fishing." The pole tip dipped and quivered.

"Set the hook, boy!"

Edu yanked. The empty hook popped out of the water and flew into the leaves. Gstan pushed off the tree, stood up, and untangled the line. "Lucky thing," he said, laughing, "we've only got one hook." He baited again with a smaller piece of meat. "Tell me more," he said, "but keep your eye on the line. Hey, are you enjoying this?"

"Very much, Mister Gstan. Dg is, too." Dg lay on his side, sleeping between them. "Com fished for adventure," Edu continued. "New places. New things. It killed him, I'm afraid." He moved on. "Govvi, she fishes for numbers. Strange, but true. Org has always loved rocks – finding them, throwing them, collecting them – so I guess you could say he fishes for them. Who'd have thought, back on the Sea Trace, when he selected a plain old rock as his personal object? Who'd have thought he'd end up running with one on his head?"

"Object?" Gstan said. "Do you have a personal object, as you say?"

"You're touching him, Mister Gstan. Dg and his watabeast collar; they're my objects." Gstan ran his finger over Dg's belly and scratched. Dg snorted contentedly in his sleep.

"And what does your muma fish for?" Gstan said. "Raise that pole up and down. Slow like. Give it a little motion. But you're doing fine. Your muma?"

"Oh, money, I guess. But she has enough money. You don't really need much to get along in Beaverton. Something else, too; she keeps reaching out, but never catching hold. I don't know. What do you fish for, Mister Gstan?"

"I fish for deals. I get a thrill closing any kind of deal. Selling lots. Selling ThinStones. Makes no difference to me. I love it." He patted Dg. And reversed himself. "Or I used to. To be perfectly honest, deal-making doesn't give me much of a kick anymore."

"You like my muma, don't you?" Edu said, laying the pole down and looking up at Gstan.

Gstan jerked in surprise. Composed himself and leaned against the tree. "I can't answer that, son."

"Why did you call me son?"

"Oh, it's just an expression, a manner of speaking. You're not my son, of course. But I do like you. I've never had a son. Never will, I guess. Too old. Oh, I'm talking too much."

"What do you like about my muma?"

"You don't give up, do you, kid? Questions, questions, questions. What we need is a strike about now, not more questions. We should have a fish or two on the bank. Lots of fish."

"Mister Gstan —"

"Look," Gstan cut him off, "you don't have to call me Mister all the time. Makes me uncomfortable."

"What would you like me to call you?"

"Gstan. Call me Gstan. Plain Gstan. Old Gstan. Your friend, Gstan. Uncle Gstan, if you like. Just not Mister, see. Just Gstan."

"Yes, sir."

"While we're talking," Gstan said, "just talking, mind you, you mentioned personal objects. Org's object. And your object – if you can call Dg here an object. Does your muma have an object, since everyone else in your family seems to have one? Or is it just you children?"

"Sure, her necklaces. While we were searching for ours, walking to Beaverton, she polished bits of driftwood and strung them together. She enjoyed it so much she made two. She never takes them off."

"Oh, those."

Their conversation drifted to other subjects, then was replaced by pleasant summer silence. They shared beaver tail for lunch, ate it all, left none for bait. Edu caught a grasshopper, impaled it on the hook, and threw it in. Dg barked at a crow in the alder and lay down again. After the grasshopper dropped off or was eaten, Edu and Dg hunted for worms but found none. They fished with a bare hook. The sun arced over the valley and hung over the Sundowns.

Edu broke the late afternoon's sleepy-warm silence. "You never asked me what I fished for. Aren't you interested?"

"I don't have to ask," Gstan said. "I'm beginning to think I know." He touched Edu's arm.

Edu took another course. "Know something? Dg lets you pet him. Do you know you're the first person besides Muma and me he's let do that? Really pet and stroke, I mean. All you want. Not even my brothers and sisters. Only a pat on the head or a swipe on the back. And they have to give him something to eat. He lets you scratch his belly, too."

Gstan grinned. "Maybe he's decided to give me a break. Temporary like."

"It's more than that Mister Gstan. Excuse me. It's more than that, just Gstan."

"Come on kid, it's late. Admit it, we've been skunked. Time to be getting on home."

33

Ziiza Goes Shopping

ZIIZA ROSE early and walked to Litti's to share the Milli report. Litti's robe was warm but she had built no morning fire; she had probably gone to meet Arbo. Ziiza returned home, blew up her own fire, and heated some meat. Then since it was still early, she walked to Beaverton Creek, filled two of Biber's water pouches, and carried them home. She washed her hair with hawberry soap, standing close to the path, not caring if early walkers and rock runners stared at her, spoke to her, or ignored her. Before dressing she beat the dust from her fur. She thought of brewing tea, but since Litti was gone one of Sister Sissi's Konkas was more appealing.

"Time to rise," Ziiza said, tickling Netti's and Govvi's feet.

Edu and Dg had gone. He had offered to help Addle get ready for Grassyknoll's fall opening. His job: trimming the grass, re-rocking the path and helping Addle greet the new students, if any. Last year Dg had assumed the role of school monitor (as he was an accomplished assistant bouncer). He would sit on the knoll-top between sonorous Addle and ever-attentive Edu. Dozers felt his nose, then his tongue, then an abrasive foot pad, what was called for. Skippers after latrine visits heard his growl or felt his teeth. He was so smart he belonged in school.

Ziiza fed the girls, bathed them, and brushed their clothes (as if they could not do it themselves). She gave their hair special attention, something she seldom had time for anymore. Netti wore hers short; Ziiza combed it carefully. Govvi's was longer; she combed, gathered, and tied it in a tail.

The three arrived at Z-sport at opening time. Sufx and Junior would check in after their workouts. Netti was soon busy supervising her makers, Govvi busy with customers. Ziiza slipped across the path for her Konka. She traded banter with the speculators waiting impatiently for Gstan's next shipment, which, according to rumors (circulated by himself), would contain "the next generation of ThinStones, the 102s." She walked to Gstan's tree-round and sipped her drink alone. Looked across the pathway at Z-sport and smiled.

We've made it. I've made it. I took a big chance, bet everything, and won. I deserve it.

She drained her cup, tossed it, and walked back. "Govvi," she said, "how many big yellows do we have in the hole?"

"Forty-five, plus some barter. I can tell you how much, exactly." Govvi squeezed her ThinStone.

"I'll take forty and the small stuff," Ziiza said, without waiting for an answer.

Govvi pulled five big yellows out of the sack and gave it to Ziiza. "We owe them to Font, Muma."

"Font can wait. Netti and I are going shopping. You're in charge." She took the bag and strode over to the work space. "Come on, Netti, we're going to have some fun." As they walked away, Ziiza added, "We'll bring you something, Govvi."

Govvi's jaw muscles bulged, ever so slightly. She turned to a customer, "That Lazy Grape looks stunning on you, ma'am. Would you like a rock to go with it?"

"Pshaw," said the woman. "You know better than that. I go to the races to see and to be seen, not to run in them."

"Yes, ma'am."

Ziiza and Netti walked quickly through H&G, heading for Murfree's, H&G's largest vend. Ziiza shook the sack; she loved the clink and clatter, big yellows against big yellows. "To heck with Font," she said. "This is our money and we're going to enjoy it. Right now. Are you ready for a new outfit, Netti girl – skirt, top, shawl, anything? Everything? The best big yellows can buy?"

"Why, sure. I guess, Muma," Netti said. She lifted the edge of her watabeast fur and examined it, as if for the first time. She ran her finger over the bare spots. Smiling broadly – the first Ziiza had seen in some time – she said, "Now that you mention it, I guess I do need something. Something that goes with this." She patted her well-worn, shoulder-strap basket and laughed.

Ziiza took the tall, patient girl's calloused hand. She wanted to ask how she was doing. Are you happy, Netti, she would ask. I know how you miss Milli. You were so close. You're keeping busy, I know. Z-sport is successful, and you are responsible for a big part of it. She would say that. So how are you sleeping? She would say that, too. What I really mean is, how are your headaches? Better, I hope. I dream about you, that big wave rolling in, smashing you against the cliff. Smashing all of us. The climb. Up the headland. Afraid you might go unconscious and never come out of it. Can't stop the dreams. They're worse than the ones about Com. Nightmares, really. And that root they sell; are you shed of it? Litti thinks you are. But really?

She contented herself with a hand squeeze, an attempt, however imperfect, to direct her love into the lonely, damaged girl.

"Strip down and kick them aside," Ziiza told Netti, when they entered Murfree's women's section. "You're not walking out of here with them. On or off." After trying on six outfits, Netti settled on a longer-length tan fur. It looked like watabeast but could not be. Could it? The elfin clerk girl "did not know." Netti looked over her shoulder and smiled.

We should do this more often.

Murfree himself waved from a discrete distance, mouthed something like, "Everything all right, ladies?" and disappeared. "That it, Netti?" Ziiza said. Netti nodded shyly. "Now bring out some really good ones," she said to the elf. "She needs something for special occasions."

"But Muma, I don't have any special occasions," Netti whispered after the girl had gone. "Haven't we spent enough already?"

"Why, Netti, we're just getting started."

Netti reluctantly chose a rich, dark brown skirt, daringly short, and a matching cape trimmed with the black tail of an exotic beast. Again, the girl knew only that it was "simply beautiful," not what it was. The ensemble came with soft slippers, unheard of in Beaverton a year ago. They moved to the jewelry section, where Netti chose malachite earrings and a hat-shell pendant. Ziiza bought a work outfit for herself. And a special occasion fur dress, a big yellow less expensive than Netti's.

"Something for Govvi?" Netti asked as they were leaving. "And Edu?"

"Yes, we should, Netti. Very thoughtful of you. And we will. But not now; we've spent almost all of our money. We have enough left for lunch. And a listen to Skedaddle. And, to top off the day, a hairdo at that new place where Wife Dragga goes. To go with these." She stroked her luxuriant beaver pelt cape, then Netti's. "It been ages since I've really enjoyed myself in H&G."

It seems like ages since *I've* enjoyed H&G, Netti mused. Skedaddle? Well, fine. Screaming Indifference. Now that was a real band. Twigg, the handsome rascal. Milli up on stage. So radiant. So wonderful. Not that I don't like the new clothes, she thought, as she clutched them fur to fur. But fancy outfits can't make up for her.

They ate carrot-root salad (recently introduced to H&G) from a walking vendor, sat under a hemlock off to the side, and listened to the Skedaddlers strum and sing their old tunes.

They've slipped a notch since the first time I heard them, but they're still a pleasure to listen to. Real music.

Like Netti, the music made Ziiza think of Screaming Indifference, and Milli, and the grandchildren she had never seen. Might never see. Or hold. Or play with.

The three-man band stopped and bent their heads together to discuss their next number. The leader tuned his instrument, plucking the strings.

A man ran past on the nearby path. More men. Women clutching skirts, running as fast as they could. Not racing. Not rock running. Running away from something? Toward something? All in the same direction. Faster runners dodged and leaped ahead of the slower ones. Some were pushed out of the way. The band started up, then stopped. The members stared. Ziiza and Netti stood up and walked toward the moving mass, now as thick as a race pack. As did the rest of the listeners; they could not help it. "What's going on?" someone asked. "Our money, our money," shouted a runner over his shoulder. The dreaded words: "Beaver shortage. . . ." The rest of his sentence trailed off in the sound of pounding feet. Ziiza gritted her teeth.

I'm not a crowd follower, but I have to find out what's going on.

"Come on, Netti," she said, taking her hand in a very different way, "this might be fun." After a few steps: "Then again, it might not."

The runners thundered down the path, beyond the thick cluster of vends around Town Hall, along the pathway toward Hill Burrow, and turned onto the narrow path to . . . Font's Bank. They piled into those already there, some so hard they fell down. The crowd spread in front of the bank, around the sides, around the back. Font stood outside his roofless shelter, erect, dignified, and speechless; his eyes reflecting the terror of money disappearing.

"Font! Font, you blackguard. I want my money! Now!" screamed the man standing next to Ziiza. A dozen picked up the cry. One was enough.

Esqq shouldered through the crowd, reached Font, shook his hand, and stepped back. He turned his head to one side then the other, smiling pleasantly. "Friends, friends," he said, in his most soothing voice. "Back away, if you will. Give Font some room. And quiet down, please. I have an announcement. Straight from Mistermayor." He did not have anything from Mistermayor, but it served to hush the angry crowd. He hurried on, knowing he did not have much time. "I assure you. Friends. Customers. I assure you. Font's Bank will honor its obligations. Will honor all obligations."

"Give us our pelts, you rascals! Now!" The speaker waved a depositor's tally. Was about to throw it, when he thought better.

"Quiet. Please. Name-calling will get us nowhere." Esqq raised his hands, then lowered them slowly, his old trick. He stared the crowd down. A crinkle of a smile tipped from the edge of his mouth. When they quieted as much as Esqq thought they would, he exposed a wall of teeth, his business smile. "Madam," he said. An elderly woman clutching a handful of big yellows responded with a who-me? gesture. "Yes, you, madam. What would you like from Font, here?"

"These big yellow beaver teeth aren't any good. Going to be a shortage this winter. I want to turn them in for the real thing: beaver meat, pelts and tails. Now the bank said —"

"Yes, I know," Esqq interrupted. "Font, take care of this good woman." Font took her by the arm and guided her inside. The people jostled and surged, ready to move in. "Ah, Barclaw," Esqq said, spotting the broad-shouldered constable pushing toward him. "Welcome to Beaverton's citadel of finance." He was putting on a masterful performance, one had to admit, greeting Barclaw, whom he was desperately happy to see, as if he had happened by on a routine look-in. In a few minutes the woman emerged with a beaver pelt, a small sack of meat, and a satisfied look on her face. "Were you paid in full, madam?" Esqq asked.

"I believe I was," she said in a crackly voice, holding up the sack. "I do believe I was." Cranky, but less hostile murmurs.

"How about me?"

"And me?"

Esqq drew himself up, showed teeth again, and raised his arms in a V. Font poked his head from behind the curtain, looked around until he saw Barclaw, then jerked the curtain shut. "Every big yellow will be redeemed," Esqq said. "Yes, every big yellow. But perhaps . . . not today." Howling angrily, they surged forward. Barclaw stood between them and Esqq. "We will pay ten customers today." Esqq said, pointing to ten people in front, one by one. "That's all today. We're closing a little early. We'll be open for business just as soon as our reserve deposits arrive. Tomorrow. Tomorrow morning. Or possibly tomorrow afternoon." He raised his hands again to quiet the protests. "If you will read your depository agreement. Line fifteen clearly states . . ."

Coo-burp. Coo-burp. Hobart stood on Bitta's head, flapping his wings and rocking. "Emergency council meeting," Bitta shouted in headline voice. "Emergency council meeting tomorrow night at Town Hall."

"Well, Netti," Ziiza said, speaking for the first time since they had arrived, "it looks bad. But it could be worse. We don't have to worry about getting our pelts out of Font; he has to worry about getting them out of us." She gave Netti a warped smile. "And what's this about a food shortage? I haven't heard anything about that, lately. And big yellows? Are they worth anything?"

Font paid all ten depositors as promised. But he used every ploy he could think of to slow the process: shuffling around, feigning misplacement, being overly solicitous, counting and recounting, "Just to be sure."

* * *

313

At six o'clock, an hour before the emergency meeting, Mistermayor told Barclaw, "The crowd's already too large. If we hold it here, they'll wreck half of H&G. Have any ideas?"

"I do," said the constable. "Yes, I do. Grassyknoll school. Council on top, looking down, the way Addle does it. Everyone in Beaverton could come. Maybe not hear, but come." He chuckled.

"Excellent," Mistermayor said. "Can you carry the council bench?" Barclaw gave a nothing-to-it shrug, hoisted the bench, turned it upside down, and balanced it on his head. "We're moving the meeting," he said to those nearby. Then in official voice: "Let's go, Barclaw."

Not only was the move necessary, it was good strategy. "Slow down, Barclaw," Mistermayor told him. "We're in no hurry." He led off and the people fell in. Then, as if reading Barclaw's mind, he said, "Don't worry, word will spread."

"Put it right here," Mistermayor said, after they had climbed the knoll. "You can stand on top, the might and muscle of Beaverton for all to see. Behold our power." He laughed nervously. Barclaw, not knowing whether he was laughing at him or the joke, took the top position and turned full circle, giving the gatherers his sternest look. "Don't let them get behind us, Barclaw," Mistermayor instructed. "And don't let them get too close. Have them sit down. Direct them with your hands. If they're on their feet, we've got problems."

Mizpark showed up, leading Friends of the Beaver, about twenty-five, mostly women. She carried a pole supporting a banner reading: Kill no Beaver. Honor our Heritage. Litti held the other end. From outward appearances all the two women had in common was their size, slim and short, and the determined looks on their faces. Other than that: youthful and wizened, demure and bristly. Polcat and the other council members came separately, each working his way up the knoll, pausing to glad-hand and reassure. Edu, sizing up the situation, led his muma and sisters around the side, then up to within hearing distance, where they met Addle, standing rigidly as if defending the sanctity of Grassyknoll from the unenlightened hordes, and daring Barclaw, of all people, to give him one more sit-down hand motion. Dg took up his monitoring station. Barclaw deputized him with a pat on the head.

"If I were to guess," Govvi said to no one in particular, "I'd say forty percent of Beaverton's here. And we've a few minutes to go. No, forty-one percent."

Mistermayor called the meeting to order, and said, "Welcome, fellow Beavertonians. We have two questions before us at this historic meeting. First, the rumored giant valley beaver shortage. Second, the excessive activity at Font's Bank, which you all know about." Shouting and objections.

Mistermayor drew himself up to his considerable height, waited them out, and said, "Friends, you all know Castor, guardian of the beaver ponds, and manager of the Beaverton meat and pelt facility. Castor, will you step to the knoll-top and make your report."

Castor, looking considerably rounder than in years past, rolled up to the council bench and stopped to catch his breath. He wore a full length beaver-pelt cloak, glossy and obviously new, a large headpiece of another animal's fur which sagged over his ear, and a magnificent string of big yellows that hung to his waist. Altogether a startling transformation from the hardy outdoor man of streams and ponds to one who looked as if he had never gotten his hands wet, let alone skinned a bloody beaver. He withdrew a pulsating, magenta-colored ThinStone from under his cloak, squeezed it as if for reassurance, and spoke: "I'm not one for thrashin' around in the pond, so I'll come right out with it. The beaver population's down, especially in ponds five and six, the two biggest ones we manage. The other twelve, we're giving them more of a look. So. . . ."

"The complete report, Castor, if you will," Mistermayor said, poking him in the back.

"So it looks like supplies of meat and pelts will be a little tight come wintertime."

"What do you mean 'tight,' you fat-bellied son of a pond sucker," screamed a man in the middle. "And speak up."

"We had a big bunch off the Sea Trace," Castor continued. "More mouths to feed. And, sorry to say, lots of poaching for big yellows. Just can't stop it. They take the big yellows, leave the rest, and go on to the next beaver. If we don't find the carcasses quick they just rot away. Sometimes they throw them in the ponds and we never find them. If that goes on much longer we could see a serious shortfall. How much I can't exactly say. It's kind of one day after another, if you know what I mean."

"Thank you, Castor. For the moment," Mistermayor said. "Any questions? Council members?"

Polcat jumped up. "With all respect, Mistermayor, I believe, as our friend Castor has alluded, we have one problem here: food and money are inextricably linked. The solution to one is the solution to the other." Mistermayor shrugged at his old rival. He's off, now, he thought, I'll never be able to shut him up. But Polcat surprised him. "Castor told me this in confidence, but a crisis is upon us, and I believe we should move forward. Castor, please share your ingenious idea with the citizens of Beaverton."

"We've been studying the ponds," Castor began, "and we were going to suggest a new management program next year. But it seems Polcat wishes to 'move forward' right now. So here goes. We've made a discovery. If we harvest all of the beavers in one pond, or many ponds, then introduce new ones all at the same time, all of the same age, prime breeding age, preliminary indications are that the population will grow much faster. Possibly twice as fast. Soon, twice as many beavers. One reason: The big old daddies don't eat the little ones before they can become big like them. We call it the Beav-enhance Pond Management Program. Beav-enhance for short."

"Pardon me, Castor," Mistermayor said. "This Beav-enhance program – let me get this straight – you kill all the beavers in an entire pond?"

"Yes sir," Castor said. "Harvest everything that lives: beavers, fish, otters, muskrats, everything. We're experimenting with draining the ponds, too. Start over from scratch."

"Harvest all? Kill everything?" Mistermayor repeated in dismay.

"He kills everything, Kills everything. Kills everything." The words passed through the rows. "Kills everything."

Then silence . . . there was nothing more to say. Mizpark and Litti stood stunned and speechless, their banner sagging. For a moment. Then Mizpark screamed, "Kill no beaver! Kill no beaver!" The Friends took up her chant. "Kill no beaver! Kill no beaver!" A few others joined in. But the crowd did not pick it up and the chant expired.

"I have an idea," Mistermayor said. "Spread out the available supplies. Licensed vends will sell beaver products only on, say, Monday, Wednesday, and Friday. Slow things down. Help the transition to other edibles." Laughter and jeers. Seeing this wasn't going anywhere, Mistermayor backed off. "Just an idea. Just an idea. But worth a look."

Ziiza, standing behind him, said to her children, "I smell something coming, kids, and I don't like it." She spotted Gstan lower on the knoll. He waved as if he had been watching her all along.

Sensing the meeting slipping out of control, Mistermayor turned to Esqq. "Lawyer Esqq, do you have anything to say?"

Esqq shook his white mane and launched his rumbling voice up the hill. "No, Mistermayor, I do not. But my friend Font does."

Font walked up the knoll, around Addle, Ziiza and company, and up to the bench. He nodded to Mistermayor, Polcat, and the members. "I wish to thank all of my depositors for their outstanding cooperation during our inconvenience," he said. "Your deposits are safe." He paused for the catcalls and taunts to die down. But mostly he saw inquisitive faces and heard sounds of approval. He continued: "As for the beaver harvest and potential food shortages during the coming winter, I say Beav-enhance looks promising. Very promising. But money is another issue. A short while ago we transitioned from barter and tail to pelts and meat." He looked at Esqq, who bowed in agreement. "That was a success, but only a step, albeit in the right direction."

"You say success. We say failure," Mizpark screamed in her best protest voice.

"In the right direction," Font continued. "Then to big yellows, as true money in hand, backed by the rest. Another forward step, even if it does not seem so now. But that was not the final step in the course of Beaverton's monetary stability. One remains." Font paused and wiped the perspiration from his forehead. The reserved banker was giving the speech of his life and doing quite well. "Beaverton, to grow strong, should, no, must, align herself with a stable monetary partner. A stronger monetary partner to stand ready to help us over the rough spots such as we are experiencing."

"Such as what, Mister banker Font?" yelled a florid-faced man with a boy on his shoulders.

"I propose sending a delegation to Swarm City. Just for. . . ."

That was as far as he got. The Beavertonians shouted him down. He attempted to explain, but could not. Mistermayor and the council members looked at each other in disbelief, and let the protests run. After announcing a postponement till the same time tomorrow, which few heard, he adjourned the meeting.

Next day Mistermayor Polcat, and the council members met informally with Font, Esqq, and Castor. That evening the council met again at Grassyknoll. But in spite of Bitta's publicity the crowd was small. Ziiza and Govvi attended; Netti, Edu, and Dg stayed home. Gstan sat on the grass next to Govvi. Mizpark and Litti came with their banner, but with fewer of last night's Friends. After people had twenty-four hours to think it over and cool down, the meeting was businesslike and brief.

Polcat moved to allow Castor to go ahead with the Beav-enhance Pond Management Program after arguing that they would have to exceed harvest limits anyway to get through the winter, and it might as well be done on an orderly, intelligent basis. It passed: four votes in favor, none against, and one abstention: again Mistermayor. For that they received an umbrella shake from Mizpark, and hoots and hisses from the Friends, who then marched away in disgust.

Mistermayor asked for a motion to send Barclaw to Swarm City, he being the only person, he noted, who had been east of the Sunups and was an experienced wintertime traveler. Polcat flew into a rage and gave an impassioned speech decrying the hated Swarm City and its infamous mayor, Sac the Magnificent. (Though he had never been there, never had met anyone who had been there, and did not know anything about their monetary system.) After hard looks by Mistermayor and the council members, Polcat stopped talking.

The junior council member rose and said, "I move that Constable Barclaw be given the temporary rank of ambassador with full powers to act for Beaverton in his best judgment. He will travel to Swarm City and evaluate their monetary system as to its stability and capacity to back up big yellows. And their willingness to cooperate. In addition, he will request emergency food, and assistance in transporting same." He smiled proudly at *same*, as if it was the legalese he was striving for. "He will leave immediately so he can cross the Sunups before they become impassible due to snow. This is declared an emergency motion and the required three-day waiting period is hereby waived." With *hereby*, the junior member positively beamed.

The motion passed, four votes in favor and one opposed, Polcat.

"No! No! No! You can't do this to Beaverton!" Polcat yelled. With that, he launched into a tirade about betrayal of everything Beaverton stood for, which, as reported by Bitta the next day, lasted far into the night. Mistermayor adjourned the meeting soon after Polcat began talking, and the members, mumbling excuses, slipped away. In a few minutes he was left talking only to his cronies.

34

Ambassador Barclaw

BEAVERTON EASED into a satisfactory autumn of chill nights, cool mornings, and sunny afternoons. Then winter, suddenly, with a cold, driving night wind and rain; the next morning found the ground covered with golden maple leaves and expired fir needles.

After what came to be called the Gasssyknoll Meeting, beaver meat, tail, and pelts continued to appear in H&G without interruption, although prices continued to rise. Font, by way of solicitous, drawn-out small talk, revised fall/winter business hours, and adding "a little something" to customers' withdrawals, managed to redeem all of the big yellows presented. The panic cycle broke.

Of course things were not right. Everyone knew it. Felt it. The malaise spread through Beaverton and hung on like a ground fog that would not lift.

Mistermayor spent most of his time monitoring beaver prices, supplies, and distribution. Worry lines formed on his face. Still, he seldom visited Castor and the ponds, could not bring himself to stick his hand in the lifeless water. He wished he had had the courage to vote no.

Mizpark and Litti organized protest marches which attracted little attention, less support, and no results. Mizpark was not one to back down or give up. Keep the spirit alive, she told the Friends, to march another day.

Z-sport slowed, but that was expected with fewer winter races. Ziiza excused Edu and Dg, told them to concentrate on school. It took Govvi only a few minutes a day to tally, so she returned to her old haunts and routines, including, Ziiza continued to suspect, trips over the hill. She also re-enrolled in Grassyknoll. Addle had grudgingly expanded his curriculum, adding an afternoon class called ThinStone Discovery. When Govvi attended, she practically taught it herself. Ziiza handled sales, mostly Lazy Grapes. She could have operated the rock balance as well, but since Sufx and Junior had nothing to do except run, eat, and flirt with the girls in H&G, she paid them half wages and let them set their own hours. As with the Sita in its slow summer she made enough to cover expenses and feed her family, but not enough to pay down Z-sport's credit line. Font did not press.

Errix Enterprises went dormant after snow blocked the pass. Leegs went on wintertime leave.

Sister Sissi's Konka Sanctuaries prospered during this time, practically the only Beaverton business that did. In a kindly gesture, so typical of her, she hired Biber to manage one of her shops. By then it was obvious his crushed leg would never heal; he would be a cripple for life. He was thrilled with the job and his new-found independence, enabling him to move out of Ziiza's and live in the back of a Sanctuary. He claimed he enjoyed serving Konkas more than brewing "the old sloozeroo." And maybe he did.

* * *

Barclaw surveyed the snowy trail to the clearing. On his left ran the broad, cold, muddy river he had followed for weeks. The last person he had met, a hunter, told him it led to Swarm City. The city lay on the north side, at the mouth, just where the river joined an even larger one. Directly ahead perched on a high bank, he saw a rude shelter of hides and mats with a fire smoldering in front, similar to those of the solitaries, mystics, and malcontents who lived apart from Beaverton, far from the valley of the Ever-faithful Daughter. To his right grew a forest of massive trees with black-brown trunks and gnarled, leafless limbs. So unlike the trees back home.

Because the trail passed close to the shelter Barclaw figured the occupant was friendly, otherwise he or she would not have put it there. So he moved forward carefully, cleared his throat, and sang "Don't Pet the Beaver," the children's ditty he had sung to entertain himself on his long, rugged walk, halfway across the New Side.

Ohhhh,
The beaver's tail is good to chew,
Whenever you are hungry.
Yoooou — caaaan,
Roast it, jerk it, eat it raw,
He even thinks it's funny.

Ohhhh,
He cuts down trees and eats the bark,
To make his tail grow longer.
Sooooo – you – can,
Roast it, jerk it, eat it raw.
You'll grow a little stronger.

Buuuut,
However nice the beaver is
To give us tasty treats,
Don't ever stroke him on his head,
Or nose or ears or feets.

Ohhhh,
Don't pet the beaver.
Don't pet the . . .

"Beavers!" A squeaky voice from the open-ended shelter. "Got none of them beavers around here. Now beat it." A man emerged from the shelter, rear end first, and stood in the snow. His head reached just to Barclaw's waist. He appeared to be on the downhill side of middle age: thin-faced, pointed beard, rotting teeth. He jumped his feet apart, pulled a knife from his belt, and glared at Barclaw with tiny black eyes. Barclaw looked down at him and said nothing. He swiped at Barclaw's belly with his knife. Did not come close. Barclaw wanted to laugh. Lift him onto his knee. Tell him a story. Or spank him. Instead he sang his song again. When he finished, the tiny man was dancing a circle in the snow.

Yes, the man told him as they shared food and fire, Swarm City was only a few days away. Barclaw probed for as much information as he could extract, then discarded most of it as unreliable. Too many extremes: plenty to eat versus starving thousands, towering public edifices versus endless slums, a tight-knit aristocracy ruling over servile masses. Swarm City could not be that different from Beaverton.

The river broadened, running through swamps and sloughs, slowing Barclaw's travel even though the snow had ended just beyond the little man's clearing. The outer fringes of what he took to be Swarm City appeared gradually, with a grungy shelter here, another there. Away in the distance he viewed a pointed tower, yellow in color. As there were no straight-line, well-kept paths, no definitive Outer Circle boundary, no stakes or stones or walls marking lots, he sighted on the tower. He did a double take as he passed a shelter straddling a mud puddle. The owner sat in front, dull-eyed and acquiescent, as if he not only did not care, but did not know he was sitting in water, did not know anything was wrong.

Few people passed. Of the few who did, no one smiled when he smiled. No one responded to his waves and cheerful greetings. He continued east, having received only grudging nods and points toward the tower in answer to his queries: "Pardon, sir. I'm a stranger. Could you direct me to the center of the city? Town Hall?" Mention of Sac the Magnificent brought blank stares and turn-aways. There was little distinction between private shelters and vends; people sold whatever they had, where they had it. Barclaw was hungry, but waded on through the mud. He had no money anyway, and no appetite for the food they offered.

From what he saw, he judged Swarm City to be two, three times as large as Beaverton, possibly larger. Possibly much larger. After walking most of the day through the depressing squalor and wondering why he came, he found his way blocked by a thick stand of evergreens, young and of uniform height, a species he had never seen, distinguished by finger-length needles and fist-sized cones. There being no opening, he walked along the tree line. The churned-up mud path showed increased use. So here he was, he guessed, in the largest settlement on the New Side, and he had never felt so isolated or alone. He came to a break in the trees, a wide path paved with stone-chip gravel. He took it, and for the first time in months he was not swimming a cold river, clambering over rocks, or walking in mud or snow. Crunch. Crunch. So this was the sound of civilization. The path rose gradually, just steeply enough so that he could not see where it led. The unnaturally uniform tree stand ended as abruptly as it had begun. The stone-chip path broke over a rise and leveled out, running across a broad, manicured grass meadow. Two hundred paces ahead it appeared to end in a mass of strange-looking structures, so tightly packed they looked like a wall. The pointed tower glowed yellow against the gray winter clouds. No muddy puddles here, no thrown-together shelters, no dilapidated humans. This low hill, Barclaw surmised, was either natural and leveled off, or built up, either way requiring a tremendous amount of labor. What happened to the rest of Swarm City each and every spring when the nearby river flooded? He hoped he would be gone before it happened.

The shelters were far different from those below. Or Beaverton's, for that matter. They were built of many different materials, he observed as he walked closer: peeled logs stuck upright in the ground, boulder piled upon boulder, closely-fitting shale slabs on edge, window openings cut into truly vertical walls. Roofs were flat or low-pitched, so low he could not see what they were made of. Amazingly, they had devised a way of stacking one dwelling on top of another. Occasionally, it seemed, three high.

Two men walked stiffly toward him crunching gravel, in step as if marching. They wore snug-fitting skin helmets with flaps covering necks and ears. Instead of furs they wore hair-less polished skins, drawn tight at the waist. Vertical wood stakes ran from shoulder to waist, then from waist to thigh, a form of armor which probably had something to do with their erect bearing. Both carried spears and had knives and clubs in their belts.

When close enough to be heard without shouting, one of the sentries, or soldiers, or guards, said. "State your business, stranger." He had a red band across the brow of his helmet, probably indicating rank.

Barclaw planted his feet and replied, "Barclaw's my name. Ambassador Extraordinary from the Sovereign Town of Beaverton. Far, far to the west of here."

The guards twirled their spears and stuck their points in the ground, the first friendly gesture Barclaw had received since leaving the crabby, then hostile, then delightful little man. "We've been expecting you, Ambassador." He said the words without smiling.

"Expecting me? How could you possibly know?"

"Sac the Magnificent knows many things."

"I guess," Barclaw mumbled.

"Be at ease, sir, and follow me." The guard spun on a foot and started toward the shelters. Barclaw followed. The other guard fell in behind.

Once through the "wall," and inside the compound, they followed a crowded winding path to a commercial district Barclaw took for Swarm City's version of H&G. The pointed structure towered over them. Four enormous poles imbedded in the ground rose ten structures high, meeting at a point. Hundreds of hides scraped clean, cut into squares and rectangles and stitched together formed a translucent cover, bottom to top. Through it Barclaw saw points of light, possibly wick burners.

The guards crunched to a stop in front of a one-level stone shelter on the edge of the commercial district. A tall man stepped from the shelter so quickly that he must have been watching for them. "Welcome to Swarm City, Ambassador," he said with an ingratiating smile. "Come in." He stepped back from the entryway and turned his hand, indicating both hospitality and command. He wore a flowing black robe. Straight, light brown hair touched his shoulders. Beardless. His limpid eyes belied shrewdness and ambition.

"I've come on an urgent mission to see the mayor," Barclaw said, "Sac, the magnificent one."

"To be sure, Ambassador. The mayor is busy at the moment. For the next few days, in fact. He sends his greetings through me, his Chief Advisor. This shelter has been reserved for you for as long as you need it: Swarm City's hospitality shelter. Mavva will attend to your needs." He gave Barclaw a hint of a smile as he pointed to a young woman standing in the shadowy back of the room. She did not move or speak. "You may walk about the city wherever you wish. Shop, eat, chat with our people. You do not need money because as a distinguished visitor your expenses are covered. Tonight, I am delighted to say, you are invited to a grand banquet and ball in your honor. In the tower." He glanced at it proudly. "Rest. Clean up. I will call for you."

For the first time in his life, Barclaw was speechless.

The Chief Advisor retreated to the entrance, turned, and said, "Mavva, prepare the Ambassador for his new clothes." Then to Barclaw: "Your journey must have been arduous, Ambassador; your clothing is in shreds."

The woman Mavva stepped into the light and stood, as if to allow Barclaw time to evaluate her, get used to her. She need not have taken so long; she was young and beautiful, barely beyond girlhood. His first thought was of Ziiza's daughter Milli, the singer. A slightly darker Milli, a finger shorter in height: black hair, knowing eyes, slender and well-formed, but subdued and businesslike, lacking Milli's liveliness and spirit. Her fruit-and-flower perfume smashed his senses.

They stared at each other, as if neither dared move. "I will clean you," she said finally. Barclaw tried to stare through her. He opened his mouth, then closed it. Expelled, trying to blow her scent away. She turned, walked into the shadow, and returned with a knife. With a few deft cuts his furs lay on the polished rock floor. He did not, could not, object. She kicked them to the edge of the fire, then flipped a piece in with her foot, just one, so as not to smother the fire. Placing her hands on his shoulders, she eased him down. Ladled water on his head. It ran over his body and onto the floor and sizzled when it reached the fire. She scooped a thick white substance from a stone crock and lathered his hair and beard. Then his back, his front, his arms, his legs. She rinsed him with clear water. When he was clean and dry she knelt, her knees touching his, and opened her top.

"Satisfactory. Very satisfactory," the Chief Advisor said as he stood over Barclaw smiling. His words woke Barclaw from an afternoon-into-evening nap, so deeply satisfying, so restorative that the desire to cover his head and go back to sleep fought with the desire to jump up and run around the room. "His clothes, Mavva. Are they ready? Do they fit?"

They left the guest shelter and walked through city center. The tower glowed yellow-orange in the night, making dual statements: overpowering majesty and delicate vulnerability. The Chief Advisor approached the opening, protected by the same uniformed guards. More stood at intervals across the front and probably around the entire tower. Inside, Barclaw shielded his eyes from the glare of an enormous central fire. Not only did the fire illuminate the structure on the outside, it reflected off the translucent skin, magnifying its effect on the inside. Smoke and ash, of which there was little, escaped through a hole in a lowered ceiling. Long platforms covered with food lined the walls. Young men, servers, stood stiffly, holding jugs and drink trays. Attendees chatted with the bored gaiety of those comfortable with events of this kind, and comfortable with their positions in the order of things. The men wore the dark flowing furs favored by the Chief Advisor. The women dressed similarly, except that their waists were pinched, and they seemed to be running an exposed shoulder competition. Barclaw blinked, drew in his breath, and put his hand on a post to steady himself.

Without signal, heads turned and the great room went silent. A short man stepped onto a platform and said, "Citizens of Swarm City," his manner implying that all of the citizens who mattered were present, "please welcome tonight's guest, Ambassador Barclaw of Beaverton. Ambassador Barclaw has traveled many weeks, months in fact, from that town of renown which we all have heard of, but few, if any, have seen." A woman tittered. The man next to her elbowed her. She covered her mouth. Her eyes laughed over her hand.

The man stepped down, then perhaps noticing Barclaw's height and size, changed his mind and stepped back upon the platform. He had a round sun-and-wind-burned face, a small nose, delicate hands, and an air of self-importance that spoke of a void that could never be filled. He wore the flowing furs of a civilian and the tight helmet of a guard, with four stripes across the brow. Also signifying rank or distinction, a red sash (which should have been shortened to fit his stature but was not) hung over his shoulder, ran diagonally across his chest and ended below the knee. He wore no beard, but had allowed a clump of facial hair to run wild between his nose and upper lip. "I am Little Sac, Commander of the Swarm City Brigade," he told Barclaw, expanding his chest, rocking on the balls of his feet, and stroking his sash.

"I'll be pleasured, Mister Little Sac," Barclaw said in his best ambassadorial voice. He wanted to say he *had* been pleasured, too, but thought better of it. He also wanted to mention Little Sac's enormous front teeth that revealed themselves when he raised his hair gate to speak. Mention their resemblance to a certain animal's teeth. He thought better of that, too. Constable Barclaw. Ambassador Barclaw. Diplomat Barclaw.

"That's *Commander* Little Sac, Ambassador," Little Sac corrected, his hair gate quivering. He recovered. Brightened. "Let's eat. And drink. I want you to meet some very special people. Come, Ambassador. Come, Chief Advisor." He jumped off the platform and strutted across the room, stopping to introduce Barclaw to men who responded with damp handshakes, restrained smiles, and mumbled cordiality. And women, who responded with interest and excitement, the kind they reserve for virile exotics. As he followed Little Sac from group to group, some of the women left their escorts and trailed behind.

"Will you have a drink, Ambassador Bar Claw?" said a lovely woman whose white-flecked black gown flared out from the slimmest of waists and whose drawn-out pronunciation of Bar and Claw suggested more than a drink.

"Why, thank you, ma'am, I'd be obliged." He winked and swiped his brow; it was very warm. "I believe I've worked up a mighty thirst." With that, Little Sac and the Chief Advisor stepped back and away, releasing Barclaw for his flight into Swarm City's high society.

The lovely woman plucked two drinks from a server's tray and handed one to Barclaw. "I'd toast your health, Ambassador," she effused, "except you seem as healthy as a man can be. Instead, to your success." She laughed and poked his thick forearm.

Barclaw grinned and slurped his drink. "Delicious," he said. "I've never tasted anything so good."

"Vin-olay," she said. "The mayor's private stock. Served only on special occasions. For special people. Like you, Ambassador." She smiled up at him, handed him another drink and said, "Now tell us about yourself." Instead of trying to monopolize him, she invited the trailing women to move closer. "Come, ladies, the Ambassador is going to tell us about far-off Beaverton. I hear you eat those dreadful beavers, tail and all. Is that true, Ambassador?"

Barclaw never made it to the food platforms. Vin-olay on an empty stomach and the attentions of a dozen beautiful and elegantly dressed women fogged his mind and loosened his tongue. He told them about beavers (omitting the unpleasantness that had prompted his journey), his family, his job as constable and storyteller, the wonders of Beaverton and the valley of the Ever-faithful Daughter, the Grand Muma River, the Sunups, the Sundowns, the coast. They should visit sometime. A server hovered behind him, refilling his cup after each hearty pull. He sang "Don't Pet the Beaver" to great applause. He launched into "How I Fought the Sita and Saved Beaverton," his all-time favorite story. He got as far as Little Binni. The lovely woman signaled for a stool, none too soon for his legs were wobbling. A musical group filed into the room, positioned themselves opposite the fire which was mercifully fading to ashes, and played dancing music. A petite woman with pink flowers in her hair pulled him to his feet. He clumped around in good humor, then stumbled back to his stool. He swiped his brow and tried to get back to his story. His eyes closed. A server broke his fall. Six guards carried him to the shelter.

Mavva began her morning chores, keeping an eye on Barclaw as he slept. When she had nothing left to do she sat by the fire staring at him. The Chief Advisor appeared at the door. She pointed. He went away. A messenger knocked and left a writing board. When Barclaw woke, well into the afternoon, Mavva read it to him. An invitation to "a small dinner party." At the lovely woman's shelter – he thought he remembered her name – in a few hours.

And so it went for five short days and five long nights. Barclaw ate, drank, laughed, danced, sang, told his stories again and again and slept late each morning. He was having the time of his life. At week's end, the Chief Advisor knew everything he wanted to know.

35

Sac the Magnificent

"MUMA, MUMA," Edu yelled as he ran toward the Z-sport vend waving a green ThinStone. "Gstan and I have discovered something. Something wonderful." Gstan caught up with him, puffing. Dg put his forepaws on Gstan's leg, drew himself upright, wagged his tail, and smiled. Or came as close to a smile as a furry creature could.

"You'll never believe it, Ziiza," Gstan said. "Never believe it. The boy asked the big question. The one nobody thought to ask. I call him Little Questions and by gosh, for once I'm right."

Ziiza smiled at both of them and ran her finger along the short hairs on Dg's muzzle. "I'm dying to know," she said warily, as if addressing two scamps with a sack full of snakes. Their smiles faded. Dg stopped wagging his tail and sat. "Oh, you're serious," she said. She sat, looked up at them, and said, "Well?" Dg rested his head in her lap.

Gstan nudged Edu. "Go ahead, boy, you discovered it."

"I was playing," Edu said, "calculating with my ThinStone. The one Gstan gave us. I thought to myself: if it can do all of these things, like calculate numbers, play games . . ." He held it up. Govvi and Netti, who had been standing back, moved closer. "All these things. So why not try talking to it? See what happens." Gstan beamed at Ziiza and mouthed *What did I tell you.* "So I squeezed and talked. Right at it. Nothing. Then I squeezed twice. Like this." He gave the ThinStone two squeezes in rapid succession. "And I let go. Quick. I don't know why, but I did. I didn't drop it or anything."

"Please, Edu," Govvi said, "can we get to the point? What happened?"

"Pardon me," Gstan said softly, "he's trying to explain. The double-squeeze is important."

Edu nodded and continued. "Did you notice the light when I squeezed? I'll do it again." He squeezed twice. The light went on, then off, then on. "It means you can talk. And when you talk, the person you are talking to knows to squeeze because their ThinStone flashes, too."

"Talk?" Ziiza said. "As in talk and listen?"

Gstan walked across to the Konka Sanctuary. When Edu saw him sit on a bench, he turned away so Gstan could not see his lips, gave his ThinStone a double-squeeze, and said, "Gstan is a good friend – and a so-so fisherman." He grinned at his muma. "He says 'check and check.' I don't hear him in my ear but I know what he says, just like games and numbers. It tells me in my head."

Gstan swaggered back and said, "'Check and check.' Do you realize," he patted Edu on the head, "what this means?" He did not wait for an answer. "All the power in these things and what do people do with them? Collect them, speculate, drive the prices up to ridiculous heights. Collect them just to own them. Lots of them. I'm not complaining; it's been great for business. And I collect them myself. But nobody really uses the number functions, the memory, the letters, not even the games much."

Govvi cleared her throat. "Excuse me."

"All right, you do, Govvi. But Z-sport is just about the only business that's junked tally boards or stick notches and converted over to ThinStone accounting. I can't even do it with Errix Enterprises. But that's just it: this is something everyone can do. And will do." He looked down. "I'm wrong. Can't do. Because we're all broke. And discouraged. And too hungry to think about miracles. So one is handed to us by this inquisitive boy. Were those guys testing us to see how long it took us to figure it out?"

"I was near Town Hall and Gstan talked to me all the way from Hill Burrow," Edu said in his most cheerful voice, trying to get everyone smiling again.

Com. Dear Com. Could ThinStone talking have saved your life? If we had only known about them in time. If they really work. If it's not some trick these two are playing on me.

"I'm hungry," Ziiza said. "Will you join us for lunch, Gstan? Maybe afterward we can practice talking on ThinStones. Sounds funny, doesn't it?"

They walked from the vend to Netti's manufacturing shelter. The flaps were down against the rain, making it dark inside. This was offset by a cozy fire, which flared up when Netti threw a handful of reed cuts on it. Notably absent were her workers. Not that rock running had faded completely. The sunshine runners' rocks sat outside their shelters awaiting spring. That was expected. Sufx, Junior, and the hard-core runners practiced but in a more relaxed manner, if you could call it that: only two or three times a week, once around instead of two, no speed work. Org ran past Z-sport occasionally. Waved, if Sufx wasn't around. Ziiza assumed he was still living with *them*, but did not know for certain. If Milli was old enough to be pledged and be a muma, then he was old enough to be on his own, however unpleasant the terms. A sad shrug for her. But she had had plenty of those.

The bright spot in Z-sport's future, as Ziiza figured and Govvi agreed, was Sister Sissi and her dedicated group. And the growing numbers they inspired. Their approach was different from the early runners and serious competitors, mostly male. These women ran for the fun of it, the joy of it, you could say. In all seasons, whatever the weather. In groups. For safety in numbers, perhaps, although there was no danger running the Circles. The pleasure of a brisk workout. Then they went to the nearest Sanctuary for the talk of the day and a hot K. Most important to Ziiza and Z-sport: all of the female rock runners wore expensive Lazy Grape competition models. Wanted to look good. The whole package. Altogether – Ziiza and crew had discussed this many times – Sister Sissi and her athletic friends had legitimized rock running. It was now as much a part of Beaverton life as going to H&G for beaver or to Town Hall for a permit.

Maybe more so. Rock runners seemed to be the only cheerful people in town. Beaverton winters were wet and cold. That was expected and coped with, with resigned good humor. That was offset by the lack of freezing weather and snowfall, for the most part, and the uplifting year-round greenery. The bank run had turned people cautious, tight with big yellows, pelts, everything. Font had not helped when he raised interest rates, the exact opposite, in Mistermayor's view, of what he should have done to help the economy.

Bitta interviewed Castor regularly. His answers grew increasingly evasive. "Coming along nicely." Or: "Looks good to me." Or: "Needs further study." The last was his favorite. But as good a reporter as she was, she could not bring herself to ask the nut question: Was Beav-enhance working? If the answer was no, then what? True, prices had doubled and most people had cut back. Beavertonians could live with that. "A test of what we are made of," the people liked to say. True, pelts-to-market were smaller and the meat lighter and tastier, indicating younger beaver. And true, Castor's men (and the poachers) were working the far-off ponds; the large, close-in ones being in "recovery stage." And true, Addle had hired old hunters and fishers to teach adult classes, another step toward turning Grassyknoll into what he despised, a trade school. Everything pointed to it, but still no one, Bitta included, dared ask: Is Beav-enhance a complete failure?

Then Barclaw, Beaverton's constable-turned-ambassador. Gone late fall into mid-winter. No word. The optimists said it was too early; he would be back by spring. Early spring? Late spring? The pessimists did not expect to see him again and delighted in speculating – eaten by wolves in the great interior (if he had gotten that far), smothered by freezing sleet while he slept (a feast for some animal when he thawed), stepped into a sink and disappeared from the face of the earth – each demise more delightful to contemplate than the previous.

All of this was on the minds of the lunchtime participants, though no one spoke of it. Or talked business. Instead, they shared a meager meal. Gstan told a joke in bad taste. Resulting in scowls. Then laughter all around. Netti gave an intricate weaving demonstration to great applause, followed by a seated half-bow and a half-smile. Sufx showed them the "amazing rock trick" he had been working on. As he ran, he tilted his head forward, allowing his rock to roll down his back and into his hands. He pitched it into the air ahead of him, ran under it, and caught it behind his back again. Govvi multiplied two enormously long numbers on her ThinStone, presumably to impress Gstan and Edu. Mild applause. Old stuff. Nobody but Govvi could verify the answer anyway.

Gstan told the story of the rainstorm last summer. The laughter began with his first words: "Shipment of wet ThinStones just in." Leegs and Old Man Haracosh had spread them on the ground to dry before auction. Dg had walked casually across from Z-sport, as if he had known exactly what he was doing. Pooped on a couple. Composed himself. Looked around. Selected some more. Pooped again. Then pulled himself around on his behind with his forepaws, soiling every last one. Lights out. Ruined. Leegs had run after him. Caught him. Would have killed him had Gstan not come along and called him off. Not funny then, at least to some, but funny now.

"I've been thinking," Ziiza said as they were breaking up and Gstan was leaving, "about something for a long time. You two boys," she said, looking at Edu and Gstan, "may have provided the missing element. Communication on ThinStones, huh? Very interesting."

* * *

Mavva leaned over Barclaw and said, "The Chief Advisor is here, Ambassador. You should get up and dress."

The Chief Advisor stood near the open-way, arms folded, drumming his fingers. Barclaw groaned, opened his eyes, smiled weakly at Mavva, closed them, and feigned snoring. She reached her hand under his beard and tickled his neck. He snorted and rolled over. The Chief Advisor walked quickly to the sleeping platform and said, "The mayor will see you, Ambassador."

"Uh, what mayor did you say?"

"Sac the Magnificent, the man you came to see."

"Oh. Right." Barclaw sat up and rubbed his eyes.

"You have a half-hour to feed him and make him presentable."

Mavva had barely finished when the Chief Advisor appeared again. Walking to the tower – Sac's palace, or whatever they called it; it certainly wasn't Town Hall – the official chatted pleasantly. At the entrance, the guards came to attention and jammed their spear points in the ground. "Does Beaverton have a standing brigade?" he asked casually, as if he did not know.

"No. Just me. I'm it," Barclaw answered. "Constable, police force, militia, brigade. We have almost no crime, no trouble. Good, solid people. Everyone loyal. No jail." He felt he could omit bank runs, beaver poaching, and unruly crowds at emergency council meetings.

Inside the tower the serving platforms around the sides were the only evidence of the grand banquet and ball a week ago. Silence. Not a person around. The huge central fire was not only out, but the ashes cleared away and the stone floor cleaned. Instead of light from within, the southeast wall glowed in mid-morning sunshine, creating a smoky light in the smokeless space. Two thick ropes hung through the vent in the ceiling, ending in spliced loops touching the floor. Beside them were piles of round, flat stones with holes in the centers.

The Chief Advisor stepped into a loop and motioned Barclaw to do the same. He jerked the rope. It went taut. Barclaw heard a creaking noise high above. The rope went slack. Tightened again. The Chief Advisor rose into the air. Barclaw's rope tightened. Creak. Creak. The noise grew to a screech and he was jerked past the Chief Advisor. A man with his foot in what must have been a loop in the other end of the rope, came down at him. Both of his arms were stuck through round stones similar to those stacked on the floor. The screeching grew louder and Barclaw rose faster. As he passed, the weighted man looked at him with empty eye sockets. And sniffed hard, like an animal. Barclaw turned away at the sight. He convulsed and threw up. The screeching stopped, and he did, too, at the top. The Chief Advisor drew up beside him.

Barclaw looked up at the smoking pole over which his rope was thrown, smoking as if to catch fire from the rope's friction. Little Sac stood on the edge of the opening laughing quietly, not particularly at him, just laughing. He extended a hooked pole to Barclaw's rope and pulled it toward him. "You can puke again if you like," Little Sac said. Before Barclaw could answer, he unhooked and let him swing out and away. Barclaw choked, belched, and heaved. One. Two. Three. Plop. He gulped air and tried again, but could not. The Chief Advisor hung on his rope, turning his head as it twisted to keep his eyes on him. Little Sac pulled them in. Barclaw stepped out of the loop, stamped the numbness from his feet, and looked around.

The room was square, with inward-sloping walls formed by the four support poles meeting high above. Each pole held an unlit torch. Woven reed mats covered the floor, similar to shelter-roof mats at home but soft to the feet. Each wall had a round opening at eye level under which was a fur-covered bench. Aside from another pile of round stones and a coil of rope, there were no other furnishings or supplies.

Sac the Magnificent reclined on a bench, his back to them, looking out of the south opening. Little Sac, the Chief Advisor, and Barclaw stood waiting for him to speak. Having surveyed that portion of Swarm City to his satisfaction, but still with his back to them, Sac said, "Shock you, did they? Ugly, what? Think nothing of them. Groins. Blind groins. Lose one or two a week. No matter. Unlimited supply."

"Ears destroyed, too," Little Sac said in an overly-loud voice, "Operate strictly by touch and smell. And can they smell!"

"Enough, Son," Sac the Magnificent said. "Let's not overdo it." He rolled, sat up, planted his feet on the floor, and looked straight through Barclaw, as if focusing on the far opening. He was small and round-faced like his son, perhaps a bit taller. Unlike his son, who but for his small stature looked the part of an outdoor commander, Sac showed paunchy, even under his white robe which was flecked with black, the reverse of the lovely woman's. No headwear. Hands pudgy. Also, unlike Little Sac, he wore no lip hair, did not have to, had no buckteeth to cover. It was in his eyes, as it often is with men of supreme ambition. Or so they appeared to Barclaw across a roomful of yellow light moving with the sway of the tower and the in-and-out pulsing of the skin covering.

Not that Barclaw was over-awed or intimidated. He was a rugged man. How else would he have made it across, alone, and in mid-winter? He was not a sophisticated man, as had been amply proven during the past week – and long before that. But he was not a stupid man either, not stupid enough to speak before being spoken to, even if his question was bursting inside. He need not have bothered.

Sac the Magnificent rose from his bench, raised an arm and said, "Sit, Ambassador. Chief Advisor. Commander. Relax." Little Sac eased himself down and dangled his feet in the opening. Barclaw and the Chief Advisor did the same.

Barclaw raised his hand. Sac's eyes flashed, then softened. "You'll get your chance, Ambassador. You'll get your chance." He paused, his power hovering in the pulsing glow. "I anticipate your question and will state just that: an alliance." He flashed pointed teeth. Lowered his voice. "I will put it as delicately as I can: You wish our help in stabilizing your floundering monetary system. You wish to negotiate a monetary alliance between Swarm City and Beaverton."

Barclaw looked at the stone floor far below and felt queasy. He pushed himself back. Looked out of a wall opening. For a cloud. A bird. Anything real.

"How does ancillary status sound to you, Ambassador? The Swarm City Central Bank elevates the Beaverton Bank to ancillary status and infuses it with hard-to-find big yellows. As many as are needed to restore confidence and stability and move Beaverton forward into the future. And everything required to back them up, give them strength. With Beaverton retaining its independence, rights, and privileges, of course. In equal measure, we will expect certain. . . . Well, that can be discussed later, Ambassador. Much later. You are traveler, a man of the world. You know how such arrangements work."

Barclaw struggled to make sense. How did Sac know about big yellows? He had not said anything, that he could remember. And it is Font's Bank. There is no "Beaverton Bank." Or is he talking banks generally? Whatever Beaverton's bank is called. Coming at him so fast. If it were not so early in the morning. If he had not stayed out so late.

Sac the Magnificent continued: "Everything is arranged. Commander Little Sac and his Brigade are ready to move. Tomorrow. With as many groins as needed. Plus extras to replace those who, shall we say, falter along the way."

Barclaw felt a twinge. He thought he saw Little Sac smirking. He was careful not to look down.

Sac the Magnificent paused for what seemed a full minute, daring anyone to breathe, let alone speak. Then in a volume Barclaw could not believe such a small man was capable of, he bellowed, "Do we have an alliance, sir?" Then softly: "You may speak."

"Why, thank you, Mayor Sac. Excuse me, Mayor Magnificent Sac. That's exactly what the council wanted. Nancillary status for our banking. As close as I can figure."

"Good, then," Sac said. "Chief Advisor. You have the agreement for Ambassador Barclaw to sign?" Then to Barclaw: "You brought your authorization with you?"

"No, sir," Barclaw said. "They just told me to go east. Gave me authority to do my best. As I see fit. So here I am. And while I'm at it, I want to thank you for your hospitality."

"I suppose we can skip that formality." Sac the Magnificent sat on the fur-covered bench, turned away, and looked out of the opening. The meeting was over.

Barclaw closed his eyes when he passed the eyeless groins on the ropes. Shuddered when heard their pitiful snorting and sniffing.

When they reached the guest shelter, the Chief Advisor looked him hard in the eye and asked, "Do you want her?"

"Want?"

"Mavva, the girl. Do you want to take her with you, Ambassador?"

"I'm married," Barclaw gasped. "Wife. Back in Beaverton."

"As I said, Ambassador," the Chief Advisor gave him a knowing, official-to-official look, "do you want her?"

* * *

Winter crocuses, white and blue. Dogwoods, first of the flowering trees. Trillium, nestled between tree roots as if for protection. Spring's vanguards had come and gone, and now the real thing: penetrating warmth when the clouds parted, and most wondrous of all, a proper length of day.

Though the winter Litti had helped Arbo classify his plant and animal specimens, preserving and storing them. To what end? When he explained, bright as she was, she still did not understand. It came down to the simple fact, she concluded, that he wanted to do it. No, that was too mild a term, *had* to do it. Because she loved him, and sharing his work brought them together, that was enough. She kept her independence by maintaining her town shelter – Arbo still refused to enter Beaverton – working with Mizpark once or twice a week, going to the day-care center occasionally, and having tea with Ziiza whenever she could. On exceptional winter days when sunny and unseasonably warm, or after a rare snowfall, she had rambled. But those days had been few. She felt that humans ought to observe a time of quiescence as did field, forest, and creature; the long wait added to the joy of the new rambling season. When it finally came.

Litti had spent the night in town. The day before she had met with Mizpark, they being all that were left of Friends of the Beaver. She could not blame the others for drifting away, they had had all they could do to feed their families and get through the winter. Protest marches and confrontations with Castor and the council were fruitless and had been discontinued. Instead, Mizpark and Litti held occasional classes in H&G, instructing whomever they could find in alternative food sources, self-reliance, and beaver meat conservation. They did not have to rail against the folly of Beav-enhance, the result was now evident. The giant valley beaver was an endangered animal, just as endangered as the watabeast, even if it was not on the list. The only bright spot was Mizpark and Litti's relationship with Mistermayor, friend of the Friends. He counseled, supported – as much as he could and remain politically viable – and supplied them with the most accurate information available.

Ziiza thought it strange that Litti was still in town at mid-morning. Strange, too, that every rose hip she crushed for tea contained a dried-up worm. "Bad year for roses?" she asked.

"Gives my tea its special flavor," Litti said, smiling. "They don't harm, you know. You could live on insects, worms, and larvae, if you had to."

"We may have to at that," Ziiza said, "if the price of beaver gets any higher."

"Yes," Litti said softly as she poked and stirred the fire. When the flames rose, she dropped her stick in and watched the fire consume it.

"What is it, Litti?" Ziiza asked, trying to act playful. Litti did not respond. Then, in a serious, somewhat alarmed voice, Ziiza repeated the words: "What is it?"

Litti looked at Ziiza with glistening eyes. "He's been acting strange again. I have fears."

What she feared, Litti went on to explain, was that the sita had returned, that Arbo had found its tracks, and that the fascination had overtaken him again. They were to meet at Water Child early this morning. But now, of all times, she was stalling, taking refuge in talk and tea.

What can I say? Ziiza asked herself. A cheerful change of subject was the best she could come up with. She had an idea, she told Litti with an exaggerated hand flourish, for a race, the biggest rock running race ever. Had been mulling it over all winter. Did not say anything because the timing had to be right. Announce it when people were down and discouraged, ready to grab onto any idea that offered diversion, fun, and hope.

Litti smiled wanly, nodded unenthusiastically, and tried to pay attention. Rock running did not interest her. Nor did competitive sports of any kind.

Yes, timing was everything, Ziiza told her. And the timing was . . . two Sundays away. Less than two weeks. Step one: talk to Mistermayor. Convince him. Obtain his backing. "Was he in a decent mood?" she inquired. Litti nodded. Then Polcat and the council. This was to be no ordinary race. It would involve the whole community. Need official sanction. A permit and much more. Govvi and Netti, Edu and Dg, Sufx and Junior? She had not told them. Word might leak out. But when they heard, they would be delighted. Swept away. Ziiza patted Litti's knee. She bounced up, realizing she had reached as high a point as she was likely to reach, and said, "Well, Litti, today's the day. The sky's clear, the sun's warm, and Beaverton's starving. Could there be a better time to visit Mistermayor?" Litti nodded, just to agree. Ziiza walked away, then returned to Litti, who had not moved, and said, "Tell me what happens, will you, Litti? Promise?"

Litti threw her untasted tea in the fire and smiled the best smile she could manage.

After Ziiza had gone, Litti walked west through H&G, turned south through the tail works and followed the path to the lifeless ponds. In the meadow, tiny flowers bloomed beneath the new grass. Buckibird and friends courted noisily. She paid her respects to Great-great-great-grandpopa Monumentree, whose limbs seemed heavy and droopy, mirroring her apprehension. She caught Water Child and followed the trail through the forest.

Litti stood at the clearing's edge, much the same as she had the first time she saw him. By habit her eyes went to the waterfall and the light green moss above. To the pool. To the outlet. Then slowly across the clearing.

Arbo was almost hidden, hunched over in the grass. He worked a long stick, laid it down, and apparently — she could not see through the grass — scooped up a handful of dirt and flung it over his shoulder. He poked, scooped, and threw. She accustomed herself to what he was doing and advanced slowly between him and Water Child to avoid being hit by flying dirt. When she had worked herself around to his side, taking care not to surprise him from behind, she said, "Hi, Arbo. What are you doing?" (Translation: Why are your hands so dirty, instead of clean and ready to make love?)

Arbo looked up, eyes wild with excitement. "Look, Litti, look." He stepped out of a shallow hole, dropped on hands and knees, and crawled through the grass. When he came to what he was looking for, he spread the grass so she could see, stuck his finger into a hole, and said, "It's back. No doubt about it."

"So, my darling," she said, trying to hold back her tears. She paused. Drew in her breath. Water Child's fall splashed behind her. "So, what are you doing?"

"I'm digging a pit. A trap. Not a hunting trap or anything like that. I'm convinced the sita has such acute senses that no one can get near him — unless he's after *them*. If I dig deep enough, wide enough, straight enough, so it takes a while to pull down the walls and climb out, maybe I'll be able to sneak up and get a look. That's all I want. A sighting. See a sita with my own eyes. Then I'll be satisfied."

Litti flung herself on his back, hugged him, kissed his neck, and hung on. Her tears ran onto his hair and down. "Don't do it, Arbo!" she cried. "Give it up!"

"No. I can't," he said, almost growling.

"I'm begging begs, Arbo," she said, sobbing. "Please give it up."

"Don't you understand? Don't you understand? I've got to do this."

She pushed away and stood. He walked back to the hole, jumped in, and picked up his stick. He poked, thrust, and pried the earth. Litti bit her finger to keep from screaming. Then, holding her cheeks between her hands, she said, "Some creatures are meant to be alone. Unseen. Unrecorded. A mystery to all people." She wiped her eyes. "That's the way of it, Arbo."

Arbo gave no indication of hearing what she had said. He grabbed a split cedar board lying beside the hole, pushed it into the loosened soil, and flung it in the air.

Litti backed away, turned, and walked into the trees.

36

Racing Towards Race Day

ZIIZA WALKED to Z-sport. She was late but it did not matter: business was slow. That will change, she thought, smiling to herself. Govvi sat by the sales counter checking her ThinStone for the umpteenth time. Or playing a game. Netti was also by herself in the manufacturing shelter, restoring the lift to a Z-Z a customer had dropped off. Govvi and Netti seldom spoke, seldom did anything together except work – at the old Sita, at Z-sport. It was not that they did not like each other. They did, in an arms-length sort of way. But that was the extent of it. Milli was gone, and as far as Netti was concerned, a part of her life had gone with her, even though she understood that Milli had found her man, and her singing, and the life she desired and deserved. Her best friend, her only friend, had vanished. Not a word after taking the pledge. Only a roundabout, second-hand message from Leegs. Months late. That hardly counted. Cool calculating Govvi a substitute? No. They had nothing in common except the same muma.

Ziiza greeted Govvi and Netti, then ambled over to Sufx and Junior who were playing catch with a Z-Z. She pinched Sufx's waist. He jumped; she had never touched him before "Just checking, Sufx, my boy. Wanted to see if you'd gone soft over the winter."

"I certainly haven't gotten fat, if that's what you mean," he replied haughtily. "Nobody in Beaverton has."

"I mean," Ziiza said, "have you been training through the bad weather? Or have you been backing off on the long runs, taking it easy, going through the motions?"

"Yeah," Junior said, pleased that Ziiza was treating Sufx as someone other than the paragon of rock running.

"I'm in shape," Sufx said. He raised his arm, made a muscle, and squeezed it with his hand. "Try that if you don't believe me. Or do you want to pinch my leg?"

Instead Ziiza spun around and grabbed for Junior's waist. He dodged her. "I've been training," he said, as if his job was at stake.

"Seen Org with a rock on top?" she asked, looking across the path at Errix, acting casual.

"Not much," Sufx said. "But he's training somewhere. You can bet on that." Junior nodded in agreement.

"Thanks, guys," she said, swinging a teasing hand at Junior.

Across the way, Gstan, who was working on his vend, called, "Hey Ziiza, got time for a Konka? I'm buying."

"No, thanks," she answered. Then, changing her mind, said, "Why yes, Gstan. I'd enjoy a small K." He bought two from the perky vend girl. He had started walking south a while back, he told her. Wanted to check on things. Leegs. Should be clear in the mountains. Had hiked for a week or so, then turned back. Too long a trip. Too tough. Something you do once, he told her. When you have to. Or don't know any better. But never again. Unless you're a Leegs. Or a maniac for punishment. And he, Gstan, was not one of those. He took his time coming back, practiced hunting and fishing and trapping, honing his survival skills.

When he stopped talking and sipped his Konka, Ziiza thanked him and excused herself, hinting at an important errand. She almost invited him to come, since brewing in the back of her mind was a part for him to play. But again she changed her mind. The timing had to be perfect.

Senior was easy to convince; there could never be too many races for him, short or long. So he and Ziiza called on Mistermayor at Town Hall. Ordinarily she would have walked in on him after noon, when the real business of the day was behind him, he had had lunch, and was a bit sleepy. But nobody was eating particularly well these days, she reasoned, so it did not matter. The sooner, the better.

Mistermayor was not as quick to grasp the race idea as Ziiza had hoped. Too many problems on his mind? Or did he simply not see what it could do for the town? "I've got a snappy name for it," she said, trying to ignite his interest. His weary glance said: You always do, Ziiza. "The B-town Run Away. B-town," she continued. "See. It's new. Nobody's called Beaverton that before. Run Away. Run away with the prizes. Run away from the pack. Get it?" She regretted *get it* as soon as the words had slipped out.

Ziiza summarized "B-town's" problems, painful as they were to talk about: the beaver meat and tail shortage (diplomatically skipping the Beav-enhance Pond Management Program); big yellow problems, the all-round low morale.

Not to mention that ripening berries, early fruits, and the summer fish runs were weeks away. Springtime into summer – she almost spoke the words – starving time. Just like on the Old Side.

"I wish I knew what happened to him," Mistermayor said; he was hardly listening.

"Huh?"

"Will we ever see Barclaw again? And if we do, what news will he bring? What *else* will he bring?"

What was bothering him, why she could not get through, was painfully clear. But this was her shot and she could not quit, could not allow the subject to drift. "This is going to be big, Mistermayor. So big I want you to announce the race. Call it. Everyone will hear you, look at you. We'll mark out a new racecourse. Have new events. More winners. Ten places instead of three. Teams, too: vend companies, town employees, any group that signs up. We need you, Mistermayor, need your support. And participation. You'll speak from a platform up a tall –"

"Oh, yes," Mistermayor said; she finally had his attention. "I'd love that. Up a tall . . . what?"

"A platform up a tall tree. Able to see the whole race. Well, most of it. Call it for those who can't see."

"I'll put it on the agenda. Brief Polcat. Something positive for a change. Leave everything to me, Ziiza." He patted her shoulder, then waved her away, looking almost enthusiastic.

Polcat caught on immediately, urged Mistermayor to call a council meeting that night. "No time to lose," he said, grasping the benefits before Mistermayor could get past his opener. "Boost our spirits. Take our minds off our troubles."

Ziiza and her Z-sport crew went to the council meeting, but were hardly needed. The passage of one afternoon's time was all it took for Mistermayor and Polcat to run away with it, so to speak. By the time the meeting started, they, and the council members were competing for Top Booster of the greatest thing to hit Beaverton – correction, B-town – since Biber's Obtuse. And who had thought up this brilliant race idea? Mistermayor? Polcat? The council, in its collective wisdom? By meeting's end, it was not entirely clear.

* * *

"Set an impossible goal, then meet it," Ziiza told her workers. In addition to their regular jobs, everyone was given two or three more. Sufx and Junior were the most enthusiastic. Added to their balancing duties, they were to sell Z-Zs and conduct novice training sessions. They could get up earlier for their own runs. Govvi, after running the numbers, was skeptical. Ziiza wanted to eliminate the entry fee for broader appeal. That, together with dropping the price of Lazy Grapes and easy credit to anyone who did not have big yellows (which was just about everyone), netted out to a huge loss on anyone's ThinStone as far as she was concerned. Ziiza listened, then assigned her to material gathering in addition to her regular sales and financial duties. Govvi accepted by not saying no. Ziiza saw Addle and wangled two weeks off for Edu and Dg – "In the service of Beaverton" – and recruited some non-running Grassyknoll students as course monitors. "Rehearsal next Sunday morning." The most "impossible" task fell to Netti: to double or triple her normal Z-Z production.

The council had approved, of course. And equally important, Mistermayor had reluctantly consented to an emergency beaver harvest to take away hunger as an excuse for non-participation. Step three was publicity. Ziiza met Bitta and Sister Sissi at the old Trace End café, now a Konka Sanctuary. Sister Sissi's cheeks glowed after her morning run. Bitta's shoulders were clean; Hobart was on his best behavior.

After explaining the race Ziiza said, "This is too big for Z-sport, Sister Sissi. We'd like Konka Sanctuaries to join as a sponsor. Not much for you to do, just put up notices, and, most importantly, make each Sanctuary a sign-up station. No entry fee. No money to handle. Just sign them up and get them committed. And give them a Z-sport coupon good for a free rock balance and a discount on a new Z-Z."

"Delighted," Sister Sissi said, thrilled with the idea – and the increased business it would generate for her Sanctuaries. "What else can I do?"

"That's about it," Ziiza said. "Times are tough and we don't want any barriers to running. Beaverton needs something to get excited about. It comes down to this: I want every person in Beaverton running in the B-town Run Away or watching it."

"And wearing a Lazy Grape," Bitta quipped.

"What's wrong with combining a civic good deed with business?" Ziiza snapped. "The question is, are you with us or not?" Before Bitta could answer she added, "Let me put it differently," she gave Bitta her most serious look, "we can't pull this off without you, Bitta. Not with our deadline less than two weeks off."

"I'm in shape," Sister Sissi said proudly. "And so are my ladies. Anyway, Ziiza, what's the hurry? Can't it wait till summer?"

"Trust me, it can't."

"I've already talked around," Bitta said. "I can't begin to tell you how excited everyone is. Think of it, the first good news in I don't know how long."

They spent the rest of the day going over details. Almost everything was new, which added to Bitta's story line. Bound to confuse: "That's not the way we did it last year." More work for Team Bitta and Hobart.

As they parted, Ziiza said, "I'll ask one last thing from both of you. And please, don't think I'm insulting your intelligence. Repetition is the key. When you've said it a hundred times, are thoroughly sick of it, don't want to hear it again – that's when it's finally sinking in."

* * *

Gstan was ready for business but had no ThinStones to sell. Leegs had not arrived. When, or if, no one knew. And no raw stone for the Hill Burrow workers to cut, polish, and shape. Trading and collecting was slow. Not that ThinStones had lost value, just that the serious collectors had completed their collections and weren't interested in trading. They still met for Konkas, trading laughs and lies instead of ThinStones. And for betting on the B-town Run Away.

"Early odds," said Wagge, Beaverton's resident bookmaker and Sanctuary habitué, "are Sufx three to one over Org. Should be higher, given his record. They surely will change as the days roll on and the bets roll in." His soft sell. He knew the gamblers could not resist and the non-gamblers would not bet under any circumstances. Any circumstances, that is, except a sure thing. Which Sufx certainly was. Wagge noted their bets on an aquamarine ThinStone, as perfect a device for bookmaking as one could imagine. Big yellows, pelts, meat, and tails in short supply did not faze the bettors; they only considered the winning side.

Yes, there certainly was a big yellow shortage. Gstan found that out when he visited Font. "Nothing to lend," Font told him glumly. "Nothing to lend until Barclaw returns. If he ever does. Even then, what news will he bring? Are they going to help us or not? Go jump in the Daughter? Or salvation?"

"Listen, Font," Gstan whispered. "I've got to borrow some big yellows. On the old credit line. I've invested all of my profits in collectible ThinStones. Done well, too. But everything I have is tied up." He looked down as if to make a calculation. "A couple of hundred. It's very important." Font made a push-away motion. "How about a hundred this week and another hundred next?"

"I'd like to," Font replied, "but for the moment I'm out of the lending business. I'm just as short as you are."

"Let me put it differently," Gstan pleaded. "I have a project that I'd rather not explain, rather it didn't get around. But it's absolutely vital. To me. I must have big yellows. Or I guess, meat, pelt, tail, any kind of old barter. Come on, Font, I'll do anything. You know I'm good for it."

"Why don't you try your trader friends?" Font replied with a shrug. "Sell a ThinStone. They're the richest ones left. If anyone is rich anymore."

"Traders talk too much," Gstan said. "Got to be confidential. I'm trusting you, Font. Not even a peep that I asked. Agreed?" Font nodded reluctantly; he was getting nervous. "I'm laying it all out," Gstan continued. "I'll secure it with Errix Enterprises and Hill Burrow. Two hundred measly big yellows. Pay you double interest. Name your price. I know you can dig them up. Somewhere."

"Pledge Errix. Hill Burrow, too. That's pretty drastic, Gstan. You really *do* want this loan. Give me a day or so to work on it."

"I'm counting on you," Gstan said, trying to make a promise out of Font's offer to try.

* * *

Bitta stood in front of Town Hall, leaning against Barclaw's round. "Hobart," she said, "let 'em have it." The yellow-headed bird lifted into the air, swooped over the H&G shoppers, let go a few white globules, causing curses or laughs depending upon how close they came, flew back and landed on her head. "Coooo-burp. Coooo-burp," he rumbled in his limited but effective vocabulary. She had their attention.

Bitta drew a breath and began: "Headline news. Headline news. First annual B-Town Run Away." This was not news in the strictest sense; the word was out after the council meeting, but Bitta always presented "news" as being fresh and exclusively from her. "Everyone is invited to run or watch the new rock running extravaganza. Here it is in a clam shell: No entry fee, courtesy of Z-sport." She waited for applause, which she got. "New racecourse; start and finish west of town. Longest race ever. Special guest announcer will be? Who other than our beloved Mistermayor. Special guest starter? Why, our star councilman, Polcat. Sign up at any Konka Sanctuary and receive a free drink, courtesy of Sister Sissi. Rebalance your rocks at Z-sport. Free. Have them autographed by Sufx, the undefeated champion. Discounts on Lazy Grapes. Does this sound like a paid advertisement? Well, it's not, folks. It's my contribution to dear old B-town."

Bitta paused to assess the crowd, which was considerable and growing. A good start. A very good start. Even though it was an older crowd and did not include many actual runners. "Best of all," she said, "this no ordinary race. The B-town Run Away offers many more places and prizes. And for the first time, teams may enter."

"What are the prizes?"

"Well, you've got me there," she said "I'll have to find out. Maybe a ribbon and a piece of beaver tail."

"If they can find any," the voice shot back. Derisive laughter.

Hobart coo-burped impatiently. He did not like to see his mistress interrupted.

All in all a good opening announcement, Bitta thought. But so many changes. So many innovations to explain. She knew Ziiza was right. She and Hobart had better pace themselves. Even *her* voice would not hold out for two weeks at this rate. In addition to her regular H&G circuit, she would have to visit the Sanctuaries at least twice a day. And roam the neighborhoods, too.

* * *

Gstan knew Ziiza was putting everything she had into the race and was determined to help. And, of course, Gstan being Gstan, and Ziiza being Ziiza, he did not want her to know. Somehow, somewhere, Font had found almost a hundred big yellows, plus a few pelts and some barter. Gstan pledged Errix and Hill Burrow as security. Font promised more in a few days, but not many; he was at his limit. (Hadn't he said that before?)

Gstan's plan was simplicity itself. The race wasn't really a race, it was a civic happening. More precisely, it was a desperate ploy to help Beaverton through a hungry, chaotic spring until things turned around. By allowing the emergency beaver harvest, Mistermayor and the council were subsidizing the Run Away. Gstan's plan was to subsidize Z-sport.

He had to be careful, very careful. First, he had Old Man Haracosh round up the laid-off stone shapers. He paid them one big yellow each for unlimited service up to race time. They were happy to get them.

"Now, boys," Gstan said, "your job is to buy Z-Zs. Lots of them. But you have to be sneaky about it." Their dull eyes lit; they liked *sneaky*. "I'll give you an allotment of money every morning. Right up to race day. Or when my supply runs out. See your friends and relatives first. Preferably those who can keep their mouths shut – if such people exist. Give them the price of a Z-Z. Have them walk over to Z-sport's vend and try on a few. Like they're really interested. Be fitted. Act fussy. Maybe walk away. Forget about rocks. Forget about running. But always, by the end of the day, buy one. They can keep them for their trouble." Gstan paused for questions, looking each one in the eye. "One more thing: no mention of my name. Or Errix. Or Hill Burrow. Or anything to connect me with it. Got that?" He thought of Ziiza and Govvi and how hard they would be to fool. Should I give them more tactics, fake reasons to throw the nosy off of the trail? Lessons in sophisticated shopping? No, he concluded, keep it simple and run the risk.

* * *

Saturday. Ziiza was busy. Govvi was busy. Edu was busy. Dg was busy. Sufx and Junior were busy. But the day before race day Netti was more than busy, she was frantic and exhausted. Sales were strong even without Gstan's stealth buyers; she could not produce Z-Zs fast enough. She had hired back all the experienced makers she could locate. Luckily, Narda the dyer was available, too.

Netti was a doer by nature, not a manager or administrator; she disliked giving orders. Her strengths were her innate sense of proportion and design, her nimble fingers, and her diligence. Saturday night she was working alone as she had every night since the rush began, filling her self-imposed quota of Z-Zs (which exceeded Ziiza's) and reworking those that did not meet her standards, when she sat back, put her hand down, and jammed a sharp rush under her fingernail. She yanked it out, but a fragment remained, impossible to remove. "Yeeee-owwww," she cried, tears shooting from her eyes. She sucked her throbbing finger. Bit the nail. Anything to stop the pain. But it only increased. A headache hit and she collapsed, sobbing and rolling on the ground.

H&G was empty. So was the Mire-root agent's outlet (Po Mire was expanding), a thicket on the south side where you had to bend over, crawl through the bushes, give a password, and turn face up for recognition. Make yourself vulnerable, so he could club you if he did not like what he saw or heard, or make his getaway if you were the law – now absent from Beaverton these many months. Had she been thinking clearly, Netti would have known as much, but she crawled in anyway. On the chance she could find a Mire-root fragment on the ground. But she found nothing. She pounded her hand on the earth in frustration. Beat the sides of her head. Beating only made her dizzy and increased the pain. She sat alone, deep in the thicket, and wept. Then Netti swiped her eyes, crawled out, and ran toward South Trail.

Po Mire found her Sunday morning huddled against the tree at the meeting place by the silver lake. His helper was a tall, full-bearded, broad-shouldered young man, with sinewy arms and long-fingered, powerful hands. His waist and hips were so slim they seemed to belong to a smaller man. He grew large again, long legs with bulging thighs and sculpted calves. Young he was, but still older than the average Miree. On Po Mire's signal, the helper slid his arms under Netti and picked her up. "Ow," she cried on the movement, waving her finger, now swollen and purple. She rocked her head back and forth, but did not open her eyes.

At the edge of the Mire, Po Mire signaled a halt. He reached into his pouch, withdrew a Mire-root and masticated it to a pulp. He spit it on his hand, then, after loading his finger, shoved it into Netti's mouth. After working her jaw, trying to unclench it, he gave up and poked it in her cheek. He motioned the man to proceed. Po Mire led, counting, turning, never hesitating until they were standing on Mire Island's soft moss.

"Why, it's Netti!" gasped a Miree when he laid her between the shelter rows. It was her old acquaintance, Braids.

Mu Mire pushed through the Mirees, sized up the situation, and acted. She scored Netti's fingernail down the middle with her knife. Bit, splitting it open. A stream of blood shot up, hopefully including the tormenting sliver. Netti shrieked. "Sorry, Netti dear," Mu Mire said. "The only way." She smiled her contrived smile and asked, "Feel better?"

Netti clutched her bloody finger and sat up. Then, noticing the Mire-root packed in her cheek, she chewed and swallowed. "Much better, thank you," she said. A dozen hands shot out offering Mire-root. She took one, placed it in her mouth, and sighed.

"One more thing," Mu Mire said when she thought the Mire-root had taken effect, "then you can sleep." She took a skin strip from her wrist, wrapped it around Netti's finger, and tied it. "When it pains you too much, twist the knot. One pain cancels the other," she fibbed. "It's the best we can do." Netti's head spun. Trees swayed. Mire meadow's pale green carpet heaved and rolled in the sunshine.

Netti woke to the sound of blue-winged swamp flies buzzing, the mid-day sun's heat turning the shelter into a bake-oven, and the far-off voices of Mirees at work. The pain in her finger was down, almost to a pleasurable tingle, having been relieved by Mu Mire's ministrations and the Mire-root. But that was not what woke her.

A hand. Fingers. They must be fingers. Patting. Stroking. "Oh! Wha —" The hand covered her mouth. "Don't be afraid," whispered a voice. A man's deep and resonant voice. The hand eased off slightly. He spread his fingers, letting her breathe, but keeping it on so he could clap down if she screamed. Then, trusting that an agreement had been reached, he said, "Netti." She tensed at her name. He removed his hand and rested it on her hair. "I'm Shulders," he said. "I carried you here. Across the Mire." He paused again, giving her opportunity to speak. She said nothing, rolled over, and squinted. "I have to talk to you, Netti," he said. "Only you. May I come closer?"

She managed a trusting, "Yes."

He scrunched across the forbidden line and lay with his head on his arms. He inhaled, evidently more agitated than she. His breath smelled of sweet mint, not at all like pungent Mire-root, but she was too fuzzy to know what to make of it. She moved her hand and felt his soft beard. "They give me the day off to sleep when I work all night," he said. He looked up and down the shelter rows; no one was around. She must leave the Mire at once, he told her; it was an evil place. Happy, contented cultivators and packers of root? Mirees against the world? Rewarded with Mu Mire and Po Mire's lavish praise? Rewarded with all of the Mire-root they needed . . . even if their "needs" increased steadily? No, Nettie, that was just the beginning. Why had she never seen an older Miree? What happens to them? How happy, how proud, how united are the song-singers? What is the real purpose of the Sunday evening processions? This evening, in case she did not know.

He was planning to escape, he told her, sliding back into his shelter in case someone came near. Realized he had to get out. Wanted her to join him before it was too late. Too late for her. With his message spoken, he relaxed and smiled broadly. His story, briefly: He had come to the Mire in a moment of weakness, after a depressing event in his life that he could not shake. Something he had thought only Mire-root could cure. He waited for her to respond, a signal that she shared his pain. Understood that he understood. Nothing. Yes, he knew of her rescue by her muma, he continued; it was a whispered part of Mire Island's lore.

Po Mire had selected him to be his packer, to carry loads across the Mire all the way to his agents and selling points. He'd gotten too fat, too lazy, too rich to do that anymore. Besides, the load sizes were increasing; they were beyond his strength. As a reward Po Mire gave him a double Mire-root ration, which he threw away, then faked chewing, faked its effects. More importantly – he lowered his voice for the ultimate confidence – he had memorized the steps across the Mire. Practiced them each trip. Just as he practiced acting the dull pack animal. "I could do it with my eyes shut," he said with satisfaction. "I know the way and I'm pure of the root. And the round greedy man and his round greedy wife have no idea."

Shulders scanned the rows again, then crawled across and laid his hand on Netti's arm. "Will you come with me, Netti?"

She felt strength in his touch. Listened to the flies buzzing in the heat. Listened to Shulders' breathing, slow, deep, and questioning. Smelled the warm shelter mats overhead.

348

37

The B-town Run Away

Zııza HAD gone to bed early Saturday night. She had asked Netti to quit, told her she had done enough. But Netti had stayed on. Getting a good night's sleep before the race is the best thing I can do, Ziiza had thought. But she could not stop the details from rolling around in her head. The minute she closed out one problem, another took its place: Are there enough Z-Zs for last-minute sales? Do we have enough course monitors? Will the place pickers be quick enough? How will Mistermayor do as an announcer? Were teams a good idea? Do we have too many places? Too few places? Will the weather hold? Will the crowd be too small? Too large? Will Sufx keep his streak alive? What about Org? Govvi did not sleep well either; she rolled around, groaning. Edu and Dg did; she knew that as she lay touching them. His chest rose and fell under her hand with calm sleeping regularity. Dg sniffed, snorted, and ran his legs through his nighttime creature adventures.

* * *

Mistermayor stepped onto the ladder's first rung. He looked up at the platform lashed to the tall tree and put his foot back down. The ground felt firm and secure. The crudely-made ladder felt wobbly and terrifying. His two spotters leaned over and taking care not to drop their ThinStones, yelled, "Come on up, Mistermayor." And, "Hey, the view is unbelievable." Mistermayor fixed his eyes on the tree, pressed his lips together, and resolutely climbed the swaying ladder. Once up, he shed his fear, surveyed the crowded racecourse, and resumed his mayoral demeanor. "Ten minutes to starting time, Mistermayor," a spotter told him. "Time to introduce the runners."

The sky was clear. An early morning chill hung in the air. Ziiza and Quord Senior had moved the starting time up to avoid the late morning heat; this race was twice a long as the others. Mistermayor looked down. The elite runners stood on the starting line flopping their hands, jumping, their rocks strategically placed ahead. Behind them, the mass of runners gathered, packed so tightly that all they could do was stand and shiver under their rocks.

The course's difficulty was its length; there were no significant hills. Mistermayor's tree was the tallest fir in a meadow west of Outer Circle. The meadow was large enough for the runners to start en masse, then sort themselves out as they ran toward the Daughter River. At the beaver works the course turned south and ran by the ponds. This would be the worst of it, as the ground was still wet. It would be quickly churned into mud by hundreds of pounding feet. Possibly the whole course would end up that way, a maddening handicap for all but the leading runners. It continued south along the Daughter, through open country, to a solitary tree, a big-leaf maple covered with pale spring leaves. The turnaround tree.

Although the spotters could see as far as the maple they could not make out details. Therefore Mistermayor's commentary would go dead, so to speak, at midpoint. Thus a rock running first: Gstan and Edu stood by the maple, ThinStones in hand, ready to relay the news. "Testing: one, two, three," Edu said, squeezing his ThinStone. "Mistermayor, can you hear me?" After a pause, "He heard me, Gstan. We're all ready. Dg's ready, too." Dg lay against the maple holding the miniature Z-Z Netti had made for him with his paws, shredding it enthusiastically.

From the turnaround tree the course doubled back (something the slower runners would come to hate, because it dramatized the distance between them and the leaders). Then back upriver. But instead of returning along the ponds, it veered around the south edge of the woods, ran to Outer Circle, and doubled back onto the meadow for a short run to the finish. Ziiza wanted the runners to burst into view as they rounded the corner.

Ziiza climbed a few steps up the ladder and surveyed the runners: nary a one without a Z-Z under his or her rock. Govvi steadied the ladder. "Five minutes till starting time," Mistermayor boomed. He introduced the elite runners. Org raised his rock when his name was called. The Bloodies screamed. But when Sufx was introduced the crowd erupted. With that, the Z-sport team (none of whom were actual Z-sport employees) jumped on top of their rocks and sang the Original Z-sport Company song:

We've got rocks on our heads
And maybe in 'em, too.
But never mind, my friend
'Cause I'm ahead of you.

Ziiza joined in the chorus. Govvi hid behind the tree. Mistermayor, high above, smiled and waved his arms, mock-leading the song.

Rock, rock, rock, rock.
Run, run, run, run.
Win, win, win, win.
Z-sport! Z-sport!
Rah! Rah! Rah!

The starting line was marked by two boulders, each waist-high on a man. Polcat the honorary starter stood on one boulder feeling for a flat spot with his toes, anxious to begin his speech. Quord Senior, the official starter, Quord Senior, the esteemed "popa of rock running," leaned on the boulder preparing to do his duty. Next to the opposite boulder that created the start and finish line stood an enormous man – or man-creature – or creature-man – two heads taller than anyone, thick-chested, long-armed, and except for his face, covered with matted black-brown hair. His head was small in proportion to his body, and his yellow eyes, which he blinked constantly as if not accustomed to the light, were smaller still. Either from fear of the man-creature or the revolting stench wafting from him, the space around him grew. The man-creature rested his hand on the boulder. On catching his odor Mistermayor looked down in amazement and said, "Stomp! Stomp! I've heard about you. But I've never seen you. Never had the pleasure." But it was race time, not Stomp time. He pointed at Polcat and said, "Take it, Polcat, it's yours."

Polcat raised his hand and waited for the expected reaction, which was not forthcoming, as every eye was on Stomp. He scowled and began: "Thank you, Mistermayor. Thank you, ladies and gentlemen, for this honor. And thank you, Ziiza, for organizing what I hope will be the first of many B-town Run Aways." Ziiza waved from the ladder. He continued: "And thank you, fellow council members, for approving this race. Beaverton has been through the most trying winter in its history. But we made it. Yes, we made it on short rations and a monetary system that leaves much to be desired." Scattered hoots and boos. "No, my friends, we, the sons and daughters of the beaver, are not licked." He paused and cocked his ear. A few eyes turned from Stomp, who stood balanced on one foot, the other sticking out behind, his arms thrust front and back as if running. No applause. "Not licked, I say. And this splendid rock running event proves it. Hungry all winter, yes. But look at these splendid athletes, trim, fit, and –"

Mistermayor circled his hand at Quord Senior in a let's-get-going motion. Senior said, "Excuse me, Polcat." Then, through a rolled-up alder bark cone, he barked: "Runners! Lift! Your! Rocks!"

Polcat paid no attention. "Athletes. The pride of Beaverton. And of the valley of the giant beaver. Strive to do yourselves proud this beautific spring morning. For I see a future for Beaverton that I will describe in detail later in my address. But first I would like to pay my respects to –"

"Get! Set!"

"Yes. I see some of you are anxious to begin. I shall be brief. First, I am pleased to announce I am nominating our own Sister Sissi as Entrepreneur of the Year for her popular Konka Sanctuary hot beverage and conversation establishments. Growing by leaps and bounds, I'm told. Although I remain a tea drinker, myself."

"Go!"

Org and Sufx leapt forward, along with Junior and the elites. The semi-competitive runners seeded just behind followed quickly. Then the mass of rock-topped humanity moved forward, first in a just-get-moving shuffle, then a walk, then a half-run, and finally full stride. The sequence repeated itself over and over, wave after wave, until everyone was moving.

Except the man-creature Stomp, who stood frozen in his artificial running position. As the runners passed from view and the cheering died down, eyes returned to him – if you could call him a him. Mistermayor leaned dangerously over the rail. Stomp blinked, turned his head, and wrapped his hairy arms around the second starting line boulder, the one opposite Polcat's. He leaned into it, rocked it, broke it free of the earth that held it. Then, with great effort (no *man* would consider trying) he hoisted it onto his shoulder, cocked his head to one side, and straightened his legs. All without a grunt or a sound. Astonished, the crowd cheered. Stomp took a halting step. Then another. Then faster, breaking into a loping, bent-kneed run, striding, striding, leaving enormous footprints, so great was his burden along with his own tremendous weight.

The first course monitor called on his ThinStone. "Can you hear me, Mistermayor?"

"I can't hear you, sir. But I read you. You're coming through in my mind, remember?" Mistermayor chuckled at his with-it commentary. "Yes, I understand. What have you got? My people are starving for news."

"Very funny, sir," said the monitor. "Anyway. Sufx just passed me, leading of course. But Org's strong, running easy, just a ways behind. Very few stopping for water. Good sign."

Mistermayor repeated this to the crowd and called J. Belly, the next monitor. (Ziiza had hired J. Belly and her troupe of belly dancers to inspire and entertain the runners.) "Lead pack's just passed," J. Belly reported. "First men's team through: Blood, Sweat, and Slooze. Rock Rage very much in contention. Stone Sober rolling. That's all. Signing off, Mistermayor. Dance time."

As Mistermayor spoke, Bitta and Hobart deep in the crowd relayed the news. Polcat, still on the other starting line boulder, continued his address.

"Lead runners now by the ponds," Mistermayor said, "Trail going to mud. This in on the women's teams: Rockettes leading Crushed Lips. Z-Z Chicks coming on strong. Yes, yes, a report from the turnaround. Gstan? What have you got? Says something strange is happening. Can't tell what. Report back soon. Back to the ponds. Uh-oh, just what I'd feared. Runners floundering in the mud. Dropped rocks. Disqualifications." Mistermayor shrugged as if to say, that's rock running for you.

He continued: "Somebody give me something on the company and nonprofit teams. Pleeeeeze. Now, what have you got? Advanced Granite Devices doing well. Probably leading their division. New Stone Age Congregation challenging the Sea Trace Survivors."

Mistermayor's winter of worry slipped away and his vigorous, voluble self returned. "Men's update: Rock Rage falling apart. Two runners down. They're out of it. Buns of Stone tightening.

"More in on the women: Konka Dregs making it nicely through the muck. Almost out. Sister Sissi herself could very well be the lead woman. Can't tell. Mud, mud, mud. Runners having trouble holding onto their rocks."

By this time the news was coming in so fast both spotters were on ThinStones, bypassing Mistermayor, yelling directly to the people below. But he had more than enough to keep him busy. "Gstan, or is it little Edu, what have you got? Giant runner he says. Never seen before. Approaching the maple tree. Enormous rock. Enormous stride. Unbelievably fast. That's Stomp, Gstan, he just showed up and jumped into the race. Unregistered. What was that? Sufx, Org, and the lead pack. Not even close. Looks like we've got an upset in the making, folks. Trouble for the favorites. And I might add for you gamblers." Mistermayor chuckled; he could not help it.

"We're getting this in real time from Gstan and little Edu at the turnaround, folks. Stomp, it has to be him, is approaching. Way ahead of everyone. The others coming off the ponds. Stomp's rounding the maple. Dg's chasing him, barking, biting his legs. 'Dg, you come back here right now!' Confusing, folks. I can't tell whether they're talking to me, to themselves, or to Dg. But hey! What did you say, Gstan? I can't believe this. Stomp didn't make the turn! He's running straight ahead. Down the river. Across the meadow. Into the forest. Gstan thinks . . . Yes, Gstan thinks . . . *He's stealing the boulder.* He's stealing the boulder, ladies and gentlemen. Stealing the boulder. That's what he wanted. The boulder. Good gracious, what if he'd won?

"Whew. That was a heart-stopper, folks. You'd think Ziiza had planned it. Anyhow we have a real race now. Sufx rounds the maple tree in first place by twenty steps. Org in second but running well. Very much in contact. They've opened up a good space between them and the pack, though. Now the pack, rounding the tree. Eight or nine. Junior in the middle. Pained look on his face.

"Women's teams update: Crushed Lips closing the gap on Rockettes. Rock Candy's still hustling. Men's teams: What's that? Stone Sober in third or fourth? Absolutely amazing. Gravel Eaters chewing it up. More on company and non-profits: Provido's Kidney Stones stuck in the middle. Grassyknoll Grads failing. Glacial Erotics grinding to a halt. Thundereggs rolling. And Banal Chatter, the Errix team, is walking, and talking, on their ThinStones. That's all they want to do: talk, talk, talk.

"Take a last sip of your Konkas, good people," Mistermayor could hardly contain his excitement, "because the leaders have left the river and are running along the woods. And can you believe, Org is gaining on Sufx. Never, in the history of rock running." (Mistermayor was fed this tidbit by a spotter.) "Org's drawing up," he continued. "Ten steps back. Sufx struggling. Yes, struggling."

Ziiza felt woozy and grabbed the ladder to steady herself. She let go. Her hands shook so violently she had to grab it again. Mistermayor high above was super-energized by the excitement and the attention focused on him. Energy draining out of her and into him? She wanted Sufx to win, carry the Z-sport banner, continue his unbeaten record. But yet . . . Org was her son, her flesh and blood. He had never won. The screams grew louder.

I've got to get away for a minute, Ziiza thought. Have to calm myself down. My heart is racing. She let go of the ladder and walked down the racecourse. The spectators, held back by ropes and course monitors, paid no attention to her. Or she to them.

"Sufx and Org, approaching," Mistermayor screamed. "On the far side. Behind the trees. Get ready for a fight to the finish."

Ziiza walked back on the meadow, sucking air, clutching her sides to keep her hands from shaking. Sweat ran down her cheeks, the excitement and the burden of a sleepless night pressing down. She saw an opening, a narrow path through the trees, stepped in, and leaned against a tree limb. She breathed deeply, slowly, then exhaled until she could expel no more. Under control now, she took a long, slow breath, lowered her head on the limb, and rested her eyes.

Crash. Snap. Crash. Ziiza snapped her head up. She rubbed her eyes as if she had fallen asleep. Footfalls. Grunting. Forced breathing of someone who cannot get enough air.. Desperate breathing . . . of a runner . . . with a rock. Covered with mud and sweat and blood. Plop, plop. His feet hit the muddy path. In an instant. He burst past her and onto the course. She blinked and realized. A cheater. A corner cutter.

Ziiza wobbled into the open. Just in time to see Sufx run by.

"Org's in the lead," Mistermayor screamed. "Coming in strong. Almost home. There's Sufx. Running hard. Can he catch him?"

Sufx had no chance. He was fast, powerful, and determined, but he was too far back. And in this mud? As he crossed the line, Org lifted his rock and pushed it in front of him. It landed with a resounding plop, splashing the finish-line huggers. The Bloodies broke through the ropes and swarmed him, hugging, pounding, kissing, licking, smearing. One count. Two counts. Sufx leaned his rock across the line and let it take him down.

High in the tree Mistermayor, at the prompting of his spotters, screamed at the crowd to stay off the course. "Stay back! Please stay back! Runners coming in. Hundreds more to finish."

As the runners streamed by, Polcat stood on his boulder talking, as he had done throughout the race. His dry voice crackled as he concluded: "And so, my friends, we close this race for glory. My congratulations to the winner, and indeed to all of the participants. For it is the participation, not the time or place that wins the day. You are all winners. And I congratulate my colleague, Mistermayor, for his thrilling step-by-step announcing. And most of all, I congratulate the people of Beaverton, of whom I am so proud." He looked around, turning full circle, waiting for a reaction. By this time, anything would do. But no one was paying attention. Seeing no other way to get down from the boulder, he jumped. As he hit, a shaft of pain shot up his leg, and he toppled inelegantly into the mud.

What remained of the lead pack streamed in, most running strong. Then in singles and doubles. The first of the teams: Blood, Sweat, and Slooze. The rest? Who could tell? Then a steady file which widened, two, three, four abreast, jostling, swinging wide, runners surging to pass just one more rival.

The finish line clogged up with exhausted but (mostly) happy runners, joyous fans, and relatives. The honor of it, finishing the longest, most demanding race in rock running history! Jettisoned rocks piled up. "Runners, runners. Please, please," Mistermayor cried, "hang onto your rocks. Take them away." The finishing runners tripped and went down, compounding the problem.

Ziiza waited next to the trees, well away from the blurry crowd, twisting her feet in the mud. "Well done. Well done. You made it." Clapping and cheering. As always, extra applause for the stragglers. When most of the cheering had stopped, she pulled a final deep breath, straightened her back, wiped her eyes, walked to the ladder, and waited until Mistermayor had quieted everyone.

He introduced Ziiza and Quord Senior for the awards presentation. Forcing smile after smile, she hung award after award – Netti-woven neck chains with agate pendants – on the place-winners' necks. Every team received one because the awards extended down to tenth place. The men's team winner: Blood, Sweat, and Slooze, as expected. The women's: Rock Candy had overtaken the early leaders. Company and nonprofit: Advanced Granite Devices.

Sister Sissi won her age group and placed second among women overall, an amazing accomplishment. (Oosa, a much younger woman, finished ahead of her.) And so Ziiza and Senior hugged and shook hands with them all: team winners, serious competitors, afterthought runners, young, old, some very old. Then the open class. Tenth place. Ninth. And on to second.

As Ziiza hung his award around his neck, Sufx whispered, "Ziiza, Ziiza, I'm sorry. So sorry. I don't know how he got in front of me. Couldn't see. Sweat and mud in my eyes. Everything. By the time I realized, he was over the line."

Ziiza's mind spun. Don't accept it, she wanted to tell him. I saw what happened. I know. Throw off your award. Grind it into the mud and walk away. File a protest with Senior. Right now. Her breath was hot on his face, the words about to spill out, but through chattering teeth, she said, "You did fine, Sufx, just fine." She stepped back and smiled at him through what were supposed to be tears of joy.

Org strode up, Hids and Grues clinging to him, pawing, licking. "Please give way," Mistermayor pleaded with the Bloodies. "Let him receive his award." They parted slightly as Ziiza approached. Org stood stiff and tall, sporting an I-won-without-a-Z-Z smirk. Ziiza shrank back as he approached; he and his Bloodies smelled as bad as Stomp. He accepted his neck chain without bending his head. Ziiza slid her hand under his bloody, matted hair and pulled until he got the message. He lowered his face and she kissed him. She stood back, forced a very hard but very necessary smile, and said, "Congratulations, Org. You've worked very hard for this." Leaving the next sentence unspoken, she turned and walked away.

38

Netti's Rescue, Again

As THE B-town Run Away progressed, Little Sac planted his foot on the bank of the North-flowing Son and raised his hand, halting the Swarm City Brigade. Barclaw, already there, turned to him and said, "We've made it, Commander. Beaverton town is just over those green hills. How beautiful they look, if you don't mind my saying so."

Little Sac's men snaked their way along the narrow trail. One by one they spread out on the bank and gazed across the water, hardly comprehending that their journey was over. The first half of it. When they had collected, Little Sac nodded an order to his trail master. The man shouted, "Lower your packs. And take care." The brigadesmen, four dozen or so, slipped their straps, let their packs fall to arms length, and set them on the ground. Of the blind groins who had started the journey, not one was present.

It took a moment for Barclaw to notice the two figures waving at them from across the river. "Pop&Jay," he said, turning to Little Sac, "knaves for sure."

"Really," replied Little Sac, who had been squinting at them all along, "I'd like to meet them."

"You will, pretty soon," Barclaw said with a disgusted turn of his mouth. "Here they come."

Pop&Jay stroked across. By this time the men were soaking their bruised and swollen feet in the cool water. And for the first time in days they were not complaining. The canoes grounded and Pop&Jay waded toward them. Barclaw hesitated, not knowing how to introduce his old adversaries. Then to his astonishment Pop walked up to Little Sac, shook his hand as if greeting an old friend, and said, "A pleasure to see you, Commander. Pleasant journey?" Barclaw's jaw dropped and hung. Little Sac glared at Pop. "Oh, yes," Pop continued. "I'm Pop and that guy stumbling up the bank there, that's Jay." He elbowed Jay in the chest when he reached them, and said, "Pop&Jay, sir, proprietors, developers, sub-dividers, marketers, surveyors, and co-mayors of Popville, which you see before you in all of its incipient splendor."

"We'll see about that," Jay muttered, playing along. Then brightening, "Please accept our hospitality."

The men shuttled across the river. They unloaded and camped, one trail shelter per Pop&Jay subdivision lot. Military discipline was relaxed for the first time in months and the men scattered to do what they liked – fish, loaf, sleep – as long as they did not use the trail over the hill. With the men occupied Little Sac called Barclaw to him and in full hearing of Pop&Jay said, "Ambassador Barclaw, I have a job for you."

Barclaw bristled; Little Sac had not given him a direct order before. Not once on the whole journey. Now in front of them, his, Popamayor's, and Mistermayor's old enemies. The disgraced ones. The banished. The pests. "Yo, Commander," was all he could think to say.

"I want a meeting in Beaverton. Tomorrow. Noon sharp. At the bank. Beaverton Bank."

"Font's Bank? But Commander. It's Mistermayor. He wants to see you first. Then the council. I thought . . ."

"Font's Bank at noon. And Ambassador, I want Beaverton's big financial players in attendance. You know who they are. Well, Font the banker knows. The officials you mentioned are welcome to attend but they are not necessary."

Barclaw looked away, not wanting Pop&Jay or Little Sac or any of the lounging brigadesmen to see the alarm in his eyes. This was not the way he had expected it to go. Not at all. Little Sac should meet with Mistermayor first. Then the council. Discuss money and food and the future. Although the painful fact was that much of the emergency food they had started with had been consumed along the way. And one by one as the food packs emptied, the groins had been cut loose from the rope-line to sniff and snort, trying to follow, only to stumble and fall back, and eventually starve and freeze. He had been powerless to interfere. Little Sac's cruelty. One against a brigade. However much it galled him, he had had to overlook it. For the greater goal, saving Beaverton.

Barclaw raised his hand to Little Sac, imitating a brigadesman's salute, and headed up the west hills. And down. Until after part of an autumn, all of a winter, and most of a spring, he stepped onto Outer Circle. Welcome to Exciting Beaverton. Well, he thought, the old sign is the same. He gave it an affectionate journey's end pat and strode into town.

"Barclaw's back! Barclaw's back!" That should have been the cry. Or something like that. But no one was around except an old woman planting her garden, who recognized him and greeted him and would have run to hug him if she could have. "They're all at the big running away," she said through broken teeth.

"What, grandmuma? I don't understand."

"The rocky race on the other side of town," she cackled. "They're all over there."

"Oh, I see." He slowed and walked and thought. When he reached H&G it was deserted, too. On Sunday. He came to his office and storytelling station. He patted it and walked on. Is this bad news or good news? He met some spectators returning from the race. "Constable Barclaw, is it you? We thought you were dead. Never expected to see you again." And they looked at him as if he were dead. "Yes, yes, the race. And you'll never believe it: Org has beaten Sufx. Fantastic finish." They did not appear to Barclaw to be starving. They were healthy-looking. And strong. And happy. Completely absorbed in this "big running away," as the old woman had called it. They swept on by. Others came, then many. H&G returned to its accustomed Sunday din. He heard Skedaddle playing. "Mistermayor?" he inquired. Yes, he announced the race, one told him. Probably still there. Polcat, too.

"Barclaw!" Mistermayor screamed when he saw him walking toward him as if in a daze. "Barclaw, you made it!" he screamed even louder. Mistermayor and Polcat rushed him, thumped his back, shook his hand. Bitta, who had been interviewing a runner, stopped speechless, trembling with excitement.

Barclaw told his story in abbreviated fashion: the long walk east, Swarm City, the pointed tower, his audience with Sac the Magnificent, the easy negotiations. Nothing about the beautiful Mavva, the parties, the blind groins, the wealthy few, the oppressed many, and Sac's absolute power. But he had to tell them about Little Sac's brigade because it was here, just over the hill. And the ultimate degradation; Little Sac wanted to meet with Font, not Mistermayor. Tomorrow at noon. They stood in silence thinking it over.

Well, Barclaw," Mistermayor said after a good long while, "You'd better see Font. Set it up. If you can find him. I didn't see him at the race."

News of Barclaw's return spread fast (but did not overcome the buzz of Org's upset), aided in great measure by Bitta the redoubtable reporter who had two sensational stories and could not stop talking. One eager listener was Govvi. Upon hearing Bitta, and confirming the rumors she had heard, she walked nonchalantly toward South Trail's intersection with Outer Circle. She turned east, walked to the Exciting sign, then up and over the hill. At Pop&Jay's she met Little Sac. She built a small fire, then a larger one for the brigadesmen, a good distance from the first. Pop&Jay, Little Sac, and Govvi talked through the moonrise, watched its reflection on the river, listened to spring chirruping sounds, and talked some more.

* * *

Miles south of Beaverton, miles south of the encampment at Pop&Jay's, Braids washed Netti's hair and rubbed her temples while slipping bits of crushed Mire-root in her mouth. Although Sunday afternoon was normally work time on Mire Island, Netti had not been assigned to a crew or any duties at all. She was in what Mu Mire called "welcome and recovery time."

"Feeling better, Netti?" Braids asked. "Do you think you can stand up for the procession? So beautiful and inspiring. I dream about it. Don't you?"

Netti smiled weakly, relieved and thankful for the rub, and said, "I've never seen it. No, never."

"You've a treat in store. Just a couple of hours off. Mu Mire and Po Mire each pick someone for private enlightenment. That's what they call it." Braids giggled. "A girl. A guy. You could get lucky."

At the end of the day the male Mirees stood, not exactly at attention but stiff, anticipatory, attentive, in front of their shelters. The females stood three paces away, facing them across the stay-away zone. Both groups had spent the day gathering flowers, water lilies mostly, and stripping off the petals.

Two Mirees, a man and a woman Netti had not seen before, picked up baskets of petals and walked slowly down the rows. As they passed, the Mirees scooped armfuls and held them to their chests. Some spilled and fluttered to the ground. Trying to remain formally upright, they kicked the stray petals in front of them so that if they could not throw them at Mu Mire and Po Mire as they passed, the pair could at least walk on them. But flower petals do not kick well. The Mirees clutched and kicked and sneaked glances toward their leaders' shelters, while the basket bearers sang the processional:

Our home,
Our protector,
One love,
Our Mire.

Our home,
Our protector,
One love,
Our Mire.

Each newly-supplied Miree picked it up. When all were singing, the bearers set their baskets down, turned, and faced the lines. Twenty-some voices sang:

Our home,
Our protector,
One love,
Our Mire.

Our home,
Our protector,
One love,
Our Mire.

Faster still and louder, running the words together:

Our home our protector one love our Mire.
Our home our protector one love our Mire.
Our home our protector one love our Mire.
Our home our protector one love our Mire.

"Stop!" screamed a basket bearer. Netti swung round to see Mu Mire and Po Mire standing, arms upraised, white ceremonial robes flung open. Po Mire stepped ahead. Then as if to make certain everyone knew what was happening they sidestepped to the opposite rows, he on the female side, she on the male. They walked forward between the rows, in step with the chant, hesitating with every verse. Petals fluttered, landing on shoulders and heads, mostly falling on the ground. When they reached the end they waited as the basket bearers re-supplied the Mirees. Mu Mire and Po Mire retraced their steps, crow eyes peering between creases of fat, appraising each Miree. The basket bearers chanted in duet:

One love,
Our Mire.
One love,
Our Mire.

Mu Mire stopped in front of a slim man, one of the youngest. Smiled. A smile of congratulation? For him? A smile of self-satisfaction? For herself? Impossible to tell. She held out her hand. He placed his trembling hand in hers. They walked toward her shelter and went inside.

Po Mire continued walking the rows like a shopper who has made up his mind but feigns interest in other goods so the vendor does not detect his itch and raise the price. Not that he had to play the game; the price would not change. Not that every Miree did not know. Except Netti, who stood, a head taller than the other females, twisting her feet, trying to disappear into the moss.

Po Mire led Netti to his shelter. As he did, the bearers walked the rows dispensing generous handfuls of Mire-root. Inside he held up a small bowl filled with root, obviously the select of the select, offering it to her. She shook her head. Seemingly taking no offense, he turned away, slipped off his robe, and shook the petals off. He swiped his head to make sure none remained. All the time he listened and waited, waited for the chattering to die down, waited for the Mirees to retire to their shelters and chew themselves into their dreams. Netti waited with him, waited for her enlightenment to begin.

Po Mire busied himself, ignoring Netti. Only after her eyes had adjusted to the dimness did she realize she had never seen a shelter as luxurious as this. Nothing in Beaverton. Not Mistermayor's. Not Sister Sissi's after she had switched from café charity to Konka Sanctuary entrepreneurship. Not Gstan's burrow after he had hit it big with ThinStones. Not Wife Dragga's. Not even her own family's shelter after Ziiza's decorating splurge. The walls, roof, even the floor, were covered with pale fur – possibly precious watabeast. She looked again at the root bowl. It sparkled with lava flower stones. A fortune right there, she thought. Cases and chests. In corners and recesses. What did they contain? Was Mu Mire's shelter as lavish as his? And why did they live separately? Or appear to do so?

Po Mire leapt on her with a swiftness that belied his corpulence. In a smooth practiced motion he pulled her fur to her waist, flung her onto his robe, and pressed his body on hers. Anticipating her scream, he covered her mouth, then kissed her cheek, her ear, her neck. He gave way slightly, exhaled putrid breath, and slipped his hand away from her mouth. Crushed her lips with his. Her hands bounced off his fat back. She clawed at him. His hands slid to her breasts. To her hips.

Her basket! She felt frantically for the shoulder strap. Bit it apart. She jerked the basket over his head. He snarled, puffed, and rolled. Netti rolled with him, wrapping the sharp-edged straps around and around his neck, cutting into rolls of sweaty flesh. She looped the straps with strong practiced fingers, pulled them tight, and tied the knot she had tied a thousand times before. She let go and flung her hands in the air, victorious – and terrified. Po Mire was under her now, beating wildly, frantically. He rolled, moaning, gasping, clawing the basket.

Netti burst through the opening and ran down the rows. Shulders lay half out of his shelter. "Shulders! Shulders!" she whispered hoarsely as she fell to her knees. She punched his arm to wake him. "You were right. I believe you. I've got to –"

"Shhhh, Netti," he said. "I'm awake. I've been waiting. Are you ready?"

Netti collapsed on him, sobbing. "My basket. I tied it on his head. He'll get it off. Soon. Please Shulders, get me out of here."

Shulders pulled a pack from the shelter, and said, "Not get *you* out, Netti. Get *us* out. We're leaving the Mire forever. My head is clear, and from the sound of you, so is yours." He took her hand and helped her up. "Quiet, now," he whispered. "Anything you want to take?" She shook her head.

They needn't have worried. Only swamp sounds and forest sounds beyond. And Po Mire thrashing around, trying to get the basket off. But the more he tugged and twisted, the tighter it became, gripping his neck in a chokehold. He stood wobbling, holding onto the shelter pole, sucking air through the basket. Netti looked, saw his dark form lurch from the shelter, stagger ahead and zigzag across the meadow. She and Shulders went to their knees and waited. After what seemed hours, they heard splashing on the root-growing side of the island.

"One, two, three. Left, one and two," Shulders counted in his deep voice, not making any attempt to keep it low. They were in the middle now without a misstep or wet leg. The moon, just up, lit the Mire in a soft gray-green. The night sounds fell, as if to assist their passage. Netti did not look back at the island; they could not be followed. She squeezed his hand. It was only then, as the moonlight threw his shadow alongside hers, that she realized how tall, how broad-shouldered he was. Yet like herself how vulnerable. And how at peace she felt. Here she was in what should have been a mad, desperate run – and she did not want it to end. "Seven, eight, nine," Shulders counted. "Right two, three. Now left, one, two. . . . " Did not want the crossing to end. Clear heads. We've got clear heads. That's what he had said. And it was true. Walking on the dangerous, undulating surface, their long shadows leading, her head *was* clear. Not only of Mire-root effect, but of headache pain. Oh, she did not think she was cured, headache-free forever. Too much to hope for. But if not that, a state of suspension. At least for the moment. She was so grateful for that.

39

Banks Run Everything

It WAS all Ziiza could do to wait until dawn Monday morning. She had not slept the night before the Run Away or the night after, the former worrying about race details, the latter worrying about Org's shortcut win. Of course she had other things to worry about: Netti's disappearance (another rescue party to the Mire?), Smoke-storm's imminent eruption (the mountain was belching and shaking; Mistermayor's lookouts had fled). Barclaw was back. What about it? Food was not a problem. They had made it through the winter. They were hungry but getting by, learning to live without beaver, going back to the old foods: field grains, berries, tree fruits, fish, and crawfish, plus seafood brought in from the coast. Not so bad. But money. Commerce and exchange. Since it was linked to the beaver, the situation could not be worse.

Ziiza turned it over and over. Org had cheated, but he was her son. If she confronted him, or went to Bitta or Senior, he would be lost to her – and she had lost enough children. On the other hand Sufx represented Z-sport, *was* Z-sport to the public, and had lost unfairly. "So Sufx is not invincible, eh?" "So old Org won bare-headed after all." "So Z-Zs are not worth it, are they?" Sufx could not lodge a protest. He had been blinded by sweat and mud, had no proof, no witness – that he knew of. If Mistermayor or the spotters or the course monitors or anyone else had noticed, they would have said something by now. But no one had.

Ziiza did not expect Litti to be home. She knew her habits, where she might be, and what she and Arbo might be doing this morning. She lay on her back, eyes tight, waiting for the morning light. Edu slept next to her, clutching Dg. Govvi had come in late. Ziiza had mumbled a good night and made nothing of it.

"You don't have to go to school today if you don't want to," Ziiza told Edu as he rose. She flopped over and pulled the robe over her head.

"Thanks, Muma, but I've been away and I miss it." He dressed, tossed Dg some food, and walked out. He liked to get to school before the others, before Addle even, to sit on top of the knoll and watch the morning open up. Predict the weather. He did his best thinking there, he said. Her youngest – her only? – boy, thinking big little boy thoughts.

Ziiza took the long way to Water Child. She wanted to spend the time, slow the trip, and above all avoid the Run Away's muddy tracks. She had had enough of that: the screaming crowd, the tension, the complexity, the effort, the uncertainty, the result.

Ziiza paid Great-great-great-grandpopa Monumentree her respects from a distance. "Good morning, Honored Monumentree." The wet meadow grass felt good slapping her ankles. In a few weeks it would slap her thighs. Where Water Child turned into the forest, she followed. The trail was in poor condition after the winter: many downed trees, fallen limbs, and shattered bushes, even though there had been no deep snows or windstorms. The slow going was all right with her.

When she entered the clearing her eyes went first to the waterfall. Then to the pool. No one. Then to a pile of dirt in the middle of the glade. She advanced. "Litti? Litti?" she called.

Litti sat next to a hole, the source of the dirt pile, bent over, rocking. "Good morning, Litti," Ziiza said. Litti mumbled faraway words. Ziiza looked into the hole and recoiled in horror. A body. No, not a body. Parts of a body. A severed leg, a slashed thigh with calf and foot attached. Ziiza flung herself onto Litti to cover the sight. Litti rocked against her. Ziiza wrapped her fur around and held her tight.

"Arbo-sita," Litti mumbled through the fur.

"Yes, Litti dear." Ziiza struggled to compose herself and said. "I know. Let's move back from the edge. So you don't see."

It was clear. At least part of it. The sita had fallen into the pit as intended, killed Arbo, clawed its way out, and run off. But what about Arbo? What had happened? How did he get into the pit? "Let's go, Litti," Ziiza said. "Away from here. There's nothing we can do for him now." She slid her arms around Litti to help her up. She was dead weight, did not move.

Litti stopped rocking, shuddered, and said, "Arbo-sita."

"Litti, tell me where we are. What's the name of this place?"

Litti looked ahead with vacant eyes.

"Litti, please. Just answer the question. Anything. Say your name."

"Arbo-sita."

It was Ziiza's turn to tremble. "If I have to drag you away from this horrible sight, so be it." She grabbed her under the arms and pulled her across the grass. "There," she said when they reached the pool, "stick your feet in the water. Listen to the waterfall." Ziiza put her arm around her and stuck her own feet in. Litti resumed rocking, her reflection vibrating on the surface.

"Litti," Ziiza said. "I would never have come, never invaded your privacy, if I didn't need to talk. Please understand."

"Arbo-sita."

"Please, Litti, you're not making sense."

"Arbo-sita," Litti mumbled on top of Ziiza's sentence.

"Maybe if I talk to you in your own voice. Will you come back? Snap out of it? I have to try. For both our sakes." She hugged Litti and rocked with her.

"Arbo-sita."

"Yes, I know, Litti. But here goes." She drew in a breath.

"Water Child," she said, imitating Litti's voice. "Water Child welcomes and soothes."

Ziiza switched to her own voice. "Org won the race yesterday, Litti. The B-town Run Away. But he cheated. I saw him. I'm the only one who did. I've said nothing, but I must do something about it. I just don't know if I can face the consequences. I can't lose another child. And I will. He's gone from sullen and distant, to rebellious, to downright hostile. Hostile to me, his very muma. You know most of that. His jealousy of Sufx goes beyond racing and winning; he hates him. He's angry with me, angry for making Sufx Z-sport's advertising hero. But I asked him first. Begged him, practically. I only asked Sufx after he refused to run with a Z-Z. His crazy idea about running pure."

Litti speeded up her rocking and stopped muttering. Ziiza let go and faced her. "Is that recognition? Litti, do you understand? I have to believe you do. I'm asking for your help. You're the one. The only one. Please tell me what to do."

"I'm thinking thinks," Ziiza said as Litti. "Honors are at stake, friend Ziiza. You must decide. And in your heart you already have."

"Thank you, Litti," Ziiza said, resuming her own voice. "Hearing it from you, it's so obvious." She stood up ankle deep in the pool and took Litti's hands. She walked her to the middle, closer to the falls. Ziiza cupped her hands, stuck them into the falls, and trickled water down Litti's back. "Water Child soothes," she said against the sound. She poured water over Litti's head, placed both hands on her slick black hair, and thought: this is the most beautiful and peaceful place I've ever seen, and only a few paces away, a sight of unbelievable ghastliness.

"Come on, Litti," Ziiza said, leading her to the bank. "Feeling better? Sit here." She pressed on Litti's shoulders and she sank to the ground. "I'll be right back." Ziiza walked to the pit. Good, she thought, glancing back at Litti sitting still, looking the other way. She scooped up a handful of dirt and threw it in. She pushed dirt over the edge with Arbo's digging board. Out of respect. She had to. For Litti. For him. She would send someone to fill in the pit later. Or maybe she would not.

Ziiza led Litti to the trail. She walked slowly, hunched over like an old woman. But she walked. Away from Water Child. She stumbled and tripped over roots and stones she had skipped over a few hours before. "And you, Litti?" Ziiza asked. "Have we helped? Water Child and me. Can you speak to me, now that we are away? Look, there's Great-great-great-grandpopa Monumentree off in the distance," she came down hard on each word, hoping to jar her out of it, "your symbol of strength and endurance. What do you say?"

"Arbo-sita."

Ziiza cringed and led her back to Beaverton.

* * *

The sight of the man's bare back took Ziiza's breath away, plates of muscle connecting his arms, deep, bumpy backbone depression, the powerful slope of his shoulders, so much so she almost overlooked the woman beside him. They sat, touching, legs drawn up, watching the path traffic in front of her shelter. "Netti!" Ziiza cried. "You're back. Are you all right?" She tugged at Litti's arm to make her speed up, but she did not respond. Ziiza left her and ran. "Why, Netti. You . . . you look wonderful."

"Muma, I would like you to meet Shulders," Netti said. He gave Ziiza an enormous grin. "Shulders, this is my muma, Ziiza."

"Well," was all Ziiza could say.

They look so right. So perfect together.

The gangly, despondent, workaday girl of a week ago – transformed. We're pledged, Muma, Ziiza expected her to say. But she did not. Going to be? She waited expectantly.

Netti looked at Ziiza serenely and said, "The short of it, Muma, is he saved me from the Mire." Shulders made a dismissive gesture and smiled again, this time sheepishly. "We're free of the Mire-root and we're going to help each other stay that way." She rubbed his arm playfully, as if embarrassed to take his hand in front of Ziiza; she had not had a man friend before. "We can talk of it later, if you like, but that's it. Oh, hello, Litti. Litti, I would like you to meet my friend, Shulders." Litti looked through them and said nothing.

"Litti," Ziiza said, "this is Netti's friend, Shulders." She spoke as if prompting a child. "What do you say, Litti?" She did not respond. Ziiza tried again. "Netti told me she was free of the Mire-root. Doesn't that make you happy?"

"Headaches much better, too," Netti added, picking up on it.

Litti opened her mouth, closed it, opened it again and said, "Arbo-sita."

"Oh, no," Ziiza said. "Oh, no." Then to Netti and Shulders: "She's had a terrible shock. It appears Arbo dug a pit to catch a sita. What he thought might be a sita. No one has seen one for years. He'd been trying to sight it for a long time. Not to capture, just to examine it, he said. But somehow he fell in. Probably. No one saw it happen. Litti found his body, or what was left of it, in the pit. The sita was gone, but there was clear evidence. Nothing else leaves claw marks like that. I've tried everything but she's still in shock. That's all she's said since I found her. 'Arbo-sita.'"

Edu and Dg appeared, back from school. He hugged Netti and shook Shulders' hand. Dg sniffed Shulders' legs and seemed to approve. "The big meeting, Muma," Edu said. "You haven't forgotten?"

"Forgotten?" Ziiza said. "How could I *not* forget with all that's gone on? Litti in shock. Netti returning before I could look for her. With this fine young man," she smiled at Shulders, could not prevent her judgment from spilling, "who rescued her." She rubbed a necklace chip, which reminded her. "Where's your basket, Netti?" But before Netti could compose an answer Ziiza turned away and said, "I must run. It's very important. At Font's Bank. So many things going on. I'm losing track. Netti, could you and Shulders look after Litti till I get back? Edu, run for Provido. Please. Right now."

"Certainly, Muma," Netti said. "Remember when Litti looked after me?"

"Where's Govvi?" Ziiza said. "She's supposed to go with me. Has anyone seen her?" Three shook their heads. One stared ahead.

* * *

Ziiza walked briskly through H&G, stopped for a Konka carry-along, and then hurried to Font's for the meeting.

"Hello, Ziiza," Gstan said, turning from talking with Font and Esqq and smiling at her. "That was a heck of a race, wasn't it? I mean even for me, distinguished turnaround commentator, and proud sponsor of the Banal Chatter racing team."

"Hello, gentlemen," Ziiza said. Then to Gstan, returning his smile: "Yes, after all our planning and work, it came off rather well, didn't it?"

For the public, anyway.

"But you know," she continued. "it seems like it was months ago, instead of yesterday."

"You look wrung out," Gstan said, almost calling her Zi.

"Wife Dragga, here." Wife Dragga planted her long legs in the path, making the point that while she was joining them, she was not *of* them. "Ziiza," she said. "Font. Esqq. I don't know why they want me here. We made it through the winter, didn't we? What do we need Swarm City for, anyway? I never did agree with that Barclaw traveling nonsense." Then, thinking she had said enough, she walked slowly in and composed her spindly self.

If Wife Dragga was put out, Mistermayor was incensed. He and the Town Hall delegation showed up well after noon, hoping the meeting would be under way, payback for Little Sac's insult. He held Polcat's arm just above the elbow, ready to squeeze if he spoke more than a word. The other councilmen followed, looking as if they had been caught bathing naked in a creek. Then came Barclaw, who after months as Little Sac's overland companion, then his messenger to the beaver eaters, had been cut loose like a groin.

Mistermayor's ploy did not work. Little Sac was late. Followed by Pop&Jay (hard looks, but no words), Govvi (chins dropped in astonishment), and eight helmeted brigadesmen. And Bitta, hanging back, not wanting to risk being ordered to leave.

Little Sac stepped up to Font as if he knew exactly whom he was addressing, raised a hand in salute and said, "Sac the Magnificent sends his personal greetings to Beaverton." He did not acknowledge Esqq, who stood beside Font, or Mistermayor, or anyone else. "I am Little Sac," he continued, "commander of the Swarm City Brigade and Sac's official representative. Just as Barclaw," he touched his helmet to Barclaw, "was your ambassador to Swarm City. And a fine job he did of it, too." Barclaw stood stiffly. "You. You out there," he said, motioning to Bitta. "Reporter person, I'll bet. With keen eye, sharp ear, and pigeon on shoulder. Come closer so you can hear." Bitta moved in. Little Sac continued: "As Sac the Magnificent understands it, Beaverton has two problems in its happy little valley. First, you are short of food. Although from the looks of it, no one seems to be starving. No one who matters, anyway."

"We're eating slim but fine," Mistermayor interrupted. "It's monetary stability. And what are those two doing here?" He glared at Pop&Jay, then looked at Barclaw as if about to give the order to run them over the hill.

"Patience, Mister Mayor," Little Sac said dismissively. "I'll get to them in a minute. My brigade is encamped over there," he pointed east, "guarding the wherewithal we transported half-way across the continent, with great difficulty, I might add, to assist you in stabilizing your banking and monetary system. At *your* request. Tie you in with Swarm City. Help with your temporary difficulty. And ultimately, we hope, form a long-lasting, mutually-beneficial relationship."

"In addition," Little Sac continued, "my brigade is guarding a large supply of big yellows, as you call them." Astonished looks. "Inject them into the system. Make everything whole again. Big yellows aplenty. And everything to back them up. No more bank runs. No more shortages. No more unpleasantness." He tapped his protruding teeth with a fingernail. "But."

Oh, yes, always the but.

"In exchange for his munificence," Little Sac looked around to see if they were sufficiently impressed with his vocabulary word, "Sac the Magnificent requests, rather requires, Font's Bank's transition to ancillary status."

"Ack, ack," Mistermayor choked. "Ancillary? Ancillary to what? Barclaw, what did you tell them? What did you agree to?"

Barclaw stepped back and looked around, seeking supporting eye contact.

Little Sac continued: "Branch, affiliate, subsidiary, call it what you will. We thought it a compliment. How about western division? Would that suit you?" He laughed a dry laugh.

"Owrrr," Mistermayor gurgled, clutching his chest as he slid to the ground. Polcat grabbed and dropped with him.

"Mistermayor! Mistermayor! Are you all right?" Ziiza shouted, rushing over. "Send for Provido! Someone! Please! He should be at my shelter., looking after Litti."

Mistermayor thumped his chest as if to restart his heart. "Forget it, Ziiza," he said. "I'm fine. I'll just sit here and listen."

With Mistermayor's seeming recovery, Little Sac pushed on: "I, Little Sac, acting for Sac the Magnificent, acting for the Swarm City Central Bank, tender an offer to buy Font's Bank." As the onlookers' jaws dropped again, he turned to Govvi and said, "How much, Miss Govvi, do you calculate would be a fair price?"

Govvi squeezed her ThinStone, and in her best business voice said, "Lot, shelter, and counter; customer deposits; accrued interest; hidden assets; non-hidden assets; loan portfolio; goodwill. One thousand, four hundred and twenty-four big yellows. Exactly."

"Thank you, Miss Govvi," Little Sac said. "But why not make it a happy 1,450. Better yet, an even 1,500. What do you say to that, banker Font? Relieved of all worry and responsibility and a rich man, too. Your answer?"

"It's not for sale," Mistermayor croaked. "It's the only bank in town. Everything depends —"

"Well. Uhh," Font stammered, his handsome face paling, his blue eyes paler still. "I didn't expect anything like this. Selling out as a condition. I'll have to think it over."

"Yes, do that," Little Sac said, smirking. "You have one minute. I didn't come all this way to haggle. Or wait."

"But I need a day or two. Talk it over with Esqq. Discuss it with the council."

"Your minute is slipping away, banker Font."

Font and Esqq turned their backs and whispered.

The council members bent over Mistermayor. "How do we stop this?" Polcat whispered.

"It's his bank," Mistermayor said, gasping. "It's too late to start controlling it now. Remember, all we were interested in before was taxing him."

Font turned and resignedly offered his hand. Little Sac shook it and said, "Wise decision, banker Font. Your big yellows will be delivered to you. Tomorrow morning. Now if you will sign here. Title to all assets and liabilities of Font's Bank." He held out two boards and a marker. Font signed both. Little Sac did the same and handed one to Font. "And here is a big yellow," he said. "Down payment. To make everything legal." He waved it so everyone could witness and dropped it in Font's hand.

The council members looked at Polcat and Mistermayor. Everything was happening too brutally fast.

"Very well," said the brigade commander, "condition of rescue met." He swept the gathering with triumphant eyes. "Moving along, for I don't have all day. Again, as authorized representative of the Swarm City Central Bank, owner of the former Font's Bank, I hereby appoint Govvi Chief Executive Officer of the western division, or whatever she wishes to call it."

Ziiza ground her teeth. Gstan dropped his ThinStone. The sharp corner hit his foot. "Owwww." He clapped his hand over his mouth. Glances exchanged. Nothing said.

Govvi stepped up. No hint of surprise. No words of thanks. This had been carefully rehearsed. "I was thinking of calling it the Magnificent Financial Group," she said demurely. Little Sac waggled his hair gate in approval. "But Western Division will do for the moment." She turned abruptly and faced Wife Dragga. "Wife Dragga," she said, "you have many loans, secured by your properties?"

"Oh, I get it," Wife Dragga said. Then curtly to Govvi, "Yes. A few. It's called leverage, my dear. I'm an investor."

"Forty-seven."

"If you say so."

"And some of your payments are behind. 'Leverage,'" Govvi's lips tightened, "as you call it, works two ways."

"Font and I have an understanding," Wife Dragga said, now with a hint of pleading in her voice.

Govvi pressed her legs together, tucked her ThinStone under her arm, and drilled Wife Dragga with hard black eyes. She stood massing her power like a storm gathering in the hills, her silence her rebuttal. She held firm until she saw Wife Dragga's arms shake, her haughty veneer crack. "You have done many favors for my family, Wife Dragga," Govvi said at last. "And some disfavors, perhaps. But I feel generous today."

Little Sac turned to his trail master and whispered behind his hand. "They were right. She's a rare find. Working the old dame over like a pro. Pushing her long, ugly face in the mud. Twisting it till she chokes. And she can't be more than nine or ten years old. A fighter – and a finisher, too."

"You have until this time tomorrow," Govvi continued, "to straighten your account."

"You're threatening me with foreclosure?" Again silence. Wife Dragga turned on her heel and stalked off with as much dignity as she could muster. As she passed Ziiza she glared and started to speak.

Ziiza held her finger to Wife Dragga's lips and said, "Our differences are in the past, Wife Dragga. I'm not competing with you anymore. Not that I ever was. We're in this together."

Ziiza watched Wife Dragga walk past a laurel hedge and disappear. Disappear under an enormous black cloud that had materialized in the sky. Smoke-storm, she thought fleetingly, then turned back to the group.

Govvi had no time to waste time on black clouds, she had some of her own to create. She turned to Gstan. "You are the owner of Errix Enterprises, one of Beaverton's largest businesses, are you not?"

"You know I am, Govvi," Gstan said stepping forward, head bowed.

"And you owe Font's Bank – if I have it correctly – and I'm sure I do – 153 big yellows. Secured by your ownership certificates."

"Yes, but I borrowed to help out. . . ." He glanced at Font. At Ziiza. Then quickly away. "Oh, forget it."

"Yours is a call loan and I'm calling it now. The bank is reorganizing. Clean tally boards through and through, as they say. Can you pay up? Now?"

"You mean for a walk-away loan like that? I don't have any big yellows. But I can pay you in ThinStones. My collection's worth thousands."

"Big yellows are the official and only medium of exchange. That's the idea. Remember? Restore monetary stability to Beaverton."

"What about it, Font?" Gstan pleaded. "You've got them. Fifteen hundred."

Font held up his big yellow. "Sure, Gstan," he said. "But I don't get any more till tomorrow. None to be had. The giant valley beaver's all played out, you know."

Little Sac turned to his man. "What a shame," he said. "All played out, eh? And who's responsible for that?"

Okay, Govvi," Gstan said. "You'll have them tomorrow. I'm clear."

"Banks don't deal in tomorrows," Govvi said icily. "Banks deal in big yellows. Big yellows in hand. Today. At least this one does."

Ziiza eyed a far-off treetop.

My clever daughter gone wrong. I've been too occupied chasing what I call my dream. Or called my dream. Didn't pay attention. Didn't see it coming. She's going to run Beaverton. And ruin her muma in the bargain.

"But . . . but . . . ," Gstan sputtered, "you just gave Wife Dragga a day."

"Perhaps if you had been first up," Govvi said with hostile sweetness. "But you weren't. Title to Errix and Hill Burrow for 300 big yellows. All debts extinguished. A fair offer in light of the circumstances."

Gstan dropped his hands in disgust. "Offer, my foot!" he barked. Then, resignedly, "Well, yes."

"Thank you," she said, her voice rising. "Now that that's done, you might as well know, Gstan, your services at Errix Enterprises are no longer required." With hardly a pause she extended her hand toward Pop, and said, "You all know Pop, formerly of Beaverton, recently of Popville-on-Son," she grinned, "now returned to Beaverton." She came down hard on the second *Beaverton*, letting the power of her position, her money, and if necessary the Swarm City Brigade encamped over the hill, sink in, daring anyone to challenge. Not Mistermayor, not Polcat, not even Barclaw, the ones responsible for Pop&Jay's banishment, blinked. "I'm appointing him President of Errix Enterprises."

Pop leaned against the bank pole, lip flapping. Ziiza eyed him. Satisfaction? Or bewilderment? She could not tell. "By all means," Pop said.

"Legal work is piling up, lawyer Esqq," Govvi said. "How would you like a full-time job as the bank's council? Of course we'll be moving to better quarters."

Eyes turned to Esqq. Was he, a Beaverton stalwart, for sale to Sac the Magnificent, Commander Little Sac, and the new Sacling, Govvi?

"I've been thinking about retiring," Esqq said, pulling at his white bush. "Moving south. Taking it easy. Maybe to Big Bay. Or beyond. Thank you for the offer Miss Govvi, but this is a job for a younger man. Or woman."

"Why, Govvi? Why?" Ziiza screamed, not able to contain herself. "Why are you doing this? To us? To Beaverton? To your own people? I don't understand." She trailed off, hot tears flowing. "I simply don't understand."

Ignoring her muma, Govvi continued. "Think it over, lawyer Esqq. I'll pay you twice what he did." She turned to Ziiza, and, looking through her, said, "Ziiza, you are the owner of the Original Z-sport Company, are you not?"

What else does this conniving child have in mind?

"And you are indebted to the former Font's Bank for 477 big yellows?"

"You know all of that," Ziiza responded wearily.

"Your loan is called. Can you pay? Today? With accrued interest, it comes to over 500." She paused in the manner of the whip-smart, pretending she needed time to calculate, and said, "Five hundred twenty-six, to be exact."

"Oh, Govvi," Ziiza cried, "I've worked so hard. Don't take it. I'm begging you. Why are you doing this to me?"

Govvi's eyes narrowed. "Why? You ask me why?" She spit the words like precisely-spaced snake bites. "In the water, Muma. You abandoned me. Let go of me. And went out for Edu. For him — and that miserable creature that caused it all. You went out and left me. Left me to drown. Left me in the water to drown."

"Govvi. Dear. How could you think that? I thought you were safe. The water shallow enough for you to make it. I had to act fast. For all of you. I'm sorry if. . . . " Ziiza covered her face to hide her tears. "And this has been festering in you all of this time?" she sobbed. "Why didn't you say anything? I could have explained."

Arms trembling, shoulders shaking, Govvi spilled her pent-up rage. "All I've done. For you. For the family. On the Sea Trace. For the Sita. For Z-sport. All taken for granted. No thanks from you. No pay. That's right, no pay. Quiet little Govvi. Dependable little Govvi. Little numbers Govvi. These men," she pointed at Pop&Jay, "gave me a big yellow. Just for making a fire. One insignificant fire." She paused, caught her breath, and screamed, "Well, they appreciate me, Muma. I'm more than a walking tally board to them. I'm Govvi. Real live Govvi. They like me. Make me laugh. And now their friend Commander Little Sac has rewarded me. With this bank." She stopped, gathered, and said, "And do you know what? Banks run everything. Even Beavertons."

Govvi looked down at her feet, her fire fading. She rubbed her red eyes and blew her nose in her hand. Wiped her hand on her fur. She gave the dumbstruck onlookers a stiff smile, as if to say: Sorry for the interruption, just some family business I had to take care of. She scuffed her foot and said primly, "Well, back to it. Now Ziiza, we'll buy you out for 300 big yellows, same as Gstan. Yes, of course you'll take it," she said, not waiting for an answer. "You have no choice. And Ziiza — are you listening? You're out. Jay, you take over Z-sport. As of now. Reporting to me, of course."

Little Sac covered his smile with his hand. "The long trip was worth it," he said to his man, giving him an unmilitary elbow poke. "We'll be heading back to civilization tomorrow. Wednesday at the latest. Job well done. Ancillary bank? Western Division? Magnificent Financial Group? Well, I don't know.

But whatever it is, we're leaving it in good, if improbable, hands – two cagy old scoundrels and a vindictive girl prodigy." The trail master smiled.

Font and Esqq stood, seemingly not knowing what to do. Two men stunned. One man rich. Possibly both. Barclaw and Polcat helped Mistermayor up – he seemed to have recovered – and they started for Town Hall. The schemers retired to the roofless office to scheme.

40

Smoke-storm

ZIIZA STUCK her aching feet in the river. "Come on," Gstan said, "let me rub. Please." She swung her legs out of the water. "I promise not to tickle," he continued, attempting to be playful and serious at the same time. He began with her left, sliding his fingers along the top and sides. He pushed slowly, soft fingers on rough feet. Then faster. He switched to the right. Fingers. Thumbs. Back to her left, where he rubbed sides and ankle with both hands. Ziiza relaxed and closed her eyes. He eased off. His thumbs felt gentle, his fingers gentler. He continued in long, slow movements.

"That's it," Ziiza sighed. "That's the spot. Yeh, the bone on the edge."

He rubbed fast and slow, fast and slow. Eased off, lighter and lighter, until his fingers barely touched. Never her soles. Never the toe void. The scar was raw and red, looked as if it had happened last week. Blood oozed from a crack. Don't these things ever heal? he thought.

Edu threw a stick in the river. "Get it, Dg," he yelled. Dg walked to the edge, stood with his forepaws in the water, and watched it swirl away downstream. "Missed it, Dg. I'll try another." But Dg was not interested.

Ziiza settled into reverie. A forest camp. As on the Sea Trace. No. Not like the Sea Trace. They were halfway between Beaverton and the Sea, maybe farther, in the Sundown Range, near the headwaters of – she struggled to remember the name – the Distant Cousin River. That was it. His massage was gentle and effective. The more she relaxed, the more she allowed her body to merge with the cool earth. The more he rubbed, stroked, touched, the better her feet felt, even the bad one. The better *she* felt. The four of them – if you counted Dg, which you had to – walking the Sundown Trail to the Sea. To Groopland resort and casino. To gamble. To have fun.

* * *

Monday, after Litti's crackup, after Netti's rescue, after Govvi's betrayal, after Sac the Magnificent's takeover, after Beaverton's humiliation, as if that were not enough for one day, Smoke-storm had erupted. Not a surprise eruption. Not a cataclysmic eruption. Just a routine five-hundred to-thousand-year eruption.

No one had heard a sound. The cloud appeared over the hills beyond the Grand Muma River looking like a thunderhead pressing in from the north. After years of watching, waiting, and fearing, Beavertonians were a mite disappointed. Was this all dreaded Smoke-storm had to offer?

But it was a sight to see. Especially the red arcs against the black cloud. Nighttime would be volcano show time. The viewpoints were soon packed with mumas, popas, and children, singles and doubles, everyone who could climb the hills. Sitting on bluffs. Balancing on branches. Smoke-storm's crown, gleaming white a few days before, bled red and orange as the earth's innards surged up and over and down. Fiery chunks – who knew how large – floated in the air, in seeming slow motion. Some faded quickly. Others continued, completing their fiery trajectories. It was as if Little Sac had scheduled a fireworks display to celebrate Beaverton's degradation.

Ziiza had not been interested in Smoke-storm's fireworks, not after what she had been through. "Go if you must," she told Edu. "But be back by midnight," she shouted as he and Dg disappeared into the crowd heading for the views. She sat behind her shelter leaning against Biber's split brew-crock, staring ahead, waiting for nightfall so she could sleep. She had tried to put Govvi out of her mind. And of course the more she tried not to think about her, the more she thought about her. And the angrier she became.

Bitta had been another Beavertonian not interested in fireworks. She had just experienced the worst day of her journalistic career. After the meeting she had walked back with Barclaw, Mistermayor, and the others, double-checking her facts. When they reached Town Hall, Barclaw sat on his storytelling round, head down, telling no stories. Mistermayor patted him on the shoulder. "I'm not blaming you for this, Barclaw," he said. "You did your best. A noble, courageous best, in my opinion. We just got clipped, that's all. Clipped."

"All right, Hobi," Bitta had said after they parted, "do your stuff." She grabbed his legs and threw him into the air. Hobart rose, coo-burping. "Good people of Beaverton," Bitta yelled in her most urgent voice, "I have news and lots of it." She paused, trying to decide what to say first. "Latest news! Latest! A startling change in yesterday's B-town Run Away." She stopped. "No, that can wait."

"Momentous business news! Historic meeting at Font's Bank. Little Sac, commander of the Swarm City Brigade, led across the snow-covered plains and through the Sunup Range by our own valiant Barclaw, in exchange for re-capitalization of Font's Bank and stabilizing our monetary system, has purchased the bank for 1,500 big yellows." She paused to catch her breath. "Not a happy seller, Font, to be sure. But, to this reporter's eyes, well compensated."

Her stream of words floated out and over H&G. A few people slowed and turned their heads. None stopped. She tugged Hobart's leg. "Fly, you lazy bird. Quit soiling my back and get to work." The pigeon rose and circled.

Bitta continued: "More! More! Ziiza's daughter Govvi will run the bank. Renamed it the Magnificent Financial Group. In honor, I suppose, of Sac the Magnificent, Mayor of Swarm City, to whom we owe our monetary rebirth." Instead of the usual mix of shoppers, lookers, walkers, and runners going every which way, almost everyone was hurrying in the same direction, east, to the hilltops for the fireworks.

"On with important news. Wife Dragga's properties threatened with foreclosure. Two of Beaverton's largest businesses, Z-sport and Errix, taken over by the bank. Loans called. Couldn't pay up. Ziiza and Gstan thrown out. Pop&Jay back in Beaverton to run them." Bitta allowed herself another editorial comment. "How the council's going to deal with that I can't imagine."

"Late-breaking news from Quord Senior. Hey, you!" Bitta yelled at a passer-by, "Stop!" She glared at his back as he walked on. "Org has disqualified himself from the B-town Run Away. Disqualified himself. Sufx will move up. His unbeaten streak continues. Yes, Org, who finished yesterday's race in first place, happened to reweigh his rock. And found it underweight. Gallant competitor that he is, he went directly to Senior and turned in his award. There will be a ceremony for Sufx tomorrow morning at the finish line. Runners and race fans invited.

"If that doesn't beat all," Bitta said, not even bothering to close her report. "The hottest news in years and nobody's interested. What's wrong, Hobi? Is it me? Am I losing it? Or is it them?"

* * *

Ziiza had woken Tuesday morning with the strangest feeling: the roof and sides of her shelter pressing in on her, the weight of a dozen robes, it seemed, plus a couple of tree trunks. "Muma," Edu said, standing outside, "it's snowing." For a person who had slept as poorly as she, this was difficult information to process. Snowing? In Beaverton, where it seldom snowed? In springtime, when it almost never snowed? She stuck her hand outside. Soon it was covered with silver-gray dust. She licked. It was certainly not cold and did not melt. She spit. The dust stuck to her tongue and mouth, and grated her teeth. She wiggled out of her almost-collapsed shelter and surveyed a uniformly gray Beaverton: pathway, yard, tree branches, shelters. Edu brushed his shoulders. Dg shook the heavy dust from his head and back. She looked over at Litti's shelter. Like hers, it was leaning and sagging.

A man and a woman with packs trudged through Ziiza's yard, making a quick detour after stumbling against her shelter. "Excuse me," he said. "Can't see the path. Can't breathe, either. Don't know where we're going to get out of this stuff, but we're going."

"Come on, Edu," Ziiza said, turning toward Litti's shelter, "let's see how they're doing." Edu and Dg jumped, eager to have something to do. Waking them up should have been fun, but it wasn't. Edu pulled on the roof, tried to lift and shake, but it would not move.

"Stop it. Go away." Netti's muffled voice. "We know what's happened. We're all right. Litti, too. We just want to sleep."

"Hey, Ziiza! Ziiza!" Gstan materialized out of the "snowfall." Like the couple who had just passed, he had a good-sized pack. Unlike the couple, he was dragging a sack as well. He covered his eyes with a hand and shook ash from his hair. "I'd like to invite," he began. "I'm getting out of here until this blows over." Self-satisfied laugh. "Going to Groopland. Walking west till I get out of this stuff. Come on. Join me. Have a little fun." He raised the sack. "You know what's in here."

"Well, I don't," Ziiza said.

"Big yellows, I'll bet," Edu chipped in. "Can Dg and I come, too?"

"Of course. You, Dg, your muma. And anyone else who wants to." He pointed at Litti's shelter.

"That's awfully nice of you, Gstan," Ziiza said. "Where do you think it ends? This gritty snow?"

"So it's agreed," he said, passing her question. "Pack up. We're off to Groopland. Sporting land. Vacation by the Sea. Maybe a permanent vacation – from Beaverton."

Netti declined Gstan's invitation. "Litti needs us," she said. "And she can't travel." Shulders, sleeping outside, raised his head, shook it, and smiled.

Ziiza had the Litti, Netti, and Shulders picture. A trio in recovery. With an odd twist of role reversal. Litti's hyphenated "Arbo-sita," delivered in a distant monotone, was frightening. When would she snap out of it? Would she ever? Netti was more than okay. Headaches under control, now that the stress of Run Away production was over. Would she succumb to the Mire-root again? Would they? And Ziiza's burning question: was he *the one*? The more she thought about it, the more she saw them together, the more she wanted it. Would they pledge? Would they help fill the void: Milli, Com, Org, Govvi? Grandchildren? Grandchildren she could see, touch, hold, play with? Selfish?

Well, so what. If caring for Litti – wounded wood sprite, greatest of hearts, greatest of friends – strengthened their bond, wouldn't that be wonderful?

Ziiza was an old hand at packing for the trail. So were Edu and Dg. Gstan sat on his pack, hands shading his eyes from the falling ash. "How many big yellows will I need?" Ziiza asked.

"Depends on how lucky you feel," he said with a twinkle and snort. "Look at it this way, we've had an incredible string of bad luck. Especially you, Ziiza." He paused for emphasis. "Now we're all choking on this ash snow that won't stop or melt or go away. But I feel a change in the air. And a change in our luck. Once we get to the coast we can forget all of this."

* * *

After Ziiza's foot rub the four walked until late afternoon. Camped next to a stream running into the Distant Cousin, now a fast-flowing river. Ziiza slowed them down and many people hurried past. Some were headed to Groopland "until this blows over and things get back to normal – if they ever do." Some carried everything they owned, said they were not coming back. "After all this, anyplace is better than Beaverton."

Wind puffs shook ash from the trees, irritating but not as bad as in town. They were over the crest. A good rain would clean things up. For now. No one knew when Smoke-storm would belch again, or what direction or how hard the wind would blow when it did, and where the ash cloud would travel. The feeder stream was gentle and bright. Gstan pulled up rocks for crawfish, while Edu waded, hand poised, waiting for the water to clear. He grabbed them behind their pincers and flung them onto the bank. Dg herded them with his paws as they tried to scuttle back to the water.

Fire building was easy. Easy in the sense that Edu had plenty of time to try again and again. They roasted crawfish, toasted bits of meat, and warmed themselves. Edu sang "Whatever It Takes," imitating everyone's voices. No one commented on its inappropriateness. Ziiza rubbed her feet, which were feeling better since they had been taking it easy.

"You know," Gstan said. "I've been thinking." He looked hard, making certain he had her attention. "It'll never work. The bank taking over Errix. Pop can't run it. Govvi, either – if you'll pardon my mentioning her name – smart as she is. Why? One guy. Silvoo. Head of the bunch that make the ThinStones. The Hieyeques. He and I have, or had, a very special arrangement. Which rose out of a very special circumstance. Which nobody in Beaverton knows anything about. Nobody."

"But hey, get this," he continued. "Leegs doesn't know, either. He's never met Silvoo. Never seen the place where they make them. Picks up the

ThinStones at a drop near the trail. Leaves them off. Has no idea where they come from. Could be anywhere. Do you know what Errix Enterprises really is? It's Silvoo and me and Leegs in-between. Brains and brains and legs. Oh, they might get a few deliveries out of him before Silvoo catches on. Then it's over."

"Are you saying you're glad it happened?" Ziiza asked incredulously.

"Now that I've put it into words, told it to you, someone who understands because she's been through something like it, I'm coming around. Yes, that's what I'm coming around to. I've got my big yellows." He rubbed the sack by his side. "I've got my ThinStone collection hidden away. Which can only grow more valuable if there are no more to be had. And I got out of Beaverton with my skin attached." He laughed. Ziiza and Edu did not.

"I kind of liked Errix Enterprises," Edu said, stroking Dg. "I thought I'd like to work there. Work for you someday. After I finished school."

"You did?" Gstan said. "Why, I'd have been delighted. But there'll be other opportunities. I'll think of something. But right now all I can think of is Groopland and the big game of chance I've heard so much about. And how I'm going to double my money."

"Or lose it," Ziiza quipped.

"That's a possibility," Gstan said. Finally everyone chuckled. "But listen to this: I don't care. I don't care. It comes, it comes. It goes, it goes. Gstan doesn't care one whit." He rested his head on locked fingers and smiled. "Look at Hill Burrow, a failure of a development. But, hey. A few rough stones from down south, some unemployed muscle boys, two dozen vacant burrows, plus Old Man Haracosh to keep an eye on things, and you've got – a ThinStone manufactory. That's ingenuity. That's. . . . Oh, forget it. And you, Ziiza? Are you coming around?"

"When you think about it," she said, leaning back, looking at the lacy light through the branches. "More specifically, when I think about the Run Away. And I've been doing a lot of thinking as I've been hobbling along."

"We've made it a long way," Edu said brightly. "Besides, what's wrong with taking our time and enjoying ourselves?"

"Mature beyond his years," Ziiza said. "Thank you, Edu. That was considerate and sweet. Now you can take the Run Away two ways. Business-wise, I mean. One, it was a huge success, kicking off the new season, boosting morale, and all of that. I can see – or could see – more races, more spectators, expanded lines. Limited edition signature Z-Zs by Sufx, for instance. On the other hand, maybe this was the peak. Nothing but downhill from now on. Rock running is healthy, exciting, and competitive. But it's also a demanding and sometimes painful sport. Requires sustained practice and conditioning.

Not to mention the right equipment." A flit of a smile. "The question I've asked myself from race one: is rock running a fad? Can it sustain itself? Was this, as Polcat said, the first annual B-town Run Away? Or was it the first and last 'annual' B-town Run Away? That was the question I would have had to face. Now I don't. But somebody does. The question of the future of rock running. And an additional one: Can Jay run the Original Z-sport Company? Because, Gstan, there's a difference from Errix. She knows everything. Oh, I'm rambling."

"Keep rambling," Gstan said. "It's good for you to talk. Good for both of us to get it out of our systems. Interesting too. Right, Edu?" He looked at the bright-eyed boy, sitting across, hugging his creature, taking it all in.

"Why speculate?" Ziiza continued. "It's not my company anymore. But for the sake of expurgatory conversation –"

"Addle would challenge you on that, Muma," Edu interrupted. "And so would I."

"So challenge. We're back to the question: What's the future of rock running?" She slapped her leg in exasperation. "Why did you get me talking about this, Gstan? I'm trying to forget about it. Especially her."

Edu sat up straight, about to ask the question that had been on his mind for days: Govvi's betrayal. Her going over to *them*. But for once he kept quiet.

"I just asked," Gstan said softly. "Besides, you said you were thinking on the trail."

"You did, Muma," Edu added, having to say something.

"I'm coming around," Ziiza continued. "I hate to admit it, but right now I'd give Z-sport less than a fifty-fifty chance . . . long term . . . even if I were running it. Much less, now. Netti's the key. She's Z-sport's underappreciated talent. In spite of another party's opinion. Will she work for *her*? Will Narda? I certainly hope not. Jay doesn't count. You know, boys, a few days after the shock of being thrown out of my own business, plus making some tracks away from ashy Beaverton, and I don't feel as bad as I think I should. Thank you, Gstan. Thank you, Edu."

"Aren't you going to thank Dg?" Edu asked.

"Thank you, Dg," she said, touching her nose to his. "Thank you for your loyalty and all you've done for my boy. And me, too."

Next day they smelled cool salt air wafting through the cedar and spruce. Going was easier, generally downhill. The travelers before them had opened the trail: snapping off branches, tossing rocks aside, trampling the trail. They emerged from the trees onto an estuarial expanse of sharp grass, hummocks, and tidal ditches. The trail went soft. Black oozing muck clung to their feet, their ankles, their legs. "Tide's coming in," Ziiza said. "This thing could be under water in an hour. Better wait till tomorrow and time it right." Gstan and Edu agreed. They retreated into the forest and made their third camp of the walk.

If this wasn't the longest day of the year, Ziiza thought, it was close to it. Plenty of daylight, leaving time to loaf around camp. Edu's fire was especially welcome as they were feeling the Sea breeze. She tossed leftover crawfish parts to some aggressive raccoons who weren't intimidated by Dg. *That* reminded her of something. More than one thing. Had they been higher up the coast, had it been a few years ago, Milli would be wading the estuary, hunting crabs on the in-coming tide. Catching them, too. Netti would be trailing her. Milli would fling crabs into the air and Netti would lunge to catch them in her basket. Ziiza could almost see them out there, tidal surges splashing against their legs, over their waists. Org would be sitting across from her, shredding cedar bark, then crushing it with his rock. Drying it by the fire. Tinder for Govvi. And little Govvi herself, hunched over her tally board, locked in her private numbers world. Com? He would be off exploring, even after the day's scouting was over, getting the lay of the land, seeking alternate trails, just in case the one across the squishy salt plain did not work out. He had to know.

She did not have to imagine what Edu and Dg would be doing. They were here, doing it. Dg growled at the raccoons from time to time, to let them know who ran the camp, but was prudent enough not to challenge. Edu poked the fire, keeping it going, asking questions. Asking her. Asking Gstan. But mostly Gstan, it seemed lately. "Where did you grow up? What were your muma and popa like? Do you have any brothers and sisters? Did you have a creature-friend like Dg when you were a boy? Was your school hard? How did you get so smart?"

"I suppose," Ziiza said after Edu had momentarily run out of questions and Gstan had momentarily run out of answers, "I should tell you something." She was surprised at the words coming out of her mouth. Surprised at what she was about to say. Thinking about the beach. And the Sea. And the Sea Trace. She plunged ahead: "To set the record straight. And to satisfy your curiosity, Gstan. And to refresh your memory, Edu. For I see before me two very curious boys." She grinned at her habit of referring to them together as boys. "I thought you might like to know what happened to Prior. My husband. That is if Edu hasn't told you."

"You told us not to talk about it, Muma. Remember? Our first day in Beaverton."

"He never mentioned anything," Gstan said. "And I never asked."

"You might think it's a long, involved story. But it isn't." She looked into the fire. "We lived on the Old Side. Everything was fine with me. I had six children to raise and that kept me more than busy. But every year just after mid-winter, groups of people passed our shelter, moving out, carrying everything they owned. Going across the ice bridge. Or ice-covered land bridge. Or whatever it is. Or was. Moving to the New Side. Your popa talked with them, walked along with them, found out everything he could. I didn't pay much attention; I was happy where we were. But after a couple of years of this, your popa got a far-away look in his eyes." Ziiza sniffled.

Gstan wanted to say something soothing, hug her, tell her not to bother continuing. But he was enthralled.

"How's this for a campfire story?" Ziiza said, wiping her nose. "They called it the New Side fever, a man's disease mostly. I knew we were going. Just a matter of time. He was waiting until you, Edu, were old enough to travel. He never said so, but that's what he was doing. Then he heard about Beaverton. Not much news came back from the New Side. They just went over and never came back. Anyway it was a special place: good climate, plenty to eat. Beautiful. Just opening up. Did things their own way. That appealed to him. Got him right here." She patted her stomach. "He couldn't stop thinking about it, talking about it: Beaverton, Beaverton, Beaverton."

"Many groups passed, and even though I thought you, Edu – and Govvi and Com, for that matter – were too young, your popa couldn't stand it. It was almost too late for that year, but we found a sizeable group and they let us join. The first weeks were the hardest. Crossing the bridge. Many turned back right there. Some died. How we made it with all of you children, I don't know. Yes, I do know: your popa's strength and determination."

Ziiza paused, giving Gstan and Edu opportunity for questions. Both looked into the fire, not daring to speak. "Anyway," she continued, "we made it. Obviously. Then it was a long walk south. Frankly, as you well know, if it weren't for the broad beaches and their clams and mussels it would have been impossible. Had it been a coast of rocky cliffs, massive headlands, and thick forests. . . . Well. And you couldn't take it easy. Stop on the way. Winter over. The best way was by canoe: faster, easier, carry more. But not many had them. Not many knew how to make them. Or had the time.

"When we camped for the night we split into family groups, each with our own fire, but close enough for safety. Or so we thought. Well, we had crossed over and walked for about a month. Were camped at the mouth of a river, ready to cross the next morning. It was raining, not hard, but enough to block the moonlight. We were a ways off the beach and into the trees. Darker still. Children asleep. So was I. Popa was on the first watch, sitting by the fire, trying to keep it going in the drizzle.

"I woke to Popa's screams: 'Back off! Back off, you beast!' The animal growled, grunted, and must have charged, because Popa screamed again, this

384

time in pain. Must have slashed or bitten him. So sudden. I jumped up, grabbed my spear, and went for it. It must have scattered the fire, because it went completely dark. I smelled burning fur. I can smell it now: sickening, sweet, terrible. I swung my spear, not knowing whether I'd hit the beast or your popa; you do crazy things like that. From then on, I don't know what happened. Except for one thing. The beast – to this day I don't know whether it was a bear, a watabeast, a sita, or something else – turned from Popa to me. Knocked me over. Growling. Snapping teeth. I must have fallen backward, because pain shot up my leg and into my head. My toe was gone, but I didn't know it then.

"I don't know how long I was unconscious. When I came to, Org and Netti were slapping me, trying to wake me up, crying, 'What happened, Muma? What happened?'"

"The beast was gone. Prior was gone. I have no way of knowing, no way of proving, but I've always believed that he sacrificed himself for us, let himself be carried away. To keep it away from the family. The most noble, most loving thing a husband and popa could do. That's my belief. I can speak of it now. Speak of it proudly."

Ziiza sucked in a long breath. "I wrapped my foot and held onto it all night. In the morning, Milli and Netti bound it up but I couldn't walk. The people in our group commiserated. For an hour or two. But our misfortune had terrified them. Made them anxious to leave. You remember that, don't you, Edu?"

"I guess so, Muma."

"We stayed for five days. Org and Com ventured as far into the forest as they dared, looking for Popa, looking for signs. Of course we hoped he would walk into camp, just like that. Finally we had to go. MeTonn picked us up, and although he was a dangerous beast himself, our time in his canoes allowed my foot to heal. Or start to. And took us farther south. If he hadn't? If, if, if. No end to the ifs."

41
Groopland

AFTER THE tide ebbed they started west on what they took to be the trail. As it turned out, they missed the trail to Groopland. Sank to their knees in the tideland muck. Two choices: Retreat again, and look for a trail through the trees. Or walk the river channel at low tide, hoping it was firm enough to support them. They chose the latter, but it was slow going. Ziiza and Gstan took turns carrying Dg. This would have been nothing for Dg back on the Sea Trace. But he was a different creature now. He tired easily, flopped on his side at each rest break, stood in streams, legs shaking, trying to decide whether he was thirsty or not.

It took all day to pick their way over the slick rocks and around the huge spruce trees swept downriver. The Distant Cousin's mud banks turned sandy; the rocky river bottom smoothed, broadened to a sandbar, and merged with the Sea. They walked along a narrow beach, backed not by forest but by rolling dunes, until they reached a small headland, a relatively easy climb. Then more dunes, spotted with shore pine. Just as Edu motioned them down a faint trail through the pines, Gstan shouted, "I think that's it!"

The sign over the entrance, barely visible in the fading light, read: Groopland Resort and Casino. And below: No Children or Creatures Allowed. Ziiza, Gstan, Edu, and Dg walked in.

"Welcome to Groopland," said the tall woman behind the counter. "I'm Foxi." She raised her voice on *Groopland* and *Foxi*, making them sound part greeting, part statement, and part question.

I'll bet you are.

Foxi was almost as tall as Wife Dragga, but the similarity ended there. Her sun-bleached hair was the fairest Ziiza had ever seen. Her nose was small, her lips full, her legs long, her body sculptured. This was not difficult to observe, as she wore only a tiny skirt that covered her hips and little else.

Her top piece was a narrow, white wrap-around fur that barely covered her breasts.

Ziiza looked at Edu, who was scanning the room. Then at Gstan. Then at Foxi. Then back at Gstan, who stared with his mouth open. She stuck her finger under his chin and raised it firmly. She waited for Gstan to speak; after all, this was his idea. He did not. "We'd like to check in," she said.

"Do you have reservations?" Foxi asked, this time a legitimate question. Ziiza looked at silent Gstan. "I guess we don't."

"Well, our shelter cottages are full up." Still the questioning lilt on *full up*, which, Ziiza noticed, had a captivating effect on men. At least the one standing next to her. Edu and Dg had walked over to a round and were watching a nattily-dressed man shaking white squares in a cup and spilling them onto the round. The other players, pressing in, reacted to each roll and spill with exaggerated cheers or exaggerated groans of disappointment. The other women employees, Ziiza noticed for the first time, wore the same skimpy, seductive tops, and the same skimpy, seductive skirts. But unlike Foxi, they were of normal height and were coarsely pretty. Edu passed his finger through spirals of greasy black smoke rising from an oil lamp.

"You can stay in the campground," Foxi continued. "I'll put you in D-11, just in from the beach. You'll have plenty of privacy." She snapped her fingers and a porter appeared. "Better have Maxwull guide you to your site. It's getting dark."

Maxwull was a skinny, big-eared, fast-mouthed young man; Ziiza pictured him as a Screaming Indifference fan. "Some of our guests eat at the casino," he said in a snooty, bored manner as they walked the beach. "Some bring their own food. Some come to gamble. Some come to watch other people gamble. Bottom fishers, I call them. Afraid to lose a little money."

"Any special instructions?" Ziiza asked, trying to sound casual, trying to sound as if she had visited the casino before. Any casino before. "The groops?"

"Groops are trained gambling fish," Maxwull explained. "Miss Foxi says we should call them 'gaming' fish. But it's plain old gambling, right? Absolutely the biggest mouths you ever saw. They come into the shallow water at the end of the surf, and kind of wait with their mouths open. You pick the one you like – they are all different: size, color, appetite – and toss some money his way. He swallows. You toss. He swallows. You toss."

"What's the point?" Edu asked. "Why would we throw our big yellows to a fish?"

"To win the Triple B of course," Maxwull said with a *you had to ask* look, "the Big Belching Blowout. When a groop collects more money than he wants – or however he figures – he blows it into the air and onto the beach.

The Triple B. The big prize. The big payoff. Could be a little. Could be a lot. Depends." He turned off the beach and led them up a dune and into the scrubby pines. "D-11," he said. "Your new home." Ziiza tipped him a big yellow. He thanked her, bit it, and left.

The walk in the Sea air snapped Gstan out of his trance. "I've never been to a casino before," he confided. "Never gambled. Except in my business ventures," he laughed, "all sure things." She gave him the you've-got-to-be-kidding smile he wanted, which he almost saw in the fading light. Although there was plenty of driftwood, they skipped the fire. Too late. Too tired.

Ziiza slept alone in her little trail shelter. Gstan wrapped up in his robe outside. (His "separate camp" had grown closer each night, until tonight all that kept him from touching her was the shelter wall.) On the other side Dg squirmed under Edu's robe, pressing against him, his nose sticking out. Edu held him tight, his hand under his collar as if to monitor his breathing and heartbeat. How things had changed. Instead of warming Edu, Edu was warming Dg. Ziiza lay on her back staring at the shelter top, pulling Sea air into her lungs. Exhaling. Pulling again. The smells. So familiar back then. Broad, endless beaches. Gorgeous sunsets – sometimes. Constantly-changing Sea. Clouds. Shoreline. Rain. Chill wind. Always chill wind. Like now, blowing through her open-ended shelter. She slid her hand under the edge and felt for Edu. "You all right?" she asked.

He found her hand and squeezed. "Yes, Muma. Good night."

"Good night, dear." Then, "Good night, Gstan." No answer; he was asleep. She said it anyway: "I'm glad I'm here."

Sea sounds poured into the tent, as if to fill the silence when she stopped talking. Not waves crashing, the dunes blocked that, but steady, distant, thunder-like sounds passing overhead and dropping down.

You never sleep like this in the valley. You sleep like this on the beach. On the Sea Trace. The sleep of utter exhaustion. Of utter peace. I'll just lie awake and think about happy times. Happy times? On the Sea Trace? No. They were desperate, fearful times. But we were a family then. Order of march. "Whatever It Takes." And we made it. All of us. Against the odds. Near drowning. Netti's accident. Way Rock. The watabeast. Mile after mile. Sore feet. Snow. All the way to Beaverton.

Edu and Dg rose first as usual, followed by Gstan. After a plunge in the Sea Edu started a beach fire. Ziiza heard them laughing and squealing. Saw them jumping around the fire, drying off. She closed her eyes, opened them, closed them, and drifted back into delicious sleep.

"Here," Gstan said, giving Edu a handful of big yellows. "Let's find a fish and go for the Big T, or whatever it's called. The spit-back prize. A little practice before your muma wakes up."

They walked toward the casino expecting to see lines of people standing in the foam-sliding surf, tossing big yellows, pelts, tail, agates, whatever they had of value. And hear the screams of the lucky few as the fishes belched. They saw no one.

"Is that a groop fish?" Edu asked. "Is that what we're looking for?"

Where the back waves hit the in-comers they saw a wide-open pink mouth, large enough to swallow Dg. The three walked into the run-out. Gstan tossed a big yellow at the mouth. It twisted in the air and fell short. The fish did not move. He tossed another. The fish leaned to the side and turned slightly, as if to sniff the big yellow as it sailed past. "Will you look at that," Gstan exclaimed. He walked closer. Edu followed. Dg stayed back. The groop did not retreat, kept its mouth open, showing hundreds of sharp teeth. "We're close enough," Gstan said. "You toss one."

Edu flipped it end over end. It went into the mouth, dead center. The mouth snapped shut. The groop spit the big yellow into the water.

"Huh! What's this?" Gstan said. "This isn't how it's supposed to work. Try again, Edu."

Edu tossed another. The groop caught. Tasted. Did not bother to spit. Let it fall out of the side of its mouth.

"Do you think it's too early?" Edu asked. "Maybe we're doing something wrong. There's nobody else here."

"Perhaps you're right, kid. Let's wake your muma and we'll all try. No. On second thought, let's grab something to eat, toast ourselves by the fire, and let her sleep as long as she wants. Her foot must not be bothering her or she would be up by now. Let her sleep."

After Ziiza had bathed and eaten, they walked until they found a dozen or so groops lined up in the surf, mouths open, waiting for their breakfast of money. The first one, the one Edu and Gstan had played with earlier, it became apparent, was a youngster. These were bigger, with mouths so large Edu and Dg could walk into them. But not receptive mouths. "You first, Ziiza," Gstan said. "Do you feel lucky? Edu and I sure don't." The result was the same: spit-backs and dribble-downs. If the groops did not swallow and collect, how could they pay the Triple B? Or any B at all?

"That's it," Gstan said. "I'm not wasting any more big yellows. Something's wrong and I'm going to find out about it."

"Enjoying your stay?" Foxi said in full questioning voice when they entered the casino, which at mid-morning was crowded with bone rollers and other "gamesters." She had on a different outfit, just as skimpy last night's, but mostly black, and as she leaned forward and placed her hands on the counter, just as revealing.

"I don't know," Gstan said, showing none of last evening's eye-popping reticence. "First of all, I thought the groop fish by the shore were the big attraction. Not these kiddy games in here. Triple Bs and all that. But no. We throw. They reject. We throw. They reject. What's the deal?"

"Oh. Yes. That," she said, her smile a little late. "Did I neglect to mention? Mention last night? We're working on the fish. Re something." She gave them more smile. Held it. She stepped back from the table and swept her hair back over her shoulders.

"Yes," Ziiza said. "'Re something.' Re what something?"

"Sort of re-positioning." Foxi hesitated as if she hoped they would leave, then said, "They've been fussy lately. Off their appetites."

"You can say that again," Gstan said with a sneer.

"What do we do?" Ziiza asked.

"Oh, relax in our lounge," Foxi said. Then, looking at Edu, "Except he's too young to enter. And," her voice took on a non-creature-loving edge, "*that* should not be on the premises at all. Play the 'kiddy games,' as you call them, sir. In the casino. And there's swimming. Beach walking. Excellent clamming. Crabbing in the Cousin. Need to brush up on your gaming skills? Hire a personal trainer. Groopland offers endless entertainment opportunities."

"Except groops," Ziiza and Gstan said in unison.

"We expect the groops to be fine," Foxi said. "Tomorrow. Monday at the latest." Questioning lit back in full force.

"You said the clamming was good," Ziiza said. "Which way on the beach?"

Foxi pointed toward their campsite.

The tide had slipped out and the beach, which had been a narrow strip along the dunes, was wide. Although the claming was just as good out from their campsite, they walked north toward the river mouth to get away from the beach walkers, who like themselves had come for groop gambling, had gotten bored with round-top games, and were taking the air.

They spread out, walking lightly, slowly, until they were spots to each other: Ziiza farthest north, Edu in the middle, Gstan closest to D-11. Dg, after sniffing some holes and taking a spout in the eye, retired to the dry sand to watch.

Again, memories of the Sea Trace. Ziiza was an experienced digger, even though the children had dug most of them on the way. She pushed up against the water line where the clams were most plentiful. Never turn your back to the Sea, she told Edu silently. Remember? She waved at him till she got his attention, then motioned *move back* with her hand. She retreated to set an example. Excellent clamming, it turned out, translated into plentiful but deep. Large clams. She dug with her hands, trying to outrace the sinking creatures.

Hard work. Hard on hands and fingernails. Hard on knees. But not so hard on feet and toes.

Fun, Ziiza thought while she dug. We are after all out of the ash fall. That made her think of Litti. And Netti. And handsome Shulders. And Org. Would he ever speak to her again? (And would he connect her to the messenger who had happened by Blood Camp? And had happened to mention that he, Org, might consider re-balancing his rock. And that he had better make certain it was underweight. And had better report it to Senior. Because if he did not, the individual who had seen him cut the corner would take care of it in a far more unpleasant manner.) Which led to far-off Milli. Then, inevitably, to Govvi. That ended it.

She flung each clam behind her, not keeping count, until she grew cold. She gathered them up and walked in – she alone had dug enough for two day's feasting – and watched Edu and Gstan. Out there.

Gstan joined her. "Well, Zi," he said. He paused, looking at her out of the corner of his eye, waiting for her to snap at *Zi*. She did not. "Bad times at good old Groopland. But I sense good times ahead." She gave him a questioning look. "Namely, a big clam dinner." He chuckled and she joined in. "What do you say I build up the fire. When I get it going, we can smash clamshells together."

"Keep an eye on Edu," Ziiza told Dg when they left for camp.

The salt-soaked driftwood burned hot, fanned by the steady Sea breeze. Gstan roasted to order: well done for Edu, medium for Ziiza, extra rare – in and out – for Dg and himself.

After dinner, marred only by sand grating on their teeth, Ziiza said, "You know, here we are in D-11, a dune pocket, a campsite we would have found barely acceptable on the Sea Trace. Remember the watabeast night in the dunes, Edu? Not only that, but we're paying for it. That's what I call progress."

"Muma?" Edu said. "Could I borrow some big yellows?"

"That's what *I* call progress," Gstan said with a sly wink.

"Borrow?" Ziiza said, "What for?"

"Since the groops aren't working. And you haven't spent many. Could I try skipping some on the water? Just to see if I can do it."

"Same as gambling," Gstan said. "You lose them anyway. But without Foxi and the fish to take their cut. Here, boy, have some of mine."

"Okay, dear. Mine, too. But not too many."

Edu walked into the low breaking waves. Dg followed until the water touched his belly and stopped.

Come on, Ziiza, Gstan said, grabbing her hand, "we've got to see this."

Edu sailed a big yellow over a wave. It stalled, dropped, and knifed into the water. He tried again, adjusting his grip. It tumbled and dropped. After ten or eleven throws he had not had a skip. He turned and looked questioningly at Ziiza and Gstan.

"Have all you want," Gstan said, holding out his sack. "This is good."

Edu threw high and low, overhand and underhand. Not even a dribble-skip-sink. "I never thought it would be this hard," he said.

"And he's an expert stone skipper," Ziiza said proudly.

"No offense, but let old Gstan show you how it's done. One little skip. Can't be that difficult. I've never been much of an outdoor guy, but I could skip a stone or two in my day. You just have to overcome the curve. And the chisel point. And the odd shape. And the ugly yellow color." He grinned at Ziiza. "And the fact that, when you think about it, big yellows are as about as different from flat skipping stones as it's possible for a shape to be. Unless they were round."

"That's the challenge, Mister Gstan," Edu said with a sniffle. "To do it when you're not supposed to be able to. Do the impossible."

"What was my name again?"

"Sorry, just Gstan."

"That's better."

Gstan threw faster and faster, harder and harder.

"Slow down, Gstan," Ziiza said. "You'll never do it that way."

"Ouch," he said. "Darn it. Pulled my shoulder. Right here." He rubbed and looked at Ziiza for sympathy.

"Poor boy."

"That's it for me," Gstan said. "When you throw to the groops you've at least got a chance of a Triple B. Or so I'm told."

Ziiza walked back to D-11 and returned with her sack. "Dip in, Edu," she said. "You've used enough of Gstan's. Mind if I try?"

"I guess I'm through, too, Muma," Edu said dejectedly. "Come on, Dg. We can watch."

"You've got to hold them just right," Gstan said. "So they sail cleanly through the air and hit the water just so."

Ziiza gave him a look and said, "Why don't you try skipping your ThinStone, Gstan? It's flat and smooth. What a beautiful sight it'd make, flying through the air, skip-skip-skipping over the water – and sink-sink-sinking into the Sea."

"Sorry."

Ziiza threw hard, overhand, underhand, backhand – and finally sidearm, the accepted stone-skipping motion. She tried the soft approach: the barest flip forward. She threw Gstan style, as hard as she could. If she could have heard them hit the water she would have heard: Clunk. Clunk. Clunk.

She stood knee deep in the surf, analyzing. Break it down. Just one skip. Do what they couldn't. Do the impossible. Hold the tip between thumb and forefinger for maximum control, she concluded. Throw sidearm, aiming down, barely. The direct approach. Shortest distance between thrower and success. *This is getting serious. I've got to limit myself.*

She counted out five in her hand. Threw one. It twisted and knifed into the water. Threw again. Same result. She turned to Gstan and Edu and held up three fingers. Clunk. Two to go. Clunk. She kissed the last big yellow for luck, held it high, and threw. Clunk.

They watched the horizon turn pink to red. Listened to the fire pop and hiss.

"Ziiza," Gstan said, "So what are your plans? I mean, Beaverton's changed, as if I had to tell you. It'll never be the same.

"Do you think I'd leave?"

"Maybe. I've considered."

"Well," she said. "I've struggled too long and too hard to let a few setbacks force me out. Beaverton's my home. Yours, too, Gstan, if you'll admit it. I'm going back. As for work, I'm through trying to make it big. Not that I couldn't. But I don't want that anymore. No pleasuring establishments. No sports. No permits. No hassles. No rent. My dream is small. I thought it up on the hobble." She looked at Gstan, waiting for his reaction. Looked for Edu's smile. "How does a small business sound? Berries and fruit in season. Netti could weave gift baskets. She and Shulders could run it. Own it, eventually. She could make hats, too. Fancy, expensive ones. Whenever she liked. I'd stay in the background. Wait on customers once in awhile. A modest vend. Well presented, of course."

"Muma," Edu said. "Aren't you getting ahead of them? Netti and Shulders, I mean."

"As I said, beyond his years." She grinned at Gstan. "But yes, Edu, I am getting ahead of them. Don't mind admitting. I said it was a dream."

"If I may be so bold," Gstan said, "I'll bet you'll be running the place in a week. And expanding. And adding lines. And hiring people."

Ziiza shrugged. "And your plans, Gstan? Since you brought it up."

"You know how we talked about Errix and Z-sport back on the trail? Problems for the new management and all that? And I said I didn't care a whit. Remember? Well, I've been thinking. Just like you, Ziiza. What I don't care a whit about is old Errix and old Hill Burrow. The bank took them — stole them, rather — and it's over and done. What I care about is my latest idea. So I make tracks down south. And, get this: instead of selling whatever Silvoo and the Hieyeques happen to be playing with at the moment — like

ThinStones — I give *them* an idea to play with. Challenge them to produce it. Challenge their ingenuity. And what, you ask, might idea this be?"

He leaned closer. "Communication," he said, looking at Edu. "Taking off with your discovery, my boy. The B-town Run Away. You and me. Out by the maple tree. Talking to Mistermayor. Talk. That's what people care about. Jabber and twaddle. A stone for talking only; that's my idea. Fit in your hand. Modern design. Rounded corners. New colors. TalkStones. Clever, what?"

"Is that what you really want?" Ziiza asked. "Walk all that way? Try to find those guys?"

"I'm wild about it. Didn't I just tell you?"

"Go through all that again? I though you said it was a one-time thing."

"Well, maybe not."

"Then what, Gstan?"

"Don't you know?"

She stared into the blowing fire, avoiding his eyes. Listened to the surf lapping on the shore. Felt the evening wind on her face. Waited.

"You, Ziiza. You," he said. "All of us. Together."

Ziiza fumbled with her necklaces, trying to separate them. Edu threw his arms around his muma. Buried his face in her middle. Dg gnawed gently on her ankle.

Acknowledgments

Many thanks to:

My wife and first reader, Carol Barrett, for her interest
and encouragement along the way.

My sister, Sylvia Troust, for her comments
and proofreading.

Robin Ireland, copy editor, Bellingham, Washington.
robinireland.com

Bob Swingle, cover designer, Lightbourne, LLC, Ashland, Oregon.
lightbourne.com

To purchase *Ziiza Moves to Beaverton*, send a check for $24.95 U.S. ($19.95 plus $5.00 shipping and handling) to:

Alder Press
P.O. Box 1503
Portland, OR 97207-1503

503-246-7983
alder@teleport.com

Alder Press does not accept credit cards.

Please include your shipping address, telephone number, and email address.

Prices and availability subject to change without notice.

See **alderpress.com** for up-to-date information.

DATE DUE

NOV 8 1976	T E S FEB 1978		
JAN 3 1977	M A S MAY 1978 MAR. 12		
B F S JUN 1977			
MAR 30 '77	B F S MAR 1980 MAY 3 1 1991		
MAR 28 '77	S F N MAR 1983 FEB 2 0 1995		
APR 4 '77 FEB 07 1988	JUL 2 4 1983 F L X APR		
	C S APR 1987 FEB 0 2 1996		
	F L X JAN		
	OCT 2 2 1994		

GA. 30336